The Monkey & the Monk

THE Monkey & THE Monk

A REVISED ABRIDGMENT OF *The Journey to the West*

Translated and Edited by Anthony C. Yu

THE UNIVERSITY OF CHICAGO PRESS

Chicago & London

The University of Chicago Press, Chicago 60637
The University of Chicago Press, Ltd., London
© 2006 by The University of Chicago
This is a revised abridgment of *The Journey to The West* originally
published in four volumes, © 1977, 1978, 1980, 1983 by The
University of Chicago
All rights reserved. Published 2006
Printed in the United States of America

14 13 12 11 10   3   4   5

ISBN-13: 978-0-226-97155-1 (cloth)
ISBN-13: 978-0-226-97156-8 (paper)
ISBN-10: 0-226-97155-4 (cloth)
ISBN-10: 0-226-97156-2 (paper)

Library of Congress Cataloging-in-Publication Data

Wu, Cheng'en, ca. 1500–ca. 1582.
   [Xi you ji. English Selections.]
   The monkey and the monk : a revised abridgment of the
journey to the west / translated and edited by Anthony C. Yu.
      p. cm.
   ISBN 0-226-97155-4 (cloth : alk. paper) —
   ISBN 0-226-97156-2 (pbk. : alk. paper)
   I. Yu, Anthony C., 1938– II. Title.
PL2697.H75E596 2006
895.1'34—dc22

                                                    2006011826

♾ The paper used in this publication meets the minimum
requirements of the American National Standard for Information
Sciences—Permanence of Paper for Printed Library Materials,
ANSI Z39.48-1992.

For James E. Miller, Jr., Michael J. Murrin, Edward Wasiolek,

and, in memoriam, Wayne C. Booth

CONTENTS

The skeletal plot of *The Journey to the West* (Chin. *Xiyouji*) was based on the famous pilgrimage of the priest Xuanzang (596?–664 CE), who traveled overland from Tang China to distant India in quest of additional Buddhist scriptures, the doctrines of which were deemed canonical to his particular division of the faith. His furtive departure from his homeland in defiance of an explicit proscription by the Tang Emperor Taizong (ca. 600–649, r. 626–649) against travel through the western frontiers at the time rendered him liable to criminal arrest and execution, but he fared much better on his return. The protracted and arduous journey lasting nearly seventeen years (627–644) won him the scriptures he desired no less than immediate imperial recognition and patronage. Installed by the emperor in the western Tang capital of Chang'an (the modern Xi'an), the pilgrim spent the remaining twenty years of his life as a master translator of Indic Buddhist texts. Together with his collaborators recruited by the imperium throughout the empire, he gave to the Chinese people in their own language seventy-five volumes or 1,341 scrolls of Buddhist writings, surpassing the accomplishment of any scripture translator in Chinese history before or since. To this day, the sites (e.g., the Big Wild-Goose Pagoda, the Xuanzang Crematorium Pagoda) and relics of his devoted labor as a cleric of the court can still be enjoyed by tourists of Xi'an.

Although the priest was by no means the only person who undertook such a lengthy peregrination in the cause of Buddhist piety, the records and accounts of his experience (by himself and his disciples after his death) encountered in Central Asia and in India made Xuanzang one of the most celebrated religious personalities in Chinese history. His own privations and sufferings during the sojourn on the Silk Road and beyond, his religious activities during each stage thereof, his irrepressible spiritual commitment and stupendous scholastic accomplishments, and the immensity of imperial favor finally bestowed all combined to transform him into a cultural hero. The profile of this hero's story in the popular and literary imagination, however, quickly departed from known historical record and events and took on characteristics all its own. Told likely by mouth and also by writing over a period of almost a millennium and in various media—the fragments, the short poetic tales, short prose fiction, developed dramas, and longer works of prose fiction—the final version that appeared as one of the proverbial four masterworks of the Ming novel had changed from the exploits of a human monk to a pilgrimage narrative fashioned as itinerant adventure, fantasy, humor, social and political satire, and serious allegory built on intricate religious syncretism. There are three significant elements in this fictive transformation of the scripture-seeking journey.

The first concerns the protagonist's personal history and disposition. In complete contrast to the historical character's attested background and experience, the account of the fictive Xuanzang evolving through dramatic and religious texts (e.g., the various "precious scrolls" appearing in late Ming times) tells of someone born and raised from the coastal region of Southeastern China. Abandoned at birth by a widowed mother abducted and raped by a bandit, the infant was raised by a Buddhist abbot and, upon reaching adulthood, succeeded in avenging a father's murder and a mother's disgrace. As told in chapters 8–13 of the present novel, Buddhist "providence" assumes a crucial role in so shaping events that they would lead eventually to the Tang emperor's selection of Xuanzang as the scripture seeker. In this rewriting of history, the intensely personal zeal of a plebian priest will be displaced by different motivations undergirding such an enormous enterprise: Buddha's compassionate wisdom in offering scriptures as a salvific gift to unenlightened, sinful Chinese in the Land of the East counterpoints the fictive pilgrim's religious devotion and political loyalism (to imperial mandate and favors). Whereas the historical journey began as a secret, transgressive act of a pious zealot, the fictive pilgrimage was foreordained by Buddha, superintended throughout by Guanyin (the most popular Goddess of Mercy in Chinese religions), and enthusiastically commissioned by the Tang emperor.

The second distinctive feature in the fictionalizing process appears when the priest took for a disciple a monkey figure, an animal guardian-attendant who was also endowed with enormous intelligence and magical powers. Though this figure's association with the pilgrim could already be found in snippets of verse as early as the twelfth century and in further development thereafter in narrative form, it remains for the hundred-chapter novel of late Ming to endow this simian character with its grandest and most attractive delineation. The importance assigned to Xuanzang's chief disciple may be seen in the fact that fully seven chapters at the beginning are devoted to relating Sun Wukong's birth and development, his training and attainment in esoteric Daoist self-cultivation, his daring exploits throughout Heaven and Hell that climax in his wreaking horrific havoc at the Celestial Palace—episodes that not only read like those of an independent tale by itself but also have been adapted in fact as such in Beijing opera and other dramatic media. Once converted to Buddhism after having been subdued and imprisoned by Buddha himself, Sun eventually became Xuanzang's most able and devoted disciple. The monkey's restless intelligence, martial and magical prowess, and almost boundless resourcefulness have reminded many a modern Chinese and foreign reader of another simian hero across cultures: Hanumat of the great Indian epic *Rāmāyaṇa*, attributed to the poet Vālmīki. Scholarship of the 1920s to the 1980s has equivocated on direct linkage of the two stories because decisive information on textual or historical influence was at first lacking. More recent research, however, has gradually but firmly uncovered possible references to various aspects of the Rama story in major Buddhist texts that had been widely circulated since their translation into Chinese. Moreover, astonishing parallels in details of description and plot in various episodes beyond mere similarity of characterization of the two monkeys (courage and prowess in battle, ability to fly, the tendency to attack their enemies through their bellies) have thus led others to doubt posited coincidence as an adequate explanation.

As Xuanzang embarked on his pilgrimage, his circle was then enlarged to encompass the fictive human priest and four disciples: the monkey, a half-human and half-pig comic (actually a Daoist god exiled from Heaven), a reformed cannibal (another Daoist pariah), and a delinquent dragon-horse as the priest's transportation. This sharp contrast between known history and the full-length novel also marks the third distinctive development in the journey's fictionalization. Whereas the former is constituted by the dedicated efforts of a lone human devotee, the latter represents the combined exertion of a community of invented figures that, in turn, may be construed variously in the story—as different aspects of a single personality, as different constitutive elements of a process (an interior journey in quest of moral self-cultivation, spiritual enlightenment, or physical longevity through alchemy), or as different kinds of individuals in a society. The world of this community, moreover, spans the entire cosmos, natural and supernatural, generated by the multicultural religious imaginaire of premodern China.

Structured throughout the long tale, the ubiquitous but unobtrusive voice of the narrator in fact provides a running, reflexive commentary—

usually through interpolated verse of many varieties and the brief prose introductions to new episodes—and gently reminds the reader of allegory's possible presence even within the fun-filled and lively depictions of cosmic battles, fantastic beings, bizarre experiences, and extraordinary feats of mental and physical bravura. To craft a story radically different from a synopsis of Buddhist history, the author has apparently made extensive use of the idioms and terminologies stemming from both the Daoist canon and an amorphous movement commonly known as "Three Religions as One (*sanjiao guiyi* or *heyi*)" that began to flourish in medieval Song China and gained widespread adherence in late imperial times among official elites, merchants, clerics of different regions, and the general populace. As articulated frequently and perhaps most pointedly in fiction and fiction commentaries of the Ming–Qing periods, the movement's syncretic discourse was verily a hermeneutics of fusion, wherein the widely disparate concepts and categories of traditional Confucianism, Daoism, and Buddhism were deliberately harmonized and unified. That this discourse was intimately known to our novel's author could be seen in lines of poetry describing a lecture by Subodhi (chapter 2), the religiously ambiguous master who first transmitted to the Monkey King the secrets of immortality and other magic powers:

> For a while he lectured on Dao;
> For a while he spoke on Chan—
> To harmonize the Three Schools is a natural thing.

The Three Schools or Lineages (*san jia*) here, of course, refer to a standard name of the three religious traditions. Another and even more decisive indication of such syncretism may be found in the very mouth of Buddha, who proclaimed at the novel's beginning (chapter 8) that his scriptures were "for the cultivation of immortality and the gate to ultimate virtue." Repeated at the end (chapters 28, 29 in the present edition) and in more expansive form, the scriptures also became "the mirror of our [Buddhist] faith . . . the source of the Three Religions." Such remarks would surely astonish real Buddhists, both historical and contemporary.

Who was the author of this narrative of such imaginative magnitude and complexity? Neither a pseudonymous editor nor the named publisher and preface writer associated with the full-length, hundred-chapter version printed in Nanjing in 1592 (generally regarded as the earliest authentic version) had provided even the merest clue to this question. Chinese scholars from the early decades of the twentieth century had begun to focus on the minor late-Ming official, Wu Cheng'en (ca. 1500–1582), as a likely candidate on the grounds that Wu was a skillful and versatile lyric poet (thus answerable to the estimated seventeen hundred–plus poems of all genres and styles enshrined in the narrative), was fond of writings and myths on the uncanny and the strange, had a reputation for excelling in satirical and humorous compositions, and was a native of the southeast coastal region of Huai'an, the peculiar dialect(s) of which had supplied the narrative with a huge amount of colloquial expressions apparent to readers since the seventeenth century. Most important of all, the *Gazetteer of Huai'an Prefecture*, compiled in the period of the Ming Tianqi reign (1621–1627), listed after Wu's name several works, among which, prominently, the title *Xiyouji* appeared, although no student of the novel since then had any clear notion as to what kind of work this *Journey to the West* was.

These arguments for Wu's authorship, certainly not to be ignored, have failed to win universal assent, and they have been repeatedly questioned by both modern Japanese and European scholarship. More recently, some Chinese scholars have turned once more to probing the history of certain branches of syncretic Daoism for possible hints of the novel's authorial identity and the context of its production. Despite anonymity in authorship, the novel since its publication has not only enjoyed vast readership among Chinese people of all regions and social strata, but its popularity has also continued to spread to other peoples and lands in the last four centuries through increased translation, adaptation in different media (illustrated books, comics, plays, Beijing and other regional operas, shadow puppet plays, radio shows, film, TV serialization, and reportedly even a contemporary Western opera in the making), and rewriting (e.g., by Timothy Mo, Maxine Hong Kingston, Mary Zimmerman, and David Henry Hwang in England and the United States).

My labor on *The Journey to the West*, begun in 1970, was doubly motivated: to rectify the acclaimed but distorted picture provided by Arthur Waley's justly popular abridgment,[1] and to redress an imbalance of criticism championed by Dr. Hu Shi, the Chinese scholar-diplomat who supplied the British translator with an influential preface. Therein, Hu asserted that "freed from all kinds of allegorical interpretations by Buddhist, Taoist, and Confucianist commentators, *Monkey* is simply a book of good humor, profound nonsense, good-natured satire, and delightful entertainment."[2] My own encounter with this marvelous work since childhood, under the kind but skillful tutelage of my late Grandfather, who used *Journey* as a

1. See *Monkey: Folk Novel of China by Wu Ch'eng-en*, trans. Arthur Waley (New York: Grove Press, 1943).

2. Ibid., 5.

textbook for teaching me Chinese during the terrible years of the Sino-Japanese war on the mainland, had long convinced me that this narrative was nothing if not one of the world's most finely wrought allegories. The thirteen years of studying and translating the text together with the subsequent decades of teaching it at Chicago and elsewhere have also made me a happy witness to the new turns in scholarly research and interpretation. The distantly collaborative result of our studies has made it clear that religion is not only crucial to the novel's conception and formation, but also that its nearly unique embodiment in this work need not clash with "good humor, profound nonsense, good-natured satire, and delightful entertainment."

My completion of the first plenary and annotated English translation of *Journey* in 1983,[3] however, was not spared from spawning its own ironies. No sooner had all four volumes of the work appeared than friends and colleagues far and near began complaining about its unwieldy length and impractical size—for general readers no less than for use in the classroom. After years of resistance to their plea for a shorter edition, I have now reached the conclusion that Professor Waley might also have had a valid perspective, although my present abridgment continues my attempt to differ from his version by providing as fully as possible all the textual features of the selected episodes. (At the head of each chapter of this volume beginning with chapter 16, the corresponding chapter number from the four-volume edition appears in square brackets.) I thank the University of Chicago Press for this opportunity to publish an abridgment, and for giving me needed technical support for revisions and conversion to the Pinyin system of romanization. I hope very much that this "reduced" version of the novel is not reductionistic, and that it will tempt the sympathetic reader to enjoy the plenitude of the full version.

Anthony C. Yu
August 2005

3. Anthony C. Yu, trans. and ed., *The Journey to the West*, 4 vols. (Chicago: University of Chicago Press, 1977–83).

ONE

The divine root being conceived, the origin appears;
The moral nature cultivated, the Great Dao is born.

The poem says:
  Before Chaos divided, Heaven tangled with Earth;
  Formless and void—this, no human had seen.
  But when Pan Gu broke up the nebula,
  Clearing began, the turbid parted from the pure.
  Humaneness supreme enfolding every life
  Enlightens all things that they become good.
  Would you know creation's merit in cyclic time?
  Read The Tale of Woes Dispersed on Journey West.

We heard that, in the order of Heaven and Earth, a single period consisted of 129,600 years. Dividing this period into twelve epochs were the twelve stems of Zi, Chou, Yin, Mao, Chen, Si, Wu, Wei, Shen, Yu, Xu, and Hai, with each epoch having 10,800 years. Considered as the horary circle, the sequence would be thus: the first sign of dawn appears in the hour of Zi, while at Chou the cock crows; daybreak occurs at Yin, and the sun rises at Mao; Chen comes after breakfast, and by Si everything is planned; at Wu the sun arrives at its meridian, and it declines westward by Wei; the evening meal comes during the hour of Shen, and the sun sinks completely at Yu; twilight sets in at Xu, and people rest by the hour of Hai. This sequence may also be understood macrocosmically. At the end of the epoch of Xu, Heaven and Earth were obscure and all things were indistinct. With the passing of 5,400 years, the beginning of Hai was the epoch of darkness. This moment was named Chaos, because there were neither human beings nor the two spheres. After another 5,400 years Hai ended, and as the creative force began to work after great perseverance, the epoch of Zi drew near and again brought gradual development. Shao Kangjie[1] said:

---

1. This is Shao Yong (1011–77), a Song scholar and an expert in the *Classic of Change*.

When winter moved to the middle of Zi,
No change occurred in the mind of Heaven.
The male principle had barely stirred,
And all things were as yet unborn.

At this point, the firmament first acquired its foundation. With another 5,400 years came the Zi epoch; the ethereal and the light rose up to form the four phenomena of the sun, the moon, the stars, and the Heavenly bodies. Hence it is said, the Heaven was created at Zi. This epoch came to its end in another 5,400 years, and the sky began to harden as the Chou epoch approached. The *Classic of Change* said:

Great was the male principle;
Supreme, the female!
They made all things,
In obedience to Heaven.

At this point, the Earth became solidified. In another 5,400 years after the arrival of the Chou epoch, the heavy and the turbid condensed below and formed the five elements of water, fire, mountain, stone, and earth. Hence it is said, the Earth was created at Chou. With the passing of another 5,400 years, the Chou epoch came to its end and all things began to grow at the beginning of the Yin epoch. The *Book of Calendar* said:

The Heavenly aura descended;
The earthly aura rose up.
Heaven and Earth copulated,
And all things were born.

At this point, Heaven and Earth were bright and fair; the yin had intercourse with the yang. In another 5,400 years, during the Yin epoch, humans, beasts, and fowls came into being, and thus the so-called three forces of Heaven, Earth, and Man were established. Hence it is said, man was born at Yin.

Following Pan Gu's construction of the universe, the rule of the Three Kings, and the ordering of the relations by the Five Emperors, the world was divided into four great continents. They were: the East Pūrvavideha Continent, the West Aparagodānīya Continent, the South Jambūdvīpa Continent, and the North Uttarakuru Continent. This book is solely concerned with the East Pūrvavideha Continent.

Beyond the ocean there was a country named Aolai. It was near a great ocean, in the midst of which was located the famous Flower-Fruit Mountain. This mountain, which constituted the chief range of the Ten Islets and formed the origin of the Three Islands, came into being after the creation of the world. As a testimonial to its magnificence, there is the following poetic rhapsody:

Its majesty commands the wide ocean;
Its splendor rules the jasper sea;
Its majesty commands the wide ocean
When, like silver mountains, the tide sweeps fishes into caves;
Its splendor rules the jasper sea
When snowlike billows send forth serpents from the deep.
On the southwest side pile up tall plateaus;
From the Eastern Sea arise soaring peaks.
There are crimson ridges and portentous rocks,
Precipitous cliffs and prodigious peaks.
Atop the crimson ridges
Phoenixes sing in pairs:
Before precipitous cliffs
The unicorn singly rests.
At the summit is heard the cry of golden pheasants;
In and out of stony caves are seen the strides of dragons:
In the forest are long-lived deer and immortal foxes.
On the trees are divine fowls and black cranes.
Strange grass and flowers never wither:
Green pines and cypresses always keep their spring.
Immortal peaches are ever fruit-bearing;
Lofty bamboos often detain the clouds.
Within a single gorge the creeping vines are dense;
The grass color of meadows all around is fresh.
This is indeed the pillar of Heaven, where a hundred rivers meet—
The Earth's great axis, in ten thousand kalpas unchanged.

There was on top of that very mountain an immortal stone, which measured thirty-six feet and five inches in height and twenty-four feet in circumference. The height of thirty-six feet and five inches corresponded to the three hundred and sixty-five cyclical degrees, while the circumference of twenty-four feet corresponded to the twenty-four solar terms of the calendar. On the stone were also nine perforations and eight holes, which corresponded to the Palaces of the Nine Constellations and the Eight Trigrams. Though it lacked the shade of trees on all sides, it was set off by epidendrums on the left and right. Since the creation of the world, it had been nourished for a long period by the seeds of Heaven and Earth and by the essences of the sun and the moon, until, quickened by divine inspiration, it became pregnant with a divine embryo. One day, it split open, giving birth to a stone egg about the size of a playing ball. Exposed to the wind, it was transformed into a stone monkey endowed with fully developed features and limbs. Having learned at once to climb and run, this monkey also bowed to the four quarters, while two beams of golden light flashed from his eyes to reach even the Palace of the Polestar. The light disturbed the Great Benevolent Sage of Heaven, the Celestial Jade Emperor of the Most Venerable Deva, who, attended by his divine ministers, was sitting in the Cloud Palace of the Golden Arches, in the Treasure Hall of the Divine Mists. Upon seeing the glimmer of the golden beams, he ordered Thousand-Mile Eye and Fair-Wind Ear to open the South Heaven Gate and to look out. At this command the two captains went out to the gate, and, having looked intently and listened clearly, they returned presently to report, "Your subjects, obeying your command to locate the beams, discovered that they came from the Flower-Fruit Mountain at the border of the small Aolai Country, which lies to the east of the East Pūrvavideha Continent. On this mountain is an immortal stone which has given birth to an egg. Exposed to the wind, it has been transformed into a monkey, who, when bowing to the four quarters, has flashed from his eyes those golden beams that reached the Palace of the Polestar. Now that he is taking some food and drink, the light is about to grow dim." With compassionate mercy the Jade Emperor declared, "These creatures from the world below are born of the essences of Heaven and Earth, and they need not surprise us."

That monkey in the mountain was able to walk, run, and leap about; he fed on grass and shrubs, drank from the brooks and streams, gathered mountain flowers, and searched out fruits from trees. He made his companions the tiger and the lizard, the wolf and the leopard; he befriended the civet and the deer, and he called the gibbon and the baboon his kin. At night he slept beneath stony ridges, and in the morning he sauntered about the caves and the peaks. Truly,

> In the mountain there is no passing of time;
> The cold recedes, but one knows not the year.

One very hot morning, he was playing with a group of monkeys under the shade of some pine trees to escape the heat. Look at them, each amusing himself in his own way by

> Swinging from branches to branches,
> Searching for flowers and fruits;
> They played two games or three
> With pebbles and with pellets;
> They circled sandy pits;
> They built rare pagodas;
> They chased the dragonflies;
> They ran down small lizards;

Bowing low to the sky,
They worshiped Bodhisattvas;
They pulled the creeping vines;
They plaited mats with grass;
They searched to catch the louse
They bit or crushed with their nails;
They dressed their furry coats;
They scraped their fingernails;
Some leaned and leaned;
Some rubbed and rubbed;
Some pushed and pushed;
Some pressed and pressed;
Some pulled and pulled;
Some tugged and tugged.
Beneath the pine forest they played without a care,
Washing themselves in the green-water stream.

So, after the monkeys had frolicked for a while, they went to bathe in the mountain stream and saw that its currents bounced and splashed like tumbling melons. As the old saying goes,

Fowls have their fowl speech,
And beasts have their beast language.

The monkeys said to each other, "We don't know where this water comes from. Since we have nothing to do today, let us follow the stream up to its source to have some fun." With a shriek of joy, they dragged along males and females, calling out to brothers and sisters, and scrambled up the mountain alongside the stream. Reaching its source, they found a great waterfall. What they saw was

A column of rising white rainbows,
A thousand fathoms of dancing waves—
Which the sea wind buffets but cannot sever,
On which the river moon shines and reposes.
Its cold breath divides the green ranges;
Its tributaries moisten the blue-green hillsides.
This torrential body, its name a cascade,
Seems truly like a hanging curtain.

All the monkeys clapped their hands in acclaim: "Marvelous water! Marvelous water! So this waterfall is distantly connected with the stream at the base of the mountain, and flows directly out, even to the great ocean." They said also, "If any of us had the ability to penetrate the curtain and find out where the water comes from without hurting himself, we would honor him as king." They gave the call three times, when suddenly the stone monkey leaped out from the crowd. He answered the challenge with a loud voice, "I'll go in! I'll go in!" What a monkey! For

Today his fame will spread wide,
His fortune arrives with the time;
He's fated to live in this place,
Sent by a king to this godly palace.

Look at him! He closed his eyes, crouched low, and with one leap he jumped straight through the waterfall. Opening his eyes at once and raising his head to look around, he saw that there was neither water nor waves inside, only a gleaming, shining bridge. He paused to collect himself and looked more carefully again: it was a bridge made of sheet iron. The water beneath it surged through a hole in the rock to reach the outside, filling in all the space under the arch. With bent body he climbed on the bridge, looking about as he walked, and discovered a beautiful place that seemed to be some kind of residence. Then he saw

Fresh mosses piling up indigo,
White clouds like jade afloat,
And luminous sheens of mist and smoke;
Empty windows, quiet rooms,
And carved flowers growing smoothly on benches;
Stalactites suspended in milky caves;
Rare blossoms voluminous over the ground.
Pans and stoves near the wall show traces of fire;
Bottles and cups on the table contain leftovers.
The stone seats and beds were truly lovable;
The stone pots and bowls were more praiseworthy.
There were, furthermore, a stalk or two of tall bamboos,
And three or five sprigs of plum flowers.
With a few green pines always draped in rain,
This whole place indeed resembled a home.

After staring at the place for a long time, he jumped across the middle of the bridge and looked left and right. There in the middle was a stone tablet on which was inscribed in regular, large letters:

The Blessed Land of Flower-Fruit Mountain,
The Cave Heaven of Water-Curtain Cave.

Beside himself with delight, the stone monkey quickly turned around to go back out and, closing his eyes and crouching again, leaped out of the water. "A great stroke of luck," he exclaimed with two loud guffaws, "a great stroke of luck." The other monkeys surrounded him and asked,

"How is it inside? How deep is the water?" The stone monkey replied, "There isn't any water at all. There's a sheet iron bridge, and beyond it is a piece of Heaven-sent property." "What do you mean that there's property in there?" asked the monkeys.

Laughing, the stone monkey said, "This water splashes through a hole in the rock and fills the space under the bridge. Beside the bridge there is a stone mansion with trees and flowers. Inside are stone ovens and stoves, stone pots and pans, stone beds and benches. A stone tablet in the middle has the inscription,

The Blessed Land of the Flower-Fruit Mountain,
The Cave Heaven of the Water-Curtain Cave.

This is truly the place for us to settle in. It is, moreover, very spacious inside and can hold thousands of the young and old. Let's all go live in there, and spare ourselves from being subject to the whims of Heaven. For we have in there

A retreat from the wind,
A shelter from the rain.
You fear no frost or snow;
You hear no thunderclap.
Mist and smoke are brightened,
Warmed by a holy light—
The pines are ever green:
Rare flowers, daily new."

When the monkeys heard that, they were delighted, saying, "You go in first and lead the way." The stone monkey closed his eyes again, crouched low, and jumped inside. "All of you," he cried, "Follow me in! Follow me in!" The braver of the monkeys leaped in at once, but the more timid ones stuck out their heads and then drew them back, scratched their ears, rubbed their jaws, and chattered noisily. After milling around for some time, they too bounded inside. Jumping across the bridge, they were all soon snatching dishes, clutching bowls, or fighting for stoves and beds—shoving and pushing things hither and thither. Befitting their stubbornly prankish nature, the monkeys could not keep still for a moment and stopped only when they were utterly exhausted. The stone monkey then solemnly took a seat above and spoke to them: "Gentlemen! 'If a man lacks trustworthiness, it is difficult to know what he can accomplish!'[2] You yourselves promised just now that whoever could get in here and leave again without hurting himself would be honored as king. Now that I have come in and gone

2. Confucius, *Analects*, 2. 22.

out, gone out and come in, and have found for all of you this Heavenly grotto in which you may reside securely and enjoy the privilege of raising a family, why don't you honor me as your king?" When the monkeys heard this, they all folded their hands on their breasts and obediently prostrated themselves. Each one of them then lined up according to rank and age, and, bowing reverently, they intoned. "Long live our great king!" From that moment, the stone monkey ascended the throne of kingship. He did away with the word "stone" in his name and assumed the title, Handsome Monkey King. There is a testimonial poem which says:

When triple spring mated to produce all things,
A divine stone was quickened by the sun and moon.
The egg changed to a monkey, perfecting the Great Way.
He took a name, matching elixir's success.
Formless, his inward shape is thus concealed;
His outer frame by action is plainly known.
In every age all persons will yield to him:
Named a king, a sage, he is free to roam.

The Handsome Monkey King thus led a flock of gibbons and baboons, some of whom were appointed by him as his officers and ministers. They toured the Flower-Fruit Mountain in the morning, and they lived in the Water-Curtain Cave by night. Living in concord and sympathy, they did not mingle with bird or beast but enjoyed their independence in perfect happiness. For such were their activities:

In the spring they gathered flowers for food and drink.
In the summer they went in quest of fruits for sustenance.
In the autumn they amassed taros and chestnuts to ward off time.
In the winter they searched for yellow-sperms³ to live out the year.

The Handsome Monkey King had enjoyed this insouciant existence for three or four hundred years when one day, while feasting with the rest of the monkeys, he suddenly grew sad and shed a few tears. Alarmed, the monkeys surrounded him bowed down and asked, "What is disturbing the Great King?" The Monkey King replied, "Though I am very happy at the moment, I am a little concerned about the future. Hence I'm distressed." The monkeys all laughed and said, "The Great King indeed does not know contentment! Here we daily have a banquet on an immortal mountain in a blessed land, in an ancient cave on a divine continent. We are not subject to the unicorn or the phoenix, nor are we governed by the rulers of mankind.

---

3. A small plant the roots of which are often used for medicinal purposes by the Chinese.

Such independence and comfort are immeasurable blessings. Why, then, does he worry about the future?" The Monkey King said, "Though we are not subject to the laws of man today, nor need we be threatened by the rule of any bird or beast, old age and physical decay in the future will disclose the secret sovereignty of Yama, King of the Underworld. If we die, shall we not have lived in vain, not being able to rank forever among the Heavenly beings?"

When the monkeys heard this, they all covered their faces and wept mournfully, each one troubled by his own impermanence. But look! From among the ranks a bareback monkey suddenly leaped forth and cried aloud, "If the Great King is so farsighted, it may well indicate the sprouting of his religious inclination. There are, among the five major divisions of all living creatures, only three species that are not subject to Yama, King of the Underworld." The Monkey King said, "Do you know who they are?" The monkey said, "They are the Buddhas, the immortals, and the holy sages; these three alone can avoid the Wheel of Transmigration as well as the process of birth and destruction, and live as long as Heaven and Earth, the mountains and the streams." "Where do they live?" asked the Monkey King. The monkey said, "They do not live beyond the world of the Jambūdvīpa for they dwell within ancient caves on immortal mountains." When the Monkey King heard this, he was filled with delight, saying, "Tomorrow I shall take leave of you all and go down the mountain. Even if I have to wander with the clouds to the corners of the sea or journey to the distant edges of Heaven, I intend to find these three kinds of people. I will learn from them how to be young forever and escape the calamity inflicted by King Yama." Lo, this utterance at once led him

To leap free of the Transmigration Net,
And be the Great Sage, Equal to Heaven.

All the monkeys clapped their hands in acclamation, saying, "Wonderful! Wonderful! Tomorrow we shall scour the mountain ranges to gather plenty of fruits, so that we may send the Great King off with a great banquet."

Next day the monkeys duly went to gather immortal peaches, to pick rare fruits, to dig out mountain herbs, and to chop yellow-sperms. They brought in an orderly manner every variety of orchids and epidendrums, exotic plants and strange flowers. They set out the stone chairs and stone tables, covering the tables with immortal wines and food. Look at the

Golden balls and pearly pellets,
Red ripeness and yellow plumpness.
Golden balls and pearly pellets are the cherries,
Their colors truly luscious.

Red ripeness and yellow plumpness are the plums,
Their taste—a fragrant tartness.
Fresh lungans
Of sweet pulps and thin skins.
Fiery lychees
Of small pits and red sacks.
Green fruits of the Pyrus are presented by the branches.
The loquats yellow with buds are held with their leaves.
Pears like rabbit heads and dates like chicken hearts
Dispel your thirst, your sorrow, and the effects of wine.
Fragrant peaches and soft almonds
Are sweet as the elixir of life:
Crisply fresh plums and strawberries
Are sour like cheese and buttermilk.
Red pulps and black seeds compose the ripe watermelons.
Four cloves of yellow rind enfold the big persimmons.
When the pomegranates are split wide,
Cinnabar grains glisten like specks of ruby:
When the chestnuts are cracked open,
Their tough brawns are hard like cornelian.
Walnut and silver almonds fare well with tea.
Coconuts and grapes may be pressed into wine.
Hazelnuts, yews, and crabapples overfill the dishes.
Kumquats, sugarcanes, tangerines, and oranges crowd the tables.
Sweet yams are baked,
Yellow-sperms overboiled,
The tubers minced with seeds of waterlily,
And soup in stone pots simmers on a gentle fire.
Mankind may boast its delicious dainties,
But what can best the pleasure of mountain monkeys.

The monkeys honored the Monkey King with the seat at the head of the table, while they sat below according to their age and rank. They drank for a whole day, each of the monkeys taking a turn to go forward and present the Monkey King with wine, flowers, and fruits. Next day the Monkey King rose early and gave the instruction, "Little ones, cut me some pinewood and make me a raft. Then find me a bamboo for the pole, and gather some fruits and the like. I'm about to leave." When all was ready, he got onto the raft by himself. Pushing off with all his might, he drifted out toward the great ocean and, taking advantage of the wind, set sail for the border of South Jambūdvīpa Continent. Here is the consequence of this journey:

The Heaven-born monkey, strong in magic might,
He left the mount and rode the raft to catch fair wind:
He drifted across the sea to seek immortals' way,
Determined in heart and mind to achieve great things.
It's his lot, his portion, to quit earthly zeals:
Calm and carefree, he'll face a lofty sage.
He'd meet, I think, a true, discerning friend:
The source disclosed, all dharma will be known.

It was indeed his fortune that, after he had boarded the wooden raft, a strong southeast wind which lasted for days sent him to the northwestern coast, the border of the South Jambūdvīpa Continent. He took the pole to test the water, and, finding it shallow one day, he abandoned the raft and jumped ashore. On the beach there were people fishing, hunting wild geese, digging clams, and draining salt. He approached them and, making a weird face and some strange antics, he scared them into dropping their baskets and nets and scattering in all directions. One of them could not run and was caught by the Monkey King, who stripped him of his clothes and put them on himself, aping the way humans wore them. With a swagger he walked through counties and prefectures, imitating human speech and human manners in the marketplaces. He rested by night and dined in the morning, but he was bent on finding the way of the Buddhas, immortals, and holy sages, on discovering the formula for eternal youth. He saw, however, that the people of the world were all seekers after profit and fame; there was not one who showed concern for his appointed end. This is their condition:

When will end this quest for fortune and fame,
This tyrant of early rising and retiring late?
Riding on mules they long for noble steeds;
By now prime ministers, they hope to be kings.
For food and raiment they suffer stress and strain,
Never fearing Yama's call to reckoning.
Seeking wealth and power to give to sons of sons,
There's not one ever willing to turn back.

The Monkey King searched diligently for the way of immortality, but he had no chance of meeting it. Going through big cities and visiting small towns, he unwittingly spent eight or nine years on the South Jambūdvīpa Continent before he suddenly came upon the Great Western Ocean. He thought that there would certainly be immortals living beyond the ocean; so, having built himself a raft like the previous one, he once again drifted across the Western Ocean until he reached the West Aparagodānīya Continent. After landing, he searched for a long time, when all at once he came upon a tall and beautiful mountain with thick forests at its base. Since he was afraid neither of wolves and lizards nor of tigers and leopards, he went straight to the top to look around. It was indeed a magnificent mountain:

A thousand peaks stand like rows of spears,
Like ten thousand cubits of screen widespread.
The sun's beams lightly enclose the azure mist;
In darkening rain, the mount's color turns cool and green.
Dry creepers entwine old trees;
Ancient fords edge secluded paths.
Rare flowers and luxuriant grass.
Tall bamboos and lofty pines.
Tall bamboos and lofty pines
For ten thousand years grow green in this blessed land.
Rare flowers and luxuriant grass
In all seasons bloom as in the Isles of the Blest.
The calls of birds hidden are near.
The sounds of streams rushing are clear.
Deep inside deep canyons the orchids interweave.
On every ridge and crag sprout lichens and mosses.
Rising and falling, the ranges show a fine dragon's pulse.[4]
Here in reclusion must an eminent man reside.

As he was looking about, he suddenly heard the sound of a man speaking deep within the woods. Hurriedly he dashed into the forest and cocked his ear to listen. It was someone singing, and the song went thus:

I watch chess games, my ax handle's rotted.
I chop at wood, zheng zheng *the sound.*
I walk slowly by the cloud's fringe at the valley's entrance.
Selling my firewood to buy some wine,
I am happy and laugh without restraint.
When the path is frosted in autumn's height,
I face the moon, my pillow the pine root.
Sleeping till dawn
I find my familiar woods.
I climb the plateaus and scale the peaks
To cut dry creepers with my ax.

When I gather enough to make a load,
I stroll singing through the marketplace

4. The dragon's pulse is one of the magnetic currents recognized by geomancers.

And trade it for three pints of rice,
With nary the slightest bickering
Over a price so modest.
Plots and schemes I do not know;
Without vainglory or attaint
My life's prolonged in simplicity.
Those I meet,
If not immortals, would be Daoists,
Seated quietly to expound the Yellow Court.

When the Handsome Monkey King heard this, he was filled with delight, saying, "So the immortals are hiding in this place." He leaped at once into the forest. Looking again carefully, he found a woodcutter chopping firewood with his ax. The man he saw was very strangely attired.

On his head he wore a wide splint hat
Of seed-leaves freshly cast from new bamboos.
On his body he wore a cloth garment
Of gauze woven from the native cotton.
Around his waist he tied a winding sash
Of silk spun from an old silkworm.
On his feet he had a pair of straw sandals,
With laces rolled from withered sedge.
In his hands he held a fine steel ax;
A sturdy rope coiled round and round his load.
In breaking pines or chopping trees
Where's the man to equal him?

The Monkey King drew near and called out: "Reverend immortal! Your disciple raises his hands." The woodcutter was so flustered that he dropped his ax as he turned to return the salutation. "Blasphemy! Blasphemy!" he said, "I, a foolish fellow with hardly enough clothes or food! How can I bear the title of immortal?" The Monkey King said, "If you are not an immortal, how is it that you speak his language?" The woodcutter said, "What did I say that sounded like the language of an immortal?" The Monkey King said, "When I came just now to the forest's edge, I heard you singing, 'Those I meet, if not immortals, would be Daoists, seated quietly to expound the *Yellow Court.*' The *Yellow Court* contains the perfected words of the Way and Virtue. What can you be but an immortal?"

Laughing, the woodcutter said, "I can tell you this much: the tune of that lyric is named 'A Court Full of Blossoms,' and it was taught to me by an immortal, a neighbor of mine. He saw that I had to struggle to make a living and that my days were full of worries; so he told me to recite the poem whenever I was troubled. This, he said, would both comfort me and rid me of my difficulties. It happened that I was anxious about something just now; so I sang the song. It didn't occur to me that I would be overheard."

The Monkey King said, "If you are a neighbor of the immortal, why don't you follow him in the cultivation of the Way? Wouldn't it be nice to learn from him the formula for eternal youth?' The woodcutter said, "My lot has been a hard one all my life. When I was young, I was indebted to my parents' nurture until I was eight or nine. As soon as I began to have some understanding of human affairs, my father unfortunately died, and my mother remained a widow. I had no brothers or sisters; so there was no alternative but for me alone to support and care for my mother. Now that my mother is growing old, all the more I dare not leave her. Moreover, my fields are rather barren and desolate, and we haven't enough food or clothing. I can't do more than chop two bundles of firewood to take to the market in exchange for a few pennies to buy a few pints of rice. I cook that myself, serving it to my mother with the tea that I make. That's why I can't practice austerities."

The Monkey King said, "According to what you have said, you are indeed a gentleman of filial piety, and you will certainly be rewarded in the future. I hope, however, that you will show me the way to the immortal's abode, so that I may reverently call upon him." "It's not far. It's not far," the woodcutter said. "This mountain is called the Mountain of Mind and Heart, and in it is the Cave of Slanting Moon and Three Stars. Inside the cave is an immortal by the name of the Patriarch Subodhi, who has already sent out innumerable disciples. Even now there are thirty or forty persons who are practicing austerities with him. Follow this narrow path and travel south for about seven or eight miles, and you will come to his home." Grabbing at the woodcutter, the Monkey King said, "Honored brother, go with me. If I receive any benefit, I will not forget the favor of your guidance." "What a boneheaded fellow you are!" the woodcutter said. "I have just finished telling you these things, and you still don't understand. If I go with you, won't I be neglecting my livelihood? And who will take care of my mother? I must chop my firewood. You go on by yourself!"

When the Monkey King heard this, he had to take his leave. Emerging from the deep forest, he found the path and went past the slope of a hill. After he had traveled seven or eight miles, a cave dwelling indeed came into sight. He stood up straight to take a better look at this splendid place, and this was what he saw:

Mist and smoke in diffusive brilliance,
Flashing lights from the sun and moon,

A thousand stalks of old cypress,
Ten thousand stems of tall bamboo.
A thousand stalks of old cypress
Draped in rain half fill the air with tender green;
Ten thousand stems of tall bamboo
Held in smoke will paint the glen chartreuse.
Strange flowers spread brocades before the door.
Jadelike grass emits fragrance beside the bridge.
On ridges protruding grow moist green lichens;
On hanging cliffs cling the long blue mosses.
The cries of immortal cranes are often heard.
Once in a while a phoenix soars overhead.
When the cranes cry,
Their sounds reach through the marsh to the distant sky.
When the phoenix soars up,
Its plume with five bright colors embroiders the clouds.
Black apes and white deer may come or hide;
Gold lions and jade elephants may leave or bide.
Look with care at this blessed, holy place:
It has the true semblance of Paradise.

He noticed that the door of the cave was tightly shut; all was quiet, and there was no sign of any human inhabitant. He turned around and suddenly perceived, at the top of the cliff, a stone slab approximately eight feet wide and over thirty feet tall. On it was written in large letters:

The Mountain of Mind and Heart;
The Cave of Slanting Moon and Three Stars.

Immensely pleased, the Handsome Monkey King said, "People here are truly honest. This mountain and this cave really do exist!" He stared at the place for a long time but dared not knock. Instead, he jumped onto the branch of a pine tree, picked a few pine seeds and ate them, and began to play.

After a moment he heard the door of the cave open with a squeak, and an immortal youth walked out. His bearing was exceedingly graceful; his features were highly refined. This was certainly no ordinary young mortal, for he had

His hair bound with two cords of silk,
A wide robe with two sleeves of wind.
His body and face seemed most distinct,
For visage and mind were both detached.
Long a stranger to all worldly things

He was the mountain's ageless boy.
Untainted even with a speck of dust,
He feared no havoc by the seasons wrought.

After coming through the door, the boy shouted, "Who is causing disturbance here?" With a bound the Monkey King leaped down from the tree,
and went up to him bowing. "Immortal boy," he said, "I am a seeker of
the way of immortality. I would never dare cause any disturbance." With
a chuckle, the immortal youth asked, "Are you a seeker of the Way?" "I
am indeed," answered the Monkey King. "My master at the house," the
boy said, "has just left his couch to give a lecture on the platform. Before
even announcing his theme, however, he told me to go out and open the
door, saying, 'There is someone outside who wants to practice austerities.
You may go and receive him.' It must be you, I suppose." The Monkey
King said, smiling, "It is I, most assuredly!" "Follow me in then," said
the boy. With solemnity the Monkey King set his clothes in order and
followed the boy into the depths of the cave. They passed rows and rows
of lofty towers and huge alcoves, of pearly chambers and carved arches.
After walking through innumerable quiet chambers and empty studios,
they finally reached the base of the green jade platform. Patriarch Subodhi
was seen seated solemnly on the platform, with thirty lesser immortals
standing below in rows. He was truly

An immortal of great ken and purest mien,
Master Subodhi, whose wondrous form of the West
Had no end or birth for the work of Double Three.
His whole spirit and breath were with mercy filled.
Empty, spontaneous, it could change at will,
His Buddha-nature able to do all things.
The same age as Heaven had his majestic frame.
Fully tried and enlightened was this grand priest.

As soon as the Handsome Monkey King saw him, he prostrated himself
and kowtowed times without number, saying, "Master! Master! I, your
pupil, pay you my sincere homage." The Patriarch said, "Where do you
come from? Let's hear you state clearly your name and country before
you kowtow again." The Monkey King said, "Your pupil came from the
Water-Curtain Cave of the Flower-Fruit Mountain, in the Aolai Country
of the East Pūrvavideha Continent." "Chase him out of here!" the Patriarch shouted. "He is nothing but a liar and a fabricator of falsehood. How
can he possibly be interested in attaining enlightenment?" The Monkey
King hastened to kowtow unceasingly and to say, "Your pupil's word is
an honest one, without any deceit." The Patriarch said, "If you are telling

the truth, how is it that you mention the East Pūrvavideha Continent? Separating that place and mine are two great oceans and the entire region of the South Jambūdvīpa Continent. How could you possibly get here?" Again kowtowing, the Monkey King said, "Your pupil drifted across the oceans and trudged through many regions for more than ten years before finding this place." The Patriarch said, "If you have come on a long journey in many stages, I'll let that pass. What is your *xing*?"[5] The Monkey King again replied," I have no *xing*. If a man rebukes me, I am not offended; if he hits me, I am not angered. In fact, I simply repay him with a ceremonial greeting and that's all. My whole life's without ill temper." "I'm not speaking of your temper," the Patriarch said, "I'm asking after the name of your parents." "I have no parents either," said the Monkey King. The Patriarch said, "If you have no parents, you must have been born from a tree." "Not from a tree," said the Monkey King, "but from a rock. I recall that there used to be an immortal stone on the Flower-Fruit Mountain. I was born the year the stone split open."

When the Patriarch heard this, he was secretly pleased, and said, "Well, evidently you have been created by Heaven and Earth. Get up and show me how you walk." Snapping erect, the Monkey King scurried around a couple of times. The Patriarch laughed and said, "Though your features are not the most attractive, you do resemble a monkey (*husun*) that feeds on pine seeds. This gives me the idea of deriving your surname from your appearance. I intended to call you by the name *Hu*. Now, when the accompanying animal radical is dropped from this word, what's left is a compound made up of the two characters, *gu* and *yue*. *Gu* means aged and *yue* means female, but an aged female cannot reproduce. Therefore, it is better to give you the surname of *Sun*. When the accompanying animal radical is dropped from this word, we have the compound of *zi* and *xi*. *Zi* means a boy and *xi* means a baby, so that the name exactly accords with the Doctrine of the Baby. So your surname will be 'Sun.'"

When the Monkey King heard this, he was filled with delight. "Splendid! Splendid!" he cried, kowtowing, "At last I know my surname. May the master be even more gracious! Since I have received the surname, let me be given also a personal name, so that it may facilitate your calling and commanding me." The Patriarch said, "Within my tradition are twelve

---

5. A pun on the words "surname" and "temper," both of which are pronounced *xing*, but are written with a different radical to the left of the Chinese graphs. The Patriarch asked for Monkey's surname, but Monkey heard it as a remark about his "temper."

characters which have been used to name the pupils according to their divisions. You are one who belongs to the tenth generation." "Which twelve characters are they?" asked the Monkey King. The Patriarch said, "They are: wide (*guang*), great (*da*), wise (*zhi*), intelligence (*hui*), true (*zhen*), conforming (*ru*), nature (*xing*), sea (*hai*), sharp (*ying*), wake-to (*wu*), complete (*yuan*), and awakening (*jue*). Your rank falls precisely on the word 'wake-to' (*wu*). You will hence be given the religious name 'Wake-to-Vacuity' (*wukong*). All right?" "Splendid! Splendid!" said the Monkey King, laughing, "henceforth I shall be called Sun Wukong." So it was thus:

> At nebula's first clearing there was no name;
> Smashing stubborn vacuity requires wake-to-vacuity.

We do not know what fruit of Daoist cultivation he succeeded in attaining afterward; let's listen to the explanation in the next chapter.

TWO

Having fully awakened to Bodhi's wondrous truths,
Cut Māra, return to the root, and fuse the primal spirit.[1]

Now we were speaking of the Handsome Monkey King, who, having received his name, jumped about joyfully and went forward to give Subodhi his grateful salutation. The Patriarch then ordered the congregation to lead Sun Wukong outdoors and to teach him how to sprinkle water on the ground and dust, and how to speak and move with proper courtesy. The company of immortals obediently went outside with Wukong, who then bowed to his fellow students. They prepared thereafter a place in the corridor where he might sleep. Next morning he began to learn from his schoolmates the arts of language and etiquette. He discussed with them the scriptures and the doctrines; he practiced calligraphy and burned incense. Such was his daily routine. In more leisurely moments he would be sweeping the grounds or hoeing the garden, planting flowers or pruning trees. gathering firewood or lighting fires, fetching water or carrying drinks. He did not lack for whatever he needed, and thus he lived in the cave without realizing that six or seven years had slipped by. One day the Patriarch ascended the platform and took his high seat. Calling together all the immortals, he began to lecture on a great doctrine. He spoke

With words so florid and eloquent
That gold lotus sprang up from the ground.
The doctrine of three vehicles he subtly rehearsed
Including even the laws' minutest tittle.
The yak's-tail waved slowly and spouted elegance:
His thunderous voice moved e'en the Ninth Heaven.
For a while he lectured on Dao;
For a while he spoke on Chan—

1. In Buddhism, *māra* has the meaning of the Destroyer, the Evil One, and the Hinderer. The Chinese term *mo* traditionally used to translate it also has the meaning of demon.

To harmonize the Three Schools [2] *is a natural thing.*
One word's elucidation in accord with truth
Leads to birthlessness and knowledge most profound.

Wukong, who was standing there and listening, was so pleased with the talk that he scratched his ear and rubbed his jaw. Grinning from ear to ear, he could not refrain from dancing on all fours! Suddenly the Patriarch saw this and called out to him, "Why are you madly jumping and dancing in the ranks and not listening to my lecture?" Wukong said, "Your pupil was devoutly listening to the lecture. But when I heard such wonderful things from my reverend master, I couldn't contain myself for joy and started to leap and prance about quite unconsciously. May the master forgive my sins!" "Let me ask you," said the Patriarch, "if you comprehend these wonderful things, do you know how long you have been in this cave?" Wukong said, "Your pupil is basically feeble-minded and does not know the number of seasons. I only remember that whenever the fire burned out in the stove, I would go to the back of the mountain to gather firewood. Finding a mountainful of fine peach trees there, I have eaten my fill of peaches seven times." The Patriarch said, "That mountain is named the Ripe Peach Mountain. If you have eaten your fill seven times, I suppose it must have been seven years. What kind of Daoist art would you like to learn from me?" Wukong said, "I am dependent on the admonition of my honored teacher. Your pupil would gladly learn whatever has a smidgen of Daoist flavor."

The Patriarch said, "Within the tradition of Dao, there are three hundred and sixty heteronomous divisions, all the practices of which may result in Illumination. I don't know which division you would like to follow." "I am dependent on the will of my honored teacher," said Wukong, "your pupil is wholeheartedly obedient." "How would it be," said the Patriarch, "if I taught you the practice of the Art division?" Wukong asked, "How would you explain the practice of the Art division?" "The practice of the Art division," said the Patriarch, "consists of summoning immortals and working the planchette, of divination by manipulating yarrow stalks, and of learning the secrets of pursuing good and avoiding evil." "Can this sort of practice lead to immortality?" asked Wukong. "Impossible! Impossible!" said the Patriarch. "I won't learn it then," Wukong said.

"How would it be," said the Patriarch again, "if I taught you the practice of the Schools division?" "What is the meaning of the Schools division?" asked Wukong. "The Schools division," the Patriarch said, "includes the

2. I.e., Confucianism, Daoism, and Buddhism.

Confucians, the Buddhists, the Daoists, the Dualists, the Mohists, and the Physicians. They read scriptures or recite prayers; they interview priests or conjure up saints and the like." "Can this sort of practice lead to immortality?" asked Wukong. The Patriarch said, "If immortality is what you desire, this practice is like setting a pillar inside a wall." Wukong said, "Master, I'm a simple fellow and I don't know the idioms of the marketplace. What's setting a pillar inside a wall?" The Patriarch said, "When people build houses and want them to be sturdy, they place a pillar as a prop inside the wall. But someday the big mansion will decay, and the pillar too will rot." "What you're saying then," Wukong said, "is that it is not long-lasting. I'm not going to learn this."

The Patriarch said, "How would it be if I taught you the practice of the Silence division?" "What's the aim of the Silence division?" Wukong asked. "To cultivate fasting and abstinence," said the Patriarch, "quiescence and inactivity, meditation and the art of cross-legged sitting, restraint of language and a vegetarian diet. There are also the practices of yoga, exercises standing or prostrate, entrance into complete stillness, contemplation in solitary confinement, and the like." "Can these activities," asked Wukong, "bring about immortality?" "They are no better than the unfired bricks on the kiln." said the Patriarch. Wukong laughed and said, "Master indeed loves to beat about the bush! Haven't I just told you that I don't know these idioms of the marketplace? What do you mean by the unfired bricks on the kiln?" The Patriarch said, "The tiles and the bricks on the kiln may have been molded into shape, but if they have not been refined by water and fire, a heavy rain will one day make them crumble." "So this too lacks permanence," said Wukong. "I don't want to learn it."

The Patriarch said, "How would it be if I taught you the practice of the Action division?" "What's it like in the Action division?" Wukong asked. "Plenty of activities," said the Patriarch, "such as gathering the yin to nourish the yang, bending the bow and treading the arrow, and rubbing the navel to pass breath. There are also experimentation with alchemical formulas, burning rushes and forging cauldrons, taking red lead, making autumn stone, and drinking bride's milk and the like." "Can such bring about long life?" asked Wukong. "To obtain immortality from such activities," said the Patriarch, "is also like scooping the moon from the water." "There you go again, Master!" cried Wukong. "What do you mean by scooping the moon from the water?" The Patriarch said, "When the moon is high in the sky, its reflection is in the water. Although it is visible therein, you cannot scoop it out or catch hold of it, for it is but an illusion." "I won't learn that either!" said Wukong.

When the Patriarch heard this, he uttered a cry and jumped down from the high platform. He pointed the ruler he held in his hands at Wukong and said to him: "What a mischievous monkey you are! You won't learn this and you won't learn that! Just what is it that you are waiting for?" Moving forward, he hit Wukong three times on the head. Then he folded his arms behind his back and walked inside, closing the main doors behind him and leaving the congregation stranded outside. Those who were listening to the lecture were so terrified that everyone began to berate Wukong. "You reckless ape!" they cried, "you're utterly without manners! The master was prepared to teach you magic secrets. Why weren't you willing to learn? Why did you have to argue with him instead? Now you have offended him, and who knows when he'll come out again?" At that moment they all resented him and despised and ridiculed him. But Wukong was not angered in the least and only replied with a broad grin. For the Monkey King, in fact, had already solved secretly, as it were, the riddle in the pot; he therefore did not quarrel with the other people but patiently held his tongue. He reasoned that the master, by hitting him three times, was telling him to prepare himself for the third watch; and by folding his arms behind his back, walking inside, and closing the main doors, was telling him to enter by the back door so that he might receive instruction in secret.

Wukong spent the rest of the day happily with the other pupils in front of the Divine Cave of the Three Stars, eagerly waiting for the night. When evening arrived, he immediately retired with all the others, pretending to be asleep by closing his eyes, breathing evenly, and remaining completely still. Since there was no watchman in the mountain to beat the watch or call the hour, he could not tell what time it was. He could only rely on his own calculations by counting the breaths he inhaled and exhaled. Approximately at the hour of Zi,[3] he arose very quietly and put on his clothes. Stealthily opening the front door, he slipped away from the crowd and walked outside. Lifting his head, he saw

The bright moon and the cool, clear dew:
In each corner was not a speck of dust.
Secluded fowls rested deep in the woods;
A brook flowed gently from its source.
The glow of darting fireflies dispersed the gloom.
Wild geese passed in calligraphic columns through the clouds.
Precisely it was the third-watch hour—
Time to seek the Truth, the Perfect Way.

3. The period from 11:00 p.m. to 1:00 a.m.

You see him following the familiar path back to the rear entrance, where he discovered that the door was, indeed, ajar. Wukong said happily, "The reverend master truly intended to give me instruction. That's why the door was left open." He reached the door in a few large strides and entered sideways. Walking up to the Patriarch's bed, he found him asleep with his body curled up, facing the wall. Wukong dared not disturb him; instead, he knelt before his bed. After a little while, the Patriarch awoke. Stretching his legs, he recited to himself:

"Hard! Hard! Hard!
The Way is most obscure!
Deem not the gold elixir a common thing.
Dark mysteries imparted to an imperfect man
Would void the words, tire the mouth, and dry the tongue!"

"Master," Wukong responded at once. "Your pupil has been kneeling here and waiting on you for a long time." When the Patriarch heard Wukong's voice, he rose and put on his clothes. "You mischievous monkey!" he exclaimed, sitting down cross-legged, "Why aren't you sleeping in front? What are you doing back here at my place?" Wukong replied, "Before the platform and the congregation yesterday, the master gave the order that your pupil, at the hour of the third watch, should come here through the rear entrance in order that he might be instructed. I was therefore bold enough to come directly to the master's bed."

When the Patriarch heard this, he was terribly pleased, thinking to himself, "This fellow is indeed an offspring of Heaven and Earth. If not, how could he solve so readily the riddle in my pot!" "There is no one here save your pupil," Wukong said. "May the master be exceedingly merciful and impart to me the way of long life. I shall never forget this gracious favor." "Since you have solved the riddle in the pot," said the Patriarch, "it is an indication that you are destined to learn, and I am glad to teach you. Come closer and listen carefully. I will impart to you the wondrous way of long life." Wukong kowtowed to express his gratitude, washed his ears, and listened most attentively, kneeling before the bed. The Patriarch said:

"This bold, secret saying that's wondrous and true:
Spare, nurse nature and life—there's nothing else.
All power resides in the semen, breath, and spirit;
Store these securely lest there be a leak.
Lest there be a leak!
Keep within the body!
Heed my teaching and the Way itself will thrive.
Hold fast the oral formulas so effective

To purge concupiscence, to reach pure cool;
To pure cool
Where the light is bright.
You'll face the elixir platform, enjoying the moon.
The moon holds the jade rabbit, the sun, the crow;
The tortoise and snake are now tightly entwined.
Tightly entwined,
Nature and life are strong.
You can plant gold lotus e'en in the midst of flames.
Squeeze the Five Phases jointly, use them back and forth—
When that's done, be a Buddha or immortal at will!"

At that moment, the very origin was revealed to Wukong, whose mind became spiritualized as happiness came to him. He carefully committed to memory all the oral formulas. After kowtowing to thank the Patriarch, he left by the rear entrance. As he went out, he saw that

The eastern sky began to pale with light,
But golden beams shone on the Westward Way.

Following the same path, he returned to the front door, pushed it open quietly, and went inside. He sat up in his sleeping place and purposely rustled the bed and the covers, crying "It's light! It's light! Get up!" All the other people were still sleeping and did not know that Wukong had received a good thing. He played the fool that day after getting up, but he persisted in what he had learned secretly by doing breathing exercises before the hour of Zi and after the hour of Wu.[4]

Three years went by swiftly, and the Patriarch again mounted his throne to lecture to the multitude. He discussed the scholastic deliberations and parables, and he discoursed on the integument of external conduct. Suddenly he asked, "Where's Wukong?" Wukong drew near and knelt down. "Your pupil's here," he said. "What sort of art have you been practicing lately?" the Patriarch asked. "Recently," Wukong said, "your pupil has begun to apprehend the nature of all things and my foundational knowledge has become firmly established." "If you have penetrated to the dharma nature to apprehend the origin," said the Patriarch, "you have, in fact, entered into the divine substance. You need, however, to guard against the danger of three calamities." When Wukong heard this, he thought for a long time and said, "The words of the master must be erroneous. I have frequently heard that when one is learned in the Way and excels in virtue, he will enjoy the same age as Heaven; fire and water cannot harm

4. The period from 11:00 a.m. to 1:00 p.m.

him and every kind of disease will vanish. How can there be this danger of three calamities?"

"What you have learned," said the Patriarch, "is no ordinary magic: you have stolen the creative powers of Heaven and Earth and invaded the dark mysteries of the sun and moon. Your success in mixing the elixir is something that the gods and the demons cannot countenance. Though your appearance will be preserved and your age lengthened, after five hundred years Heaven will send down the calamity of thunder to strike you. Hence you must be intelligent and wise enough to avoid it ahead of time. If you can escape it, your age will indeed equal that of Heaven; if not, your life will thus be finished. After another five hundred years Heaven will send down the calamity of fire to burn you. That fire is neither natural nor common fire; its name is the Fire of Yin, and it arises from within the soles of your feet to reach even the cavity of your heart, reducing your entrails to ashes and your limbs to utter ruin. The arduous labor of a millennium will then have been made completely superfluous. After another five hundred years the calamity of wind will be sent to blow at you. It is not the wind from the north, south, east, or west; nor is it one of the winds of four seasons; nor is it the wind of flowers, willows, pines, and bamboos. It is called the Mighty Wind, and it enters from the top of the skull into the body, passes through the midriff and penetrates the nine apertures. The bones and the flesh will be dissolved and the body itself will disintegrate. You must therefore avoid all three calamities."

When Wukong heard this, his hair stood on end, and, kowtowing reverently, he said, "I beg the master to be merciful and impart to me the method to avoid the three calamities. To the very end, I shall never forget your gracious favor." The Patriarch said, "It is not, in fact, difficult, except that I cannot teach you because you are somewhat different from other people." "I have a round head pointing to Heaven," said Wukong, "and square feet walking on Earth. Similarly, I have nine apertures and four limbs, entrails and cavities. In what way am I different from other people?" The Patriarch said, "Though you resemble a man, you have much less jowl." The monkey, you see, has an angular face with hollow cheeks and a pointed mouth. Stretching his hand to feel himself, Wukong laughed and said, "The master does not know how to balance matters! Though I have much less jowl than human beings, I have my pouch, which may certainly be considered a compensation."

"Very well, then," said the Patriarch, "what method of escape would you like to learn? There is the Art of the Heavenly Ladle, which numbers thirty-six transformations, and there is the Art of the Earthly Multitude, which numbers seventy-two transformations." Wukong said, "Your pupil is always eager to catch more fishes, so I'll learn the Art of the Earthly Multitude." "In that case," said the Patriarch, "come up here, and I'll pass on the oral formulas to you." He then whispered something into his ear, though we do not know what sort of wondrous secrets he spoke of. But this Monkey King was someone who, knowing one thing, could understand a hundred! He immediately learned the oral formulas and, after working at them and practicing them himself, he mastered all seventy-two transformations.

One day when the Patriarch and the various pupils were admiring the evening view in front of the Three Stars Cave, the master asked, "Wukong, has that matter been perfected?" Wukong said, "Thanks to the profound kindness of the master, your pupil has indeed attained perfection; I now can ascend like mist into the air and fly." The Patriarch said, "Let me see you try to fly." Wishing to display his ability, Wukong leaped fifty or sixty feet into the air, pulling himself up with a somersault. He trod on the clouds for about the time of a meal and traveled a distance of no more than three miles before dropping down again to stand before the Patriarch. "Master," he said, his hands folded in front of him, "this is flying by cloud-soaring." Laughing, the Patriarch said, "This can't be called cloud-soaring! It's more like cloud-crawling! The old saying goes, 'The immortal tours the North Sea in the morning and reaches Cangwu by night.' If it takes you half a day to go less than three miles, it can't even be considered cloud-crawling."

"What do you mean," asked Wukong, "by saying, 'The immortal tours the North Sea in the morning and reaches Cangwu by night'?" The Patriarch said, "Those who are capable of cloud-soaring may start from the North Sea in the morning, journey through the East Sea, the West Sea, the South Sea, and return again to Cangwu. Cangwu refers to Lingling in the North Sea. It can be called true cloud-soaring only when you can traverse all four seas in one day." "That's truly difficult!" said Wukong, "truly difficult!" "Nothing in the world is difficult," said the Patriarch; "only the mind makes it so." When Wukong heard these words, he kowtowed reverently and implored the Patriarch, "Master, if you do perform a service for someone, you must do it thoroughly. May you be most merciful and impart to me also this technique of cloud-soaring. I would never dare forget your gracious favor." The Patriarch said, "When the various immortals want to soar on the clouds, they all rise by stamping their feet. But you're not like them. When I saw you leave just now, you had to pull yourself up by jumping. What I'll do now is to teach you the cloud-somersault in accordance with your form." Wukong again prostrated himself and pleaded with him, and the Patriarch gave him an oral formula, saying,

"Make the magic sign, recite the spell, clench your fist tightly, shake your body, and when you jump up, one somersault will carry you a hundred and eight thousand miles." When the other people heard this, they all giggled and said, "Lucky Wukong! If he learns this little trick, he can become a dispatcher for someone to deliver documents or carry circulars. He'll be able to make a living anywhere!"

The sky now began to darken, and the master went back to the cave dwelling with his pupils. Throughout the night, however, Wukong practiced ardently and mastered the technique of cloud-somersault. From then on, he had complete freedom, blissfully enjoying his state of long life.

One day early in the summer, the disciples were gathered under the pine trees for fellowship and discussion. They said to him, "Wukong, what sort of merit did you accumulate in another incarnation that led the master to whisper in your ear, the other day, the method of avoiding the three calamities? Have you learned everything?" "I won't conceal this from my various elder brothers," Wukong said, laughing. "Owing to the master's instruction in the first place and my diligence day and night in the second, I have fully mastered the several matters!" "Let's take advantage of the moment," one of the pupils said. "You try to put on a performance and we'll watch." When Wukong heard this, his spirit was aroused and he was most eager to display his powers. "I invite the various elder brothers to give me a subject," he said. "What do you want me to change into?" "Why not a pine tree?" they said. Wukong made the magic sign and recited the spell; with one shake of his body he changed himself into a pine tree. Truly it was

Thickly held in smoke through all four seasons,
Its chaste fair form soars straight to the clouds.
With not the least likeness to the impish monkey,
It's all frost-tried and snow-tested branches.

When the multitude saw this, they clapped their hands and roared with laughter, everyone crying, "Marvelous monkey! Marvelous monkey!" They did not realize that all this uproar had disturbed the Patriarch, who came running out of the door, dragging his staff. "Who is creating this bedlam here?" he demanded. At his voice the pupils immediately collected themselves, set their clothes in order, and came forward. Wukong also changed back into his true form, and, slipping into the crowd, he said, "For your information, Reverend Master, we are having fellowship and discussion here. There is no one from outside causing any disturbance." "You were all yelling and screaming," said the Patriarch angrily, "and were behaving in a manner totally unbecoming to those practicing cultivation. Don't you know that those in the cultivation of Dao resist

Opening their mouths lest they waste their breath and spirit,
Or moving their tongues lest they provoke arguments?

Why are you all laughing noisily here?" "We dare not conceal this from the master," the crowd said. "Just now we were having fun with Wukong, who was giving us a performance of transformation. We told him to change into a pine tree, and he did indeed become a pine tree! Your pupils were all applauding him and our voices disturbed the reverend teacher. We beg his forgiveness."

"Go away, all of you," the Patriarch said. "You, Wukong, come over here! I ask you what sort of exhibition were you putting on, changing into a pine tree? This ability you now possess, is it just for showing off to people? Suppose you saw someone with this ability. Wouldn't you ask him at once how he acquired it? So when others see that you are in possession of it, they'll come begging. If you're afraid to refuse them, you will give away the secret; if you don't, they may hurt you. You are actually placing your life in grave jeopardy." "I beseech the master to forgive me," Wukong said kowtowing. "I won't condemn you," said the Patriarch, "but you must leave this place." When Wukong heard this, tears fell from his eyes. "Where am I to go, Teacher?" he asked. "From wherever you came," the Patriarch said, "you should go back there." "I came from the East Pūrvavideha Continent," Wukong said, his memory jolted by the Patriarch, "from the Water-Curtain Cave of the Flower-Fruit Mountain in the Aolai Country." "Go back there quickly and save your life," the Patriarch said. "You cannot possibly remain here!" "Allow me to inform my esteemed teacher," said Wukong, properly penitent, "I have been away from home for twenty years, and I certainly long to see my subjects and followers of bygone days again. But I keep thinking that my master's profound kindness to me has not yet been repaid. I, therefore, dare not leave." "There's nothing to be repaid," said the Patriarch. "See that you don't get into trouble and involve me: that's all I ask."

Seeing that there was no other alternative, Wukong had to bow to the Patriarch and take leave of the congregation. "Once you leave," the Patriarch said, "you're bound to end up evildoing. I don't care what kind of villainy and violence you engage in, but I forbid you ever to mention that you are my disciple. For if you but utter half the word, I'll know about it; you can be assured, wretched monkey, that you'll be skinned alive. I will break all your bones and banish your soul to the Place of Ninefold Darkness, from which you will not be released even after ten thousand afflictions!" "I will never dare mention my master," said Wukong. "I'll say that I've learned this all by myself." Having thanked the Patriarch, Wukong turned away, made the magic sign, pulled himself up, and performed the cloud-somersault. He headed straight toward the East Pūrvavideha, and in less than an hour he could already see the Flower-Fruit Mountain and the Water-Curtain Cave. Rejoicing secretly, the Handsome Monkey King said to himself:

> *"I left weighed down by bones of mortal stock.*
> *The Dao attained makes light both body and frame.*
> *'Tis this world's pity that none firmly resolves*
> *To learn such mystery that by itself is plain.*
> *'Twas hard to cross the seas in former time.*
> *Returning this day, I travel with ease.*
> *Words of farewell still echo in my ears.*
> *I ne'er hope to see so soon the eastern depths!"*

Wukong lowered the direction of his cloud and landed squarely on the Flower-Fruit Mountain. He was trying to find his way when he heard the call of cranes and the cry of monkeys; the call of cranes reverberated in the Heavens, and the cry of monkeys moved his spirit with sadness. "Little ones," he called out, "I have returned!" From the crannies of the cliff, from the flowers and bushes, and from the woods and trees, monkeys great and small leaped out by the tens of thousands and surrounded the Handsome Monkey King. They all kowtowed and cried, "Great King! What laxity of mind! Why did you go away for such a long time and leave us here longing for your return like someone hungering and thirsting? Recently, we have been brutally abused by a monster, who wanted to rob us of our Water-Curtain Cave. Out of sheer desperation, we fought hard with him. And yet all this time, that fellow has plundered many of our possessions, kidnaped a number of our young ones, and given us many restless days and nights watching over our property. How fortunate that our great king has returned! If the great king had stayed away another year or so, we and the entire mountain cave would have belonged to someone else!"

Hearing this, Wukong was filled with anger. "What sort of a monster is this," he cried, "that behaves in such a lawless manner? Tell me in detail and I will find him to exact vengeance." "Be informed, Great King," the monkeys said, kowtowing, "that the fellow calls himself the Monstrous King of Havoc, and he lives north of here." Wukong said, "From here to his place, how great is the distance?" The monkeys said, "He comes like the cloud and leaves like the mist, like the wind and the rain, like lightning and thunder. We don't know how great the distance is." "In that case," said Wukong, "go and play for a while and don't be afraid. Let me go and find him."

Dear Monkey King! He leaped up with a bound and somersaulted all the way northward until he saw a tall and rugged mountain. What a mountain!

Its penlike peak stands erect;
Its winding streams flow unfathomed and deep.
Its penlike peak, standing erect, cuts through the air;
Its winding streams, unfathomed and deep, reach diverse sites on earth.
On two ridges flowers rival trees in exotic charm;
At various spots pines match bamboos in green.
The dragon on the left
Seems docile and tame;
The tiger on the right
Seems gentle and meek.
Iron oxen[5]
On occasion are seen plowing.
Gold-coin flowers are frequently planted.
Rare fowls make melodious songs;
The phoenix stands facing the sun.
Rocks worn smooth and shiny
By water placid and bright
Appear by turns grotesque, bizarre, and fierce.
In countless numbers are the world's famous mountains
Where flowers bloom and wither; they flourish and die.
What place resembles this long-lasting scene
Wholly untouched by the four seasons and eight epochs?
This is, in the Three Regions, the Mount of Northern Spring,
The Water-Belly Cave, nourished by the Five Phases.

The Handsome Monkey King was silently viewing the scenery when he heard someone speaking. He went down the mountain to find who it was, and he discovered the Water-Belly Cave at the foot of a steep cliff. Several imps who were dancing in front of the cave saw Wukong and began to run away. "Stop!" cried Wukong. "You can use the words of your mouth to communicate the thoughts of my mind. I am the lord of the Water-Curtain Cave in the Flower-Fruit Mountain south of here. Your Monstrous King of Havoc, or whatever he's called, has repeatedly bullied my young ones, and I have found my way here with the specific purpose of settling matters with him."

5. Oxen made of cast iron were placed in streams or fields; farmers used them as a charm to prevent floods.

Hearing this, the imps darted into the cave and cried out, "Great King, a disastrous thing has happened!" "What sort of disaster?" asked the Monstrous King. "Outside the cave," said the imps, "there is a monkey who calls himself the lord of the Water-Curtain Cave in the Flower-Fruit Mountain. He says that you have repeatedly bullied his young ones and that he has come to settle matters with you." Laughing, the Monstrous King said, "I have often heard those monkeys say that they have a great king who has left the family to practice self-cultivation. He must have come back. How is he dressed, and what kind of weapon does he have?" "He doesn't have any kind of weapon," the imps said. "He is bare-headed, wears a red robe with a yellow sash, and has a pair of black boots on. He looks like neither a monk nor a layman, neither a Daoist nor an immortal. He is out there making demands with naked hands and empty fists." When the Monstrous King heard this, he ordered, "Get me my armor and my weapon." These were immediately brought out by the imps, and the Monstrous King put on his breastplate and helmet, grasped his scimitar, and walked out of the cave with his followers. "Who is the lord of the Water-Curtain Cave?" he cried with a loud voice. Quickly opening wide his eyes to take a look, Wukong saw that the Monstrous King

Wore on his head a black gold helmet
Which gleamed in the sun;
And on his body a dark silk robe
Which swayed in the wind;
Lower he had on a black iron vest
Tied tightly with leather straps;
His feet were shod in finely carved boots,
Grand as those of warriors great.
Ten spans—the width of his waist;
Thirty feet—the height of his frame;
He held in his hands a sword;
Its blade was fine and bright.
His name: the Monster of Havoc
Of most fearsome form and look.

"You have such big eyes, reckless monster, but you can't even see old Monkey!" the Monkey King shouted. When the Monstrous King saw him, he laughed and said, "You're not four feet tall, nor are you thirty years old; you don't even have weapons in your hands. How dare you be so insolent, looking for me to settle accounts?" "You reckless monster!" cried Wukong. "You are blind indeed! You think I'm small, not knowing that it's hardly difficult for me to become taller; you think I'm without weapon, but my two hands can drag the moon down from the edge of Heaven. Don't be afraid; just have a taste of old Monkey's fist!" He leaped into the air and aimed a blow smack at the monster's face. Parrying the blow with his hand, the Monstrous King said, "You are such a midget and I'm so tall; you want to use your fist but I have my scimitar. If I were to kill you with it, I would be a laughingstock. Let me put down my scimitar, and we'll see how well you can box." "Well said, fine fellow," replied Wukong. "Come on!"

The Monstrous King shifted his position and struck out. Wukong closed in on him, hurtling himself into the engagement. The two of them pummeled and kicked, struggling and colliding with each other. Now it's easy to miss on a long reach, but a short punch is firm and reliable. Wukong jabbed the Monstrous King in the short ribs, hit him on his chest, and gave him such heavy punishment with a few sharp blows that the monster stepped aside, picked up his huge scimitar, aimed it straight at Wukong's head, and slashed at him. Wukong dodged, and the blow narrowly missed him. Seeing that his opponent was growing fiercer, Wukong now used the method called the Body beyond the Body. Plucking a handful of hairs from his own body and throwing them into his mouth, he chewed them to tiny pieces and then spat them into the air. "Change!" he cried, and they changed at once into two or three hundred little monkeys encircling the combatants on all sides. For you see, when someone acquires the body of an immortal, he can project his spirit, change his form, and perform all kinds of wonders. Since the Monkey King had become accomplished in the Way, every one of the eighty-four thousand hairs on his body could change into whatever shape or substance he desired. The little monkeys he had just created were so keen of eye and so swift of movement that they could be wounded by neither sword nor spear. Look at them! Skipping and jumping, they rushed at the Monstrous King and surrounded him, some hugging, some pulling, some crawling in between his legs, some tugging at his feet. They kicked and punched; they yanked at his hair and poked at his eyes; they pinched his nose and tried to sweep him completely off his feet, until they tangled themselves into confusion.

Meanwhile Wukong succeeded in snatching the scimitar, pushed through the throng of little monkeys, and brought the scimitar down squarely onto the monster's skull, cleaving it in two. He and the rest of the monkeys then fought their way into the cave and slaughtered all the imps, young and old. With a shake, he collected his hair back onto his body, but there were some monkeys that did not return to him. They were the little monkeys kidnaped by the Monstrous King from the Water-Curtain Cave.

"Why are you here?" asked Wukong. The thirty or fifty of them all said tearfully, "After the Great King went away to seek the way of immortality, the monster menaced us for two whole years and finally carried us off to this place. Don't these utensils belong to our cave? These stone pots and bowls were all taken by the creature." "If these are our belongings," said Wukong, "move them out of here." He then set fire to the Water-Belly Cave and reduced it to ashes. "All of you," he said to them, "follow me home." "Great King," the monkeys said, "when we came here, all we felt was wind rushing past us, and we seemed to float through the air until we arrived here. We don't know the way. How can we go back to our home?" Wukong said, "That's a magic trick of his. But there's no difficulty! Now I know not only one thing but a hundred! I'm familiar with that trick too. Close your eyes, all of you, and don't be afraid."

Dear Monkey King. He recited a spell, rode for a while on a fierce wind, and then lowered the direction of the cloud. "Little ones," he cried, "open your eyes!" The monkeys felt solid ground beneath their feet and recognized their home territory. In great delight, every one of them ran back to the cave along the familiar roads and crowded in together with those waiting in the cave. They then lined up according to age and rank and paid tribute to the Monkey King. Wine and fruits were laid out for the welcome banquet. When asked how he had subdued the monster and rescued the young ones, Wukong presented a detailed rehearsal, and the monkeys broke into unending applause. "Where did you go, Great King?" they cried. "We never expected that you would acquire such skills!"

"The year I left you all," Wukong said, "I drifted with the waves across the Great Eastern Ocean and reached the West Aparagodānīya Continent. I then arrived at the South Jambūdvīpa Continent, where I learned human ways, wearing this garment and these shoes. I swaggered along with the clouds for eight or nine years, but I had yet to learn the Great Art. I then crossed the Great Western Ocean and reached the West Aparagodānīya Continent.[6] After searching for a long time, I had the good fortune to discover an old Patriarch, who imparted to me the formula for enjoying the same age as Heaven, the secret of immortality." "Such luck is hard to meet even after ten thousand afflictions!" the monkeys said, all congratulating him. "Little ones," Wukong said, laughing again, "Another delight is that our entire family now has a name."

"What is the name of the great king?"

"My surname is Sun," replied Wukong, "and my religious name is

6. An inconsistency in the text.

Wukong." When the monkeys heard this, they all clapped their hands and shouted happily, "If the great king is Elder Sun, then we are all Junior Suns, Suns the Third, small Suns, tiny Suns—the Sun Family, the Sun Nation, and the Sun Cave!" So they all came and honored Elder Sun with large and small bowls of coconut and grape wine, of divine flowers and fruits. It was indeed one big happy family! Lo,

The surname is one, the self's return'd to its source.

This glory awaits—a name recorded in Heaven!

We do not know what the result was and how Wukong fared in this territory; let's listen to the explanation in the next chapter.

THREE

The Four Seas and the Thousand Mountains all bow to submit;
From Ninefold Darkness ten species' names are removed.

Now we were speaking of the Handsome Monkey King's triumphant return to his home country. After slaying the Monstrous King of Havoc and wresting from him his huge scimitar, he practiced daily with the little monkeys the art of war, teaching them how to sharpen bamboos for making spears, how to file wood for making swords, how to arrange flags and banners, how to go on patrol, how to advance or retreat, and how to pitch camp. For a long time he played thus with them. Suddenly he grew quiet and sat down, thinking out loud to himself, "The game we are playing here may turn out to be something quite serious. Suppose we disturb the rulers of humans or of fowls and beasts, and they become offended; suppose they say that these military exercises of ours are subversive, and raise an army to destroy us. How can we meet them with our bamboo spears and wooden swords? We must have sharp swords and fine halberds. But what can be done at this moment?" When the monkeys heard this, they were all alarmed. "The great king's observation is very sound," they said, "but where can we obtain these things?" As they were speaking, four older monkeys came forward, two female monkeys with red buttocks and two bareback gibbons. Coming to the front, they said, "Great King, to be furnished with sharp-edged weapons is a very simple matter." "How is it simple?" asked Wukong. The four monkeys said, "East of our mountain, across two hundred miles of water, is the boundary of the Aolai Country. In that country there is a king who has numberless men and soldiers in his city, and there are bound to be all kinds of metalworks there. If the great king goes there, he can either buy weapons or have them made. Then you can teach us how to use them for the protection of our mountain, and this will be the stratagem for assuring ourselves of perpetuity." When Wukong heard this, he was filled with delight. "Play here, all of you," he said. "Let me make a trip."

Dear Monkey King! He quickly performed his cloud-somersault and crossed the two hundred miles of water in no time. On the other side he did indeed discover a city with broad streets and huge marketplaces, countless houses and numerous arches. Under the clear sky and bright sun, people were coming and going constantly. Wukong thought to himself, "There must be ready-made weapons around here. But going down there to buy a few pieces from them is not as good a bargain as getting them by magic." He therefore made the magic sign and recited a spell. Facing the ground on the southwest, he took a deep breath and then blew it out. At once it became a mighty wind, hurtling pebbles and rocks through the air. It was truly terrifying:

> Thick clouds in vast formation moved o'er the world;
> Black fog and dusky vapor darkened the Earth;
> Waves churned in seas and rivers, affrighting fishes and crabs;
> Boughs broke in mountain forests, wolves and tigers taking flight.
> Traders and merchants were gone from stores and shops.
> No single man was seen at sundry marts and malls.
> The king retreated to his chamber from the royal court.
> Officials, martial and civil, returned to their homes.
> This wind toppled Buddha's throne of a thousand years
> And shook to its foundations the Five-Phoenix Tower.

The wind arose and separated the king from his subjects in the Aolai Country. Throughout the various boulevards and marketplaces, every family bolted the doors and windows and no one dared go outside. Wukong then lowered the direction of his cloud and rushed straight through the imperial gate. He found his way to the armory, knocked open the doors, and saw that there were countless weapons inside. Scimitars, spears, swords, halberds, battle-axes, scythes, whips, rakes, drumsticks, drums, bows, arrows, forks, and lances—every kind was available. Highly pleased, Wukong said to himself, "How many pieces can I possibly carry by myself? I'd better use the magic of body division to transport them." Dear Monkey King! He plucked a handful of hairs, chewed them to pieces in his mouth, and spat them out. Reciting the spell, he cried, "Change!" They changed into thousands of little monkeys, which snatched and grabbed the weapons. Those that were stronger took six or seven pieces, the weaker ones two or three pieces, and together they emptied out the armory. Wukong then mounted the cloud and performed the magic of displacement by calling up a great wind, which carried all the little monkeys back to their home.

We tell you now about the various monkeys, both great and small, who were playing outside the cave of the Flower-Fruit Mountain. They suddenly heard the sound of wind and saw in midair a huge horde of monkeys approaching, the sight of which made them all flee in terror and hide. In a moment, Wukong lowered his cloud and, shaking himself, collected the pieces of hair back onto his body. All the weapons were piled in front of the mountain. "Little ones," he shouted, "come and receive your weapons." The monkeys looked and saw Wukong standing alone on level ground. They came running to kowtow and ask what had happened. Wukong then recounted to them how he had made use of the mighty wind to transport the weapons. After expressing their gratitude, the monkeys all went to grab at the scimitars and snatch at the swords, to wield the axes and scramble for spears, to stretch the bows and mount the arrows. Shouting and screaming, they played all day long.

The following day, they marched in formation as usual. Assembling the monkeys, Wukong found that there were forty-seven thousand of them. This assembly greatly impressed all the wild beasts of the mountain— wolves, insects, tigers, leopards, mouse deer, fallow deer, river deer, foxes, wild cats, badgers, lions, elephants, apes, bears, antelopes, boars, musk-oxen, chamois, green one-horn buffaloes, wild hares, and giant mastiffs. Led by the various demon kings of no fewer than seventy-two caves, they all came to pay homage to the Monkey King. Henceforth they brought annual tributes and answered the roll call made every season. Some of them joined in the maneuvers; others supplied provisions in accordance with their rank. In an orderly fashion, they made the entire Flower-Fruit Mountain as strong as an iron bucket or a city of metal. The various de-mon kings also presented metal drums, colored banners, and helmets. The hurly-burly of marching and drilling went on day after day.

While the Handsome Monkey King was enjoying all this, he suddenly said to the multitude, "You all have become adept with the bow and ar-row and proficient in the use of weapons. But this scimitar of mine is truly cumbersome, not at all to my liking. What can I do?" The four elder monkeys came forward and memorialized, "The great king is a divine sage, and therefore it is not fit for him to use an earthly weapon. We do not know, however, whether the great king is able to take a journey through water?" "Since I have known the Way," said Wukong, "I have the abil-ity of seventy-two transformations. The cloud-somersault has unlimited power. I am familiar with the magic of body concealment and the magic of displacement. I can find my way to Heaven or I can enter the Earth. I can walk past the sun and the moon without casting a shadow, and I can penetrate stone and metal without hindrance. Water cannot drown me, nor fire burn me. Is there any place I can't go to?" "It's a good thing that the great king possesses such powers," said the four monkeys, "for the water below this sheet iron bridge of ours flows directly into the Dragon Palace of the Eastern Ocean. If you are willing to go down there, Great King, you will find the old Dragon King, from whom you may request some kind of weapon. Won't that be to your liking?" Hearing this, Wukong said with delight, "Let me make the trip!"

Dear Monkey King! He jumped to the bridgehead and employed the magic of water restriction. Making the magic sign with his fingers, he leaped into the waves, which parted for him, and he followed the waterway straight to the bottom of the Eastern Ocean. As he was walking, he suddenly ran into a yakṣa[1] on patrol, who stopped him with the question, "What divine sage is this who comes pushing through the water? Speak plainly so that I can announce your arrival." Wukong said, "I am the Heaven-born sage Sun Wukong of the Flower-Fruit Mountain, a near neighbor of your old Dragon King. How is it that you don't recognize me?" When the yakṣa heard this, he hurried back to the Water-Crystal Palace to report. "Great King," he said, "there is outside a Heaven-born sage of the Flower-Fruit Mountain named Sun Wukong. He claims that he is a near neighbor of yours, and he is about to arrive at the palace." Aoguang, the Dragon King of the Eastern Ocean, arose immediately; accompanied by dragon sons and grandsons, shrimp soldiers and crab generals, he came out for the reception. "High Immortal," he said, "please come in!" They went into the palace for proper introduction, and after offering Wukong the honored seat and tea, the king asked, "When did the high immortal become accomplished in the Way, and what kind of divine magic did he receive?" Wukong said, "Since the time of my birth, I have left the family to practice self-cultivation. I have now acquired a birthless and deathless body. Recently I have been teaching my children how to protect our mountain cave, but unfortunately I am without an appropriate weapon. I have heard that my noble neighbor, who has long enjoyed living in this green-jade palace and its shell portals, must have many divine weapons to spare. I came specifically to ask for one of them."

When the Dragon King heard this, he could hardly refuse. So he ordered a perch commander to bring out a long-handled scimitar, and presented it to his visitor. "Old Monkey doesn't know how to use a scimitar," said Wukong. "I beg you to give me something else." The Dragon King then commanded a whiting lieutenant together with an eel porter to carry out

---

1. A *yakṣa* is generally thought of in Indian religions as a demon in the earth, the air, or the lower heavens. They can be violent and malignant, but in this novel, they seem to be associated much more with the oceans.

a nine-pronged fork. Jumping down from his seat, Wukong took hold of it and tried a few thrusts. He put it down, saying, "Light! Much too light! And it doesn't suit my hand. I beg you to give me another one." "High Immortal," said the Dragon King, laughing, "won't you even take a closer look? This fork weighs three thousand six hundred pounds." "It doesn't suit my hand," Wukong said, "it doesn't suit my hand!" The Dragon King was becoming rather fearful; he ordered a bream admiral and a carp brigadier to carry out a giant halberd, weighing seven thousand two hundred pounds. When he saw this, Wukong ran forward and took hold of it. He tried a few thrusts and parries and then stuck it in the ground, saying, "It's still light! Much too light!" The old Dragon King was completely unnerved. "High Immortal," he said, "there's no weapon in my palace heavier than this halberd." Laughing, Wukong said, "As the old saying goes, 'Who worries about the Dragon King's lacking treasures!' Go and look some more, and if you find something I like, I'll offer you a good price." "There really aren't any more here," said the Dragon King.

As they were speaking, the dragon mother and her daughter slipped out and said, "Great King, we can see that this is definitely not a sage with meager abilities. Inside our ocean treasury is that piece of rare magic iron by which the depth of the Heavenly River[2] is fixed. These past few days the iron has been glowing with a strange and lovely light. Could this be a sign that it should be taken out to meet this sage?" "That," said the Dragon King, "was the measure with which the Great Yu[3] fixed the depths of rivers and oceans when he conquered the Flood. It's a piece of magic iron, but of what use could it be to him?" "Let's not be concerned with whether he could find any use for it," said the dragon mother. "Let's give it to him, and he can do whatever he wants with it. The important thing is to get him out of this palace!" The old Dragon King agreed and told Wukong the whole story. "Take it out and let me see it," said Wukong. Waving his hands, the Dragon King said, "We can't move it! We can't even lift it! The high immortal must go there himself to take a look." "Where is it?" asked Wukong. "Take me there."

The Dragon King accordingly led him to the center of the ocean treasury, where all at once they saw a thousand shafts of golden light. Pointing to the spot, the Dragon King said, "That's it—the thing that is glowing." Wukong girded up his clothes and went forward to touch it: it was an iron

2. Heavenly River is the Chinese name for the Milky Way.

3. The Great Yu was the putative founder of the Xia dynasty (ca. 2205 BCE) and the mythic conqueror of the Flood in China.

rod more than twenty feet long and as thick as a barrel. Using all his might, he lifted it with both hands, saying, "It's a little too long and too thick. It would be more serviceable if it were somewhat shorter and thinner." Hardly had he finished speaking when the treasure shrunk a few feet in length and became a layer thinner. "Smaller still would be even better," said Wukong, giving it another bounce in his hands. Again the treasure became smaller. Highly pleased, Wukong took it out of the ocean treasury to examine it. He found a golden hoop at each end, with solid black iron in between. Immediately adjacent to one of the hoops was the inscription, "The Compliant Golden-Hooped Rod. Weight: thirteen thousand five hundred pounds." He thought to himself in secret delight, "This treasure, I suppose, must be most compliant with one's wishes." As he walked, he was deliberating in his mind and murmuring to himself, bouncing the rod in his hands, "Shorter and thinner still would be marvelous!" By the time he took it outside, the rod was no more than twenty feet in length and had the thickness of a rice bowl.

See how he displayed his power now! He wielded the rod to make lunges and passes, engaging in mock combat all the way back to the Water-Crystal Palace. The old Dragon King was so terrified that he shook with fear, and the dragon princes were all panic-stricken. Sea-turtles and tortoises drew in their necks; fishes, shrimps, and crabs all hid themselves. Wukong held the treasure in his hands and sat in the Water-Crystal Palace. Laughing, he said to the Dragon King, "I am indebted to my good neighbor for his profound kindness." "Please don't mention it," said the Dragon King. "This piece of iron is very useful," said Wukong, "but I have one further statement to make." "What sort of statement does the high immortal wish to make?" asked the Dragon King. Wukong said, "Had there been no such iron, I would have let the matter drop. Now that I have it in my hands, I can see that I am wearing the wrong kind of clothes to go with it. What am I to do? If you have any martial apparel, you might as well give me some too. I would thank you most heartily." "This, I confess, is not in my possession," said the Dragon King. Wukong said, "A solitary guest will not disturb two hosts. Even if you claim that you don't have any, I shall never walk out of this door." "Let the high immortal take the trouble of going to another ocean," said the Dragon King. "He might turn up something there." "To visit three homes is not as convenient as sitting in one," said Wukong, "I beg you to give me one outfit." "I really don't have one," said the Dragon King, "for if I did, I would have presented it to you." "Is that so?" said Wukong. "Let me try the iron on you!" "High Immortal," the Dragon King said nervously, "don't ever raise your hand!

Don't ever raise your hand! Let me see whether my brothers have any and we'll try to give you one." "Where are your honored brothers?" asked Wukong. "They are," said the Dragon King, "Aoqin, Dragon King of the Southern Ocean; Aoshun, Dragon King of the Northern Ocean; and Aorun, Dragon King of the Western Ocean." "Old Monkey is not going to their places," said Wukong. "For as the common saying goes, 'Three in bond can't compete with two in hand.' I'm merely requesting that you find something casual here and give it to me. That's all." "There's no need for the high immortal to go anywhere," said the Dragon King. "I have in my palace an iron drum and a golden bell. Whenever there is any emergency, we beat the drum and strike the bell and my brothers are here shortly." "In that case," said Wukong, "go beat the drum and strike the bell." The turtle general went at once to strike the bell, while the tortoise marshal came to beat the drum.

Soon after the drum and the bell had sounded, the Dragon Kings of the Three Oceans got the message and arrived promptly, all congregating in the outer courtyard. "Elder Brother," said Aoqin, "what emergency made you beat the drum and strike the bell?" "Good Brother," answered the old Dragon, "it's a long story! We have here a certain Heaven-born sage from the Flower-Fruit Mountain, who came here and claimed to be my near neighbor. He subsequently demanded a weapon; the steel fork I presented he deemed too small, and the halberd I offered too light. Finally he himself took that piece of rare, divine iron by which the depth of the Heavenly River was fixed and used it for mock combat. He is now sitting in the palace and also demanding some sort of battle dress. We have none of that here. So we sounded the drum and the bell to invite you all to come. If you happen to have some such outfit, please give it to him so that I can send him out of this door!"

When Aoqin heard this, he was outraged. "Let us brothers call our army together," he said, "and arrest him. What's wrong with that?" "Don't talk about arresting him!" the old Dragon said, "don't talk about arresting him! That piece of iron—a small stroke with it is deadly and a light tap is fatal! The slightest touch will crack the skin and a small rap will injure the muscles!" Aorun, the Dragon King of the Western Ocean, said, "Second elder brother should not raise his hand against him. Let us rather assemble an outfit for him and get him out of this place. We can then present a formal complaint to Heaven, and Heaven will send its own punishment." "You are right," said Aoshun, the Dragon King of the Northern Ocean, "I have here a pair of cloud-treading shoes the color of lotus root." Aorun, the Dragon King of the Western Ocean said, "I brought along a cuirass of chainmail made of yellow gold." "And I have a cap with erect phoenix plumes, made of red gold," said Aoqin, the Dragon King of the Southern Ocean. The old Dragon King was delighted and brought them into the Water-Crystal Palace to present the gifts. Wukong duly put on the gold cap, the gold cuirass, and cloud-treading shoes, and, wielding his compliant rod, he fought his way out in mock combat, yelling to the dragons, "Sorry to have bothered you!" The Dragon Kings of the Four Oceans were outraged, and they consulted together about filing a formal complaint, of which we make no mention here.

Look at that Monkey King! He opened up the waterway and went straight back to the head of the sheet iron bridge. The four old monkeys were leading the other monkeys and waiting beside the bridge. They suddenly beheld Wukong leaping out of the waves: there was not a drop of water on his body as he walked onto the bridge, all radiant and golden. The various monkeys were so astonished that they all knelt down, crying, "Great King, what marvels! What marvels!" Beaming broadly, Wukong ascended his high throne and set up the iron rod right in the center. Not knowing any better, the monkeys all came and tried to pick the treasure up. It was rather like a dragonfly attempting to shake an ironwood tree: they could not budge it an inch! Biting their fingers and sticking out their tongues, every one of them said, "O Father, it's so heavy! How did you ever manage to bring it here?" Wukong walked up to the rod, stretched forth his hands, and picked it up. Laughing, he said to them, "Everything has its owner. This treasure has presided in the ocean treasury for who knows how many thousands of years, and it just happened to glow recently. The Dragon King only recognized it as a piece of black iron, though it is also said to be the divine rarity which fixed the bottom of the Heavenly River. All those fellows together could not lift or move it, and they asked me to take it myself. At first, this treasure was more than twenty feet long and as thick as a barrel. After I struck it once and expressed my feeling that it was too large, it grew smaller. I wanted it smaller still, and again it grew smaller. For a third time I commanded it, and it grew smaller still! When I looked at it in the light, it had on it the inscription, 'The Compliant Golden-Hooped Rod. Weight: thirteen thousand five hundred pounds.' Stand aside, all of you. Let me ask it to go through some more transformations."

He held the treasure in his hands and called out, "Smaller, smaller, smaller!" and at once it shrank to the size of a tiny embroidery needle, small enough to be hidden inside the ear. Awe-struck, the monkeys cried, "Great King! Take it out and play with it some more." The Monkey King took it out from his ear and placed it on his palm. "Bigger, bigger, bigger!" he shouted, and again it grew to the thickness of a barrel and more than twenty feet long. He became so delighted playing with it that he jumped onto the bridge and walked out of the cave. Grasping the treasure in his hands, he began to perform the magic of cosmic imitation. He bent over and cried, "Grow!" and at once grew to be ten thousand feet tall, with a head like the Tai Mountain and a chest like a rugged peak, eyes like lightning and a mouth like a blood bowl, and teeth like swords and halberds. The rod in his hands was of such a size that its top reached the thirty-third Heaven and its bottom the eighteenth layer of Hell. Tigers, leopards, wolves, and crawling creatures, all the monsters of the mountain and the demon kings of the seventy-two caves, were so terrified that they kowtowed and paid homage to the Monkey King in fear and trembling. Presently he revoked his magical appearance and changed the treasure back into a tiny embroidery needle stored in his ear. He returned to the cave dwelling, but the demon kings of the various caves were still frightened, and they continued to come to pay their respects.

At this time, the banners were unfurled, the drums sounded, and the brass gongs struck loudly. A great banquet of a hundred delicacies was given, and the cups were filled to overflowing with the fruit of the vines and the juices of the coconut. They drank and feasted for a long time, and they engaged in military exercises as before. The Monkey King made the four old monkeys mighty commanders of his troops by appointing the two female monkeys with red buttocks as marshals Ma and Liu, and the two bareback gibbons as generals Beng and Ba. The four mighty commanders, moreover, were entrusted with all matters concerning fortification, pitching camps, reward, and punishment. Having settled all this, the Monkey King felt completely at ease to soar on the clouds and ride the mist, to tour the four seas and disport himself in a thousand mountains. Displaying his martial skill, he made extensive visits to various heroes and warriors; performing his magic, he made many good friends. At this time, moreover, he entered into fraternal alliance with six other monarchs: the Bull Monster King, the Dragon Monster King, the Garuda Monster King, the Giant Lynx King, the Macaque King, and the Orangutan King. Together with the Handsome Monkey King, they formed a fraternal order of seven. Day after day they discussed civil and military arts, exchanged wine cups and goblets, sang and danced to songs and strings. They gathered in the morning and parted in the evening; there was not a single pleasure that they overlooked, covering a distance of ten thousand miles as if it were but the span of their own courtyard. As the saying has it,

One nod of the head goes farther than three thousand miles;
One twist of the torso covers more than eight hundred.

One day, the four mighty commanders had been told to prepare a great banquet in their own cave, and the six kings were invited to the feast. They killed cows and slaughtered horses; they sacrificed to Heaven and Earth. The various imps were ordered to dance and sing, and they all drank until they were thoroughly drunk. After sending the six kings off, Wukong also rewarded the leaders great and small with gifts. Reclining in the shade of pine trees near the sheet iron bridge, he fell asleep in a moment. The four mighty commanders led the crowd to form a protective circle around him, not daring to raise their voices. In his sleep the Handsome Monkey King saw two men approach with a summons with the three characters "Sun Wukong" written on it. They walked up to him and, without a word, tied him up with a rope and dragged him off. The soul of the Handsome Monkey King was reeling from side to side. They reached the edge of a city. The Monkey King was gradually coming to himself, when he lifted up his head and suddenly saw above the city an iron sign bearing in large letters the three words "Region of Darkness." The Handsome Monkey King at once became fully conscious. "The Region of Darkness is the abode of Yama, King of Death," he said. "Why am I here?" "Your age in the World of Life has come to an end," the two men said. "The two of us were given this summons to arrest you." When the Monkey King heard this, he said, "I, old Monkey himself, have transcended the Three Regions and the Five Phases; hence I am no longer under Yama's jurisdiction. Why is he so confused that he wants to arrest me?" The two summoners paid scant attention. Yanking and pulling, they were determined to haul him inside. Growing angry, the Monkey King whipped out his treasure. One wave of it turned it into the thickness of a rice bowl; he raised his hands once, and the two summoners were reduced to hash. He untied the rope, freed his hands, and fought his way into the city, wielding the rod. Bull-headed demons hid in terror, and horse-faced demons fled in every direction. A band of ghost soldiers ran up to the Palace of Darkness, crying, "Great Kings! Disaster! Disaster! Outside there's a hairy-faced thunder god fighting his way in!"

Their report alarmed the Ten Kings of the Underworld so much that they quickly straightened out their attire and went out to see what was happening. Discovering a fierce and angry figure, they lined up according to their ranks and greeted him with loud voices: "High Immortal, tell us your name. High Immortal, tell us your name." "I am the Heaven-born sage Sun Wukong from the Water-Curtain Cave in the Flower-Fruit

Mountain," said the Monkey King, "what kind of officials are you?" "We are the Emperors of Darkness," answered the Ten Kings, bowing, "the Ten Kings of the Underworld." "Tell me each of your names at once," said Wukong, "or I'll give you a drubbing."

The Ten Kings said, "We are: King Qinguang, King of the Beginning River, King of the Song Emperor, King of Avenging Ministers, King Yama, King of Equal Ranks, King of the Tai Mountain, King of City Markets, King of the Complete Change, and King of the Turning Wheel."

"Since you have all ascended the thrones of kingship," said Wukong, "you should be intelligent beings, responsible in rewards and punishments. Why are you so ignorant of good and evil? Old Monkey has acquired the Tao and attained immortality. I enjoy the same age as Heaven, and I have transcended the Three Regions and leapt clear of the Five Phases. Why, then, did you send men to arrest me?"

"High Immortal," said the Ten Kings, "let your anger subside. There are many people in this world with the same name and surname. Couldn't the summoners have made a mistake?" "Nonsense! Nonsense!" said Wukong. "The proverb says, 'Magistrates err, clerks err, but the man with the warrant never errs!'⁴ Quick, get out your register of births and deaths, and let me have a look."

When the Ten Kings heard this, they invited him to go into the palace to see for himself. Holding his compliant rod, Wukong went straight up to the Palace of Darkness and, facing south, sat down in the middle. The Ten Kings immediately had the judge in charge of the records bring out his books for examination. The judge, who did not dare tarry, hastened into a side room and brought out five or six books of documents and the ledgers on the ten species of living beings. He went through them one by one—short-haired creatures, furry creatures, winged creatures, crawling creatures, and scaly creatures—but he did not find his name. He then proceeded to the file on monkeys. You see, though this monkey resembled a human being, he was not listed under the names of men; though he resembled the short-haired creatures, he did not dwell in their kingdoms; though he resembled other animals, he was not subject to the unicorn; and though he resembled flying creatures, he was not governed by the phoenix. He had, therefore, a separate ledger, which Wukong examined himself. Under the heading "Soul 1350" he found the name Sun Wukong recorded, with the description: "Heaven-born Stone Monkey. Age: three hundred and forty-two years. A good end." Wukong said, "I really don't

4. Arthur Waley's translation is so apt that I have simply quoted it here.

remember my age. All I want is to erase my name. Bring me a brush." The judge hurriedly fetched the brush and soaked it in heavy ink. Wukong took the ledger on monkeys and crossed out all the names he could find in it. Throwing down the ledger, he said, "That's the end of the account, the end of the account! Now I'm truly not your subject." Brandishing his rod, he fought his way out of the Region of Darkness. The Ten Kings did not dare approach him. They went instead to the Green Cloud Palace to consult the Bodhisattva King Kṣitigarbha and made plans to report the incident to Heaven, which does not concern us for the moment.

While our Monkey King was fighting his way out of the city, he was suddenly caught in a clump of grass, and stumbled. Waking up with a start, he realized that it was all a dream. As he was stretching himself, he heard the four mighty commanders and the various monkeys crying with a loud voice, "Great King! How much wine did you imbibe? You've slept all night long. Aren't you awake yet?" "Sleeping is nothing to get excited about," said Wukong, "but I dreamed that two men came to arrest me, and I didn't perceive their intention until they brought me to the outskirts of the Region of Darkness. Showing my power, I protested right up to the Palace of Darkness and argued with the Ten Kings. I went through our ledger of births and deaths and crossed out all our names. Those fellows have no hold over us now." The various monkeys all kowtowed to express their gratitude. From that time onward there were many mountain monkeys who did not grow old, for their names were not registered in the Underworld. When the Handsome Monkey King finished his account of what had happened, the four mighty commanders reported the story to the demon kings of various caves, who all came to tender their congratulations. Only a few days had passed when the six sworn brothers also came to congratulate him, all of them delighted about the cancellation of the names. We shall not elaborate here on their joyful gathering.

We shall turn instead to the Great Benevolent Sage of Heaven, the Celestial Jade Emperor of the Most Venerable Deva, who was holding court one day in the Treasure Hall of Divine Mists, the Cloud Palace of Golden Arches. The divine ministers, civil and military, were just gathering for the morning session when suddenly the Daoist immortal Qiu Hongzhi announced, "Your Majesty, outside the Translucent Palace, Aoguang, the Dragon King of the Eastern Ocean, is awaiting your command to present a memorial to the Throne." The Jade Emperor gave the order to have him brought forth, and Aoguang was led into the Hall of Divine Mists. After he had paid his respects, a divine page boy in charge of documents received the memorial, and the Jade Emperor read it from the beginning. The memorial said:

> From the lowly water region of the Eastern Ocean at the East Pūrvavideha Continent, the small dragon subject, Aoguang, humbly informs the Wise Lord of Heaven, the Most Eminent High God and Ruler, that a bogus immortal, Sun Wukong, born of the Flower-Fruit Mountain and resident of the Water-Curtain Cave, has recently abused your small dragon, gaining a seat in his water home by force. He demanded a weapon, employing power and intimidation; he asked for martial attire, unleashing violence and threats. He terrorized my water kinsmen, and scattered turtles and tortoises. The Dragon of the Southern Ocean trembled; the Dragon of the Western Ocean was filled with horror; the Dragon of the Northern Ocean drew back his head to surrender; and your subject Aoguang flexed his body to do obeisance. We presented him with the divine treasure of an iron rod and the gold cap with phoenix plumes; giving him also a chain-mail cuirass and cloud-treading shoes, we sent him off courteously. But even then he was bent on displaying his martial prowess and magical powers, and all he could say to us was "Sorry to have bothered you!" We are indeed no match for him, nor are we able to subdue him. Your subject therefore presents this petition and humbly begs for imperial justice. We earnestly beseech you to dispatch the Heavenly host and capture this monster, so that tranquility may be restored to the oceans and prosperity to the Lower Region. Thus we present this memorial.

When the Holy Emperor had finished reading, he gave the command: "Let the Dragon God return to the ocean. We shall send our generals to arrest the culprit." The old Dragon King gratefully touched his forehead to the ground and left. From below the Immortal Elder Ge, the Divine Teacher, also brought forth the report. "Your Majesty, the Minister of Darkness, King Qinguang, supported by the Bodhisattva King Kṣitigarbha, Pope of the Underworld, has arrived to present his memorial." The jade girl in charge of communication came from the side to receive this document, which the Jade Emperor also read from the beginning. The memorial said:

> The Region of Darkness is the nether region proper to Earth. As Heaven is for gods and Earth for ghosts, so life and death proceed in cyclic succession. Fowls are born and animals die; male and female, they multiply. Births and transformations, the male begotten of the procreative female—such

is the order of Nature, and it cannot be changed. But now appears Sun Wukong, a Heaven-born baneful monkey from the Water-Curtain Cave in the Flower-Fruit Mountain, who practices evil and violence, and resists our proper summons. Exercising magic powers, he utterly defeated the ghostly messengers of Ninefold Darkness; exploiting brute force, he terrorized the Ten Merciful Kings. He caused great confusion in the Palace of Darkness; he abrogated by force the Register of Names, so that the category of monkeys is now beyond control, and inordinately long life is given to the simian family. The wheel of transmigration is stopped, for birth and death are eliminated in each kind of monkey. Your poor monk therefore risks offending your Heavenly authority in presenting this memorial. We humbly beg you to send forth your divine army and subdue this monster, to the end that life and death may once more be regulated and the Underworld rendered perpetually secure. Respectfully we present this memorial.

When the Jade Emperor had finished reading, he again gave a command: "Let the Lord of Darkness return to the Underworld. We shall send our generals to arrest this culprit." King Qinguang also touched his head to the ground gratefully and left.

The Great Heavenly Deva called together his various immortal subjects, both civil and military, and asked, "When was this baneful monkey born, and in which generation did he begin his career? How is it that he has become so powerfully accomplished in the Great Art?" Scarcely had he finished speaking when, from the ranks, Thousand-Mile Eye and Fair-Wind Ear stepped forward. "This monkey," they said, "is the Heaven-born stone monkey of three hundred years ago. At that time he did not seem to amount to much, and we do not know where he acquired the knowledge of self-cultivation these last few years and became an immortal. Now he knows how to subdue dragons and tame tigers, and thus he is able to annul by force the Register of Death." "Which one of you divine generals," asked the Jade Emperor, "wishes to go down there to subdue him?"

Scarcely had he finished speaking when the Long-Life Spirit of the Planet Venus came forward from the ranks and prostrated himself. "Highest and Holiest," he said, "within the three regions, all creatures endowed with the nine apertures can, through exercise, become immortals. It is not surprising that this monkey, with a body nurtured by Heaven and Earth, a frame born of the sun and moon, should achieve immortality, seeing that his head points to Heaven and his feet walk on Earth, and that he feeds on the dew and the mist. Now that he has the power to subdue dragons and tame tigers, how is he different from a human being? Your subject therefore makes so bold as to ask Your Majesty to remember the compassionate grace of Creation and issue a decree of pacification. Let him be summoned to the Upper Region and given some kind of official duties. His name will be recorded in the Register and we can control him here. If he is receptive to the Heavenly decree, he will be rewarded and promoted hereafter; but if he is disobedient to your command, we shall arrest him forthwith. Such an action will spare us a military expedition in the first place, and, in the second, permit us to receive into our midst another immortal in an orderly manner."

The Jade Emperor was highly pleased with this statement, and he said, "We shall follow the counsel of our minister." He then ordered the Star Spirit of Songs and Letters to compose the decree, and delegated the Gold Star of Venus to be the viceroy of peace. Having received the decree, the Gold Star went out of the South Heaven Gate, lowered the direction of his hallowed cloud, and headed straight for the Flower-Fruit Mountain and the Water-Curtain Cave. He said to the various little monkeys, "I am the Heavenly messenger sent from above. I have with me an imperial decree to invite your great king to go to the Upper Region. Report this to him quickly!" The monkeys outside the cave passed the word along one by one until it reached the depth of the cave. "Great King," one of the monkeys said, "there's an old man outside bearing a document on his back. He says that he is a messenger sent from Heaven, and he has an imperial decree of invitation for you." Upon hearing this, the Handsome Monkey King was exceedingly pleased. "These last two days," he said, "I was just thinking about taking a little trip to Heaven, and the Heavenly messenger has already come to invite me!" The Monkey King quickly straightened out his attire and went to the door for the reception. The Gold Star came into the center of the cave and stood still with his face toward the south. "I am the Gold Star of Venus from the West," he said. "I came down to Earth, bearing the imperial decree of pacification from the Jade Emperor, and invite you to go to Heaven to receive an immortal appointment." Laughing, Wukong said, "I am most grateful for the Old Star's visit." He then gave the order: "Little ones, prepare a banquet to entertain our guest." The Gold Star said, "As a bearer of imperial decree, I cannot remain here long. I must ask the Great King to go with me at once. After your glorious promotion, we shall have many occasions to converse at our leisure." "We are honored by your presence," said Wukong; "I am sorry that you have to leave with empty hands!" He then called the four mighty commanders together for this admonition: "Be diligent in teaching and drilling the young ones. Let me go up to Heaven to take a look and to see whether I can have you all brought up there too to live with me." The four mighty commanders indicated their obedience. This Monkey King mounted the cloud with the Gold Star and rose up into the sky. Truly

He ascends the high rank of immortals from the sky;
His name's enrolled in cloud columns and treasure scrolls.

We do not know what sort of rank or appointment he received; let's listen to the explanation in the next chapter.

FOUR

Appointed as a Bima, how could he be content?;
Named Equal to Heaven, he's still unpacified.

The Gold Star of Venus left the depths of the cave dwelling with the Handsome Monkey King, and together they rose by mounting the clouds. But the cloud-somersault of Wukong, you see, is no common magic; its speed is tremendous. Soon he left the Gold Star far behind and arrived first at the South Heaven Gate. He was about to dismount from the cloud and go in when the Devarāja Virūḍhaka leading Pang, Liu, Kou, Bi, Deng, Xin, Zhang, and Tao, the various divine heroes, barred the way with spears, scimitars, swords, and halberds and refused him entrance. The Monkey King said, "What a deceitful fellow that Gold Star is! If old Monkey has been invited here, why have these people been ordered to use their swords and spears to bar my entrance?" He was protesting loudly when the Gold Star arrived in haste. "Old man," said Wukong angrily to his face, "why did you deceive me? You told me that I was invited by the Jade Emperor's decree of pacification. Why then did you get these people to block the Heaven Gate and prevent my entering?" "Let the Great King calm down," the Gold Star said, laughing. "Since you have never been to the Hall of Heaven before, nor have you been given a name, you are quite unknown to the various Heavenly guardians. How can they let you in on their own authority? Once you have seen the Heavenly Deva, received an appointment, and had your name listed in the Immortal Register, you can go in and out as you please. Who would then obstruct your way?" "If that's how it is," said Wukong, "it's all right. But I'm not going in by myself." "Then go in with me," said the Gold Star, pulling him by the hand.

As they approached the gate, the Gold Star called out loudly, "Guardians of the Heaven Gate, lieutenants great and small, make way! This person is an immortal from the Region Below, whom I have summoned by the imperial decree of the Jade Emperor." The Devarāja Virūḍhaka and the various divine heroes immediately lowered their weapons and stepped aside, and the Monkey King finally believed what he had been told. He walked slowly inside with the Gold Star and looked around. For it was truly

His first ascent to the Region Above,
His sudden entrance into the Hall of Heaven,
Where ten thousand shafts of golden light whirled as a coral rainbow,
And a thousand layers of hallowed air diffused mist of purple.
Look at that South Heaven Gate!
Its deep shades of green
From glazed tiles were made;
Its radiant battlements
Adorned with treasure jade.
On two sides were posted scores of celestial sentinels,
Each of whom, standing tall beside the pillars,
Carried bows and clutched banners.
All around were sundry divine beings in golden armor,
Each of them holding halberds and whips,
Or wielding scimitars and swords.
Impressive may be the outer court;
Overwhelming is the sight within!
In the inner halls stood several huge pillars
Coiled around with red-whiskered dragons whose scales of gold gleamed in the
*   sun.*
There were, moreover, a few long bridges;
Above them crimson-headed phoenixes circled with soaring plumes of many
*   hues.*
Bright mist shimmered in the light of the sky.
Green fog descending obscured the stars.
Thirty-three Heavenly mansions were found up here,
With names like the Scattered Cloud, the Vaiśrvaṇa, the Pāncavidyā, the
*   Suyāma, the Nirmāṇarati . . .*[1]
On the roof of every mansion the ridge held a stately golden beast.
There were also the seventy-two treasure halls,
With names like the Morning Assembly, the Transcendent Void, the Precious
*   Light, the Heavenly King, the Divine Minister . . .*
In every hall beneath the pillars stood rows of jade unicorn.

1. The verse here is alluding to the Indra heaven with its thirty-three summits and to the six heavens of desire.

On the Platform of Canopus,[2]
There were flowers unfading in a thousand millennia;
Beside the oven for refining herbs,
There were exotic grasses growing green for ten thousand years.
He went before the Tower of Homage to the Sage,
Where he saw robes of royal purple gauze
Brilliant as stars refulgent,
Caps the shape of hibiscus,
Resplendent with gold and precious stones,
And pins of jade and shoes of pearl,
And purple sashes and golden ornaments.
When the golden bells swayed to their striking,
The memorial of the Three Judges[3] would cross the vermilion courtyard;
When the drums of Heaven were sounded,
Ten thousand sages of the royal audience would honor the Jade Emperor.
He went, too, to the Treasure Hall of Divine Mists
Where nails of gold penetrated frames of jade,
And colorful phoenixes danced atop scarlet doors.
Here were covered bridges and winding corridors
Displaying everywhere openwork carvings most elegant;
And eaves crowding together in layers three and four,
On each of which reared up phoenixes and dragons.
There was high above
A round dome big, bright, and brilliant—
Its shape, a huge gourd of purple gold,
Below which guardian goddesses hung out their fans
And jade maidens held up their immortal veils.
Ferocious were the sky marshals overseeing the court;
Dignified, the divine officials protecting the Throne.
There at the center, on a crystal platter,
Tablets of the Great Monad Elixir were heaped;
And rising out of the cornelian vases
Were several branches of twisting coral.
So it was that
Rare goods of every order were found in Heaven's Hall,
And nothing like them on Earth could ever be seen—

2. The Star of Long Life in Chinese mythology.
3. Special judges in the Underworld, traditionally robed in red, blue, and green.

Those golden arches, silver coaches, and that Heavenly house,
Those coralline blooms and jasper plants with their buds of jade.
The jade rabbit passed the platform to adore the king.
The golden crow flew by to worship the sage.
Blessed was the Monkey King coming to this Heavenly realm,
He who was not mired in the filthy soil of man.

The Gold Star of Venus led the Handsome Monkey King to the Treasure Hall of Divine Mists, and, without waiting for further announcement, they went into the imperial presence. While the Star prostrated himself, Wukong stood erect by him. Showing no respect, he cocked his ear only to listen to the report of the Gold Star. "According to your decree," said the Gold Star, "your subject has brought the bogus immortal." "Which one is the bogus immortal?" asked the Jade Emperor graciously. Only then did Wukong bow and reply, "None other than old Monkey!" Blanching with horror, the various divine officials said, "That wild ape! Already he has failed to prostrate himself before the Throne, and now he dares to come forward with such an insolent reply as 'None other than old Monkey'! He is worthy of death, worthy of death!" "That fellow Sun Wukong is a bogus immortal from the Region Below," announced the Jade Emperor, "and he has only recently acquired the form of a human being. We shall pardon him this time for his ignorance of court etiquette." "Thank you, Your Majesty," cried the various divine officials. Only then did the Monkey King bow deeply with folded hands and utter a cry of gratitude. The Jade Emperor then ordered the divine officials, both civil and military, to see what vacant appointment there might be for Sun Wukong to receive. From the side came the Star Spirit of Wuqu, who reported, "In every mansion and hall everywhere in the Palace of Heaven, there is no lack of ministers. Only at the imperial stables is a supervisor needed." "Let him be made a Bimawen,"[4] proclaimed the Jade Emperor. The various subjects again shouted their thanks, but Monkey only bowed deeply and gave a loud whoop of gratitude. The Jade Emperor then sent the Star Spirit of Jupiter to accompany him to the stables.

The Monkey King went happily with the Star Spirit of Jupiter to the stables in order to assume his duties. The Star Spirit then returned to his own mansion. At the stables, he gathered together the deputy and assistant supervisors, the accountants and stewards, and other officials both great

---

4. In Chinese folklore, the monkey is said to be able to ward off sickness from horses. This title is a pun on the words *bi* (to avoid, to keep off), *ma* (horse), and *wen* (pestilence, plague).

and small and made thorough investigation of all the affairs of the stables.
There were about a thousand celestial horses,[5] and they were all

Hualius *and* Chizhis
Lu'ers *and* Xianlis,
Consorts of Dragons and Purple Swallows,
Folded Wings and Suxiangs,
Juetis *and Silver Hooves,*
Yaoniaos *and Flying Yellows.*
Chestnuts and Faster-than-Arrows,
Red Hares and Speedier-than-Lights,
Leaping Lights and Vaulting Shadows,
Rising Fogs and Triumphant Yellows,
Wind Chasers and Distance Breakers.
Flying Pinions and Surging Airs,
Rushing Winds and Fiery Lightnings.
Copper Sparrows and Drifting Clouds,
Dragonlike piebalds and Tigerlike pintos,
Dust Quenchers and Purple Scales,
And Ferghanas from the Four Corners.
Like the Eight Steeds and Nine Stallions
They have no rivals within a thousand miles!
Such are these fine horses.
Every one of which
Neighs like the wind and gallops like thunder to show a mighty spirit.
They tread the mist and mount the clouds with unflagging strength.

Our Monkey King went through the lists and made a thorough inspection of the horses. Within the imperial stables, the accountants were in
charge of getting supplies; the stewards groomed and washed the horses,
chopped hay, watered them, and prepared their food; and the deputies and
assistants saw to the overall management. Never resting, the Bima oversaw
the care of the horses, fussing with them by day and watching over them
diligently by night. Those horses that wanted to sleep were stirred up and
fed; those that wanted to gallop were caught and placed in the stalls. When

5. In this poem, which is exceedingly difficult to translate, the author has made
use of numerous lists of horses associated with the emperors Zhou Muwang (ca.
1001–942 BCE), Qin Shi Huangdi (221–209 BCE), and Han Wendi (179–57 BCE). To
construct the poem, some names are used merely for their tonal effects (e.g., *chizhi*
and *yaoniao*), while others have ostensible meanings as well. My translation attempts
to approximate the original.

the celestial horses saw him, they all behaved most properly and they were so well cared for that their flanks became swollen with fat.

More than half a month soon went by, and on one leisurely morning, the various department ministers gave a banquet to welcome him and congratulate him. While they were drinking happily, the Monkey King suddenly put down his cup and asked: "What sort of rank is this Bimawen of mine?" "The rank and the title are the same," they said. "But what ministerial grade is it?" "It does not have a grade," they said. "If it does not have a grade," said the Monkey King, "I suppose it must be the very highest." "Not at all," they replied, "it can only be called 'the unclassified'!" The Monkey King said, "What do you mean by 'the unclassified'?" "It is really the meanest level," they said. "This kind of minister is the lowest of the low ranks; hence he can only look after horses. Take the case of Your Honor, who, since your arrival, have been so diligent in discharging your duties. If the horses are fattened, you will only earn yourself a 'Fairly Good!' If they look at all thin, you will be roundly rebuked. And if they are seriously hurt or wounded, you will be prosecuted and fined."

When the Monkey King heard this, fire leaped up from his heart. "So that's the kind of contempt they have for old Monkey!" he cried angrily, gnashing his teeth. "At the Flower-Fruit Mountain I was honored as king and patriarch. How dare they trick me into coming to look after horses for them? If horse tending is such a menial service, reserved only for the young and lowly, how did they intend to treat me? I won't do this anymore! I won't do this anymore! I'm leaving right now!" With a crash, he kicked over his official desk and took out the treasure from his ear. One wave of his hand and it had the thickness of a rice bowl. Delivering blows in all directions, he fought his way out of the imperial stables and went straight to the South Heaven Gate. The various celestial guardians, knowing that he had been officially appointed a Bimawen, did not dare stop him and allowed him to fight his way out of the Heaven Gate.

In a moment, he lowered the direction of his cloud and returned to the Flower-Fruit Mountain. The four mighty commanders were seen drilling troops with the Monster Kings of various caves. "Little ones," this Monkey King cried in a loud voice, "old Monkey has returned!" The flock of monkeys all came to kowtow and received him into the depths of the cave dwelling. As the Monkey King ascended his throne, they busily prepared a banquet to welcome him. "Receive our congratulations, Great King," they said. "Having gone to the region above for more than ten years, you must be returning in success and glory." "I have been away for only half a month," said the Monkey King. "How can it be more than ten years?"

"Great King," said the various monkeys, "you are not aware of time and season when you are in Heaven. One day in Heaven above is equal to a year on Earth. May we ask the Great King what ministerial appointment he received?"

"Don't mention that! Don't mention that!" said the Monkey King, waving his hand. "It embarrasses me to death! That Jade Emperor does not know how to use talent. Seeing the features of old Monkey, he appointed me to something called the Bimawen, which actually means taking care of horses for him. It's a job too low even to be classified! I didn't know this when I first assumed my duties, and so I managed to have some fun at the imperial stables. But when I asked my colleagues today, I discovered what a degraded position it was. I was so furious that I knocked over the banquet they were giving me and rejected the title. That's why I came back down." "Welcome back!" said the various monkeys, "welcome back! Our Great King can be the sovereign of this blessed cave dwelling with the greatest honor and happiness. Why should he go away to be someone's stable boy?" "Little ones," they cried, "send up the wine quickly and cheer up our Great King."

As they were drinking wine and conversing happily, someone came to report: "Great King, there are two one-horned demon kings outside who want to see you." "Show them in," said the Monkey King. The demon kings straightened out their attire, ran into the cave, and prostrated themselves. "Why did you want to see me?" asked the Handsome Monkey King. "We have long heard that the Great King is receptive to talents," said the demon kings, "but we had no reason to request your audience. Now we learn that our Great King has received a divine appointment and has returned in success and glory. We have come, therefore, to present the Great King with a red and yellow robe for his celebration. If you are not disdainful of the uncouth and the lowly and are willing to receive us plebeians, we shall serve you as dogs or as horses." Highly pleased, the Monkey King put on the red and yellow robe while the rest of them lined up joyfully and did homage. He then appointed the demon kings to be the Vanguard Commanders, Marshals of the Forward Regiments. After expressing their thanks, the demon kings asked again, "Since our Great King was in Heaven for a long time, may we ask what kind of appointment he received?" "The Jade Emperor belittles the talented," said the Monkey King. "He only made me something called the Bimawen." Hearing this, the demon kings said again, "Great King has such divine powers! Why should you take care of horses for him? What is there to stop you from assuming the rank of the Great Sage, Equal to Heaven?" When the Monkey King heard these words, he could not conceal his delight, shouting repeatedly, "Bravo! Bravo!" "Make me a banner immediately," he ordered the four mighty commanders, "and inscribe on it in large letters, 'The Great Sage, Equal to Heaven.' Erect a pole to hang it on. From now on, address me only as the Great Sage, Equal to Heaven, and the title Great King will no longer be permitted. The Monster Kings of the various caves will also be informed so that it will be known to all." Of this we shall speak no further.

We now refer to the Jade Emperor, who held court the next day. The Heavenly Preceptor Zhang was seen leading the deputy and the assistant of the imperial stables to come before the vermilion courtyard. "Your Majesty," they said prostrating themselves, "the newly appointed Bimawen, Sun Wukong, objected to his rank as being too low and left the Heavenly Palace yesterday in rebellion." As they were saying this, the Devarāja Virūḍhaka leading the various celestial guardians from the South Heaven Gate, also made the report, "The Bimawen for reasons unknown to us has walked out of the Heaven Gate." When the Jade Emperor heard this, he made the proclamation: "Let the two divine commanders and their followers return to their duties. We shall send forth celestial soldiers to capture this monster." From among the ranks, Devarāja Li, who was the Pagoda Bearer, and his Third Prince Naṭa came forward and presented their request, saying, "Your Majesty, though your humble subjects are not gifted, we await your authorization to subdue this monster." Delighted, the Jade Emperor appointed Pagoda Bearer Devarāja Li Jing to be grand marshal for subduing the monster, and promoted Third Prince Naṭa to be the great deity in charge of the Three-Platform Assembly of the Saints. They were to lead an expeditionary force at once for the Region Below.

Devarāja Li and Naṭa kowtowed to take leave and went back to their own mansion. After reviewing the troops and their captains and lieutenants, they appointed Mighty-Spirit God to be Vanward Commander, the Fish-Belly General to bring up the rear, and the General of the Yakṣas to urge the troops on. In a moment they left by the South Heaven Gate and went straight to the Flower-Fruit Mountain. A level piece of land was selected for encampment, and the order was then given to the Mighty-Spirit God to provoke battle. Having received his order and having buckled and knotted his armor properly, the Mighty-Spirit God grasped his spreading-flower ax and came to the Water-Curtain Cave. There in front of the cave he saw a great mob of monsters, all of them wolves, insects, tigers, leopards, and the like; they were all jumping and growling, brandishing their swords and waving their spears. "Damnable beasts!" shouted the Mighty-Spirit God. "Hurry and tell the Bimawen that I, a great general from Heaven, have by the authorization of the Jade Emperor come to subdue him. Tell him to come out quickly and surrender, lest all of you be annihilated!"

Running pell-mell into the cave, those monsters shouted the report, "Disaster! Disaster!" "What sort of disaster?" asked the Monkey King. "There's a celestial warrior outside," said the monsters, "who claims the title of an imperial envoy. He says he came by the holy decree of the Jade Emperor to subdue you, and he orders you to go out quickly and surrender, lest we lose our lives." Hearing this, the Monkey King commanded, "Get my battle dress!" He quickly donned his red gold cap, pulled on his yellow gold cuirass, slipped on his cloud-treading shoes, and seized the compliant golden-hooped rod. He led the crowd outside and set them up in battle formation. The Mighty-Spirit God opened wide his eyes and stared at this magnificent Monkey King:

> The gold cuirass worn on his body was brilliant and bright;
> The gold cap on his head also glistened in the light.
> In his hands was a staff, the golden-hooped rod,
> That well became the cloud-treading shoes on his feet.
> His eyes glowered strangely like burning stars.
> Hanging past his shoulders were two ears, forked and hard.
> His remarkable body knew many ways of change,
> And his voice resounded like bells and chimes.
> This Bimawen of pointed mouth and gaping teeth
> Set high his aim to be the Sage, Equal to Heaven.

"Lawless ape," the Mighty-Spirit God roared powerfully, "do you recognize me?" When the Great Sage heard these words, he asked quickly, "What sort of dull-witted deity are you? Old Monkey has yet to meet you! State your name at once!" "Fraudulent simian," cried the Mighty-Spirit, "what do you mean, you don't recognize me! I am the Celestial General of Mighty-Spirit, the Vanward Commander and subordinate to Devarāja Li, the Pagoda Bearer, from the divine empyrean. I have come by the imperial decree of the Jade Emperor to receive your submission. Strip yourself of your apparel immediately and yield to the Heavenly grace, so that this mountainful of creatures can avoid execution. If you dare but utter half a 'No,' you will be reduced to powder in seconds!"

When the Monkey King heard those words, he was filled with anger. "Reckless simpleton!" he cried. "Stop bragging and wagging your tongue! I would have killed you with one stroke of my rod, but then I would have no one to communicate my message. So, I'll spare your life for the moment. Get back to Heaven quickly and inform the Jade Emperor that he has no regard for talent. Old Monkey has unlimited abilities. Why did he ask me to mind horses for him? Take a good look at the words on this banner. If I am promoted according to its title, I will lay down my arms, and the cosmos will then be fair and peaceable. But if he does not agree to my demand, I'll fight my way up to the Treasure Hall of Divine Mists, and he won't even be able to sit on his dragon throne!" When the Mighty-Spirit God heard these words, he opened his eyes wide and faced the wind. He did indeed see a tall pole outside the cave; on the pole hung a banner bearing in large letters the words "The Great Sage, Equal to Heaven."

The Mighty-Spirit God laughed scornfully three times and jeered, "Lawless ape! How fatuous can you be, and how arrogant! So you want to be the Great Sage, Equal to Heaven! Be good enough to take a bit of my ax first!" Aiming at his head, he hacked at him, but, being a knowledgeable fighter, the Monkey King was not unnerved. He met the blow at once with his golden-hooped rod, and this exciting battle was on.

The rod was named Compliant;
The ax was called Spreading Flower.
The two of them, meeting suddenly,
Did not yet know their weakness or strength;
But ax and rod
Clashed left and right.
One concealed secret powers most wondrous;
The other vaunted openly his vigor and might.
They used magic—
Blowing out cloud and puffing up fog;
They stretched their hands,
Splattering mud and spraying sand.
The might of the celestial battler had its way:
But the Monkey King's power of change knew no bounds.
The rod uplifted seemed a dragon playing in water;
The ax arrived as a phoenix slicing through flowers.
Mighty-Spirit, though his name was known throughout the world,
In prowess truly could not match the other one.
The Great Sage whirling lightly his iron staff
Could numb the body with one stroke on the head.

The Mighty-Spirit God could oppose him no longer and allowed the Monkey King to aim a mighty blow at his head, which he hastily sought to parry with his ax. With a crack the ax handle split in two, and Mighty-Spirit turned swiftly to flee for his life. "Imbecile! Imbecile!" laughed the Monkey King, "I've already spared you. Go and report my message at once!"

Back at the camp, the Mighty-Spirit God went straight to see the Pagoda Bearer Devarāja. Huffing and puffing, he knelt down saying, "The Bimawen indeed has great magic powers! Your unworthy warrior cannot prevail against him. Defeated, I have come to beg your pardon." "This fellow has blunted our will to fight," said Devarāja Li angrily. "Take him out and have him executed!" From the side came Prince Naṭa, who said, bowing deeply, "Let your anger subside, Father King, and pardon for the moment the guilt of Mighty-Spirit. Permit your child to go into battle once, and we shall know the long and short of the matter." The Devarāja heeded the admonition and ordered Mighty-Spirit to go back to his camp and await trial.

This Prince Naṭa, properly armed, leaped from his camp and dashed to the Water-Curtain Cave. Wukong was just dismissing his troops when he saw Naṭa approaching fiercely. Dear Prince!

Two boyish tufts barely cover his skull.
His flowing hair has yet to reach the shoulders.
A rare mind, alert and intelligent.
A noble frame, pure and elegant.
He is indeed the unicorn son from Heaven above,
Truly immortal as the phoenix of mist and smoke.
This seed of dragon has by nature uncommon features.
His tender age shows no relation to any worldly kin.
He carries on his body six kinds of magic weapons.
He flies, he leaps; he can change without restriction.
Now by the golden-mouth proclamation of the Jade Emperor
He is appointed to the Assembly: its name, the Three Platforms.[6]

Wukong drew near and asked, "Whose little brother are you, and what do you want, barging through my gate?" "Lawless monstrous monkey!" shouted Naṭa. "Don't you recognize me? I am Naṭa, third son of the Pagoda Bearer Devarāja. I am under the imperial commission of the Jade Emperor to come and arrest you." "Little prince," said Wukong laughing, "your baby teeth haven't even fallen out, and your natal hair is still damp! How dare you talk so big? I'm going to spare your life, and I won't fight you. Just take a look at the words on my banner and report them to the Jade Emperor above. Grant me this title, and you won't need to stir your forces. I will submit on my own. If you don't satisfy my cravings, I will surely fight my way up to the Treasure Hall of Divine Mists."

6. The Three Platforms are the offices of Daoist Star Spirits, which are said to correspond to the Three Officials in imperial government.

Lifting his head to look, Naṭa saw the words "Great Sage, Equal to Heaven." "What great power does this monstrous monkey possess," said Naṭa, "that he dares claim such a title? Fear not! Swallow my sword." "I'll just stand here quietly," said Wukong, "and you can take a few hacks at me with your sword." Young Naṭa grew angry. "Change!" he yelled loudly, and he changed at once into a fearsome person having three heads and six arms. In his hands he held six kinds of weapons: a monster-stabbing sword, a monster-cleaving scimitar, a monster-binding rope, a monster-taming club, an embroidered ball, and a fiery wheel. Brandishing these weapons, he mounted a frontal attack. "This little brother does know a few tricks!" said Wukong, somewhat alarmed by what he saw. "But don't be rash. Watch my magic!" Dear Great Sage! He shouted, "Change!" and he too transformed himself into a creature with three heads and six arms. One wave of the golden-hooped rod and it became three staffs, which were held with six hands. The conflict was truly earth-shaking and made the very mountains tremble. What a battle!

The six-armed Prince Naṭa.
The Heaven-born Handsome Stone Monkey King.
Meeting, each met his match
And found each to be from the same source.
One was consigned to come down to Earth.
The other in guile disturbed the universe.
The edge of the monster-stabbing sword was quick;
The keen, monster-cleaving scimitar alarmed demons and gods;
The monster-binding rope was like a flying snake;
The monster-taming club was like the head of a wolf;
The lightning-propelled fiery wheel was like darting flames;
Hither and thither the embroidered ball rotated.
The three compliant rods of the Great Sage
Protected the front and guarded the rear with care and skill.
A few rounds of bitter contest revealed no victor,
But the prince's mind would not so easily rest.
He ordered the six kinds of weapon to change
Into hundreds and thousands of millions, aiming for the head.
The Monkey King, undaunted, roared with laughter loud,
And wielded his iron rod with artful ease:
One turned to a thousand, a thousand to ten thousand,
Filling the sky as a swarm of dancing dragons,
And shocked the Monster Kings of sundry caves into shutting their doors.
Demons and monsters all over the mountain hid their heads.

The angry breath of divine soldiers was like oppressive clouds.
The golden-hooped iron rod whizzed like the wind.
On this side,
The battle cries of celestial fighters appalled everyone;
On that side,
The banner-waving of monkey monsters startled each person.
Growing fierce, the two parties both willed a test of strength.
We know not who was stronger and who weaker.

Each displaying his divine powers, the Third Prince and Wukong battled for thirty rounds. The six weapons of that Prince changed into a thousand and ten thousand pieces; the golden-hooped rod of Sun Wukong into ten thousand and a thousand. They clashed like raindrops and meteors in the air, but victory or defeat was not yet determined. Wukong, however, proved to be the one swifter of eye and hand. Right in the midst of the confusion, he plucked a piece of hair and shouted, "Change!" It changed into a copy of him, also wielding a rod in its hands and deceiving Naṭa. His real person leaped behind Naṭa and struck his left shoulder with the rod. Naṭa, still performing his magic, heard the rod whizzing through the air and tried desperately to dodge it. Unable to move quickly enough, he took the blow and fled in pain. Breaking off his magic and gathering up his six weapons, he returned to his camp in defeat.

Standing in front of his battle line, Devarāja Li saw what was happening and was about to go to his son's assistance. The prince, however, came to him first and gasped, "Father King! The Bimawen is truly powerful. Even your son of such magical strength is no match for him! He has wounded me in the shoulder." "If this fellow is so powerful," said the Devarāja, turning pale with fright, "how can we beat him?" The prince said, "In front of his cave he has set up a banner bearing the words 'The Great Sage, Equal to Heaven.' By his own mouth he boastfully asserted that if the Jade Emperor appointed him to such a title, all troubles would cease. If he were not given this name, he would surely fight his way up to the Treasure Hall of Divine Mists!" "If that's the case," said the Devarāja, "let's not fight with him for the moment. Let us return to the region above and report these words. There will be time then for us to send for more celestial soldiers and take this fellow on all sides." The prince was in such pain that he could not do battle again; he therefore went back to Heaven with the Devarāja to report, of which we speak no further.

Look at that Monkey King returning to his mountain in triumph! The monster kings of seventy-two caves and the six sworn brothers all came to congratulate him, and they feasted jubilantly in the blessed cave dwelling.

He then said to the six brothers, "If little brother is now called the Great Sage, Equal to Heaven, why don't all of you assume the title of Great Sage also?" "Our worthy brother's words are right!" shouted the Bull Monster King from their midst, "I'm going to be called the Great Sage, Parallel with Heaven." "I shall be called the Great Sage, Covering the Ocean," said the Dragon Monster King. "I shall be called the Great Sage, United with Heaven," said the Garuda Monster King. "I shall be called the Great Sage, Mover of Mountains," said the Giant Lynx King. "I shall be called the Telltale Great Sage," said the Macaque King. "And I shall be called the God-Routing Great Sage," said the Orangutan King. At that moment, the seven Great Sages had complete freedom to do as they pleased and to call themselves with whatever titles they liked. They had fun for a whole day and then dispersed.

Now we return to the Devarāja Li and the Third Prince, who, leading the other commanders, went straight to the Treasure Hall of Divine Mists to give this report: "By your holy decree your subjects led the expeditionary force down to the Region Below to subdue the baneful immortal, Sun Wukong. We had no idea of his enormous power, and we could not prevail against him. We beseech Your Majesty to give us reinforcements to wipe him out." "How powerful can we expect one baneful monkey to be," asked the Jade Emperor, "that reinforcements are needed?" "May Your Majesty pardon us from an offense worthy of death!" said the prince, drawing closer. "That baneful monkey wielded an iron rod; he defeated first the Mighty-Spirit God and then wounded the shoulder of your subject. Outside the door of his cave he had set up a banner bearing the words 'The Great Sage, Equal to Heaven.' He said that if he were given such a rank, he would lay down his arms and come to declare his allegiance. If not, he would fight his way up to the Treasure Hall of Divine Mists."

"How dare this baneful monkey be so insolent!" exclaimed the Jade Emperor, astonished by what he had heard. "We must order the generals to have him executed at once!" As he was saying this, the Gold Star of Venus came forward again from the ranks and said, "The baneful monkey knows how to make a speech, but he has no idea what's appropriate and what isn't. Even if reinforcements are sent to fight him, I don't think he can be subdued right away without taxing our forces. It would be better if Your Majesty were greatly to extend your mercy and proclaim yet another decree of pacification. Let him indeed be made the Great Sage, Equal to Heaven; he will be given an empty title, in short, rank without compensation." "What do you mean by rank without compensation?" said the Jade Emperor. The Gold Star said, "His name will be Great Sage,

Equal to Heaven, but he will not be given any official duty or salary. We shall keep him here in Heaven so that we may put his perverse mind at rest and make him desist from his madness and arrogance. The universe will then be calm and the oceans tranquil again." Hearing these words, the Jade Emperor said, "We shall follow the counsels of our minister." He ordered the mandate to be made up and the Gold Star to bear it hence.

The Gold Star left through the South Heaven Gate once again and headed straight for the Flower-Fruit Mountain. Outside the Water-Curtain Cave things were quite different from the way they had been the previous time. He found the entire region filled with the awesome and bellicose presence of every conceivable kind of monster, each one of them clutching swords and spears, wielding scimitars and staffs. Growling and leaping about, they began to attack the Gold Star the moment they saw him. "You, chieftains, hear me," said the Gold Star, "let me trouble you to report this to your Great Sage. I am the Heavenly messenger sent by the Lord above, and I bear an imperial decree of invitation." The various monsters ran inside to report, "There is an old man outside who says that he is a Heavenly messenger from the region above, bearing a decree of invitation for you." "Welcome! Welcome!" said Wukong. "He must be that Gold Star of Venus who came here last time. Although it was a shabby position they gave me when he invited me up to the region above, I nevertheless made it to Heaven once and familiarized myself with the ins and outs of the celestial passages. He has come again this time undoubtedly with good intentions." He commanded the various chieftains to wave the banners and beat the drums, and to draw up the troops in receiving order. Leading the rest of the monkeys, the Great Sage donned his cap and his cuirass, over which he tossed the red and yellow robe, and slipped on the cloud shoes. He ran to the mouth of the cave, bowed courteously, and said in a loud voice, "Please come in, Old Star! Forgive me for not coming out to meet you."

The Gold Star strode forward and entered the cave. He stood facing south and declared, "Now I inform the Great Sage. Because the Great Sage has objected to the meanness of his previous appointment and absented himself from the imperial stables, the officials of that department, both great and small, reported the matter to the Jade Emperor. The proclamation of the Jade Emperor said at first, 'All appointed officials advance from lowly positions to exalted ones. Why should he object to that arrangement?' This led to the campaign against you by Devarāja Li and Naṭa. They were ignorant of the Great Sage's power and therefore suffered defeat. They reported back to Heaven that you had set up a banner which made known your desire to be the Great Sage, Equal to Heaven. The various martial officials still wanted to deny your request. It was this old man who, risking offense, pleaded the case of the Great Sage, so that he might be invited to receive a new appointment, and without the use of force. The Jade Emperor accepted my suggestion; hence I am here to invite you." "I caused you trouble last time," said Wukong, laughing, "and now I am again indebted to you for your kindness. Thank you! Thank you! But is there really such a rank as the Great Sage, Equal to Heaven, up there?" "I made certain that this title was approved," said the Gold Star, "before I dared come with the decree. If there is any mishap, let this old man be held responsible."

Wukong was highly pleased, but the Gold Star refused his earnest invitation to stay for a banquet. He therefore mounted the hallowed cloud with the Gold Star and went to the South Heaven Gate, where they were welcomed by the celestial generals and guardians with hands folded at their breasts. Going straight into the Treasure Hall of Divine Mists, the Gold Star prostrated himself and memorialized, "Your subject, by your decree, has summoned here Bimawen Sun Wukong." "Have that Sun Wukong come forward," said the Jade Emperor. "I now proclaim you to be the Great Sage, Equal to Heaven, a position of the highest rank. But you must indulge no more in your preposterous behavior." Bowing deeply, the monkey uttered a great whoop of thanks. The Jade Emperor then ordered two building officials, Zhang and Lu, to erect the official residence of the Great Sage, Equal to Heaven, to the right of the Garden of Immortal Peaches. Inside the mansion, two departments were established, named "Peace and Quiet" and "Serene Spirit," both of which were full of attending officials. The Jade Emperor also ordered the Star Spirits of Five Poles[7] to accompany Wukong to assume his post. In addition, two bottles of imperial wine and ten clusters of golden flowers were bestowed on him, with the order that he must keep himself under control and make up his mind to indulge no more in preposterous behavior. The Monkey King obediently accepted the command and went that day with the Star Spirits to assume his post. He opened the bottles of wine and drank them all with his colleagues. After seeing the Star Spirits off to their own palaces, he settled down in complete contentment and delight to enjoy the pleasures of Heaven, without the slightest worry or care. Truly

His name divine, forever recorded in the Long–Life Book
And kept from falling into saṃsāra, will long be known.

We do not know what took place hereafter; let's listen to the explanation in the next chapter.

7. These are also Daoist deities.

FIVE

Disrupting the Peach Festival, the Great Sage steals elixir;
With revolt in Heaven, many gods try to seize the fiend.

Now we must tell you that the Great Sage, after all, was a monkey monster; in truth, he had no knowledge of his title or rank, nor did he care for the size of his salary. He did nothing but place his name on the Register. At his official residence he was cared for night and day by the attending officials of the two departments. His sole concern was to eat three meals a day and to sleep soundly at night. Having neither duties nor worries, he was free and content to tour the mansions and meet friends, to make new acquaintances and form new alliances at his leisure. When he met the Three Pure Ones,[1] he addressed them as "Your Reverence"; and when he ran into the Four Emperors, he would say, "Your Majesty." As for the Nine Luminaries, the Generals of the Five Quarters the Twenty-Eight Constellations, the Four Devarājas, the Twelve Horary Branches, the Five Elders of the Five Regions, the Star Spirits of the entire Heaven, and the numerous gods of the Milky Way,[2] he called them all brother and treated them in a fraternal manner. Today he toured the east, and tomorrow he wandered west. Going and coming on the clouds, he had no definite itinerary.

Early one morning, when the Jade Emperor was holding court, the Daoist immortal Xu Jingyang stepped from the ranks and went forward to memorialize, kowtowing, "The Great Sage, Equal to Heaven, has no

1. The Three Pure Ones, the highest gods of the Daoist Pantheon, are: the Jade-Pure Honorable Divine of the Origin (Yuqing yuanshi tianzun), the Exalted-Pure Honorable Divine of Spiritual Treasures (Shangqing lingbao tianzun), and the Primal-Pure Honorable Divine of Moral Virtue (Taiqing daode tianzun, also named Taiqing taishang laojun). The last one is the name of the deified Laozi.

2. All of these are deities of the Daoist Pantheon, developed and expanded from the early medieval period down to the time of the Ming. The various deities are a syncretic assembly of those appropriated from Indic Buddhism and of those local and transregional figures in territorial China. Some of those figures antedated the rise of organized Daoism in the second century CE.

duties at present and merely dawdles away his time. He has become quite chummy with the various Stars and Constellations of Heaven, calling them his friends regardless of whether they are his superiors or subordinates, and I fear that his idleness may lead to roguery. It would be better to give him some assignment so that he will not grow mischievous." When the Jade Emperor heard these words, he sent for the Monkey King at once, who came amiably. "Your Majesty," he said, "what promotion or reward did you have in mind for old Monkey when you called him?" "We perceive," said the Jade Emperor, "that your life is quite indolent, since you have nothing to do, and we have decided therefore to give you an assignment. You will temporarily take care of the Garden of Immortal Peaches. Be careful and diligent, morning and evening." Delighted, the Great Sage bowed deeply and grunted his gratitude as he withdrew.

He could not restrain himself from rushing immediately into the Garden of Immortal Peaches to inspect the place. A local spirit from the garden stopped him and asked, "Where is the Great Sage going?" "I have been authorized by the Jade Emperor," said the Great Sage, "to look after the Garden of Immortal Peaches. I have come to conduct an inspection." The local spirit hurriedly saluted him and then called together all the stewards in charge of hoeing, watering, tending peaches, and cleaning and sweeping. They all came to kowtow to the Great Sage and led him inside. There he saw

Radiantly young and lovely,
On every trunk and limb—
Radiantly young and lovely blossoms filling the trees,
And fruits on every trunk and limb weighing down the stems.
The fruits, weighing down the stems, hang like balls of gilt:
The blossoms, filling the trees, form tufts of rouge.
Ever they bloom, and ever fruit-bearing, they ripen in a thousand years;
Not knowing winter or summer, they lengthen out to ten thousand years.
Those that first ripen glow like faces reddened with wine,
While those half-grown ones
Are stalk-held and green-skinned.
Encased in smoke their flesh retains their green,
But sunlight reveals their cinnabar grace.
Beneath the trees are rare flowers and exotic grass
Which colors, unfading in four seasons, remain the same.
The towers, the terraces, and the studios left and right
Rise so high into the air that often cloud covers are seen.

Not planted by the vulgar or the worldly of the Dark City,
They are grown and tended by the Queen Mother of the Jade Pool.[3]

The Great Sage enjoyed this sight for a long time and then asked the local spirit, "How many trees are there?" "There are three thousand six hundred," said the local spirit. "In the front are one thousand two hundred trees with little flowers and small fruits. These ripen once every three thousand years, and after one taste of them a man will become an immortal enlightened in the Way, with healthy limbs and a lightweight body. In the middle are one thousand two hundred trees of layered flowers and sweet fruits. They ripen once every six thousand years. If a man eats them, he will ascend to Heaven with the mist and never grow old. At the back are one thousand two hundred trees with fruits of purple veins and pale yellow pits. These ripen once every nine thousand years and, if eaten, will make a man's age equal to that of Heaven and Earth, the sun and the moon." Highly pleased by these words, the Great Sage that very day made thorough inspection of the trees and a listing of the arbors and pavilions before returning to his residence. From then on, he would go there to enjoy the scenery once every three or four days. He no longer consorted with his friends, nor did he take any more trips.

One day he saw that more than half of the peaches on the branches of the older trees had ripened, and he wanted very much to eat one and sample its novel taste. Closely followed, however, by the local spirit of the garden, the stewards, and the divine attendants of the Equal to Heaven Residence, he found it inconvenient to do so. He therefore devised a plan on the spur of the moment and said to them, "Why don't you all wait for me outside and let me rest a while in this arbor?" The various immortals withdrew accordingly. That Monkey King then took off his cap and robe and climbed up onto a big tree. He selected the large peaches that were thoroughly ripened and, plucking many of them, ate to his heart's content right on the branches. Only after he had his fill did he jump down from the tree. Pinning back his cap and donning his robe, he called for his train of followers to return to the residence. After two or three days, he used the same device to steal peaches to gratify himself once again.

One day the Lady Queen Mother decided to open wide her treasure chamber and to give a banquet for the Grand Festival of Immortal Peaches, which was to be held in the Palace of the Jasper Pool. She ordered the

3. Sometimes called the Lady Queen Mother (Wangmu niangniang), or the Queen Mother of the West (Xi Wangmu), she is the highest goddess of Daoism. Her official residence is the Palace of the Jasper Pool on Mount Kunlun in Tibet.

various Immortal Maidens—Red Gown, Blue Gown, White Gown, Black Gown, Purple Gown, Yellow Gown, and Green Gown—to go with their flower baskets to the Garden of Immortal Peaches and pick the fruits for the festival. The seven maidens went to the gate of the garden and found it guarded by the local spirit, the stewards, and the ministers from the two departments of the Equal to Heaven Residence. The girls approached them, saying, "We have been ordered by the Queen Mother to pick some peaches for our banquet." "Divine maidens," said the local spirit, "please wait a moment. This year is not quite the same as last year. The Jade Emperor has put in charge here the Great Sage, Equal to Heaven, and we must report to him before we are allowed to open the gate." "Where is the Great Sage?" asked the maidens. "He is in the garden," said the local spirit. "Because he is tired, he is sleeping alone in the arbor." "If that's the case," said the maidens, "let us go and find him, for we cannot be late." The local spirit went into the garden with them; they found their way to the arbor but saw no one. Only the cap and the robe were left in the arbor, but there was no person to be seen. The Great Sage, you see, had played for a while and eaten a number of peaches. He had then changed himself into a figure only two inches high and, perching on the branch of a large tree, had fallen asleep under the cover of thick leaves. "Since we came by imperial decree," said the Seven-Gown Immortal Maidens, "how can we return empty-handed, even though we cannot locate the Great Sage?" One of the divine officials said from the side, "Since the divine maidens have come by decree, they should wait no longer. Our Great Sage has a habit of wandering off somewhere, and he must have left the garden to meet his friends. Go and pick your peaches now, and we shall report the matter for you." The Immortal Maidens followed his suggestion and went into the grove to pick their peaches.

They gathered two basketfuls from the trees in front and filled three more baskets from the trees in the middle. When they went to the trees at the back of the grove, they found that the flowers were sparse and the fruits scanty. Only a few peaches with hairy stems and green skins were left, for the fact is that the Monkey King had eaten all the ripe ones. Looking this way and that, the Seven Immortal Maidens found on a branch pointing southward one single peach that was half white and half red. The Blue Gown Maiden pulled the branch down with her hand, and the Red Gown Maiden, after plucking the fruit, let the branch snap back up into its position. This was the very branch on which the transformed Great Sage was sleeping. Startled by her, the Great Sage revealed his true form and whipped out from his ear the golden-hooped rod. One wave and it had the thickness of a rice bowl. "From what region have you come, monsters," he cried, "that you have the gall to steal my peaches?" Terrified, the Seven Immortal Maidens knelt down together and pleaded, "Let the Great Sage calm himself! We are not monsters, but the Seven-Gown Immortal Maidens sent by the Lady Queen Mother to pluck the fruits needed for the Grand Festival of Immortal Peaches, when the treasure chamber is opened wide. We just came here and first saw the local spirit of the garden, who could not find the Great Sage. Fearing that we might be delayed in fulfilling the command of the Queen Mother, we did not wait for the Great Sage but proceeded to pluck the peaches. We beg you to forgive us."

When the Great Sage heard these words, his anger changed to delight. "Please arise, divine maidens," he said. "Who is invited to the banquet when the Queen Mother opens wide her treasure chamber?" "The last festival had its own set of rules," said the Immortal Maidens, "and those invited were: the Buddha, the Bodhisattvas, the holy monks, and the arhats of the Western Heaven; Kuan-yin from the South Pole; the Holy Emperor of Great Mercy of the East; the Immortals of Ten Continents and Three Islands; the Dark Spirit of the North Pole; the Great Immortal of the Yellow Horn from the Imperial Center. These were the Elders from the Five Quarters. In addition, there were the Star Spirits of the Five Poles, the Three Pure Ones, the Four Deva Kings, the Heavenly Deva of the Great Monad, and the rest from the Upper Eight Caves. From the Middle Eight Caves there were the Jade Emperor, the Nine Heroes, the Immortals of the Seas and Mountains; and from the Lower Eight Caves, there were the Pope of Darkness and the Terrestrial Immortals. The gods and devas, both great and small, of every palace and mansion, will be attending this happy Festival of the Immortal Peaches."

"Am I invited?" asked the Great Sage, laughing. "We haven't heard your name mentioned," said the Immortal Maidens. "I am the Great Sage, Equal to Heaven," said the Great Sage. "Why shouldn't I, old Monkey, be made an honored guest at the party?" "Well, we told you the rule for the last festival," said the Immortal Maidens, "but we do not know what will happen this time." "You are right," said the Great Sage, "and I don't blame you. You all just stand here and let old Monkey go and do a little detection to find out whether he's invited or not."

Dear Great Sage! He made a magic sign and recited a spell, saying to the various Immortal Maidens, "Stay! Stay! Stay!" This was the magic of immobilization, the effect of which was that the Seven-Gown Immortal Maidens all stood wide-eyed and transfixed beneath the peach trees. Leaping out of the garden, the Great Sage mounted his hallowed cloud and headed straight for the Jasper Pool. As he journeyed, he saw over there

A skyful of holy mist with sparkling light,
And sacred clouds of five colors passing unendingly.
The cries of white cranes resounded in the nine Heavens;
The fine color of red blossoms spread through a thousand leaves.
Right in this midst an immortal now appeared
With a face of natural beauty and features most distinguished.
His spirit glowed like a rainbow dancing in the air.
From his waist hung the list untouched by birth or death.
His name, the Great Joyful Immortal of Naked Feet,
Going to the Peach Festival, he would add to his age.

That Great Immortal of Naked Feet ran right into the Great Sage, who, his head bowed, was just devising a plan to deceive the real immortal. Since he wanted to go in secret to the festival, he asked, "Where is the Venerable Wisdom going?" The Great Immortal said, "On the kind invitation of the Queen Mother, I am going to the happy Festival of Immortal Peaches." "The Venerable Wisdom has not yet learned of what I'm about to say," said the Great Sage. "Because of the speed of my cloud-somersault, the Jade Emperor has sent old Monkey out to all five thoroughfares to invite people to go first to the Hall of Perfect Light for a rehearsal of ceremonies before attending the banquet." Being a sincere and honest man, the Great Immortal took the lie for the truth, though he protested, "In years past we rehearsed right at the Jasper Pool and expressed our gratitude there. Why do we have to go to the Hall of Perfect Light for rehearsal this time before attending the banquet?" Nonetheless, he had no choice but to change the direction of his hallowed cloud and go straight to the hall.

Treading the cloud, the Great Sage recited a spell and, with one shake of his body, changed into the form of the Great Immortal of Naked Feet. It did not take him very long before he reached the treasure chamber. He stopped his cloud and walked softly inside. There he found

Swirling waves of ambrosial fragrance,
Dense layers of holy mist,
A jade terrace decked with ornaments,
A chamber full of the life force,
Ethereal shapes of the phoenix soaring and the argus rising,
And undulant forms of gold blossoms with stems of jade.
Set upon there were the Screen of Nine Phoenixes in Twilight,
The Beacon Mound of Eight Treasures and Purple Mist,
A table inlaid with five-color gold,
And a green jade pot of a thousand flowers.
On the tables were dragon livers and phoenix marrow,

Bear paws and the lips of apes.
Most tempting was every item of the hundred delicacies,
And most succulent the color of every kind of fruit and food.

Everything was laid out in an orderly fashion, but no deity had yet arrived for the feast. Our Great Sage could not make an end of staring at the scene when he suddenly felt the overpowering aroma of wine. Turning his head, he saw, in the long corridor to the right, several wine-making divine officials and grain-mashing stewards. They were giving directions to the few Daoists charged with carrying water and the boys who took care of the fire in washing out the barrels and scrubbing the jugs. For they had already finished making the wine, rich and mellow as the juices of jade. The Great Sage could not prevent the saliva from dripping out of the corner of his mouth, and he wanted to have a taste at once, except that the people were all standing there. He therefore resorted to magic. Plucking a few hairs, he threw them into his mouth and chewed them to pieces before spitting them out. He recited a spell and cried "Change!" They changed into many sleep-inducing insects, which landed on the people's faces. Look at them, how their hands grow weak, their heads droop, and their eyelids sink down. They dropped their activities, and all fell sound asleep. The Great Sage then took some of the rare delicacies and choicest dainties and ran into the corridor. Standing beside the jars and leaning on the barrels, he abandoned himself to drinking. After feasting for a long time, he became thoroughly drunk, but he turned this over in his mind, "Bad! Bad! In a little while, when the invited guests arrive, won't they be indignant with me? What will happen to me once I'm caught? I'd better go back home now and sleep it off!"

Dear Great Sage! Reeling from side to side, he stumbled along solely on the strength of wine, and in a moment he lost his way. It was not the Equal to Heaven Residence that he went to, but the Tushita Palace. The moment he saw it, he realized his mistake. "The Tushita Palace is at the uppermost of the thirty-three Heavens," he said, "the Griefless Heaven which is the home of the Most High Laozi. How did I get here? No matter, I've always wanted to see this old man but have never found the opportunity. Now that it's on my way, I might as well pay him a visit." He straightened out his attire and pushed his way in, but Laozi was nowhere to be seen. In fact, there was not a trace of anyone. The fact of the matter was that Laozi, accompanied by the Aged Buddha Dīpaṁkara, was giving a lecture on the tall, three-storied Red Mound Elixir Platform. The various divine youths, commanders, and officials were all attending the lecture, standing on both sides of the platform. Searching around, our Great Sage went all the way to the alchemical room. He found no one but saw fire burning in an oven beside the hearth, and around the oven were five gourds in which finished elixir was stored. "This thing is the greatest treasure of immortals," said the Great Sage happily. "Since old Monkey has understood the Way and comprehended the mystery of the Internal's identity with the External, I have also wanted to produce some golden elixir on my own to benefit people. While I have been too busy at other times even to think about going home to enjoy myself, good fortune has met me at the door today and presented me with this! As long as Laozi is not around, I'll take a few tablets and try the taste of something new." He poured out the contents of all the gourds and ate them like fried beans.

In a moment, the effect of the elixir had dispelled that of the wine, and he again thought to himself, "Bad! Bad! I have brought on myself calamity greater than Heaven! If the Jade Emperor has knowledge of this, it'll be difficult to preserve my life! Go! Go! Go! I'll go back to the Region Below to be a king." He ran out of the Tushita Palace and, avoiding the former way, left by the West Heaven Gate, making himself invisible by the magic of body concealment. Lowering the direction of his cloud, he returned to the Flower-Fruit Mountain. There he was greeted by flashing banners and shining spears, for the four mighty commanders and the monster kings of seventy-two caves were engaging in a military exercise. "Little ones," the Great Sage called out loudly, "I have returned!" The monsters dropped their weapons and knelt down, saying, "Great Sage! What laxity of mind! You left us for so long, and did not even once visit us to see how we were doing." "It's not that long!" said the Great Sage. "It's not that long!" They walked as they talked, and went deep inside the cave dwelling. After sweeping the place clean and preparing a place for him to rest, and after kowtowing and doing homage, the four mighty commanders said, "The Great Sage has been living for over a century in Heaven. May we ask what appointment he actually received?"

"I recall that it's been but half a year," said the Great Sage, laughing. "How can you talk of a century?" "One day in Heaven," said the commanders, "is equal to one year on Earth." The Great Sage said, "I am glad to say that the Jade Emperor this time was more favorably disposed toward me, and he did indeed appoint me Great Sage, Equal to Heaven. An official residence was built for me, and two departments—Peace and Quiet, and Serene Spirit—were established, with bodyguards and attendants in each department. Later, when it was found that I carried no responsibility, I was asked to take care of the Garden of Immortal Peaches. Recently the Lady Queen Mother gave the Grand Festival of Immortal Peaches, but she did not invite me. Without waiting for her invitation, I went first to the Jasper Pool and secretly consumed the food and wine. Leaving that place, I staggered into the palace of Laozi and finished up all the elixir stored in five gourds. I was afraid that the Jade Emperor would be offended, and so I decided to walk out of the Heaven Gate."

The various monsters were delighted by these words, and they prepared a banquet of fruits and wine to welcome him. A stone bowl was filled with coconut wine and presented to the Great Sage, who took a mouthful and then exclaimed with a grimace, "It tastes awful! Just awful!" "The Great Sage," said Beng and Ba, the two commanders, "has grown accustomed to tasting divine wine and food in Heaven. Small wonder that coconut wine now seems hardly delectable. But the proverb says, 'Tasty or not, it's water from home!'" "And all of you are, 'related or not, people from home'!" said the Great Sage. "When I was enjoying myself this morning at the Jaspar Pool, I saw many jars and jugs in the corridor full of the juices of jade, which you have never savored. Let me go back and steal a few bottles to bring down here. Just drink half a cup, and each one of you will live long without growing old." The various monkeys could not contain their delight. The Great Sage immediately left the cave and, with one somersault, went directly back to the Festival of Immortal Peaches, again using the magic of body concealment. As he entered the doorway of the Palace of the Jasper Pool, he saw that the wine makers, the grain mashers, the water carriers, and the fire tenders were still asleep and snoring. He took two large bottles, one under each arm, and carried two more in his hands. Reversing the direction of his cloud, he returned to the monkeys in the cave. They held their own Festival of Immortal Wine, with each one drinking a few cups, which incident we shall relate no further.

Now we tell you about the Seven-Gown Immortal Maidens, who did not find a release from the Great Sage's magic of immobilization until a whole day had gone by. Each one of them then took her flower basket and reported to the Queen Mother, saying, "We are delayed because the Great Sage, Equal to Heaven, imprisoned us with his magic." "How many baskets of immortal peaches have you gathered?" asked the Queen Mother. "Only two baskets of small peaches, and three of medium-sized peaches," said the Immortal Maidens, "for when we went to the back of the grove, there was not even half a large one left! We think the Great Sage must have eaten them all. As we went looking for him, he unexpectedly made his appearance and threatened us with violence and beating. He also questioned us about who had been invited to the bnquet, and we gave him a thorough account of the last festival. It was then that he bound us with a spell, and we didn't know where he went. It was only a moment ago that we found release and so could come back here."

When the Queen Mother heard these words, she went immediately to the Jade Emperor and presented him with a full account of what had taken place. Before she finished speaking, the group of wine makers together with the various divine officials also came to report: "Someone unknown to us has vandalized the Festival of Immortal Peaches. The juice of jade, the eight dainties, and the hundred delicacies have all been stolen or eaten up." Four royal preceptors then came up to announce, "The Supreme Patriarch of Dao has arrived." The Jade Emperor went out with the Queen Mother to greet him. Having paid his respects to them, Laozi said, "There are, in the house of this old Daoist, some finished Golden Elixir of Nine Turns, which are reserved for the use of Your Majesty during the next Grand Festival of Cinnabar. Strange to say, they have been stolen by some thief, and I have come specifically to make this known to Your Majesty." This report stunned the Jade Emperor. Presently the officials from the Equal to Heaven Residence came to announce, kowtowing, "The Great Sage Sun has not been discharging his duties of late. He went out yesterday and still has not yet returned. Moreover, we do not know where he went." These words gave the Jade Emperor added anxiety.

Next came the Great Immortal of Naked Feet, who prostrated himself and said, "Yesterday, in response to the Queen Mother's invitation, your subject was on his way to attend the festival when he met by chance the Great Sage, Equal to Heaven. The Sage said to your subject that Your Majesty had ordered him to send your subject first to the Hall of Perfect Light for a rehearsal of ceremonies before attending the banquet. Your subject followed his direction and duly went to the hall. But I did not see the dragon chariot and the phoenix carriage of Your Majesty, and therefore hastened to come here to wait upon you."

More astounded than ever, the Jade Emperor said, "This fellow now falsifies imperial decrees and deceives my worthy ministers! Let the Divine Minister of Detection quickly locate his whereabouts!" The minister received his order and left the palace to make a thorough investigation. After obtaining all the details, he returned presently to report, "The person who has so profoundly disturbed Heaven is none other than the Great Sage, Equal to Heaven." He then gave a repeated account of all the previous incidents, and the Jade Emperor was furious. He at once commanded the Four Great Devarājas to assist Devarāja Li and Prince Naṭa. Together, they called up the Twenty-Eight Constellations, the Nine Luminaries, the

Twelve Horary Branches, the Fearless Guards of Five Quarters, the Four
Temporal Guardians, the Stars of East and West, the Gods of North and
South, the Deities of the Five Mountains and the Four Rivers, the Star
Spirits of the entire Heaven, and a hundred thousand celestial soldiers.
They were ordered to set up eighteen sets of cosmic net, to journey to the
Region Below, to encircle completely the Flower-Fruit Mountain, and
to capture the rogue and bring him to justice. All the deities immediately
alerted their troops and departed from the Heavenly Palace. As they left,
this was the spectacle of the expedition:

Yellow with dust; the churning wind concealed the dark'ning sky:
Reddish with clay, the rising fog o'erlaid the dusky world.
Because an impish monkey insulted the Highest Lord,
The saints of all Heaven descended to this mortal Earth.
Those Four Great Devarājas,
Those Fearless Guards of Five Quarters—
Those Four Great Deva Kings made up the main command;
Those Fearless Guards of Five Quarters moved countless troops.
Li, the Pagoda Bearer, gave orders from the army's center,
With the fierce Naṭa as the captain of his vanward forces.
The Star of Rāhu, at the forefront, made the roll call;
The Star of Ketu, noble and tall, brought up the rear:
Sōma, the moon, displayed a spirit most eager;
Āditya, the sun, was all shining and radiant.
Heroes of special talents were the Stars of Five Phases.
The Nine Luminaries most relished a good battle.
The Horary Branches of Zi, Wu, Mao, and Yao—
They were all celestial guardians of titanic strength.
To the east and west, the Five Plagues and the Five Mountains!
To the left and right, the Six Gods of Darkness and the Six Gods of Light!
Above and below, the Dragon Gods of the Four Rivers!
And in tightest formation, the Twenty-Eight Constellations!
Citrā, Svātī, Viśākhā, and Anurādhā were the captains.
Revatī, Aśvinī, Apabharaṇī, and Kṛttikā knew combat well.
Uttara-Aṣāḍhā, Abhijit, Śravaṇā, Śraviṣṭha, Pūrva-Proṣṭhapada, Uttara-
*   Proṣṭhapada,*
Rohiṇī, Mūlabarhaṇī, Pūrva-Aṣāḍhā—every one an able star!
Punarvasu, Tiṣya, Aśleṣā, Meghā, Pūrva-Phalgunī, and Hastā—
All brandished swords and spears to show their power.
Stopping the cloud and lowering the mist they came to this mortal world
And pitched their tents before the Mountain of Flower and Fruit.

The poem says:

> Many are the forms of the changeful Heaven-Born Monkey King!
> Snatching wine and stealing elixir, he revels in his mountain lair.
> Since he has wrecked the Grand Festival of Immortal Peaches,
> A hundred thousand soldiers of Heaven now spread the net of God.

Devarāja Li now gave the order for the celestial soldiers to pitch their tents, and a cordon was drawn so tightly around the Flower-Fruit Mountain that not even water could escape! Moreover, eighteen sets of cosmic net were spread out above and below the region, and the Nine Luminaries were then ordered to go into battle. They led their troops and advanced to the cave, in front of which they found a troop of monkeys, both great and small, prancing about playfully. "Little monsters over there," cried one of the Star Spirits in a severe voice, "where is your Great Sage? We are Heavenly deities sent here from the Region Above to subdue your rebellious Great Sage. Tell him to come here quickly and surrender. If he but utters half a 'No,' all of you will be executed." Hastily the little monsters reported inside, "Great Sage, disaster! Disaster! Outside there are nine savage deities who claim that they are sent from the Region Above to subdue the Great Sage." Our Great Sage was just sharing the Heavenly wine with the four mighty commanders and the monster kings of seventy-two caves. Hearing this announcement, he said in a most nonchalant manner,

> "If you have wine today, get drunk today;
> Mind not the troubles in front of your door!"

Scarcely had he uttered this proverb when another group of imps came leaping and said, "Those nine savage gods are trying to provoke battle with foul words and nasty language." "Don't listen to them," said the Great Sage, laughing.

> "Let us seek today's pleasure in poetry and wine,
> And cease asking when we may achieve glory or fame."

Hardly had he finished speaking when still another flock of imps arrived to report, "Father, those nine savage gods have broken down the door, and are about to fight their way in!" "The reckless, witless deities!" said the Great Sage angrily. "They really have no manners! I was not about to quarrel with them. Why are they abusing me to my face?" He gave the order for the One-Horn Demon King to lead the monster kings of seventy-two caves to battle, adding that old Monkey and the four mighty commanders would follow in the rear. The Demon King swiftly led his troops of ogres to go out to fight, but they were ambushed by the Nine Luminaries and pinned down right at the head of the sheet iron bridge.

At the height of the melee, the Great Sage arrived. "Make way!" he yelled, whipping out his iron rod. One wave of it and it was as thick as a rice bowl and about twelve feet long. The Great Sage plunged into battle, and none of the Nine Luminaries dared oppose him. In a moment, they were all beaten back. When they regrouped themselves again in battle formation, the Nine Luminaries stood still and said, "You senseless Bimawen! You are guilty of the ten evils. You first stole peaches and then wine, utterly disrupting the Grand Festival of Immortal Peaches. You also robbed Laozi of his immortal elixir, and then you had the gall to plunder the imperial winery for your personal enjoyment. Don't you realize that you have piled up sin upon sin?" "Indeed," said the Great Sage, "these several incidents did occur! But what do you intend to do now?" The Nine Luminaries said, "We received the golden decree of the Jade Emperor to lead our troops here to subdue you. Submit at once, and spare these creatures from being slaughtered. If not, we shall level this mountain and overturn this cave!" "How great is your magical power, silly gods," retorted the Great Sage angrily, "that you dare to mouth such foolhardy words? Don't go away! Have a taste of old Monkey's rod!" The Nine Luminaries mounted a joint attack, but the Handsome Monkey King was not in the least intimidated. He wielded his golden-hooped rod, parrying left and right, and fought the Nine Luminaries until they were thoroughly exhausted. Every one of them turned around and fled, his weapons trailing behind him. Running into the tent at the center of their army, they said to the Pagoda Bearer Devarāja, "That Monkey King is indeed an intrepid warrior! We cannot withstand him, and have returned defeated." Devarāja Li then ordered the Four Great Devarājas and the Twenty-Eight Constellations to go out together to do battle. Without displaying the slightest panic, the Great Sage also ordered the One-Horn Demon King, the monster kings of seventy-two caves, and the four mighty commanders to range themselves in battle formation in front of the cave. Look at this all-out battle! It was truly terrifying with

The cold, soughing wind,
The dark, dreadful fog.
On one side, the colorful banners fluttered;
On the other, lances and halberds glimmered.
There were row upon row of shining helmets,
And coat upon coat of gleaming armor.
Row upon row of helmets shining in the sunlight
Resembled silver bells whose chimes echoed in the sky;
Coat upon coat of gleaming armor rising clifflike in layers
Seemed like glaciers crushing the earth.
The giant scimitars

Flew and flashed like lightning;
The mulberry-white spears,
Could pierce even mist and cloud!
The crosslike halberds
And tiger-eye lashes
Were arranged like thick rows of hemp;
The green swords of bronze
And four-sided shovels
Crowded together like trees in a dense forest.
Curved bows, crossbows, and stout arrows with eagle plumes,
Short staffs and snakelike lances—all could kill or maim.
That compliant rod, which the Great Sage owned,
Kept tossing and turning in this battle with gods.
They fought till the air was rid of birds flying by;
Wolves and tigers were driven from within the mount;
The planet was darkened by hurtling rocks and stones,
And the cosmos bedimmed by flying dust and dirt.
The clamor and clangor disturbed Heaven and Earth;
The scrap and scuffle alarmed both demons and gods.

Beginning with the battle formation at dawn, they fought until the sun sank down behind the western hills. The One-Horn Demon King and the monster kings of seventy-two caves were all taken captive by the forces of Heaven. Those who escaped were the four mighty commanders and the troop of monkeys, who hid themselves deep inside the Water-Curtain Cave. With his single rod, the Great Sage withstood in midair the Four Great Devarājas, Li the Pagoda Bearer, and Prince Naṭa and battled with them for a long time. When he saw that evening was approaching, the Great Sage plucked a handful of hairs, threw them into his mouth, and chewed them to pieces. He spat them out, crying, "Change!" They changed at once into many thousands of Great Sages, each employing a golden-hooped rod! They beat back Prince Naṭa and defeated the Five Devarājas. In triumph the Great Sage collected back his hairs and hurried back to his cave. Soon, at the head of the sheet iron bridge, he was met by the four mighty commanders leading the rest of the monkeys. As they kowtowed to receive him they cried three times, sobbing aloud, and then they laughed three times, hee-heeing and ho-hoing. The Great Sage said, "Why do you all laugh and cry when you see me?" "When we fought with the Deva Kings this morning," said the four mighty commanders, "the monster kings of seventy-two caves and the One-Horn Demon King were all taken captive by the gods. We were the only ones who managed to escape alive, and that is why we cried. Now we see that the Great Sage has returned unharmed and triumphant, and so we laugh as well."

"Victory and defeat," said the Great Sage, "are the common experiences of a soldier. The ancient proverb says,

You may kill ten thousand of your enemies,
But you will lose three thousand of your allies!

Moreover, those chieftains who have been captured are tigers and leopards, wolves and insects, badgers and foxes, and the like. Not a single member of our own kind has been hurt. Why then should we be disconsolate? Although our adversaries have been beaten back by my magic of body division, they are still encamped at the foot of our mountain. Let us be most vigilant, therefore, in our defense. Have a good meal, rest well, and conserve your energy. When morning comes, watch me perform a great magic and capture some of these generals from Heaven, so that our comrades may be avenged." The four mighty commanders drank a few bowls of coconut wine with the host of monkeys and went to sleep peacefully. We shall speak no more of them.

When those Four Devarājas retired their troops and stopped their fighting, each one of the Heavenly commanders came to report his accomplishment. There were those who had captured lions and elephants and those who had apprehended wolves, crawling creatures, and foxes. Not a single monkey monster, however, had been seized. The camp was then secured, a great tent was pitched, and those commanders with meritorious services were rewarded. The soldiers in charge of the cosmic nets were ordered to carry bells and were given passwords. They encircled the Flower-Fruit Mountain to await the great battle of the next day, and each soldier everywhere diligently kept his watch. So this is the situation:

The impish monkey in rebellion disturbs Heaven and Earth.
But the net is spread and open, ready night and day.

We do not know what took place after the next morning; let's listen to the explanation in the next chapter.

SIX

Guanyin, attending the banquet, inquires into the affair;
The Little Sage, exerting his power, subdues the Great Sage.

For the moment we shall not tell you about the siege of the gods or the
Great Sage at rest. We speak instead of the Great Compassionate Deliverer,
the Efficacious Bodhisattva Guanyin from the Potalaka Mountain of the
South Sea. Invited by the Lady Queen Mother to attend the Grand Festival
of Immortal Peaches, she arrived at the treasure chamber of the Jasper Pool
with her senior disciple, Hui'an. There they found the whole place desolate
and the banquet tables in utter disarray. Although several members of the
Heavenly pantheon were present, none was seated. Instead, they were all
engaged in vigorous exchanges and discussions. After the Bodhisattva had
greeted the various deities, they told her what had occurred. "Since there
will be no festival," said the Bodhisattva, "nor any raising of cups, all of
you might as well come with this humble cleric to see the Jade Emperor."
The gods followed her gladly, and they went to the entrance to the Hall of
Perfect Light. There the Bodhisattva was met by the Four Heavenly Preceptors and the Immortal of Naked Feet, who recounted how the celestial
soldiers, ordered by an enraged Jade Emperor to capture the monster, had
not yet returned. The Bodhisattva said, "I would like to have an audience
with the Jade Emperor. May I trouble one of you to announce my arrival?"
The Heavenly Preceptor Qiu Hongji went at once into the Treasure Hall
of Divine Mists and, having made his report, invited Guanyin to enter.
Laozi then took the upper seat with the Emperor, while the Lady Queen
Mother was in attendance behind the throne.

The Bodhisattva led the crowd inside. After paying homage to the
Jade Emperor, they also saluted Laozi and the Queen Mother. When each
of them was seated, she asked, "How is the Grand Festival of Immortal
Peaches?" "Every year when the festival has been given," said the Jade
Emperor, "we have thoroughly enjoyed ourselves. This year it has been
completely ruined by a baneful monkey, leaving us with nothing but an invitation to disappointment." "Where did this baneful monkey come from?"

asked the Bodhisattva. "He was born of a stone egg on top of the Flower-Fruit Mountain of the Aolai Country of the East Pūrvavideha Continent," said the Jade Emperor. "At the moment of his birth, two beams of golden light flashed immediately from his eyes, reaching as far as the Palace of the Polestar. We did not think much of that, but he later became a monster, subduing the Dragon and taming the Tiger as well as eradicating his name from the Register of Death. When the Dragon Kings and the Kings of the Underworld brought the matter to our attention, we wanted to capture him. The Star of Long Life, however, observed that all the beings of the three regions which possessed the nine apertures could attain immortality. We therefore decided to educate and nurture the talented monkey and summoned him to the Region Above. He was appointed to the post of Bimawen at the imperial stables, but, taking offense at the lowliness of his position, he left Heaven in rebellion. We then sent Devarāja Li and Prince Naṭa to ask for his submission by proclaiming a decree of pacification. He was brought again to the Region Above and was appointed the Great Sage, Equal to Heaven—a rank without compensation. Since he had nothing to do but to wander east and west, we feared that he might cause further trouble. So he was asked to look after the Garden of Immortal Peaches. But he broke the law and ate all the large peaches from the oldest trees. By then, the banquet was about to be given. As a person without salary he was, of course, not invited; nonetheless, he plotted to deceive the Immortal of Naked Feet and managed to sneak into the banquet by assuming the Immortal's appearance. He finished off all the divine wine and food, after which he also stole Laozi's elixir and took away a considerable quantity of imperial wine for the enjoyment of his mountain monkeys. Our mind has been sorely vexed by this, and we therefore sent a hundred thousand celestial soldiers with cosmic nets to capture him. We haven't yet received today's report on how the battle is faring."

When the Bodhisattva heard this, she said to Disciple Hui'an, "You must leave Heaven at once, go down to the Flower-Fruit Mountain, and inquire into the military situation. If the enemy is engaged, you can lend your assistance; in any event, you must bring back a factual report." The Disciple Hui'an straightened out his attire and mounted the cloud to leave the palace, an iron rod in his hand. When he arrived at the mountain, he found layers of cosmic net drawn tightly and sentries at every gate holding bells and shouting passwords. The encirclement of the mountain was indeed watertight! Hui'an stood still and called out, "Heavenly sentinels, may I trouble you to announce my arrival? I am Prince Mokṣa, second son of Devarāja Li, and I am also Hui'an, senior disciple of Guanyin of South Sea.

I have come to inquire about the military situation." The divine soldiers of the Five Mountains at once reported this beyond the gate. The consellations Aquarius, Pleiades, Hydra, and Scorpio then conveyed the message to the central tent. Devarāja Li issued a directorial flag, which ordered the cosmic nets to be opened and entrance permitted for the visitor. Day was just dawning in the east as Hui'an followed the flag inside and prostrated himself before the Four Great Devarājas and Devarāja Li.

After he had finished his greetings, Devarāja Li said, "My child, where have you come from?" "Your untutored son," said Hui'an, "accompanied the Bodhisattva to attend the Festival of Immortal Peaches. Seeing that the festival was desolate and the Jasper Pool laid waste, the Bodhisattva led the various deities and your untutored son to have an audience with the Jade Emperor. The Jade Emperor spoke at length about Father and King's expedition to the Region Below to subdue the baneful monkey. Since no report has returned for a whole day and neither victory nor defeat has been ascertained, the Bodhisattva ordered your untutored son to come here to find out how things stand." "We came here yesterday to set up the encampment," said Devarāja Li, "and the Nine Luminaries were sent to provoke battle. But this fellow made a grand display of his magical powers, and the Nine Luminaries all returned defeated. After that, I led the troops personally to confront him, and the fellow also brought his forces into formation. Our hundred thousand celestial soldiers fought with him until evening, when he retreated from the battle by using the magic of body division. When we recalled the troops and made our investigation, we found that we had captured some wolves, crawling creatures, tigers, leopards, and the like. But we did not even catch half a monkey monster! And today we have not yet gone into battle."

As he was saying all this, someone came from the gate of the camp to report, "That Great Sage, leading his band of monkey monsters, is shouting for battle outside." The Four Devarājas, Devarāja Li, and the prince at once made plans to bring out the troops, when Mokṣa said, "Father King, your untutored son was told by the Bodhisattva to come down here to acquire information. She also told me to give you assistance should there be actual combat. Though I am not very talented, I volunteer to go out now and see what kind of a Great Sage this is!" "Child," said the Devarāja, "since you have studied with the Bodhisattva for several years, you must, I suppose, have some powers! But do be careful!"

Dear prince! Grasping the iron rod with both hands, he tightened up his embroidered garment and leaped out of the gate. "Who is the Great Sage, Equal to Heaven?" he cried. Holding high his compliant rod, the Great

Sage answered, "None other than old Monkey here! Who are you that you dare question me?" "I am Mokṣa, the second prince of Devarāja Li," said Mokṣṣa. "At present I am also the disciple of Bodhisattva Guanyin, a defender of the faith before her treasure throne. And my religious name is Hui'an." "Why have you left your religious training at South Sea and come here to see me?" said the Great Sage. "I was sent by my master to inquire about the military situation," said Mokṣa. "Seeing what a nuisance you have made of yourself, I have come specifically to capture you." "You dare to talk so big?" said the Great Sage. "But don't run away! Have a taste of old Monkey's rod!" Mokṣa was not at all frightened and met his opponent squarely with his own iron rod. The two of them stood before the gate of the camp at mid-mountain, and what a magnificent battle they fought!

Though one rod is pitted against another, the iron's quite different;
Though this weapon couples with the other, the persons are not the same.
The one called the Great Sage is an apostate primordial immortal;
The other is Guanyin's disciple, truly heroic and proud.
The all-iron rod, pounded by a thousand hammers,
Is made by the Six Gods of Darkness and the Six Gods of Light.
The compliant rod fixes the depth of Heaven's river,
A thing divine ruling the oceans with its magic might.
The two of them in meeting have found their match;
Back and forth they battle in endless rounds.
From this one the rod of stealthy hands,
Savage and fierce,
Around the waist stabs and jabs swiftly as the wind;
From the other the rod, doubling as a spear
Driving and relentless,
Lets up not a moment its parrying left and right.
On this side the banners flare and flutter;
On the other the war drums roll and rattle.
Ten thousand celestial fighters circle round and round.
The monkey monsters of a whole cave stand in rows and rows.
Weird fog and dark cloud spread throughout the earth.
The fume and smoke of battle reach even Heaven's Palace.
Yesterday's battle was something to behold.
Still more violent is the contest today.
Envy the Monkey King, for he's truly able:
Moksa's defeated—he's fleeing for his life!

Our Great Sage battled Hui'an for fifty or sixty rounds until the prince's arms and shoulders were sore and numb and he could fight no longer. After one final, futile swing of his weapon, he fled in defeat. The Great Sage then gathered together his monkey troops and stationed them securely outside the entrance of the cave. At the camp of the Devarāja, the celestial soldiers could be seen receiving the prince and making way for him to enter the gate. Panting and puffing, he ran in and gasped out to the Four Devarājas, Pagoda Bearer Li, and Naṭa, "That Great Sage! What an ace! Great indeed is his magical power! Your son cannot overcome him and has returned defeated." Shocked by the sight, Devarāja Li at once wrote a memorial to the Throne to request further assistance. The demon king Mahābāli and Prince Mokṣa were sent to Heaven to present the document.

The two of them dared not linger. They crashed out of the cosmic nets and mounted the holy mist and hallowed cloud. In a moment they reached the Hall of Perfect Light and met the Four Heavenly Preceptors, who led them into the Treasure Hall of Divine Mists to present their memorial. Hui'an also saluted the Bodhisattva, who asked him, "What have you found out about the situation?" "When I reached the Flower-Fruit Mountain by your order," said Hui'an, "I opened the cosmic nets by my call. Seeing my father, I told him of my master's intentions in sending me. Father King said, 'We fought a battle yesterday with that Monkey King but managed to take from him only tigers, leopards, lions, elephants, and the like. We did not catch a single one of his monkey monsters.' As we were talking, he again demanded battle. Your disciple used the iron rod to fight him for fifty or sixty rounds, but I could not prevail against him and returned to the camp defeated. Thus father had to send the demon king Mahābāli and your pupil to come here for help." The Bodhisattva bowed her head and pondered.

We now tell you about the Jade Emperor, who opened the memorial and found a message asking for assistance. "This is rather absurd!" he said laughing. "Is this monkey monster such a wizard that not even a hundred thousand soldiers from Heaven can vanquish him? Devarāja Li is again asking for help. What division of divine warriors can we send to assist him?" Hardly had he finished speaking when Guanyin folded her hands and said to him, "Your Majesty, let not your mind be troubled! This humble cleric will recommend a god who can capture the monkey." "Which one would you recommend?" said the Jade Emperor. "Your Majesty's nephew," said the Bodhisattva, "the Immortal Master of Illustrious Sagacity Erlang, who is living at the mouth of the River of Libations in the Guan Prefecture and enjoying the incense and oblations offered to him from the Region Below. In former days he himself slew six monsters. Under his command are the Brothers of Plum Mountain and twelve hundred plant-headed deities, all possessing great magical powers. However, he will agree only to special assignments and will not obey any general summons. Your Majesty may want to send an edict transferring his troops to the scene of the battle and requesting his assistance. Our monster will surely be captured." When the Jade Emperor heard this, he immediately issued such an edict and ordered the demon king Mahābāli to present it.

Having received the edict, the demon king mounted a cloud and went straight to the mouth of the River of Libations. It took him less than half an hour to reach the temple of the Immortal Master. Immediately the demon magistrates guarding the doors made this report inside: "There is a messenger from Heaven outside who has arrived with an edict in his hand." Erlang and his brothers came out to receive the edict, which was read before burning incense. The edict said:

> The Great Sage, Equal to Heaven, a monstrous monkey from the Flower-Fruit Mountain, is in revolt. At the Palace he stole peaches, wine, and elixir, and disrupted the Grand Festival of Immortal Peaches. A hundred thousand Heavenly soldiers with eighteen sets of cosmic nets were dispatched to surround the mountain and capture him, but victory has not yet been secured. We therefore make this special request of our worthy nephew and his sworn brothers to go to the Flower-Fruit Mountain and assist in destroying this monster. Following your success will be lofty elevation and abundant reward.

In great delight the Immortal Master said, "Let the messenger of Heaven go back. I will go at once to offer my assistance with drawn sword." The demon king went back to report, but we shall speak no further of that.

This Immortal Master called together the Six Brothers of Plum Mountain: they were Kang, Zhang, Yao, and Li, the four grand marshals, and Guo Shen and Zhi Jian, the two generals. As they congregated before the court, he said to them, "The Jade Emperor just now sent us to the Flower-Fruit Mountain to capture a monstrous monkey. Let's get going!" Delighted and willing, the brothers at once called out the divine soldiers under their command. With falcons mounted and dogs on leashes, with arrows ready and bows drawn, they left in a violent magic wind and crossed in a moment the great Eastern Ocean. As they landed on the Flower-Fruit Mountain, they saw their way blocked by dense layers of cosmic net. "Divine commanders guarding the cosmic nets, hear us," they shouted. "We are specially assigned by the Jade Emperor to capture the monstrous monkey. Open the gate of your camp quickly and let us through." The various deities conveyed the message to the inside, level by level. The Four Devarājas and Devarāja Li then came out to the gate of the camp to receive them. After they had exchanged greetings, there were questions about the military situation, and the Devarāja gave them a thorough briefing. "Now that I, the Little Sage, have come," said the Immortal Master, laughing, "he will have to engage in a contest of transformations with his adversary. You gentlemen make sure that the cosmic nets are tightly drawn on all sides, but leave the top uncovered. Let me try my hand in this contest. If I lose, you gentlemen need not come to my assistance, for my own brothers will be there to support me. If I win, you gentlemen will not be needed in tying him up either; my own brothers will take care of that. All I need is the Pagoda Bearer Devarāja to stand in midair with his imp-reflecting mirror. If the monster should be defeated, I fear that he may try to flee to a distant locality. Make sure that his image is clearly reflected in the mirror, so that we don't lose him." The Devarājas set themselves up in the four directions, while the Heavenly soldiers all lined up according to their planned formations.

With himself as the seventh brother, the Immortal Master led the four grand marshals and the two generals out of the camp to provoke battle. The other warriors were ordered to defend their encampment with vigilance, and the plant-headed deities were ordered to have the falcons and dogs ready for battle. The Immortal Master went to the front of the Water-Curtain Cave, where he saw a troop of monkeys neatly positioned in an array that resembled a coiled dragon. At the center of the array was the banner bearing the words "The Great Sage, Equal to Heaven." "That audacious monster!" said the Immortal Master. "How dare he assume the rank 'Equal to Heaven'?" "There's no time for praise or blame," said the Six Brothers of Plum Mountain. "Let's challenge him at once!" When the little monkeys in front of the camp saw the Immortal Master, they ran quickly to make their report. Seizing his golden-hooped rod, straightening out his golden cuirass, slipping on his cloud-treading shoes, and pressing down his red-gold cap, the Monkey King leaped out of the camp. He opened his eyes wide to stare at the Immortal Master, whose features were remarkably refined and whose attire was most elegant. Truly, he was a man of

> Features most comely and noble mien,
> With ears reaching his shoulders and eyes alert and bright.
> A cap of the Three Mountains' Phoenix flying crowned his head,
> And a pale yellow robe of goose-down he wore on his frame.
> His boots of gold threads matched the hoses of coiling dragons.
> Eight emblems like flower clusters adorned his belt of jade.

From his waist hung the pellet bow of new moon shape.
His hands held a lance with three points and two blades.
He once axed open the Peach Mountain to save his mother.
He struck with a single pellet two phoenixes of Zongluo.
He slew the Eight Monsters, and his fame spread wide;
He made as chivalric allies the Plum Mountain's Seven Sages.
A lofty mind, he scorned being a relative of Heaven. 阿罔怀 鼠乙, 不同作 以向诔. 临心.
His proud nature led him to live near the River of Libations.
This is the Kind and Magnanimous Sage from the City of Chi;
Skilled in boundless transformations, his name's Erlang.

When the Great Sage saw him, he lifted high his golden-hooped rod with gales of laughter and called out, "What little warrior are you and where do you come from, that you dare present yourself here to provoke battle?" "You must have eyes but no pupils," shouted the Immortal Master, "if you don't recognize me! I am the maternal nephew of the Jade Emperor, Erlang, the King of Illustrious Grace and Spirit by imperial appointment. I have received my order from above to arrest you, the rebellious Bimawen ape. Don't you know that your time has come?" "I remember," said the Great Sage, "that the sister of the Jade Emperor some years ago became enamored of the Region Below; she married a man by the name of Yang and had a son by him. Are you that boy who was reputed to have cleaved open the Peach Mountain with his ax? I would like to rebuke you roundly, but I have no grudge against you. I can hit you with this rod of mine too, but I'd like to spare your life! A little boy like you, why don't you hurry back and ask your Four Great Devarājas to come out?" When the Immortal Master heard this, he grew very angry and shouted, "Reckless ape! Don't you dare be so insolent! Take a sample of my blade!" Swerving to dodge the blow, the Great Sage quickly raised his golden-hooped rod to engage his opponent. What a fine fight there was between the two of them:

Erlang, the God of Illustrious Kindness,
And the Great Sage, Equal to Heaven!
The former, haughty and high-minded, defied the Handsome Monkey King.
The latter, not knowing his man, would crush a stalwart foe.
Suddenly these two met,
And both desired a match—
They had never known which was the better man;
Today they'll learn who's strong and who's weak!
The iron rod seemed a flying dragon,
And the lance divine a dancing phoenix:
Left and right they struck,

Attacking both front and back.
The Six Brothers of Plum Mountain filled one side with their awesome
    presence,
While the four generals, like Ma and Liu, took command on the other side.
All worked as one to wave the flags and beat the drums;
All assisted the battle by cheering and sounding the gong.
Those two sharp weapons sought a chance to hurt,
But the thrusts and parries slacked not one whit.
The golden-hooped rod, that wonder of the sea,
Could change and fly to gain a victory.
A little lag and your life is over!
A tiny slip and your luck runs out!

The Immortal Master fought the Great Sage for more than three hundred rounds, but the result still could not be determined. The Immortal Master, therefore, summoned all his magical powers; with a shake, he made his body a hundred thousand feet tall. Holding with both hands the divine lance of three points and two blades like the peaks that cap the Hua Mountain, this green-faced, saber-toothed figure with scarlet hair aimed a violent blow at the head of the Great Sage. But the Great Sage also exerted his magical power and changed himself into a figure having the features and height of Erlang. He wielded a compliant golden-hooped rod that resembled the Heaven-supporting pillar on top of Mount Kunlun to oppose the god Erlang. This vision so terrified the marshals, Ma and Liu, that they could no longer wave the flags, and so appalled the generals, Beng and Ba, that they could use neither scimitar nor sword. On the side of Erlang, the Brothers Kang, Zhang, Yao, Li, Guo Shen, and Zhi Jian gave the order to the plant-headed deities to let loose the falcons and dogs and to advance upon those monkeys in front of the Water-Curtain Cave with mounted arrows and drawn bows. The charge, alas,

Dispersed the four mighty commanders of monkey imps
And captured two or three thousand numinous fiends!

Those monkeys dropped their spears and abandoned their armor, forsook their swords and threw away their lances. They scattered in all directions—running, screaming, scuttling up the mountain, or scrambling back to the cave. It was as if a cat at night had stolen upon resting birds: they darted up as stars to fill the sky. The Brothers thus gained a complete victory, of which we shall speak no further.

Now we were telling you about the Immortal Master and the Great Sage, who had changed themselves into forms which imitated Heaven and Earth. As they were doing battle, the Great Sage suddenly perceived that the monkeys of his camp were put to rout, and his heart grew faint. He changed out of his magic form, turned around, and fled, dragging his rod behind him. When the Immortal Master saw that he was running away, he chased him with great strides, saying, "Where you going? Surrender now, and your life will be spared!" The Great Sage did not stop to fight anymore but ran as fast as he could. Near the cave's entrance, he ran right into Kang, Zhang, Yao, and Li, the four grand marshals, and Guo Shen and Zhi Jian, the two generals, who were at the head of an army blocking his way. "Lawless ape!" they cried, "where do you think you're going?" Quivering all over, the Great Sage squeezed his golden-hooped rod back into an embroidery needle and hid it in his ear. With a shake of his body, he changed himself into a small sparrow and flew to perch on top of a tree. In great agitation, the six Brothers searched all around but could not find him. "We've lost the monkey monster! We've lost the monkey monster!" they all cried.

As they were making all that clamor, the Immortal Master arrived and asked, "Brothers, where did you lose him in the chase?" "We just had him boxed in here," said the gods, "but he simply vanished." Scanning the place with his phoenix eye wide open, Erlang at once discovered that the Great Sage had changed into a small sparrow perched on a tree. He changed out of his magic form and took off his pellet bow. With a shake of his body, he changed into a sparrow hawk with outstretched wings, ready to attack its prey. When the Great Sage saw this, he darted up with a flutter of his wings; changing himself into a cormorant, he headed straight for the open sky. When Erlang saw this, he quickly shook his feathers and changed into a huge ocean crane, which could penetrate the clouds to strike with its bill. The Great Sage therefore lowered his direction, changed into a small fish, and dove into a stream with a splash. Erlang rushed to the edge of the water but could see no trace of him. He thought to himself, "This simian must have gone into the water and changed himself into a fish, a shrimp, or the like. I'll change again to catch him." He duly changed into a fish hawk and skimmed downstream over the waves. After a while, the fish into which the Great Sage had changed was swimming along with the current. Suddenly he saw a bird that looked like a green kite though its feathers were not entirely green, like an egret though it had small feathers, and like an old crane though its feet were not red. "That must be the transformed Erlang waiting for me," he thought to himself. He swiftly turned around and swam away after releasing a few bubbles. When Erlang saw this, he said, "The fish that released the bubbles looks like a carp though its tail is not red, like a perch though there are no patterns on its scales, like a snake fish though there are no stars on its head, like a bream though its gills have no bristles. Why does it move away the moment it sees me? It must be the transformed monkey himself!" He swooped toward the fish and snapped at it with his beak. The Great Sage shot out of the water and changed at once into a water snake: he swam toward shore and wriggled into the grass along the bank. When Erlang saw that he had snapped in vain and that a snake had darted away in the water with a splash, he knew that the Great Sage had changed again. Turning around quickly, he changed into a scarlet-topped gray crane, which extended its beak like sharp iron pincers to devour the snake. With a bounce, the snake changed again into a spotted bustard stand-ing by itself rather stupidly amid the water-pepper along the bank. When Erlang saw that the monkey had changed into such a vulgar creature—for the spotted bustard is the basest and most promiscuous of birds, mating indiscriminately with phoenixes, hawks, or crows—he refused to approach him. Changing back into his true form, he went and stretched his bow to the fullest. With one pellet he sent the bird hurtling.

The Great Sage took advantage of this opportunity, nonetheless. Roll-ing down the mountain slope, he squatted there to change again—this time into a little temple for the local spirit. His wide-open mouth became the entrance, his teeth the doors, his tongue the Bodhisattva, and his eyes the windows. Only his tail he found to be troublesome, so he stuck it up in the back and changed it into a flagpole. The Immortal Master chased him down the slope, but instead of the bustard he had hit he found only a little temple. He opened his phoenix eye quickly and looked at it carefully. Seeing the flagpole behind it, he laughed and said, "It's the ape! Now he's trying to deceive me again! I have seen plenty of temples before but never one with a flagpole behind it. This must be another of that animal's tricks. Why should I let him lure me inside where he can bite me once I've entered? First I'll smash the windows with my fist! Then I'll kick down the doors!"

The Great Sage heard this and said in dismay, "How vicious! The doors are my teeth and the windows my eyes. What am I going to do with my eyes smashed and my teeth knocked out?" Leaping up like a tiger, he disap-peared again into the air. The Immortal Master was looking all around for him when the four grand marshals and the two generals arrived together. "Elder Brother," they said, "have you caught the Great Sage?" "A moment ago," said the Immortal Master laughing, "the monkey changed into a temple to trick me. I was about to smash the windows and kick down the doors when he vanished out of sight with a leap. It's all very strange! Very strange!" The Brothers were astonished, but they could find no trace of him in any direction.

"Brothers," said the Immortal Master, "keep a lookout down here. Let me go up there to find him." He swiftly mounted the clouds and rose up into the sky, where he saw Devarāja Li holding high the imp-reflecting mirror and standing on top of the clouds with Naṭa. "Devarāja," said the Immortal Master, "have you seen the Monkey King?" "He hasn't come up here," said the Devarāja, "I have been watching him in the mirror."

After telling them about the duel in magic and transformations and the captivity of the rest of the monkeys, the Immortal Master said, "He finally changed into a temple. Just as I was about to attack him, he got away." When Devarāja Li heard these words, he turned the imp-reflecting mirror all the way around once more and looked into it. "Immortal Master," he said, roaring with laughter. "Go quickly! Quickly! That monkey used his magic of body concealment to escape from the cordon and he's now heading for the mouth of your River of Libations."

We now tell you about the Great Sage, who had arrived at the mouth of the River of Libations. With a shake of his body, he changed into the form of Holy Father Erlang. Lowering the direction of his cloud, he went straight into the temple, and the demon magistrates could not tell that he was not the real Erlang. Every one of them, in fact, kowtowed to receive him. He sat down in the middle and began to examine the various offerings; the three kinds of sacrificial meat brought by Li Hu, the votive offering of Zhang Long, the petition for a son by Zhao Jia, and the request for healing by Qian Bing. As he was looking at these, someone made the report, "Another Holy Father has arrived!" The various demon magistrates went quickly to look and were terror-stricken, one and all. The Immortal Master asked, "Did a so-called Great Sage, Equal to Heaven, come here?" "We haven't seen any Great Sage," said the demon magistrates. "But another Holy Father is in there examining the offerings." The Immortal Master crashed through the door; seeing him, the Great Sage revealed his true form and said, "There's no need for the little boy to strive anymore! Sun is now the name of this temple!"

The Immortal Master lifted his divine lance of three points and two blades and struck, but the Monkey King with agile body was quick to move out of the way. He whipped out that embroidery needle of his, and with one wave caused it to take on the thickness of a rice bowl. Rushing forward, he engaged Erlang face to face. Starting at the door of the temple, the two combatants fought all the way back to the Flower-Fruit Mountain, treading on clouds and mists and shouting insults at each other. The Four Devarājas and their followers were so startled by their appearance that they stood guard with even greater vigilance, while the grand marshals joined the Immortal Master to surround the Handsome Monkey King. But we shall speak of them no more.

We tell you instead about the demon king Mahābāli, who, having requested the Immortal Master and his Six Brothers to lead their troops to subdue the monster, returned to the Region Above to make his report. Conversing with the Bodhisattva Guanyin, the Queen Mother, and the various divine officials in the Hall of Divine Mists, the Jade Emperor said, "If Erlang has already gone into battle, why has no further report come back today?" Folding her hands, Guanyin said, "Permit this humble cleric to invite Your Majesty and the Patriarch of Dao to go outside the South Heaven Gate, so that you may find out personally how things are faring." "That's a good suggestion," said the Jade Emperor. He at once sent for his imperial carriage and went with the Patriarch, Guanyin, the Queen Mother, and the various divine officials to the South Heaven Gate, where the cortege was met by celestial soldiers and guardians. They opened the gate and peered into the distance; there they saw cosmic nets on every side manned by celestial soldiers, Devarāja Li and Naṭa in midair holding high the imp-reflecting mirror, and the Immortal Master and his Brothers encircling the Great Sage in the middle and fighting fiercely. The Bodhisattva opened her mouth and addressed Laozi: "What do you think of Erlang, whom this humble cleric recommended? He is certainly powerful enough to have the Great Sage surrounded, if not yet captured. I shall now help him to achieve his victory and make certain that the enemy will be taken prisoner."

"What weapon will the Bodhisattva use," asked Laozi, "and how will you assist him?" "I shall throw down my immaculate vase which I use for holding my willow sprig," said the Bodhisattva. "When it hits that monkey, at least it will knock him over, even if it doesn't kill him. Erlang, the Little Sage, will then be able to capture him."

"That vase of yours," said Laozi, "is made of porcelain. It's all right if it hits him on the head. But if it crashed on the iron rod instead, won't it be shattered? You had better not raise your hands; let me help him win." The Bodhisattva said, "Do you have any weapon?"

"I do, indeed," said Laozi. He rolled up his sleeve and took down from his left arm an armlet, saying, "This is a weapon made of red steel, brought into existence during my preparation of elixir and fully charged with theurgical forces. It can be made to transform at will; indestructible by fire or water, it can entrap many things. It's called the diamond cutter or the diamond snare. The year when I crossed the Hangu Pass, I depended on it a great deal for the conversion of the barbarians, for it was practically my bodyguard night and day. Let me throw it down and hit him." After saying this, Laozi hurled the snare down from the Heaven Gate; it went tumbling down into the battlefield at the Flower-Fruit Mountain and landed smack on the Monkey King's head. The Monkey King was engaged in a bitter struggle with the Seven Sages and was completely unaware of this weapon which had dropped from the sky and hit him on the crown of his head. No longer able to stand on his feet, he toppled over. He managed to scramble up again and was about to flee, when the Holy Father Erlang's small hound dashed forward and bit him in the calf. He was pulled down for the second time and lay on the ground cursing, "You brute! Why don't you go and do your master in, instead of coming to bite old Monkey?" Rolling over quickly, he tried to get up, but the Seven Sages all pounced on him and pinned him down. They bound him with ropes and punctured his breastbone with a knife, so that he could transform no further.

Laozi retrieved his diamond snare and requested the Jade Emperor to return to the Hall of Divine Mists with Guanyin, the Queen Mother, and the rest of the Immortals. Down below the Four Great Deva Kings and Devarāja Li all retired their troops, broke camp, and went forward to congratulate Erlang, saying, "This is indeed a magnificent accomplishment by the Little Sage!" "This has been the great blessing of the Heavenly Devas," said the Little Sage, "and the proper exercise of their divine authority. What have I accomplished?" The Brothers Kang, Zhang, Yao, and Li said, "Elder Brother need have no further discussion. Let us take this fellow up to the Jade Emperor to see what will be done with him." "Worthy Brothers," said the Immortal Master, "you may not have a personal audience with the Jade Emperor because you have not received any divine appointment. Let the celestial guardians take him into custody. I shall go with the Devarāja to the Region Above to make our report, while all of you make a thorough search of the mountain here. After you have cleaned it out, go back to the River of Libations. When I have our deeds recorded and received our rewards, I shall return to celebrate with you." The four grand marshals and the two generals followed his bidding. The Immortal Master then mounted the clouds with the rest of the deities, and they began their triumphal journey back to Heaven, singing songs of victory all the way. In a little while, they reached the outer court of the Hall of Perfect Light, and the Heavenly preceptor went forward to memorialize to the Throne, saying, "The Four Great Devarājas have captured the monstrous monkey, the Great Sage, Equal to Heaven. They await the command of Your Majesty." The Jade Emperor then gave the order that the demon king Mahābāli and the celestial guardians take the prisoner to the monster execution block, where he was to be cut to small pieces. Alas, this is what happens to

Fraud and impudence, now punished by the Law;
Heroics grand will fade in the briefest time!

We do not know what will become of the Monkey King; let's listen to the explanation in the next chapter.

SEVEN

From the Eight Trigrams Brazier the Great Sage escapes;
Beneath the Five Phases Mountain, Mind Monkey is stilled.[1]

Fame and fortune,
All predestined;
One must ever shun a guileful heart.
Rectitude and truth,
The fruits of virtue grow both long and deep.
A little presumption brings on Heaven's wrath:
Though yet unseen, it will surely come in time.
Ask the Lord of the East[2] *for why*
Such pains and perils now appear:
Because pride has sought to scale the limits,
Ignoring hierarchy to flout the law.

We were telling you about the Great Sage, Equal to Heaven, who was taken by the celestial guardians to the monster execution block, where he was bound to the monster-subduing pillar. They then slashed him with a scimitar, hewed him with an ax, stabbed him with a spear, and hacked him with a sword, but they could not hurt his body in any way. Next, the Star Spirit of the South Pole ordered the various deities of the Fire Department to burn him with fire, but that, too, had little effect. The gods of the Thunder Department were then ordered to strike him with thunderbolts, but not a single one of his hairs was destroyed. The demon king Mahābāli and the others therefore went back to report to the Throne, saying, "Your Majesty, we don't know where this Great Sage has acquired such power to protect his body. Your subjects slashed him with a scimitar and hewed him with an ax; we also struck him with thunder and burned him with fire. Not a single one of his hairs was destroyed. What shall we do?"

1. The phrase "the Monkey of the Mind and the Hose of the Will" (*xinyuan yima*) is made up of metaphors commonly used in Buddhist writings.
2. Possibly a reference to the Sun God.

When the Jade Emperor heard these words, he said, "What indeed can we do to a fellow like that, a creature of that sort?" Laozi then came forward and said, "That monkey ate the immortal peaches and drank the imperial wine. Moreover, he stole the divine elixir and ate five gourdfuls of it, both raw and cooked. All this was probably refined in his stomach by the Samādhi fire[3] to form a single solid mass. The union with his constitution gave him a diamond body which cannot be quickly destroyed. It would be better, therefore, if this Daoist takes him away and places him in the Brazier of Eight Trigrams, where he will be smelted by high and low heat. When he is finally separated from my elixir, his body will certainly be reduced to ashes." When the Jade Emperor heard these words, he told the Six Gods of Darkness and the Six Gods of Light to release the prisoner and hand him over to Laozi, who left in obedience to the divine decree. Meanwhile, the illustrious Sage Erlang was rewarded with a hundred gold blossoms, a hundred bottles of imperial wine, a hundred pellets of elixir, together with rare treasures, lustrous pearls, and brocades, which he was told to share with his brothers. After expressing his gratitude, the Immortal Master returned to the mouth of the River of Libations, and for the time being we shall speak of him no further.

Arriving at the Tushita Palace, Laozi loosened the ropes on the Great Sage, pulled out the weapon from his breastbone, and pushed him into the Brazier of Eight Trigrams. He then ordered the Daoist who watched over the brazier and the page boy in charge of the fire to blow up a strong flame for the smelting process. The brazier, you see, was of eight compartments corresponding to the eight trigrams of Qian, Kan, Gen, Zhen, Xun, Li, Kun, and Dui. The Great Sage crawled into the space beneath the compartment which corresponded to the Xun trigram. Now Xun symbolizes wind; where there is wind, there is no fire. However, wind could churn up smoke, which at that moment reddened his eyes, giving them a permanently inflamed condition. Hence they were sometimes called Fiery Eyes and Diamond Pupils.

Truly time passed by swiftly, and the forty-ninth day arrived imperceptibly.[4] The alchemical process of Laozi was perfected, and on that day he came to open the brazier to take out his elixir. The Great Sage at the time was covering his eyes with both hands, rubbing his face and shedding

---

3. Samādhi fire: the fire that is said to consume the body of Buddha when he enters Nirvāṇa. But in the syncretic religious milieu of vernacular fiction, this fire is possessed by many fighters or warriors who have attained immortality (including a Daoist deity like Erlang), and it is often used as a weapon.

4. In religious Daoism, seven is regarded as a sacred number; a perfected cycle often is calculated on the basis of seven times seven.

tears. He heard noises on top of the brazier and, opening his eyes, suddenly saw light. Unable to restrain himself, he leaped out of the brazier and kicked it over with a loud crash. He began to walk straight out of the room, while a group of startled fire tenders and guardians tried desperately to grab hold of him. Every one of them was overthrown; he was as wild as a white brow tiger in a fit, a one-horn dragon with a fever. Laozi rushed up to clutch at him, only to be greeted by such a violent shove that he fell head over heels while the Great Sage escaped. Whipping the compliant rod out from his ear, he waved it once in the wind and it had the thickness of a rice bowl. Holding it in his hands, without regard for good or ill, he once more careened through the Heavenly Palace, fighting so fiercely that the Nine Luminaries all shut themselves in and the Four Devarājas disappeared from sight. Dear Monkey Monster! Here is a testimonial poem for him. The poem says:

> This cosmic being fully fused with nature's gifts
> Passes with ease through ten thousand toils and tests.
> Vast and motionless like the One Great Void,
> Perfect, quiescent, he's named the Primal Depth.
> Long refined in the brazier, he's no mercury or lead,
> Just the very immortal, living above all things.
> Forever transforming, he changes still;
> The three refuges and five commandments he all rejects.

Here is another poem:

> As light supernal fills the boundless space,
> So, too, that rod behaves accordingly.
> It lengthens or shortens as a man would wish;
> Upright or prostrate, it grows or shrinks at will.

And another:

> A monkey's changed body weds the human mind.
> Mind is a monkey—this, the sense profound.
> The Great Sage, Equal to Heaven, is no false thought.
> How could the post of Bima justly show his gifts?
> Horse works with Monkey would mean both Mind and Will
> Must firmly be harnessed and not be ruled without.
> All things back to Nirvāṇa follow this one truth—
> In league with Tathāgata to live beneath twin trees.[5]

This time our Monkey King had no respect for persons great or small; he lashed out this way and that with his iron rod, and not a single deity could

5. The twin Sāl trees in the grove in which Śākyamuni entered Nirvāṇa.

withstand him. He fought all the way into the Hall of Perfect Light and was
approaching the Hall of Divine Mists, where fortunately Wang Lingguan,
aide to the Immortal Master of Adjuvant Holiness, was on duty. He saw the
Great Sage advancing recklessly and went forward to bar his way, holding
high his golden whip. "Wanton monkey," he cried, "where are you going?
I am here, so don't you dare be insolent!" The Great Sage did not wait for
further utterance; he raised his rod and struck at once, while Lingguan met
him also with brandished whip. The two of them charged into each other
in front of the Hall of Divine Mists. What a fight that was between

A red-blooded patriot of enormous fame,
And a rebel in Heaven with notorious name!
The saint and the sinner gladly do this fight,
To test the skills of two warriors brave.
Though the rod is brutal
And the whip is fleet,
How can the hero, upright and just, forbear?
This one is a supreme god of vengeance with thunderous voice;
The other, the Great Sage, Equal to Heaven, a monstrous ape.
The golden whip and the iron rod used by the two
Are both weapons divine from the House of God.
At the Treasure Hall of Divine Mists this day they show their might,
Displaying each his prowess most admirably.
This one brashly seeks to take the Big Dipper Palace.
The other with all his strength defends the sacred realm.
In bitter strife relentless they show their power;
Moving back and forth, whip or rod has yet to score.

The two of them fought for some time, and neither victory nor defeat
could yet be determined. The Immortal Master of Adjuvant Holiness,
however, had already sent word to the Thunder Department, and thirty-
six thunder deities were summoned to the scene. They surrounded the
Great Sage and plunged into a fierce battle. The Great Sage was not in the
least intimidated; wielding his compliant rod, he parried left and right
and met his attackers to the front and to the rear. In a moment he saw that
the scimitars, lances, swords, halberds, whips, maces, hammers, axes, gilt
bludgeons, sickles, and spades of the thunder deities were coming thick
and fast. So with one shake of his body he changed into a creature with six
arms and three heads. One wave of the compliant rod and it turned into
three; his six arms wielded the three rods like a spinning wheel, whirling
and dancing in their midst. The various thunder deities could not approach
him at all. Truly his form was

Tumbling round and round,
Bright and luminous;
A form everlasting, how imitated by men?
He cannot be burned by fire.
Can he ever be drowned in water?
A lustrous pearl of maṇi[6] he is indeed,
Immune to all the spears and the swords.
He could be good;
He could be bad;
Present good and evil he could do at will.
He'd be an immortal, a Buddha, if he's good;
Wickedness would coat him with hair and horn.
Endlessly changing he runs amok in Heaven,
Not to be seized by fighting lords or thunder gods.

At the time the various deities had the Great Sage surrounded, but they could not close in on him. All the hustle and bustle soon disturbed the Jade Emperor, who at once sent the Wandering Minister of Inspection and the Immortal Master of Blessed Wings to go to the Western Region and invite the aged Buddha to come and subdue the monster.

The two sages received the decree and went straight to the Spirit Mountain. After they had greeted the Four Vajra-Buddhas and the Eight Bodhisattvas in front of the Treasure Temple of Thunderclap, they asked them to announce their arrival. The deities therefore went before the Treasure Lotus Platform and made their report. Tathāgata at once invited them to appear before him, and the two sages made obeisance to the Buddha three times before standing in attendance beneath the platform. Tathāgata asked, "What causes the Jade Emperor to trouble the two sages to come here?"

The two sages explained as follows: "Some time ago there was born on the Flower-Fruit Mountain a monkey who exercised his magic powers and gathered to himself a troop of monkeys to disturb the world. The Jade Emperor threw down a decree of pacification and appointed him a Bimawen, but he despised the lowliness of that position and left in rebellion. Devarāja Li and Prince Naṭa were sent to capture him, but they were unsuccessful, and another proclamation of amnesty was given to him. He was then made the Great Sage, Equal to Heaven, a rank without compensation. After a while he was given the temporary job of looking after the Garden of Immortal Peaches, where almost immediately he stole the peaches. He also went to the Jasper Pool and made off with the food

6. Known for its luster, this pearl is said to give sight to the blind.

and wine, devastating the Grand Festival. Half-drunk, he went secretly into the Tushita Palace, stole the elixir of Laozi, and then left the Celestial Palace in revolt. Again the Jade Emperor sent a hundred thousand Heavenly soldiers, but he was not to be subdued. Thereafter Guanyin sent for the Immortal Master Erlang and his sworn brothers, who fought and pursued him. Even then he knew many tricks of transformation, and only after he was hit by Laozi's diamond snare could Erlang finally capture him. Taken before the Throne, he was condemned to be executed; but, though slashed by a scimitar and hewn by an ax, burned by fire and struck by thunder, he was not hurt at all. After Laozi had received royal permission to take him away, he was refined by fire, and the brazier was not opened until the forty-ninth day. Immediately he jumped out of the Brazier of Eight Trigrams and beat back the celestial guardians. He penetrated into the Hall of Perfect Light and was approaching the Hall of Divine Mists when Wang Lingguan, aide to the Immortal Master of Adjuvant Holiness, met and fought with him bitterly. Thirty-six thunder generals were ordered to encircle him completely, but they could never get near him. The situation is desperate, and for this reason, the Jade Emperor sent a special request for you to defend the Throne."

When Tathāgata heard this, he said to the various bodhisattvas, "All of you remain steadfast here in the chief temple, and let no one relax his meditative posture. I have to go exorcise a demon and defend the Throne."

Tathāgata then called Ānanda and Kāśyapa , his two venerable disciples, to follow him. They left the Thunderclap Temple and arrived at the gate of the Hall of Divine Mists, where they were met by deafening shouts and yells. There the Great Sage was being beset by the thirty-six thunder deities. The Buddhist Patriarch gave the dharma-order: "Let the thunder deities lower their arms and break up their encirclement. Ask the Great Sage to come out here and let me ask him what sort of divine power he has." The various warriors retreated immediately, and the Great Sage also threw off his magical appearance. Changing back into his true form, he approached angrily and shouted with ill humor, "What region are you from, monk, that you dare stop the battle and question me?" Tathāgata laughed and said, "I am Śākyamuni, the Venerable One from the Western Region of Ultimate Bliss . I have heard just now about your audacity, your wildness, and your repeated acts of rebellion against Heaven. Where were you born, and in which year did you succeed in acquiring the Way? Why are you so violent and unruly?" The Great Sage said, "I was

Born of Earth and Heaven, immortal divinely fused,
An old monkey hailing from the Flower-Fruit Mount.

I made my home in the Water-Curtain Cave;
Seeking friend and teacher, I learned the Great Mystery.
Perfected in the many arts of ageless life,
I learned to change in ways boundless and vast.
Too narrow the space I found on that mortal earth:
I set my mind to live in the Green Jade Sky.
In Divine Mists Hall none should long reside,
For king may follow king in the reign of man.
If might is honor, let them yield to me.
Only he is hero who dares to fight and win!"

When the Buddhist Patriarch heard these words, he laughed aloud in scorn. "A fellow like you," he said, "is only a monkey who happens to become a spirit. How dare you be so presumptuous as to want to seize the honored throne of the Exalted Jade Emperor? He began practicing religion when he was very young, and he has gone through the bitter experience of one thousand seven hundred and fifty kalpas, with each kalpa lasting a hundred and twenty-nine thousand six hundred years. Figure out yourself how many years it took him to rise to the enjoyment of his great and limitless position! You are merely a beast who has just attained human form in this incarnation. How dare you make such a boast? Blasphemy! This is sheer blasphemy, and it will surely shorten your allotted age. Repent while there's still time and cease your idle talk! Be wary that you don't encounter such peril that you will be cut down in an instant, and all your original gifts will be wasted."

"Even if the Jade Emperor has practiced religion from childhood," said the Great Sage, "he should not be allowed to remain here forever. The proverb says, 'Many are the turns of kingship, and next year the turn will be mine!' Tell him to move out at once and hand over the Celestial Palace to me. That'll be the end of the matter. If not, I shall continue to cause disturbances and there'll never be peace!" "Besides your immortality and your transformations," said the Buddhist Patriarch, "what other powers do you have that you dare to usurp this hallowed region of Heaven?" "I've plenty of them!" said the Great Sage. "Indeed, I know seventy-two transformations and a life that does not grow old through ten thousand kalpas. I know also how to cloud-somersault, and one leap will take me a hundred and eight thousand miles. Why can't I sit on the Heavenly throne?"

The Buddhist Patriarch said, "Let me make a wager with you. If you have the ability to somersault clear of this right palm of mine, I shall consider you the winner. You need not raise your weapon in battle then, for I shall ask the Jade Emperor to go live with me in the West and let you have the Celestial Palace. If you cannot somersault out of my hand, you can go back to the Region Below and be a monster. Work through a few more kalpas before you return to cause more trouble."

When the Great Sage heard this, he said to himself, snickering, "What a fool this Tathāgata is! A single somersault of mine can carry old Monkey a hundred and eight thousand miles, yet his palm is not even one foot across. How could I possibly not jump clear of it?" He asked quickly, "You're certain that your decision will stand?" "Certainly it will," said Tathāgata. He stretched out his right hand, which was about the size of a lotus leaf. Our Great Sage put away his compliant rod and, summoning his power, leaped up and stood right in the center of the Patriarch's hand. He said simply, "I'm off!" and he was gone—all but invisible like a streak of light in the clouds. Training the eye of wisdom on him, the Buddhist Patriarch saw that the Monkey King was hurtling along relentlessly like a whirligig.

As the Great Sage advanced, he suddenly saw five flesh-pink pillars supporting a mass of green air. "This must be the end of the road," he said. "When I go back presently, Tathāgata will be my witness and I shall certainly take up residence in the Palace of Divine Mists." But he thought to himself, "Wait a moment! I'd better leave some kind of memento if I'm going to negotiate with Tathāgata." He plucked a hair and blew a mouthful of magic breath onto it, crying, "Change!" It changed into a writing brush with extra thick hair soaked in heavy ink. On the middle pillar he then wrote in large letters the following line: "The Great Sage, Equal to Heaven, has made a tour of this place." When he had finished writing, he retrieved his hair, and with a total lack of respect he left a bubbling pool of monkey urine at the base of the first pillar. He reversed his cloud-somersault and went back to where he had started. Standing on Tathāgata's palm, he said, "I left, and now I'm back. Tell the Jade Emperor to give me the Celestial Palace."

"You pisshead ape!" scolded Tathāgata. "Since when did you ever leave the palm of my hand?" The Great Sage said, "You are just ignorant! I went to the edge of Heaven, and I found five flesh-pink pillars supporting a mass of green air. I left a memento there. Do you dare go with me to have a look at the place?" "No need to go there," said Tathāgata. "Just lower your head and take a look." When the Great Sage stared down with his fiery eyes and diamond pupils, he found written on the middle finger of the Buddhist Patriarch's right hand the sentence, "The Great Sage, Equal to Heaven, has made a tour of this place." A pungent whiff of monkey urine came from the fork between the thumb and the first finger. Astonished, the Great Sage said, "Could this really happen? Could this really happen?

I wrote those words on the pillars supporting the sky. How is it that they now appear on his finger? Could it be that he is exercising the magic power of foreknowledge without divination? I won't believe it! I won't believe it! Let me go there once more!"

Dear Great Sage! Quickly he crouched and was about to jump up again, when the Buddhist Patriarch flipped his hand over and tossed the Monkey King out of the West Heaven Gate. The five fingers were transformed into the Five Phases of metal, wood, water, fire, and earth. They became, in fact, five connected mountains, named Five-Phases Mountain, which pinned him down with just enough pressure to keep him there. The thunder deities, Ānanda, and Kāśyapa all folded their hands and cried in acclamation:

"Praise be to virtue! Praise be to virtue!
He learned to be human, born from an egg that year,
Aiming to cultivate the authentic Way's fruit.
His was a fine place by ten thousand kalpas unmoved.
But one day he changed, expending vim and strength.
Craving high place, he flouted Heaven's reign,
Mocked sages, stole pills, and broke the great relations.
Evil, full to the brim, now meets its retribution.
We know not when he may hope to find release."

After the Buddhist Patriarch Tathāgata had vanquished the monstrous monkey, he at once called Ānanda and Kāśyapa to return with him to the Western Paradise. At that moment, however, Tianpeng and Tianyou, two celestial messengers, came running out of the Treasure Hall of Divine Mists and said, "We beg Tathāgata to wait a moment, please! Our Lord's grand carriage will arrive momentarily." When the Buddhist Patriarch heard these words, he turned around and waited with reverence. In a moment he did indeed see a chariot drawn by eight colorful phoenixes and covered by a canopy adorned with nine luminous jewels. The entire cortege was accompanied by the sound of wondrous songs and melodies, chanted by a vast celestial choir. Scattering precious blossoms and diffusing fragrant incense, it came up to the Buddha, and the Jade Emperor offered his thanks, saying, "We are truly indebted to your mighty dharma for vanquishing that monster. We beseech Tathāgata to remain for one brief day, so that we may invite the immortals to join us in giving you a banquet of thanks." Not daring to refuse, Tathāgata folded his hands to thank the Jade Emperor, saying, "Your old monk came here at your command, Most Honorable Deva. Of what power may I boast, really? I owe my success entirely to the excellent fortune of Your Majesty and the various deities. How can I be worthy of your thanks?" The Jade Emperor then ordered the various deities from the Thunder Department to send invitations abroad to the Three Pure Ones, the Four Ministers, the Five Elders, the Six Women Officials, the Seven Stars, the Eight Poles, the Nine Luminaries, and the Ten Capitals. Together with a thousand immortals and ten thousand sages, they were to come to the thanksgiving banquet given for the Buddhist Patriarch. The Four Great Imperial Preceptors and the Divine Maidens of Nine Heavens were told to open wide the golden gates of the Jade Capital, the Treasure Palace of Primal Secret, and the Five Lodges of Penetrating Brightness. Tathāgata was asked to be seated high on the Numinous Terrace of Seven Treasures, and the rest of the deities were then seated according to rank and age before a banquet of dragon livers, phoenix marrow, juices of jade, and immortal peaches.

In a little while, the Jade-Pure Honorable Divine of the Origin, the Exalted-Pure Honorable Divine of Spiritual Treasures, the Primal-Pure Honorable Divine of Moral Virtue, the Immortal Masters of Five Influences, the Star Spirits of Five Constellations, the Three Ministers, the Four Sages, the Nine Luminaries, the Left and Right Assistants, the Devarāja, and Prince Naṭa all marched in leading a train of flags and canopies in pairs. They were all holding rare treasures and lustrous pearls, fruits of longevity and exotic flowers to be presented to the Buddha. As they bowed before him, they said, "We are most grateful for the unfathomable power of Tathāgata, who has subdued the monstrous monkey. We are grateful, too, to the Most Honorable Deva, who is having this banquet and asked us to come here to offer our thanks. May we beseech Tathāgata to give this banquet a name?"

Responding to the petition of the various deities, Tathāgata said, "If a name is desired, let this be called 'The Great Banquet for Peace in Heaven.'" "What a magnificent name!" the various Immortals cried in unison. "Indeed, it shall be the Great Banquet for Peace in Heaven." When they finished speaking, they took their seats separately, and there was the pouring of wine and exchanging of cups, pinning of corsages and playing of zithers. It was indeed a magnificent banquet, for which we have a testimonial poem. The poem says:

That Feast of Peaches Immortal disturbed by the ape
Is now surpassed by this Banquet for Peace in Heaven.
Dragon flags and phoenix chariots stand glowing in halos bright,
As standards and blazing banners whirl in hallowed light.
Sweet are the tunes of immortal airs and songs,
Noble the sounds of panpipes and double flutes of jade.

Incense ambrosial surrounds this assembly of saints.
The world is tranquil. May the Holy Court be praised!

As all of them were feasting happily, the Lady Queen Mother also led a host of divine maidens and immortal singing-girls to come before the Buddha, dancing with nimble feet. They bowed to him, and she said, "Our Festival of Immortal Peaches was ruined by that monstrous monkey. We are beholden to the mighty power of Tathāgata for the enchainment of this mischievous ape. In the celebration during this Great Banquet for Peace in Heaven, we have little to offer as a token of our thanks. Please accept, however, these few immortal peaches plucked from the large trees by our own hands." They were truly

Half red, half green, and spouting aroma sweet,
Of luscious roots immortal, and ten thousand years old.
Pity those fruits planted at the Wuling Spring![7]
How do they equal the marvels of Heaven's home:
Those tender ones of purple veins so rare in the world,
And those of matchless sweetness with pale yellow pits?
They lengthen your age, prolong your life, and change your frame.
He who has the luck to eat them will never be the same.

After the Buddhist Patriarch had pressed together his hands to thank the Queen Mother, she ordered the immortal singing-girls and the divine maidens to sing and dance. All the immortals at the banquet applauded enthusiastically. Truly there were

Whorls of Heavenly incense filling the seats,
And profuse array of divine petals and stems.
Jade capital and golden arches in what great splendor!
How priceless, too, the strange goods and rare treasures!
Every pair had the same age as Heaven.
Every set increased through ten thousand kalpas.
Mulberry fields or vast oceans, let them shift and change.
He who lives here has neither grief nor fear.

The Queen Mother commanded the immortal maidens to sing and dance, as wine cups and goblets clinked together steadily. After a little while, suddenly

A wondrous fragrance came to meet the nose,
Rousing Stars and Planets in that great hall.
The gods and the Buddha put down their cups.

---

7. Wuling: a prefecture located in the town of Changde in modern Hunan province. The brook was made famous by literary treatments of the peach forest there.

Raising his head, each waited with his eyes.
There in the air appeared an aged man,
Holding a most luxuriant long-life plant.
His gourd had elixir of ten thousand years.
His book listed names twelve millennia old.
Sky and earth in his cave knew no constraint.
Sun and moon were perfected in his vase.
He roamed the Four Seas in joy serene,
And made the Ten Islets his tranquil home.
Getting drunk often at the Peaches Feast
He woke; the moon shone brightly as of old.
He had a long head, short frame, and large ears.
His name: Star of Long Life from South Pole.

After the Star of Long Life had arrived and had greeted the Jade Emperor, he also went up to thank Tathāgata, saying, "When I first heard that the baneful monkey was being led by Laozi to the Tushita Palace to be refined by alchemical fire, I thought peace was surely secured. I never suspected that he could still escape, and it was fortunate that Tathāgata in his goodness had subdued this monster. When I got word of the thanksgiving banquet, I came at once. I have no other gifts to present to you but these purple agaric, jasper plant, jade-green lotus root, and golden elixir." The poem says:

Jade-green lotus and golden drug are given to Śākya.
Like the sands of Ganges is the age of Tathāgata.
The brocade of the three wains is calm, eternal bliss.[8]
The nine-grade garland is a wholesome, endless life.[9]
The true master of the Mādhyamika School
Dwells in the Heaven of both form and emptiness.
The great earth and cosmos all call him Lord.
His sixteen-foot diamond frame's great in blessing and age.[10]

Tathāgata accepted the thanks cheerfully, and the Star of Long Life went to his seat. Again there was pouring of wine and exchanging of cups. The Great Immortal of Naked Feet also arrived. After prostrating himself before the Jade Emperor, he too went to thank the Buddhist Patriarch, saying,

8. The three wains are the three vehicles drawn by a goat, a deer, and an ox to convey the living across the cycles of births and deaths to the shores of Nirvāṇa.

9. "Nine-grade" refers to the nine classes or grades of rewards in the Pure Land.

10. Buddha's transformed (deified) body is said to be sixteen feet, the same height as his earthly body.

"I am profoundly grateful for your dharma which subdued the baneful monkey. I have no other things to convey my respect but two magic pears and some fire dates, which I now present to you." The poem says:

The Naked-Feet Immortal brought fragrant pears and dates
To give to Amitābha, whose count of years is long.
Firm as a hill is his Lotus Platform of Seven Treasures;
Brocadelike is his Flower Seat of Thousand Gold adorned.
No false speech is this—his age equals Heaven and Earth;
Nor is this a lie—his luck is great as the sea.
Blessing and long life reach in him their fullest scope,
Dwelling in that Western Region of calm, eternal bliss.

Tathāgata again thanked him and asked Ānanda and Kāśyapa to put away the gifts one by one before approaching the Jade Emperor to express his gratitude for the banquet. By now, everyone was somewhat tipsy. A Spirit Minister of Inspection then arrived to make the report, "The Great Sage is sticking out his head!" "No need to worry," said the Buddhist Patriarch. He took from his sleeve a tag on which were written in gold letters the words *Oṁ maṇi padme hūṁ*. Handing it over to Ānanda, he told him to stick it on the top of the mountain. This deva received the tag, took it out of the Heaven Gate, and stuck it tightly on a square piece of rock at the top of the Mountain of Five Phases. The mountain immediately struck root and grew together at the seams, though there was enough space for breathing and for the prisoner's hands to crawl out and move around a bit. Ānanda then returned to report, "The tag is tightly attached."

Tathāgata then took leave of the Jade Emperor and the deities, and went with the two devas out of the Heaven Gate. Moved by compassion, he recited a divine spell and called together a local spirit and the Fearless Guards of Five Quarters to stand watch over the Five-Phases Mountain. They were told to feed the prisoner with iron pellets when he was hungry and to give him melted copper to drink when he was thirsty. When the time of his chastisement was fulfilled, they were told, someone would be coming to deliver him. So it is that

The brash, baneful monkey in revolt against Heaven
Is brought to submission by Tathāgata.
He drinks melted copper to endure the seasons,
And feeds on iron pellets to pass the time.
Tried by this bitter misfortune sent from the Sky,
He's glad to be living, though in a piteous lot.
If this hero is allowed to struggle anew,
He'll serve Buddha in future and go to the West.

Another poem says:

Prideful of his power once the time was ripe,
He tamed dragon and tiger, exploiting wily might.
Stealing peaches and wine, he roamed the House of Heaven.
He found trust and favor in the Capital of Jade.
He's now imprisoned, for his evil's full to the brim.
By the good stock[11] unfailing his spirit will rise again.
If he's indeed to escape Tathāgata's hands,
He must await the holy monk from the Tang Court.

We do not know in what month or year hereafter the days of his penance will be fulfilled; let's listen to the explanation in the next chapter.

---

11. Good stock: the Buddhist idea of the good seeds sown by a virtuous life which will bring future rewards.

EIGHT

Our Sovereign Buddha makes scriptures to impart ultimate bliss;
Guanyin receives the decree to go up to Chang'an.[1]

Ask the site of meditation
Why even numberless exercise
Would lead only to empty old age!
Polishing bricks to make mirrors,
Hoarding snow to use as foodstuff—
How many youths are thus deceived;
A feather swallows the great ocean?
A mustard seed contains the Sumeru?
The Golden Dhūta is gently smiling.[2]
Enlightened, one transcends the ten stages[3] and three vehicles.[4]
The sluggards must join the four creatures and six ways.[5]
Who has heard below the Thoughtless Cliff,
Beneath the Shadowless Tree,
The cuckoo's one call greeting the dawn of spring?

1. Capital of the Tang (618–906), renamed Xi'an in modern times, it is located in Shanxi Province.

2. One of Śākyamuni's principal disciples who was also chief of the ascetics before the enlightenment. The reference alludes to a famous tale of how only one disciple of the Buddha understood his esoteric teaching on *Chan* (Zen) principles by smiling at Buddha's gift of a single flower. Twenty-eight generations later, the mystery passed down by this disciple allegedly reached China as Zen Buddhism.

3. Ten stages: part of the different stages taught by different schools of Buddhism on the process of how a bodhisattva might develop into a Buddha.

4. Three vehicles: differently explained by various exponents, the three vehicles usually refer to the three means of conveyance that carry sentient beings across the cycles of birth and death or mortality to reach the shores of Ultimate Bliss or Nirvāna.

5. The four creatures are those born of the womb or stomach, of eggs, of moisture (i.e., worms and fishes), and those which evolve or metamorphose in different forms (i.e., insects). The six ways point to the sixfold path of reincarnation or transmigration.

Perilous are the roads at Caoxi,[6]
Dense are the clouds on Vulture Peak;[7]
Here the voice of any old friend is mute.
At a ten thousand–foot waterfall
Where a five-petal lotus unfolds,
An old temple hangs its incense-draped curtains—
In that hour,
Once you break through to the origin,
You'll see the Dragon King's three jewels.[8]

The tune of this lyric is named the "Slow Su Wu." We shall now tell you about our Sovereign Buddha Tathāgata, who took leave of the Jade Emperor and returned to the Treasure Monastery of Thunderclap. All the three thousand buddhas, the five hundred arhats, the eight diamond kings, and the countless bodhisattvas held temple pennants, embroidered canopies, rare treasures, and immortal flowers, forming an orderly array before the Spirit Mountain and beneath the two Śāla Trees to welcome him. Tathāgata stopped his hallowed cloud and said to them: I have

With incomparable prajñā[9]
Looked through the three regions.
The fundamental nature of all things
Will finally come to naught.
Equally empty is immateriality,
For nothing of independent nature exists.
The extirpation of the wily monkey,
This event none can comprehend.
Name, birth, death, and origin—
Such are the characteristics of all things.

When he had finished speaking, he beamed forth the śārī light,[10] which filled the air with forty-two white rainbows, connected end to end from north to south. Seeing this, the crowd bowed down and worshiped.

In a little while, Tathāgata gathered together the holy clouds and blessed fog, ascended the lotus platform of the highest rank, and sat down sol-

6. A stream in Guangdong Province where, in the Tang, the Sixth Patriarch of Zen Huineng taught.

7. A place said to be frequented by the Buddha, and where the *Lotus sūtra* was preached.

8. Three jewels or three treasures: a reference to the Buddha, the dharma, and the saṅgha.

9. Wisdom and understanding.

10. Śārī or satrīra is usually associated with the relics of Buddha.

emnly. Those three thousand buddhas, five hundred arhats, eight diamond kings, and four bodhisattvas folded their hands and drew near. After bowing down, they asked, "The one who caused disturbance in Heaven and ruined the Peach Festival, who was he?" "That fellow," said Tathāgata, "was a baneful monkey born in the Flower-Fruit Mountain. His wickedness was beyond all bounds and defied description. The divine warriors of the entire Heaven could not bring him to submission. Though Erlang caught him and Laozi tried to refine him with fire, they could not hurt him at all. When I arrived, he was just making an exhibition of his might and prowess in the midst of the thunder deities. When I stopped the fighting and asked about his antecedents, he said that he had magic powers, knowing how to transform himself and how to cloud-somersault, which would carry him a hundred and eight thousand miles at a time. I made a wager with him to see whether he could leap clear of my hand. I then grabbed hold of him while my fingers changed into the Mountain of Five Phases, which had him firmly pinned down. The Jade Emperor opened wide the golden doors of the Jade Palace, invited me to sit at the head table, and gave a Banquet for Peace in Heaven to thank me. It was only a short while ago that I took leave of the Throne to come back here." All were delighted by these words. After they had expressed their highest praise for the Buddha, they withdrew according to their ranks; they went back to their several duties and enjoyed the *bhūtatathatā*.[11] Truly it is the scene of

Holy mist encompassing Tianzhu,[12]
Rainbow light enclosing the Honored One,
Who is called the First in the West,
The King of the Formlessness School.[13]
Here often black apes are seen presenting fruits.
Tailed-deer holding flowers in their mouths,
Blue phoenixes dancing,
Colorful birds singing,
The spirit tortoise boasting of his age,
And the divine crane picking agaric.
They enjoy in peace the Pure Land's Jetavana,[14]
The Dragon Palace, and worlds vast as Ganges' sands.
Every day the flowers bloom;

11. The permanent reality underlying all phenomena.
12. Tianzhu: the traditional Chinese name for India.
13. I.e., the Mādhyamika School.
14. A park near Śrāvastī, said to be a favorite resort of Śākyamuni.

Every hour the fruits ripen.
They practice silence to return to the Real.
They meditate to reach the right fruition.
They do not die nor are they born.
No growth is there, nor any decrease.
Mist and smoke wraithlike may come and go.
No seasons intrude, nor are years remembered.

The poem says:

All the movements are easy and free;
There is neither fear nor sorrow here.
Fields of Ultimate Bliss are flat and wide.
This world's region has no autumn or spring.

As the Buddhist Patriarch lived in the Treasure Monastery of the Thunderclap in the Spirit Mountain, he called together one day the various buddhas, arhats, guardians, bodhisattvas, diamond kings, and mendicant monks and nuns and said to them. "We do not know how much time has passed here since I subdued the wily monkey and pacified Heaven, but I suppose at least half a millennium has gone by in the worldly realm. As this is the fifteenth day of the first month of autumn, I have prepared a treasure bowl filled with a hundred varieties of exotic flowers and a thousand kinds of rare fruit. I would like to share them with all of you in celebration of the Feast of the Ullambana Bowl.[15] How about it?" Every one of them folded his hands and paid obeisance to the Buddha three times to receive the festival. Tathāgata then ordered Ānanda to take the flowers and fruits from the treasure bowl, and Kāśyapa was asked to distribute them. All were thankful, and they presented poems to express their gratitude.

[Ed.: *Three poems are omitted here.*]

After the bodhisattvas had presented their poems, they invited Tathāgata to disclose the origin and elucidate the source. Tathāgata gently opened his benevolent mouth to expound the great dharma and to proclaim the truth. He lectured on the wondrous doctrines of the three vehicles, the five skandhas,[16] and the *Śūraṅgama Sūtra*. As he did so, celestial dragons were seen circling above and flowers descended like rain in abundance. It was truly thus:

The Chan mind shines bright like a thousand rivers' moon;
True nature's pure and great as an unclouded sky.

When Tathāgata had finished his lecture, he said to the congregation, "I have watched the Four Great Continents, and the morality of their inhabit-

---

15. The Feast of All Souls, celebrated in China by both Daoists and Buddhists.

16. A reference to the five substances or components of an intelligent being like a human. They are form, reception, thought, action, and cognition.

ants varies from place to place. Those living on the East Pūrvavideha revere Heaven and Earth, and they are straightforward and peaceful. Those on the North Uttarakuru, though they love to destroy life, do so out of the necessity of making a livelihood. Moreover, they are rather dull of mind and lethargic in spirit, and they are not likely to do much harm. Those of our West Aparagodānīya are neither covetous nor prone to kill; they control their humor and temper their spirit. There is, to be sure, no illuminate of the first order, but everyone is certain to attain longevity. Those who reside in the South Jambūdvīpa, however, are prone to practice lechery and delight in evildoing, indulging in much slaughter and strife. Indeed, they are all caught in the treacherous field of tongue and mouth, in the wicked sea of slander and malice. However, I have three baskets of true scriptures which can persuade man to do good." Upon hearing these words, the various bodhisattvas folded their hands and bowed down. "What are the three baskets of authentic scriptures," they asked, "that Tathāgata possesses?"

Tathāgata said, "I have one collection of vinaya, which speaks of Heaven; one collection of śāstras, which tells of the Earth; and one collection of sūtras, which redeems the damned. Altogether the three collections of scriptures contain thirty-five divisions written in fifteen thousand one hundred forty-four scrolls. They are the scriptures for the cultivation of immortality; they are the gate to ultimate virtue. I myself would like to send these to the Land of the East; but the creatures in that region are so stupid and so scornful of the truth that they ignore the weighty elements of our Law and mock the true sect of Yoga. Somehow we need a person with power to go to the Land of the East and find a virtuous believer. He will be asked to experience the bitter travail of passing through a thousand mountains and ten thousand waters to come here in quest of the authentic scriptures, so that they may be forever implanted in the east to enlighten the people. This will provide a source of blessings great as a mountain and deep as the sea. Which one of you is willing to make such a trip?"

At that moment, the Bodhisattva Guanyin came near the lotus platform and paid obeisance three times to the Buddha, saying, "Though your disciple is untalented, she is willing to go to the Land of the East to find a scripture pilgrim." Lifting their heads to look, the various buddhas saw that the Bodhisattva had

A mind perfected in the four virtues,[17]
A golden body filled with wisdom,

17. They differ according to different traditions. In Confucianism, they refer to filial piety, fraternal submission, fidelity, and trustworthiness. In Buddhism, they sometimes refer to permanence, joy, the reality of the self, and purity.

Fringes of dangling pearls and jade,
Scented bracelets set with lustrous treasures,
Dark hair piled smoothly in a coiled-dragon bun,
And elegant sashes lightly fluttering as phoenix quills.
Her green jade buttons
And white silk robe
Bathed in holy light;
Her velvet skirt
And golden cords
Wrapped by hallowed air.
With brows of new moon shape
And eyes like two bright stars,
Her jadelike face beams natural joy,
And her ruddy lips seem a flash of red.
Her immaculate vase overflows with nectar from year to year,
Holding sprigs of weeping willow green from age to age.
She disperses the eight woes;
She redeems the multitude;
She has great compassion;
Thus she rules on the Tai Mountain
And lives at the South Sea.
She saves the poor, searching for their voices,
Ever heedful and solicitous,
Ever wise and efficacious.
Her orchid heart delights in green bamboos;
Her chaste nature loves the wisteria.
She is the merciful ruler of the Potalaka Mountain,
The Living Guanyin from the Cave of Tidal Sound.

When Tathāgata saw her, he was most delighted and said to her, "No other person is qualified to make this journey. It must be the Honorable Guanyin of mighty magic powers—she's the one to do it!" "As your disciple departs for the east," said the Bodhisattva, "do you have any instructions?"

"As you travel," said Tathāgata, "you are to examine the way carefully. Do not journey high in the air, but remain at an altitude halfway between mist and cloud so that you can see the mountains and waters and remember the exact distance. You will then be able to give close instructions to the scripture pilgrim. Since he may still find the journey difficult, I shall also give you five talismans." Ordering Ānanda and Kāśyapa to bring out an embroidered cassock and a nine-ring priestly staff, he said to the Bodhisattva, "You may give this cassock and this staff to the scripture pilgrim. If he is firm in his intention to come here, he may put on the cassock and it will protect him from falling back into the wheel of transmigration. When he holds the staff, it will keep him from meeting poison or harm." The Bodhisattva bowed low to receive the gifts. Tathāgata then took out also three fillets and handed them to the Bodhisattva, saying, "These treasures are called the tightening fillets, and though they are all alike, their uses are not the same. I have a separate spell for each of them: the Golden, the Constrictive, and the Prohibitive Spell. If you encounter on the way any monster who possesses great magic powers, you must persuade him to learn to be good and to follow the scripture pilgrim as his disciple. If he is disobedient, this fillet may be put on his head, and it will strike root the moment it comes into contact with the flesh. Recite the particular spell which belongs to the fillet and it will cause the head to swell and ache so painfully that he will think his brains are bursting. That will persuade him to come within our fold."

After the Bodhisattva had bowed to the Buddha and taken her leave, she called Disciple Hui'an to follow her. This Hui'an, you see, carried a huge iron rod which weighed a thousand pounds. He followed the Bodhisattva closely and served her as a powerful bodyguard. The Bodhisattva made the embroidered cassock into a bundle and placed it on his back; she hid the golden fillets, took up the priestly staff, and went down the Spirit Mountain. Lo, this one journey will result in

A Buddha son returning to keep his primal vow.
The Gold Cicada Elder will clasp the candana.[18]

The Bodhisattva went to the bottom of the hill, where she was received at the door of the Yuzhen Daoist Temple by the Great Immortal of Golden Head. The Bodhisattva was presented with tea, but she did not dare linger long, saying, "I have received the dharma-decree of Tathāgata to look for a scripture pilgrim in the Land of the East." The Great Immortal said, "When do you expect the scripture pilgrim to arrive?" "I'm not sure," said the Bodhisattva. "Perhaps in two or three years' time he'll be able to get here." So she took leave of the Great Immortal and traveled at an altitude halfway between cloud and mist in order that she might remember the way and the distance. We have a testimonial poem for her that says:

A search through ten thousand miles—no need to say!
To state who will be found is no easy thing.
Has not seeking someone been just like this?

18. A kind of sandalwood from southern India.

What's been my whole life, was that a mere chance?
We preach the Dao, our method turns foolish
When saying meets no belief; we preach in vain.
To find some percipient I'd yield liver and gall.
There's affinity, I think, lying straight ahead.

As the mentor and her disciple journeyed, they suddenly came upon a large body of Weak Water, for this was the region of the Flowing Sand River.[19] "My disciple," said the Bodhisattva, "this place is difficult to cross. The scripture pilgrim will be of temporal bones and mortal stock. How will he be able to get across?" "Teacher," said Hui'an, "how wide do you suppose this river is?" The Bodhisattva stopped her cloud to take a look, and she saw that

In the east it touches the sandy coast;
In the west it joins the barbaric states;
In the south it reaches even Wuyi;[20]
In the north it approaches the Tartars.
Its width is eight hundred miles,
And its length must measure many thousand more.
The water flows as if Earth is heaving its frame.
The current rises like a mountain rearing its back.
Outspread and immense;
Vast and interminable.
The sound of its towering billows reaches distant ears.
The raft of a god cannot come here,
Nor can a leaf of the lotus stay afloat.
Lifeless grass in the twilight drifts along the crooked banks.
Yellow clouds conceal the sun to darken the long dikes.
Where can one find the traffic of merchants?
Has there been ever a shelter for fishermen?
On the flat sand no wild geese descend;
From distant shores comes the crying of apes.
Only the red smartweed flowers know this scene,
Basking in the white duckweed's fragile scent.

The Bodhisattva was looking over the river when suddenly a loud splash was heard, and from the midst of the waves leaped an ugly and ferocious monster. He appeared to have

19. Weak Water (*ruoshui*) is a river located in northwestern China (now Kansu Province), and the entire region has the name of Flowing Sand (*liusha*).
20. "Wuyi" refers to Wuyishanli, or Arachosia.

A green, though not too green,
And black, though not too black,
Face of gloomy complexion;
A long, though not too long,
And short, though not too short,
Sinewy body with naked feet.
His gleaming eyes
Shone like two lights beneath the stove.
His mouth, forked at the corners,
Was like a butcher's bloody bowl.
With teeth protruding like swords and knives,
And red hair all disheveled,
He bellowed once and it sounded like thunder,
While his legs sprinted like whirling wind.

Holding in his hands a priestly staff, that fiendish creature ran up the bank and tried to seize the Bodhisattva. He was opposed, however, by Hui'an, who wielded his iron rod, crying, "Stop!" but the fiendish creature raised his staff to meet him. So the two of them engaged in a fierce battle beside the Flowing Sand River which was truly terrifying.

The iron rod of Mokṣa
Displays its power to defend the Law;
The monster-taming staff of the creature
Labors to show its heroic might.
Two silver pythons dance along the river's bank.
A pair of godlike monks charge each other on the shore.
This one plies his talents as the forceful lord of Flowing Sand.
That one, to attain great merit, protects Guanyin by strength.
This one churns up foam and stirs up waves.
That one belches fog and spits out wind.
The stirred-up foams and waves darken Heaven and Earth.
The spat-out fog and wind make dim both sun and moon.
The monster-taming staff of this one
Is like a white tiger emerging from the mountain;
The iron rod of that one
Is like a yellow dragon lying on the way.
When used by one,
This weapon spreads open the grass and finds the snake.
When let loose by the other,
That weapon knocks down the kite and splits the pine.
They fight until the darkness thickens

Save for the glittering stars,
And the fog looms up
To obscure both sky and land.
This one, long a dweller in the Weak Water, is uniquely fierce.
That one, newly leaving the Spirit Mountain, seeks his first win.

Back and forth along the river the two of them fought for twenty or thirty rounds without either prevailing, when the fiendish creature stilled the other's iron rod and asked, "What region do you come from, monk, that you dare oppose me?" "I'm the second son of the Pagoda Bearer Devarāja," said Mokṣa, "Mokṣa, Disciple Hui'an. I am serving as the guardian of my mentor, who is looking for a scripture pilgrim in the Land of the East. What kind of monster are you that you dare block our way?" "I remember," said the monster, suddenly recognizing his opponent, "that you used to follow the Guanyin of the South Sea and practice austerities there in the bamboo grove. How did you get to this place?" "Don't you realize," said Mokṣa, "that she is my mentor—the one over there on the shore?"

When the monster heard these words, he apologized repeatedly. Putting away his staff, he allowed Mokṣa to grasp him by the collar and lead him away. He lowered his head and bowed low to Guanyin, saying, "Bodhisattva, please forgive me and let me submit my explanation. I am no monster; I am rather the Curtain-Raising Marshal who waits upon the phoenix chariot of the Jade Emperor at the Divine Mists Hall. Because I carelessly broke a crystal cup at one of the Festivals of Immortal Peaches, the Jade Emperor gave me eight hundred lashes, banished me to the Region Below, and changed me into my present shape. Every seventh day he sends a flying sword to stab my breast and side more than a hundred times before it leaves me. Hence my present wretchedness! Moreover, the hunger and cold are unbearable, and I am driven every few days to come out of the waves and find a traveler for food. I certainly did not expect that my ignorance would today lead me to offend the great, merciful Bodhisattva."

"Because of your sin in Heaven," said the Bodhisattva, "you were banished. Yet the taking of life in your present manner can surely be said to be adding sin to sin. By the decree of Buddha, I am on my way to the Land of the East to find a scripture pilgrim. Why don't you come into my fold, take refuge in good works, and follow the scripture pilgrim as his disciple when he goes to the Western Heaven to ask Buddha for the scriptures? I'll order the flying sword to stop piercing you. At the time when you achieve merit, your sin will be expiated and you will be restored to your former position. How do you feel about that?" "I'm willing," said the monster, "to seek refuge in right action." He said also, "Bodhisattva, I have devoured countless human beings at this place. There have even been a number of scripture pilgrims here, and I ate all of them. The heads of those I devoured I threw into the Flowing Sand, and they sank to the bottom, for such is the nature of this water that not even goose down can float on it. But the skulls of the nine pilgrims floated on the water and would not sink. Regarding them as something unusual, I chained them together with a rope and played with them at my leisure. If this becomes known, I fear that no other scripture pilgrim will want to come this way. Won't it jeopardize my future?"

"Not come this way? How absurd!" said the Bodhisattva. "You may take the skulls and hang them round your neck. When the scripture pilgrim arrives, there will be a use for them." "If that's the case," said the monster, "I'm now willing to receive your instructions." The Bodhisattva then touched the top of his head and gave him the commandments.[21] The sand was taken to be a sign, and he was given the surname "Sha" and the religious name "Wujing,"[22] and that was how he entered the Gate of Sand.[23] After he had seen the Bodhisattva on her way, he washed his heart and purified himself; he never took life again but waited attentively for the arrival of the scripture pilgrim.

So the Bodhisattva parted with him and went with Mokṣa toward the Land of the East. They traveled for a long time and came upon a high mountain, which was covered by miasma so foul that they could not ascend it on foot. They were just about to mount the clouds and pass over it when a sudden blast of violent wind brought into view another monster of most ferocious appearance. Look at his

Lips curled and twisted like dried lotus leaves;
Ears like rush-leaf fans and hard, gleaming eyes;
Gaping teeth as sharp as a fine steel file's;
A long mouth wide open like a fire pot.
A gold cap is fastened with bands by the cheek.
Straps on his armor seem like scaleless snakes.
He holds a rake—a dragon's out-stretched claws;
From his waist hangs a bow of half-moon shape.

21. It was Buddha's custom to lay his hand on top of his disciple's head while teaching him.

22. *Sha* means sand, and *Wujing* means "he who awakes to purity."

23. A pun on his religious name, as the Gate of Sand refers to the sand of the River Ganges: hence Buddhism.

His awesome presence and his prideful mien
Defy the deities and daunt the gods.

He rushed up toward the two travelers and, without regard for good or ill, lifted the rake and brought it down hard on the Bodhisattva. But he was met by Disciple Hui'an, who cried with a loud voice, "Reckless monster! Desist from such insolence! Look out for my rod!" "This monk," said the monster, "doesn't know any better! Look out for my rake!" The two of them clashed together at the foot of the mountain to discover who was to be the victor. It was a magnificent battle!

The monster is fierce.
Hui'an is powerful.
The iron rod jabs at the heart;
The muckrake swipes at the face.
Spraying mud and splattering dust darken Heaven and Earth;
Flying sand and hurling rocks scare demons and gods.
The nine-teeth rake,
All burnished,
Loudly jingles with double rings;
The single rod,
Black throughout,
Leaps and flies in both hands.
This one is the prince of a Devarāja;
That one is the spirit of a grand marshal.
This one defends the faith at Potalaka;
That one lives in a cave as a monster.
Meeting this time they rush to fight,
Not knowing who shall lose and who shall win.

At the very height of their battle, Guanyin threw down some lotus flowers from midair, separating the rod from the rake. Alarmed by what he saw, the fiendish creature asked, "What region are you from, monk, that you dare to play this 'flower-in-the-eye' trick on me?" "Cursed beast of fleshly eyes and mortal stock!" said Mokṣa. "I am the disciple of the Bodhisattva from South Sea, and these are lotus flowers thrown down by my mentor. Don't you recognize them?" "The Bodhisattva from South Sea?" asked the fiend. "Is she Guanyin who sweeps away the three calamities and rescues us from the eight disasters?" "Who else," said Mokṣa, "if not she?" The fiend threw away his muckrake, lowered his head, and bowed, saying, "Venerable brother! Where is the Bodhisattva? Please be so good as to introduce me to her." Mokṣa raised his head and pointed upward, saying, "Isn't she up there?" "Bodhisattva!" the fiend kowtowed toward her and cried with a loud voice, "Pardon my sin! Pardon my sin!"

Guanyin lowered the direction of her cloud and came to ask him, "What region are you from, wild boar who has become a spirit or old sow who has become a fiend, that you dare bar my way?" "I am neither a wild boar," said the fiend, "nor am I an old sow! I was originally the Marshal of the Heavenly Reeds in the Heavenly River.[24] Because I got drunk and dallied with the Goddess of the Moon, the Jade Emperor had me beaten with a mallet two thousand times and banished me to the world of dust. My true spirit was seeking the proper home for my next incarnation when I lost my way, passed through the womb of an old sow, and ended up with a shape like this! Having bitten the sow to death and killed the rest of the litter, I took over this mountain ranch and passed my days eating people. Little did I expect to run into the Bodhisattva. Save me, I implore you! Save me!"

"What is the name of this mountain?" asked the Bodhisattva.

"It's called the Mountain of the Blessed Mound," said the fiendish creature, "and there is a cave in it by the name of Cloudy Paths. There was a Second Elder Sister Luan originally in the cave. She saw that I knew something of the martial art and therefore asked me to be the head of the family, following the so-called practice of 'standing backward in the door.'[25] After less than a year, she died, leaving me to enjoy the possession of her entire cave. I have spent many days and years at this place, but I know no means of supporting myself and I pass the time eating people. I implore the Bodhisattva to pardon my sin." The Bodhisattva said, "There is an old saying: 'If you desire to have a future, act with reverence for the future.' You have already transgressed in the Region Above, and yet you have not changed your violent ways but indulge in the taking of life. Don't you know that both crimes will be punished?" "The future! The future!" said the fiend. "If I listen to you, I might as well feed on the wind! The proverb says, 'If you follow the law of the court, you'll be beaten to death; if you follow the law of Buddha, you'll be starved to death!' Let me go! Let me go! I would much prefer catching a few travelers and munching on the plump and juicy lady of the family. Why should I care about two crimes, three crimes, a thousand crimes, or ten thousand crimes?" "There is a saying," said the Bodhisattva, "'Heaven helps those who have good intentions.' If you are willing to return to the fruits of truth, there will be means to sustain your body. There are five kinds of grain in this world and they all can relieve hunger. Why do you need to pass the time by feeding on human beings?"

24. Marshal of the Heavenly Reeds (Tianpeng yuanshuai) is one of the Four Sages in the Daoist pantheon, high-ranking aides to the Jade Emperor.

25. A colloquialism of the Huai'an region, referring to a man living in the woman's house after marriage.

When the fiend heard these words, he was like one who woke from a dream, and he said to the Bodhisattva, "I would very much like to follow the truth. But 'since I have offended Heaven, even my prayers are of little avail.'"[26] "I have received the decree from Buddha to go to the Land of the East to find a scripture pilgrim," said the Bodhisattva. "You can follow him as his disciple and make a trip to the Western Heaven; your merit will cancel out your sins, and you will surely be delivered from your calamities." "I'm willing. I'm willing," promised the fiend with enthusiasm. The Bodhisattva then touched his head and gave him the instructions. Pointing to his body as a sign, she gave him the surname "Zhu" and the religious name "Wuneng."[27] From that moment on, he accepted the commandment to return to the real. He fasted and ate only a vegetable diet, abstaining from the five forbidden viands and the three undesirable foods[28] so as to wait single-mindedly for the scripture pilgrim.

The Bodhisattva and Mokṣa took leave of Wuneng and proceeded again halfway between cloud and mist. As they were journeying, they saw in midair a young dragon calling for help. The Bodhisattva drew near and asked, "What dragon are you, and why are you suffering here?" The dragon said, "I am the son of Aorun, Dragon King of the Western Ocean. Because I inadvertently set fire to the palace and burned some of the pearls therein, my father the king memorialized to the Heavenly Court and charged me with grave disobedience. The Jade Emperor hung me in the sky and gave me three hundred lashes, and I shall be executed in a few days. I beg the Bodhisattva to save me."

When Guanyin heard these words, she rushed with Mokṣa up to the South Heaven Gate. She was received by Qiu and Zhang, the two Divine Preceptors, who asked her, "Where are you going?" "This humble cleric needs to have an audience with the Jade Emperor," said the Bodhisattva. The two Divine Preceptors promptly made the report, and the Jade Emperor left the hall to receive her. After presenting her greetings, the Bodhisattva said, "By the decree of Buddha, this humble cleric is journeying to the Land of the East to find a scripture pilgrim. On the way I met a mischievous dragon hanging in the sky. I have come specially to beg you to spare his life and grant him to me. He can be a good means of

26. The monster here is quoting the words of Confucius in *Analects* 3.13.

27. *Zhu* means pig or hog, and *Wuneng* means "he who awakes to power."

28. According to various Buddhist teachings, the five forbidden viands may refer to spices (leeks, garlic, onion, green onion, and scallion) or to kinds of meat (the flesh of horse, dog, bullock, goose, and pigeon). The three undesirable foods, prohibited by Daoism, are wild goose, dog, and black fish.

transportation for the scripture pilgrim." When the Jade Emperor heard these words, he at once gave the decree of pardon, ordering the Heavenly sentinels to release the dragon to the Bodhisattva. The Bodhisattva thanked the Emperor, while the young dragon also kowtowed to the Bodhisattva to thank her for saving his life and pledged obedience to her command. The Bodhisattva then sent him to live in a deep mountain stream with the instruction that when the scripture pilgrim should arrive, he was to change into a white horse and go to the Western Heaven. The young dragon obeyed the order and hid himself, and we shall speak no more of him for the moment.

The Bodhisattva then led Mokṣa past the mountain, and they headed again toward the Land of the East. They had not traveled long before they suddenly came upon ten thousand shafts of golden light and a thousand layers of radiant vapor. "Teacher," said Mokṣa, "that luminous place must be the Mountain of Five Phases. I can see the tag of Tathāgata imprinted on it." "So, beneath this place," said the Bodhisattva, "is where the Great Sage, Equal to Heaven, who disturbed Heaven and the Festival of Immortal Peaches, is being imprisoned." "Yes, indeed," said Mokṣa. The mentor and her disciple ascended the mountain and looked at the tag, on which was inscribed the divine words *Oṁ maṇi padme hūṁ*. When the Bodhisattva saw this, she could not help sighing, and composed the following poem:

> *I rue the impish ape not heeding the Law,*
> *Who let loose wild heroics in bygone years.*
> *His mind puffed up, he wrecked the Peach Banquet*
> *And boldly stole in Tushita Palace.*
> *He found no worthy match in ten thousand troops;*
> *Through ninefold Heaven he displayed his power.*
> *Imprisoned now by Sovereign Tathāgata,*
> *When will he be free to show once more his might?*

As mentor and disciple were speaking, they disturbed the Great Sage, who shouted from the base of the mountain, "Who is up there on the mountain composing verses to expose my faults?" When the Bodhisattva heard those words, she came down the mountain to take a look. There beneath the rocky ledges were the local spirit, the mountain god, and the Heavenly sentinels guarding the Great Sage. They all came and bowed to receive the Bodhisattva, leading her before the Great Sage. She looked and saw that he was pinned down in a kind of stone box: though he could speak, he could not move his body. "You whose name is Sun," said the Bodhisattva, "do you recognize me?"

The Great Sage opened wide his fiery eyes and diamond pupils and nodded. "How could I not recognize you?" he cried. "You are the Mighty Deliverer, the Great Compassionate Bodhisattva Guanyin from the Potalaka Mountain of the South Sea. Thank you, thank you for coming to see me! At this place every day is like a year, for not a single acquaintance has ever come to visit me. Where did you come from?"

"I have received the decree from Buddha," said the Bodhisattva, "to go to the Land of the East to find a scripture pilgrim. Since I was passing through here, I rested my steps briefly to see you."

"Tathāgata deceived me," said the Great Sage, "and imprisoned me beneath this mountain. For over five hundred years already I have not been able to move. I implore the Bodhisattva to show a little mercy and rescue old Monkey!" "Your sinful karma is very deep," said the Bodhisattva. "If I rescue you, I fear that you will again perpetrate violence, and that will be bad indeed." "Now I know the meaning of penitence," said the Great Sage. "So I entreat the Great Compassion to show me the proper path, for I am willing to practice cultivation." Truly it is that

One wish born in the heart of man
Is known throughout Heaven and Earth.
If vice or virtue lacks reward,
Unjust must be the universe.

When the Bodhisattva heard those words, she was filled with pleasure and said to the Great Sage, "The scripture says, 'When a good word is spoken, an answer will come from beyond a thousand miles; but when an evil word is spoken, there will be opposition from beyond a thousand miles.' If you have such a purpose, wait until I reach the Great Tang Nation in the Land of the East and find the scripture pilgrim. He will be told to come and rescue you, and you can follow him as a disciple. You shall keep the teachings and hold the rosary to enter our gate of Buddha, so that you may again cultivate the fruits of righteousness. Will you do that?" "I'm willing, I'm willing," said the Great Sage repeatedly.

"If you are indeed seeking the fruits of virtue," said the Bodhisattva, "let me give you a religious name." "I have one already," said the Great Sage, "and I'm called Sun Wukong." "There were two persons before you who came into our faith," said the delighted Bodhisattva, "and their names, too, are built on the word 'Wu.' Your name will agree with theirs perfectly, and that is splendid indeed. I need not give you any more instruction, for I must be going." So our Great Sage, with manifest nature and enlightened mind, returned to the Buddhist faith, while our Bodhisattva, with attention and diligence, sought the divine monk.

She left the place with Mokṣa and proceeded straight to the east; in a few days they reached Chang'an of the Great Tang Nation. Forsaking the mist and abandoning the cloud, mentor and disciple changed themselves into two wandering monks covered with scabby sores[29] and went into the city. It was already dusk. As they walked through one of the main streets, they saw a temple of the local spirit. They both went straight in, alarming the spirit and the demon guards, who recognized the Bodhisattva. They kowtowed to receive her, and the local spirit then ran quickly to report to the city's guardian deity, the god of the soil, and the spirits of various temples of Chang'an. When they learned that it was the Bodhisattva, they all came to pay homage, saying, "Bodhisattva, please pardon us for being tardy in our reception." "None of you," said the Bodhisattva, "should let a word of this leak out! I came here by the special decree of Buddha to look for a scripture pilgrim. I would like to stay just for a few days in one of your temples, and I shall depart when the true monk is found." The various deities went back to their own places, but they sent the local spirit off to the residence of the city's guardian deity so that the teacher and the disciple could remain incognito in the spirit's temple. We do not know what sort of scripture pilgrim was found. Let's listen to the explanation in the next chapter.

29. In vernacular Chinese literature, the mendicant monk with scabby sores or leprosy is frequently a holy man in disguise.

NINE

Chen Guangrui, going to his post, meets disaster;
Monk River Float, avenging his parents, repays their kindness.

We now tell you about the city of Chang'an in the great nation in Shanxi Province which was the place that kings and emperors from generation to generation had made their capital. Since the periods of Zhou, Qin, and Han,

> *Three counties of flowers bloomed like brocade,*
> *And eight rivers flowed encircling the city.*

It was truly a land of great scenic beauty. At this time the emperor Taizong of the Great Tang dynasty was on the throne, and the name of his reign was Zhenguan. He had been ruling now for thirteen years, and the cyclical name of the year was Jisi. The whole land was at peace: people came bearing tributes from eight directions, and the inhabitants of the whole world called themselves his subjects.

One day Taizong ascended his throne and assembled his civil and military officials. After they had paid him homage, the prime minister Wei Zheng left the ranks and came forward to memorialize to the Throne, saying, "Since the world now is at peace and tranquility reigns everywhere, we should follow the ancient custom and establish sites for civil examinations, so that we may invite worthy scholars to come here and select those talents who will best serve the work of administration and government." "Our worthy subject has voiced a sound principle in his memorial," said Taizong. He therefore issued a summons to be proclaimed throughout the empire: in every prefecture, county, and town, those who were learned in the Confucian classics, who could write with ease and lucidity, and who had passed the three sessions of examination, regardless of whether they were soldiers or peasants, would be invited to go to Chang'an to take the imperial examination.

This summons reached the place Haizhou, where it was seen by a certain man named Chen E (with the courtesy name of Guangrui), who then went straight home to talk to his mother, whose maiden name was Zhang. "The court," he said, "has sent a yellow summons, declaring in these southern provinces that there will be examinations for the selection of the worthy and the talented. Your child wishes to try out at such an examination, for if I manage to acquire an appointment, or even half a post, I would become more of a credit to my parents, magnify our name, give my wife a title, benefit my son, and bring glory to this house of ours. Such is the aspiration of your son: I wish to tell my mother plainly before I leave." "My son," said she of the Zhang family, "an educated person 'learns when he is young, but leaves when he is grown.' You should indeed follow this maxim. But as you go to the examination, you must be careful on the way, and, when you have secured a post, come home quickly." So Kuangjui gave instructions for his family page to pack his bags, took leave of his mother, and began his journey. When he reached Chang'an, the examination site had just been opened, and he went straight in. He took the preliminary tests, passed them, and went to the court examination, where in three sessions on administrative policy he took first place, receiving the title "zhuangyuan," the certificate of which was signed by the Tang emperor's own hand. As was the custom, he was led through the streets on horseback for three days.

The procession at one point passed by the house of the chief minister, Yin Kaishan, who had a daughter named Wenjiao, nicknamed Mantangjiao (A Hall of Loveliness). She was not yet married, and at this time she was just about to throw down an embroidered ball from high up on a festooned tower in order to select her spouse. It happened that Chen Guangrui was passing by the tower down below. When the young maiden saw Guangrui's outstanding appearance and knew that he was the recent zhuangyuan of the examinations, she was very pleased. She threw down the embroidered ball, which just happened to hit the black gauze hat of Guangrui. Immediately, lively music of pipes and flutes could be heard throughout the area as scores of maids and serving-girls ran down from the tower, took hold of the bridle of Guangrui's horse, and led him into the residence of the chief minister for the wedding. The chief minister and his wife at once came out of their chambers, called together the guests and the master of ceremonies, and gave the girl to Guangrui as his bride. Together, they bowed to Heaven and Earth; then husband and wife bowed to each other, before bowing to the father- and mother-in-law.

The chief minister then gave a big banquet and everyone feasted merrily for a whole evening, after which the two of them walked hand in hand into the bridal chamber. At the fifth watch early next morning, Taizong took his seat in the Treasure Hall of Golden Chimes as civil and military officials attended the court. Taizong asked, "What appointment should the new zhuangyuan receive?" The prime minister Wei Zheng said, "Your subject has discovered that within our territory there is a vacancy at Jiangzhou. I beg my Lord to grant him this post." Taizong at once made him governor of Jiangzhou and ordered him to leave without delay. After thanking the emperor and leaving the court, Guangrui went back to the house of the chief minister to inform his wife. He took leave of his father- and mother-in-law and proceeded with his wife to the new post at Jiangzhou.

As they left Chang'an and went on their journey, the season was late spring:

A soft wind blew to green the willows;
A fine rain spotted to redden the flowers.

As his home was on the way, Guangrui returned to his house where husband and wife bowed together to his mother, Lady Zhang. "Congratulations, my son," said she of the Zhang family, "you even came back with a wife!" "Your child," said Guangrui, "relied on the power of your blessing and was able to attain the undeserved honor of zhuangyuan. By imperial command I was making a tour of the streets when, as I passed by the mansion of Chief Minister Yin, I was hit by an embroidered ball. The chief minister kindly gave his daughter to your child to be his wife, and His Majesty appointed him governor of Jiangzhou. I have returned to take you with me to the post." She of the Zhang family was delighted and packed at once for the journey.

They had been on the road for a few days when they came to stay at the Inn of Ten Thousand Flowers, kept by a certain Liu Xiaoer. She of the Zhang family suddenly became ill and said to Guangrui, "I don't feel well at all. Let's rest here for a day or two before we journey again." Guangrui obeyed. Next morning there was a man outside the inn holding a golden carp for sale, which Guangrui bought for a string of coins. He was about to have it cooked for his mother when he saw that the carp was blinking its eyes vigorously. In astonishment, Guangrui said, "I have heard that when a fish or a snake blinks its eyes in this manner, that's the sure sign that it's not an ordinary creature!" He therefore asked the fisherman, "Where did you catch this fish?" "I caught it," said the fisherman, "from the river Hong, some fifteen miles from this district." Accordingly, Guangrui sent the fish live back to the river and returned to the inn to tell his mother about it. "It is a good deed to release living creatures from captivity," said she of the Zhang family. "I am very pleased." "We have stayed in this inn now for three days," said Guangrui. "The imperial command is an urgent one. Your child intends to leave tomorrow, but he would like to know whether mother has fully recovered." She of the Zhang family said, "I'm still not well, and the heat on the journey at this time of year, I fear, will only add to my illness. Why don't you rent a house for me to stay here temporarily and leave me an allowance? The two of you can proceed to your new post. By autumn, when it's cool, you can come fetch me." Guangrui discussed the matter with his wife; they duly rented a house for her and left some cash with her, after which they took leave and left.

They felt the fatigue of traveling, journeying by day and resting by night, and they soon came to the crossing of the Hong River, where two boatmen, Liu Hong and Li Biao, took them into their boat. It happened that Guangrui was destined in his previous incarnation to meet this calamity, and so he had to come upon these fated enemies of his. After ordering the houseboy to put the luggage on the boat, Guangrui and his wife were just about to get aboard when Liu Hong noticed the beauty of Lady Yin, who had a face like a full moon, eyes like autumnal water, a small, cherrylike mouth, and a tiny, willowlike waist. Her features were striking enough to sink fishes and drop wild geese, and her complexion would cause the moon to hide and put the flowers to shame. Stirred at once to cruelty, he plotted with Li Biao; together they punted the boat to an isolated area and waited until the middle of the night. They killed the houseboy first, and then they beat Guangrui to death, pushing both bodies into the water. When the lady saw that they had killed her husband, she made a dive for the water, but Liu Hong threw his arms around her and caught her. "If you consent to my demand," he said, "everything will be all right. If you do not, this knife will cut you in two!" Unable to think of any better plan, the lady had to give her consent for the time being and yielded herself to Liu Hong. The thief took the boat to the south bank, where he turned the boat over to the care of Li Biao. He himself put on Guangrui's cap and robe, took his credentials, and proceeded with the lady to the post at Jiangzhou.

We should now tell you that the body of the houseboy killed by Liu Hong drifted away with the current. The body of Chen Guangrui, however, sank to the bottom of the water and stayed there. A yakṣa on patrol at the mouth of the Hong River saw it and rushed into the Dragon Palace. The Dragon King was just holding court when the yakṣa entered to report, saying, "A scholar has been beaten to death at the mouth of the Hong River by some unknown person, and his body is now lying at the bottom of the water." The Dragon King had the corpse brought in and laid before him. He took a careful look at it and said, "But this man was my benefactor! How could he have been murdered? As the common saying goes, 'Kindness should be paid by kindness.' I must save his life today so that I may repay the kindness of yesterday." He at once issued an official dispatch, sending a yakṣa to deliver it to the municipal deity and local spirit of Hongzhou, and asked for the soul of the scholar so that his life might be saved. The municipal deity and the local spirit in turn ordered the little demons to hand over the soul of Chen Guangrui to the yakṣa, who led the soul back to the Water Crystal Palace for an audience with the Dragon King.

"Scholar," asked the Dragon King, "what is your name? Where did you come from? Why did you come here, and for what reason were you beaten to death?" Guangrui saluted him and said, "This minor student is named Chen E, and my courtesy name is Guangrui. I am from the Hongnong district of Haizhou. As the unworthy zhuangyuan of the recent session of examination, I was appointed by the court to be governor of Jiangzhou, and I was going to my post with my wife. When I took a boat at the river, I did not expect the boatman, Liu Hong, to covet my wife and plot against me. He beat me to death and tossed out my body. I beg the Great King to save me." Hearing these words, the Dragon King said, "So, that's it! Good sir, the golden carp that you released earlier was myself. You are my benefactor. You may be in dire difficulty at the moment, but is there any reason why I should not come to your assistance?" He therefore laid the body of Guangrui to one side, and put a preservative pearl in his mouth so that his body would not deteriorate but be reunited with his soul to avenge himself in the future. He also said, "Your true soul may remain temporarily in my Water Bureau as an officer." Guangrui kowtowed to thank him, and the Dragon King prepared a banquet to entertain him, but we shall say no more about that.

We now tell you that Lady Yin hated the bandit Liu so bitterly that she wished she could devour his flesh and sleep on his skin! But because she was with child and did not know whether it would be a boy or a girl, she had no alternative but to yield reluctantly to her captor. In a little while they arrived at Zhiangzhou; the clerks and the lictors all came to meet them, and all the subordinate officials gave a banquet for them at the governor's mansion. Liu Hong said, "Having come here, a student like me is utterly dependent on the support and assistance of you gentlemen." "Your Honor," replied the officials, "is first in the examinations and a major talent. You will, of course, regard your people as your children; your public declarations will be as simple as your settlement of litigation is fair. We subordinates are all dependent on your leadership, so why should you be unduly modest?" When the official banquet ended, the people all left.

Time passed by swiftly. One day, Liu Hong went far away on official business, while Lady Yin at the mansion was thinking of her mother-in-law and her husband and sighing in the garden pavilion. Suddenly she was seized by tremendous fatigue and sharp pains in her belly. Falling unconscious to the ground, she gave birth to a son. Presently she heard someone whispering in her ear: "Mantangjiao, listen carefully to what I have to say. I am the Star Spirit of South Pole, who sends you this son by the express command of the Bodhisattva Guanyin. One day his name will be known far and wide, for he is not to be compared with an ordinary mortal. But when the bandit Liu returns, he will surely try to harm the child, and you must take care to protect him. Your husband has been rescued by the Dragon King; in the future both of you will meet again even as son and mother will be reunited. A day will come when wrongs will be redressed and crimes punished. Remember my words! Wake up! Wake up!" The voice ceased and departed. The lady woke up and remembered every word; she clasped her son tightly to her but could devise no plan to protect him. Liu Hong then returned and wanted to have the child killed by drowning the moment he saw him. The lady said, "Today it's late already. Allow him to live till tomorrow and then have him thrown into the river."

It was fortunate that Liu Hong was called away by urgent business the next morning. The lady thought to herself: "If this child is here when that bandit returns, his life is finished! I might as well abandon him now to the river, and let life or death take its own course. Perhaps Heaven, taking pity on him, will send someone to his rescue and to have him cared for. Then we may have a chance to meet again." She was afraid, however, that future recognition would be difficult; so she bit her finger and wrote a letter with her blood, stating in detail the names of the parents, the family history, and the reason for the child's abandonment. She also bit off a little toe from the child's left foot to establish a mark of his identity. Taking one of her own inner garments she wrapped the child and took him out of the mansion when no one was watching. Fortunately the mansion was not far from the river. Reaching the bank, the lady burst into tears and wailed long and loud. She was about to toss the child into the river when she caught sight of a plank floating by the river bank. At once she prayed to Heaven, after which she placed the child on the plank and tied him securely to it with some rope. She fastened the letter written in blood to his chest, pushed the plank out into the water, and let it drift away. With tears in her eyes, the lady went back to the mansion, but we shall say no more of that.

Now we shall tell you about the boy on the plank, which floated with the current until it came to a standstill just beneath the Temple of Gold Mountain. The abbot of this temple was called Monk Faming. In the cultivation and comprehension of truth, he had attained already the wondrous secret of birthlessness. He was sitting in meditation when all at once he heard a baby crying. Moved by this, he went quickly down to the river to have a look, and discovered the baby lying there on a plank at the edge of the water. Hurriedly the abbot lifted him out of the water. When he read the letter in blood fastened to his chest, he learned of the child's origin. He then gave him the baby name River Float and arranged for someone to nurse and care for him, while he himself kept the letter written in blood safely hidden. Time passed by like an arrow, and the seasons like a weaver's shuttle; River Float soon reached his eighteenth year. The abbot had his hair shaved and asked him to join in the practice of austerities, giving him the religious name Xuanzang. Having had his head touched and having received the prohibitions, Xuanzang pursued the Way with great determination.

One day in late spring, the various monks gathered in the shade of pine trees were discussing the canons of Zen and debating the fine points of the mysteries. One feckless monk, who happened to have been completely outwitted by Xuanzang's questions, shouted angrily, "You damnable beast! You don't even know your own name, and you are ignorant of your own parents! Why are you still hanging around here playing tricks on people?" When Xuanzang heard such language of rebuke, he went into the temple and knelt before the master, saying with tears flowing from his eyes, "Though a human being born into this world receives his natural endowments from the forces of yin and yang and from the Five Phases, he is always nurtured by his parents. How can there be a person in this world who has no father or mother?" Repeatedly and piteously he begged for the names of his parents. The abbot said, "If you truly wish to seek your parents, you may follow me to my cell." Xuanzang duly followed him to his cell, where, from the top of a heavy crossbeam, the abbot took down a small box. Opening the box, he took out a letter written in blood and an inner garment and gave them to Xuanzang. Only after he had unfolded the letter and read it did Xuanzang learn the names of his parents and understand in detail the wrongs that had been done them.

When Xuanzang had finished reading, he fell weeping to the floor, saying, "How can anyone be worthy to bear the name of man if he cannot avenge the wrongs done to his parents? For eighteen years, I have been ignorant of my true parents, and only this day have I learned that I have a mother! And yet, would I have even reached this day if my master had not saved me and cared for me? Permit your disciple to go seek my mother. Thereafter, I will rebuild this temple with an incense bowl on my head, and repay the profound kindness of my teacher." "If you desire to seek your mother," said the master, "you may take this letter in blood and the inner garment with you. Go as a mendicant monk to the private quarters at the governor's mansion of Jiangzhou. You will then be able to meet your mother."

Xuanzang followed the words of his master and went to Jiangzhou as a mendicant monk. It happened that Liu Hong was out on business, for Heaven had planned that mother and child should meet. Xuanzang went straight to the door of the private quarters of the governor's mansion to beg for alms. Lady Yin, you see, had had a dream the night before in which she saw a waning moon become full again. She thought to herself, "I have no news from my mother-in-law; my husband was murdered by this bandit; my son was thrown into the river. If by chance someone rescued him and had him cared for, he must be eighteen by now. Perhaps Heaven wished us to be reunited today. Who can tell?"

As she was pondering the matter in her heart, she suddenly heard someone reciting the scriptures outside her residence and crying repeatedly, "Alms! Alms!" At a convenient moment, the lady slipped out and asked him, "Where did you come from?" "Your poor monk," said Xuanzang, "is the disciple of Faming, abbot of the Temple of Gold Mountain." "So you are the disciple of the abbot of that temple?" She asked him into the mansion and served him some vegetables and rice. Watching him closely, she noticed that in speech and manner he bore a remarkable resemblance to her husband. The lady sent her maid away and then asked, "Young master! Did you leave your family as a child or when you grew up? What are your given name and your surname? Do you have any parents?" "I did not leave my family when I was young," replied Xuanzang, "nor did I do so when I grew up. To tell you the truth, I have a wrong to avenge great as the sky, an enmity deep as the sea. My father was a murder victim, and my mother was taken by force. My master the abbot Faming told me to seek my mother in the governor's mansion of Jiangzhou." "What is your mother's surname?" asked the lady. "My mother's surname is Yin," said Xuanzang, "and her given name is Wenjiao. My father's surname is Chen and his given name is Guangrui. My nickname is River Float, but my religious name is Xuanzang."

"I am Wenjiao," said the lady, "but what proof have you of your identity?" When Xuanzang heard that she was his mother, he fell to his knees and wept most grievously. "If my own mother doesn't believe me," he said, "you may see the proof in this letter written in blood and this inner garment." Wenjiao took them in her hands, and one look told her that they were the real things. Mother and child embraced each other and wept.

Lady Yin then cried, "My son, leave at once!" "For eighteen years I have not known my true parents," said Xuanzang, "and I've seen my mother for the first time only this morning. How could your son bear so swift a separation?" "My son," said the lady, "leave at once, as if you were on fire! If that bandit Liu returns, he will surely take your life. I shall pretend to be ill tomorrow and say that I must go to your temple and fulfill a vow I made in a previous year to donate a hundred pairs of monk shoes. At that time I shall have more to say to you." Xuanzang followed her bidding and bowed to take leave of her.

We were speaking of Lady Yin, who, having seen her son, was filled with both anxiety and joy. The next day, under the pretext of being sick, she lay on her bed and would take neither tea nor rice. Liu Hong returned to the mansion and questioned her. "When I was young," said Lady Yin, "I vowed to donate a hundred pairs of monk shoes. Five days ago, I dreamed that a monk demanded those shoes of me, holding a knife in his hand. From then on, I did not feel well." "Such a small matter!" said Liu Hong. "Why didn't you tell me earlier?" He at once went up to the governor's hall and gave the order to his stewards Wang and Li that a hundred families of the city were each to bring in a pair of monk shoes within five days. The families obeyed and completed their presentations. "Now that we have the shoes," said Lady Yin to Liu Hong, "what kind of temple do we have nearby that I can go to fulfill my vow?" Liu Hong said, "There is a Temple of Gold Mountain here in Jiangzhou as well as a Temple of Burned Mountain. You may go to whichever one you choose." "I have long heard," said the lady, "that the Temple of Gold Mountain is a very good one. I shall go there." Liu Hong at once gave the order to his stewards Wang and Li to prepare a boat. Lady Yin took a trusted companion with her and boarded the boat. The boatmen poled it away from the shore and headed for the Temple of Gold Mountain.

We now tell you about Xuanzang, who returned to the temple and told the abbot Faming what had happened. The next day, a young housemaid arrived to announce that her mistress was coming to the temple to fulfill a vow she had made. All the monks came out of the temple to receive her. The lady went straight inside to worship the Bodhisattva and to give a great vegetarian banquet. She ordered the housemaid to put the monk shoes and stockings in trays and have them brought into the main ceremonial hall. After the lady had again worshiped with extreme devoutness, she asked the abbot Faming to distribute the gifts to the various monks before they dispersed. When Xuanzang saw that all the monks had left and that there was no one else in the hall, he drew near and knelt down. The lady asked him to remove his shoes and stockings, and she saw that there was, indeed, a small toe missing from his left foot. Once again, the two of them embraced and wept. They also thanked the abbot for his kindness in fostering the youth.

Faming said, "I fear that the present meeting of mother and child may become known to that wily bandit. You must leave speedily so that you may avoid any harm." "My son," the lady said, "let me give you an incense ring. Go to Hongzhou, about fifteen hundred miles northwest of here, where you will find the Ten Thousand Flowers Inn. Earlier we left an aged woman there whose maiden name is Zhang and who is the true mother of your father. I have also written a letter for you to take to the capital of the Tang emperor. To the left of the Golden Palace is the house of Chief Minister Yin, who is the true father of your mother. Give my letter to your maternal grandfather, and ask him to request the Tang emperor to dispatch men and horses to have this bandit arrested and executed, so that your father may be avenged. Only then will you be able to rescue your old mother. I dare not linger now, for I fear that that knave may be offended by my returning late." She went out of the temple, boarded the boat, and left.

Xuanzang returned weeping to the temple. He told his master everything and bowed to take leave of him immediately. Going straight to Hongzhou, he came to the Ten Thousand Flowers Inn and addressed the innkeeper, Liu Xiaoer, saying, "In a previous year there was an honored guest here by the name of Chen whose mother remained at your inn. How is she now?" "Originally," said Liu Xiaoer, "she stayed in my inn. Afterwards she went blind, and for three or four years did not pay me any rent. She now lives in a dilapidated potter's kiln near the Southern Gate, and every day she goes begging on the streets. Once that honored guest had left, he was gone for a long time, and even now there is no news of him whatever. I can't understand it."

When Xuanzang had heard this, he went at once to the dilapidated potter's kiln at the Southern Gate and found his grandmother. The grandmother said, "Your voice sounds very much like that of my son Chen Guangrui." "I'm not Chen Guangrui," said Xuanzang, "but only his son! Lady Wenjiao is my mother." "Why didn't your father and mother come back?" asked the grandmother. "My father was beaten to death by bandits," said Xuanzang, "and one of them forced my mother to be his wife." "How did you know where to find me?" asked the grandmother. "It was my mother," answered Xuanzang, "who told me to seek my grandmother. There's a letter from mother here and there's also an incense ring."

The grandmother took the letter and the incense ring and wept without restraint. "For merit and reputation," she said, "my son came to this! I thought that he had turned his back on righteousness and had forgotten parental kindness. How should I know that he was murdered! Fortunately, Heaven remembered me at least in pity, and this day a grandson has come to seek me out."

"Grandmother," asked Xuanzang, "how did you go blind?" "Because I thought so often about your father," said the grandmother. "I waited for him daily, but he did not return. I wept until I was blind in both eyes." Xuanzang knelt down and prayed to Heaven, saying, "Have regard of Xuanzang who, at the age of eighteen, has not yet avenged the wrong done to his parents. By the command of my mother, I came this day to find my grandmother. If Heaven would take pity on my sincerity, grant that the eyes of my grandmother regain their sight." When he finished his petition, he licked the eyes of his grandmother with the tip of his tongue. In a moment, both eyes were licked open and they were as of old. When the grandmother saw the youthful monk, she said, "You're indeed my grandson! Why, you are just like my son Guangrui!" She felt both happy and sad. Xuanzang led his grandmother out of the kiln and went back to Liu Xiaoer's inn, where he rented a room for her to stay. He also gave her some money, saying, "In a little more than a month's time, I'll be back."

Taking leave of his grandmother, he went straight to the capital and found his way to the house of the chief minister Yin on the eastern street of the imperial city. He said to the porter, "This little monk is a kinsman who has come to visit the chief minister." The porter made the report to the chief minister, who replied, "I'm not related to any monk!" But his wife said, "I dreamed last night that my daughter Mantangjiao came home. Could it be that our son-in-law has sent us a letter?" The chief minister therefore had the little monk shown to the living room. When he saw the chief minister and his wife, he fell weeping to the floor. Taking a letter from within the folds of his robe, he handed it over to the chief minister. The chief minister opened it, read it from beginning to end, and wept without restraint. "Your Excellency, what is the matter?" asked his wife. "This monk," said the chief minister, "is our grandson. Our son-in-law, Chen Guangrui, was murdered by bandits, and Mantangjiao was made the wife of the murderer by force." When the wife heard this, she too wept inconsolably.

"Let our lady restrain her grief," said the chief minister. "Tomorrow morning I shall present a memorial to our Lord. I shall lead the troops myself to avenge our son-in-law." Next day, the chief minister went into court to present his memorial to the Tang emperor, which read:

> The son-in-law of your subject, the zhuangyuan Chen Guangrui, was proceeding to his post at Jiangzhou with members of his family. He was beaten to death by the boatman Liu Hong, who then took our daughter by force to be his wife. He pretended to be the son-in-law of your subject and usurped his post for many years. This is indeed a shocking and tragic incident. I beg Your Majesty to dispatch horses and men at once to exterminate the bandits.

The Tang emperor saw the memorial and became exceedingly angry. He immediately called up sixty thousand imperial soldiers and ordered the chief minister Yin to lead them forth. The chief minister took the decree and left the court to make the roll call for the troops at the barracks. They proceeded immediately toward Jiangzhou, journeying by day and resting by night, and they soon reached the place. Horses and men pitched camps on the north shore, and that very night, the chief minister summoned with golden tablets the Subprefect and County Judge of Jiangzhou to his camp. He explained to the two of them the reason for the expedition and asked for their military assistance. They then crossed the river and, before the sky was light, had the mansion of Liu Hong completely surrounded. Liu Hong was still in his dreams when at the shot of a single cannon and the unisonous roll of drums, the soldiers broke into the private quarters of the mansion. Liu Hong was seized before he could offer any resistance. The chief minister had him and the rest of the prisoners bound and taken to the field of execution, while the rest of the soldiers pitched camp outside the city.

Taking a seat in the great hall of the mansion, the chief minister invited the lady to come out to meet him. She was about to do so but was overcome by shame at seeing her father again, and wanted to hang herself right there. Xuanzang learned of this and rushed inside to save his mother. Falling to his knees, he said to her, "Your son and his grandfather led the troops here to avenge father. The bandit has already been captured. Why does mother want to die now? If mother were dead, how could your son possibly remain alive?" The chief minister also went inside to offer his consolation. "I have heard," said the lady, "that a woman follows her spouse to the grave. My husband was murdered by this bandit, causing me dreadful grief. How could I yield so shamefully to the thief? The child I was carrying—that was my sole lease on life which helped me bear my humiliation! Now that my son is grown and my old father has led troops to avenge our wrong, I who am the daughter have little face left for my reunion. I can only die to repay my husband!"

"My child," said the chief minister, "you did not alter your virtue according to prosperity or adversity. You had no choice! How can this be regarded as shame!" Father and daughter embraced, weeping; Xuanzang, too, could not contain his emotion. Wiping away his tears, the chief minister said, "The two of you must sorrow no more. I have already captured the culprit, and I must now dispose of him." He got up and went to the execution site, and it happened that the Subprefect of Jiangzhou had also apprehended the pirate, Li Biao, who was brought by sentinels to the same place. Highly pleased, the chief minister ordered Liu Hong and Li Biao to be flogged a hundred times with large canes. Each signed an affidavit, giving a thorough account of the murder of Chen Guangrui. First Li Biao was nailed to a wooden ass, and after it had been pushed to the market place, he was cut to pieces and his head exposed on a pole for all to see. Liu Hong was then taken to the crossing at the Hong River, to the exact spot where he had beaten Chen Guangrui to death. The chief minister, the lady, and Xuanzang all went to the bank of the river, and as libations they offered the heart and liver of Liu Hong, which had been gouged out from him live. Finally, an essay eulogizing the deceased was burned.

Facing the river the three persons wept without restraint, and their sobs were heard down below in the water region. A yakṣa patrolling the waters brought the essay in its spirit form to the Dragon King, who read it and at once sent a turtle marshal to fetch Guangrui. "Sir," said the king, "Congratulations! Congratulations! At this moment, your wife, your son, and your father-in-law are offering sacrifices to you at the bank of the river. I am now letting your soul go so that you may return to life. We are also presenting you with a pearl of wish fulfillment, two rolling-pan pearls, ten bales of mermaid silk, and a jade belt with lustrous pearls.[1] Today you will enjoy the reunion of husband and wife, mother and son." After Guangrui had given thanks repeatedly, the Dragon King ordered a yakṣa to escort his body to the mouth of the river and there to return his soul. The yakṣa followed the order and left.

1. The various pearls named in this sentence are all taken from Chinese lore and legend on the object, while mermaid silk is said to be raw silk spun and sold by mermaids. Pearls in literary writings, especially in classical poetry, are a familiar symbol for tears. The pearls and silk as aquatic symbols here are thus used deliberately because Chen Guangrui is revived from a watery grave. A bale is eighteen Chinese feet in length.

We tell you now about Lady Yin, who, having wept for some time for her husband, would have killed herself again by plunging into the water if Xuanzang had not desperately held on to her. They were struggling pitifully when they saw a dead body floating toward the river bank. The lady hurriedly went forward to look at it. Recognizing it as her husband's body, she burst into even louder wailing. As the other people gathered around to look, they suddenly saw Guangrui unclasping his fists and stretching his legs. The entire body began to stir, and in a moment he clambered up to the bank and sat down, to the infinite amazement of everyone. Guangrui opened his eyes and saw Lady Yin, the chief minister Yin, his father-in-law, and a youthful monk, all weeping around him. "Why are you all here?" said Guangrui.

"It all began," said Lady Yin, "when you were beaten to death by bandits. Afterwards your unworthy wife gave birth to this son, who is fortunate enough to have been brought up by the abbot of the Gold Mountain Temple. The abbot sent him to meet me, and I told him to go seek his maternal grandfather. When father heard this, he made it known to the court and led troops here to arrest the bandits. Just now we took out the culprit's liver and heart live to offer to you as libations, but I would like to know how my husband's soul is able to return to give him life." Guangrui said, "That's all on account of our buying the golden carp, when you and I were staying at the Inn of Ten Thousand Flowers. I released that carp, not knowing that it was none other than the Dragon King of this place. When the bandits pushed me into the river thereafter, he was the one who came to my rescue. Just now he was also the one who gave me back my soul as well as many precious gifts, which I have here with me. I never even knew that you had given birth to this boy, and I am grateful that my father-in-law has avenged me. Indeed, bitterness has passed and sweetness has come! What unsurpassable joy!"

When the various officials heard about this, they all came to tender their congratulations. The chief minister then ordered a great banquet to thank his subordinates, after which the troops and horses on the very same day began their march homeward. When they came to the Inn of Ten Thousand Flowers, the chief minister gave order to pitch camp. Guangrui went with Xuanzang to the Inn of Liu to seek the grandmother, who happened to have dreamed the night before that a withered tree had blossomed. Magpies behind her house were chattering incessantly as well. She thought to herself, "Could it be that my grandson is coming?" Before she had finished talking to herself, father and son arrived together. The youthful monk pointed to her and said, "Isn't this my grandmother?" When Guangrui saw his aged mother, he bowed in haste; mother and son embraced and wept without restraint for a while. After recounting to each other what had happened, they paid the innkeeper his bill and set out again for the capital. When they reached the chief minister's residence, Guangrui, his wife, and his mother all went to greet the chief minister's wife, who was overjoyed. She ordered her servants to prepare a huge banquet to celebrate the occasion. The chief minister said, "This banquet today may be named the Festival of Reunion, for truly our whole family is rejoicing."

Early next morning, the Tang emperor held court, during which time the chief minister Yin left the ranks to give a careful report on what had taken place. He also recommended that a talent like Guangrui's be used in some important capacity. The Tang emperor approved the memorial, and ordered that Chen E be promoted to Subchancellor of the Grand Secretariat so that he could accompany the court and carry out its policies. Xuanzang, determined to follow the way of Zen, was sent to practice austerities at the Temple of Infinite Blessing. Some time after this, Lady Yin calmly committed suicide after all, and Xuanzang went back to the Gold Mountain Temple to repay the kindness of abbot Faming. We do not know how things went thereafter; let's listen to the explanation in the next chapter.

The Old Dragon King, in foolish schemes, transgresses Heaven's decrees;
Prime Minister Wei sends a letter to an official of the dead.

For the time being, we shall make no mention of Guangrui serving in his post and Xuanzang practicing austerities. We tell you now about two worthies who lived on the banks of the river Jing outside the city of Chang'an: a fisherman by the name of Zhang Shao and a woodman by the name of Li Ding. The two of them were scholars who had passed no official examination, mountain folks who knew how to read. One day in the city of Chang'an, after they had sold the wood on the one's back and the carp in the other's basket, they went into a small inn and drank until they were slightly tipsy. Each carrying a bottle, they followed the bank of the Jing River and walked slowly back. "Brother Li," said Zhang Shao, "in my opinion those who strive for fame will lose their lives on account of fame; those who live in quest of fortune will perish because of riches; those who have titles sleep embracing a tiger; and those who receive official favors walk with snakes in their sleeves. When you think of it, their lives cannot compare with our carefree existence, close to the blue mountains and fair waters. We cherish poverty and pass our days without having to quarrel with fate."

"Brother Zhang," said Li Ding, "there's a great deal of truth in what you say. But your fair waters cannot match my blue mountains." "On the contrary," said Zhang Shao, "your blue mountains cannot match my fair waters, in testimony of which I offer a lyric to the tune of 'Butterflies Enamored of Flowers' that says:

On ten thousand miles of misty waters in a tiny boat
I lean to the silent, solitary sail,
Surrounded by the sound of the mermaid-fish.
My mind cleansed, my care purged, for here's little wealth or fame;
In leisure I pick the stems of bulrushes and reeds.
To count the seagulls: that's pleasure to be told!
At willowed banks and reeded bays

My wife and children join my joyous laugh.
I sleep most soundly as wind and wave recede;
No shame, no glory, nor any misery."

Li Ding said, "Your fair waters are not as good as my blue mountains. I also have as testimony a lyric poem to the tune of 'Butterflies Enamored of Flowers' that says:

At a dense forest's pine-seeded corner
I hear, wordless, the oriole—
Its deft tongue's a tuneful pipe.
Pale reds and bright greens announce the warmth of spring;
Summer comes abruptly; so passes time.
Then autumn arrives (for it's an easy change)
With fragrant golden flowers
Most worthy of our joy;
And cold winter enters, swift as a finger snaps.
Ruled by no one, I'm free in all four climes."

[Ed.: *The lengthy exchange of poems in the narrative by the fisherman and wood-man, in different tunes and styles, is omitted here.*]

The two of them thus recited poems and songs and composed linking-verses. Arriving at the place where their ways parted, they bowed to take leave of each other. "Elder Brother Li," said Zhang Shao, "take care as you go on your way. When you climb the mountains, be wary of the tiger. If you were harmed, I would find, as the saying goes, 'one friend missing on the street tomorrow.'" When Li Ding heard these words, he grew very angry saying, "What a scoundrel you are! Good friends would even die for each other! But you, why do you say such unlucky things to me? If I'm to be harmed by a tiger, your boat will surely capsize in the river." "I'll never capsize my boat in the river," said Zhang Shao. "As there are unexpected storms in the sky,'" said Li Ding, "'so there is sudden weal or woe on earth.' What makes you so sure that you won't have an accident?" "Elder Brother Li," said Zhang Shao, "you say this because you have no idea what may befall you in your business, whereas I can predict what'll happen in my kind of business. And I assure you that I won't have any accident." "The kind of living you pick up on the waters," said Li Ding, "is an exceedingly treacherous business. You have to take chances all the time. How can you be so certain about your future?"

"Here's something you don't know about," said Zhang Shao. "In this city of Chang'an, there's a fortune teller who plies his trade on the West Gate Street. Every day I give him a golden carp as a present, and he consults the sticks in his sleeve for me. I follow his instructions when I lower my nets, and I've never missed in a hundred times. Today I went again to buy his prediction; he told me to set my nets at the east bend of the Jing River and to cast my line from the west bank. I know I'll come back with a fine catch of fishes and shrimps. When I go up to the city tomorrow, I'll sell my catch and buy some wine, and then I'll get together with you again, old brother." The two men then parted.

There is, however, a proverb: "What is said on the road is heard in the grass." For you see, it happened that a yakṣa on patrol in the Jing River overheard the part of the conversation about not having missed a hundred times. He dashed back to the Water Crystal Palace and hastily reported to the Dragon King, shouting, "Disaster! Disaster!" "What sort of disaster?" asked the Dragon King.

"Your subject," said the yakṣa, "was patrolling the river and overheard a conversation between a woodman and a fisherman. Before they parted, they said something terrible. According to the fisherman, there is a fortune teller on West Gate Street in the city of Chang'an who is most accurate in his calculations. Everyday the fisherman gives him a carp, and he then consults the sticks in his sleeve, with the result that the fisherman has not missed once in a hundred times when he casts his line! If such accurate calculations continue, will not all our water kin be exterminated? Where will you find any more inhabitants for the watery region who will toss and leap in the waves to enhance the majesty of the Great King?"

The Dragon King became so angry that he wanted to take the sword and go at once up to Chang'an to slay the fortune teller. But his dragon sons and grandsons, the shrimp and crab ministers, the samli counselor, the perch Subdirector of the Minor Court, and the carp President of the Board of Civil Office all came from the side and said to him, "Let the Great King restrain his anger. The proverb says, 'Don't believe everything you hear.' If the Great King goes forth like this, the clouds will accompany you and the rains will follow you. We fear that the people of Chang'an will be terrified and Heaven will be offended. Since the Great King has the power to appear or disappear suddenly and to transform into many shapes and sizes, let him change into a scholar. Then go to the city of Chang'an and investigate the matter. If there is indeed such a person, you can slay him without delay; but if there is no such person, there is no need then to harm innocent people." The Dragon King accepted their suggestion; he abandoned his sword and dismissed the clouds and the rains. Reaching the river bank, he shook his body and changed into a white-robed scholar, truly with

Features most virile,
A stature towering;

A stride most stately—
So orderly and firm.
His speech exalts Kong and Meng;
His manner embodies Zhou and Wen.[1]
He wears a silk robe of the color of jade;
His casual head-wrap's shaped like the letter one.[2]

Coming out of the water, he strode to the West Gate Street in the city of Chang'an. There he found a noisy crowd surrounding someone who was saying in a lofty and self-assured manner, "Those born under the Dragon will follow their fate; those under the Tiger will collide with their physiognomies. The branches Yin, Chen, Si, and Hai may be said to fit into the grand scheme, but I fear your birthday may clash with the Planet Jupiter." When the Dragon King heard this, he knew that he had come upon the fortune teller's place. Walking up to it and pushing the people apart, he peered inside to see

Four walls of exquisite writings;
A room full of brocaded paintings;
Smoke unending from the treasure duck;[3]
And such pure water in a porcelain vase.
On both sides are mounted Wang Wei's paintings;
High above his seat hangs the Guigu form.[4]
The ink slab from Duanxi,[5]
The golden smoke ink,
Both match the great brush of frostiest hair;
The crystal balls,
Guo Pu's numbers,[6]
Neatly face new classics of soothsaying.

1. The four proper names mentioned in these two lines refer to Confucius (Kong Qiu), Mencius (Meng Ke), the Duke of Zhou (Zhou Gong), and King Wen (King Wen, putative founder of the Zhou dynasty).

2. Unlike the Arabic numeral one, the Chinese graph for one is a single horizontal stroke. Thus the headwrap is quite flat as used in the traditional attire of a student or scholar.

3. An incense burner.

4. Guigu or Guiguzi (Master of the Ghostly Valley) was a legendary strategist and expert diviner of antiquity.

5. Duanxi, a stream in Guangdong Province famous for its stones that can be turned into fine ink slabs.

6. Famous poet of the Jin (265–419 CE) who was also known to be a master occultist.

He knows the hexagrams well;
He's mastered the eight trigrams;
He perceives the laws of Heaven and Earth;
He discerns the ways of demons and gods.
One tray before him fixes the cosmic hours;
His mind clearly orders all planets and stars.
Truly those things to come
And those things past
He beholds as in a mirror;
Which house will rise
And which will fall
He foresees like a god.
He knows evil and decrees the good;
He prescribes death and predicts life.
His pronouncements quicken the wind and rain;
His brush alarms both spirits and gods.
His shop sign has letters to declare his name;
This divine diviner, Yuan Shoucheng.

Who was this man? He was actually the uncle of Yuan Tiankang, president of the Imperial Board of Astronomy in the present dynasty. The gentleman was truly a man of extraordinary appearance and elegant features; his name was known throughout the great country and his art was considered the highest in Chang'an. The Dragon King went inside the door and met the Master; after exchanging greetings, he was invited to take the seat of honor while a boy served him tea. The Master asked, "What would you like to know?" The Dragon King said, "Please forecast the weather." The Master consulted his sticks and made his judgment:

Clouds hide the hilltop
And fog shrouds the tree.
The rain you'd divine
Tomorrow you'll see.

"At what hour will it rain tomorrow, and how much rain will there be?" said the Dragon King. "At the hour of the Dragon the clouds will gather," said the Master, "and thunder will be heard at the hour of the Serpent. Rain will come at the hour of the Horse and reach its limit at the hour of the Sheep.[7] There will be altogether three feet, three inches, and forty-eight drops of rain." "You had better not be joking now," said the

7. The hours of Dragon, Serpent, Horse, and Sheep are 7–9 a.m., 9–11 a.m., 11 a.m.–1 p.m., and 1–3 p.m.

Dragon King, laughing. "If it rains tomorrow and if it is in accordance with the time and the amount you prophesied, I shall present you with fifty taels of gold as my thanks. But if it does not rain, or if the amount and the hours are incorrect, I tell you truly that I shall come and break your front door to pieces and tear down your shop sign. You will be chased out of Chang'an at once so that you may no longer seduce the multitude." "You may certainly do that," said the Master amiably. "Good-bye for now. Please come again tomorrow after the rain."

The Dragon King took leave and returned to his water residence. He was received by various aquatic deities, who asked, "How was the Great King's visit to the soothsayer?" "Yes, yes, yes," said the Dragon King, "there is indeed such a person, but he's a garrulous fortune teller. I asked him when it would rain, and he said tomorrow; I asked him again about the time and the amount, and he told me that clouds would gather at the hour of the Dragon, thunder would be heard at the hour of the Serpent, rain would come at the hour of the Horse and would reach its limit at the hour of the Sheep. Altogether there would be three feet, three inches, and forty-eight drops of water. I made a wager with him: if it is as he said, I'll reward him with fifty taels of gold. If there is the slightest error, I'll break down his shop and chase him away, so that he will not be permitted to seduce the multitude at Chang'an." "The Great King is the supreme commander of the eight rivers," said the water kin laughing, "the great Dragon Deity in charge of rain. Whether there is going to be rain or not, only the Great King knows that. How dare he speak so foolishly? That soothsayer is sure to lose!"

While the dragon sons and grandsons were laughing at the matter with the fish and crab officials, a voice was heard suddenly in midair announcing, "Dragon King of the Jing River, receive the imperial command." They raised their heads to look and saw a golden-robed guardian holding the decree of the Jade Emperor and heading straight for the water residence. The Dragon King hastily straightened out his attire and burned incense to receive the decree. After he had made his delivery, the guardian rose into the air and left. The Dragon King opened the decree, which said:

We bid the Eight-Rivers Prince
To call up thunder and rain;
Pour out tomorrow your grace
To benefit Chang'an's race.

The instructions regarding the hours and the amount of rain written on the decree did not even differ in the slightest from the soothsayer's prediction. So overwhelmed was the Dragon King that his spirit left him and his soul fled, and only after a while did he regain consciousness. He said to his water kinsmen, "There is indeed an intelligent creature in the world of dust! How well he comprehends the laws of Heaven and Earth! I'm bound to lose to him!"

"Let the Great King calm himself," said the samli counselor. "Is it so difficult to get the better of the fortune teller? Your subject here has a little plan which will silence that fellow for good." When the Dragon King asked what the plan was, the counselor said, "If the rain tomorrow misses the timing and the amount specified by a mere fraction, it will mean that his prediction is not accurate. Won't you have won? What's there to stop you then from tearing up his shop sign and putting him on the road?" The Dragon King took his counsel and stopped worrying.

The next day he ordered the Duke of Wind, the Lord of Thunder, the Boy of Clouds, and the Mother of Lightning to go with him to the sky above Chang'an. He waited until the hour of the Serpent before spreading the clouds, the hour of the Horse before letting loose the thunder, the hour of the Sheep before releasing the rain, and only by the hour of the Monkey did the rain stop.[8] There were only three feet and forty drops of water, since the times were altered by an hour and the amount was changed by three inches and eight drops.

After the rain, the Dragon King dismissed his followers and came down from the clouds, transformed once again into a scholar dressed in white. He went to the West Gate Street and crashed into Yuan Shoucheng's shop. Without a word of explanation, he began to smash the shop sign, the brushes, and the ink slab to pieces. The Master, however, sat on his chair and remained unmoved; so the Dragon King unhinged the door and threatened to hit him with it, crying, "You're nothing but a bogus prophet of good and evil, an imposter who deludes the minds of the people! Your predictions are incorrect; your words are patently false! What you told me about the time and quantity of today's rain was utterly inaccurate, and yet you dare sit so smugly and so high on your seat? Leave here at once before you are executed!" Still Yuan Shoucheng was not at all intimidated. He lifted up his head and laughed scornfully. "I'm not afraid!" he said. "Not in the least! I'm not guilty of death, but I fear that you have committed a mortal crime. You can fool other people, but you can't fool me! I recognize you all right: you are not a white-robed scholar but the Dragon King of the Jing River. By altering the times and holding back the quantity of rain, you have disobeyed the decree of the Jade Emperor and transgressed

8. The hour of the Monkey is 3–5 p.m.

the law of Heaven. On the dragon execution block you won't escape the knife! And here you are, railing at me!"

When the Dragon King heard these words, his heart trembled and his hair stood on end. He dropped the door quickly, tidied his clothes, and knelt before the Master saying, "I beg the Master not to take offense. My previous words were spoken in jest; little did I realize that my prank would turn out to be such a serious crime. Now I have indeed transgressed the law of Heaven. What am I to do? I beseech the Master to save me. If you won't, I'll never let you go!" "I can't save you," said Shoucheng, "I can only point out to you what may be a way of life." "I'm willing to be instructed," said the Dragon.

The Master said, "You are to be executed tomorrow by the human judge, Wei Zheng, at the third quarter past the hour of noon. If you want to preserve your life, you must go quickly to plead your case before the present emperor Tang Taizong, for Wei Zheng is the prime minister before his throne. If you can win the emperor's favor, you'll be spared." Hearing this, the Dragon took leave with tears in his eyes. Soon the red sun sank down and the moon arose. You see

> Smoke thickens on purple mountains as homing crows tire;
> Travelers on distant journeys head for inns;
> Young wild geese at fords rest on field and sand.
> The silver stream appears
> To hasten the time floats.
> Lights flare in a lone village from dying flames:
> Wind sweeps the burner to clear Daoist yard of smoke
> As man fades away in the butterfly dream.
> The moon moves floral shadows up the garden's rails.
> The stars are rife
> As water clocks strike;
> So swiftly the gloom deepens that it's midnight.

Our Dragon King of the Jing River did not even return to his water home; he waited in the air until it was about the hour of the Rat,[9] when he descended from the clouds and mists and came to the gate of the palace. At this time the Tang emperor was just having a dream about taking a walk outside the palace in the moonlight, beneath the shades of flowers. The Dragon suddenly assumed the form of a human being and went up to him. Kneeling, he cried out, "Your Majesty, save me, save me!" "Who are you?" asked Taizong. "We would be glad to save you." "Your Majesty is the true dragon," said the Dragon King, "but I am an accursed one. Because I have

---

9. The hour of the Rat is 11 p.m.–1 a.m.

disobeyed the decree of Heaven, I am to be executed by a worthy subject of Your Majesty, the human judge Wei Zheng. I have therefore come here to plead with you to save me." "If Wei Zheng is to be the executioner," said Taizong, "we can certainly save you. You may leave and not worry." The Dragon King was delighted and left after expressing his gratitude.

We tell you now about Taizong, who, having awakened, was still turning over in his mind what he had dreamed. Soon it was three-fifths past the hour of the fifth watch, and Taizong held court for his ministers, both civil and martial. You see

> *Smoke shrouding the phoenix arches;*
> *Incense clouding the dragon domes;*
> *Light shimmering as the silk screens move;*
> *Clouds brushing the feather-trimmed flags;*
> *Rulers and lords harmonious as Yao and Shun;*
> *Rituals and music solemn as Han's and Zhou's.*
> *The attendant lamps,*
> *The court-maiden fans*
> *Show their colors in pairs;*
> *From peacock screens*
> *And unicorn halls*
> *Light radiates everywhere.*
> *Three cheers for long life!*
> *A wish for reign everlasting!*
> *When a whip cracks three times,*
> *The caps and robes will bow to the Crown.*
> *Brilliant the palatial blooms, endued by Heaven's scent;*
> *Pliant the bank willows, sung and praised by court music.*
> *The screens of pearl,*
> *The screens of jade,*
> *Are drawn high by golden hooks:*
> *The dragon-phoenix fan,*
> *The mountain-river fan,*
> *Rest on top of the royal carriage.*
> *The civil lords are noble and refined;*
> *The martial lords, strong and valiant.*
> *The imperial path divides the ranks:*
> *The vermilion court aligns the grades.*
> *The golden seal and purple sashes bearing the three signs[10]*
> *Will last for millions of years as Heaven and Earth.*

10. The three signs: the sun, the moon, and the stars.

After the ministers had paid their homage, they all went back to standing in rows according to their rank. The Tang emperor opened his dragon eyes to look at them one by one: among the civil officials were Fang Xuanling, Du Ruhui, Xu Shizhi, Xu Jingzong, and Wang Guei; and among the military officials were Ma Sanbao, Duan Zhixian, Yin Kaishan, Cheng Yaojin, Liu Hongzhi, Hu Jingde, and Qin Shubao. Each one of them was standing there in a most solemn manner, but the prime minister Wei Zheng was not to be seen anywhere. The Tang emperor asked Xu Shizhi to come forward and said to him, "We had a strange dream last night: there was a man who paid homage to us, calling himself the Dragon King of the Jing River. He said that he had disobeyed the command of Heaven and was supposed to be executed by the human judge Wei Zheng. He implored us to save him, and we gave our consent. Today only Wei Zheng is absent from the ranks. Why is that?" "This dream may indeed come true," answered Shizhi, "and Wei Zheng must be summoned to court immediately. Once he arrives, let Your Majesty keep him here for a whole day and not permit him to leave. After this day, the dragon in the dream will be saved." The Tang emperor was most delighted: he gave the order at once to have Wei Zheng summoned to court.

We speak now of prime minister Wei Zheng, who studied the movement of the stars and burned incense at his home that evening. He heard the cries of cranes in the air and saw there a Heavenly messenger holding the golden decree of the Jade Emperor, which ordered him to execute in his dream the old dragon of the Jing River at precisely the third quarter past the noon hour. Having thanked the Heavenly grace, our prime minister prepared himself in his residence by bathing himself and abstaining from food; he was also sharpening his magic sword and exercising his spirit, and therefore he did not attend court. He was terribly flustered when he saw the royal officer on duty arriving with the summons. Not daring, however, to disobey the emperor's command, he had to dress quickly and follow the summons into court, kowtowing and asking for pardon before the throne. The Tang emperor said, "We pardoned indeed our worthy subject."

At that time the various ministers had not yet retired from the court, and only after Wei Zheng's arrival was the curtain drawn up for the court's dismissal. Wei Zheng alone was asked to remain; he rode the golden carriage with the emperor to enter the chamber for relaxation, where he discussed with the emperor tactics for making the empire secure and other affairs of state. When it was just about midway between the hour of the Serpent and the hour of the Horse, the emperor asked the royal attendants to bring out a large chess set, saying, "We shall have a game with our worthy subject." The various concubines took out the chessboard and set it on the imperial table. After expressing his gratitude, Wei Zheng set out to play chess with the Tang emperor, both of them moving the pieces step by step into positions. It was completely in accordance with the instruction of the *Chess Classic*:

> The way of chess exalts discipline and caution; the most powerful pieces should remain in the center, the weakest ones at the flanks, and the less powerful ones at the corners. This is a familiar law of the chess player. The law says: "You should rather lose a piece than an advantage. When you strike on the left, you must guard your right; when you attack in the rear, you must watch your front. Only when you have a secure front will you also have a rear, and only if you have a secure rear will you maintain your front. The two ends cannot be separated, and yet both must remain flexible and not be encumbered. A broad formation should not be too loose, while a tight position should not be constricted. Rather than clinging on to save a single piece, it is better to sacrifice it in order to win; rather than moving without purpose, it is better to remain stationary in order to be self-supportive. When your adversary outnumbers you, your first concern is to survive; when you outnumber your adversary, you must strive to exploit your force. He who knows how to win will not prolong his fight; he who is a master of positions will not engage in direct combat; he who knows how to fight will not suffer defeat; and he who knows how to lose will not panic. For chess begins with proper engagement but ends in unexpected victory. If your enemy, even without being threatened, is bringing up his reinforcement, it is a sign of his intention to attack; if he deserts a small piece without trying to save it, he may be stalking a bigger piece. If he moves in a casual manner, he is a man without thoughts; response without thought is the way to defeat. The *Classic of Poetry* says: Approach with extreme caution as if facing a deep canyon. Such is the meaning thereof."

The poem says:
> *The chessboard's the earth; the pieces are the sky;*
> *The colors are light and dark as the whole universe.*
> *When playing reaches that skillful, subtle stage,*
> *Boast and laugh with the old Immortal of Chess.*

The two of them, emperor and subject, played chess until three quarters past the noon hour, but the game was not yet finished. Suddenly Wei Zheng put his head on the table and fell fast asleep. Taizong laughed and said, "Our worthy subject truly has worn himself out for the state and exhausted his strength on behalf of the empire. He has therefore fallen asleep in spite of himself." Taizong allowed him to sleep on and did not arouse him. In a little while, Wei Zheng awoke and prostrated himself on the ground saying, "Your subject deserves ten thousand deaths! Your subject deserves ten thousand deaths! Just now I lost consciousness for no reason at all. I beg Your Majesty's pardon for such insult against the emperor."

"What insult is there?" said Taizong. "Arise! Let us forget the old game and start a new one instead." Wei Zheng expressed his gratitude. As he put his hand on a piece, a loud clamor was heard outside the gate. It was occasioned by the ministers Qin Shubao and Xu Mougong, who arrived with a dragon head dripping with blood. Throwing it in front of the emperor, they said, "Your Majesty, we have seen seas turn shallow and rivers run dry, but a thing as strange as this we have never even heard of." Taizong arose with Wei Zheng and said, "Where did this thing come from?" "South of the Thousand-Step Corridor," replied Shubao and Mougong, "at the crossroads, this dragon head fell from the clouds. Your lowly subjects dare not withhold it from you."

In alarm, the Tang emperor asked Wei Zheng, "What's the meaning of this?" Turning to kowtow to him, Wei Zheng said, "This dragon was executed just now by your subject in his dream." When the Tang emperor heard this, he was seized with fear and said, "When our worthy minister was sleeping, I did not see any movement of body or limb, nor did I perceive any scimitar or sword. How could you have executed this dragon?" Wei Zheng replied, "My lord, although

My body was before my master,
I left Your Majesty in my dream;
My body before my master faced the unfinished game,
With dim eyes fully closed;
I left Your Majesty in my dream to ride the blessed cloud,
With spirit most eager and alert.
That dragon on the dragon execution block
Was bound up there by celestial hosts.
Your subject said,
'For breaking Heaven's law,
You are worthy of death.
Now by Heaven's command,
I end your wretched life.'
The dragon listened in grief;
Your subject bestirred his spirit;

The dragon listened in grief,
Retrieving claws and scales to await his death;
Your subject bestirred his spirit,
Lifting robe and taking step to hold high his blade.
With one loud crack the knife descended;
And thus the head of the dragon fell from the sky."

When Taizong heard these words, he was filled with both sadness and delight. The delight was caused by his pride in having a minister as good as Wei Zheng. If he had worthies of this kind in his court, he thought, need he worry about the security of his empire? He was saddened, however, by the fact that he had promised in his dream to save the dragon, and he had not anticipated that the creature would be killed in this manner. He had to force himself to give the order to Shubao that the dragon head be hung on display at the market, so that the populace of Chang'an might be informed. Meanwhile, he rewarded Wei Zheng, after which the various ministers dispersed.

That night he returned to his palace in deep depression, for he kept remembering the dragon in the dream crying and begging for his life. Little did he expect that the turn of events would be such that the dragon still could not escape calamity. Having thought about the matter for a long time, he became physically and mentally drained. At about the hour of the second watch, the sound of weeping was heard outside the door of the palace, and Taizong became even more fearful. He was sleeping fitfully when he saw our Dragon King of the Jing River holding his head dripping with blood in his hand, and crying in a loud voice: "Tang Taizong! Give me back my life! Give me back my life! Last night you were full of promises to save me. Why did you order a human judge in the daytime to have me executed? Come out, come out! I am going to argue this case with you before the King of the Underworld." He seized Taizong and would neither let go nor desist from his protestation. Taizong could not say a word; he could only struggle until perspiration covered his entire body. Just at the moment when it seemed that nothing could separate them, fragrant clouds and colorful mists appeared from the south. A Daoist priestess came forward and waved a willow twig. That headless dragon, still mourning and weeping, left at once toward the northwest. For you see, this was none other than the Bodhisattva Guanyin, who by the decree of Buddha was seeking a scripture pilgrim in the Land of the East. She was staying in the temple of the local spirit at the city of Chang'an when she heard in the night the weeping of demons and the crying of spirits. So she came specially to drive the accursed dragon away and to rescue the emperor. That dragon went directly to the court of the Underworld to file suit, of which we shall say no more.

We now tell you about Taizong, who, when he awoke, could only yell aloud, "Ghost! Ghost!" He so terrified the queens of three palaces, the concubines of six chambers, and the attending eunuchs that they remained sleepless for the entire night. Soon it was the fifth watch, and all the officials of the court, both civil and military, were waiting for an audience outside the gate. They waited until dawn, but the emperor did not appear, and every one of them became apprehensive and restless. Only after the sun was high in the sky did a proclamation come out saying, "We are not feeling too well. The ministers are excused from court." Five or six days went by swiftly, and the various officials became so anxious that they were about to enter the court without summons and inquire after the Throne. Just then the queen mother gave the order to have the physician brought into the palace, and so the multitude waited at the gate of the court for some news. In a little while, the physician came out and he was questioned by them about the emperor's illness. "The pulse of His Majesty is irregular," said the physician, "for it is weak as well as rapid. He blabbers about seeing ghosts. I also perceive that there were ten movements and one rest, but there is no breath left in his viscera. I am afraid that he will pass away within seven days." When the various ministers heard this statement, they paled with fright.

In this state of alarm, they again heard that Taizong had summoned Xu Mougong, Huguo Gong, and Yuchi Gong to appear before him. The three ministers hurried into the auxiliary palace, where they prostrated themselves. Speaking somberly and with great effort, Taizong said, "My worthy subjects, since the age of nineteen I have been leading my army in expeditions to the four corners of the Earth. I have experienced much hardship throughout the years, but I have never encountered any kind of strange or weird thing. This day, however, I have seen ghosts!"

"When you established your empire," said Yuchi Gong, "you had to kill countless people. Why should you fear ghosts?" "You may not believe it," said Taizong, "but outside this bedroom of mine at night, there are bricks thrown and spirits screaming to a degree that is truly unmanageable. In the daytime it's not too bad, but it's intolerable at night!" "Let Your Majesty be relieved," said Shubao, "for this evening your subject and Jingde[11] will stand guard at the palace gate. We shall see what sort of ghostly business

11. Jingde: frequently the name of Yuchi Gong in vernacular Chinese fiction. He was a famous general originally from Central Asia serving at the Tang court.

there is." Taizong agreed to the proposal, and Mougong and the other ministers retired after expressing their gratitude.

That evening the two ministers, in full battle dress and holding golden bludgeon and battle-ax, stood guard outside the palace gate. Dear generals! Look how they are attired:

They wore on their heads bright glimmering golden helmets,
And on their bodies cuirasses of dragon scales.
Their jeweled breastplates glow like hallowed clouds:
With lion knots tightly drawn,
And silk sashes newly spun.
This one had phoenix eyes staring into the sky to frighten the stars:
The other had brown eyes glowering like lightning and shining like the moon.
They were once warriors of greatest merit;
But now they became for all time the guardians of the gates,
In all ages the protectors of the home.

The two generals stood beside the door for the entire night and did not see the slightest disturbance. That night Taizong rested peacefully in the palace; when morning came he summoned the two generals before him and thanked them profusely, saying, "Since falling ill, I haven't been able to sleep for days, and only last night did I manage to get some rest because of your presence. Let our worthy ministers retire now for some rest so that we may count on your protection once again at night." The two generals left after expressing their gratitude, and for the following two or three nights their standing guard brought continued peace. However, the royal appetite diminished and the illness became more severe. Taizong, moreover, could not bear to see the two generals overworked. So once again he called Shubao, Jingde, the ministers Du and Fang into the palace, saying to them, "Though I got some rest these past two days, I have imposed on the two generals the hardship of staying up all night. I wish to have portraits made of both of them by a skilled painter and have these pasted on the door, so that the two generals will be spared any further labor. How about it?" The various ministers obeyed; they selected two portrait painters, who made pictures of the two generals in their proper battle attire. The portraits were then mounted near the gate, and no incident occurred during the night.

So it was for two or three days, until the loud rattling of bricks and tiles was again heard at the rear gate of the palace. At dawn the emperor called together the various ministers, saying to them, "For the past few days there have been, happily, no incidents at the front of the palace, but last night the noises at the back door were such that they nearly frightened me to death." Mougong stepped forward and said, "The disturbances at the front door were driven off by Jingde and Shubao. If there is disturbance at the rear gate, then Wei Zheng ought to stand guard." Taizong approved the suggestion and ordered Wei Zheng to guard the rear door that night. Accepting the charge, Wei donned his full court regalia that evening; holding the sword with which he had slain the dragon, he stood at attention before the rear gate of the palace. What splendid heroic stature! Look how he is attired:

A turban of green satin swathed his brow:
On his brocaded robe a jade belt hung from his waist;
Windblown, the sleeves of his crane-skinned gown fluttered like drifting snow.
He surpassed even the divine figures of Lu and Shu.
His feet were shod in black boots supple and smooth.
In his hands was a sharp blade, fierce and keen.
With glaring eyes he looked all around.
What goblin or demon would dare approach?

A whole night went by and no ghost appeared. But though there were no incidents at either the front or the rear gate, the emperor's condition worsened. One day the queen mother sent for all the ministers to discuss funeral arrangements. Taizong himself also summoned Xu Mougong to his bedside to entrust to him the affairs of state, committing the crown prince to the minister's care as Liu Bei did to Zhuge Liang. When he had finished speaking, he bathed and changed his garments, waiting for his time to come. Wei Zheng then stepped out from the side and tugged the royal garment with his hand, saying, "Let Your Majesty be relieved. Your subject knows something which will guarantee long life for Your Majesty."

"My illness," said Taizong, "has reached the irremediable stage; my life is in danger. How can you preserve it?" "Your subject has a letter here," said Wei, "which I submit to Your Majesty to take with you to Hell and give to the Judge of the Underworld, Jue."

"Who is Cui Jue?" asked Taizong.

"Cui Jue," said Wei, "was the subject of the deceased emperor, your father: at first he was the district magistrate of Cizhou, and subsequently he was promoted to vice-president of the Board of Rites. When he was alive, he was an intimate friend and sworn brother of your subject. Now that he is dead, he has become a judge in the capital of the Underworld, having in his charge the chronicles of life and death in the region of darkness. He meets with me frequently, however, in my dreams. If you go there presently and hand this letter to him, he will certainly remember his obligation toward your lowly subject and allow Your Majesty to return here. Surely your soul will return to the human world, and your royal countenance will once more grace the capital." When Taizong heard these words, he took the letter in his hands and put it in his sleeve; with that, he closed his eyes and died. Those queens and concubines from three palaces and six chambers, the crown prince and the two rows of civil and military officials, all put on their mourning garb to mourn him, as the imperial coffin lay in state at the Hall of the White Tiger, but we shall say no more about that. We do not know how the soul of Taizong came back; let's listen to the explanation in the next chapter.

ELEVEN

Having toured the Underworld, Taizong returns to life;
Having presented melons and fruits, Liu Quan marries again.

The poem says:
  A hundred years pass by like flowing streams;
  Like froth and foam a lifetime's work now seems.
  Yesterday faces had a peach's glow;
  Today the temples float up flakes of snow.
  Termites disband—illusion then you'll learn!
  Cuckoos call gravely for your early return.
  Secret good works will always life prolong.
  Virtue's not needy for Heav'n's care is strong.

We now tell you about Taizong, whose soul drifted out of the Tower of
Five Phoenixes. Everything was blurred and indistinct. It seemed to him
that a company of imperial guardsmen was inviting him to a hunting
party, to which Taizong gladly gave his consent and went off with them.
They had journeyed for a long time when suddenly all the men and horses
vanished from sight. He was left alone, walking the deserted fields and
desolate plains. As he was anxiously trying to find his way back, he heard
someone from beyond calling in a loud voice: "Great Tang Emperor, come
over here! Come over here!" Taizong heard this and looked up. He saw
that the man had

  A black gauze cap on his head;
  Rhinoceros horns around his waist.
  Soft bands dangled from the black gauze hat on his head:
  Golden buckles enhanced the rhinoceros horns around his waist.
  He held an ivory tablet shrouded by blessed mist;
  He wore a silk robe encircled by holy light.
  On his feet was a pair of white-soled boots
  To walk the clouds and climb the fog;
  He carried near his heart a book of life and death,
  Which determined one's fate.

His hair, loose and luxuriant, haloed his head:
His beard floated and danced around his jaws.
He was once a Tang prime minister:
Now he handled cases to serve the King of Hades.

Taizong walked toward him, and the man, kneeling at the side of the road, said to him, "Your Majesty, please pardon your subject for neglecting to meet you at a greater distance." "Who are you," asked Taizong, "and for what reason did you come to meet me?" The man said, "Half a month ago, your lowly subject met in the Halls of Darkness the Dragon Ghost of the Jing River, who was filing suit against Your Majesty for having him executed after promising to save him. So the great king Qinguang of the first chamber immediately sent demon messengers to arrest you and bring you to trial before the Three Tribunes. Your subject learned of this and therefore came here to receive you. I did not expect to come late today, and I beg you to forgive me."

"What is your name," said Taizong, "and what is your rank?" "When your lowly subject was alive," said that man, "he served on Earth before the previous emperor as the district magistrate of Cizhou. Afterwards I was appointed vice-president of the Board of Rites. My surname is Cui and my given name is Jue. In the Region of Darkness I hold a judgeship in the Capital of Death." Taizong was very glad; he went forward and held out his royal hands to raise the man up, saying, "I am sorry to have inconvenienced you. Wei Zheng who serves before my throne, has a letter for you. I'm glad that we have a chance to meet here." The judge expressed his gratitude and asked where the letter was. Taizong took it out of his sleeve and handed it over to Cui Jue, who received it, bowing, and then opened it and read:

Your unworthily beloved brother Wei Zheng sends with bowed head this letter to the Great Judge, my sworn brother the Honorable Mr. Cui. I recall our former goodly society, and both your voice and your countenance seem to be present with me. Several years have hastened by since I last heard your lofty discourse. I could only prepare a few vegetables and fruits to offer to you as sacrifices during the festive times of the year, though I do not know whether you have enjoyed them or not. I am grateful, however, that you have not forgotten me, and that you have revealed to me in my dreams that you, my elder brother, have ascended to an even higher office. Unfortunately, the worlds of Light and Darkness are separated by a gulf wide as the Heavens, so that we cannot meet face to face. The reason that I am writing you now is the sudden demise of my emperor, the accomplished

Taizong, whose case, I suppose, will be reviewed by the Three Tribunes, so that he will certainly be given the opportunity to meet you. I earnestly beseech you to remember our friendship while you were living and grant me the small favor of allowing His Majesty to return to life. This will be a very great favor to me, for which I thank you once more.

After reading the letter, the judge said with great delight, "The execution of the old dragon the other day by the human judge Wei is already known to your subject, who greatly admires him for this deed. I am, moreover, indebted to him for looking after my children. Since he has written such a letter now, Your Majesty need have no further concern. Your lowly subject will make certain that you will be returned to life, to ascend once more your throne of jade." Taizong thanked him.

As the two of them were speaking, they saw in the distance two young boys in blue robes holding banners and flags and calling out, "The King of the Underworld has an invitation for you." Taizong went forward with Judge Cui and the two boys. He suddenly saw a huge city, and on a large plaque above the city gate was the inscription in gold letters, "The Region of Darkness, The Gate of Spirits." Waving the banners, the blue robes led Taizong into the city. As they walked along, they saw at the side of the street the emperor's predecessor Li Yuan, his elder brother Jiancheng, and his deceased brother Yuanji, who came toward them, shouting, "Here comes Shimin! Here comes Shimin!" The brothers clutched at Taizong and began beating him and threatening vengeance. Having no place to dodge, the emperor fell into their clutch; and only when Judge Cui called a blue-faced, hook-tusked demon to drive them away could he escape and continue his journey.

They had traveled no more than a few miles when they arrived at a towering edifice with green tiles. This building was truly magnificent. You see

Lightly ten thousand folds of colored mists pile high;
Dimly a thousand strands of crimson brume appear.
Heads of wild beasts rear up from the eaves aglow.
Lambent roof tiles in pairs rise in tiers of five.
Rows of red-gold nails bore deeply into doors;
Crosswise, white jade slabs form the sills.
Windows near the lights release luminous smoke.
The screens, the curtains, flash like fiery bolts.
High-rising towers reach to the azure sky.
Criss-crossing hallways join the treasure rooms.
Fragrant clouds from ornate tripods line the royal robes;

Fires of scarlet silk lanterns brighten the portals' leaves.
On the left, hordes of fierce Bull-heads stand;
On the right, gangs of gruesome Horse-faces hover.
To greet the dead, to guide the ghosts, the gold placards turn;
To lead the souls, to call the spirits, the white silk descends.
It bears this name: The Central Gate of Hell,
The Hall of Darkness of the Princes of Hades.

As Taizong was looking at the place, there came from within the tinkling of girdle jade, the mysterious fragrance of divine incense, and two pairs of torch candles followed by the Ten Kings of the Underworld coming down the steps. The Ten Kings were: King Qinguang, King of the Beginning River, King of the Song Emperor, King of Avenging Ministers, King Yama, King of Equal Ranks, King of the Tai Mountain, King of City Markets, King of Complete Change, and King of the Turning Wheel. Coming out of the Treasure Hall of Darkness, they bowed to receive Taizong, who, feigning modesty, declined to lead the way. The Ten Kings said, "Your Majesty is the emperor of men in the World of Light, whereas we are but the kings of spirits in the World of Darkness. Such are indeed our appointed stations, so why should you defer to us?" "I'm afraid that I have offended all of you," said Taizong, "so how can I dare to speak of observing the etiquette of ghosts and men, of Light and Darkness?" Only after much protestation did Taizong proceed into the Hall of Darkness. After he had greeted the Ten Kings properly, they sat down according to the places assigned to hosts and guests.

After a little while, King Qinguang folded his hands in front of him and came forward, saying, "The Dragon Spirit of the Jing River accuses Your Majesty of having him slain after promising to save him. Why?" "I did promise him that nothing would happen," said Taizong, "when the old dragon appealed to me in my dream at night. He was guilty, you know, and was condemned to be executed by the human judge Wei Zheng. It was to save him that I invited Wei Zheng to play chess with me, not anticipating that Wei Zheng could have performed the execution in his dream! That was indeed a miraculous stratagem devised by the human judge, and, after all, the dragon was also guilty of a mortal offense. I fail to see how I am to blame." When the Ten Kings heard these words, they replied, bowing, "Even before that dragon was born, it was already written on the Book of Death held by the Star of South Pole that he should be slain by a human judge. We have known this all along, but the dragon lodged his complaint here and insisted that Your Majesty be brought down so that his case might be reviewed by the Three Tribunes. We have already sent him on his way to his next incarnation through the Wheel of Transmigration. We regret, however, that we have caused Your Majesty the inconvenience of this journey, and we beg your pardon for pressing you to come here."

When they had finished speaking, they ordered the judge in charge of the Books of Life and Death to bring out the records quickly so that they could ascertain what the allotted time of the emperor was to be. Judge Cui went at once to his chamber and examined, one by one, the ages pre-ordained for all the kings in the world that were inscribed in the books. Startled when he saw that the Great Tang Emperor Taizong of the South Jambūdvīpa Continent was destined to die in the thirteenth year of the period Zhenguan, he quickly dipped his big brush in thick ink and added two strokes before presenting the book. The Ten Kings took one look and saw that "thirty-three years" was written beneath the name Taizong. They asked in alarm: "How long has it been since Your Majesty was enthroned?" "It has been thirteen years," said Taizong. "Your Majesty need have no worry," said King Yama, "for you still have twenty years of life. Now that your case has been clearly reviewed, we can send you back to the World of Light." When Taizong heard this, he bowed to express his gratitude as the Ten Kings ordered Judge Cui and Grand Marshal Chu to accompany him back to life.

Taizong walked out of the Hall of Darkness and asked, saluting the Ten Kings once again, "What's going to happen to those living in my palace?" "Everyone will be safe," said the Ten Kings, "except your younger sister. It appears that she will not live long." "When I return to the World of Light," said Taizong, bowing again to thank them, "I have very little that I can present you as a token of my gratitude. Perhaps I can send you some melons or other kinds of fruit?" Delighted, the Ten Kings said, "We have eastern and western melons here, but we lack southern melons."[1] "The moment I get back," said Taizong, "I shall send you some." They bowed to each other with hands folded, and parted.

The marshal took the lead, holding a flag for guiding souls, while Judge Cui followed behind to protect Taizong. They walked out of the Region of Darkness, and Taizong saw that it was not the same road. He asked the judge, "Are we going on the wrong way?" "No," said the judge, "for this is how it is in the Region of Darkness: there is a way for you to come, but there is no way out. Now we must send Your Majesty off from the region

---

1. Eastern melon is actually winter melon, or white gourd, the name here being a pun since east and winter (*dong*) are homonyms. Western and southern melons are watermelons and pumpkins respectively.

of the Wheel of Transmigration, so that you can make a tour of Hell as well as be sent on your way to reincarnation." Taizong had little alternative but to follow their lead.

They had gone only a few miles when they came upon a tall mountain. Dark clouds touched the ground around it, and black mists shrouded the sky. "Mr. Cui," said Taizong, "what mountain is this?" The judge said, "It's the Mountain of Perpetual Shade in the Region of Darkness." "How can we go there?" asked Taizong fearfully. "Your Majesty need not worry," said the judge, "for your subjects are here to guide you." Shaking and quaking, Taizong followed the two of them and ascended the slope. He raised his head to look around and saw that

Its shape was both craggy and curvate,
And its form was even more tortuous.
Rugged like the Shu peaks;
Tall like the Lu summits;
It was not a famed mountain in the World of Light,
But a treacherous place in the Region of Darkness.
Thickets of thorns sheltered monsters;
Tiers of stone ridges harbored demons.
No sound of fowl or beast came to one's ears;
Only ghosts or griffins walked before one's eyes.
The howling cold wind;
The endless black mist—
The howling cold wind was the huffing of infernal hosts;
The endless black mist was the puffing of demonic troops.
There was no scenic splendor though one looked high and low;
All was desolation when one stared left and right.
At that place there were mountains
And peaks,
And summits,
And caves,
And streams;
Only no grass grew on the mountains;
No peaks punctured the sky;
No travelers scaled the summits;
No clouds ever entered the caves;
No water flowed in the streams.
They were all specters on the shores,
And bogies beneath the cliffs.
The phantoms huddled in the caves,

And lost souls hid on the floors of streams.
All around the mountain,
Bull-heads and Horse-faces wildly clamored;
Half hidden and half in sight,
Hungry ghosts and needy souls frequently wept.
The judge in quest of souls,
In haste and fury delivered his summons;
The guard who chased the spirits,
Snorted and shouted to present his papers.
The Swift of Foot:
A boiling cyclone!
The Soul Snatcher:
A spreading dark mist!

Had he not trusted in the judge's protection, Taizong would have never made it across this Mountain of Perpetual Shade.

As they proceeded, they came to a place where there were many halls and chambers; everywhere they turned, melancholy cries blasted their ears and grotesque sights struck terror in their hearts. "What is this place?" asked Taizong again. "The Eighteenfold Hell behind the Mountain of Perpetual Shade," said the judge. "What is that?" said Taizong. The judge replied, "Listen to what I have to say:

The Hell of the Rack,
The Hell of Gloomy Guilt,
The Hell of the Fiery Pit:
All such sorrow,
All such desolation,
Are caused by a thousand sins committed in the life before;
They all come to suffer after they die.
The Hell of Hades,
The Hell of Tongue-Pulling,
The Hell of Skin-Shredding:
All those weeping and wailing,
All those pining and mourning,
Await the traitors, the rebels, and the Heaven baiters;
He of Buddha-mouth and serpent-heart will end up here.
The Hell of Grinding,
The Hell of Pounding,
The Hell of Crushing;
With frayed skin and torn flesh,
Gaping mouths and grinding teeth,

These are they who cheat and lie to work injustice,
Who fawn and flatter to deceive.
The Hell of Ice,
The Hell of Mutilation,
The Hell of Evisceration:
With grimy face and matted hair,
Knitted brow and doleful look,
These are they who fleece the simple with weights unjust,
And so bring ruin upon themselves.
The Hell of Boiling Oil,
The Hell of Grim Darkness,
The Hell of the Sword Mountain:
They shake and quake;
They sorrow and pine:
For oppressing the righteous by violence and fraud
They now must cower in their lonely pain.
The Hell of the Pool of Blood,
The Hell of Avīci.[2]
The Hell of Scales and Weights:
All the skins peeled and bones exposed,
The limbs cut and the tendons severed,
Are caused by murder stemming from greed,
The taking of life of both humans and beasts.
Their fall has no reversal in a thousand years—
Eternal perdition without release.
Each is firmly bound and tightly tied,
Shackled by both ropes and cords.
The slightest move brings on the Red-hair demons,
The Black-face demons,
With long spears and sharp swords;
The Bull-head demons,
The Horse-face demons,
With iron spikes and bronze gavels,
They strike till faces contort and blood flows down,
But cries to Earth and Heaven find no response.
So it is that man ought not his own conscience betray,
For gods have knowledge, who could get away?

2. The lowest and deepest of the eight hot hells in Buddhism.

Thus vice and virtue will at last be paid:
It differs only in coming soon or late."

When Taizong heard these words, he was terror-stricken.

They went on for a little while and came upon a group of demon soldiers, each holding banners and flags and kneeling beside the road. "The
Guards of the Bridges have come to receive you," they said. The judge
ordered them to make way and proceeded to lead Taizong across a golden
bridge. Looking to one side, Taizong saw another silver bridge, on which
there were several travelers who seemed to be persons of principle and
rectitude, justice and honesty. They too were led by banners and flags.
On the other side was another bridge, with icy wind churning around it
and bloody waves seething below. The continuous sound of weeping and
wailing could be heard. "What is the name of that bridge?" asked Taizong.
"Your Majesty," said the judge, "it is the Bridge with No Alternative.
When you reach the World of Light, you must have this recorded for
posterity. For below the bridge there is nothing but

A vast body of surging water;
A strait and treacherous path;
Like bales of raw silk flowing down the Long River,
Or the Pit of Fire floating up to Earth,
This cold air, oppressive, this bone-piercing chill;
This foul stench both irksome and nauseous.
The waves roll and swirl;
No boat comes or goes to ferry men across;
With naked feet and tangled hair
Those moving here and there are all damned spirits.
The bridge is a few miles long
But only three spans wide.
Its height measures a hundred feet;
Below, a thousand fathoms deep.
On top are no railways for hands to hold;
Beneath you have man-seizing savage fiends
Who, bound by cangues and locks,
Will fight to flee the perilous stream.
Look at those ferocious guardians beside the bridge
And those damned souls in the river—how truly wretched!
On branches and twigs
Clothes of green, red, yellow, and purple silk hang;
Below the precipice
Strumpets crouch for having abused their own in-laws.

Iron dogs and brass serpents will strive to feed on them.
Their fall's eternal—there is no way out."

The poem says:

Ghosts are heard wailing; demons often cry
As waves of blood rise ten thousand feet high.
Horse-faces and Bull-heads by countless scores
This Naihe Bridge most grimly fortify.

While Taizong and his guides were speaking, the several Guardians of
the Bridge went back to their station. Terrified by his vision, Taizong could
only nod his head in silent horror. He followed the judge and the Grand
Marshal across the River of No Alternative and the bitter Realm of the
Bloody Bowl. Soon they arrived at the City of the Dead, where clamoring
voices were heard proclaiming distinctly, "Li Shimin has come! Li Shimin
has come!" When Taizong heard all this shouting, his heart shook and his
gall quivered. Then he saw a throng of spirits, some with backs broken by
the rack, some with severed limbs, and some headless, who barred his way
and shouted together, "Give us back our lives! Give us back our lives!" In
terror Taizong tried desperately to flee and hide, at the same time crying,
"Mr. Cui, save me! Mr. Cui, save me!"

"Your Majesty," said the judge, "these are the spirits of various princes
and their underlings, of brigands and robbers from sundry places. Through
works of injustice, both theirs and others', they perished and are now cut
off from salvation because there is none to receive them or care for them.
Since they have no money or belongings, they are ghosts abandoned to
hunger and cold. Only if Your Majesty can give them some money will
I be able to offer you deliverance." "I came here," said Taizong, "with
empty hands. Where can I get money?"

"Your Majesty," said the judge, "there is in the World of the Living
a man who has deposited great sums of gold and silver in our Region of
Darkness. You can use your name for a loan, and your lowly judge will
serve as your voucher; we shall borrow a roomful of money from him
and distribute it among the hungry ghosts. You will then be able to get
past them." "Who is this man?" asked Taizong. "He's a man from the
Kaifeng District in Henan Province," said the judge. "His given name is
Liang and his surname is Xiang. He has thirteen rooms of gold and silver
down here. If Your Majesty borrows from him, you can repay him when
you return to the World of Light." Highly pleased and more than willing
to use his name for the loan, Taizong at once signed a note for the judge.
He borrowed a roomful of gold and silver, and the grand marshal was
asked to distribute the money among the ghosts. The judge also instructed

them, saying, "You may divide up these pieces of silver and gold among yourselves and use them accordingly. Let the Great Tang Father pass, for he still has a long time to live. By the solemn word of the Ten Kings I am accompanying him to return to life. When he reaches the world of the living, he has been instructed to hold a Grand Mass of Land and Water for your salvation.[3] So don't start any more trouble." When the ghosts heard these words and received the silver and gold, they obeyed and turned back. The judge ordered the grand marshal to wave the flag for guiding souls, and led Taizong out of the City of the Dead. They set out again on a broad and level path, leaving quickly with light, airy steps.

They traveled for a long time and arrived at the junction of the Six-fold Path of Transmigration. They saw some people who rode the clouds wearing embroidered capes, and some with Daoist amulets of gold fish dangling from their waists; there were in fact monks, nuns, Daoists, and secular persons, and all varieties of beasts and fowls, ghosts and spirits. In an unending stream they all ran beneath the Wheel of Transmigration to enter each into a predestined path. "What is the meaning of this?" asked the Tang emperor. "Your Majesty," said the judge, "as your mind is enlightened to perceive the pervasive immanence of the Buddha-nature in all things, you must remember this and proclaim it in the World of the Living. This is called the Sixfold Path of Transmigration. Those who perform good works will ascend to the way of the immortals; those who remain patriotic to the end will advance to the way of nobility; those who practice filial piety will be born again into the way of blessing; those who are just and honest will enter once more into the way of humans; those who cherish virtue will proceed to the way of riches; those who are vicious and violent will fall back into the way of demons." When the Tang emperor heard this, he nodded his head and sighed, saying,

"Ah, how truly good is goodness!
To do good will never bring illness!
In a good heart always abide.
On a good way your door fling wide.
Let no evil thoughts arise,
And all mischief you must despise.
Don't say there's no retribution,
For gods have their disposition."

The judge accompanied the Tang emperor up to the very entrance to the way of nobility before he prostrated himself and called out, "Your Majesty,

---

3. The Mass, which offered food for both water and land spirits, was a Buddhist ritual said to have been inaugurated by Emperor Wu of the Liang (r. 502–549).

this is where you must proceed, and here your humble judge will take leave of you. I am asking Grand Marshal Zhu to accompany you a little further." The Tang emperor thanked him, saying, "I'm sorry, sir, that you have had to travel such great distance on my account." "When Your Majesty returns to the World of Light," said the judge, "be very certain that you celebrate the Grand Mass of Land and Water so that those wretched, homeless souls may be delivered. Please do not forget! Only if there is no murmuring for vengeance in the Region of Darkness will there be the prosperity of peace in your World of Light. If there are any wicked ways in your life, you must change them one by one, and you must teach your subjects far and wide to do good. You may be assured then that your empire will be firmly established, and that your fame will go down to posterity." The Tang emperor promised to grant each one of the judge's requests.

Having parted from Judge Cui, he followed Grand Marshal Zhu and entered the gate. The grand marshal saw inside a black-maned bay horse complete with rein and saddle. Lending the emperor assistance from left and right, he quickly helped him mount it. The horse shot forward like an arrow, and soon they reached the bank of the Wei River, where a pair of golden carps could be seen frolicking on top of the waves. Pleased by what he saw, the Tang emperor reined in his horse and stopped to watch. "Your Majesty," said the grand marshal, "let's hurry and get you back into your city while there is still time." But the emperor persisted in his indulgence and refused to go forward. The grand marshal grabbed one of his legs and shouted, "You still won't move? What are you waiting for?" With a loud splash, he was pushed off his horse into the Wei River, and thus he left the Region of Darkness and returned to the World of Light.

We shall now tell you about those who served before the Throne in the Tang dynasty. Xu Mougong, Qin Shubao, Hu Jingde, Duan Zhixian, Ma Sanbao, Cheng Yaojin, Gao Shilian, Li Shiji, Fang Xuanling, Du Ruhui, Xiao Yu, Fu Yi, Zhang Daoyuan, Zhang Shiheng, and Wang Guei constituted the two groups of civil and military officials. They gathered with the crown prince of the Eastern Palace, the queen, the ladies of the court, and the chief steward in the Hall of the White Tiger for the imperial mourning. At the same time, they were talking about issuing the obituary proclamation for the whole empire and crowning the prince as emperor. From one side of the hall, Wei Zheng stepped forward and said, "All of you, please refrain from doing anything hasty. If you alarm the various districts and cities, you may bring about something undesirable and unexpected. Let's wait here for another day, for our lord will surely come back to life."

"What nonsense you are talking, Prime Minister Wei," said Xu Jing-zong, coming from below, "for the ancient proverb says, 'Just as spilled water cannot be retrieved, so a dead man can never return!' Why do you mouth such empty words to vex our minds? What reason do you have for this?" "To tell you the truth, Mr. Xu," said Wei Zheng, "I have been instructed since my youth in the arts of immortality. My calculations are most accurate, and I promise you that His Majesty will not die."

As they were talking, they suddenly heard a loud voice crying in the coffin, "You've drowned me! You've drowned me!" It so startled the civil and military officials, and so terrified the queen and the ladies, that every one of them had

A face brown as autumnal mulberry leaves,
A body limp as the willow of early spring.
The legs of the crown prince buckled,
He could not hold the mourning staff to finish his rites.
The soul of the steward left him,
He could not wear the mourning cap to show his grief.
The matrons collapsed;
The ladies pitched sideways;
The matrons collapsed
Like weak hibiscus blasted by savage wind.
The ladies pitched sideways
Like lilies overwhelmed by sudden rain.
The petrified lords—
Their bones and tendons feeble—
Trembled and shook,
All dumb and awe-struck.
The whole White-Tiger Hall was like a bridge with broken beams;
The funeral stage resembled a temple wrecked.

Every person attending the court ran away, and no one dared approach the coffin. Only the upright Xu Mougong, the rational Prime Minister Wei, the courageous Qin Qiong, and the impulsive Jingde came forward and took hold of the coffin. "Your Majesty," they cried, "if there's something bothering you, tell us about it. Don't play ghost and terrify your relatives!"

Then, however, Wei Zheng said, "He's not playing ghost. His Majesty is coming back to life! Get some tools, quick!" They opened the top of the coffin and saw indeed that Taizong was sitting up inside, still shouting, "You've drowned me! Who bailed me out?" Mougong and the rest of them went forward to lift him up, saying, "Don't be afraid, Your Majesty, and wake up. Your subjects are here to protect you." Only then did the Tang emperor open his eyes and say, "How I suffered just now! I barely escaped attack by spiteful demons from the Region of Darkness, only to encounter death by drowning!" "Have no fear, Your Majesty," said the ministers. "What kind of calamity occurred in the water?" "I was riding a horse," the Tang emperor said, "when we came near the Wei River where two fishes were playing. That deceitful Grand Marshal Zhu pushed me off my horse into the river, and I was almost drowned."

"His Majesty is still not entirely free from the influences of the dead," said Wei Zheng. He quickly ordered from the imperial dispensary medicinal broth designed to calm his spirit and fortify his soul. They also prepared some rice gruel, and only after taking such nourishments once or twice did he become his old self again, fully regaining his living senses. A quick calculation revealed that the Tang emperor had been dead for three days and nights and then returned to life to rule again. We have thus a testimonial poem:

> From ancient times how oft the world has changed!
> History is full of kingdoms that rise and fall.
> Countless were the wonders of Zhou, Han, and Jin.
> Which could match King Tang's from death to life recall?

By then it was dusk; the various ministers withdrew after they had seen the emperor retire. Next day, they took off their mourning garb and changed into their court attire: everyone had on his red robe and black cap, his purple sash and gold medal, waiting outside the gate to be summoned to court. We now tell you about Taizong, who, having received the medicine prescribed for calming his spirit and fortifying his soul, and having taken the rice broth several times, was carried into his bedchamber by his attendants. He slept soundly that whole night, and when he arose at dawn, his spirit was fully revived. Look how he was attired:

> He donned a tall, royal cap;
> He wore a dark ocher robe;
> He put on a belt of green jade from Blue Mountain;
> He trod a pair of empire-building carefree boots.
> His stunning looks
> Surpassed anyone in court:
> With power to spare
> He resumed his reign.
> What a great Tang emperor of justice and truth,
> The Majestic Li who rose again from the dead!

The Tang emperor went up to the Treasure Hall of the Golden Carriage and gathered together the two groups of civil and military officials, who, after shouting "Long live the emperor" three times, stood in attention according to rank and file. Then they heard this loud announcement: "If there is any business, come forth and make your memorial; if there is no business, you are dismissed from court."

From the east came [the row of civil officials] and from the west [came the row of military officials]; they all went forward and prostrated themselves before the steps of white jade. "Your Majesty," they said, "may we inquire how you awoke from your slumber which lasted so long?"

"On that day, after we had received the letter from Wei Zheng," said Taizong, "we felt that our soul had departed from these halls, having been invited by the imperial guardsmen to join a hunting party. As we were traveling, the men and horses both disappeared, whereupon my father, the former emperor, and my deceased brothers came to hassle us. We would not have been able to escape them had it not been for the arrival of someone in black cap and robe; this man happened to be the judge Cui Jue, who managed to send my deceased brothers away. We handed Wei Zheng's letter over to him, and as he was reading it, some boys in blue came to lead us with flags and banners to the Hall of Darkness, where we were met by the Ten Kings of the Underworld. They told us of the Jing River Dragon, who accused us of having him slain after promising to save him. We in turn explained to them what happened, and they assured us that our case had been jointly reviewed by the Three Tribunes. Then they asked for the Chronicles of Life and Death to examine what was to be our allotted age. Judge Cui presented his books, and King Yama, after checking them, said that Heaven had assigned us a portion of thirty-three years. Since we had ruled for only thirteen years, we were entitled to twenty more years of living. So Grand Marshal Zhu and Judge Cui were ordered to send us back here. We took leave of the Ten Kings and promised to thank them with gifts of melons and other fruits. After our departure from the Hall of Darkness, we encountered in the Underworld all those who were treasonous to the state and disloyal to their parents, those who practiced neither virtue nor righteousness, those who squandered the five grains, those who cheated openly or in secret, those who indulged in unjust weights and measurements—in sum, the rapists, the thieves, the liars, the hypocrites, the wantons, the deviates, the connivers, and the lawbreakers. They were all suffering from various tortures by grinding, burning, pounding, sawing, frying, boiling, hanging, and skinning. There were tens of thousands of them, and we could not make an end of this ghastly sight. Thereafter we passed by the City of the Dead, filled with the souls of brigands and bandits from all over the Earth, who came to block our path. Fortunately, Judge Cui was willing to vouch for us, and we could then borrow a roomful of

gold and silver from Old Man Xiang of Henan to buy off the spirits before we could proceed once more. We finally parted after Judge Cui had
repeatedly instructed us that when we returned to the World of Light we
were to celebrate a Grand Mass of Land and Water for the salvation of
those orphaned spirits. After leaving the Sixfold Path of Transmigration,
Grand Marshal Zhu asked us to mount a horse so swift it seemed to be
flying, and brought me to the bank of the Wei River. As we were enjoying the sight of two fishes playing in the water, he grabbed our legs and
pushed us into the river. Only then did we come back to life." When the
various ministers heard these words, they all praised and congratulated
the emperor. A notice was also sent out to every town and district in the
empire, and all the officials presented gratulatory memorials, which we
shall mention no further.

We shall now tell you about Taizong, who proclaimed a general amnesty
for the prisoners in the empire. Moreover, he asked for an inventory of
those convicted of capital crimes, and the judge from the Board of Justice
submitted some four hundred names of those awaiting death by beheading or hanging. Taizong granted them one year's leave to return to their
families, so that they could settle their affairs and put their property in
order before going to the marketplace to receive their just deserts. The
prisoners all thanked him for such grace before departing. After issuing
another edict for the care and welfare of orphans, Taizong also released
some three thousand court maidens and concubines from the palace and
married them off to worthy military officers. From that time on, his reign
was truly a virtuous one, to which we have a testimonial poem:

Great is the virtue of the Great Tang Ruler!
Surpassing Sage Kings, he makes his people prosper.
Five hundred convicts may now leave the prison;
Three thousand maidens find release from the palace.
The empire's officials all wish him long life.
The ministers at court all give him high praise.
Such good heart, once stirred, the Heavens should bless,
And pass such weal to seventeen generations.

After releasing the court maidens and convicts, Taizong also issued
another proclamation to be posted throughout the empire. The proclamation read:

The cosmos, though vast,
Is brightly surveyed by the sun and the moon;
The world, though immense,
Approves not villains in Heaven or on Earth.

If your intent is trickery,
Even this life will bring retribution;
If your giving exceeds receiving,
There's blessing not only in the life hereafter.
A thousand clever designs
Are not as living according to one's duties;
Ten thousand men of violence
Cannot compare with one frugal and content.
If you're bent on good works and mercy,
Need you read the sūtras with diligence?
If you intend to harm others,
Even the learning of Buddha is vain!

From that time on, there was not a single person in the empire who did not practice virtue.

Meanwhile, another notice was posted asking for a volunteer to take the melons and other fruits to the Region of Darkness. At the same time, a roomful of gold and silver from the treasury was sent with the Imperial Duke of Khotan, Hu Jingde, to the Kaifeng District of Henan so that the debt to Xiang Liang could be repaid. After the notice had been posted for some days, a worthy came forth to volunteer his life for the mission. He was originally from Zunzhou; his surname was Liu and his given name Quan, and he belonged to a family of great wealth. The reason he came forward was that his wife, Li Cuilian, happened to have given a gold hairpin from her head, by way of alms, to a monk in front of their house. When Liu Quan chided her for her indiscretion in flaunting herself outside their home, Li became so upset that she promptly hanged herself, leaving behind her a pair of young children, who wept piteously day and night. Liu Quan was so filled with remorse by the sight of them that he was willing to leave life and property to take the melons to hell. He therefore took down the royal notice and came to see the Tang emperor. The emperor ordered him to go to the Lodge of the Golden Pavilion, where a pair of southern melons were put on his head, some money in his sleeve, and some medicine in his mouth.

So Liu Quan died by taking poison. His soul, still bearing the fruits on his head, arrived at the Gate of Spirits. The demon guardian at the door shouted, "Who are you, that you dare to come here?" "By the imperial command of the Great Tang Emperor Taizong," said Liu Quan, "I came here especially to present melons and other fruits for the enjoyment of the Ten Kings of the Underworld." The demon guardian received him amiably and led him to the Treasure Hall of Darkness. When he saw King

Yama, he presented the melons saying, "By order of the Tang emperor, I came from afar to present these melons as a token of thanks for the gracious hospitality of the Ten Kings." Highly pleased, King Yama said, "That Emperor Taizong is certainly a man of his word!" He accepted the melons and proceeded to ask the messenger about his name and his home. "Your humble servant," said Liu Quan, "resided originally in Junzhou; my surname is Liu and my given name is Quan. Because my wife hanged herself, leaving no one to care for our children, I decided to leave home and children and sacrifice my life for the country by helping my emperor to take these melons here as a thank-offering."

When the Ten Kings heard these words, they asked at once for Li, the wife of Liu Quan; she was brought in by the demon guardian, and wife and husband had a reunion before the Hall of Darkness. They conversed about what had happened and also thanked the Ten Kings for this meeting. King Yama, moreover, examined the Books of Life and Death and found that both husband and wife were supposed to live to a ripe old age. He quickly ordered the demon guardian to take them back to life, but the guardian said, "Since Li Cuilian has been back in the World of Darkness for many days, her body no longer exists. To whom should her soul attach herself?"

"The emperor's sister, Li Yuying," said King Yama, "is destined to die very soon. Borrow her body right away so that this woman can return to life." The demon guardian obeyed the order and led Liu Quan and his wife out of the Region of Darkness to return to life. We do not know how the two of them returned to life; let's listen to the explanation in the next chapter.

TWELVE

The Tang emperor, firm in sincerity, convenes the Grand Mass;
Guanyin, revealing herself, converts Gold Cicada.

We were telling you about the demon guardian who was leading Liu Quan and his wife out of the Region of Darkness. Accompanied by a swirling dark wind, they went directly back to Chang'an of the great nation. The demon pushed the soul of Liu Quan into the Golden Court Pavilion Lodge, but the soul of Cuilian was brought into the inner court of the royal palace. Just then the Princess Yuying was walking beneath the shadows of flowers along a path covered with green moss. The demon guardian crashed right into her and pushed her to the ground; her living soul was snatched away and the soul of Cuilian was pushed into Yuying's body instead. The demon guardian then returned to the Region of Darkness, and we shall say no more about that.

We now tell you that the maidservants of the palace, both young and old, when they saw that Yuying had fallen and died, ran quickly to the Hall of the Golden Chimes and reported the incident to the queen, saying, "The princess has fallen and died!" Horrified, the queen reported it to Taizong. When Taizong heard the news, he nodded, sighing, and said, "So this has come to pass indeed! We did ask the King of Darkness whether the old and young of our family would be safe or not. He said, 'They will all be safe, but I fear that your royal sister will not live long.' Now his word is fulfilled." All the inhabitants of the palace came to mourn her, but when they reached the spot where she had fallen, they saw that the princess was breathing. "Stop weeping! Stop weeping!" said the Tang emperor. "Don't startle her!" He went forward and lifted her head with the royal hand, crying out, "Wake up, royal sister!" Our princess suddenly turned over and cried, "Husband, walk slowly! Wait for me!" "Sister," said Taizong, "we are all here." Lifting her head and opening her eyes to look around, the princess said, "Who are you that you dare touch me?" "This is your royal brother," said Taizong, "and your sister in-law." "Where do I have any royal brother and sister-in-law?" asked the princess. "My family is Li, and my maiden name is Li Cuilian.

My husband's surname is Liu and his given name is Quan; both of us are from Junzhou. Because I pulled a golden hairpin to give to a monk outside our home as alms three months ago, my husband rebuked me for walking indiscreetly out of our doors and thus violating the etiquette appropriate to a woman. He scolded me, and I became so enraged that I hanged myself with a white silk cord, leaving behind a pair of children who wept night and day. On account of my husband, who was sent by the Tang emperor to the Region of Darkness to present melons, King Yama took pity on us and allowed us both to return to life. He was walking ahead; I could not keep up with him, tripped, and fell. How rude you all are! Not knowing my name, how dare you touch me!" When Taizong heard these words, he said to his attendants, "I suppose my sister was knocked senseless by the fall. She's babbling!" He ordered that Yuying be helped into the palace and medicine be brought in from the court dispensary.

As the Tang emperor went back to the court, one of his assistants came forward to report, saying, "Your Majesty, the man Liu Quan, who went to present the melons, has returned to life. He is now outside the gate, awaiting your order." Greatly startled, the Tang emperor at once gave the order for Liu Quan to be brought in, who then prostrated himself before the red-lacquered courtyard. Taizong asked him, "How did the presentation of melons come off?" "Your subject," said Liu Quan, "bore the melons on his head and went straight to the Gate of Spirits. I was led to the Hall of Darkness, where I met the Ten Kings of the Underworld. I presented the melons and spoke at length about the sincere gratitude of my lord. King Yama was most delighted, and he complimented Your Majesty profusely, saying, 'That Taizong emperor is indeed a man of virtue and a man of his word!'" "What did you happen to see in the Region of Darkness?" asked the Tang emperor. "Your subject did not travel far," said Liu Quan, "and I did not see much. I only heard King Yama questioning me on my native village and my name. Your subject therefore gave him a full account of how I abandoned home and children because of my wife's suicide and volunteered for the mission. He quickly sent for a demon guardian, who brought in my wife, and we were reunited at the Hall of Darkness. Meanwhile, they also examined the Books of Life and Death and told us that we both should live to a ripe old age. The demon guardian was dispatched to see us back to life. Your subject walked ahead, but my wife fell behind. I am grateful that I am now returned to life, but I do not know where my wife has gone." Alarmed, the Tang emperor asked, "Did King Yama say anything about your wife?" "He didn't say much," said Liu Quan. "I only heard the demon guardian's exclamation that Li Cuilian had been dead for so long that her body no longer existed. King Yama said, 'The royal sister, Li Yuying, should die shortly. Let Cuilian borrow the body of Yuying so that she may return to life.' Your subject has no knowledge of who that royal sister is and where she resides, nor has he made any attempt to locate her."

When the Tang emperor heard this report, he was filled with delight and said to the many officials around him, "When we took leave of King Yama, we questioned him with regard to the inhabitants of the palace. He said that the old and the young would all be safe, though he feared that our sister would not live long. Just now our sister Yuying fell dying beneath the flowers. When we went to her assistance, she regained her consciousness momentarily, crying, 'Husband, walk slowly! Wait for me!' We thought that her fall had knocked her senseless, as she was babbling like that. But when we questioned her carefully, she said exactly what Liu Quan now tells us." "If Her Royal Highness passed away momentarily, only to say these things after she regained consciousness," said Wei Zheng, "this means that there is a real possibility that Liu Quan's wife has returned to life by borrowing another person's body. Let us invite the princess to come out, and see what she has to tell us." "We just asked the court dispensary to send in some medicine," said the Tang emperor, "and we don't know what's happening." Some ladies of the court were sent to fetch the princess, and they found her inside, screaming, "Why do I need to take any medicine? How can this be my house? Ours is a clean, cool house of tiles; it's not like this one, yellow as if it had jaundice, and with such gaudy appointments! Let me out! Let me out!"

She was still shouting when four or five ladies and two or three eunuchs took hold of her and led her outside to the court. The Tang emperor said, "Do you recognize your husband?" "What are you talking about?" said Yuying. "The two of us were pledged to each other since childhood as husband and wife. I bore him a boy and a girl. How could I not recognize him?" The Tang emperor asked one of the palatial officials to help her go down from the Treasure Hall. The princess went right before the steps of white jade, and when she saw Liu Quan, she grabbed him, saying, "Husband, where have you been? You didn't even wait for me! I tripped and fell, and then I was surrounded by all these crazy people, talking nonsense! What do you have to say to this?" Liu Quan heard that she was speaking like his wife, but the person he saw certainly did not resemble her, and he dared not acknowledge her to be his own. The Tang emperor said,

"Indeed,
Men have seen mountains cracking, or the gaping of earth;
But none has seen the living exchanged for the dead!"

What a just and kindly ruler! He took his sister's toilet boxes, garments, and jewelry and bestowed them all on Liu Quan; it was as if the man was provided with a dowry. He was, moreover, exempted forever from having to engage in any compulsory service to the Crown, and was told to take the royal sister back to his home. So, husband and wife together expressed their gratitude before the steps and returned happily to their village. We have a poem in testimony:

> How long, how short—man has his span of years;
> He lives and dies, each foreordained by fate.
> Liu Quan presented melons and returned to life;
> In someone's body so did Li, his mate.

The two of them took leave of the emperor, went directly back to Junzhou, and saw that both house and children were in good order. They never ceased thereafter to proclaim the rewards of virtue, but we shall speak of them no further.

We now tell you about Yuchi Gong, who took a huge load of gold and silver and went to see Xiang Liang at the Kaifeng District in Henan. It turned out that the man made his living by selling water, while his wife, whose surname was Zhang, sold pottery in front of their home. Whatever money they made, they kept only enough for their subsistence, giving all the rest either as alms to the monks or as gifts to the dead by purchasing paper money and burning it. They thus built up enormous merit; for though they were poor folks in the World of Light, they were, in fact, leading citizens for whom jade and gold were laid up in the other world. When Yuchi Gong came to their door with the gold and silver, Papa Xiang and Mama Xiang were terror-stricken. And when they also saw the district officials with their horses and carriages assembling outside their thatched hut, the aged couple were dumbfounded. They knelt on the floor and kowtowed without ceasing. "Old folks, please arise," said Yuchi Gong. "Though I am an imperial official, I came here with this gold and silver to repay you by order of my king." Shaking and quaking, the man said, "Your lowly servant has never lent money to others. How dare we accept such inexplicable wealth?"

"I have found out," said Yuchi Gong, "that you are indeed a poor fellow. But you have also given alms to feed the monks. Whatever exceeds your necessities you have used to purchase paper money, which you burned in dedication to the Region of Darkness. You have thus accumulated a vast fortune down below. Our emperor, Taizong, returned to life after being dead for three days; he borrowed a roomful of gold and silver from you while he was in the Region of Darkness, and we are returning the exact sum to you. Please count your money accordingly so that we may make our report back to the emperor." Xiang Liang and his wife, however, remained adamant. They raised their hands to Heaven and cried, "If your lowly servants accepted this gold and silver, we should die quickly. We might have been given credit for burning paper cash, but this is a secret unknown to us. Moreover, what evidence do we have that our Father, His Majesty, borrowed our money in some other world? We simply dare not accept this." "His Majesty told us," said Yuchi Gong, "that he received the loan from you because Judge Cui vouched for him, and he could bear testimony. So please accept this." "Even if I were to die," said Xiang Liang, "I could not accept the gift."

Seeing that they persisted in their refusal, Yuchi Gong had no alternative but to send someone back to report to the Throne. When Taizong saw the report and learned that Xiang Liang had refused to accept the gold and silver, he said, "They are truly virtuous elders!" He issued a decree at once that Hu Jingde should use the money to erect a temple, to build a shrine, and to support the religious services that would be performed in them. The old couple, in other words, would be repaid in this manner. The decree went out to Jingde, who, having expressed his gratitude, facing the capital, proclaimed its content for all to know. He used the money to purchase a lot of about fifty acres not needed either by the military authorities or the people. A temple was erected on this piece of land and named the Royal Xiangguo Temple. To the left of it there was also a shrine dedicated to Papa and Mama Xiang, with a stone inscription stating that the buildings were erected under the supervision of Yuchi Gong. This is the Great Xiangguo Temple still standing today.

The work was finished and reported; Taizong was exceedingly pleased. He then gathered many officials together in order that a public notice be issued to invite monks for the celebration of the Grand Mass of Land and Water, so that those orphaned souls in the Region of Darkness might find salvation. The notice went throughout the empire, and officials of all regions were asked to recommend monks illustrious for their holiness to go to Chang'an for the Mass. In less than a month's time, the various monks from the empire had arrived. The Tang emperor ordered the court historian, Fu Yi, to select an illustrious priest to take charge of the ceremonies. When Fu Yi received the order, however, he presented a memorial to the Throne which attempted to dispute the worth of Buddha. The memorial said:

> The teachings of the Western Territory deny the relations of ruler and subject, of father and son. With the doctrines of the Three Ways and the Sixfold Path, they beguile and seduce the foolish and the simpleminded.

They emphasize the sins of the past in order to ensure the felicities of the future. By chanting in Sanskrit, they seek a way of escape. We submit, however, that birth, death, and the length of one's life are ordered by nature; but the conditions of public disgrace or honor are determined by human volition. These phenomena are not, as some philistines would now maintain, ordained by Buddha. The teachings of Buddha did not exist in the time of the Three Kings and the Five Emperors, and yet those rulers were wise, their subjects loyal, and their reigns long-lasting. It was not until the period of Emperor Ming in the Han dynasty that the worship of foreign gods was established, but this meant only that priests of the Western Territory were permitted to propagate their faith. The event, in fact, represented a foreign intrusion in China, and the teachings are hardly worthy to be believed.

When Taizong saw the memorial, he had it distributed among the various officials for discussion. At that time the prime minister Xiao Yu came forward and prostrated himself to address the Throne, saying, "The teachings of Buddha, which have flourished in several previous dynasties, seek to exalt the good and to restrain what is evil. In this way they are covertly an aid to the nation, and there is no reason why they should be rejected. For Buddha after all is also a sage, and he who spurns a sage is himself lawless. I urge that the dissenter be severely punished."

Taking up the debate with Xiao Yu, Fu Yi contended that propriety had its foundation in service to one's parents and ruler. Yet Buddha forsook his parents and left his family; indeed, he defied the Son of Heaven all by himself, just as he used an inherited body to rebel against his parents. Xiao Yu, Fu Yi went on to say, was not born in the wilds, but by his adherence to this doctrine of parental denial, he confirmed the saying that an unfilial son had in fact no parents. Xiao Yu, however, folded his hands in front of him and declared, "Hell was established precisely for people of this kind." Taizong thereupon called on the Lord High Chamberlain, Zhang Daoyuan, and the President of the Grand Secretariat, Zhang Shiheng, and asked how efficacious the Buddhist exercises were in the procurement of blessings. The two officials replied, "The emphasis of Buddha is on purity, benevolence, compassion, the proper fruits, and the unreality of things. It was Emperor Wu of the Northern Zhou dynasty who set the Three Religions in order. The Chan Master, Da Hui, also had extolled those concepts of the dark and the distant. Generations of people revered such saints as the Fifth Patriarch, who became man, or the Bodhidharma, who appeared in his sacred form; none of them proved to be inconspicuous in grace and power. Moreover, it has been held since antiquity that the Three Religions are most honorable, not to be destroyed or abolished. We beseech, therefore, Your Majesty to exercise your clear and sagacious judgment." Highly pleased, Taizong said, "The words of our worthy subjects are not unreasonable. Anyone who disputes them further will be punished." He thereupon ordered Wei Zheng, Xiao Yu, and Zhang Daoyuan to invite the various Buddhist priests to prepare the site for the Grand Mass and to select from among them someone of great merit and virtue to preside over the ceremonies. All the officials then bowed their heads to the ground to thank the emperor before withdrawing. From that time also came the law that any person who denounces a monk or Buddhism will have his arms broken.

Next day the three court officials began the process of selection at the Mountain-River Platform, and from among the priests gathered there they chose an illustrious monk of great merit. "Who is this person?" you ask.

Gold Cicada was his former divine name.
As heedless he was of the Buddha's talk,
He had to suffer in this world of dust,
To fall in the net by being born a man.
He met misfortune as he came to Earth,
And evildoers even before his birth.
His father: Chen, a zhuangyuan from Haizhou.
His mother's sire: chief of this dynasty's court.
Fated by his natal star to fall in the stream,
He followed tide and current, chased by mighty waves.
At Gold Mountain, the island, he had great fortune;
For the abbot, Qian'an, raised him up.
He met his true mother at age eighteen,
And called on her father at the capital.
A great army was sent by Chief Kaishan
To stamp out the vicious crew at Hongzhou.
The zhuangyuan Guangrui escaped his doom:
Son united with sire—how worthy of praise!
They saw the king to receive his favor;
Their names resounded in Lingyan Tower.
Declining office, he wished to be a monk,
To seek at Hongfu Temple the Way of Truth,
A former child of Buddha, nicknamed River Float,
Had a religious name of Chen Xuanzang.

So that very day the multitude selected the priest Xuanzang, a man who had been a monk since childhood, who maintained a vegetarian diet, and who had received the commandments the moment he left his mother's womb. His maternal grandfather was Yin Kaishan, one of the chief army commanders of the present dynasty. His father, Chen Guangrui, had taken the prize of zhuangyuan and was appointed Grand Secretary of the Wenyuan Chamber. Xuanzang, however, had no love for glory or wealth, being dedicated wholly to the pursuit of Nirvāṇa. Their investigations revealed that he had an excellent family background and the highest moral character. Not one of the thousands of classics and sūtras had he failed to master; none of the Buddhist chants and hymns was unknown to him. The three officials led Xuanzang before the Throne. After going through elaborate court ritual, they bowed to report, "Your subjects, in obedience to your holy decree, have selected an illustrious monk by the name of Chen Xuanzang." Hearing the name, Taizong thought silently for a long time and said, "Can Xuanzang be the son of Grand Secretary Chen Guangrui?" Child River Float kowtowed and replied, "That is indeed your subject." "This is a most appropriate choice," said Taizong, delighted. "You are truly a monk of great virtue and devotion. We therefore appoint you the Grand Expositor of the Faith, Supreme Vicar of Priests." Xuanzang touched his forehead to the ground to express his gratitude and to receive his appointment. He was given, furthermore, a cassock of knitted gold and five colors, a Vairocana hat, and the instruction diligently to seek out all worthy monks and to rank all these ācāryas[1] in order. They were to follow the imperial decree and proceed to the Temple of Transformation,[2] where they would begin the ceremony after selecting a propitious day and hour.

Xuanzang bowed again to receive the decree and left. He went to the Temple of Transformation and gathered many monks together; they made ready the beds, built the platforms, and rehearsed the music. A total of one thousand two hundred worthy monks, young and old, were chosen, who were further separated into three divisions, occupying the rear, middle, and front portions of the hall. All the preparations were completed and everything was put in order before the Buddhas. The third day of the ninth month of that same year was selected as the lucky day, when a Grand Mass of Land and Water lasting forty-nine days (in accordance with the number seven times seven) would begin. A memorial was presented to Taizong, who went with all his relatives and officials, both civil and military, to the Mass on that day to burn incense and listen to the lecture. We have a poem as testimony. The poem says:

1. A spiritual master or preceptor, used frequently in Chinese writings as a synonym for a Buddhist priest.
2. *Anpapādaka*, meaning direct metamorphosis or birth by transformation.

When the year-star of Zhenguan reached thirteen,
The king called his people to hear the Sacred Books.
The boundless Law was performed at a plot of truth;
Cloud, fog, and light filled the Great Promise Hall.
By grace and the king's edict they met at this grand temple;
Gold Cicada cast his shell, changed by the bounteous West.
He spread wide the good works to save the damned,
And held fast his faith to preach the Three Modes of Life.[3]

In the thirteenth year of the Zhenguan period, when the year stood at *jisi* and the ninth month at *jiaxu*, on the third day and at the auspicious hour of *gueimao*, Chen Xuanzang, the Great Expositor-Priest, gathered together one thousand two hundred illustrious monks. They met at the Temple of Transformation in the city of Chang'an to expound the various holy sūtras. After holding court early that morning, the emperor led many officials both military and civil and left the Treasure Hall of Golden Chimes by phoenix carriages and dragon chariots. They came to the temple to listen to the lectures and raise incense. How does the imperial cortege appear? Truly it comes with

A sky full of blessed air
And ten thousand shafts of hallowed light.
The favorable wind blows gently;
The omnific sun shines brightly.
A thousand lords with girdle-jade walk in front and rear.
The many flags of guardsmen stand both left and right.
Those holding gilt bludgeons,
And halberds and axes,
March in pairs and pairs;
The red silk lanterns,
The royal incense urn,
Move in solemnity.
The dragons fly and the phoenixes dance;
The falcons soar and the eagles take wing.
Most holy is the king and upright;
Most principled are the lords and true.
They increase our bliss by a thousand years, surpassing Yu and Shun;
They secure peace of ten thousand ages, rivaling Yao and Tang.
We also see the curve-handled umbrella,
And robes with rolling dragons—

3. I.e., the past, the present, and the future lives.

Their glare lighting up each other;
The jade joined-rings,
The phoenix fans,
Waving through holy mist.
Those caps of pearls and belts of jade;
The purple sashes and medals of gold.
A thousand rows of soldiers protect the Throne;
Two lines of marshals uphold the carriage.
This emperor, cleansed and sincere, bows to the Buddha,
Glad to raise incense and seek virtue's fruit.

The grand cortege of the Tang emperor soon arrived in front of the temple. The emperor ordered a halt to the music, left the carriages, and led many officials in the worship of Buddha by taking up burning incense sticks in their hands. After bowing three times holding the incense, they raised their heads and looked around them. This was indeed a splendid religious hall. You see

Dancing flags and banners;
Bright, gleaming sunshades.
Dancing flags and banners
Fill the air with strands of flashing colored mists.
Bright, gleaming sunshades
Glow in the sun as fiery bolts.
Imposing, the gold image of Lokājyeṣṭha;[4]
Most awesome, the jade features of the arhats.
Divine flowers fill the vases.
Sandal wood incense burn in the urns.
The divine flowers filling the vases
Adorn the temple with a brilliant forest of brocade.
The sandalwood incense burning in the urns
Covers the clear sky with waves of fragrant clouds.
Piled high on red trays are fruits in season.
On colored counters, mounds of cakes and sweets rest.
Rows of noble priests chant the holy sūtras
To save from their afflictions those orphaned souls.

Taizong and his officials each lifted the incense; they also worshiped the golden body of the Buddha and paid homage to the arhats. Thereafter, the Master of the Law, Chen Xuanzang, the Grand Expositor of the Faith, led the various monks to greet the Tang emperor. After the ceremony, they

4. The most honorable one of the world.

went back to their seats according to their rank and station. The priest then presented Taizong with the proclamation for the deliverance of the orphaned souls. It read:

> The supreme virtue is vast and endless, for Buddhism is founded upon Nirvāṇa. The spirit of the pure and the clean circulates freely and flows everywhere in the Three Regions. There are a thousand changes and ten thousand transformations, all regulated by the forces of yin and yang. Boundless and vast indeed are the substance, the function, the true nature, and the permanence of such phenomena. But look at those orphaned souls, how worthy they are of our pity and commiseration! Now by the holy command of Taizong, we have selected and assembled various priests, who will engage in meditation and in the proclamation of the Law. Flinging wide the gates of salvation and setting in motion many vessels of mercy, we would deliver you, the multitudes, from the Sea of Woe and save you from perdition and from the Sixfold Path. You will be led to return to the way of truth and to enjoy the bliss of Heaven. Whether it be by motion, rest, or nonactivity, you will be united with, and become, pure essences. Therefore make use of this noble occasion, for you are invited to the pleasures of the celestial city. Take advantage of our Grand Mass so that you may find release from Hell's confinement, ascend quickly and freely to ultimate bliss, and travel without restraint in the Region of the West.

The poem says:
An urn of immortal incense.
Some scrolls of salvific power.
As we proclaim this boundless Law,
Receive now Heaven's endless grace.
All your guilt and crime abolished,
You lost souls may leave your prison.
May our nation be firmly blessed
With peace long and all-embracing.

Highly pleased by what he read, Taizong said to the monks, "Be firm, all of you, in your devotion, and do not slack in your service to Buddha. After the achievement of merit and after each has received his blessing, we shall reward you handsomely. Be assured that you will not have labored in vain." The twelve hundred monks all touched their foreheads to the ground to express their gratitude. After the three vegetarian meals of the day, the Tang emperor returned to the palace to wait for the formal celebration of the mass seven days hence, when he would again be invited to raise incense. As dusk was about to fall, the various officials all retired. What sort of evening was this? Look at

> The long stretch of clear sky as twilight dims,
> As specks of jackdaw drop to their perch late.
> People grow quiet, the city full of lights:
> Now's the time for Chan monks to meditate.

We have told you about the scenery of the night. The next morning the Master of the Law again ascended his seat and gathered the monks to recite their sūtras, but we shall say no more about that.

We shall now tell you about the Bodhisattva Guanyin of the Potalaka Mountain in the South Sea, who, since receiving the command of Tathāgata, was searching in the city of Chang'an for a worthy person to be the seeker of scriptures. For a long time, however, she did not encounter anyone truly virtuous. Then she learned that Taizong was extolling merit and virtue and selecting illustrious monks to hold the Grand Mass. When she discovered, moreover, that the chief priest and celebrant was the monk Child River Float, who was a child of Buddha born from paradise and who happened also to be the very elder whom she had sent to this incarnation, the Bodhisattva was exceedingly pleased. She immediately took the treasures bestowed by Buddha and carried them out with Mokṣa to sell them on the main streets of the city. "What were these treasures?" you ask. There were the embroidered cassock with rare jewels and the nine-ring priestly staff. But she kept hidden the Golden, the Constrictive, and the Prohibitive Fillets for use in a later time, putting up for sale only the cassock and the priestly staff.

Now in the city of Chang'an there was one of those foolish monks who had not been selected to participate in the Grand Mass but who happened to possess a few strands of pelf. Seeing the Bodhisattva, who had changed herself into a monk covered with scabs and sores, bare-footed and bare-headed, dressed in rags, and holding up for sale the glowing cassock, he approached and asked, "You filthy monk, how much do you want for your cassock?" "The price of the cassock," said the Bodhisattva, "is five thousand taels of silver; for the staff, two thousand." The foolish monk laughed and said, "This filthy monk is mad! A lunatic! You want seven thousand taels of silver for two such common articles? They are not worth that much even if wearing them would make you immortal or turn you into a buddha. Take them away! You'll never be able to sell them!" The Bodhisattva did not bother to argue with him; she walked away and proceeded on her journey with Mokṣa.

After a long while, they came to the Eastern Flower Gate and ran right into the chief minister Xiao Yu, who was just returning from court. His outriders were shouting to clear the streets, but the Bodhisattva boldly refused to step aside. She stood on the street holding the cassock and met the chief minister head on. The chief minister pulled in his reins to look at this bright, luminous cassock, and asked his subordinates to inquire about the price of the garment. "I want five thousand taels for the cassock," said the Bodhisattva, "and two thousand for the staff." "What is so good about them," said Xiao Yu, "that they should be so expensive?" "This cassock," said the Bodhisattva, "has something good about it, and something bad, too. For some people it may be very expensive, but for others it may cost nothing at all."

"What's good about it," asked Xiao Yu, "and what's bad about it?"

"He who wears my cassock," said the Bodhisattva, "will not fall into perdition, will not suffer in Hell, will not encounter violence, and will not meet tigers and wolves. That's how good it is! But if the person happens to be a foolish monk who relishes pleasures and rejoices in iniquities, or a priest who obeys neither the dietary laws nor the commandments, or a worldly fellow who attacks the sūtras and slanders the Buddha, he will never even get to see my cassock. That's what's bad about it!" The chief minister asked again, "What do you mean, it will be expensive for some and not expensive for others?" "He who does not follow the Law of Buddha," said the Bodhisattva, "or revere the Three Jewels will be required to pay seven thousand taels if he insists on buying my cassock and my staff. That's how expensive it'll be! But if he honors the Three Jewels, rejoices in doing good deeds, and obeys our Buddha, he is a person worthy of these things. I shall willingly give him the cassock and the staff to establish an affinity of goodness with him. That's what I meant when I said that for some it would cost nothing."

When Xiao Yu heard these words, his face could not hide his pleasure, for he knew that this was a good person. He dismounted at once and greeted the Bodhisattva ceremoniously, saying, "Your Holy Eminence, please pardon whatever offense Xiao Yu might have caused. Our Great Tang Emperor is a most religious person, and all the officials of his court are like-minded. In fact, we have just begun a Grand Mass of Land and Water, and this cassock will be most appropriate for the use of Chen Xuanzang, the Grand Expositor of the Faith. Let me go with you to have an audience with the Throne."

The Bodhisattva was happy to comply with the suggestion. They turned around and went into the Eastern Flower Gate. The Custodian of the Yellow Door went inside to make the report, and they were summoned to the

Treasure Hall, where Xiao Yu and the two monks covered with scabs and sores stood below the steps. "What does Xiao Yu want to report to us?" asked the Tang emperor. Prostrating himself before the steps, Xiao Yu said, "Your subject going out of the Eastern Flower Gate met by chance these two monks, selling a cassock and a priestly staff. I thought of the priest, Xuanzang, who might wear this garment. For this reason, we asked to have an audience with Your Majesty."

Highly pleased, Taizong asked for the price of the cassock. The Bodhisattva and Mokṣa stood at the foot of the steps but did not bow at all. When asked the price of the cassock, the Bodhisattva replied, "Five thousand taels for the cassock and two thousand for the priestly staff." "What's so good about the cassock," said Taizong, "that it should cost so much?" The Bodhisattva said:

"Of this cassock,
A dragon which wears but one shred
Will miss the woe of being devoured by the great roc;
Or a crane on which one thread is hung
Will transcend this world and reach the place of the gods.
Sit in it:
Ten thousand gods will salute you!
Move with it:
Seven Buddhas will follow you!
This cassock was made of silk drawn from ice silkworm
And threads spun by skilled craftsmen.
Immortal girls did the weaving;
Divine maidens helped at the loom.
Bit by bit, the parts were sewn and embroidered.
Stitch by stitch, it arose—a brocade from the heddle,
Its pellucid weave finer than ornate blooms.
Its colors, brilliant, emit precious light.
Wear it, and crimson mist will surround your frame.
Doff it, and see the colored clouds take flight.
Outside the Three Heavens' door its primal light was seen;
Before the Five Mountains its magic aura grew.
Inlaid are layers of lotus from the West,
And hanging pearls shine like planets and stars.
On four corners are pearls which glow at night;
On top stays fastened an emerald.
Though lacking the all-seeing primal form,
It's held by Eight Treasures all aglow.

This cassock
You keep folded at leisure;
You wear it to meet sages.
When it's kept folded at leisure,
Its rainbowlike hues cut through a thousand wrappings.
When you wear it to meet sages,
All Heaven takes fright—both demons and gods!
On top are the ṛddhi pearl,
The māṇi pearl,
The dust-clearing pearl,
The wind-stopping pearl.
There are also the red cornelian,
The purple coral,
The luminescent pearl,
The Śāriputra.
They rob the moon of its whiteness;
They match the sun in its redness.
In waves its divine aura imbues the sky;
In flashes its brightness lifts up its perfection.
In waves its divine aura imbues the sky,
Flooding the Gate of Heaven.
In flashes its brightness lifts up its perfection,
Lighting up the whole world.
Shining upon the mountains and the streams,
It wakens tigers and leopards;
Lighting up the isles and the seas,
It moves dragons and fishes.
Along its edges hang two chains of melted gold,
And joins the collars a ring of snow-white jade.
The poem says:
The august Three Jewels, this venerable Truth—
It judges all Four Creatures on the Sixfold Path.
The mind enlightened knows and holds God's Law and man's;
The soul illumined can transmit the lamp of wisdom.
The solemn guard of one's body is Vajradhātu;[5]
Like ice in a jade pitcher is the purified mind.
Since Buddha caused this cassock to be made,
Which of ten thousand kalpas can harm a monk?"

5. The golden or diamond element in the universe, signifying the indestructible and active wisdom of Vairocana.

When the Tang emperor, who was up in the Treasure Hall, heard these words, he was highly pleased. "Tell me, priest," he asked again, "What's so good about the nine-ring priestly staff?" "My staff," said the Bodhisattva, "has on it

Nine joined-rings made of iron and set in bronze,
And nine joints of vine immortal ever young.
When held, it scorns the sight of aging bones;
It leaves the mount to return with fleecy clouds.
It roamed through Heaven with the Fifth Patriarch;
It broke Hell's gate where Lo Bo sought his Mom.[6]
Not soiled by the filth of this red-dust world,
It gladly trails the god-monk up Mount Jade."[7]

When the Tang emperor heard these words, he gave the order to have the cassock spread open so that he might examine it carefully from top to bottom. It was indeed a marvelous thing! "Venerable Elder of the Great Law," he said, "we shall not deceive you. At this very moment we have exalted the Religion of Mercy and planted abundantly in the fields of blessing. You may see many priests assembled in the Temple of Transformation to perform the Law and the sūtras. In their midst is a man of great merit and virtue, whose religious name is Xuanzang. We wish, therefore, to purchase these two treasure objects from you to give them to him. How much do you really want for these things?" Hearing these words, the Bodhisattva and Mokṣa folded their hands and gave praise to the Buddha. "If he is a man of virtue and merit," she said to the Throne, bowing, "this humble cleric is willing to give them to him. I shall not accept any money." She finished speaking and turned at once to leave. The Tang emperor quickly asked Xiao Yu to hold her back. Standing up in the Hall, he bowed low before saying, "Previously you claimed that the cassock was worth five thousand taels of silver, and the staff two thousand. Now that you see we want to buy them, you refuse to accept payment. Are you implying that we would bank on our position and take your possession by force? That's absurd! We shall pay you according to the original sum you asked for; please do not refuse it."

Raising her hands for a salutation, the Bodhisattva said, "This humble cleric made a vow before, stating that anyone who reveres the Three Treasures, rejoices in virtue, and submits to our Buddha will be given these

6. Lo Bo: the Chinese name for Mahāmaudgalyāyana, one of the chief disciples of Śākyamuni, who was famous for his journey to Hell to save his mother from the marauding hungry ghosts.

7. Another abode of the Lady Queen Mother of the West.

treasures free. Since it is clear that Your Majesty is eager to magnify virtue, to rest in excellence, and to honor our Buddhist faith by having an illustrious monk proclaim the Great Law, it is my duty to present these gifts to you. I shall take no money for them. They will be left here and this humble cleric will take leave of you." When the Tang emperor saw that she was so insistent, he was very pleased. He ordered the Court of Banquets to prepare a huge vegetarian feast to thank the Bodhisattva, who firmly declined that also. She left amiably and went back to her hiding place at the Temple of the Local Spirit, which we shall mention no further.

We tell you now about Taizong, who held a noon court and asked Wei Zheng to summon Xuanzang to an audience. That Master of the Law was just leading the monks in chanting sūtras and reciting *geyas*.[8] When he heard the emperor's decree, he left the platform immediately and followed Wei Zheng to come before the Throne. "We have greatly troubled our Master," said Taizong, "to render exemplary good works, for which we have hardly anything to offer you in thanks. This morning Xiao Yu came upon two monks who were willing to present us with a brocaded cassock with rare treasures and a nine-ring priestly staff. We therefore call specially for you so that you may receive them for your enjoyment and use." Xuanzang kowtowed to express his thanks.

"If our Master of the Law is willing," said Taizong, "please put the garment on for us to have a look." The priest accordingly shook open the cassock and draped it on his body, holding the staff in his hands. As he stood before the steps, ruler and subjects were all delighted. Here was a true child of Tathāgata! Look at him:

His looks imposing, how elegant and fine!
This robe of Buddha fits him like a glove!
Its splendor, most lustrous, spills over the world;
Its radiant colors imbue the universe.
Up and down are set rows of shining pearls.
Back and front thread layers of golden cords.
Brocade gilds the robe's edges all around,
With patterns embroidered most varied and rare.
Shaped like Eight Treasures are the thread-made frogs.
A gold ring joins the collars with velvet loops.
It shows on top and bottom Heaven's ranks,
And stars, great and small, are placed left and right.
Great is the fortune of Xuanzang, the priest,

8. A metrical piece, one of the twelve classes of sūtras in Hīnayāna Buddhism.

Now most deserving of this precious thing.
He seems a living arhat from the West,
Or even better than its true elite.
Holding his staff, with all its nine rings clanging,
Benevolent in his Vairocana hat,
He's a true child of Buddha, it's no idle tale!
Nor is it false that he the Bodhi matched.

The various officials, both civil and military, stood before the steps and shouted "Bravo!" Taizong could not have been more pleased, and he told the Master of the Law to keep his cassock on and the staff in his hands. Two regiments of honor guards were ordered to accompany him along with many other officials. They left the gate of the court and proceeded on the main streets toward the temple, and the whole entourage gave the impression that a zhuangyuan was making a tour of the city. The procession was a stirring sight indeed! The merchants and tradesmen in the city of Chang'an, the princes and noblemen, the men of ink and letters, the grown men and the little girls—they all vied to get a good view. Everyone exclaimed, "What a priest! He is truly a living arhat descended to Earth, a live bodhisattva coming to the world!" Xuanzang went right to the temple where he was met by all the monks leaving their seats. The moment they saw him wearing that cassock and holding the staff, they all said that King Kṣitigarbha had arrived! Everyone bowed to him and waited on him left and right. Going up to the main hall, Xuanzang lighted incense to honor the Buddha, after which he spoke of the emperor's favor to the multitude. Thereafter, each went back to his assigned seat, and soon the fiery orb sank westward. So it was

Sunset, and mist hid trees and grasses,
As the capital's first chimes rang out.
Zheng-zheng *they struck thrice, and human traffic ceased;*
The streets back and front soon grew quiet.
Though lights burned bright at First Temple,
The lone hamlet was noiseless and still.
The monk in silence tended the sūtras yet—
Ready to tame demons, to train his spirit.

Time went by like the snapping of fingers, and the formal celebration of the Grand Mass on the seventh day was to take place. Xuanzang presented the Tang emperor with a memorial, inviting him to raise the incense. News of these good works was circulating throughout the empire. Upon receiving the notice, Taizong sent for his carriage and led many of his officials, both civil and military, as well as his relatives and the ladies of the court, to the temple. All the people of the city—young and old, nobles and commoners—went along also to hear the preaching. At the same time, the Bodhisattva said to Mokṣa, "Today is the formal celebration of the Grand Mass, the first seventh of seven such occasions. It's about time for you and me to join the crowd. First, we want to see how the mass is going; second, we want to find out whether Gold Cicada is worthy of my treasures; and third, we can discover what division of Buddhism he is preaching about." The two of them thereupon went to the temple; and so it is that

Affinity will help old comrades meet
As perfection returns to this holy seat.

As they walked inside the temple to look around, they discovered that such a place in the capital of a great nation indeed surpassed the Ṣaḍ-varṣa,[9] or even the Jetavana Garden of the Śrāvastī. It was truly a lofty temple of Caturdiśaḥ,[10] resounding with divine music and Buddhist chants. Our Bodhisattva went directly to the side of the platform of many treasures and beheld a form truly resembling the enlightened Gold Cicada. The poem says:

All things were pure with not a spot of dust.
Xuanzang of the Great Law sat high on stage.
Lost souls, redeemed, approached the place unseen;
The city's highborn came to hear the Law.
You give when time's ripe: this intent's far-reaching.
You die as you please, the Canon door's open.
As they heard him rehearse the Boundless Law,
Young and old were glad and comforted.

Another poem says:

Since she made a tour of this holy site,
She met a friend unlike all other men.
They spoke of the present and of countless things—
Of merit and trial in this world of dust.
The cloud of Law extends to shroud the hills;
The net of Truth spread wide to fill all space.
Examine your lives and return to God,
For Heaven's grace is rife as falling blooms.

On the platform, that Master of the Law recited for a while the Sūtra of Life and Deliverance for the Dead; he then lectured for a while on the Heavenly Treasure Chronicle for Peace in the Nation, after which he preached for a while

9. The sexennial assembly of Buddha's disciples.
10. Name of a famous Buddhist monastery.

on the *Scroll on Merit and Self-Cultivation*. The Bodhisattva drew near and thumped her hands on the platform, calling out in a loud voice, "Hey, monk! You only know how to talk about the teachings of the Little Vehicle. Don't you know anything about the Great Vehicle?" When Xuanzang heard this question, he was filled with delight. He turned and leaped down from the platform, raised his hands and saluted the Bodhisattva, saying, "Venerable Teacher, please pardon your pupil for much disrespect. I only know that the priests who came before me all talk about the teachings of the Little Vehicle. I have no idea what the Great Vehicle teaches." "The doctrines of your Little Vehicle," said the Bodhisattva, "cannot save the damned by leading them up to Heaven; they can only mislead and confuse mortals. I have in my possession Tripitaka, three collections of the Great Vehicle Laws of Buddha, which are able to send the lost to Heaven, to deliver the afflicted from their sufferings, to fashion ageless bodies, and to break the cycles of coming and going."

As they were speaking, the officer in charge of incense and the inspection of halls went to report to the emperor, saying, "The Master was just in the process of lecturing on the wondrous Law when he was pulled down by two scabby mendicants, babbling some kind of nonsense." The king ordered them to be arrested, and the two monks were taken by many people and pushed into the hall in the rear. When the monk saw Taizong, she neither raised her hands nor made a bow; instead, she lifted her face and said, "What do you want of me, Your Majesty?" Recognizing her, the Tang emperor said, "Aren't you the monk who brought us the cassock the other day?" "I am," said the Bodhisattva. "If you have come to listen to the lecture," said Taizong, "you may as well take some vegetarian food. Why indulge in this wanton discussion with our Master and disturb the lecture hall, delaying our religious service?"

"What that Master of yours was lecturing on," said the Bodhisattva, "happens to be the teachings of the Little Vehicle, which cannot lead the lost up to Heaven. In my possession is the Tripitaka, the Great Vehicle Law of Buddha, which is able to save the damned, deliver the afflicted, and fashion the indestructible body." Delighted, Taizong asked eagerly, "Where is your Great Vehicle Law of Buddha?" "At the place of our lord, Tathāgata," said the Bodhisattva, "in the Great Temple of Thunderclap, located in India of the Great Western Heaven. It can untie the knot of a hundred enmities; it can dispel unexpected misfortunes." "Can you remember any of it?" said Taizong. "Certainly," said the Bodhisattva. Taizong was overjoyed and said, "Let the Master lead this monk to the platform to begin a lecture at once."

Our Bodhisattva led Mokṣa and flew up onto the high platform. She then trod on the hallowed clouds to rise up into the air and revealed her true salvific form, holding the pure vase with the willow branch. At her left stood the virile figure of Mokṣa carrying the rod. The Tang emperor was so overcome that he bowed to the sky and worshiped, as civil and military officials all knelt on the ground and burned incense. Throughout the temple, there was not one of the monks, nuns, Taoists, secular persons, scholars, craftsmen, and merchants, who did not bow down and exclaim, "Dear Bodhisattva! Dear Bodhisattva!" We have a song as a testimony. They saw only

Auspicious mist in diffusion
And dharmakāya[11] *veiled by holy light.*
In the bright air of ninefold Heaven
A lady immortal appeared.
That Bodhisattva
Wore on her head a cap
Fastened by leaves of gold
And set with flowers of jade,
With tassels of dangling pearls,
All aglow with golden light.
On her body she had
A robe of fine blue silk,
Lightly colored
And simply fretted
By circling dragons
And soaring phoenixes.
Down in front was hung
A pair of fragrant girdle-jade,
Which glowed with the moon
And danced with the wind,
Overlaid with precious pearls
And with imperial jade.
Around her waist was tied
An embroidered velvet skirt
Of ice-worm silk
And piped in gold,
In which she topped the colored clouds

11. The true, spiritual form or "body," the embodiment of essential Buddha-hood.

And crossed the jasper sea.
Before her she led
A cockatoo with red beak and yellow plumes,
Which had roamed the Eastern Ocean
And throughout the world
To foster deeds of mercy and filial piety.
She held in her hands
A grace-dispensing and world-sustaining precious vase,
In which was planted
A twig of pliant willow,
That could moisten the blue sky,
And sweep aside all evil—
All clinging fog and smoke.
Her jade rings joined the embroidered loops,
And gold lotus grew thick beneath her feet.
In three days how often she came and went:
This very Guanshiyin[12] who saves from pain and woe.

So pleased by the vision was Tang Taizong that he forgot about his empire; so enthralled were the civil and military officials that they completely ignored court etiquette. Everyone was chanting, "Namo Bodhisattva Guanshiyin!"

Taizong at once gave the order for a skilled painter to sketch the true form of the Bodhisattva. No sooner had he spoken than a certain Wu Daozi was selected, who could portray gods and sages and was a master of the noble perspective and lofty vision. (This man, in fact, was the one who would later paint the portraits of meritorious officials in the Lingyan Tower.) Immediately he opened up his magnificent brush to record the true form. The hallowed clouds of the Bodhisattva gradually drifted away, and in a little while the golden light disappeared. From midair came floating down a slip of paper on which were plainly written several lines in the style of the *gāthā*:

We greet the great Ruler of Tang
With scripts most sublime of the West.
The way: a hundred and eight thousand miles.
Seek earnestly this Mahāyāna.
These Books, when they reach your fair state,
Can redeem damned spirits from Hell.

12. The full name of Guanyin, meaning in popular understanding, "she who hearkens to the voices of the world."

If someone is willing to go,
He'll become a Buddha of gold.

When Taizong saw the *gāthā*, he said to the various monks: "Let's stop the Mass. Wait until I have sent someone to bring back the scriptures of the Great Vehicle. We shall then renew our sincere effort to cultivate the fruits of virtue." Not one of the officials disagreed with the emperor, who then asked in the temple, "Who is willing to accept our commission to seek scriptures from Buddha in the Western Heaven?" Hardly had he finished speaking when the Master of the Law stepped from the side and saluted him, saying, "Though your poor monk has no talents, he is ready to perform the service of a dog and a horse. I shall seek these true scriptures on behalf of Your Majesty, that the empire of our king may be firm and everlasting." Highly pleased, the Tang emperor went forward to raise up the monk with his royal hands, saying, "If the Master is willing to express his loyalty this way, undaunted by the great distance or by the journey over mountains and streams, we are willing to become bond brothers with you." Xuanzang touched his forehead to the ground to express his gratitude. Being indeed a righteous man, the Tang emperor went at once before Buddha's image in the temple and bowed to Xuanzang four times, addressing him as "our brother and holy monk."

Deeply moved, Xuanzang said, "Your Majesty, what ability and what virtue does your poor monk possess that he should merit such affection from your Heavenly Grace? I shall not spare myself in this journey, but I shall proceed with all diligence until I reach the Western Heaven. If I do not attain my goal, or the true scriptures, I shall not return to our land even if I have to die. I would rather fall into eternal perdition in Hell." He thereupon lifted the incense before Buddha and made that his vow. Highly pleased, the Tang emperor ordered his carriage back to the palace to wait for the auspicious day and hour, when official documents could be issued for the journey to begin. And so the Throne withdrew as everyone dispersed.

Xuanzang also went back to the Temple of Great Blessing. The many monks of that temple and his several disciples, who had heard about the quest for the scriptures, all came to see him. They asked, "Is it true that you have vowed to go to the Western Heaven?" "It is," said Xuanzang. "O Master," one of his disciples said, "I have heard people say that the way to the Western Heaven is long, filled with tigers, leopards, and all kinds of monsters. I fear that there will be departure but no return for you, as it will be difficult to safeguard your life."

"I have already made a great vow and a profound promise," said Xuanzang, "that if I do not acquire the true scriptures, I shall fall into eternal perdition in Hell. Since I have received such grace and favor from the king, I have no alternative but to serve my country to the utmost of my loyalty. It is true, of course, that I have no knowledge of how I shall fare on this journey or whether good or evil awaits me." He said to them again, "My disciples, after I leave, wait for two or three years, or six or seven years. If you see the branches of the pine trees within our gate pointing eastward, you will know that I am about to return. If not, I shall not be coming back." The disciples all committed his words firmly to memory.

The next morning Taizong held court and gathered all the officials together. They wrote up the formal rescript stating the intent to acquire scriptures and stamped it with the seal of free passage. The President of the Imperial Board of Astronomy then came with the report, "Today the positions of the planets are especially favorable for men to make a journey of great length." The Tang emperor was most delighted. Thereafter the Custodian of the Yellow Gate also made a report, saying, "The Master of the Law awaits your pleasure outside the court." The emperor summoned him up to the treasure hall and said, "Royal Brother, today is an auspicious day for the journey, and your rescript for free passage is ready. We also present you with a bowl made of purple gold for you to collect alms on your way. Two attendants have been selected to accompany you, and a horse will be your means of travel. You may begin your journey at once."

Highly pleased, Xuanzang expressed his gratitude and received his gifts, not displaying the least desire to linger. The Tang emperor called for his carriage and led many officials outside the city gate to see him off. The monks in the Temple of Great Blessing and the disciples were already waiting there with Xuanzang's winter and summer clothing. When the emperor saw them, he ordered the bags to be packed on the horses first, and then asked an officer to bring a pitcher of wine. Taizong lifted his cup to toast the pilgrim saying, "What is the byname of our Royal Brother?" "Your poor monk," said Xuanzang, "is a person who has left the family. He dares not assume a byname." "The Bodhisattva said earlier," said Taizong, "that there were three collections of scriptures in the Western Heaven. Our Brother can take that as a byname and call himself Tripitaka. How about it?" Thanking him, Xuanzang accepted the wine and said, "Your Majesty, wine is the first prohibition of priesthood. Your poor monk has practiced abstinence since birth." "Today's journey," said Taizong, "is not to be compared with any ordinary event. Please drink one cup of this dietary wine, and accept our good wishes that go along with the toast." Xuanzang dared not refuse; he took the wine and was about to drink, when he saw

Taizong stoop down to scoop up a handful of dirt with his fingers and sprinkle it in the wine. Tripitaka had no idea what this gesture meant.

"Dear Brother," said Taizong, laughing, "how long will it take you to come back from this trip to the Western Heaven?" "Probably in three years time," said Tripitaka, "I'll be returning to our noble nation." "The years are long and the journey is great," said Taizong. "Drink this, Royal Brother, and remember: Treasure a handful of dirt from your home, but love not ten thousand taels of foreign gold." Then Tripitaka understood the meaning of the handful of dirt sprinkled in his cup; he thanked the emperor once more and drained the cup. He went out of the gate and left, as the Tang emperor returned in his carriage. We do not know what will happen to him on this journey; let's listen to the explanation in the next chapter.

THIRTEEN

In the Den of Tigers, the Gold Star brings deliverance;
At Double-Fork Ridge, Boqin detains the monk.

> *The rich Tang ruler issued a decree,*
> *Deputing Xuanzang to seek the source of Chan.*
> *He bent his mind to find the Dragon Den,*
> *With firm resolve to climb the Vulture Peak.*[1]
> *Through how many states did he roam beyond his own?*
> *Through clouds and hills he passed ten thousand times.*
> *He now leaves the Throne to go to the West;*
> *He'll keep law and faith to reach the Great Void.*

We shall now tell you about Tripitaka, who, on the third day before the fifteenth of the ninth month in the thirteenth year of the period Zhenguan, was sent off by the Tang emperor and many officials from outside the gate of Chang'an. For a couple of days his horse trotted without ceasing, and soon they reached the Temple of the Law Gate. The abbot of that temple led some five hundred monks on both sides to receive him and took him inside. As they met, tea was served, after which a vegetarian meal was presented. Soon after the meal, dusk fell, and thus

> *Shadows moved to the Star River's nearing pulse;*
> *The moon was bright without a speck of dust.*
> *The wild geese called from the distant sky,*
> *And washing flails beat from nearby homes.*
> *As birds returned to perch on withered trees,*
> *The Chan monks conversed in their Sanskrit tones.*
> *On rush mats placed upon a single bunk,*
> *They sat until halfway through the night.*

Beneath the lamps the various monks discussed Buddhist doctrines and the purpose of seeking scriptures in the Western Heaven. Some pointed

---

1. Vulture Peak: *Gṛdhrakūṭa*, a place supposedly frequented by the Buddha and where the *Lotus sūtra* was preached. The full name of the mountain is Spirit Vulture Mountain.

out that the waters were wide and the mountains very high; others mentioned that the roads were crowded with tigers and leopards; still others
maintained that the precipitous peaks were difficult to scale; and another
group insisted that the vicious monsters were hard to subdue. Tripitaka,
however, kept his mouth shut tightly, but he pointed with his finger to
his own heart and nodded his head several times. Not perceiving what he
meant, the various monks folded their hands and asked, "Why did the
Master of the Law point to his heart and nod his head?" "When the mind
is active," Tripitaka replied, "all kinds of *māra* come into existence; when
the mind is extinguished, all kinds of *māra* will be extinguished. This disciple has already made an important vow before Buddha in the Temple of
Transformation, and he has no alternative but to fulfill it with his whole
heart. If I go, I shall not turn aside until I have reached the Western Heaven,
seen Buddha, and acquired the scriptures so that the Wheel of the Law
will be turned to us[2] and the kingdom of our lord will be secured forever."
When the various monks heard this statement, everyone congratulated and
commended him, saying, "A loyal and valiant master!" They praised him
unceasingly as they escorted him to bed.

Soon

The bamboos struck down the setting moon
And the cocks crew to gather the clouds of dawn

The various monks arose and prepared some tea and the morning meal.
Xuanzang put on his cassock and went to worship Buddha in the main hall.
"Your disciple, Chen Xuanzang," he said, "is on his way to seek scriptures
in the Western Heaven. But my fleshly eyes are dim and unperceptive and
do not recognize the true form of the living Buddha. Now I wish to make
a vow: that throughout this journey I shall burn incense whenever I come
upon a temple, I shall worship Buddha whenever I meet a Buddha, and I shall
sweep a pagoda whenever I reach a pagoda. May our Buddha be merciful and
soon reveal to me his Diamond Body sixteen feet tall. May he grant me the
true scriptures so that they may be preserved in the Land of the East."

He finished his prayer and went back to the hall for the vegetarian meal,
after which his two attendants made ready the saddle and urged him to
begin his journey. Going out of the temple's gate, Tripitaka took leave of
the monks, who grieved to see him go. They accompanied him for ten miles
before turning back, tears in their eyes, as Tripitaka proceeded directly
toward the West. It was the time of late autumn. You see

2. The Wheel of the Law is *dharmacakra*, the truth of Buddha able to vanquish all
evil and all resistance. It rolls on from man to man and from age to age.

Trees growing bare in hamlets as rush petals break;
From every maple column the red leaves fall.
Few are the trekkers through paths of mist and rain.
The fair chrysanthemums,
The sharp mountain rocks,
Cold streams and cracked lilies all make one sad.
Snow falls from a frosty sky on rushes and reeds.
One duck at dusk descends in the distant void.
Clouds o'er the wilds move through the gathering gloom.
The swallows depart;
The wild geese appear—
Their cries, though loud, are halting and forlorn.

After traveling for several days, master and disciples arrived at the city of Gongzhou. They were met at once by the various municipal officials of that city, where they spent the night. The next morning they set off again, taking food and drink along the way, resting by night and journeying by day. In two or three days, they arrived at the District of Hezhou, which formed the border of the Great Tang Empire. When the garrison commander of the border as well as the local monks and priests heard that the Master of the Law, a bond brother of the emperor, was on his way to the Western Heaven to see Buddha by royal commission, they received the travelers with due reverence. Some chief priests then invited them to spend the night at Fuyuan Temple, where every resident cleric came to pay respect to the pilgrims. Dinner was served, after which the two attendants were told to feed the horses well, for the Master wanted to leave before dawn. At the first crowing of the cock, he called for his attendants and aroused the monks of that temple. They hastened to prepare tea and breakfast, after which the pilgrims departed from the border. As he was somewhat impatient to get going, the Master arose a trifle too early. The fact is that this was late autumn, when cocks crow rather early—at about the time of the fourth watch. Facing the clear frost and the bright moon, the three of them (the horse made up the fourth member of the team) journeyed for some twenty or thirty miles, when they came upon a mountain range. It soon became exceedingly difficult for them to find their way. As they had to poke around in the grass to look for a path, they began to worry that they might be heading in the wrong direction. In that very anxious moment, they suddenly tripped; all three of them as well as the horse tumbled into a deep pit. Tripitaka was terrified; his companions all shook with fear. They were still trembling when they heard voices shouting, "Seize them! Seize them!" A violent wind swept by, and a mob of fifty or sixty ogres appeared, who seized Tripitaka with his companions and hauled them out of the pit. Quivering and shivering, the Master of the Law stole a glance around and saw a ferocious Monster King seated up on high. Truly he had

A figure most awesomely bold,
A face most distinctly fierce.
Light flashed from his lightninglike eyes;
All quaked at his thunderous voice.
His sawlike teeth jutted outward,
Like fangs they emerged from his jaws.
Brocade wrapped his body around,
And coiling stripes covered his spine.
They saw flesh through sparse, steely whiskers.
Keen-edged were his claws like sharp swords.
Even Huang Gong of Donghai would fear[3]
This white-browed King of Mount South.

Tripitaka was so frightened that his spirit left him, while the bones of his followers grew weak and their tendons turned numb. The Monster King shouted for them to be bound, and the various ogres tied up all three of them with ropes. They were being prepared to be eaten when a clamor was heard outside the camp. Someone came in to report: "The Bear Mountain Lord and the Steer Hermit have arrived." Hearing this, Tripitaka looked up. The first one to come in was a swarthy fellow. "How did he look?" you ask.

He seemed valiant and courageous,
With body both tough and brawny.
His great strength could ford the waters.
He prowled the woods, flaunting his power.
Ever a good omen in dreams,[4]
He showed now his forceful features.
He could break or climb the green trees,
And predicted when winter was near.
Truly he was most clever.
Hence Mountain Lord was his name.

Following behind him was another husky fellow. "How did he look?" you ask.

3. Huang Gong, a man of the Han period and a native of Donghai (in modern Jiangsu Province), was reputedly a tamer of tigers.

4. From antiquity, the dream of a bear had been interpreted by the Chinese as a sign of the imminent birth of a male child.

A cap of twin horns rugged,
And a humpback most majestic.
His green robe showed his calm nature,
He walked with a slumberous gait.
He came from a father named Bull;
His mother's name proper was Cow.
A great boon to people who plowed,
He was thus called the Steer Hermit.

The two creatures swaggered in, and the Monster King hurried out to receive them. The Bear Mountain Lord said, "You are in top form, General Yin. Congratulations! Congratulations!" "General Yin looks better than ever," said the Steer Hermit. "It's marvelous! It's marvelous!" "And you two gentlemen, how have you been these days?" asked the Monster King. "Just maintaining my idleness," said the Mountain Lord. "Just keeping up with the times," said the Hermit. After these exchanges, they sat down to chat some more.

Meanwhile, one of Tripitaka's attendants was bound so tightly that he began to moan pitifully. "How did these three get here?" asked the swarthy fellow. "They practically presented themselves at the door!" said the Monster King. "Can they be used for the guests' dinner?" asked the Hermit, laughing. "By all means!" said the Monster King. "Let's not finish them all up," said the Mountain Lord. "We'll dine on two of them and leave one over." The Monster King agreed. He called his subordinates at once to have the attendants eviscerated and their carcasses carved up; their heads, hearts, and livers were to be presented to the guests, the limbs to the host, and the remaining portions of flesh and bone to the rest of the ogres. The moment the order was given, the ogres pounced on the attendants like tigers preying on sheep: munching and crunching, they devoured them in no time at all. The priest nearly died of fear, for this, you see, was his first bitter ordeal since his departure from Chang'an.

As he was nursing his horror, light began to grow in the east. The two monsters did not retire until dawn. Saying, "We're beholden to your generous hospitality today. Permit us to repay in kind in another time," they left together. Soon the sun rose high in the sky, but Tripitaka was still in a stupor, unable to discern which way was north, south, east, or west. In that half-dead condition, he suddenly saw an old man approaching, holding a staff in his hands. Walking up to Tripitaka, the man waved his hands and all the ropes snapped. He then blew on Tripitaka, and the monk began to revive. Falling on the ground, he said, "I thank the aged father for saving the life of this poor monk!" "Get up," the old man said, returning his salute, "have you lost anything?"

"The followers of your poor monk," said Tripitaka, "have been eaten by the monsters. I have no idea where my horse is or my luggage." "Isn't that your horse over there with the two bundles?" asked the old man, pointing with his staff. Tripitaka turned around and discovered that his belongings had indeed remained untouched. Somewhat relieved, he asked the old man, "Aged father, what is this place? How do you happen to be here?" "It is called the Double-Fork Ridge, a place infested with tigers and wolves. How did you manage to get here?" "At the first crow of the cock," said Tripitaka, "your poor monk left the District of Hezhou. Little did I realize that we had risen too early, and we lost our way tramping through fog and dew. We came upon this Monster King so exceedingly ferocious that he captured me and my two followers. There was also a swarthy fellow called the Bear Mountain Lord and a husky fellow called the Steer Hermit. They arrived and addressed the Monster King as General Yin. All three of them devoured my two followers and retired only at dawn. I have no idea where I accrued the fortune and merit that caused the aged father to rescue me here."

"That Steer Hermit," said the old man, "is a wild bull spirit; the Mountain Lord, a bear spirit; and General Yin, a tiger spirit. The various ogres are all demons of mountains and trees, spirits of strange beasts and wolves. Because of the primal purity of your nature, they cannot devour you. Follow me now, and I shall lead you on your way." Tripitaka could not be more thankful. Fastening the bundles on the saddle and leading his horse, he followed the old man out of the pit and walked toward the main road. He tied the horse to the bushes beside the path and turned to thank the aged father. At that moment a gentle breeze swept by, and the old man rose into the air and left, riding on a white crane with a crimson head. As the wind subsided, a slip of paper fluttered down, with four lines of verse written on it:

> I am the Planet Venus from the West,
> Who came to save you by special request,
> Some pupils divine will come to your aid.
> Blame not the scriptures for hardships ahead.

When Tripitaka read this, he bowed toward the sky saying, "I thank the Gold Star for seeing me through this ordeal." After that, he led his horse off again on his lonely and melancholy journey. On this ridge truly you have

> Cold and soughing, the wind of the rain forest;
> Purling and gurgling, the water of the brooklets;
> Fragrant and musky, wild flowers in bloom;

In clutters and clumps, rough rocks piled high;
Chattering and clattering, the apes and the deer;
In rank and file, the musk and the fallow deer.
Chirping and cooing, birds frequently call.
Silent and still, not one man is in sight.
That master
Shivers and quivers to his anxious mind.
This dear horse,
Scared and nervous, can barely raise his legs.

Ready to abandon his body and sacrifice his life, Tripitaka started up
that rugged mountain. He journeyed for half a day, but not a single human
being or dwelling was in sight. He was gnawed by hunger and disheartened
by the rough road. In that desperate moment, he saw two fierce tigers
growling in front of him and several huge snakes circling behind him; vicious creatures appeared on his left and strange beasts on his right. As he
was all by himself, Tripitaka had little alternative but to submit himself
to the will of Heaven. As if to complete his helplessness, his horse's back
was sagging and its legs were buckling; it went to its knees and soon lay
prostrate on the ground. He could budge it neither by beating nor by
tugging. With hardly an inch of space to stand on, our Master of the Law
was in the depths of despair, thinking that certain death would be his fate.
We can tell you, however, that though he was in danger, help was on its
way. For just as he thought he was about to expire, the vicious creatures
began to scatter and the monstrous beasts fled; the fierce tigers vanished
and the huge snakes disappeared. When Tripitaka looked further ahead,
he saw a man coming over the mountain slope with a steel trident in his
hands and bow and arrows at his waist. He was indeed a valiant figure!
Look at him:

He had on his head a cap
Of leopard skin, spotted and artemisia-white;
He wore on his body a robe
Of lamb's wool with dark silk brocade.
Around his waist was tied a lion king belt,
And on his feet he wore tall boots of suede.
His eyes were staring like those of a hanged man.
With wild beard, he looked like a fierce god!
A bow and poisoned arrows hung on him.
He held a huge trident of the finest steel.
His voice like thunder appalled the mountain cats,
And wild pheasants trembled at his truculence.

When Tripitaka saw him draw near, he knelt at the side of the path and called out, his hands clasped in front of him, "Great king, save me! Great king, save me!" The fellow came up to Tripitaka and put down his trident. Raising up the monk with his hands, he said, "Don't be afraid, Elder, for I'm not a wicked man. I'm a hunter living in this mountain; my surname is Liu and my given name is Boqin. I also go by the nickname of Senior Guardian of the Mountain. I came here to find some animals to eat, not expecting to run into you. I hope I didn't scare you."

"Your poor monk," said Tripitaka, "is a cleric who has been sent by his Majesty, the Tang emperor, to seek scriptures from Buddha in the Western Heaven. When I arrived here a few moments ago, I was surrounded by tigers, wolves, and snakes, so that I could not proceed. But when the creatures saw you coming they all scattered, and you have thus saved my life. Many thanks! Many thanks!" "Since I live here and my livelihood depends on killing a few tigers and wolves," said Boqin, "or catching a few snakes and reptiles, I usually frighten the wild beasts away. If you have come from the Tang empire, you are actually a native here, for this is still Tang territory and I am a Tang subject. You and I both live off the land belonging to the king, so that we are in truth citizens of the same nation. Don't be afraid. Follow me. You may rest your horse at my place, and I shall see you off in the morning." Tripitaka was filled with delight when he heard these words, and he led his horse to follow the hunter.

They passed the slope and again heard the howling of the wind. "Sit here, Elder," said Boqin, "and don't move. The sound of that wind tells me that a mountain cat is approaching. I'll take him home so that I can make you a meal of him." When Tripitaka heard this, his heart hammered and his gall quivered and he became rooted to the ground. Grasping his trident, that Guardian strode forward and came face to face with a great striped tiger. Seeing Boqin, he turned and fled. Like a crack of thunder, the Guardian bellowed, "Cursed beast! Where will you flee?" When the tiger saw him pressing near, he turned with flailing claws to spring at him, only to be met by the Guardian with uplifted trident. Tripitaka was so terrified that he lay paralyzed on the grass. Since leaving his mother's belly, when had he ever witnessed such violent and dangerous goings-on? The Guardian went after that tiger to the foot of the slope, and it was a magnificent battle between man and beast. You see

Raging resentment,
And churning whirlwind.
In raging resentment
The mighty Guardian's hair pushed up his cap;

Like churning whirlwind
The striped prince belched dust, displaying his strength.
This one bared its teeth and wielded its paws;
That one stepped sideways, yet turning to fight.
The trident reached skyward, reflecting the sun.
The striped tail stirred up both fog and cloud.
This one stabbed madly at the breast of his foe;
That one, facing him would swallow him whole.
Stay away and you may live out your years.
Join the fray and you'll meet Yama, the king!
You hear the roar of the striped prince
And the harsh cries of the Guardian.
The roar of the striped prince
Shook mountains and streams to terrify birds and beasts;
The harsh cries of the Guardian
Unlocked the Heavens to make the stars appear.
The gold eyeballs of this one protruded,
And wrath burst from the bold heart of that one.
Lovable was Liu the Mountain Guardian;
Praiseworthy was this king of the wild beasts.
So tiger and man fought, each craving life—
A little slower, and one forfeits his soul!

The two of them fought for about an hour, and as the paws of the tiger began to slow and his torso to slacken, he was downed by the Guardian's trident stabbing him through the chest. A pitiful sight it was! The points of the trident pierced the heart, and at once the ground was covered with blood. The Guardian then dragged the beast by the ear up the road. What a man! He hardly panted, nor did his face change color. He said to Tripitaka, "We're lucky! We're lucky! This mountain cat should be sufficient for a day's food for the elder." Applauding him unceasingly, Tripitaka said, "The Guardian is truly a mountain god!" "What ability do I have," said Boqin, "that I merit such acclaim? This is really the good fortune of the father. Let's go. I'd like to skin him quickly so that I can cook some of his meat to entertain you." He held the trident in one hand and dragged the tiger with the other, leading the way while Tripitaka followed him with his horse. They walked together past the slope and all at once came upon a mountain village, in front of which

Old trees soared skyward,
And roads were filled with wild creepers.
In countless canyons the wind was cool;

On many ridges were strange sounds and sights.
One path's wild blooms, whose scent clung to one's body;
A few poles of bamboo and what memorable green!
The portal of grass,
The wattle-fenced yard—
A picture to paint or sketch.
The stone-slab bridge,
The white-earth walls—
How charming indeed, and rare!
Now in the wistful face of autumn,
The air was cool and brisk,
By the wayside yellow leaves fell;
Over the peaks the white clouds drifted.
In thinly-grown woods the wild fowls twittered,
And young dogs yelped outside the village gate.

When Boqin reached the door of his house, he threw down the dead tiger and called, "Little ones, where are you?" Out came three or four houseboys, all rather unattractive and mean-looking, who hauled the tiger inside. Boqin told them to skin it quickly and prepare it for the guest. He then turned around to welcome Tripitaka into his dwelling, and as they greeted each other, Tripitaka thanked him again for the great favor of saving his life. "We are fellow countrymen," said Boqin, "and there's little need for you to thank me." After they had sat down and drunk tea, an old woman with someone who appeared to be her daughter-in-law came out to greet Tripitaka. "This is my mother, and this my wife," said Boqin. "Pray ask your parent to take the honored seat," said Tripitaka, "and let your poor monk pay his respects." "Father is a guest coming from great distance," said the old woman. "Please relax and don't stand on ceremony." "Mother," said Boqin, "he has been sent by the Tang emperor to seek scriptures from Buddha in the Western Heaven. He met your son just now at the ridge. Since we are fellow countrymen, I invited him to the house to rest his horse. Tomorrow I shall see him on his way." When she heard these words, the old woman was very pleased. "Good! Good! Good!" she said. "The timing couldn't be better, even if we had planned to invite him. For tomorrow happens to be the anniversary of your late father's death. Let us invite the elder to perform some good deeds and recite an appropriate passage of scripture. We shall see him off day after tomorrow." Although he was a tiger slayer, a so-called "Guardian of the Mountain," our Liu Boqin had a good deal of filial feeling for his mother. When he heard what she said, he immediately wanted to prepare the incense and the paper money, so that Tripitaka might be asked to stay.

As they talked, the sky began to darken. The servants brought chairs and a table and set out several dishes of well-cooked tiger meat, steaming hot. Boqin invited Tripitaka to begin, telling him that rice would follow. "O dear!" said Tripitaka, his hands folded. "To tell you the truth, I have been a monk since leaving my mother's womb, and I have never eaten any meat." Hearing this, Boqin reflected a while. He then said, "Elder, for generations this humble family has never kept a vegetarian diet. We could, I suppose, find some bamboo shoots and wood ears and prepare some dried vegetables and bean cakes, but they would all be cooked with the fat of deer or tigers. Even our pots and pans are grease-soaked! What am I to do? I must ask the elder's pardon." "Don't fret," said Tripitaka. "Enjoy the food yourself. Even if I were not to eat for three or four days, I could bear the hunger. But I dare not break the dietary commandment." "Suppose you starve to death," said Boqin, "what then?" "I am indebted to the Heavenly kindness of the Guardian," said Tripitaka, "for saving me from the packs of tigers and wolves. Starving to death is better than being food for a tiger."

When Boqin's mother heard this, she cried, "Son, stop such idle talk with the elder. Let me prepare a vegetarian dish to serve him." "Where would you get such a dish?" said Boqin. "Never mind. I'll fix it," said his mother. She asked her daughter-in-law to take down a small cooking pan and heat it until much of the grease had burned off. They washed and scrubbed the pan again and again and then put it back on the stove and boiled some water in it. Taking some elm leaves from the mountain, they made soup with it, after which they cooked some rice with yellow millet mixed with Indian corn. They also prepared two bowls of dried vegetables and brought it all out to the table. "Elder," the aged mother said to Tripitaka, "please have some. This is the cleanest and purest food that my daughter-in-law and I have ever prepared." Tripitaka left his seat to thank her before sitting down again. Boqin removed himself to another place; dishes and bowls full of unsauced and unsalted tiger meat, musk-deer meat, serpent meat, fox flesh, rabbit, and strips of cured venison were set before him. To keep Tripitaka company, he sat down and was about to pick up his chopsticks when he saw Tripitaka fold his hands and begin to recite something. Startled, Boqin dared not touch his chopsticks; he jumped up instead and stood to one side. Having uttered no more than a few phrases, Tripitaka said to him, "Please eat." "You are a priest who likes to recite short scriptures," said Boqin. "That was not scripture," said Tripitaka, "only a prayer to be said before meals." "You people who leave your families," said Boqin, "are particular about everything! Even for a meal you have to mumble something!"

They ate their dinner and the dishes and bowls were taken away. Evening was setting in when Boqin led Tripitaka out of the main hall to go for a walk at the back of the dwelling. They passed through a corridor and arrived at a straw shed. Pushing open the door, they walked inside, where they found several heavy bows and some quivers of arrows hanging on the walls. Two pieces of tiger skin, stinking and blood-stained, were draped across the cross beams, and a number of spears, knives, tridents, and rods were stuck into the ground at one corner. There were two seats in the middle of the shed, and Boqin invited Tripitaka to sit for a moment. Seeing that the place was so gruesome and putrid, Tripitaka dared not linger. They soon left the shed and walked further back to a huge garden, where there seemed to be no end of thick clumps of chrysanthemum piling their gold and stands of maple hoisting their crimson. With a loud rustle, more than a dozen fat deer and a large herd of musk deer jumped out. Calm and mild-mannered, they were not at all frightened at the sight of human beings. Tripitaka said, "You must have tamed these animals." "Like the people in your city of Chang'an," said Boqin, "where the affluent store up wealth and treasures and the landlords gather rice and grain, so we hunters must keep some of these wild beasts to prepare against dark days. That's all!" As they walked and conversed, it grew dark, and they returned to the house to rest.

As soon as the members of the family, young and old, arose next morning, they went to prepare vegetarian food to serve to the priest, who was then asked to begin his recitations. Having first washed his hands, the priest went to the ancestral hall with the Guardian to burn incense. Only after he had bowed to the house shrine did Tripitaka beat on his wooden fish and recite first the true sentences for the purification of the mouth, and then the divine formula for the purification of mind and body. He went on to the *Sūtra for the Salvation of the Dead*, after which Boqin requested him to compose in writing a specific prayer for the deliverance of the deceased. He then took up the *Diamond Sūtra* and the *Guanyin Sūtra*, each of which was given a loud and clear recitation. After lunch, he recited several sections from the *Lotus Sūtra* and the *Amitāyus Sūtra*, before finishing with the *Peacock Sūtra* and a brief recounting of the story of Buddha healing a bhikṣu.[5] Soon it was evening again. All kinds of incense were burned together with the various paper horses, images of the deities, and the prayer for the deliverance of the deceased. The Buddhist service was thus completed, and each person retired.

5. A mendicant monk.

We shall now tell you about the soul of Boqin's father, verily a ghost redeemed from perdition, who came to his own house and appeared to all the members of his family in a dream. "It was difficult," he said, "for me to escape my bitter ordeals in the Region of Darkness, and for a long time I could not attain salvation. Fortunately, the holy monk's recitations have now expiated my sins. King Yama has ordered someone to send me to the rich land of China, where I may ssume my next incarnation in a noble family. All of you, therefore, must take care to thank the elder, and see that you are not negligent in any way. Now I leave you." So it is that

There is, in all things, a solemn purpose:
To save the dead from perdition and pain.

When the whole family awoke from the dream, the sun was already rising in the east. The wife of Boqin said, "Guardian, I dreamed last night that father came to the house. He said that it was difficult for him to escape his bitter ordeals in the Region of Darkness, and that for a long time he could not attain salvation. Fortunately, the holy monk's recitations have now expiated his sins, and King Yama has ordered someone to send him to the rich land of China where he may assume his next incarnation in a noble family. He told us to take care to thank the elder and not be negligent in any way. After he had finished speaking, he drifted away, despite my plea for him to stay. I woke up and it was all a dream!" "I had a dream also," said Boqin, "one exactly like yours! Let's get up and talk to mother about this." The two of them were about to do so when they heard the old mother calling, "Boqin, come here. I want to talk to you." They went in and found the mother sitting up in bed. "Son," she said, "I had a happy dream last night. I dreamed that your father came to the house saying that, thanks to the redemptive work of the elder, his sins had been expiated. He is on his way to the rich land of China, where he will assume his next incarnation in a noble family." Husband and wife laughed uproariously. Boqin said, "Your daughter-in-law and I both had this dream, and we were just coming to tell you. Little did we expect that mother's call also had to do with this dream." They therefore called on every member of the family to express their gratitude and prepare the monk's horse for travel. They came bowing before the priest and said, "We thank the elder for providing life and deliverance for our deceased father, for which we can never repay you sufficiently." "What has this poor monk accomplished," said Tripitaka, "that merits such gratitude?"

Boqin gave a thorough account of the dream that the three of them had had, and Tripitaka was also very pleased. A vegetarian meal was again served, and a tael of silver was presented as a token of their gratitude.

Tripitaka refused to accept so much as a penny, though the whole family begged him earnestly. He only said, "If, in compassion, you can escort me on the first part of my way, I shall ever be grateful for such kindness." Boqin and his mother and wife had little alternative but hastily to prepare some biscuits from unrefined flour, which Tripitaka was glad to accept. Boqin was told to escort him as far as possible. Obeying his mother's bidding, the Guardian also ordered several houseboys to join them, each bringing hunting equipment and weapons. They walked to the main road, and there seemed to be no end to the scenic splendor of the mountains and peaks.

When they had traveled for half a day, they came upon a huge mountain so tall and rugged that it truly seemed to touch the blue sky. In a little while the whole company reached the foot of the mountain, and the Guardian began to ascend it as if he were walking on level ground. Halfway up, Boqin turned around and stood still at the side of the road, saying, "Elder, please go on yourself. I must now take leave of you and turn back." When Tripitaka heard these words, he rolled down from his saddle and said, "I beg you to escort me a little further." "You do not realize, Elder," said Boqin, "that this mountain is called the Mountain of Two Frontiers; the eastern half belongs to our Great Tang domain, but the western half is the territory of the Tartars. The tigers and wolves over there are not my subjects, nor should I cross the border. You must proceed by yourself." Tripitaka became fearful; he stretched out his hands and clutched at the sleeves of the hunter, tears pouring from his eyes. It was at this tender moment of farewell that there came from beneath the mountain a thunderous voice crying, "My master has come! My master has come!" Tripitaka was dumbfounded, and Boqin trembled. We do not know who was crying; let's listen to the explanation in the next chapter.

FOURTEEN

Mind Monkey returns to the Right;
The Six Robbers vanish from sight.[1]

Mind is the Buddha and the Buddha is Mind;
Both Mind and Buddha are important things.
If you perceive there's neither Mind nor Thing,
Yours is the dharmakāya of True Mind.
The dharmakāya
Has no shape or form:
One pearl-like radiance holding myriad things.
The bodiless body is the body true;
And real form is that form which has no form.
There's no form, no void, no no-emptiness;
No coming, no leaving, no pariṇāmanā;[2]
No contrast, no sameness, no being or nonbeing:
No giving, no taking, no hopeful craving.
Light efficacious is in and out the same.
Buddha's whole realm is in a grain of sand.
A grain of sand the chiliocosm holds;
One mind or body's like ten thousand things.
To know this you must grasp the No-mind Spell;
Unclogged and taintless is the karma pure.
Do not the many acts of good or ill:
This is true submission to Śākyamuni.

We were telling you about Tripitaka and Boqin, who, in fear and alarm, again heard the cry: "My Master has come!" The various houseboys said, "It must be the old ape in that stone box beneath the mountain who is

1. The six robbers or *cauras* refer to the six senses of the body, which impede enlightenment: hence they appear in this chapter's allegory as bandits.
2. The term literally means to turn toward. It also refers to the bestowal of merit by one being on another.

shouting." "It's he! It's he!" said the Guardian. Tripitaka asked, "Who is this old ape?" "The ancient name of this mountain," said the Guardian, "was the Mountain of Five Phases. It was changed to the Mountain of the Two Frontiers as a result of our Great Tang ruler's western campaigns to secure his empire. A few years ago, I heard from my elders that during the time when Wang Mang usurped the throne of the Ham emperor, this mountain fell from Heaven with a divine monkey clamped beneath it. He feared neither heat nor cold, and he took neither food nor drink. He had been watched and guarded by the spirits of the Earth, who fed him iron balls when he was hungry and juices of bronze when he was thirsty. He has lasted from that time until now, surviving both cold and hunger. He must be the one who is making all this noise. Don't be afraid, Elder. Let's go down the mountain to take a look."

Tripitaka had to agree and led his horse down the mountain. They had traveled only a few miles when they came upon a stone box in which there was indeed a monkey who, with his head sticking out, was waving his hands wildly and crying, "Master, why have you taken so long to get here? Welcome! Welcome! Get me out, and I'll protect you on your way to the Western Heaven!" The priest went forward to look more closely at him. "How does he look?" you ask.

A pointed mouth and hollow cheeks;
Two diamond pupils and fiery eyes.
Lichens had piled on his head;
Wisteria grew in his ears.
At his temples there was more green grass than hair;
Beneath his chin, moss instead of a beard.
With mud on his brow,
And earth in his nose,
He looked most desperate!
His fingers coarse
And calloused palms
Were caked in filth and dirt!
Luckily, his eyes could still roll about,
And the apish tongue, articulate.
Though in speech he had great ease,
His body he could not move.
He was the Great Sage Sun of five hundred years ago.
Today his ordeal ends, he leaves the net of Heaven.

Undeniably a courageous person, that Guardian Liu went up to the creature and pulled away some of the grass at his temples and some of the moss beneath his chin. He asked, "What do you have to say?" "Nothing to you," said the monkey, "but ask that master to come up here. I have a question for him." "What's your question?" asked Tripitaka. "Are you someone sent by the great king of the Land of the East to go seek scriptures in the Western Heaven?" asked the monkey. "I am," said Tripitaka. "Why do you ask?" "I am the Great Sage, Equal to Heaven," said the monkey, "who greatly disturbed the Heavenly Palace five hundred years ago. Because of my sin of rebellion and disobedience, I was imprisoned here by the Buddha. Some time ago, a certain Bodhisattva Guanyin had received the decree of Buddha to go to the Land of the East in quest of a scripture pilgrim. I asked her to give me some help, and she persuaded me not to engage again in violence. I was told to believe in the Law of Buddha and faithfully to protect the scripture pilgrim on his way to worship Buddha in the West, for there would be a goodly reward reserved for me when such merit is achieved. I have therefore been maintaining my vigilance night and day, waiting for the Master to come to rescue me. I'm willing to protect you in your quest of scriptures and become your disciple."

When Tripitaka heard these words, he was filled with delight and said, "Though you have this good intention, because of the Bodhisattva's instruction, of entering our Buddhist fold, I have neither ax nor drill. How can I free you?" "No need for ax or drill," said the monkey. "If you are willing to rescue me, I'll be able to get out." Tripitaka said, "I'm willing, but how can you get out?" "On top of this mountain," said the monkey, "there is a tag stamped with the golden letters of our Buddha Tathāgata. Go up there and lift up the tag. Then I'll come out." Tripitaka agreed, and turned to Boqin, imploring him, "Guardian, come with me up the mountain." "Do you think he's speaking the truth?" asked Boqin. "It's the truth!" the monkey shouted. "I dare not lie!"

Boqin had no choice but to call his houseboys to lead the horses. He himself supported Tripitaka with his hands, and they again started up the tall mountain. Tugging at creepers and vines, they finally arrived at the highest peak, where they beheld ten thousand shafts of golden light and a thousand folds of hallowed air. There was a huge square slab of stone, on which was taped a seal with the golden letters, *Oṁ maṇi padme hūṁ*. Tripitaka approached the stone and knelt down; he looked at the golden letters and kowtowed several times to the stone. Then, facing the West, he prayed: "Your disciple, Chen Xuanzang, was specifically commanded to seek scriptures from you. If it is so ordained that he should be my disciple, let me lift up those golden letters so that the divine monkey may find release and join me at the Spirit Mountain. If he is not predestined to be my disciple, if he is only a cruel monster trying to deceive me and to bring misfortune to our enterprise, let me not lift up this tape." He kowtowed again after he had prayed. Going forward, with the greatest of ease he took down the golden letters. A fragrant wind swept by immediately and blew the tag out of his hands into the air as a voice called out, "I am the prison guard of the Great Sage. Today his ordeal is completed, and my colleagues and I are returning this seal to Tathāgata." Tripitaka, Boqin, and their followers were so terrified that they fell on the ground and bowed toward the sky. They then descended from the tall mountain and came back to the stone box, saying to the monkey, "The tag has been lifted. You may come out." Delighted, the monkey said, "Master, you had better walk away from here so that I can come out. I don't want to frighten you."

When Boqin heard this, he led Tripitaka and the rest of the company to walk back eastward for five or six miles. Again they heard the monkey yelling, "Further still! Further still!" So Tripitaka and the others went still further until they had left the mountain. All at once came a crash so loud that it was as if the mountain was cracking and the earth splitting wide open; everyone was awe-struck. The next moment the monkey was already in front of Tripitaka's horse; completely naked, he knelt down and cried, "Master, I'm out!" He bowed four times toward Tripitaka, and then, jumping up, he said to Boqin respectfully, "I thank Elder Brother for taking the trouble of escorting my master. I'm grateful also for your shaving the grass from my face." Having thanked him, he went at once to put the luggage in order so that it could be tied onto the horse's back. When the horse saw him, its torso slackened and its legs stiffened. In fear and trembling, it could hardly stand up. For you see, that monkey had been a Bimawen, who used to look after dragon horses in the celestial stables. His authority was such that horses of Earth inevitably would fear him when they saw him.

When Tripitaka saw that the monkey was truly a person of good intentions, someone who truly resembled those who had embraced the Buddhist faith, he called to him, "Disciple, what is your surname?" "My surname is Sun," said the Monkey King. "Let me give you a religious name," said Tripitaka, "so that it will be convenient to address you." "This noble thought of the master is deeply appreciated," said the Monkey King, "but I already have a religious name. I'm called Sun Wukong." "It exactly fits the emphasis of our denomination," said Tripitaka, delighted. "But look at you, you look rather like a little *dhūta*.[3] Let me give you a nickname and

---

3. Literally, the word means shaken, shaken off, or cleansed. It points to the practice of asceticism as an antidote to worldly attachments. Hence it is also used in the Chinese vernacular as a name for any mendicant.

call you Pilgrim Sun.⁴ How's that?" "Good! Good!" said Wukong. So from then on, he was also called Pilgrim Sun.

When Boqin saw that Pilgrim Sun was definitely preparing to leave, he turned to speak respectfully to Tripitaka, saying, "Elder, you are fortunate to have made an excellent disciple here. Congratulations! This person should be most fit to accompany you. I must take leave of you now." Bowing to thank him, Tripitaka said, "I cannot thank you enough for all your kindness. Please be certain to thank your dear mother and wife when you return to your house. I have caused you all great inconvenience, and I shall thank you again on my way back." Boqin returned his salutation, and they parted.

We shall now tell you about Pilgrim Sun, who asked Tripitaka to mount his horse. He himself, stark naked, carried the luggage on his back and led the way. In a little while, as they were passing the Mountain of Two Frontiers, they saw a fierce tiger approaching, growling and waving its tail. Tripitaka, sitting on his horse, became alarmed, but Pilgrim, walking at the side of the road, was delighted. "Don't be afraid, Master," he said, "for he's here to present me with some clothes." He put down the luggage and took a tiny needle out of his ears. One wave of it facing the wind, and it became an iron rod with the thickness of a rice bowl. He held it in his hands and laughed, saying, "I haven't used this treasure for over five hundred years! Today I'm taking it out to bag a little garment for myself." Look at him! He strode right up to the tiger, crying, "Cursed beast! Where do you think you're going?" Crouching low, the tiger lay prone on the dust and dared not move. Pilgrim Sun aimed the rod at its head, and one stroke caused its brain to burst out like ten thousand red petals of peach blossoms, and the teeth to fly out like so many pieces of white jade. So terrified was our Chen Xuanzang that he fell off his horse. "O God! O God!" he cried, biting his fingers. "When Guardian Liu overcame that striped tiger the other day, he had to do battle with him for almost half a day. But without even fighting today, Sun Wukong reduces the tiger to pulp with one blow of his rod. How true is the saying, 'For the strong, there's always someone stronger'!"

"Master," said Pilgrim as he returned dragging the tiger, "sit down for a while, and wait till I have stripped him of his clothes. When I put them on, we'll start off again." "Where does he have any clothes?" said Tripitaka. "Don't mind me, Master," said Pilgrim, "I have my own plan." Dear Monkey King! He pulled off one strand of hair and blew a mouthful of

4. Literally, the Chinese term *xingzhe* means a novice who practices austerities or asceticism, and also a mendicant.

magic breath onto it, crying, "Change!" It changed into a sharp, curved knife, with which he ripped open the tiger's chest. Slitting the skin straight down, he then ripped it off in one piece. He chopped away the paws and the head, cutting the skin into one square piece. He picked it up and tried it for size, and then said, "It's a bit too large; one piece can be made into two." He took the knife and cut it again into two pieces; he put one of these away and wrapped the other around his waist. Ripping off a strand of rattan from the side of the road, he firmly tied on this covering for the lower part of his body. "Master," he said, "let's go! Let's go! When we reach someone's house, we will have sufficient time to borrow some threads and a needle to sew this up." He gave his iron rod a squeeze and it changed back into a tiny needle, which he stored in his ear. Throwing the luggage on his back, he asked his Master to mount the horse.

As they set off, the monk asked him, "Wukong, how is it that the iron rod you used to slay the tiger has disappeared?" "Master," said Pilgrim laughing, "you have no idea what that rod of mine really is. It was acquired originally from the Dragon Palace in the Eastern Ocean. It's called the Precious Divine Iron for Guarding the Heavenly River, and another name of it is the Compliant Golden-Hooped Rod. At the time when I revolted against Heaven, I depended on it a great deal; for it could change into any shape or form, great or small, according to my wish. Just now I had it changed into a tiny embroidery needle, and it's stored that way in my ear. When I need it, I'll take it out." Secretly pleased by what he heard, Tripitaka asked again: "Why did that tiger become completely motionless when it saw you? How do you explain the fact that it simply let you hit it?" "To tell you the truth," said Wukong, "even a dragon, let alone this tiger, would behave itself if it saw me! I, old Monkey, possess the ability to subdue dragons and tame tigers, and the power to overturn rivers and stir up oceans. I can look at a person's countenance and discern his character; I can listen merely to sounds and discover the truth. If I want to be big, I can fill the universe; if I want to be small, I can be smaller than a piece of hair. In sum, I have boundless ways of transformation and incalculable means of becoming visible or invisible. What's so strange, then, about my skinning a tiger? Wait till we come to some real difficulties—you'll see my talents then!" When Tripitaka heard these words, he was more relieved than ever and urged his horse forward. So master and disciple, the two of them, chatted as they journeyed, and soon the sun sank in the west. You see

Soft glow of the fading twilight,
And distant clouds slowly returning.
On every hill swells the chorus of birds;

In flocks they seek shelter in the woods.
Wild beasts in couples and pairs,
In packs and groups they trek homeward.
The new moon, hooklike, breaks the spreading gloom
With ten thousand stars luminous.

Pilgrim said, "Master, let's move along, for it's getting late. There are dense clumps of trees over there, and I suppose there must be a house or village too. Let's hurry over there and ask for lodging." Urging his horse forward, Tripitaka went straight up to a house and dismounted. Pilgrim threw down the bag and went to the door, crying, "Open up! Open up!" An old man came to the door, leaning on a cane. When he pulled open the creaking door, he was panic-stricken by the hideous appearance of Pilgrim, who had the tiger skin around his waist and looked like a thunder god. He began to shout, "A ghost! A ghost!" and other such foolish words. Tripitaka drew near and took hold of him, saying, "Old Patron, don't be afraid. He is my disciple, not a ghost." Only when he looked up and saw the handsome features of Tripitaka did the old man stand still. "Which temple are you from," he asked, "and why are you bringing such a nasty character to my door?" "I am a poor monk from the Tang court," said Tripitaka, "on my way to seek scriptures from Buddha in the Western Heaven. We were passing through here and it was getting late; that is why we made so bold as to approach your great mansion and beg you for a night's lodging. We plan to leave tomorrow before it's light, and we beseech you not to deny our request."

"Though you may be a Tang man," the old man said, "that nasty character is certainly no Tang man!" "Old fellow!" cried Wukong in a loud voice, "you really can't see, can you? The Tang man is my master, and I am his disciple. Of course, I'm no sugar man[5] or honey man! I am the Great Sage, Equal to Heaven! The members of your family should recognize me. Moreover, I have seen you before."

"Where have you seen me before?" "When you were young," said Wukong, "didn't you gather firewood before my eyes? Didn't you haul vegetables before my face?" The old man said, "That's nonsense! Where did you live? And where was I, that I should have gathered firewood and hauled vegetables before your eyes?" "Only my son would talk nonsense!" said Wukong. "You really don't recognize me! Take a closer look! I am the Great Sage in the stone box of this Mountain of Two Frontiers." "You do look somewhat like him," said the old man, half recognizing the figure be-

5. A pun: sugar in Chinese is also expressed by the phoneme *tang*.

fore him, "but how did you get out?" Wukong thereupon gave a thorough account of how the Bodhisattva had converted him and how she had asked him to wait for the Tang monk to lift the tag for his deliverance.

After that, the old man bowed deeply and invited Tripitaka in, calling for his aged wife and his children to come out and meet the guests. When he told them what had happened, everyone was delighted. Tea was then served, after which the old man asked Wukong, "How old are you, Great Sage?" "And how old are you?" said Wukong. "I have lived foolishly for a hundred and thirty years!" said the old man. "You are still my great-great-great-great-grandson!" said Pilgrim. "I can't remember when I was born, but I have spent over five hundred years underneath this mountain." "Yes, yes," said the old man. "I remember my great-grandfather saying that when this mountain dropped from the sky, it had a divine ape clamped underneath it. To think that you should have waited until now for your freedom! When I saw you in my childhood, you had grass on your head and mud on your face, but I wasn't afraid of you then. Now without mud on your face and grass on your head, you seem a bit thinner. And with that huge piece of tiger skin draped around your waist, what great difference is there between you and a demon?"

When the members of his family heard this remark, they all roared with laughter. Being a rather decent fellow, that old man at once ordered a vegetarian meal to be prepared. Afterwards Wukong said, "What is your family name?" "Our humble family," said the old man, "goes by the name of Chen." When Tripitaka heard this, he left his seat to salute him, saying, "Old Patron, you and I share the same illustrious ancestors." "Master," said Pilgrim, "your surname is Tang. How can it be that you and he share the same illustrious ancestors?" Tripitaka said, "The surname of my secular family is also Chen, and I come from the Juxian Village, in the Hongnong District of Haizhou in the Tang domain. My religious name is Chen Xuan-zang. Because our Great Tang Emperor Taizong made me his brother by decree, I took the name Tripitaka and used Tang as my surname. Hence I'm called the Tang monk." The old man was very pleased to hear that they had the same surname.

"Old Chen," said Pilgrim, "I must trouble your family some more, for I haven't taken a bath for five hundred years! Please go and boil some water so that my master and I, his disciple, can wash ourselves. We shall thank you all the more when we leave." The old man at once gave the order for water to be boiled and basins to be brought in with several lamps. As master and disciple sat before the lamps after their baths, Pilgrim said, "Old Chen, I still have one more favor to ask of you. Can you lend me a needle and some thread?" "Of course, of course," said the old man. One of the amahs was told to fetch the needle and thread, which were then handed over to Pilgrim. Pilgrim, you see, had the keenest sight; he noticed that Tripitaka had taken off a shirt made of white cloth and had not put it on again after his bath. Pilgrim grabbed it and put it on himself. Taking off his tiger skin, he sewed the hems together using a "horse-face fold"[6] and fastened it round his waist again with the strand of rattan. He paraded in front of his master saying, "How does old Monkey look today compared with the way he looked yesterday?" "Very good," said Tripitaka, "very good! Now you do look like a pilgrim! If you don't think that the shirt is too worn or old, you may keep it." "Thanks for the gift!" said Wukong respectfully. He then went out to find some hay to feed the horse, after which master and disciple both retired with the old man and his household.

Next morning Wukong arose and woke up his master to get ready for the journey. Tripitaka dressed himself while Wukong put their luggage in order. They were about to leave when the old man brought in washing water and some vegetarian food, and so they did not set out until after the meal. Tripitaka rode his horse with Pilgrim leading the way; they journeyed by day and rested by night, taking food and drink according to their needs. Soon it was early winter. You see

Frost-blighted maples and the wizened trees;
Few verdant pine and cypress still on the ridge.
Budding plum blossoms spread their gentle scent.
The brief, warm day—
A Little Spring gift![7]
But dying lilies yield to the lush wild tea.
A cold bridge struggles against an old tree's bough,
And gurgling water flows in the winding brook.
Gray clouds, snow-laden, float throughout the sky.
The strong, cold wind
Tears at the sleeve!
How does one bear this chilly might of night?

Master and disciple had traveled for some time when suddenly six men jumped out from the side of the road with much clamor, all holding long spears and short swords, sharp blades and strong bows. "Stop, monk!" they cried. "Leave your horse and drop your bag at once, and we'll let

6. A colloquialism in the southern dialects which refers to the making of a folded lining. The term is still used in Cantonese.

7. The tenth month of the lunar year is often referred to as Little Spring.

you pass on alive!" Tripitaka was so terrified that his soul left him and his spirit fled; he fell from his horse, unable to utter a word. But Pilgrim lifted him up, saying, "Don't be alarmed, Master. It's nothing really, just some people coming to give us clothes and a travel allowance!" "Wukong," said Tripitaka, "you must be a little hard of hearing! They told us to leave our bag and our horse, and you want to ask them for clothes and a travel allowance?" "You just stay here and watch our belongings," said Pilgrim, "and let old Monkey confront them. We'll see what happens." Tripitaka said, "Even a good punch is no match for a pair of fists, and two fists can't cope with four hands! There are six big fellows over there, and you are such a tiny person. How can you have the nerve to confront them?"

As he always had been audacious, Pilgrim did not wait for further discussion. He walked forward with arms folded and saluted the six men, saying, "Sirs, for what reason are you blocking the path of this poor monk?" "We are kings of the highway," said the men, "philanthropic mountain lords. Our fame has long been known, though you seem to be ignorant of it. Leave your belongings at once, and you will be allowed to pass. If you but utter half a no, you'll be chopped to pieces!" "I have been also a great hereditary king and a mountain lord for centuries," said Pilgrim, "but I have yet to learn of your illustrious names." "So you really don't know!" one of them said. "Let's tell you then: one of us is named Eye That Sees and Delights; another, Ear That Hears and Rages; another Nose That Smells and Loves; another, Tongue That Tastes and Desires; another, Mind That Perceives and Covets; and another, Body That Bears and Suffers." "You are nothing but six hairy brigands," said Wukong laughing, "who have failed to recognize in me a person who has left the family, your proper master. How dare you bar my way? Bring out the treasures you have stolen so that you and I can divide them into seven portions. I'll spare you then!" Hearing this, the robbers all reacted with rage and amusement, covetousness and fear, desire and anxiety. They rushed forward crying, "You reckless monk! You haven't a thing to offer us, and yet you want us to share our loot with you!" Wielding spears and swords, they surrounded Pilgrim and hacked away at his head seventy or eighty times. Pilgrim stood in their midst and behaved as if nothing were happening.

"What a monk!" said one of the robbers. "He really does have a hard head!" "Passably so!" said Pilgrim laughing. "But your hands must be getting tired from all that exercise; it's about time for old Monkey to take out his needle for a little entertainment." "This monk must be an acupuncture man in disguise," said the robber. "We're not sick! What's all this about using a needle?" Pilgrim reached into his ear and took out a tiny embroidery needle; one wave of it in the wind and it became an iron rod with the thickness of a rice bowl. He held it in his hands, saying, "Don't run! Let old Monkey try his hand on you with this rod!" The six robbers fled in all directions, but with great strides he caught up with them and rounded all of them up. He beat every one of them to death, stripped them of their clothes, and seized their valuables. Then Pilgrim came back smiling broadly and said, "You may proceed now, Master. Those robbers have been exterminated by old Monkey." △

"That's a terrible thing you have done!" said Tripitaka. "They may have been strong men on the highway, but they would not have been sentenced to death even if they had been caught and tried. If you have such abilities, you should have chased them away. Why did you slay them all? How can you be a monk when you take life without cause? We who have left the family should

Keep ants out of harm's way when we sweep the floor,
And put shades on lamps for the love of moths.

How can you kill them just like that, without regard for black or white? You showed no mercy at all! It's a good thing that we are here in the mountains, where any further investigation will be unlikely. But suppose someone offends you when we reach a city and you act with violence again, hitting people indiscriminately with that rod of yours, would I be able to remain innocent and get away scot-free?"

"Master," said Wukong, "if I hadn't killed them, they would have killed you!" Tripitaka said, "As a priest, I would rather die than practice violence. If I were killed, there would be only one of me, but you slaughtered six persons. How can you justify that? If this matter were brought before a judge, and even if your old man were the judge, you certainly would not be able to justify your action." "To tell you the truth, Master," said Pilgrim, "when I, old Monkey, was king on the Flower-Fruit Mountain five hundred years ago, I killed I don't know how many people. I would not have been a Great Sage, Equal to Heaven, if I had lived by what you are saying." "It's precisely because you had neither scruples nor self-control," said Tripitaka, "unleashing your waywardness on Earth and perpetrating outrage in Heaven, that you had to undergo this ordeal of five hundred years. Now that you have entered the fold of Buddhism, if you still insist on practicing violence and indulge in the taking of life as before, you are not worthy to be a monk, nor can you go to the Western Heaven. You're wicked! You're just too wicked!"

Now this monkey had never in all his life been able to tolerate scolding. When he heard Tripitaka's persistent reprimand, he could not suppress the flames leaping up in his heart. "If that's what you think," he said, "if you think I'm not worthy to be a monk, nor can I go to the Western Heaven, you needn't bother me further with your nagging! I'll leave and go back!" Before Tripitaka had time to reply, Pilgrim was already so enraged that he leaped into the air, crying only, "Old Monkey's off!" Tripitaka quickly raised his head to look, but the monkey had already disappeared, trailed only by a swishing sound fast-fading toward the East. Left by himself, the priest could only shake his head and sigh, "That fellow! He's so unwilling to be taught! I only said a few words to him. How could he vanish without a trace and go back just like that? Well! Well! Well! It must be also that I am destined not to have a disciple or any other companion, for now I couldn't even call him or locate him if I wanted to. I might as well go on by myself!" So, he was prepared to

> Lay down his life and go toward the West,
> To be his own master and on none rely.

The priest had little alternative but to pack up his bag and put it on the horse, which he did not even bother to mount. Holding his staff in one hand and the reins in the other, he set off sadly toward the West. He had not traveled far when he saw an old woman before him on the mountain road, holding a silk garment and a cap with a floral design. When Tripitaka saw her approach, he hastened to pull his horse aside for her to pass. "Elder, where do you come from," asked the old woman, "and why are you walking here all by yourself?" Tripitaka said, "Your child was sent by the Great King of the Land of the East to seek true scriptures from the living Buddha in the Western Heaven." "The Buddha of the West," said the old woman, "lives in the Great Temple of Thunderclap in the territory of India, and the journey there is a hundred and eight thousand miles long. You are all by yourself, with neither a companion nor a disciple. How can you possibly think of going there?" "A few days ago," said Tripitaka, "I did pick up a disciple, a rather unruly and headstrong character. I scolded him a little, but he refused to be taught, and disappeared." The old woman said, "I have here a silk shirt and a flower cap inlaid with gold, which used to belong to my son. He had been a monk for only three days when unfortunately he died. I have just finished mourning him at the temple, where I was given these things by his master to be kept in his memory. Father, since you have a disciple, I'll give the shirt and the cap to you." "I'm most grateful for your lavish gifts," said Tripitaka, "but my disciple has left. I dare not take them." "Where did he go?" said the old woman. Tripitaka said, "I heard a swishing sound heading toward the East." "My home is not too far away in the east," said the old woman, "and he may be going there. I have a spell which is called the True Words for Controlling the Mind, or the Tight-Fillet Spell. You must memorize it secretly; commit it firmly to your memory, and don't let anyone learn of it. I'll try to catch up with him and persuade him to come back and follow you. When he returns, give him the shirt and the cap to wear; and if he again refuses to obey you, recite the spell silently. He will not dare do violence or leave you again."

On hearing these words, Tripitaka bowed his head to thank her. The old woman changed herself into a shaft of golden light and vanished toward the east. Then Tripitaka realized that it was the Bodhisattva Guanyin who had taught him the True Words; he hurriedly picked up a few pinches of earth with his fingers and scattered them like incense, bowing reverently toward the East. He then took the shirt and the cap and hid them in his bag. Sitting beside the road, he began to recite the True Words for Controlling the Mind. After a few times, he knew it thoroughly by heart, but we shall speak no more of him for the time being.

We now tell you about Wukong, who, having left his master, headed straight toward the Eastern Ocean with a single cloud-somersault. He stopped his cloud, opened up a path in the water, and went directly to the Water Crystal Palace. Learning of his arrival, the Dragon King came out to welcome him. After they had exchanged greetings and sat down, the Dragon King said, "I heard recently that the ordeal of the Great Sage had been completed, and I apologize for not having congratulated you yet. I suppose you have again taken occupancy in your immortal mountain and returned to the ancient cave." "I was so inclined," said Wukong, "but I became a monk instead." "What sort of a monk?" said the Dragon King. "I was indebted to the Bodhisattva of South Sea," said Pilgrim, "who persuaded me to do good and seek the truth. I was to follow the Tang monk from the Land of the East to go worship Buddha in the West. Since entering the fold of Buddhism, I was given also the name 'Pilgrim.'" "That is indeed praiseworthy!" said the Dragon King. "You have, as we say, left the wrong and followed the right; you have been created anew by setting your mind on goodness. But if that's the case, why are you not going toward the West, but are returning eastward instead?"

Pilgrim laughed and said, "That Tang monk knows nothing of human nature! There were a few ruffians who wanted to rob us, and I slew them all. But that Tang monk couldn't stop nagging me, telling me over and over how wrong I was. Can you imagine old Monkey putting up with that sort of tedium? I just left him! I was on my way back to my mountain when I decided to come visit you and ask for a cup of tea." "Thanks for coming!

Thanks for coming!" said the Dragon King. At that moment, the Dragon sons and grandsons presented them with aromatic tea.

When they had finished the tea, Pilgrim happened to turn around and saw hanging behind him on the wall a painting on the "Presentation of Shoes at Yi Bridge." "What's this all about?" asked Pilgrim. The Dragon King said, "The incident depicted in the painting took place some time after you were born, and you may not recognize what it was, the threefold presentation of shoes at Yi Bridge." "What do you mean by the threefold presentation of shoes?" asked Pilgrim.

"The immortal in the painting," said the Dragon King, "was named Huang Shigong, and the young man kneeling in front of him was called Zhang Liang.[8] Shigong was sitting on the Yi Bridge when suddenly one of his shoes fell off and dropped under the bridge. He asked Zhang Liang to fetch it, and the young man quickly did so, putting it back on for him as he knelt there. This happened three times. Since Zhang Liang did not display the slightest sign of pride or impatience, he won the affection of Shigong, who imparted to him that night a celestial manual and told him to support the house of Han. Afterwards, Zhang Liang 'made his plans sitting in a military tent to achieve victories a thousand miles away.'[9] When the Han dynasty was established, he left his post and went into the mountains, where he followed the Daoist Red Pine Seed and became enlightened in the way of immortality. Great Sage, if you do not accompany the Tang monk, if you are unwilling to exercise diligence or to accept instruction, you will remain a bogus immortal after all. Don't think that you'll ever acquire the Fruits of Truth."

Wukong listened to these words and fell silent for some time. The Dragon King said, "Great Sage, you must make the decision yourself. It's unwise to allow momentary comfort to jeopardize your future." "Not another word!" said Wukong. "Old Monkey will go back to accompany him, that's all!" Delighted, the Dragon King said, "If that's your wish, I dare not detain you. Instead, I ask the Great Sage to show his mercy at once and not permit his master to wait any longer." When Pilgrim heard this exhortation to leave, he bounded right out of the oceanic region; mounting the clouds, he left the Dragon King.

8. One of the three master tacticians who assisted Liu Bang in establishing the Han.

9. A quotation from the *Records of History* by the Han historian, Sima Qian. The sentence was part of a compliment to Zhang Liang by Liu Bang himself, and the saying has been used in posterity as a hyperbolic description of the talents of a good strategist.

On his way he ran right into the Bodhisattva of South Sea. "Sun Wu-kong," said the Bodhisattva, "why did you not listen to me and accompany the Tang monk? What are you doing here?" Pilgrim was so taken aback that he saluted her on top of the clouds. "I'm most grateful for the kind words of the Bodhisattva," he said. "A monk from the Tang court did appear, lifted the seal, and saved my life. I became his disciple, but he blamed me for being too violent. I walked out on him for a little while, but I'm going back right now to accompany him." "Go quickly then," said the Bodhisattva, "before you change your mind again." They finished speaking and each went on his way. In a moment, our Pilgrim saw the Tang monk sitting dejectedly at the side of the road. He approached him and said, "Master, why are you not on the road? What are you doing here?" "Where have you been?" said Tripitaka, looking up. "Your absence has forced me to sit here and wait for you, not daring to walk or move." Pilgrim said, "I just went to the home of the old Dragon King at the Eastern Ocean to ask for some tea."

"Disciple," said Tripitaka, "those who have left the family should not lie. It was less than an hour since you left me, and you claim to have had tea at the home of the Dragon King?" "To tell you the truth," said Pilgrim, laughing, "I know how to cloud-somersault, and a single somersault will carry me a hundred and eight thousand miles. That's why I can go and return in no time at all." Tripitaka said, "Because I spoke to you a little sharply, you were offended and left me in a rage. With your ability, you could go and ask for some tea, but a person like me has no other prospect but to sit here and endure hunger. Do you feel comfortable about that?" "Master," said Pilgrim, "if you're hungry, I'll go beg some food for you." "There's no need to beg," said Tripitaka, "for I still have in my bag some dried goods given to me by the mother of Guardian Liu. Fetch me some water in that bowl. I'll eat some food and we can start out again."

Pilgrim went to untie the bag and found some biscuits made of unrefined flour, which he took out and handed over to the master. He then saw light glowing from a silk shirt and a flower cap inlaid with gold. "Did you bring this garment and cap from the Land of the East?" he asked. "I wore these in my childhood," said Tripitaka nonchalantly. "If you wear the hat, you'll know how to recite scriptures without having to learn them; if you put on the garment, you'll know how to perform rituals without having to practice them." "Dear Master," said Pilgrim, "let me put them on." "They may not fit you," said Tripitaka, "but if they do, you may wear them." Pilgrim thereupon took off his old shirt made of white cloth and put on the silk shirt, which seemed to have been made especially for him.

Then he put on the cap as well. When Tripitaka saw that he had put on the cap, he stopped eating the dried goods and began to recite the Tight-Fillet Spell silently.

"Oh, my head!" cried Pilgrim. "It hurts! It hurts!" The master went through the recitation several times without ceasing, and the pain was so intense that Pilgrim was rolling on the ground, his hands gripping the flower cap inlaid with gold. Fearing that he might break the gold fillet, Tripitaka stopped reciting and the pain ceased. Pilgrim touched his head with his hand and felt that it was tightly bound by a thin metal band; it could be neither pulled off nor ripped apart, for it had, as it were, taken root on his head. Taking the needle out of his ear, he rammed it inside the fillet and started prying madly. Afraid that he might break the fillet with his prying, Tripitaka started his recitation again, and Pilgrim's head began to hurt once more. It was so painful that he did cartwheels and somersaults: his face and even his ears turned red; his eyes bulged; and his body grew weak. When the master saw his appearance, he was moved to break off his recitation, and the pain stopped as before. "My head," said Pilgrim, "the master has put a spell on it." "I was just saying the Tight-Fillet Sūtra," said Tripitaka. "Since when did I put a spell on you?" "Recite it some more and see what happens," said Pilgrim. Tripitaka accordingly began to recite, and the Pilgrim immediately started to hurt. "Stop! Stop!" he cried. "I hurt the moment you begin to recite. How do you explain that?" "Will you listen now to my instructions?" said Tripitaka. "Yes, I will," said Pilgrim. "And never be unruly again?" "I dare not," said Pilgrim.

Although he said that with his mouth, Pilgrim's mind was still devising evil. One wave of the needle and it had the thickness of a rice bowl; he aimed it at the Tang monk and was about to slam it down on him. The priest was so startled that he went through the recitation two or three more times. Falling to the ground, the monkey threw away the iron rod and could not even raise his hands. "Master," he said, "I've learned my lesson! Stop! Please stop!" "How dare you be so reckless," said Tripitaka, "that you should want to strike me?" "I wouldn't dare strike you," said Pilgrim, "but let me ask you something. Who taught you this magic?" "It was an old woman," said Tripitaka, "who imparted it to me a few moments ago." Growing very angry, Pilgrim said, "You needn't say anything more! The old woman had to be that Guanshiyin! Why did she want me to suffer like this? I'm going to South Sea to beat her up!"

"If she had taught me this magic," said Tripitaka, "she had to know it even before I did. If you go looking for her, and she starts her recitation, won't you be dead?" Pilgrim saw the logic of this and dared not remove himself. Indeed, he had no alternative but to kneel in contrition and plead with Tripitaka, saying, "Master, this is her method of controlling me, allowing me no alternative but to follow you to the West. I'll not go to bother her, but you must not regard this spell as a plaything for frequent recitation either! I'm willing to accompany you without ever entertaining the thought of leaving again." "If that's so," said Tripitaka, "help me onto the horse and let's get going." At that point, Pilgrim gave up all thoughts of disobedience or rebellion. Eagerly he tugged at his silk shirt and went to gather the luggage together, and they headed again toward the West. We do not know what is to be told after their departure; let's listen to the explanation in the next chapter.

FIFTEEN

At Serpent Coil Mountain, the gods give secret protection;
At Eagle Grief Stream, the Horse of the Will is reined.

We were telling you about Pilgrim, who ministered to the Tang monk faithfully as they journeyed westward. They traveled for several days under the frigid sky of midwinter; a cold wind was blowing fiercely, and slippery icicles hung everywhere. What they traversed were

A tortuous path of hanging gorges and cliffs,
A parlous range tiered with summits and peaks.

As Tripitaka was riding along on his horse, his ears caught the distant sound of a torrent. He turned to ask: "Wukong, where is that sound coming from?" Pilgrim said, "The name of this place, I recall, is Serpent Coil Mountain, and there is an Eagle Grief Stream in it. I suppose that's where it's coming from." Before they had finished their conversation, they arrived at the bank of the stream. Tripitaka reined in his horse and looked around. He saw

A bubbling cold stream piercing through the clouds,
Its limpid current reddened by the sun.
Its splatter in night rain stirs quiet vales;
Its colors glow at dawn to fill the air.
Wave after wave seems like flying chips of jade,
Their deep roar resonant as the clear wind.
It flows to join one vast stretch of smoke and tide,
Where gulls are lost with egrets but no fishers bide.

Master and disciple were looking at the stream, when there was a loud splash in midstream and a dragon emerged. Churning the waters, it darted toward the bank and headed straight for the priest. Pilgrim was so startled that he threw away the luggage, hauled the master off his horse, and turned to flee with him at once. The dragon could not catch up with them, but it swallowed the white horse, harness and all, with one gulp before losing itself again in the water. Pilgrim carried his master to high ground and left the priest seated there; then he returned to fetch the horse and the luggage. The load of bags was still there, but the horse was nowhere to be seen. Placing the luggage in front of his master, he said, "Master, there's not a trace of that cursed dragon, which has frightened away our horse." "Disciple," said Tripitaka, "how can we find the horse again?" "Relax! Relax!" said Pilgrim. "Let me go and have a look!"

He whistled once and leaped up into the air. Shading his fiery eyes and diamond pupils with his hand, he peered in all four directions, but there was not the slightest trace of the horse. Dropping down from the clouds, he made his report, saying, "Master, our horse must have been eaten by that dragon. It's nowhere to be seen!" "Disciple," said Tripitaka, "how big a mouth does that creature have that he can swallow a horse, harness and all? It must have been frightened away instead, probably still running loose somewhere in the valley. Please take another look." Pilgrim said, "You really have no conception of my ability. This pair of eyes of mine in daylight can discern good and evil within a thousand miles; at that distance, I can even see a dragonfly when it spreads its wings. How can I possibly miss something as big as a horse?" "If it has been eaten," said Tripitaka, "how am I to proceed? Pity me! How can I walk through those thousand hills and ten thousand waters?" As he spoke, tears began to fall like rain. When Pilgrim saw him crying, he was infuriated and began to shout: "Master, stop behaving like a namby-pamby! Sit here! Just sit here! Let old Monkey find that creature and ask him to give us back our horse. That'll be the end of the matter." Clutching at him, Tripitaka said, "Disciple, where do you have to go to find him? Wouldn't I be hurt if he should appear from somewhere after you are gone? How would it be then if both man and horse should perish?" At these words, Pilgrim became even more enraged. "You're a weakling! Truly a weakling!" he thundered. "You want a horse to ride on, and yet you won't let me go. You want to sit here and grow old, watching our bags?"

As he was yelling angrily like this, he heard someone calling out in mid-air: "Great Sage Sun, don't be annoyed. And stop crying, Royal Brother of Tang. We are a band of deities sent by the Bodhisattva Guanyin to give secret protection to the scripture pilgrim." Hearing this, the priest hastily bowed to the ground. "Which divinities are you?" asked Pilgrim. "Tell me your names, so that I can check you off the roll." "We are the Six Gods of Darkness and the Six Gods of Light," they said, "the Guardians of Five Points, the Four Sentinels, and the Eighteen Protectors of Monasteries. Every one of us waits upon you in rotation." "Which one of you will begin today?" asked Pilgrim. "The Gods of Darkness and Light," they said, "to be followed by the Sentinels and the Protectors. We Guardians of Five

Points, with the exception of the Golden-Headed Guardian, will be here somewhere night and day." "That being the case," said Pilgrim, "those not on duty may retire, but the first Six Gods of Darkness, the Day Sentinel, and the Guardians should remain to protect my master. Let old Monkey go find that cursed dragon in the stream and ask him for our horse." The various deities obeyed. Only then did Tripitaka feel somewhat relieved as he sat on the cliff and told Pilgrim to be careful. "Just don't worry," said Pilgrim. Dear Monkey King! He tightened the belt around his silk shirt, hitched up his tiger-skin kilt, and went straight toward the gorge of the stream holding the golden-hooped iron rod. Standing halfway between cloud and fog, he cried loudly on top of the water, "Lawless lizard! Give me back my horse! Give me back my horse!"

We now tell you about the dragon, who, having eaten the white horse of Tripitaka, was lying on the bottom of the stream, subduing his spirit and nourishing his nature. When he heard someone demanding the horse with abusive language, however, he could not restrain the fire leaping up in his heart and he jumped up quickly. Churning the waves, he darted out of the water, saying, "Who dares to insult me here with his big mouth?" Pilgrim saw him and cried ferociously, "Don't run away! Give me back my horse!" Wielding his rod, he aimed at the beast's head and struck, while the dragon attacked with open jaws and dancing claws. The battle between the two of them before the stream was indeed a fierce one. You see

The dragon extending sharp claws:
The monkey lifting his rod.
The whiskers of this one hung like white jade threads;
The eyes of that one shone like red-gold lamps.
The mouth beneath the whiskers of that one belched colored mists:
The iron rod in the hands of this one moved like a fierce wind.
That one was a cursed son who brought his parents grief;
This one was a monster who defied the gods on high.
Both had to suffer because of their plight.
They now want to win, so each displays his might.

Back and forth, round and round, they fought for a long time, until the dragon grew weak and could fight no longer. He turned and darted back into the water; plunging to the bottom of the stream, he refused to come out again. The Monkey King heaped insult upon insult, but the dragon only pretended to be deaf.

Pilgrim had little choice but to return to Tripitaka, saying, "Master, that monster made his appearance as a result of my tongue-lashing. He fought with me for a long time before taking fright and running. He's hiding in the water now and refuses to come out again." "Do you know for certain that it was he who ate my horse?" said Tripitaka. "Listen to the way you talk!" said Pilgrim. "If he hadn't eaten it, would he be willing to face me and answer me like that?" "The time you killed the tiger," said Tripitaka, "you claimed that you had the ability to tame dragons and subdue tigers. Why can't you subdue this one today?" As the monkey had a rather low tolerance for any kind of provocation, this single taunt of Tripitaka so aroused him that he said, "Not one word more! Let me go and show him who is master!"

With great leaps, our Monkey King bounded right to the edge of the stream. Using his magic of overturning seas and rivers, he transformed the clear, limpid water of the Eagle Grief Stream into the muddy currents of the Yellow River during high tide. The cursed dragon in the depth of the stream could neither sit nor lie still for a single moment. He thought to himself: "Just as 'Blessing never repeats itself, so misfortune never comes singly!' It has been barely a year since I escaped execution by Heaven and came to bide my time here, but now I have to run into this wretched monster who is trying to do me harm." Look at him! The more he thought about the matter, the more irritated he became. Unable to bear it any longer, he gritted his teeth and leaped out of the water, crying, "What kind of monster are you, and where do you come from, that you want to oppress me like this?" "Never mind where I come from," said Pilgrim. "Just return the horse, and I'll spare your life." "I've swallowed your horse into my stomach," said the dragon, "so how am I to throw it up? What are you going to do if I can't return it to you?" Pilgrim said, "If you don't give back the horse, just watch for this rod. Only when your life is made a payment for my horse will there be an end to this matter!" The two of them again waged a bitter struggle below the mountain ridge. After a few rounds, however, the little dragon just could not hold out any longer; shaking his body, he changed himself into a tiny water snake and wriggled into the marshes.

The Monkey King came rushing up with his rod and parted the grass to look for the snake, but there was not a trace of it. He was so exasperated that the spirits of the Three Worms in his body exploded[1] and smoke

1. According to religious Daoism, the Three Worms are spirits resident in different parts of the human body: the head, the chest, and the abdomen (in certain texts, the feet are mentioned as a variant location). These spirits are regarded as variously connected to human appetites and desires and thus must be subdued through ritual and the practice of austerities.

began to appear from his seven apertures. He recited a spell beginning with the letter *oṃ* and summoned the local spirit and the mountain god of that region. The two of them knelt before him, saying, "The local spirit and the mountain god have come to see you." "Stick out your shanks," said Pilgrim, "and I'll greet each of you with five strokes of my rod just to relieve my feelings." "Great Sage," they pleaded, "please be more lenient and allow your humble subjects to tell you something." "What have you got to say?" said Pilgrim. "The Great Sage has been in captivity for a long time," said the two deities, "and we had no knowledge of when you were released. That's why we have not been here to receive you, and we beg you to pardon us." "All right," said Pilgrim, "I won't hit you. But let me ask you something. Where did that monstrous dragon in the Eagle Grief Stream come from, and why did he devour my master's white horse?" "We have never known the Great Sage to have a master," the two deities said, "for you have always been a first-rank primordial immortal who submits neither to Heaven nor to Earth. What do you mean by your master's horse?" Pilgrim said, "Of course you didn't know about this. Because of my contemptuous behavior toward Heaven, I had to suffer for this five hundred years. I was converted by the kindly persuasion of Bodhisattva Guanyin, who had the true monk from the Tang court rescue me. As his disciple, I was to follow him to the Western Heaven to seek scriptures from Buddha. We passed through this place, and my master's white horse was lost."

"So, that's how it is!" said the two deities. "There has never been anything evil about this stream, except that it is both broad and deep, and its water is so clear that you can see right to the bottom. Large fowls such as crows or eagles are hesitant to fly over it; for when they see their own reflections in the clear water, they are prone to mistake them for other birds of their own flock and throw themselves into the stream. Whence the name, the Steep Eagle Grief Stream. Some years ago, on her way to look for a scripture pilgrim, Bodhisattva Guanyin rescued a dragon and sent him here. He was told to wait for the scripture pilgrim and was forbidden to do any evil or violence. Only when he is hungry is he permitted to come up to the banks to feed on birds or antelopes. How could he be so ignorant as to offend the Great Sage!" Pilgrim said, "At first, he wanted to have a contest of strength with me and managed only a few bouts. Afterwards he would not come out even when I abused him. Only when I used the magic of overturning seas and rivers and stirred up the water did he appear again, and then he still wanted to fight. He really had no idea how heavy my rod was! When finally he couldn't hold out any longer, he changed himself into a water snake and wriggled into the grass. I rushed up there to look for him, but there was no trace of him." "You may not know, Great Sage," said the local spirit, "that there are countless holes and crevices along these banks, through which the stream is connected with its many tributaries. The dragon could have crawled into any one of these. But there's no need for the Great Sage to get angry trying to look for him. If you want to capture this creature, all you need do is to ask Guanshiyin to come here; then he'll certainly surrender."

When Pilgrim heard this, he called the mountain god and the local spirit to go with him to see Tripitaka to give an account of what had happened. "If you need to send for the Bodhisattva," said Tripitaka, "when will you be able to return? How can this poor monk endure the cold and hunger?" He had hardly finished speaking when the Golden-Headed Guardian called out from midair, "Great Sage, you needn't leave. Your humble subject will go fetch the Bodhisattva." Pilgrim was very pleased, shouting, "Thanks for taking all that trouble! Go quickly!" The Guardian mounted the clouds swiftly and headed straight for South Sea; Pilgrim asked the mountain god and the local spirit to protect his master and the Day Sentinel to find some vegetarian food, while he himself went back to patrol the stream, and we shall say no more of that.

We now tell you about the Golden-Headed Guardian, who mounted the clouds and soon arrived at South Sea. Descending from the auspicious light, he went straight to the purple bamboo grove of the Potalaka Mountain, where he asked the various deities in golden armor and Mokṣa to announce his arrival. The Bodhisattva said, "What have you come for?" "The Tang monk lost his horse at the Eagle Grief Stream of the Serpent Coil Mountain," said the Guardian, "and the Great Sage Sun was placed in a terrible dilemma. He questioned the local deities, who claimed that a dragon sent by the Bodhisattva to that stream had eaten it. The Great Sage, therefore, sent me to request the Bodhisattva to go and subdue that cursed dragon, so that he might get back his horse." Hearing this, the Bodhisattva said, "That creature was originally the son of Aorun of the Western Ocean. Because in his carelessness he set fire to the palace and destroyed the luminous pearls hanging there, his father accused him of subversion, and he was condemned to die by the Heavenly Tribunal. It was I who personally sought pardon from the Jade Emperor for him, so that he might serve as a means of transportation for the Tang monk. I can't understand how he could swallow the monk's horse instead. But if that's what happened. I'll have to get over there myself." The Bodhisattva left her lotus platform and went out of the divine cave. Mounting the auspicious luminosity with the Guardian, she crossed the South Sea. We have a testimonial poem which says:

> Buddha proclaimed the Tripitaka Supreme
> Which the Goddess declared throughout Chang'an:
> Those great, wondrous truths could reach Heaven and Earth;
> Those wise, true words could save the spirits damned.
> They caused Gold Cicada to cast again his shell.
> They moved Xuanzang to mend his ways anew.
> By blocking his path at Eagle Grief Stream,
> The dragon son came home[2] in a horse's form.

The Bodhisattva and the Guardian soon arrived at the Serpent Coil Mountain. They stopped the hallowed clouds in midair and saw Pilgrim Sun down below, shouting abuses at the bank of the stream. The Bodhisattva asked the Guardian to fetch him. Lowering his clouds, the Guardian went past Tripitaka and headed straight for the edge of the stream, saying to Pilgrim, "The Bodhisattva has arrived." When Pilgrim heard this, he jumped quickly into the air and yelled at her: "You, so-called Teacher of the Seven Buddhas and the Founder of the Faith of Mercy! Why did you have to use your tricks to harm me?" "You impudent stableman, ignorant red-buttocks!" said the Bodhisattva. "I went to considerable effort to find a scripture pilgrim, whom I carefully instructed to save your life. Instead of thanking me, you are finding fault with me!" "You saved me all right!" said Pilgrim. "If you truly wanted to deliver me, you should have allowed me to have a little fun with no strings attached. When you met me the other day above the ocean, you could have chastened me with a few words, telling me to serve the Tang monk with diligence, and that would have been enough. Why did you have to give him a flower cap, and have him deceive me into wearing it so that I would suffer? Now the fillet has taken root on old Monkey's head. And you even taught him this so-called 'Tight-Fillet Spell' which he recites again and again, causing endless pain in my head! You haven't harmed me, indeed!" The Bodhisattva laughed and said, "O, Monkey! You are neither attentive to admonition nor willing to seek the fruit of truth. If you are not restrained like this, you'll probably mock the authority of Heaven again without regard for good or ill. If you create troubles as you did before, who will be able to control you? It's only through this bit of adversity that you will be willing to enter our gate of Yoga."

"All right," said Pilgrim, "I'll consider the matter my hard luck. But

2. Came home: literally, returned to the Real.

why did you take that condemned dragon and send him here so that he could become a spirit and swallow my master's horse? It's your fault, you know, if you allow an evildoer to perpetrate his villainies some more!" "I went personally to plead with the Jade Emperor," said the Bodhisattva, "to have the dragon stationed here so that he could serve as a means of transportation for the scripture pilgrim. Those mortal horses from the Land of the East, do you think that they could walk through ten thousand waters and a thousand hills? How could they possibly hope to reach the Spirit Mountain, the land of Buddha? Only a dragon-horse could make that journey!" "But right now he's so terribly afraid of me," said Pilgrim, "that he refuses to come out of his hiding place. What can we do?" The Bodhisattva said to the Guardian, "Go to the edge of the stream and say, 'Come out, Third Prince Jade Dragon of the Dragon-king Aorun. The Bodhisattva from South Sea is here.' He'll come out then."

The Guardian went at once to the edge of the stream and called out twice. Churning the waters and leaping across the waves, the little dragon appeared and changed at once into the form of a man. He stepped on the clouds and rose up into the air; saluting the Bodhisattva, he said, "I thank the Bodhisattva again for saving my life. I've waited here a long time, but I've heard no news of the scripture pilgrim." Pointing to Pilgrim, the Bodhisattva said, "Isn't he the eldest disciple of the scripture pilgrim?" When he saw him, the little dragon said, "Bodhisattva, he's my adversary. I was hungry yesterday and ate his horse. We fought over that, but he took advantage of his superior strength and defeated me; in fact, he so abused me that I dared not show myself again. But he has never mentioned a word about scripture seeking." "You didn't bother to ask my name," said Pilgrim. "How did you expect me to tell you anything?" The little dragon said, "Didn't I ask you, 'What kind of a monster are you and where do you come from?' But all you did was shout, 'Never mind where I come from; just return my horse!' Since when did you utter even half the word 'Tang'?" "That monkey," said the Bodhisattva, "is always relying on his own abilities! When has he ever given any credit to other people? When you set off this time, remember that there are others who will join you. So when they ask you, by all means mention first the matter of scripture seeking; they will submit to you without causing you further trouble."

Pilgrim received this word of counsel amiably. The Bodhisattva went up to the little dragon and plucked off the shining pearls hanging around his neck. She then dipped her willow branch into the sweet dew in her vase and sprinkled it all over his body; blowing a mouthful of magic breath on him, she cried, "Change!" The dragon at once changed into a horse with hair of exactly the same color and quality as that of the horse he had swallowed. The Bodhisattva then told him, "You must overcome with utmost diligence all the cursed barriers. When your merit is achieved, you will no longer be an ordinary dragon; you will acquire the true fruit of a golden body." Holding the bit in his mouth, the little dragon humbly accepted the instruction. The Bodhisattva told Wukong to lead him to Tripitaka, saying, "I'm returning across the ocean." Pilgrim took hold of her and refused to let go, saying, "I'm not going on! I'm not going on! The road to the West is so treacherous! If I have to accompany this mortal monk, when will I ever get there? If I have to endure all these miseries, I may well lose my life. What sort of merit do you think I'll achieve? I'm not going! I'm not going!"

"In years past, before you reached the way of humanity," said the Bodhisattva, "you were most eager to seek enlightenment. Now that you have been delivered from the chastisement of Heaven, how could you become slothful again? The truth of Nirvāṇa in our teaching can never be realized without faith and perseverance. If on your journey you should come across any danger that threatens your life, I give you permission to call on Heaven, and Heaven will respond; to call on Earth, and Earth will prove efficacious. In the event of extreme difficulty, I myself will come to rescue you. Come closer, and I shall endow you with one more power." Plucking three leaves from her willow branch, the Bodhisattva placed them at the back of Pilgrim's head, crying, "Change!" They changed at once into three hairs with lifesaving power. She said to him: "When you find yourself in a helpless and hopeless situation, you may use these according to your needs, and they will deliver you from your particular affliction." After Pilgrim had heard all these kind words, he thanked the Bodhisattva of Great Mercy and Compassion. With scented wind and colored mists swirling around her, the Bodhisattva returned to Potalaka.

Lowering the direction of his cloud, Pilgrim tugged at the mane of the horse and led him to Tripitaka, saying, "Master, we have a horse!" Highly pleased by what he saw, Tripitaka said, "Disciple, how is it that the horse has grown a little fatter and stronger than before? Where did you find him?" "Master, you are still dreaming!" said Pilgrim. "Just now the Golden-Headed Guardian managed to bring the Bodhisattva here, and she transformed the dragon of the stream into our white horse. Except for the missing harness, the color and hair are all same, and old Monkey has pulled him here." "Where is the Bodhisattva?" said Tripitaka, greatly surprised. "Let me go and thank her." "By this time," said Pilgrim, "the Bodhisattva has probably arrived at South Sea; there's no need to bother about that." Picking up a few pinches of earth with his fingers and scattering them like incense, Tripitaka bowed reverently toward the South. He then got up and prepared to leave again with Pilgrim.

Having dismissed the mountain god and the local spirit and given instructions to the Guardians and the Sentinels, Pilgrim asked his master to mount. Tripitaka said, "How can I ride a horse without harness? Let's find a boat to cross this stream, and then we can decide what to do." "This master of mine is truly impractical!" said Pilgrim. "In the wilds of this mountain, where will you find a boat? Since the horse has lived here for a long time, he must know the water's condition. Just ride him like a boat and we'll cross over." Tripitaka had no choice but to follow his suggestion and climbed onto the barebacked horse; Pilgrim took up the luggage and they arrived at the edge of the stream. Then they saw an old fisherman punting downstream toward them in an old wooden raft. When Pilgrim caught sight of him, he waved his hands and called out: "Old fisherman, come here! Come here! We come from the Land of the East to seek scriptures. It's difficult for my master to cross, so please take us over." When the fisherman heard these words, he quickly punted the raft up to the bank. Asking his master to dismount, Pilgrim helped Tripitaka onto the raft before he embarked the horse and the luggage. That old fisher punted the raft away, and like an arrow in the wind, they crossed the steep Eagle Grief Stream swiftly and landed on the western shore. Tripitaka told Pilgrim to untie a bag and take out a few Tang pennies to give to the old fisherman. With a shove of his pole, the old fisherman pulled away, saying, "I don't want any money." He drifted downstream and soon disappeared from sight. Feeling very much obliged, Tripitaka kept folding his hands to express his gratitude. "Master," said Pilgrim, "you needn't be so solicitous. Don't you recognize him? He is the Water God of this stream. Since he didn't come to pay his respects to old Monkey, he was about to get a beating. It's enough that he is now spared from that. Would he dare take any money!" The Master was only half-believing him when he climbed onto the barebacked horse once again; following Pilgrim, he went up to the main road and set off again toward the West. It would be like this that they

Through the vast Thusness reach the other shore,
And climb with hearts unfeigned the Spirit Mount.

Master and disciple journeyed on, and soon the fiery sun sank westward as the sky gradually darkened. You see

Clouds hazy and aimless,
A mountain moon dim and gloomy.
The sky, all frost-colored, makes you cold;

The wind, howling around, pierces your frame.
One bird is lost midst the pale, wide sandbars,
As twilight glows where the distant hills are low.
A thousand trees roar in the sparse woodland;
A lonely ape cries on a barren summit.
No traveler is seen on this long road
When boats from afar return for the night.

As Tripitaka, riding his horse, peered into the distance, he suddenly saw something like a hamlet beside the road. "Wukong," he said, "there's a house ahead of us. Let's ask for lodging there and travel again tomorrow." Raising his head to take a look, Pilgrim said, "Master, it's no ordinary house." "Why not?" said Tripitaka. "If it were an ordinary house," said Pilgrim, "there would be no flying fishes or reclining beasts decorating the ridge of its roof. That must be a temple or a monastery." While they were speaking, master and disciple arrived at the gate of the building. Dismounting, Tripitaka saw on top of the gate three large characters: Lishe Shrine. They walked inside, where they were met by an old man with some beads hanging around his neck. He came forward with hands folded, saying, "Master, please take a seat." Tripitaka hastily returned his salutation and then went to the main hall to bow to the holy images. The old man called a youth to serve tea, after which Tripitaka asked him, "Why is this shrine named Lishe?"

The old man said, "This region belongs to the Hamil Kingdom of the western barbarians. There is a village behind the shrine, which was built from the piety of all its families. The 'Li' refers to the land owned by the whole village, and the 'She' is the God of the Soil. During the days of spring sowing, summer plowing, autumn harvesting, and winter storing, each of the families would bring the three beasts,[3] flowers, and fruits to sacrifice at the shrine, so that they might be blessed with good luck in all four seasons, a rich harvest of the five grains, and prosperity in raising the six domestic creatures."[4] When Tripitaka heard these words, he nodded his head to show his approval, saying, "This is truly like the proverb: 'Even three miles from home there are customs entirely distinct.' The families in our region do not practice such good works." Then the old man asked, "Where is the honorable home of the master?" "Your poor monk," said Tripitaka, "happens to have been sent by the royal decree from the Great Tang Nation in the East to go to seek scriptures from Buddha in the

---

3. The cow, the sheep, and the pig.
4. The cow, the sheep, the pig, the dog, the chicken, and the horse.

Western Heaven. It was getting rather late when I passed your esteemed edifice. I therefore came to your holy shrine to ask for a night's lodging. I'll leave as soon as it gets light." The old man was delighted and kept saying, "Welcome! Welcome!" He called the youth again to prepare a meal, which Tripitaka ate with gratitude.

As usual, Pilgrim was extremely observant. Noticing a rope for hanging laundry tied under the eaves, he walked over to it and pulled at it until it snapped in two. He then used the piece of rope to tie up the horse. "Where did you steal this horse?" said the old man laughing. "Old man," said Pilgrim angrily, "watch what you are saying! We are holy monks going to worship Buddha. How could we steal horses?" "If you didn't steal it," said the old man laughing, "why is there no saddle or rein, so that you have to rip up my clothesline?"

"This rascal is always so impulsive," said Tripitaka apologetically. "If you wanted to tie up the horse, why didn't you ask the old gentleman properly for a rope? Why did you have to rip up his clothesline? Sir, please don't be angry! Our horse, to tell you the truth, is not a stolen one. When we approached the Eagle Grief Stream yesterday from the east, I had a white horse complete with harness. Little did we anticipate that there was a condemned dragon in the stream who had become a spirit, and who swallowed my horse in one gulp, harness and all. Fortunately, my disciple has some talents, and he was able to bring the Bodhisattva Guanyin to the stream to subdue the dragon. She told him to assume the form of my original white horse, so that he could carry me to worship Buddha in the Western Heaven. It has barely been one day since we crossed the stream and arrived at your holy shrine. We haven't had time to look for a harness."

"Master, you needn't worry," said the old man. "An old man like me loves to tease, but I had no idea your esteemed disciple was so serious about everything! When I was young, I had a little money, and I too loved to ride. But over the years I had my share of misfortunes: deaths in the family and fires in the household have not left me much. Thus I am reduced to being a caretaker here in the shrine, looking after the fires and incense, and dependent on the goodwill of the patrons in the village back there for a living. I still have in my possession a harness which I have always cherished, and which even in this poverty I couldn't bear to sell. But since hearing your story, how even the Bodhisattva delivered the divine dragon and made him change into a horse to carry you, I feel that I must not withhold from giving either. I shall bring the harness tomorrow and present it to the master, who, I hope, will be pleased to accept it." When Tripitaka heard this, he thanked him repeatedly. Before long, the youth brought in the evening meal, after which lamps were lit and the beds prepared. Everyone then retired.

Next morning, Pilgrim arose and said, "Master, that old caretaker promised last night to give us the harness. Ask him for it. Don't spare him." He had hardly finished speaking when the old man came in with a saddle, together with pads, reins, and the like. Not a single item needed for riding a horse was lacking. He set them down in the corridor, saying, "Master, I am presenting you with this harness." When Tripitaka saw it, he accepted it with delight and asked Pilgrim to try the saddle on the horse. Going forward. Pilgrim took up the accoutrements and examined them piece by piece. They were indeed some magnificent articles, for which we have a testimonial poem. The poem says:

> The carved saddle shines with studs of silver stars.
> The precious seat glows with bright threads of gold.
> The pads are stacks of fine-spun woolen quilts.
> The reins are three bands of purple cords of silk.
> The bridle's leather straps are shaped like flowers.
> The flaps have gold-etched forms of dancing beasts.
> The rings and bit are made of finest steel.
> And waterproof tassels hang on both sides.

Secretly pleased, Pilgrim put the saddle on the back of the horse, and it seemed to have been made to measure. Tripitaka bowed to thank the old man, who hastily raised him up, saying, "It's nothing! What do you need to thank me for?" The old man did not ask them to stay any longer; instead, he urged Tripitaka to mount. The priest came out of the gate and climbed into the saddle, while Pilgrim followed, hauling the luggage. The old man then took a whip out from his sleeve, with a handle of rattan wrapped in strips of leather, and the strap knitted with cords made of tiger ligaments. He stood by the side of the road and presented it with hands uplifted, saying, "Holy Monk, I have a whip here which I may as well give you." Tripitaka accepted it on his horse, saying, "Thanks for your donation! Thanks for your donation!"

Even as he was saying this, the old man vanished. The priest turned around to look at the Lishe Shrine, but it had become just a piece of level ground. From the sky came a voice saying, "Holy Monk, I'm sorry not to have given you a better reception! I am the local spirit of Potalaka Mountain, who was sent by the Bodhisattva to present you with the harness. You two must journey to the West with all diligence. Do not be slothful in any moment." Tripitaka was so startled that he fell off his horse and bowed toward the sky, saying, "Your disciple is of fleshly eyes and mortal stock, and he does not recognize the holy visage of the deity. Please forgive me. I beseech you to convey my gratitude to the Bodhisattva." Look at him! All he could do was to kowtow toward the sky without bothering to count how many times! By the side of the road the Great Sage Sun reeled with laughter, the Handsome Monkey King broke up with hilarity. He came up and tugged at his master, saying, "Master, get up! He is long gone! He can't hear you, nor can he see your kowtowing. Why keep up this adoration?" "Disciple," said the priest, "when I kowtowed like that, all you could do was to stand snickering by the side of the road, with not even a bow. Why?" "You wouldn't know, would you?" said Pilgrim. "For playing a game of hide-and-seek like that with us, he really deserves a beating! But for the sake of the Bodhisattva, I'll spare him, and that's something already! You think he dares accept a bow from old Monkey? Old Monkey has been a hero since his youth, and he doesn't know how to bow to people! Even when I saw the Jade Emperor and Laozi, I just gave them my greeting, that's all!" "Blasphemy!" said Tripitaka. "Stop this idle talk! Let's get going without further delay." So the priest got up and prepared to set off again toward the West. . . . We do not know what took place thereafter; let's listen to the explanation in the next chapter.

At the Guanyin Hall the Tang monk escapes his ordeal;[1]
At the Gao Village the Great Sage disposes of the monster.

[Having recovered the stolen cassock with the help of the Bodhisattva Guanyin, Tripitaka and his disciple left the Guanyin Hall to set out again on their journey.] As Pilgrim led the way forward, it was the happiest time of spring. You see

The horse making light tracks on grassy turfs;
Gold threads of willow swaying with fresh dew.
Peaches and apricots fill the forest gay.
Creepers grow with vigor along the way.
Pairs of sun-warmed ducks rest on sandy banks;
The brook's fragrant flowers tame the butterflies.
Thus autumn goes, winter fades, and spring's half gone;
When will merit be made and the True Writ found?

Master and disciple traveled for some six or seven days in the wilderness. One day, when it was getting late, they saw a village in the distance. "Wukong," said Tripitaka, "look! There's a village over there. How about asking for lodging for the night before we travel again tomorrow?" "Let's wait until I have determined whether it is a good or bad place before we decide," said Pilgrim. The master pulled in the reins as Pilgrim stared intently at the village. Truly there were

Dense rows of bamboo fences;
Thick clusters of thatched huts.
Skyscraping wild trees faced the doorways;
The winding brooklet reflected the houses.
Willows by the path unfurled their lovely green;
Fragrant were the flowers blooming in the yard.
At this time of twilight fast fading,

---

1. The first line of this couplet summarizes the ending of the previous episode that has been omitted here.

The birds chattered everywhere in the woods.
As kitchen smoke arose,
Cattle returned on every lane and path.
You saw, too, well-fed pigs and chickens sleeping by the house's edge,
And the old, sotted neighbor coming with a song.

After surveying the area, Pilgrim said, "Master, you may proceed. It appears to be a village of good families, where it will be appropriate for us to seek shelter." The priest urged the white horse on, and they arrived at the beginning of a lane heading into the village, where they saw a young man wearing a cotton head-wrap and a blue jacket. He had an umbrella in his hand and a bundle on his back; his trousers were rolled up, and he had on his feet a pair of straw sandals with three loops. He was striding along the street in a resolute manner when Pilgrim grabbed him, saying, "Where are you going? I have a question for you: what is this place?" Struggling to break free, the man protested: "Isn't there anyone else here in the village? Why must you pick me for your question?" "Patron," said Pilgrim genially, "don't get upset. 'Helping others is in truth helping yourself.' What's so bad about your telling me the name of this place? Perhaps I can help you with your problems." Unable to break out of Pilgrim's grip, the man was so infuriated that he jumped about wildly. "I'm licked, licked!" he cried. "No end to the grievances I have suffered at the hands of my family elders and I still have to run into this baldheaded fellow and suffer such indignity from him!" "If you have the ability to pry open my hand," said Pilgrim, "I'll let you go." The man twisted left and right without any success: it was as if he had been clamped tight with a pair of iron tongs. He became so enraged that he threw away his bundle and his umbrella; with both hands, he rained blows and scratches on Pilgrim. With one hand steadying his luggage, Pilgrim held off the man with the other, and no matter how hard the man tried, he could not scratch or even touch Pilgrim at all. The more he fought, the firmer was Pilgrim's grip, so that the man was utterly exasperated.

"Wukong," said Tripitaka, "isn't someone coming over there? You can ask someone else. Why hang onto him like that? Let the man go." "Master, you don't understand," said Pilgrim laughing. "If I ask someone else, all the fun will be gone. I have to ask him if, as the saying goes, 'there's going to be any business'!" Seeing that it was fruitless to struggle any more, the man said finally, "This place is called the Mr. Gao Village in the territory of the Kingdom of Tibet. Most of the families here in the village are surnamed Gao, and that's why the village is so called. Now, please let me go." "You are hardly dressed for a stroll in the neighborhood," said Pilgrim, "so tell me the truth. Where are you going, and what are you doing anyway? Then I'll let you go."

The man had little alternative but to speak the truth. "I'm a member of the family of old Mr. Gao, and my name is Gao Cai. Old Mr. Gao has a daughter, his youngest, in fact, who is twenty years old and not yet betrothed. Three years ago, however, a monster-spirit seized her and kept her as his wife. Having a monster as his son-in-law bothered old Mr. Gao terribly; he said, 'My daughter having a monster as her spouse can hardly be a lasting arrangement. First, my family's reputation is ruined, and second, I don't even have any in-laws with whom we can be friends.' All that time he wanted to have this marriage annulled, but the monster absolutely refused; he locked the daughter up instead in the rear building and would not permit her to see her family for nearly half a year. The old man, therefore, gave me several taels of silver and told me to find an exorcist to capture the monster. Since then, I have hardly rested my feet; I managed to turn up three or four persons, all worthless monks and impotent Daoists. None of them could subdue the monster. A short while ago I received a severe scolding for my incompetence, and with only half an ounce more of silver as a travel allowance, I was told to find a capable exorcist this time. I didn't expect to run into you, my unlucky star, and now my journey is delayed. That's what I meant by the grievances I had suffered in and out of the family, and that's why I was protesting just now. I didn't know you had this trick of holding people, which I couldn't overcome. Now I have told you the truth, please let me go."

"It's really your luck," said Pilgrim, "coupled with my vocation: they fit like the numbers four and six when you throw the dice! You needn't travel far, nor need you waste your money. We are not worthless monks or impotent Daoists, for we really do have some abilities; we are most experienced, in fact, in capturing monsters. As the saying goes, 'You have now not only a caring physician, but now you have cured your eyes as well!' Please take the trouble of returning to the head of your family and tell him that we are holy monks sent by the Throne in the Land of the East to go worship Buddha in the Western Heaven and acquire scriptures. We are most capable of seizing monsters and binding fiends." "Don't mislead me," said Gao Cai, "for I've had it up to here! If you are deceiving me and really don't have the ability to take the monster, you will only cause me more grievances." Pilgrim said, "I guarantee that you won't be harmed in any way. Lead me to the door of your house." The man could not think of a better alternative; he picked up his bundle and umbrella and turned to lead master and disciple to the door of his house. "You two elders," he said, "please rest yourselves for a moment against the hitching posts here. I'll go in to report to my master." Only then did Pilgrim release him. Putting down the luggage and dismounting from the horse, master and disciple stood and waited outside the door.

Gao Cai walked through the main gate and went straight to the main hall in the center, but it just happened that he ran right into old Mr. Gao. "You thick-skinned beast!" railed Mr. Gao. "Why aren't you out looking for an exorcist? What are you doing back here?" Putting down his bundle and umbrella, Gao Cai said, "Let me humbly inform my lord. Your servant just reached the end of the street and ran into two monks: one riding a horse and the other hauling a load. They caught hold of me and refused to let go, asking where I was going. At first I absolutely refused to tell them, but they were most insistent and I had no means of freeing myself. It was only then that I gave them a detailed account of my lord's affairs. The one who was holding me was delighted, saying that he would arrest the monster for us." "Where did they come from?" said old Mr. Gao. "He claimed to be a holy monk, the brother of the emperor," said Gao Cai, "who was sent from the Land of the East to go worship Buddha in the Western Heaven and acquire scriptures." "If they are monks who have come from such a great distance," said old Mr. Gao, "they may indeed have some abilities. Where are they now?" "Waiting outside the front door," said Gao Cai.

Hurriedly that old Mr. Gao changed his clothes and came out with Gao Cai to extend his welcome, crying, "Your Grace!" When Tripitaka heard this, he turned quickly, and his host was already standing in front of him. That old man had on his head a dark silk wrap; he wore a robe of Sichuan silk brocade in spring-onion white with a dark green sash, and a pair of boots made of rough steer hide. Smiling affably, he addressed them saying, "Honored Priests, please accept my bow!" Tripitaka returned his greeting, but Pilgrim stood there unmoved. When the old man saw how hideous he looked, he did not bow to him. "Why don't you say hello to me?" demanded Pilgrim. Somewhat alarmed, the old man said to Gao Cai: "Young man! You have really done me in, haven't you? There is already an ugly monster in the house that we can't drive away. Now you have to fetch this thunder-spirit to cause me more troubles!"

"Old Gao," said Pilgrim, "it's in vain that you have reached such old age, for you have hardly any discernment! If you want to judge people by appearances, you are utterly wrong! I, old Monkey, may be ugly, but I have some abilities. I'll capture the monster for your family, exorcise the fiend, apprehend that son-in-law of yours, and get your daughter back. Will that be good enough? Why all these mutterings about appearances!" When the old man heard this, he trembled with fear, but he managed to pull himself together sufficiently to say, "Please come in!" At this invitation, Pilgrim led the white horse and asked Gao Cai to pick up their luggage so that Tripitaka could go in with them. With no regard for manners, he tethered the horse on one of the pillars and drew up a weather-beaten lacquered chair for his master to be seated. He pulled over another chair and sat down himself on one side. "This little priest," said old Mr. Gao, "really knows how to make himself at home!" "If you are willing to keep me here for half a year," said Pilgrim, "then I'll truly feel at home!"

After they were seated, old Mr. Gao asked: "Just now my little one said that you two honored priests came from the Land of the East?" "Yes," said Tripitaka. "Your poor monk was commissioned by the court to go to the Western Heaven to seek scriptures for Buddha. Since we have reached your village, we would like to ask for lodging for the night. We plan to leave early tomorrow morning." "So the two of you wanted lodging?" said old Mr. Gao. "Then why did you say you could catch monsters?" "Since we are asking for a place to stay," said Pilgrim, "we thought we might as well catch a few monsters, just for fun! May we ask how many monsters there are in your house?" "My God!" exclaimed old Mr. Gao, "How many monsters could we feed? There's only this one son-in-law, and we have suffered enough from him!" "Tell me everything about the monster," said Pilgrim, "how he came to this place, what sort of power he has, and so forth. Start from the beginning and don't leave out any details. Then I can catch him for you."

"From ancient times," said old Mr. Gao, "this village of ours has never had any troubles with ghosts, goblins, or fiends; in fact, my sole misfortune consists of not having a son. I had three daughters born to me: the eldest is named Fragrant Orchid; the second one, Jade Orchid; and the third, Green Orchid. The first two since their youth had been promised to people belonging to this same village, but I had hoped that the youngest would take a husband who would stay with our family and consent to have his children bear our name. Since I have no son, he would in fact become my heir and look after me in my old age. Little did I expect that about three years ago a fellow would turn up who was passably good-looking. He said that he came from the Fuling Mountain and that his surname was Zhu (Hog). Since he had neither parents nor brothers, he was willing to be taken in as a son-in-law, and I accepted him, thinking that someone with no other family attachment was exactly the right sort of person. When he first came into our family, he was, I must confess, fairly industrious and well-behaved. He worked hard to loosen the earth and plow the fields without even using a buffalo; and when he harvested the grains, he did the reaping without sickle or staff. He came home late in the evening and started early again in the morning, and to tell you the truth, we were quite happy with him. The only trouble was that his appearance began to change."

"In what way?" asked Pilgrim. "Well," said old Mr. Gao, "when he first came, he was a stout, swarthy fellow, but afterwards he turned into an idiot with huge ears and a long snout, with a great tuft of bristles behind his head. His body became horribly coarse and hulking. In short, his whole appearance was that of a hog! And what an enormous appetite! For a single meal, he has to have three to five bushels of rice: a little snack in the morning means over a hundred biscuits or rolls. It's a good thing he keeps a vegetarian diet; if he liked meat and wine, the property and estate of this old man would be consumed in half a year!" "Perhaps it's because he's a good worker," said Tripitaka, "that he has such a good appetite." "Even that appetite is a small problem!" said old Mr. Gao. "What is most disturbing is that he likes to come riding the wind and disappears again astride the fog; he kicks up stones and dirt so frequently that my household and my neighbors have not had a moment's peace. Then he locked up my little girl, Green Orchid, in the back building, and we haven't seen her for half a year and don't know whether she's dead or alive. We are certain now that he is a monster, and that's why we want to get an exorcist to drive him away." "There's nothing difficult about that," said Pilgrim. "Relax, old man! Tonight, I'll catch him for you, and I'll demand that he sign a document of annulment and return your daughter. How's that?" Immensely pleased, old Mr. Gao said, "My taking him in was a small thing, when you consider how he has ruined my good reputation and how many relatives of ours he had alienated! Just catch him for me. Why bother about a document; Please, just get rid of him for me." Pilgrim said, "It's simple! When night falls, you'll see the result!"

The old man was delighted; he asked at once for tables to be set and a vegetarian feast to be prepared. When they had finished the meal, evening was setting in. The old man asked: "What sort of weapons and how many people do you need? We'd better prepare soon." "I have my own weapon," replied Pilgrim. The old man said, "The only thing the two of you have is that priestly staff, hardly something you can use to battle the monster," whereupon Pilgrim took an embroidery needle out of his ear, held it in his hands, and waving it once in the wind, changed it into a golden-hooped rod with the thickness of a rice bowl. "Look at this rod," he said to old

Mr. Gao, "how does it compare with your weapons? Think it'll do for the monster?" "Since you have a weapon," said old Mr. Gao again, "do you need some attendants?" "No need for any attendants," said Pilgrim. "All I ask for is some decent elderly persons to keep my master company and talk with him, so that I may feel free to leave him for a while. I'll catch the monster for you and make him promise publicly to leave, so that you will be rid of him for good." The old man at once asked his houseboy to send for several intimate friends and relatives, who soon arrived. After they were introduced, Pilgrim said, "Master, you may feel quite safe sitting here. Old Monkey is off!"

Look at him! Lifting high his iron rod, he dragged old Mr. Gao along saying, "Lead me to the back building where the monster is staying so that I may have a look." The old man indeed took him to the door of the building in the rear. "Get a key quickly!" said Pilgrim. "Take a look yourself," said old Mr. Gao. "If I could use a key on this lock. I wouldn't need you." Pilgrim laughed and said, "Dear old man! Though you are quite old, you can't even recognize a joke! I was just teasing you a little, and you took my words literally." He went forward and touched the lock: it was solidly welded with liquid copper. Annoyed, Pilgrim smashed open the door with one terrific blow of his rod and found it was pitch black inside. "Old Gao," said Pilgrim, "go give your daughter a call and see if she is there inside." Summoning up his courage, the old man cried, "Miss Three!" Recognizing her father's voice, the girl replied faintly, "Papa! I'm over here!" His golden pupils ablaze, Pilgrim peered into the dark shadows. "How does she look?" you ask. You see that

Her cloudlike hair is unkempt and unbrushed;
Her jadelike face is grimy and unwashed.
Though her nature refined is unchanged,
Her lovely image is weary and wan.
Her cherry lips seem completely bloodless,
And her body is both crooked and bent.
Knitted in sorrow
The moth-brows are pallid;
Weakened by weight loss,
The speaking voice is faint.

She came forward, and when she saw that it was old Mr. Gao, she clutched at him and began to wail.

"Stop crying! Stop crying!" said Pilgrim. "Let me ask you: where is the monster?" "I don't know where he has gone," said the girl. "Nowadays he leaves in the morning and comes back only after nightfall. Surrounded by cloud and fog, he comes and goes without ever letting me know where he is. Since he has learned that father is trying to drive him away, he takes frequent precautions; that's why he comes only at night and leaves in the morning." "No need to talk anymore," Pilgrim said. "Old Man! Take your beloved daughter to the building in front, and then you can spend all the time you want with her. Old Monkey will be here waiting for him; if the monster doesn't show up, don't blame me. But if he comes at all, I'll pull out the weeds of your troubles by the roots!" With great joy, old Mr. Gao led his daughter to the front building. Exercising his magic might, Pilgrim shook his body and changed at once into the form of that girl, sitting all by herself to wait for the monster. In a little while, a gust of wind swept by, kicking up dust and stones. What a wind!

At first it was a breeze gentle and light.
Thereafter it became gusty and strong.
A light, gentle breeze that could fill the world!
A strong, gusty wind that nothing else could stop!
Flowers and willow snapped like shaken hemp;
Trees and plants were felled like uprooted crops.
It stirred up streams and seas, cowing ghosts and gods.
It fractured rocks and mountains, awing Heaven and Earth.
Flower-nibbling deer lost their homeward trail.
Fruit-picking monkeys all were gone astray.
The seven-tiered pagoda crashed on Buddha's head.
Flags on eight sides damaged the temple's top.
Gold beams and jade pillars were rooted up.
Like flocks of swallow flew the roofing tiles.
The boatman lifted his oars to make a vow,
Eager to have his livestock sacrificed.
The local spirit abandoned his shrine.
Dragon kings from four seas made humble bows.
At sea the ship of yakṣa ran aground,
While half of Great Wall's rampart was blown down.

When the violent gust of wind had gone by, there appeared in midair a monster who was ugly indeed. With his black face covered with short, stubby hair, his long snout and huge ears, he wore a cotton shirt that was neither quite green nor quite blue. A sort of spotted cotton handkerchief was tied round his head. Said Pilgrim, smiling to himself, "So, I have to do business with a thing like this!" Dear Pilgrim! He neither greeted the monster, nor did he speak to him; he lay on the bed instead and pretended to be sick, moaning all the time. Unable to tell the true from the false, the monster walked into the room and, grabbing his "spouse," he at once demanded a kiss. "He really wants to sport with old Monkey!" said Pilgrim, smiling to himself. Using a holding trick, he caught the long snout of that monster and gave it a sudden, violent twist, sending him crashing to the floor with a loud thud. Picking himself up, the monster supported himself on the side of the bed and said, "Sister, how is it that you seem somewhat annoyed with me today? Because I'm late, perhaps?" "I'm not annoyed!" said Pilgrim. "If not," said that monster, "why did you give me such a fall?" "How can you be so boorish," said Pilgrim, "grabbing me like that and wanting to kiss me? I don't feel very well today; under normal conditions I would have been up waiting for you and would have opened the door myself. You may take off your clothes and go to sleep."

The fiend did not suspect anything and took off his clothes. Pilgrim jumped up and sat on the chamber pot, while the fiend climbed into bed. Groping around, he could not feel anyone and called out: "Sister, where have you gone? Please take off your clothes and go to sleep." "You go to sleep first," said Pilgrim, "for I have to wait until I've dropped my load." The fiend indeed loosened his clothes and stayed in bed. Suddenly Pilgrim gave out a sigh, saying, "My luck's pretty low!" "What's bothering you?" said the monster. "What do you mean, your luck's pretty low? It's true that I have consumed quite a bit of food and drink since I entered your family, but I certainly did not take them as free meals. Look at the things I did for your family: sweeping the grounds and draining the ditches, hauling bricks and carrying tiles, building walls and pounding mortar, plowing the fields and raking the earth, planting seedlings of rice and wheat—in short, I took care of your entire estate. Now what you have on your body happens to be brocade, and what you wear as ornaments happens to be gold. You enjoy the flowers and fruits of four seasons, and you have fresh vegetables for the table in all eight periods. Whatever makes you so dissatisfied that you have to sigh and lament, saying your luck's pretty low?"

"It isn't quite as you say," said Pilgrim. "Today my parents gave me a severe scolding over the partition wall, throwing bricks and tiles into this place." "What were they scolding you for?" asked the monster. Pilgrim said, "They said that since we have become husband and wife, you are in fact a son-in-law in their family but one who is completely without manners. A person as ugly as you is unpresentable: you can't meet your brothers-in-law, nor can you greet the other relatives. Since you come with the clouds and leave with the fog, we really don't know what family you belong to and what your true name is. In fact, you have ruined our family's reputation and defiled our heritage. That was what they rebuked me for, and that's why I'm upset." "Though I am somewhat homely," said the monster, "it's no great problem if they insist on my being more handsome. We discussed these matters before when I came here, and I entered your family fully with your father's consent. Why did they bring it up again today? My family is located in the Cloudy Paths Cave of Fuling Mountain; my surname is based on my appearance. Hence I am called Zhu (Hog), and my official name is Ganglie (Stiff Bristles). If they ever ask you again, tell them what I have told you."

"This monster is quite honest," said Pilgrim to himself, secretly pleased. "Without torture, he has already made a plain confession; with his name and location clearly known, he will certainly be caught, regardless of what may happen." Pilgrim then said to him: "My parents are trying to get an exorcist here to arrest you." "Go to sleep! Go to sleep!" said the monster, laughing. "Don't mind them at all! I know as many transformations as the number of stars in the Heavenly Ladle, and I own a nine-pronged muckrake. Why should I fear any exorcist, monk, or Daoist priest? Even if your old man were pious enough to be able to get the Monster-Routing Patriarch to come down from the Ninefold Heaven, I could still claim to have been an old acquaintance of his. And he wouldn't dare do anything to me." "But they were saying that they hoped to invite someone by the name of Sun," said Pilgrim, "the so-called Great Sage, Equal to Heaven, who caused havoc in the Celestial Palace five hundred years ago. They were going to ask him to come catch you." When the monster heard this name, he became rather alarmed. "If that's true," he said, "I'm leaving. We can't live as a couple anymore!" "Why do you have to leave so suddenly?" asked Pilgrim. "You may not know," said the monster, "that that Bimawen who caused such turmoil in Heaven has some real abilities. I fear that I am no match for him, and losing my reputation is not my form!"

When he had finished speaking, he slipped on his clothes, opened the door, and walked right out. Pilgrim grabbed him, and with one wipe of his own face he assumed his original form, shouting: "Monster, where do you think you're going? Take a good look and see who I am!" The monster turned around and saw the protruding teeth, the gaping mouth, the fiery eyes, the golden pupils, the pointed head, and the hairy face of Pilgrim—virtually a living thunder god! He was so horrified that his hands became numb and his feet grew weak. With a loud ripping sound, he tore open his shirt and broke free of Pilgrim's clutch by changing into a violent wind. Pilgrim rushed forward and struck mightily at the wind with his iron rod; the monster at once transformed himself into myriad shafts of flaming light and fled toward his own mountain. Mounting the clouds,

Pilgrim pursued him, crying, "Where are you running to? If you ascend to Heaven, I'll chase you to the Palace of the Polestar, and if you go down into the Earth, I'll follow you into the heart of Hell!" Good Heavens! We do not know where the chase took them to or what was the outcome of the fight. Let's listen to the explanation in the next chapter.

At Cloudy Paths Cave, Wukong takes in Bajie;
At Pagoda Mountain, Tripitaka receives the Heart Sūtra.

We were telling you about the flaming light of the monster, which was fleeing, while the Great Sage riding the rosy clouds followed right behind. As they were thus proceeding, they came upon a tall mountain, where the monster gathered together the fiery shafts of light and resumed his original form. Racing into a cave, he took out a nine-pronged muckrake to fight. "Lawless monster!" shouted Pilgrim. "What region are you from, fiend, and how do you know old Monkey's names? What abilities do you have? Make a full confession quickly and your life may be spared!" "So you don't know my powers!" said that monster. "Come up here and brace yourself! I'll tell you!

> *My mind was dim since the time of youth;*
> *Always I loved my indolence and sloth.*
> *Neither nursing nature nor seeking long life,*[1]
> *I passed my days deluded and confused.*
> *I met a true immortal suddenly*
> *Who sat and spoke to me of heat and cold.*[2]
> *'Repent,' he said, 'and cease your worldly way:*
> *From taking life accrues a boundless curse.*
> *One day when the Great Limit ends your lot,*
> *For eight woes and three ways*[3] *you'll grieve too late!'*

1. Seeking long life: literally, cultivating authenticity or realized immortality (*xiuzhen*).

2. Heat and cold: though the phrase *hanwen* may refer to weather and thus it may point to the exchange of conventional greetings in this conversation, the terms can also be references to alchemical processes inside or outside the body.

3. The eight woes (*banan*) refer to eight conditions or states of being (the state of hells, the state of animals, the state of hungry ghosts, the states of being deaf, blind, and dumb, the state of no affliction, and the state of the intermediate period between a Buddha and his successor) that make it difficult for one to see Buddha or

I listened and turned my will to mend my ways:
I heard, repented, and sought the wondrous rune.
By fate my teacher he became at once,
Pointing out passes key to Heav'n and Earth.
To get the Great Pill of Nine Cyclic Turns,
My work incessant went on night and day.[4]
It reached the Mud-Pill Palace of my crown
And the Jetting-Spring Points beneath my feet.
With kidney-brine flooding the Floral Pool,
My Cinnabar Field was thus warmly nursed.
Baby and virgin mated as yin and yang;
Lead and mercury mixed as sun and moon.
In concord Li-dragon and Kan-tiger used,
The spirit turtle sucked dry the gold crow's blood.
Three flowers joined on top, the root reclaimed;
Five breaths faced their source and all freely flowed.
My merit done, I ascended on high,
Met by pairs of immortals from the sky.
Radiant pink clouds arose beneath my feet;
With light, sound frame I faced the Golden Arch.
The Jade Emperor gave a banquet for gods
Who sat in rows according to their ranks.
Made a marshal of the Celestial Stream,
I took command of both sailors and ships.
Because Queen Mother gave the Peaches Feast—
When she met her guests at the Jasper Pool—
My mind turned hazy for I got dead drunk,
A shameless rowdy reeling left and right.
Boldly I barged through the Vast Cold Palace[5]
Where the charming fairy beckoned me in.
When I saw her face that would snare one's soul,
My carnal itch of old could not be stopped!
Without regard for manners or for rank,

---

hear his law. The three ways are that of fire, where one is burned in hell; of blood, which is the realm of predatory animals; and of the sword, with which hungry ghosts are tortured.

4. What follows in the next eight lines are allusions to the various processes of internal or physiological alchemy.

5. A poetic name for the mythic palace on the moon.

I grabbed Miss Chang'e[6] asking her to bed.
For three or four times she rejected me:
Hiding east and west, she was sore annoyed.
My passion sky-high I roared like thunder,
Almost toppling the arch of Heaven's gate.
Inspector General told the Emperor Jade;
I was destined that day to meet my fate.
The Vast Cold completely enclosed airtight
Left me no way to run or to escape.
Then I was caught by the various gods,
Undaunted still, for wine was in my heart.
Bound and taken to see the Emperor Jade,
By law I should have been condemned to death.
It was Venus the Gold Star, Mr. Li,
Who left the ranks and knelt to beg for me.
My punishment changed to two thousand blows,
My flesh was torn; my bones did almost crack.
Alive! I was banished from Heaven's gate
To make my home beneath the Fuling Mount.
An errant womb's my sinful destination:
Stiff-Bristle Hog's my worldly appellation!"

When Pilgrim heard this, he said, "So you are actually the Water God of the Heavenly Reeds, who came to earth. Small wonder you knew old Monkey's name." "Curses!" cried the monster. "You Heaven-defying Bimawen! When you caused such turmoil that year in Heaven, you had no idea how many of us had to suffer because of you. And here you are again to make life miserable for others! Don't give me any lip! Have a taste of my rake!" Pilgrim, of course, was unwilling to be tolerant; lifting high his rod, he struck at the monster's head. The two of them thus began a battle in the middle of the mountain, in the middle of the night. What a fight!

Pilgrim's gold pupils blazed like lightning;
The monster's round eyes flashed like silver blooms.
This one spat out colored fog:
That one spouted crimson mist.
The spouted crimson mist lit up the dark;
The colored fog spat out made bright the night.
The golden-hooped rod;
The nine-pronged muckrake.

6. Chang'e: the immortal goddess who resides in the moon.

Two true heroes most worthy of acclaim:
One was the Great Sage descended to earth;
One was a Marshal who came from Heaven.
That one, for indecorum, became a monster;
This one, to flee his ordeal, bowed to a monk.
The rake lunged like a dragon wielding his claws:
The rod came like a phoenix darting through flowers.
That one said: "Your breaking up a marriage is like patricide!"
This one said: "You should be arrested for raping a young girl!"
Such idle words!
Such wild clamor!
Back and forth the rod blocked the rake.
They fought till dawn was about to break,
When the monster's two arms felt sore and numb.

From the time of the second watch, the two of them fought until it was growing light in the east. That monster could hold out no longer and fled in defeat. He changed once more into a violent gust of wind and went straight back to his cave, shutting the doors tightly and refusing to come out. Outside the cave, Pilgrim saw a large stone tablet, which had on it the inscription "Cloudy Paths Cave." By now, it was completely light. Realizing that the monster was not going to come out, Pilgrim thought to himself: "I fear that Master may be anxiously waiting for me. I may as well go back and see him before returning here to catch the monster." Mounting the clouds, he soon arrived at Old Gao village.

We shall now tell you about Tripitaka, who chatted about past and present with the other elders and did not sleep all night. He was just wondering why Pilgrim had not shown up, when suddenly the latter dropped down into the courtyard. Straightening out his clothes and putting away his rod. Pilgrim went up to the hall, crying, "Master! I've returned!" The various elders hurriedly bowed low, saying, "Thank you for all the trouble you have been to!" "Wukong, you were gone all night," said Tripitaka. "If you captured the monster, where is he now?" "Master," said Pilgrim, "that monster is no fiend of this world, nor is he a strange beast of the mountains. He is actually the incarnation of the Marshal of the Heavenly Reeds. Because he took the wrong path of rebirth, his appearance assumed the form of a wild hog: but actually his spiritual nature has not been extinguished. He said that he derived his surname from his appearance, and he went by the name of Zhu Ganglie. When I attacked him with my rod in the rear building, he tried to escape by changing into a violent gust of wind; I then struck at the wind, and he changed into shafts of flaming light and retreated to his mountain cave. There he took out a nine-pronged muckrake to do battle with old Monkey for a whole night. Just now when it grew light, he could fight no longer and fled into the cave, shutting the doors tightly and not coming out any more. I wanted to break down the door to finish him off, but I was afraid that you might be waiting here anxiously. That's why I came back first to give you some news."

When he had finished speaking, old Mr. Gao came forward and knelt down, saying, "Honored Priest, I have no alternative but to say this. Though you have chased him away, he might come back here after you leave. What should we do then? I may as well ask you to do us the favor of apprehending him, so that we shall not have any further worries. This old man, I assure you, will not be ungrateful or unkind; there will be a generous reward for you. I shall ask my relatives and friends to witness the drawing up of a document, whereby I shall divide my possessions and my property equally with you. All I want is to pluck up the trouble by the root, so that the pure virtue of our Gao family will not be tainted."

"Aren't you being rather demanding, old man?" said Pilgrim, laughing. "That monster did tell me that, although he has an enormous appetite and has consumed a good deal of food and drink from your family, he has also done a lot of good work for you. Much of what you were able to accumulate these last few years you owe to his strength, so that he really hasn't taken any free meals from you. Why ever do you want to have him driven away? According to him, he is a god who has come down to earth and who has helped your family earn a living. Moreover, he has not harmed your daughter in any way. Such a son-in-law, I should think, would be a good match for your daughter and your family. So, what's all this about ruining your family's reputation and damaging your standing in the community? Why not really accept him as he is?"

"Honored Priest," said old Mr. Gao, "though this matter may not offend public morals, it does leave us with a bad name. Like it or not, people will say, 'The Gao family has taken in a monster as a son-in-law!' How can one stand remarks of that kind?" "Wukong," said Tripitaka, "if you have worked for him all this while, you might as well see him through to a satisfactory conclusion." Pilgrim said, "I was testing him a little, just for fun. This time when I go, I'll apprehend the monster for certain and bring him back for you all to see. Don't worry, old Gao! Take good care of my master. I'm off!"

He said he was off, and the next instant he was completely out of sight. Bounding up that mountain, he arrived at the cave's entrance; a few strokes of the iron rod reduced the doors to dust. "You overstuffed coolie!" he shouted, "Come out quickly and fight with old Monkey!" Huffing and puffing, the monster was lying in the cave and trying to catch his breath. When he heard his doors being struck down and heard himself called "an overstuffed coolie," he could not control his wrath. Dragging his rake, he pulled himself together and ran out. "A Bimawen like you," he yelled, "is an absolute pest! What have I done to you that you have to break my doors to pieces? Go and take a look at the law: a man who breaks someone's door and enters without permission may be guilty of trespassing, a crime punishable by death!" "Idiot!" said Pilgrim laughing. "I may have broken down the door, but my case is still a defensible one. But you, you took a girl from her family by force—without using the proper matchmakers and witnesses, without presenting the proper gifts of money and wine. If you ask me, you are the one guilty of a capital crime!" "Enough of this idle talk," said the monster, "and watch out for old Hog's rake!" Parrying the rake with his rod, Pilgrim said, "Isn't that rake of yours just something you use as a regular farm hand to plow the fields or plant vegetables for the Gao family? Why on earth should I fear you?"

"You have made a mistake!" said the monster. "Is this rake a thing of this world? Just listen to my recital:

This is divine ice steel greatly refined,
Polished so highly that it glows and shines.
Laozi wielded the large hammer and tong;
Mars added himself charcoals piece by piece.
Five Kings of Five Quarters applied their schemes;
Twelve Gods of Time expended all their skills.
They made nine prongs like dangling teeth of jade,
And brass rings were cast with dropping gold leaves.
Decked with five stars and six brightnesses,
Its frame conformed to eight spans and four climes.
Its whole length set to match the cosmic scheme
Accorded with yinyang, *with the sun and moon.*
Six-Diagram Gods followed Heaven's rules;[7]
Eight-Trigram Stars stood in ranks and files;
They named this the High Treasure Golden Rake,
A gift for Jade Emperor to guard his court.
Since I learned to be a great immortal,
Becoming someone with longevity,
I was made Marshal of the Heavenly Reeds

7. Deities deriving from the *Classic of Change.*

And given this rake, a sign of royal grace.
When it's held high, there'll be bright flames and light;
When it's brought low, strong wind blows down white snow.
The warriors of Heaven all fear it;
The Ten Kings of Hell all shrink from it.
Are there such weapons among mankind?
In this wide world there's no such fine steel.
It changes its form after my own wish,
Rising and falling after my command.
I've kept it with me for several years,
A daily comrade I never parted from.
I've stayed with it right through the day's three meals,
Nor left it when I went to sleep at night.
I brought it along to the Peaches Feast,
And with it I attended Heaven's court.
Since I wrought evil relying on wine,
Since trusting my strength I displayed my fraud,
Heaven sent me down to this world of dust,
Where in my next life I would sin some more.
With wicked mind I ate men in my cave,
Pleased to be married at the Gao Village.
This rake can overturn sea dragons' and turtles' lairs
And rake up mountain dens of tigers and wolves.
All other weapons there's no need to name,
Only my rake is the most fitting one
To win in battle, for it's no hard thing!
And making merit? It need not be said!
You may have a bronze head, an iron brain, and a full steel frame.
I'll rake till your soul melts and your spirit leaks!"

When Pilgrim heard these words, he put away his iron rod and said, "Don't brag too much, Idiot! Old Monkey will stretch out his head right here, and you can give him a blow. See if his soul melts and his spirit leaks!" The monster did indeed raise his rake high and bring it down with all his might; with a loud bang, the rake made sparks as it bounced back up. But the blow did not make so much as a scratch on Pilgrim's head. The monster was so astounded that his hands turned numb and his feet grew weak. He mumbled, "What a head! What a head!" "You didn't know about this, did you?" said Pilgrim. "When I caused such turmoil in Heaven by stealing the magic pills, the immortal peaches, and the imperial wine, I was captured by the Little Sage Erlang and taken to the Polestar Palace. The various celestial beings chopped me with an ax, pounded me with a bludgeon, cut me with a scimitar, jabbed me with a sword, burned me with fire, and struck me with thunder—all this could not hurt me one whit. Then I was taken by Laozi and placed in his eight-trigram brazier, in which I was refined by divine fire until I had fiery eyes and diamond pupils, a bronze head and iron arms. If you don't believe me, give me some more blows and see whether it hurts me at all."

"Monkey," said the monster, "I remember that at the time you were causing trouble in Heaven, you lived in the Water-Curtain Cave of the Flower-Fruit Mountain, in the Aolai Country of the East Pūrvavideha Continent. Your name hasn't been heard of for a long time. How is it that you suddenly turn up at this place to oppress me? Could my father-in-law have gone all that way to ask you to come here?" "Your father-in-law did not go to fetch me," said Pilgrim. "It's old Monkey who turned from wrong to right, who left the Daoist to follow the Buddhist. I am now accompanying the royal brother of the Great Tang Emperor in the Land of the East, whose name is Tripitaka, Master of the Law. He is on his way to the Western Heaven to seek scriptures from Buddha. We passed through the Gao Village and asked for lodging; old man Gao then brought up the subject of his daughter and asked me to rescue her and to apprehend you, you overstuffed coolie!"

Hearing this, the monster threw away his muckrake and said with great affability, "Where is the scripture pilgrim? Please take the trouble of introducing me to him." "Why do you want to see him?" asked Pilgrim. The monster said, "I was a convert of the Bodhisattva Guanshiyin, who commanded me to keep a vegetarian diet here and to wait for the scripture pilgrim. I was to follow him to the Western Heaven to seek scriptures from the Buddha, so that I might atone for my sins with my merit and regain the fruits of Truth. I have been waiting for a number of years without receiving any further news. Since you have been made his disciple, why didn't you mention the search for scriptures in the first place? Why did you have to unleash your violence and attack me right at my own door?"

"Don't try to soften me with deception," said Pilgrim, "thinking that you can escape that way. If you are truly sincere about accompanying the Tang monk, you must face Heaven and swear that you are telling the truth. Then I'll take you to see my master." At once the monster knelt down and kowtowed as rapidly as if he were pounding rice with his head. "Amitābha," he cried, "Namo Buddha! If I am not speaking the truth in all sincerity, let me be punished as one who has offended Heaven—let me be hewn to pieces!"

Hearing him swear such an oath, Pilgrim said, "All right! You light a fire and burn up this place of yours; then I'll take you with me." The monster accordingly dragged in bunches of rushweed and thorns and lighted the fire; the Cloudy Paths Cave soon looked like a derelict potter's kiln. "I have no other attachment," he said to Pilgrim. "You can take me away." "Give me your muckrake and let me hold it," said Pilgrim, and our monster at once handed it over. Yanking out a piece of hair, Pilgrim blew onto it and cried "Change!" It changed into a three-ply hemp rope with which he prepared to tie up the monster's hands. Putting his arms behind his back, the monster did nothing to stop himself from being bound. Then Pilgrim took hold of his ear and dragged him along, crying, "Hurry! Hurry!" "Gently, please!" pleaded the monster. "You are holding me so roughly, and my ear is hurting!" "I can't be any gentler," said Pilgrim, "for I can't worry about you now. As the saying goes, 'A good pig is held roughly!' After you have seen my master and proved your worth, I'll let you go." Rising up to a distance halfway between cloud and fog, they headed straight for the Gao Family Village. We have a poem as a testimony:[8]

> Strong is metal's nature to vanquish wood:
> Mind Monkey has the Wood Dragon subdued.
> With metal and wood both obedient as one,
> All their love and virtue will grow and show.
> One guest and one host[9] there's nothing between;
> Three matings, three unions—there's great mystery![10]
> Nature and feelings gladly fused as Last and First:[11]
> Both will surely be enlightened in the West.

In a moment they had arrived at the village. Grasping the rake and pulling at the monster's ear, Pilgrim said, "Look at the one sitting in a most dignified

8. This poem is the first of the novel's many passages in which the relations of the pilgrims one to another are depicted allegorically by the terms of the Five Phases (*wuxing*).

9. In alchemical lore, lead is sometimes regarded as host (*zhu*) and mercury as the guest (*ke* or *bin*), and vice versa.

10. According to *yinyang* theorists, three matings (*sanjiao*) refer to the intercourse of pneumatics (*qi*) of the *yin* (darkness, female), the *yang* (light, male), and *tian* (Heaven, sky); nothing can be created if one is lacking. Later, the idea is expanded to the correlation of the Five Phases with the cycles of the year, the month, and the day, which is also thus called three unions (*sanhe*).

11. Last and First: literally, *zhen* (to determine, divine) and *yuan* (the primary, the initial), two of the four "attributes" assigned to the first hexagram (*qian* or *jian*) that opens the text of the *Classic of Change*. Thus the combination in this line may point again to the conjoining of opposites, an idea fundamental to alchemical theories.

manner up there in the main hall: that's my master." When old Mr. Gao and his relatives suddenly saw Pilgrim dragging by the ear a monster who had his hands bound behind his back, they all gladly left their seats to meet them in the courtyard. The old man cried, "Honored Priest! There's that son-in-law of mine." Our monster went forward and fell on his knees, kowtowing to Tripitaka and saying, "Master, your disciple apologizes for not coming to meet you. If I had known earlier that my master was staying in my father-in-law's house, I would have come at once to pay my respects, and none of these troubles would have befallen me." "Wukong," said Tripitaka, "how did you manage to get him here to see me?" Only then did Pilgrim release his hold. Using the handle of the rake to give the monster a whack, he shouted, "Idiot! Say something!" The monster gave a full account of how the Bodhisattva had converted him. Greatly pleased, Tripitaka said at once, "Mr. Gao, may I borrow your incense table?" Old Mr. Gao took it out immediately, and Tripitaka lighted the incense after purifying his hands. He bowed toward the south, saying, "I thank the Bodhisattva for her holy grace!" The other elders all joined in the worship by adding incense, after which Tripitaka resumed his seat in the main hall and asked Wukong to untie the monster. Pilgrim shook his body to retrieve his hair, and the rope fell off by itself. Once more the monster bowed to Tripitaka, declaring his intention to follow him to the West, and then bowed also to Pilgrim, addressing him as "elder brother" since he was the senior disciple.

"Since you have entered my fold," said Tripitaka, "and have decided to become my disciple, let me give you a religious name so that I may address you properly." "Master," said the monster, "the Bodhisattva already laid hands on my head and gave me the commandments and a religious name, which is Zhu Wuneng." "Good! Good!" said Tripitaka, laughing. "Your elder brother is named Wukong and you are called Wuneng; your names are well in accord with the emphasis of our denomination." "Master," said Wuneng, "since I received the commandments from the Bodhisattva, I was completely cut off from the five forbidden viands and the three undesirable foods. I maintained a strict vegetarian diet in my father-in-law's house, never touching any forbidden food. Now that I have met my master today, let me be released from my vegetarian vow." "No, no!" said Tripitaka. "Since you have not eaten the five forbidden viands and the three undesirable foods, let me give you another name. Let me call you Bajie."[12] Delighted, Idiot said, "I shall obey my master." For this reason, he was also called Zhu Bajie.

12. Bajie: i.e., eight proscriptions. These are the first eight of the ten commandments in Buddhism forbidding killing, stealing, sexual immorality, lying, the use

When old Mr. Gao saw the happy ending of this whole affair, he was more delighted than ever. He ordered his houseboys immediately to prepare a feast to thank the Tang monk. Bajie went forward and tugged at him, saying, "Papa, please ask my humble wife to come out and greet the grand-dads and uncles. How about it?" "Worthy brother!" said Pilgrim laughing. "Since you have embraced Buddhism and become a monk, please don't ever mention 'your humble wife' again. There may be a married Daoist in this world, but there's no such monk, is there? Let's sit down, rather, and have a nice vegetarian meal. We'll have to start off soon for the West."

Old Mr. Gao set the tables in order and invited Tripitaka to take the honored seat in the middle: Pilgrim and Bajie sat on both sides while the relatives took the remaining seats below. Mr. Gao opened a bottle of dietary wine and filled a glass: he sprinkled a little of the wine on the ground to thank Heaven and Earth before presenting the glass to Tripitaka. "To tell you the truth, aged sir," said Tripitaka, "this poor monk has been a vegetarian from birth. I have not touched any kind of forbidden food since childhood." "I know the reverend teacher is chaste and pure," said old Mr. Gao, "and I did not dare bring forth any forbidden foodstuff. This wine is made for those who maintain a vegetarian diet: there's no harm in your taking a glass." "I just don't dare use wine," said Tripitaka. "for the prohibition of strong drink is a monk's first commandment." Alarmed, Wuneng said, "Master, though I kept a vegetarian diet, I didn't cut out wine." "Though my capacity is not great," said Wukong, "and I'm not able to handle more than a crock or so, I haven't discontinued the use of wine either." "In that case," said Tripitaka, "you two brothers may take some of this pure wine. But you are not permitted to get drunk and cause trouble." So the two of them took the first round before taking their seats again to enjoy the feast. We cannot tell you in full what a richly laden table that was, and what varieties of delicacies were presented.

After master and disciples had been feted, old Mr. Gao took out a red lacquered tray bearing some two hundred taels of gold and silver in small pieces, which were to be presented to the three priests for travel expenses. There were, moreover, three outer garments made of fine silk. Tripitaka said, "We are mendicants who beg for food and drink from village to village. How could we accept gold, silver, and precious clothing?" Coming forward and stretching out his hand, Pilgrim took a handful of the money, saying, "Gao Cai, yesterday you took the trouble to bring my master here,

---

of cosmetics and other personal comforts (e.g., a fine bed), strong drink, the use of dancing and music, and eating out of regulation hours. The last two deal with specific forbidden foods and the rule for fasting.

with the result that we made a disciple today. We have nothing to thank you with. Take this as remuneration for being a guide; perhaps you can use it to buy a few pairs of straw sandals. If there are any more monsters, turn them over to me and I'll truly be grateful to you." Gao Cai took the money and kowtowed to thank Pilgrim for his reward. Old Mr. Gao then said, "If the masters do not want the silver and gold, please accept at least these three simple garments, which are but small tokens of our goodwill." "If those of us who have left the family," said Tripitaka again, "accept the bribe of a single strand of silk, we may fall into ten thousand kalpas from which we may never recover. It is quite sufficient that we take along the leftovers from the table as provisions on our way." Bajie spoke up from the side: "Master, Elder Brother, you may not want these things. But I was a son-in-law in this household for several years, and the payment for my services should be worth more than three stones of rice! Father, my shirt was torn by Elder Brother last night; please give me a cassock of blue silk. My shoes are worn also, so please give me a good pair of new shoes." When old Mr. Gao heard that, he dared not refuse; a new pair of shoes and a cassock were purchased at once so that Bajie could dispose of the old attire.

Swaggering around, our Bajie spoke amiably to old Mr. Gao, saying, "Please convey my humble sentiments to my mother-in-law, my great-aunt, my second aunt, and my uncle-in-law, and all my other relatives. Today I am going away as a monk, and please do not blame me if I cannot take leave of them in person. Father, do take care of my better half. If we fail in our quest for scriptures, I'll return to secular life and live with you again as your son-in-law." "Coolie!" shouted Pilgrim. "Stop babbling nonsense!" "It's no nonsense," said Bajie. "Sometimes I fear that things may go wrong, and then I could end up unable either to be a monk or to take a wife, losing out on both counts." "Less of this idle conversation!" said Tripitaka. "We must hurry up and leave." They therefore packed their luggage, and Bajie was told to carry the load with a pole. Tripitaka rode on the white horse, while Pilgrim led the way with the iron rod across his shoulders. The three of them took leave of old Mr. Gao and his relatives and headed toward the West. We have a poem as testimony:

The earth's mist-shrouded, the trees appear tall.
The Buddha-son of Tang Court ever toils.
He eats in need rice begged from many homes;
He wears when cold a robe patched a thousandfold.
Hold fast at the breast the Horse of the Will!
The Mind-Monkey is sly—let him not wail!

Nature one with feelings, causes all joined—
The moon's full of gold light is the hair shorn.[13]

The three of them proceeded toward the West, and for about a month it was an uneventful journey. When they crossed the boundary of Tibet, they looked up and saw a tall mountain. Tripitaka reined in his horse and said, "Wukong, Wuneng, there's a tall mountain ahead. We must approach it with care." "It's nothing!" said Bajie. "This mountain is called the Pagoda Mountain and a Crow's Nest Chan Master lives there, practicing austerities. Old Hog has met him before." "What's his business?" said Tripitaka. "He's fairly accomplished in the Way," said Bajie, "and he once asked me to practice austerities with him. But I didn't go, and that was the end of the matter." As master and disciple conversed, they soon arrived at the mountain. What a splendid mountain! You see

South of it, blue pines, jade-green junipers;
North of it, green willows, red peach trees.
A clamorous din:
The mountain fowls are conversing.
A fluttering dance:
Immortal cranes fly in unison.
A dense fragrance:
The flowers in a thousand colors.
A manifold green:
Diverse plants in forms exotic.
In the stream there's water bubbling and green;
Before the cliff, petals of blessed cloud afloat.
Truly a place of rare beauty, a well-secluded spot;
Silence is all, not a man to be seen.

As the master sat on his horse, peering into the distance, he saw on top of the fragrant juniper tree a nest made of dried wood and grass. To the left, muskdeer carried flowers in their mouths; to the right, mountain monkeys were presenting fruits. At the top of the tree, blue and pink phoenixes sang together, soon to be joined by a congregation of black cranes and brightly colored pheasants. "Isn't that the Crow's Nest Chan Master?" asked Bajie, pointing. Tripitaka urged on his horse and rode up to the tree.

We now tell you about that Chan Master, who, seeing the three of

13. Hair shorn: the phrase refers to a story in which one Old Man Wang (Wang Weng) attained physical longevity in stages. At the last, when since his time of birth he went through five times during which his hair was shorn or fell off and apparently grew back again, he realized immortality.

them approach, left his nest and jumped down from the tree. Tripitaka dismounted and prostrated himself. Raising him up with his hand, the Chan Master said, "Holy Monk, please arise! Pardon me for not coming to meet you." "Old Chan Master," said Bajie, "please receive my bow!" "Aren't you the Zhu Ganglie of the Fuling Mountain?" asked the Chan Master, startled. "How did you have the good fortune to journey with the holy monk?" "A few years back," said Bajie, "I was beholden to the Bodhisattva Guanyin for persuading me to follow him as a disciple." "Good! Good! Good!" said the Chan Master, greatly pleased. Then he pointed to Pilgrim and asked: "Who is this person?" "How is it that the old Chan recognizes him," said Pilgrim, laughing, "and not me?" "Because I haven't had the pleasure of meeting you," said the Chan Master. Tripitaka said, "He is my eldest disciple, Sun Wukong." Smiling amiably, the Chan Master said, "How impolite of me!"

Tripitaka bowed again and asked about the distance to the Great Thunderclap Temple of the Western Heaven. "It's very far away! Very far away!" said the Chan Master. "What's more, the road is a difficult one, filled with tigers and leopards." With great earnestness. Tripitaka asked again, "Just how far is it?" "Though it may be very far," answered the Chan Master, "you will arrive there one day. But all those *māra* hindrances along the way are hard to dispel. I have a Heart Sūtra here in this scroll; it has fifty-four sentences containing two hundred and seventy characters. When you meet these *māra* hindrances, recite the sūtra and you will not suffer any injury or harm." Tripitaka prostrated himself on the ground and begged to receive it, whereupon the Chan Master imparted the sūtra by reciting it orally. The sūtra said:

Heart Sūtra of the Great Perfection of Wisdom
When the Bodhisattva Guanzizai[14] was moving in the deep course of the Perfection of Wisdom, she saw that the five heaps[15] were but emptiness, and she transcended all sufferings. Śāriputra, form is no different from emptiness, emptiness no different from form; form is emptiness, and emptiness is form. Of sensations, perceptions, volition, and consciousness, the same is also true. Śāriputra, it is thus that all dharmas are but empty appearances, neither produced nor destroyed, neither defiled nor pure, neither

14. Guanzizai: Guanyin, the Onlooking Lord.
15. The five aggregates or elements constitutive of the human person: physical phenomena related to the senses, sensation or reception from stimuli, discernment or perception, decision or volition, and cognition and consciousness.

increasing nor decreasing. This is why in emptiness there are no forms and no sensations, perceptions, volition, or consciousness; no eye, ear, nose, tongue, body, or mind; no form, sound, smell, taste, touch, or object of mind. There is no realm of sight [and so forth], until we reach the realm of no mind-consciousness; there is no ignorance, nor is there extinction of ignorance [and so forth], until we reach the stage where there is no old age and death, nor is there the extinction of old age and death; there is no suffering, annihilation, or way; there is no cognition or attainment. Because there is nothing to be attained, the mind of the Bodhisattva, by virtue of reliance upon the Perfection of Wisdom, has no hindrances: no hindrances, and therefore, no terror or fear; he is far removed from error and delusion, and finally reaches Nirvāṇa. All the Buddhas of the three worlds[16] rely on the Perfection of Wisdom, and that is why they attain the ultimate and complete enlightenment. Know, therefore, that the Perfection of Wisdom is a great divine spell, a spell of great illumination, a spell without superior, and a spell without equal. It can do away with all sufferings—such is the unvarnished truth. Therefore, when the Spell of the Perfection of Wisdom is to be spoken, say this spell: "Gate! Gate! Pāragate! Pārasaṃgate! Bodhisvāhā!"[17]

Now because that master of the law from the Tang Court was spiritually prepared, he could remember the Heart Sūtra after hearing it only once. Through him, it has come down to us this day. It is the comprehensive classic for the cultivation of Truth, the very gateway to becoming a Buddha.

After the transmission of the sūtra, the Chan Master trod on the cloudy luminosity and was about to return to his crow's nest. Tripitaka, however, held him back and earnestly questioned him again about the condition of the road to the West. The Chan Master laughed and said:

"The way is not too hard to walk;
Try listening to what I say.
A thousand hills and waters deep;
Places full of goblins and snags;
When you reach those sky-touching cliffs,
Fear not and put your mind at rest.
Crossing the Rub Ear Precipice,
You must walk with steps placed sideways.

16. Three worlds: the past, present, and future ones.
17. The quotation says: "Gone, gone, gone beyond, completely gone beyond! O what an awakening! All hail!"

Take care in the Black Pine Forest;
Fox-spirits will likely bar your way.
Griffins will fill the capitals;
Monsters all mountains populate;
Old tigers sit as magistrates;
Graying wolves act as registrars.
Lions, elephants—all called kings!
Leopards, tigers are coachmen all!
A wild pig totes a hauling pole;
You'll meet ahead a water sprite.
An old stone ape of many years
Now nurses over there his spite!
Just ask that acquaintance of yours:
Well he knows the way to the West."

Hearing this, Pilgrim laughed with scorn and said, "Let's go. Don't ask him, ask me! That's enough!" Tripitaka did not perceive what he meant. The Chan Master, changing into a beam of golden light, went straight up to his crow's nest, while the priest bowed toward him to express his gratitude. Enraged, Pilgrim lifted his iron rod and thrust it upward violently, but garlands of blooming lotus flowers were seen together with a thousand-layered shield of blessed clouds. Though Pilgrim might have the strength to overturn rivers and seas, he could not catch hold of even one strand of the crow's nest. When Tripitaka saw this, he pulled Pilgrim back, saying, "Wukong, why are you jabbing at the nest of a bodhisattva like him?" "For leaving like that after abusing both my brother and me," said Pilgrim. "He was speaking of the way to the Western Heaven," said Tripitaka. "Since when did he abuse you?" "Didn't you get it?" asked Pilgrim. "He said, 'A wild pig totes a hauling pole,' and insulted Bajie: 'An old stone ape of many years' ridiculed old Monkey. How else would you explain that?" "Elder Brother," said Bajie, "don't be angry. This Chan Master does know the events of past and future. Let's see if his statement, 'You'll meet ahead a water sprite,' will be fulfilled or not. Let's spare him and leave." Pilgrim saw the lotus flowers and auspicious fog near the nest, and he had little alternative than to ask his master to mount so that they could descend from the mountain and proceed toward the West. Lo, their journey

Thus shows that in man's world pure leisure is rare,
But evils and ogres are rife in the hills!

We really do not know what took place in the journey ahead; let's listen to the explanation in the next chapter.

Bajie fights fiercely at the Flowing-Sand River;
Moksa by order receives Wujing's submission.

Now we tell you about the Tang monk and his disciples, the three travellers, who proceeded toward the West through a vast level plain. Time went by swiftly, and summer yielded to the arrival of autumn. All they saw were some

Cold cicadas sing on dying willows
As the Great Fire roll toward the West.

As they proceeded, they came upon a huge and turbulent river, its waves surging and splashing. "Disciples," exclaimed Tripitaka, "look at that vast expanse of water in front of us. Why are there no boats in sight? How can we get across?" Taking a close look, Bajie said, "It's very turbulent, too rough for any boat!" Pilgrim leaped into the air and peered into the distance, shading his eyes with his hand. Even he became somewhat frightened and said, "Master, it's very difficult! Very difficult! If old Monkey wishes to cross this river, he need only make one twist of his body and he will reach the other shore. But for you, Master, it's impossible to get across." "I can't even see the other shore from here," said Tripitaka. "Really, how wide is it?" "It's just about eight hundred miles wide," said Pilgrim. "Elder Brother," said Bajie, "how could you determine its width just like that?" "To tell you the truth, Worthy Brother," said Pilgrim, "these eyes of mine can determine good or evil up to a thousand miles away in daylight. Just now when I was up in the air, I could not tell how long the river was, but I could make out its width to be at least eight hundred miles." Sighing anxiously, the elder pulled back his horse and suddenly discovered on the shore a slab of stone. When the three of them drew closer to have a look, they saw three words written in seal-script, "Flowing-Sand River," below which there were also four lines written in regular style. It read:

These Flowing-Sand metes, eight hundred wide;
These Weak Waters, three thousand deep.
A goose feather cannot stay afloat;
A rush petal will sink to the bottom.

As master and disciples were reading the inscription, the waves in the river suddenly rose like tall mountains, and with a loud splash from the midst of the waters a monster sprang out. Looking most savage and hideous, he had

A head full of wild and flamelike hair;
A pair of bright, round eyes which shone like lamps;
A bluish face which seemed neither black nor green;
An old dragon's voice like thunderclap or drum.
He wore a cape of light yellow goose down.
Two strands of white reeds tied around his waist.
Beneath his chin nine skulls were strung and hung;
His hands held an awesome priestly staff.

Like a cyclone, the fiend rushed up to the shore and went straight for the Tang monk. Pilgrim was so taken aback that he grabbed his master and dashed for high ground to make the escape. Putting down the pole, Bajie whipped out his rake and brought it down hard on the monster. The fiend used his staff to parry the blow, and so the two of them began to unleash their power on the bank of the Flowing-Sand River. This was some battle!

The nine-pronged rake;
The fiend-routing staff;
These two met in battle on the river shore.
This one was the Marshal of Heavenly Reeds;
That one was the Curtain-Raising Captain by the Throne.
In years past they met in Divine Mists Hall;
Today they fought and waged a test of might.
From this one the rake went out like a dragon stretching its claws;
From that one the staff blocked the way like a sharp-tusked elephant.
They stood with their limbs outstretched;
Each struck at the other's rib cage.
This one raked madly, heedless of head or face;
That one struck wildly without pause or rest.
This one was a man-eating spirit, long a lord of Flowing-Sand;
That one was a Way-seeking fighter upholding Law and Faith.

Closing in again and again, the two of them fought for twenty rounds, but neither emerged the victor.

The Great Sage meanwhile was standing there to protect the Tang monk. As he held the horse and guarded the luggage, he became so aroused by the sight of Bajie engaging that fiend that he ground his teeth and rubbed his hands vehemently. Finally he could not restrain himself: whipping out the rod, he said, "Master, sit here and don't be afraid. Let old Monkey go play with him a little." The master begged in vain for him to stay, and with a loud whoop he leaped forward. The monster, you see, was just having a grand time fighting with Bajie, the two of them so tightly locked in combat that nothing seemed able to part them. Pilgrim, however, rushed up to the monster and delivered a terrific blow at his head with his iron rod. The monster was so shaken that he jumped aside: turning around he dove straight into the Flowing-Sand River and disappeared. Bajie was so upset that he leaped about wildly, crying, "Elder Brother! Who asked you to come? The monster was gradually weakening and was finding it difficult to parry my rake. Another four or five rounds and I would have captured him. But when he saw how fierce you were, he fled in defeat. Now, what shall we do?" "Brother," said Pilgrim laughing, "to tell you the truth, since defeating the Yellow Wind Fiend a month ago, I have not played with my rod all this time after leaving the mountain. When I saw how delicious your fight with him was, I couldn't stand the itch beneath my feet! That's why I jumped up here to play a little with him. That monster doesn't know how to play, and I suppose that's the reason for his departure."

Holding hands and teasing each other, the two of them returned to the Tang monk. "Did you catch the monster?" asked the Tang monk. "He didn't last out the fight," said Pilgrim, "and he scrambled back to the water in defeat." "Disciple," said Tripitaka, "since this monster has probably lived here a long time, he ought to know the deep and the shallow parts of the river. After all, such a boundless body of weak water, and not a boat in sight—we need someone who is familiar with the region to lead us across." "Exactly!" said Pilgrim. "As the proverb says, 'He who's near cinnabar becomes red, and he who's near ink turns black.' The monster living here must have a good knowledge of the water. When we catch him, we should not slay him, but just make him take Master across the river before we dispose of him." "Elder Brother," said Bajie, "no need for further delay. You go ahead and catch him, while old Hog guards our master."

"Worthy Brother," said Pilgrim with a laugh, "In this case I've really nothing to brag about, for I'm just not comfortable doing business in water. If all I do is walk around down there, I still have to make the magic sign and recite the water-repelling spell before I can move anywhere. Or else I have to change into a water creature like a fish, shrimp, crab, or turtle before going in. If it were a matter of matching wits in the high mountains or up in the clouds, I know enough to deal with the strangest and most difficult situation. But doing business in water somewhat cramps my style!"

"When I was Marshal of the Heavenly River in former years," said Bajie, "I commanded a naval force of eighty thousand men, and I acquired some knowledge of that element. But I fear that that monster may have some relatives down there in his den, and I won't be able to withstand him if his seventh and eighth cousins all come out. What will happen to me then if they grab me?" "If you go into the water to fight him," said Pilgrim, "don't tarry. Make sure, in fact, that you feign defeat and entice him out here. Then old Monkey will help you." "Right you are," said Bajie, "I'm off!" He took off his blue silk shirt and his shoes; holding the rake with both hands, he divided the waters to make a path for himself. Using the ability he had developed in bygone years, he leaped through billows and waves and headed for the bottom of the river.

We now tell you about that monster, who went back to his home in defeat. He had barely caught his breath when he heard someone pushing water, and as he rose to take a look, he saw Bajie pushing his way through with his rake. That monster lifted his staff and met him face to face, crying, "Monk, watch where you are going or you'll receive a blow from this!" Using the rake to block the blow, Bajie said, "What sort of a monster are you that you dare to bar our way?" "So you don't recognize me," said the monster. "I'm no demon or fiend, nor do I lack a name or surname." "If you are no demon or fiend," said Bajie, "why do you stay here and take human lives? Tell me your name and surname, and I'll spare your life." The monster said:

"*My spirit was strong since the time of birth.*
I had made a tour of the whole wide world,
Where my fame as a hero became well known—
A gallant type emulated by all.
Through countless nations I went as I pleased;
Over lakes and seas I freely roamed.
To learn the Way I crossed the edge of Heaven;
To find a teacher I stumped this great earth.
For years my clothes and alms bowl went with me:
Not one day was I ever lax in spirit.
For scores of times I cruised cloudlike the earth
And walked everywhere a hundred times.
Only then a true immortal I did meet,
Who showed me the Great Path of Golden Light.
I seized the baby and the fair girl first[1]

---

1. As in Bajie's previous verse autobiography, the monster here is referring to his experience of self-cultivation by means of physiological alchemy.

Then released wood mother and the squire of gold.
Bright Hall's kidney-brine flooded the Floral Pool;
The Tower's liver-fire plunged to the heart.
Three thousand merits done, I saw Heaven's face
And reverently bowed to the Hall of Light.
Then the Jade Emperor exalted me;
The Curtain-Raising Captain he made me.
An honored one in South Heaven Gate,
I was much esteemed at Divine Mists Hall.
I hung at my waist the Tiger-Headed Shield:
I held in my hands the Fiend-Routing Staff.
Just like the sunlight my gold helmet shone;
My body's armor flashed like radiant mists.
I was chief of the guardians of the Throne:
I was first among attendants of the court.
When Queen Mother gave the Festival of Peach—
She served her guests at Jasper Pool a feast—
I dropped and broke a crystal glass of jade,
And souls from all the hosts of Heaven fled.
Jade Emperor grew mightily enraged;
Hands clasped, he faced his counsel on the left.
Stripped of my hat, my armor, and my rank,
I was taken bodily to the block.
Only the Great Immortal of Naked Feet
Came from the ranks and begged to have me freed.
Pardoned from death and with my sentence stayed,
I was banished to the shores of Flowing-Sand.
Sated, I lie wearily in the stream;
Famished, I churn the waves to find my feed.
The woodsman sees me and his life is gone;
The fishers face me and they soon perish.
From first to last I've eaten many men;
I've sinned, repeatedly, taking human lives.
Since you dare to work violence at my door,
My stomach this day has its fondest hopes!
Don't say you're too coarse to be eaten now.
I'll catch you, and look, that's my minced meat sauce!"

Terribly angered by what he heard, Bajie shouted: "You brazen thing! You haven't the slightest perception! Old Hog is tempting enough to make people's mouths water, and you dare say that I'm coarse, that I'm to be chopped up for a chopped meat sauce! Come to think of it, you would like to consider me a piece of tough old bacon! Watch your manners and swallow this rake of your ancestor!" When the monster saw the rake coming, he used the style of "the phoenix nodding its head" to dodge the blow. The two of them thus fought to the surface of the water, each one treading the waters and waves. This conflict was somewhat different from the one before. Look at

> The Curtain-Raising Captain,
> The Marshal of Heavenly Reeds:
> Each showing most admirably his magic might.
> This one waved above his head the fiend-routing staff:
> That one moved the rake as swiftly as his hand.
> The vaulting waves rocked hills and streams;
> The surging tide the cosmos dimmed.
> Savage like Jupiter wielding banners and flags!
> Fierce like Hell's envoy upsetting sacred tops!
> This one guarded the Tang monk devotedly;
> That one, a water fiend, perpetrated his crimes.
> The rake's one stroke would leave nine red marks:
> The staff's one blow would dissolve man's soul.
> They strove to win the fight;
> They struggled to prevail.
> All in all for the scripture pilgrim's sake,
> They vented their fury without restraint.
> They brawled till carps and perches lost their newborn scales,
> And youthful shells of turtles, big and small, were hurt.
> Red shrimps and purple crabs all lost their lives;
> The sundry gods of water all bowed to Heaven!
> You heard only the waves rolled and crashed like thunderclaps.
> The world was astounded: sun and moon were dark!

The two of them fought for two hours, and neither prevailed. It was like

> A brass pan meeting an iron broom,
> A jade gong facing a golden bell.

We now tell you about the Great Sage, who was standing guard beside the Tang monk. With bulging eyes he watched them fighting on the water, but he dared not lift his hands. Finally, Bajie made a half-hearted blow with his rake and, feigning defeat, turned to flee toward the eastern shore. The monster gave chase and was about to reach the river bank when our Pilgrim could no longer restrain himself. He abandoned his master, whipped out the iron rod, leaped to the river side and struck at the monster's head. Fearing to face him, the monster swiftly dove back into the river. "You

Bimawen!" shouted Bajie. "You impulsive ape! Can't you be a bit more patient? You could have waited until I led him up to high ground and then blocked his path to the river. We would have caught him then. Now he has gone back in, and when do you think he'll come out again?" "Idiot," said Pilgrim laughing, "stop shouting! Let's go talk to Master first."

Bajie went with Pilgrim back to high ground to Tripitaka. "Disciple," said Tripitaka, bowing, "you must be tired!" "I won't complain about my fatigue," said Bajie. "Let's subdue the monster and take you across the river; only then would our plan be completely realized." Tripitaka said, "How did the battle go with the monster just now?" "He was just about my equal," said Bajie, "and we fought to a draw. But then I feigned defeat and he chased me up to the bank. When he saw Elder Brother lifting his rod, however, he fled." "So what are we going to do?" asked Tripitaka. "Master, relax!" said Pilgrim. "Let's not worry now, for it's getting late. You sit here on the cliff and let old Monkey go beg some vegetarian food. Take some rest after you eat, and we'll find a solution tomorrow." "You are right," said Bajie. "Go, and come back quickly."

Pilgrim swiftly mounted the clouds and went north to beg a bowl of vegetarian food from some family to present to his master. When the master saw him return so soon, he said, "Wukong, let us go to that household which gave us the food and ask them how we may cross this river. Isn't this better than fighting the monster?" With a laugh, Pilgrim said, "That household is quite far from here, about six or seven thousand miles, no less! How could the people there know about the water? What's the use of asking them?" "You are fibbing again, Elder Brother!" said Bajie. "Six or seven thousand miles, how could you cover that distance so quickly?" "You have no idea," said Pilgrim, "about the capacity of my cloud-somersault, which with one leap can cover a hundred and eight thousand miles. For the six or seven thousand here, all I have to do is to nod my head and stretch my waist, and that's a round trip already! What's so hard about that?" "Elder Brother," said Bajie, "if it's so easy, all you need to do is to carry Master on your back: nod your head, stretch your waist, and jump across. Why continue to fight this monster?" "Don't you know how to ride the clouds?" asked Pilgrim. "Can't you carry him across the river?"

"The mortal nature and worldly bones of Master are as heavy as the Tai Mountain," Bajie said. "How could my cloud-soaring bear him up? It has to be your cloud-somersault." "My cloud-somersault is essentially like cloud-soaring," said Pilgrim, "the only difference being that I can cover greater distances more rapidly. If you can't carry him, what makes you think I can? There's an old proverb which says:

Move Mount Tai: it's light as mustard seeds.
Lift a man and you won't leave the red dust!

Take this monster here: he can use spells and call upon the wind, pushing and pulling a little, but he can't carry a human into the air. And if it's this kind of magic, old Monkey knows every trick well, including becoming invisible and making distances shorter. But it is required of Master to go through all these strange territories before he finds deliverance from the sea of sorrows; hence even one step turns out to be difficult. You and I are only his protective companions, guarding his body and life, but we cannot exempt him from these woes, nor can we obtain the scriptures all by ourselves. Even if we had the ability to go and see Buddha first, he would not bestow the scriptures on you and me. Remember the adage:

What's easily gotten
Is soon forgotten."

When Idiot heard these words, he accepted them amiably as instruction. Master and disciples ate some of the simply prepared vegetarian food before resting on the eastern shore of the Flowing-Sand River.

Next morning, Tripitaka said, "Wukong, what are we going to do today?" "Not much," said Pilgrim, "except that Bajie must go into the water again." "Elder Brother," said Bajie, "you only want to stay clean, but you have no hesitation making me go into the water." "Worthy Brother," said Pilgrim, "this time I'll try not to be impulsive. I'll let you trick him into coming up here, and then I'll block his retreat along the river bank. We must capture him." Dear Bajie! Wiping his face, he pulled himself together. Holding the rake in both hands, he walked to the edge of the river, opened up a path in the water, and went to the monster's home as before. The monster had just wakened from his sleep when he heard the sound of water. Turning quickly to look, he saw Bajie approaching with the rake. He leaped out at once and barred the way, shouting, "Slow down! Watch out for my staff!" Bajie lifted his rake to parry the blow, saying, "What sort of mourning staff do you have there that you dare ask your ancestor to watch out for it?" "A fellow like you," said the monster, "wouldn't recognize this!

For years my staff has enjoyed great fame,
At first an evergreen in the moon.
Wu Gang² cut down from it one huge limb:

---

2. Wu Gang: supposedly an immortal of the Han period, who took up residence in the moon. There he tried frequently to cut down a cassia tree, only to have it grow again once it was felled.

Lu Ban[3] then made it, using all his skills.
Within the hub's one solid piece of gold:
Outside it's wrapped by countless pearly threads.
It's called the treasure staff for crushing fiends,
Ever placed in Divine Mists to rout the ogres.
Since I was appointed a captain great,
The Jade Emperor gave it to me to use.
It lengthens or shortens after my desire;
It grows thick or thin with my command.
It went to guard the Throne at the Peaches Feast:
It served at court in Heaven's world above.
On duty it saw the many sages bowed,
And immortals, too, when the screen was raised.
A divine weapon of transcendent power,
It's no mere human fighting piece.
Since I was banished from the gate of Heaven,
It roamed with me at will beyond the seas.
Perhaps it is not right for me to boast,
But swords and spears of man can't match this staff.
Look at that old, rusted muckrake of yours:
Fit only for hoeing fields and raking herbs!"

"You unchastened brazen thing!" said Bajie laughing. "Never mind whether it's fit for hoeing fields! One little touch and you won't even know how to begin putting bandages or ointment on nine bleeding holes! Even if you are not killed, you will grow old with chronic infection!" The monster raised his hands and again fought with Bajie from the bottom of the river up to the surface of the water. This battle was even more different from the first one. Look at them

Wielding the treasure staff.
Striking with muckrake;
They would not speak as if they were estranged.
Since wood mother constrained the spatula,[4]
The two engaged in a combat fierce.
No win or loss;

3. Reputedly a craftsman of marvelous skills in the Spring and Autumn period who was subsequently venerated by carpenters and builders as their patron deity.

4. Spatula: *daoguei*, the spatula or knifelike instrument which the alchemists use to separate or measure their chemicals or herbs. In the narrative, it is used as a metaphor for Sha Wujing.

With determined minds
They churned up waves and billows to fight a war.
How could this one control his bitter rage;
That one found unbearable his pain.
Rake and staff went back and forth to show their might;
The water rolled like poison in Flowing-Sand.
They huffed and puffed!
They worked and worked!
All because Tripitaka must face the West.
The muckrake so ferocious!
The staff used with such ease!
This one made a grab to pull him up the shore;
That one sought to seize and drown him in the stream.
They roared like thunder, stirring dragon and fish.
Gods and ghosts cowered as the Heavens grew dim.

This time they fought back and forth for thirty rounds, and neither one proved to be the stronger. Again Bajie pretended to be defeated and fled, dragging his rake. Kicking up the waves, the monster gave chase and they reached the edge of the river. "Wretch!" cried Bajie. "Come up here! We can fight better on solid ground up here." "You are just trying to trick me into going up there," shouted the monster, "so that you can bring out your assistant. You come down here, and we can fight in the water." The monster, you see, had become wise; he refused to go up to the bank and remained near the edge of the water to argue with Bajie. When Pilgrim saw that the monster refused to leave the water, he was highly irritated, and all he could think of was to catch him at once. "Master," he said, "you sit here. Let me give him a taste of the 'ravenous eagle seizing his prey.'" He somersaulted into the air and then swooped down onto the monster, who was still bickering with Bajie. When he heard the sound of the wind, he turned quickly and discovered Pilgrim hurtling down from the clouds. Putting away his staff, he dove into the water and disappeared. Pilgrim stood on the shore and said to Bajie: "Brother, that monster is catching on! He refuses to come up now. What shall we do?" "It's hard, terribly hard!" said Bajie. "I just can't beat him—even when I summoned up the strength of my milk-drinking days! We are evenly matched!" "Let's go talk to Master," said Pilgrim.

The two of them went up again to high ground and told the Tang monk everything. "If it's so difficult," said the Elder, tears welling up in his eyes, "how can we ever get across?" "Master, please don't worry," said Pilgrim. "It is hard for us to cross with this monster hiding deep in the river. So, don't fight with him any more, Bajie; just stay here and protect Master. I'm going to make a trip up to South Sea." "Elder Brother," said Bajie, "what do you want to do at South Sea?" Pilgrim said, "This business of seeking scriptures originated from the Bodhisattva Guanyin; the one who delivered us from our ordeals was also the Bodhisattva Guanyin. Today our path is blocked at this Flowing-Sand River and we can't proceed. Without her, how can we ever solve our problem? Let me go ask her to help us: it's much better than doing battle with this monster." "You have a point there, Elder Brother," said Bajie. "When you get there, please convey my gratitude to her for her kindly instructions in the past." "Wukong," said Tripitaka, "if you want to go see the Bodhisattva, you needn't delay. Go, and hurry back."

Pilgrim catapulted into the air with his cloud-somersault and headed for the South Sea. Ah! It did not even take him half an hour before he saw the scenery of the Potalaka Mountain. In a moment, he dropped down from his somersault and arrived at the edge of the purple bamboo grove, where he was met by the Spirits of the Twenty-Four Ways. They said to him, "Great Sage, what brings you here?" "My master faces an ordeal," said Pilgrim, "which brings me here specially to see the Bodhisattva." "Please take a seat," said the spirits, "and allow us to make the announcement." One of the spirits who was on duty went to the entrance of the Tidal-Sound Cave, announcing, "Sun Wukong wishes to have an audience with you." The Bodhisattva was leaning on the rails by the Treasure Lotus Pool, looking at the flowers with the Pearl-Bearing Dragon Princess. When she heard the announcement, she went back to the cave, opened the door, and asked that he be shown in. With great solemnity, the Great Sage prostrated himself before her.

"Why are you not accompanying the Tang monk?" asked the Bodhisattva. "For what reason did you want to see me again?" "Bodhisattva," said Pilgrim, looking up at her, "my master took another disciple at the Gao Village, to whom you had given the religious name of Wuneng. After crossing the Yellow Wind Ridge, we have now arrived at the Flowing-Sand River eight hundred miles wide, a body of weak water, which is difficult for Master to get across. There is, moreover, a monster in the river who is quite accomplished in the martial arts. We are grateful to Wuneng, who fought in the water with him three times but could not beat him. The monster is, in fact, blocking our path and we cannot get across. That is why I have come to see you, hoping you will take pity and grant us deliverance." "Monkey," said the Bodhisattva, "are you still acting so smug and self-sufficient that you refuse to disclose the fact that you are in the service of the Tang monk?" "All we had intended to do," said Pilgrim, "was to catch the monster and make him take Master across the river. I am not too good at doing business in the water; so, Wuneng went down alone to his lair to look for him, and they had some conversation. I presume the matter of scripture seeking was not mentioned."

"That monster in the Flowing-Sand River," said the Bodhisattva, "happens to be the incarnation of the Curtain-Raising Captain, who was also brought into the faith by my persuasion when I told him to accompany those on their way to acquire scriptures. Had you been willing to mention that you were a scripture pilgrim from the Land of the East, he would not have fought you; he would have yielded instead." Pilgrim said: "That monster is afraid to fight now; he refuses to come up to the shore and is hiding deep in the water. How can we bring him to submission? How can my master get across this body of weak water?"

The Bodhisattva immediately called for Hui'an. Taking a little red gourd from her sleeves, she handed it over to him, saying, "Take this gourd and go with Sun Wukong to the Flowing-Sand River. Call 'Wujing,' and he'll come out at once. You must first take him to submit to the Tang monk. Next, string together those nine skulls of his and arrange them according to the position of the Nine Palaces. Put this gourd in the center, and you will have a dharma vessel ready to ferry the Tang monk across the boundary formed by the Flowing-Sand River." Obeying the instructions of his master, Hui'an left the Tidal-Sound Cave with the Great Sage carrying the gourd. As they departed the purple bamboo grove in compliance with the holy command, we have a testimonial poem:

The Five Phases well balanced as Heaven's Truth,
He can recognize his former master.
The self's refined, the base's set for wondrous use;
Discerning good and evil he can see the cause.
Metal returns to nature—of the same kind are both.
Wood asks for mercy for they're all related.
The two-earths[5] completes the merit to reach the great void.
As water and fire are blended without a speck of dust.

In a little while the two of them lowered their clouds and arrived at the Flowing-Sand River. Recognizing the disciple Mokṣa, Zhu Bajie led his master to receive him. After bowing to Tripitaka, Mokṣa then greeted Bajie, who said, "I was grateful to be instructed by Your Reverence so that I could meet the Bodhisattva. I have indeed obeyed the Law, and I am

5. Two-earths: an anagrammatic pun on one of the graphs making up the character for spatula.

happy recently to have entered the gate of Buddhism. Since we have been constantly on the road, I have yet to thank you. Please forgive me." "Let's forget about these fancy conversations," said Pilgrim. "We must go and call that fellow." "Call whom?" said Tripitaka. Pilgrim said, "Old Monkey saw the Bodhisattva and gave her an account of what happened. The Bodhisattva told me that this monster in the Flowing-Sand River happened to be the incarnation of the Curtain-Raising Captain. Because he had sinned in Heaven, he was banished to this river and became a monster. But he was converted by the Bodhisattva, who had told him to accompany you to the Western Heaven. Since we did not mention the matter of seeking scriptures, he fought us bitterly. Now the Bodhisattva has sent Mokṣa with this gourd, which that fellow will turn into a dharma vessel to take you across the river." When Tripitaka heard these words, he bowed repeatedly to Mokṣa, saying, "I beseech Your Reverence to act quickly." Holding the gourd and treading half on cloud and half on fog, Mokṣa moved directly above the surface of the Flowing-Sand River. He cried with a loud voice, "Wujing! Wujing! The scripture pilgrim has been here for a long time. Why have you not submitted?"

We now tell you about that monster who, fearful of the Monkey King, had gone back to the bottom of the river to rest in his den. When he heard someone call him by his religious name, he knew that it had to be the Bodhisattva Guanyin. And when he heard, moreover, that the scripture pilgrim had arrived, he no longer feared the ax or the halberd. Swiftly he leaped out of the waves and saw that it was the disciple Mokṣa. Look at him! All smiles, he went forward and bowed, saying, "Your Reverence, forgive me for not coming to meet you. Where is the Bodhisattva?" "My teacher did not come," said Mokṣa, "but she sent me to tell you to become the disciple of the Tang monk without delay. You are to take the skulls around your neck and this gourd, and to fashion with them a dharma vessel according to the position of the Nine Palaces so that he may be taken across this body of weak water." "Where is the scripture pilgrim?" asked Wujing. Pointing with his finger, Mokṣa said, "Isn't he the one sitting on the eastern shore?"

Wujing caught sight of Bajie and said, "I don't know where that lawless creature came from! He fought with me for two whole days, never once saying a word about seeking scriptures." When he saw Pilgrim, he said again. "That customer is his assistant, and a formidable one too! I'm not going over there!" "That is Zhu Bajie," said Mokṣa, "and that other one is Pilgrim Sun, both disciples of the Tang monk and both converted by the Bodhisattva. Why fear them? I'll escort you to the Tang monk." Only then did Wujing put away his precious staff and straighten his yellow silk shirt.

He jumped ashore and knelt before Tripitaka, saying, "Master, your disciple has eyes but no pupils, and he failed to recognize your noble features. I have greatly offended you, and I beg you to pardon me." "You bum!" said Bajie. "Why did you not submit in the first place? Why did you only want to fight with me? What do you have to say for yourself?" "Brother," said Pilgrim laughing, "don't berate him. It's really our fault for not mentioning that we were seeking scriptures, and we didn't tell him our names." "Are you truly willing to embrace our faith?" said the elder. "Your disciple was converted by the Bodhisattva," said Wujing. "Deriving my surname from the river, she gave me the religious name Sha Wujing. How could I be unwilling to take you as my master?" "In that case," said Tripitaka, "Wukong may bring over the sacred razor and shave off his hair." The Great Sage indeed took the razor and shaved Wujing's head, after which he came again to do homage to Tripitaka, Pilgrim, and Bajie, thus becoming the youngest disciple of the Tang monk. When Tripitaka saw that he comported himself very much like a monk, he gave him the nickname of Sha Monk. "Since you have embraced the faith," said Mokṣa, "there's no need for further delay. You must build the dharma vessel at once."

Not daring to delay, Wujing took off the skulls around his neck and strung them up with a rope after the design of the Nine Palaces, placing the gourd in the middle. He then asked his master to leave the shore, and our elder thus embarked on the dharma vessel. As he sat in the center, he found it to be as sturdy as a little boat. He was, moreover, supported by Bajie on his left and Wujing on his right, while Pilgrim Sun, leading the dragon-horse, followed in the rear, treading half on cloud and half on fog. Above their heads Mokṣa also took up his post to give them added protection. In this way our master of the Law was safely ferried across the boundary of the Flowing-Sand River: with the wind calm and waves quiet he crossed the weak water. It was truly as fast as flying or riding an arrow, for in a little while he reached the other shore, having been delivered from the mighty waves. He did not drag up mud or water, and happily both his hands and feet remained dry. In sum, he was pure and clean without engaging in any activity. When master and disciples reached solid ground again, Mokṣa descended from the auspicious clouds. As he took back his gourd, the nine skulls changed into nine curls of dark wind and vanished. Tripitaka bowed to thank Mokṣa and also gave thanks to the Bodhisattva. So it was that Mokṣa went straight back to the South Sea, while Tripitaka mounted his horse to go to the West. We do not know how long it took them to achieve the right fruit of scripture acquisition; let's listen to the explanation in the next chapter.

Tripitaka does not forget his origin;
The Four Sages test the priestly mind.

A long journey westward is his decree,
As frosted blooms fall in autumn's mild breeze.
Tie up the sly ape, don't loosen the ropes!
Hold back the mean horse, and don't use the whip!
Wood mother, metal squire—they mix themselves.
Yellow hag and red son are all the same.[1]
Bite open the iron ball—there's mystery true:
Perfection and wisdom will come to you.

The principal aim of this chapter is to make clear that the quest for scriptures is essentially the same as the need to attend to the fundamentals in one's life. We now tell you about master and disciples, the four of them, who, having awakened to the suchness of all things, broke the lock of dust asunder. Leaping clear from the flowing sand of the sea of nature, they were completely rid of any hindrance and proceeded westward on the main road. They passed through countless green hills and blue waters: they saw wild grass and untended flowers in endless arrays. Time was swift indeed and soon it was autumn again. You see

Maple leaves red all over the mountain;
Golden blooms prevail over the night-wind.
The old cicada's song turns languid;
The sad cricket ever voices his plaint.
Cracked lotus leaves like green silk fans;

1. Yellow hag: the secretion of the spleen in internal alchemy is so called (*huangpo*), and it is considered vital to the nourishment of the other viscera. In the narrative, the term is frequently used to designate Sha Monk. Red child or red boy (*chizi*) in literary Chinese refers usually to the newborn infant because of its color. In internal alchemy, however, the formation of the baby can refer to the state of achieved physical immortality, and it is in this sense that the term is occasionally used in the narrative to identify Tripitaka.

Oranges tangy like balls of gold.
Lovely, those rows of wild geese,
Spreading dots in the distant sky.

As they journeyed, it was getting late again. "Disciples," said Tripitaka, "it's getting late. Where shall we go to spend the night?" "Master," said Pilgrim, "what you said is not quite right. Those who have left home dine on the winds and rest beside the waters; they sleep beneath the moon and lie on the frost; in short, any place can be their home. Why ask where we should spend the night?" "Elder Brother," said Zhu Bajie, "all you seem to care about is making progress on the journey, and you've no concern for the burdens of others. Since crossing the Flowing-Sand River, we have been doing nothing but scale mountains and peaks, and hauling this heavy load is becoming rather hard on me. Wouldn't it be much more reasonable to look for a house where we can ask for some tea and rice, and try to regain our strength?"

"Idiot," said Pilgrim, "your words sound as if you begrudge this whole enterprise. If you think that you are still back in the Gao Village, where you can enjoy the comfort which comes to you without your exerting yourself, then you won't make it! If you have truly embraced the faith of Buddhism, you must be willing to endure pain and suffering; only then will you be a true disciple." "Elder Brother," said Bajie, "how heavy do you think this load of luggage is?" Pilgrim said, "Brother, since you and Sha Monk joined us, I haven't had a chance to pole it. How would I know its weight?" "Ah! Elder Brother," said Bajie, "just count the things here:

Four yellow rattan mats;
Long and short, eight ropes in all.
To guard agains dampness and rain,
There are blankets—three, four layers!
The flat pole's too slippery, perhaps?
You add nails on nails at both ends!
Cast in iron and copper, the nine-ringed priestly staff.
Made of bamboo and rattan, the long, large cloak.

With all this luggage, you should pity old Hog, who has to walk all day carrying it! You only are the disciple of our master: I've been made into a long-term laborer!"

"Idiot!" said Pilgrim with a laugh, "to whom are you complaining?" "To you. Elder Brother," said Bajie. "If you're making complaints to me," said Pilgrim, "you've made a mistake! Old Monkey is solely concerned with Master's safety, whereas you and Sha Monk have the special responsibility of looking after the luggage and the horse. If you ever slack off, you'll get a good whipping in the shanks from this huge rod!" "Elder Brother," said Bajie, "don't mention whipping, for that only means taking advantage of others by brute force. I realize that you have a proud and haughty nature, and you are not about to pole the luggage. But look how fat and strong the horse is that Master is riding: he's only carrying one old monk. Make him take a few pieces of luggage, for the sake of fraternal sentiment!" "So you think he's a horse!" said Pilgrim. "He's no earthly horse, for he is originally the son of Aorun, the Dragon King of the Western Ocean. Because he set fire to the palace and destroyed some of its pearls, his father charged him with disobedience and he was condemned by Heaven. He was fortunate to have the Bodhisattva Guanyin save his life, and he was placed in the Eagle Grief Stream to await Master's arrival. At the appropriate time, the Bodhisattva also appeared personally to take off his scales and horns and to remove the pearls around his neck. It was then that he changed into this horse to carry Master to worship Buddha in the Western Heaven. This is a matter of achieving merit for each one of us individually, and you shouldn't bother him."

When Sha Monk heard these words, he said, "Elder Brother, is he really a dragon?" "Yes," said Pilgrim. Bajie said, "Elder Brother, I have heard an ancient saying that a dragon can breathe out clouds and mists, kick up dust and dirt, and he even has the ability to leap over mountains and peaks, the divine power to stir up rivers and seas. How is it that he is walking so slowly at the moment?" "You want him to move swiftly?" said Pilgrim. "I'll make him do that. Look!" Dear Great Sage! He shook his golden-hooped rod once, and there were ten thousand shafts of colorful lights! When that horse saw the rod, he was so afraid that he might be struck by it that he moved his four legs like lightning and darted away. As his hands were weak, the master could not restrain the horse from this display of its mean nature. The horse ran all the way up a mountain cliff before slowing down to a trot. The master finally caught his breath, and that was when he discovered in the distance several stately buildings beneath some pine trees. He saw

Doors draped by hanging cedars:
Houses beside a green hill;
Pine trees fresh and straight.
And some poles of mottled bamboo.
By the fence wild chrysanthemums glow with the frost:
By the bridge, reflections of orchids redden the stream.
Walls of white plaster;
And fences brick-laid.
A great hall, how noble and august:

A tall house, so peaceful and clean.
No oxen or sheep are seen, nor hens or dogs.
After autumn's harvest the farm chores must be light.

As the master held on to the saddle and slowly surveyed the scenery, Wukong and his brothers arrived. "Master," said Wukong, "you didn't fall off the horse?" "You brazen ape!" scolded the elder. "You were the one who frightened the horse! It's a good thing I managed to stay on him!" Attempting to placate him with a smile, Pilgrim said, "Master, please don't scold me. It all began when Zhu Bajie said that the horse was moving too slowly: so I made him hurry a little." Because he tried to catch up with the horse, Idiot ran till he was all out of breath, mumbling to himself, "I'm done, done! Look at this belly of mine, and the slack torso! Already the pole is so heavy that I can hardly carry it. Now I'm given the additional bustle and toil of running after this horse!" "Disciples," said the elder, "look over there: there's a small village where we may perhaps ask for lodging." When Pilgrim heard these words, he looked up and saw that it was covered by auspicious clouds and hallowed mists. He knew then that this place had to be a creation of buddhas or immortals, but he dared not reveal the Heavenly secret. He only said replied: "Fine! Fine! Let's go ask for shelter."

Quickly dismounting, the elder discovered that the towered entrance gate was decorated with carved lotus designs and looped slits in the woodwork; its pillars were carved and its beams gilded. Sha Monk put down the luggage, while Bajie led the horse, saying, "This must be a family of considerable wealth!" Pilgrim would have gone in at once, but Tripitaka said, "No, you and I are priests, and we should behave with circumspection. Don't ever enter a house without permission. Let's wait until someone comes out, and then we may request lodging politely." Bajie tied up the horse and sat down, leaning against the wall. Tripitaka sat on one of the stone drums while Pilgrim and Sha Monk seated themselves at the foot of the gate. They waited for a long time, but no one came out. Impatient by nature, Pilgrim leaped up after a while and ran inside the gate to have a look. There were, in fact, three large halls facing south, each with its curtains highly drawn up. Above the door screen hung a horizontal scroll painting with motifs of long life and rich blessings. And pasted on the gold lacquered pillars on either side was this new year couplet written on bright red paper:

Frail willows float like gossamer, the low bridge at dusk:
Snow dots the fragrant plums, a small yard in the spring.

In the center hall, there was a small black lacquered table, its luster half gone, bearing an old bronze urn in the shape of a beast. There were six straight-backed chairs in the main hall, while hanging screens were mounted on the walls east and west just below the roof.

As Pilgrim was glancing at all this furtively, the sound of footsteps suddenly came from behind the door to the rear, and out walked a middle-aged woman who asked in a seductive voice, "Who are you, that you dare enter a widow's home without permission?" The Great Sage was so taken aback that he could only murmur his reply: "This humble monk came from the Great Tang in the Land of the East, having received the royal decree to seek scriptures from Buddha in the West. There are four of us altogether. As we reached your noble region, it became late, and we therefore approached the sacred abode of the old Bodhisattva to seek shelter for the night." Smiling amiably, the woman said, "Elder, where are your other three companions? Please invite them to come in." "Master," shouted Pilgrim in a loud voice, "you are invited to come in." Only then did Tripitaka enter with Bajie and Sha Monk, who was leading the horse and carrying the luggage as well. The woman walked out of the hall to greet them, where she was met by the furtive, wanton glances of Bajie. "How did she look?" you ask.

She wore a gown of mandarin green and silk brocade,
Topped by a light pink vest,
To which was fastened a light yellow embroidered skirt;
Her high-heeled, patterned shoes glinted beneath.
A black lace covered her stylish coiffure,
Nicely matching the twin-colored braids like dragons coiled.
Her ivory palace-comb, gleaming red and halcyon-blue,
Supported two gold hair-pins set aslant.
Her half-grey tresses swept up like phoenix wings;
Her dangling earrings had rows of precious pearls.
Still lovely even without powder or rouge,
She had charm and beauty like one fair youth.

When the woman saw the three of them, she became even more amiable and invited them with great politeness into the main hall. After they had exchanged greetings one after the other, the pilgrims were told to be seated for tea to be served. From behind the screen a young maid with two tufts of flowing locks appeared, holding a golden tray with several white-jade cups. There were

Fragrant tea wafting warm air,
Strange fruits spreading fine aroma.

That lady rolled up her colorful sleeves and revealed long, delicate fingers like the stalks of spring onions; holding high the jade cups, she passed the tea to each one of them, bowing as she made the presentation. After the tea, she gave instructions for vegetarian food to be prepared. "Old Bodhi-sattva," said Tripitaka bowing, "what is your noble surname? And what is the name of your esteemed region?" The woman said, "This belongs to the West Aparagodānīya Continent. My maiden surname is Jia (Unreal), and the surname of my husband's family is Mo (Nonexisting). Unfortunately, my in-laws died prematurely, and my husband and I inherited our ancestral fortune, which amounted to more than ten thousand taels of silver and over fifteen thousand acres of prime land. It was fated, however, that we should have no son, having given birth only to three daughters. The year before last, it was my great misfortune to lose my husband also, and I was left a widow. This year my mourning period is completed, but we have no other relatives beside mother and daughters to inherit our vast property and land. I would have liked to marry again, but I find it difficult to give up such wealth. We are delighted, therefore, that the four of you have arrived, for we four, mother and daughters, would like very much to ask you to become our spouses. I do not know what you will think of this proposal."

When Tripitaka heard these words, he turned deaf and dumb; shutting his eyes to quiet his mind, he fell silent and gave no reply. The woman said, "We own over three hundred acres of paddies, over four hundred and sixty acres of dried fields, and over four hundred and sixty acres of orchards and forests. We have over a thousand head of yellow water buffalo, herds of mules and horses, countless pigs and sheep. In all four quarters, there are over seventy barns and haystacks. In this household there is grain enough to feed you for more than eight or nine years, silk that you could not wear out in a decade, gold and silver that you might spend for a lifetime. What could be more delightful than our silk sheets and curtains, which can render spring eternal? Not to mention those who wear golden hairpins standing in rows! If all of you, master and disciples, are willing to change your minds and enter the family of your wives, you will be most comfortable, having all these riches to enjoy. Will that not be better than the toil of the journey to the West?" Like a dumb and stupid person, Tripitaka refused to utter a word.

The woman said, "I was born in the hour of the Cock, on the third day of the third month, in the year Dinghai. As my deceased husband was three years my senior, I am now forty-five years old. My eldest daughter, named Zhenzhen, is twenty; my second daughter, Aiai, is eighteen; and my youngest daughter, Lianlian, is sixteen. None of them has been betrothed to anyone. Though I am rather homely, my daughters fortunately are rather good-looking. Moreover, each of them is well trained in needlework and the feminine arts. And because we had no son, my late husband brought them up as if they were boys, teaching them some of the Confucian classics when they were young as well as the art of writing verse and couplets. So, although they reside in a mountain home, they are not vulgar or uncouth persons; they would make suitable matches, I dare say, for all of you. If you elders can put away your inhibitions and let your hair grow again, you can at once become masters of this household. Are not the silk and brocade that you will wear infinitely better than the porcelain almsbowl and black robes, the straw sandals and grass hats?"

Sitting aloft in the seat of honor, Tripitaka was like a child struck by lightning, a frog smitten by rain. With eyes bulging and rolling upward, he could barely keep himself from keeling over in his chair. But Bajie, hearing of such wealth and such beauty, could hardly quell the unbearable itch in his heart! Sitting on his chair, he kept turning and twisting as if a needle were pricking him in the ass. Finally he could restrain himself no longer. Walking forward, he tugged at his master, saying, "Master! How can you completely ignore what the lady has been saying to you? You must try to pay some attention." Jerking back his head, the priest gave such a hostile shout that Bajie backed away hurriedly. "You cursed beast!" he bellowed. "We are people who have left home. How can we possibly allow ourselves anymore to be moved by riches and tempted by beauty?" With a laugh the woman said, "Oh dear, dear! Tell me, what's so good about those who leave home?" "Lady Bodhisattva," said Tripitaka, "tell me what is so good about those of you who remain at home?" "Please take a seat, elder," said the woman, "and let me tell you the benefits in the life of those of us who remain at home. If you ask what they are, this poem will make them abundantly clear.

When spring fashions appear I wear new silk;
Pleased to watch summer lilies I change to lace.
Autumn brings fragrant rice-wine newly brewed.
In winter's heated rooms my face glows with wine.
I may enjoy the fruits of all four climes
And every dainty of eight seasons, too.
The silk sheets and quilts of the bridal eve
Best the mendicant's life of Buddhist chants."

Tripitaka said, "Lady Bodhisattva, you who remain in the home can enjoy riches and glory; you have things to eat, clothes to wear, and children by your side. That is undeniably a good life, but you do not know that there are some benefits in the life of those of us who have left home. If you ask what they are, this poem will make them abundantly clear.

The will to leave home is no common thing:
You must tear down the old stronghold of love!
No cares without, tongue and mouth are at peace;
Your body within has good yin and yang.
When merit's done, you face the Golden Arch
And go back, mind enlightened, to your Home.
It beats the life of lust for household meat:
You rot with age, one stinking bag of flesh!"

When the woman heard these words, she grew terribly angry, saying, "How dare you to be so insolent, you brazen monk! If I had had no regard for the fact that you have come from the Land of the East. I would have sent you away at once. Here I was trying to ask you, with all sincerity, to enter our family and share our wealth, and you insult me instead. Even though you have received the commandments and made the vow never to return to secular life, at least one of your followers could become a member of our family. Why are you being so legalistic?"

Seeing how angry she had become, Tripitaka was intimidated and said, "Wukong, why don't you stay here." Pilgrim said, "I've been completely ignorant in such matters since the time I was young. Let Bajie stay." "Elder Brother," said Bajie, "don't play tricks on people. Let's all have some further discussion." "If neither of you is willing," said Tripitaka, "I'll ask Wujing to stay." "Listen to the way Master is speaking!" said Sha Monk. "Since I was converted by the Bodhisattva and received the commandments from her, I've been waiting for you. It has been scarcely two months since you took me as your disciple and gave me your teachings, and I have yet to acquire even half an inch of merit. You think I would dare seek such riches! I will journey to the Western Heaven even if it means my death! I'll never engage in such perfidious activities!" When the woman saw them refusing to remain, she quickly walked behind the screen and slammed the door to the rear. Master and disciples were left outside, and no one came out again to present tea or rice. Exasperated, Bajie began to find fault with the Tang monk, saying, "Master, you really don't know how to handle these matters! In fact, you have ruined all our chances by the way you spoke! You could have been more flexible and given her a vague reply so that she would at least have given us a meal. We would at least have enjoyed a pleasant evening, and whether we would be willing to stay tomorrow or not would have been for us to decide. Now the door is shut and no one is going to come out. How are we going to last through the night in the midst of these empty ashes and cold stoves?"

"Second Brother," said Wujing, "why don't you stay here and become her son-in-law." Bajie said, "Brother, don't play tricks on people. Let's discuss the matter further." "What's there to discuss?" said Pilgrim. "If you are willing, Master and that woman will become in-laws, and you will be the son-in-law who lives in the girl's home. With such riches and such treasures in this family, you will no doubt be given a huge dowry and a nice banquet to greet the kinsfolk, which all of us can also enjoy. Your return to secular life here will in fact benefit both parties concerned." "You can say that all right," said Bajie, "but for me it's a matter of fleeing the secular life only to return to secular life, of leaving my wife only to take another wife."

"So, Second Brother already has a wife?" said Sha Monk. "You didn't realize," Pilgrim said, "that originally he was the son-in-law of Mr. Gao of the Old Gao Village, in the Kingdom of Tibet. Since I defeated him, and since he had earlier received the commandments from the Bodhisattva, he had little choice but to follow the priestly vocation. That's the reason he abandoned his former wife to follow Master and to go worship Buddha in the Western Heaven. I suppose he has felt the separation keenly and has been brooding on it for some time. Just now, when marriage was mentioned, he must have been sorely tempted. Idiot, why don't you become the son-in-law of this household? Just make sure that you make a few extra bows to old Monkey, and you won't be reprimanded!" "Nonsense! Nonsense!" said Idiot. "Each one of us is tempted, but you only want old Hog to be embarrassed. The proverb says, 'A monk is the preta of sensuality,' and which one of us can truly say that he doesn't want this? But you have to put on a show, and your histrionics have ruined a good thing. Now we can't even get a drop of tea or water, and no one is tending the lamps or fires. We may last through the night, but I doubt that the horse can: he has to carry someone tomorrow and walk again, you know. If he goes hungry for a night, he might be reduced to a skeleton. You people sit here, while old Hog goes to graze the horse." Hastily, Idiot untied the reins and pulled the horse outside. "Sha Monk," said Pilgrim, "you stay here and keep Master company. I'll follow him and see where he is going to graze the horse." "Wukong," said Tripitaka, "you may go and see where he's going, but don't ridicule him." "I won't," said Pilgrim. The Great Sage walked out of the main hall, and with one shake of his body he changed into a red dragonfly. He flew out of the front gate and caught up with Bajie.

Idiot pulled the horse out to where there was grass, but he did not graze him there. Shouting and whooping, he chased the horse instead to the rear of the house, where he found the woman standing outside the door with three girls, enjoying the sight of some chrysanthemums. When mother and daughters saw Bajie approaching, the three girls slipped inside the house at once, but the woman stood still beside the door and said, "little elder, where are you going?" Our Idiot threw away the reins and went up to greet her with a most friendly "Hello!" Then he said, "Mama, I came to graze the horse." "Your master is much too squeamish," said the woman. "If he took a wife in our family, he would be much better off, wouldn't he, than being a mendicant trudging to the West?" "Well, they all have received the command of the Tang emperor," said Bajie with a laugh, "and they haven't the courage to disobey the ruler's decree. That's why they are unwilling to do this thing. Just now they were all trying to play tricks on me in the front hall, and I was somewhat embarrassed because I was afraid that Mama would find my long snout and large ears too offensive." "I don't, really." said the woman, "and since we have no master of the house, it's better to take one than none at all. But I do fear that my daughters may find you somewhat unattractive." "Mama," said Bajie, "please instruct your noble daughters not to choose their men that way. Others may be more handsome, but they usually turn out to be quite useless. Though I may be ugly, I do live by certain principles." "And what are they?" said the woman. Bajie said,

"Though I may be somewhat ugly,
I can work quite diligently.
A thousand acres of land, you say?
No need for oxen to plow it.
I'll go over it once with my rake,
And the seeds will grow in season.
When there's no rain I can make rain.
When there's no wind I'll call for wind.
If the house is not tall enough.
I'll build you a few stories more.
If the grounds are not swept I'll give them a sweep.
If the gutter's not drained I'll draw it for you.
All things both great and small around the house
I am able to do most readily."

"If you can work around the house," said the woman, "you should discuss the matter again with your master. If there's no great inconvenience, we'll take you." "No need for further discussion," said Bajie, "for he's no genuine parent of mine. Whether I want to do this or not is for me to decide." "All right, all right," said the woman. "Let me talk to my girls first." She slipped back inside immediately and slammed the rear door shut. Bajie did not graze the horse there either, but led it back to the front. Little did he realize, however, that Great Sage Sun had heard everything. With wings outstretched, the Great Sage flew back to see the Tang monk, changing back into his original form. "Master," he said, "Wuneng is leading the horse back here." "Of course he's leading the horse," said the Tang monk, "for if he doesn't, it may run away in a fit of mischief." Pilgrim started to laugh and gave a thorough account of what the woman and Bajie had said, but Tripitaka did not know whether to believe him or not.

In a little while Idiot arrived and tied up the horse. "Have you grazed him?" asked the elder. "There's not much good grass around here," said Bajie, "so it's really no place to graze a horse." "It may not be a place to graze the horse," said Pilgrim, "but is it a place to lead a horse?"[2] When Idiot heard this question, he knew that his secret was known. He lowered his head and turned it to one side; with pouting lips and wrinkled brows, he remained silent for a long time. Just then, they heard the side door open with a creak, and out came a pair of red lanterns and a pair of portable incense burners. There were swirling clouds of fragrance and the sounds of tinkling girdle-jade, when the woman walked out leading her three daughters. Zhenzhen, Aiai, and Lianlian were told to bow to the scripture pilgrims, and as they did so, standing in a row at the main hall, they appeared to be most beautiful indeed. Look at them!

> Each mothlike eyebrow painted halcyon-blue:
> Each pretty face aglow with springlike hues.
> What beguiling, empire-shaking beauty!
> What ravishing, heart-jolting charm!
> Their filigreed headgears enhance their grace;
> Silk sashes afloat, they seem wholly divine.
> Like ripe cherries their lips part, half-smiling,
> As they walk slowly and spread their orchid-scent.
> Their heads full of pearls and jade
> Atop countless hairpins slightly trembling.
> Their bodies full of delicate aroma,
> Shrouded by exquisite robes of fine golden thread.
> Why speak of lovely ladies of the South,
> Or the good looks of Xizi?[3]
> They look like the fairy ladies descending from the Ninefold Heaven,
> Or the Princess Chang'e leaving her Lunar Palace.

2. "To lead a horse": a Chinese metaphor for a marriage go-between.

3. Xizi: the legendary beauty and concubine of King Fucha of the ancient kingdom of Wu.

When he saw them, Tripitaka lowered his head and folded his hands in front of him, while the Great Sage became dumb and mute and Sha Monk turned away completely. But look at that Zhu Bajie! With eyes unblinking, a mind filled with lust, and passion fast rising, he murmured huskily: "What an honor it is to have the presence of you immortal ladies! Mama, please ask your dear sisters to leave." The three girls went behind the screen, leaving the pair of lanterns behind. The woman said, "Have you four elders made up your mind which one of you shall be betrothed to my daughters?" "We have discussed the matter," said Wujing, "and we have decided that the one whose surname is Zhu shall enter your family." "Brother," said Bajie, "please don't play any tricks on me. Let's discuss the matter further." "What's there to discuss?" said Pilgrim. "You have already made all the arrangements with her at the back door, and even call her 'Mama.' What's there to discuss any more? Master can be the in-law for the groom while this woman here will give away the bride; old Monkey will be the witness, and Sha monk the go-between. There's no need even to consult the almanac, for today happens to be the most auspicious and lucky day. You come here and bow to Master, and then you can go inside and become her son-in-law." "Nothing doing! Nothing doing!" said Bajie. "How can I engage in this kind of business?"

"Idiot!" said Pilgrim. "Stop this fakery! You have addressed her as 'Mama' for countless times already! What do you mean by 'nothing doing'? Agree to this at once, so that we may have the pleasure of enjoying some wine at the wedding." He caught hold of Bajie with one hand and pulled at the woman with the other, saying, "Mother-in-law, take your son-in-law inside." Somewhat hesitantly, Idiot started to shuffle inside, while the woman gave instructions to a houseboy, saying, "Take out some tables and chairs and wipe them clean. Prepare a vegetarian dinner to serve these three relatives of ours. I'm leading our new master inside." She further gave instructions for the cook to begin preparation for a wedding banquet to be held next morning. The houseboys then left to tell the cook. After the three pilgrims had eaten their meal, they retired to the guest rooms, and we shall say no more of them for the moment.

We now tell you about Bajie, who followed his mother-in-law and walked inside. There were row upon row of doorways and chambers with tall thresholds, causing him constantly to stumble and fall. "Mama," said Idiot, "please walk more slowly. I'm not familiar with the way here, so you must guide me a little." The woman said, "These are all the storerooms, the treasuries, the rooms where the flour is ground. We have yet to reach the kitchen." "What a huge house!" said Bajie. Stumbling along a winding course, he walked for a long time before finally reaching the inner chamber of the house. "Son-in-law," said the woman, "since your brother said that today is a most auspicious and lucky day, I have taken you in. In all this hurry, we have not had the chance of consulting an astrologer, nor have we been prepared for the proper wedding ceremony of worshiping Heaven and Earth and of spreading grains and fruits on the bridal bed. Right now, why don't you kowtow eight times toward the sky?" "You are right, Mama," said Bajie. "You take the upper seat also, and let me bow to you a few times. We'll consider that my worship of Heaven and Earth as well as my gesture of gratitude to you. Doing these two things at once will save me some trouble." "All right, all right," said his mother-in-law, laughing, "you are indeed a son-in-law who knows how to fulfill your household duties with the least effort. I'll sit down, and you can make your bows."

The candles on silver candlesticks were shining brightly throughout the hall as Idiot made his bows. Afterwards he said, "Mama, which one of the dear sisters do you plan to give me?" "That's my dilemma," said his mother-in-law. "I was going to give you my eldest daughter, but I was afraid of offending my second daughter. I was going to give you my second daughter, but I was afraid then of offending my third daughter. And if I were to give you my third daughter, I fear that my eldest daughter may be offended. That's why I cannot make up my mind." "Mama," said Bajie, "if you want to prevent strife, why not give them all to me? That way, you will spare yourself a lot of bickering that can destroy the harmony of the family." "Nonsense!" said his mother-in-law. "You mean you alone want to take all three of my daughters?" "Listen to what you're saying, Mama!" said Bajie. "Who doesn't have three or four concubines nowadays? Even if you have a few more daughters, I'll gladly take them all. When I was young, I learned how to be long-lasting in the arts of love. You can be assured that I'll render satisfactory service to every one of them." "That's no good! That's no good!" said the woman. "I have a large handkerchief here, with which you can cover your head, blindfold yourself, and determine your fated marriage that way. I'm going to ask my daughters to walk past you, and the one you can catch with your hands will be betrothed to you." Idiot accepted her suggestion and covered his head with his handkerchief. We have a testimonial poem which says:

> The fool knows not the true causes of things
> Beauty's sword can in secret the self destroy.
> Proper rites have long been fixed by the Duke of Zhou,
> But a bridegroom today still covers his head!

After Idiot had tied himself up properly, he said, "Mama, ask the dear sisters to come out." "Zhen, Aiai, Lianlian," cried his mother-in-law, "you all come out and determine your fated marriage, so that one of you may be given to this man." With the sounds of girdle-jade and the fragrance of orchids, it seemed that some fairy ladies had suddenly appeared. Idiot indeed stretched forth his hands to try to catch hold of one of the girls, but though he darted about madly this way and that, he could not lay hands on anyone on either side of him. It seemed to him, to be sure, that the girls were making all kinds of movement around him, but he could not grab a single one of them. He lunged toward the east and wrapped his arms around a pillar; he made a dive toward the west and slammed into a wooden partition. Growing faint from rushing about like that, he began to stumble and fall all over the place—tripping on the threshold in front of him, smashing into the brick wall behind him! Fumbling and tumbling around, he ended up sitting on the floor with a bruised head and a swollen mouth. "Mama," he cried, panting heavily, "you have a bunch of slippery daughters! I can't catch a single one of them! What am I to do? What am I to do?" Taking off his blindfold, the woman said, "Son-in-law, it's not that my daughters are slippery; it's just that they are all very modest. Each defers to the other so that she may take you." "If they are unwilling to take me, Mama," said Bajie, "why don't you take me instead?" "Dear son-in-law," said the woman, "you really have no regard for age or youth, when you even want your mother-in-law! My three daughters are really quite talented, for each one of them has woven a silk undershirt studded with pearls. Try them on, and the one whose shirt fits you will take you in." "Fine! Fine! Fine!" said Bajie. "Bring out all three undershirts and let me try them on. If all fit me, they can all have me." The woman went inside and took out one undershirt, which she handed over to Bajie. Taking off his blue silk shirt, Idiot took up the undergarment and draped it over his body at once. Before he had managed to tie the strings, however, he suddenly fell to the floor. The undershirt, you see, had changed into several pieces of rope which had him tightly bound. As he lay there in great pain, the women vanished.

We now tell you about Tripitaka, Pilgrim, and Sha Monk, who woke up when it began to grow light in the East. As they opened their eyes, they discovered that all the noble halls and buildings had vanished. There were neither carved beams nor gilded pillars, for the truth of the matter is that they had all been sleeping in a forest of pines and cedars. In a panic, the elder began to shout for Pilgrim, and Sha Monk also cried: "Elder Brother, we are finished! We have met some ghosts!" The Great Sage Sun, however, realized fully what had happened. Smiling gently, he said, "What are you talking about?" "Look where we've been sleeping!" cried the elder. "It's pleasant enough in this pine forest," said Pilgrim, "but I wonder where that Idiot is going through his ordeal." "Who is going through an ordeal?" asked the elder. Pilgrim answered with a laugh. "The women of that household happened to be some bodhisattvas from somewhere, who had waited for us to teach us a lesson. They must have left during the night, but unfortunately Zhu Bajie has to suffer." When Tripitaka heard this, he quickly folded his hands to make a bow. Then they saw a slip of paper hanging on an old cedar tree, fluttering in the wind. Sha Monk quickly took it down for his master to read. On it was written the following eight-line poem:

> Though the old Dame of Li Shan had no desire,
> Guanyin invited her to leave the mount.
> Mañjuśri and Viśvabhadra, too, were guests
> Who took in the woods the form of maidens fair.
> The holy monk's virtuous and truly chaste,
> But Bajie's profane, loving things mundane.
> Henceforth he must repent with quiet heart,
> For if he's slothful, the way will be hard.

As the elder, Pilgrim and Sha Monk recited this poem aloud, they heard a loud call from deep in the woods: "Master, the ropes are killing me! Save me, please! I'll never dare do this again!" "Wukong," said Tripitaka, "is it Wuneng who is calling us?" "Yes," said Sha Monk. "Brother," said Pilgrim, "don't bother about him. Let us leave now." "Though Idiot is stupid and mischievous," said Tripitaka, "he is at least fairly honest, and he has arms strong enough to carry the luggage. Let's have some regard for the Bodhisattva's earlier intention, let's rescue him so that he may continue to follow us. I doubt that he'll ever dare do this again." Sha Monk thereupon rolled up the bedding and put the luggage in order, after which Great Sage Sun untied the horse to lead the Tang monk into the woods to see what had happened. Ah! So it is that

> You must take care in the pursuit of truth
> To purge desires, and you'll enter the Real.

Entering the forest, they found Idiot tied to a tree.[4] He was screaming continuously because of the unbearable pain. Pilgrim approached him and said to him, laughing, "Dear son-in-law! It's getting rather late, and you still haven't got around to performing the proper ceremony of thanking

---

4. The rest of the chapter is taken from the beginning of chapter 24 in the full-length edition.

your parents or announcing your marriage to Master. You are still having a grand old time playing games here! Hey! Where's your mama? Where's your wife? What a dear son-in-law, all bound and beaten!" When Idiot heard such ridicule, he was so mortified that he clenched his teeth to try to endure the pain without making any more noise. Sha Monk, however, could not bear to look at him; he put down the luggage and went forward to untie the ropes. After he was freed, Idiot could only drop to his knees and kowtow toward the sky, for he was filled with shame. For him we have as a testimony this lyric to the tune of "Moon Over West River":

Eros is a sword injurious:
Live by it and you will be slain.
The lady so fair and lovely at sixteen
Is more vicious than a yakṣa.
You have but one principal sum;
You can't add profit to your purse.
Guard and keep well your precious capital
Which you must not squander and waste.

Scooping up some dirt and scattering it like incense, Bajie bowed to the sky. "Did you recognize those bodhisattvas at all?" said Pilgrim. "I was in a stupor, about to faint," said Bajie. "How could I recognize anyone?" Pilgrim then handed him the slip of paper. When Bajie saw the gāthā, he was more embarrassed than ever. "Second Brother does have all the luck," said Sha Monk with a laugh, "for you have attracted these four bodhisattvas here to become your wives!" "Brother," said Bajie, "let's not ever mention that again! It's blasphemy! From now on, I'll never dare do such foolish things again. Even if it breaks my bones, I'll carry the pole and luggage to follow Master to the West." "You are speaking sensibly at last," said Tripitaka.

Pilgrim then led his master and the two brothers up the main road. We do not know what sort of good or evil was in store for them; let's listen to the explanation in the next chapter.

The dharma-body in primary cycle meets the force of the cart;
The mind, righting monstrous deviates, crosses the spine-ridge pass.

The poem says:
> *To seek scriptures and freedom they go to the West,*
> *An endless toil through countless mounts of fame.*
> *The days fly by like darting hares and crows;*
> *As petals fall and birds sing the seasons go.*
> *A little dust—the eye reveals three thousand worlds;*
> *The priestly staff—its head has seen four hundred isles.*
> *They feed on wind and rest on dew to seek their goal,*
> *Not knowing which day they may all return.*

We were telling you about Tripitaka Tang and his disciples, who found the main road to the West. Truly they had to face the wind and brave the snow, to be capped by the moon and cloaked by the stars. They journeyed for a long time and soon it was the time of early spring. You see

> *The cycled return of triple yang;*[1]
> *The radiance of all things.*
> *The cycled return of triple yang*
> *Makes all Heavens beguiling like a painted scroll;*
> *The radiance of all things*
> *Means flowers spread brocade through all the earth.*
> *The plums fade to a few specks of snow;*
> *The grains swell with the valley clouds.*
> *Ice breaks gradually and mountain streams flow;*
> *Seedlings sprout completely and unparched.*
> *Truly it is that*
> *The God of the Year rides forth;*

1. Triple yang: a metaphor for the first month of the lunar calendar, it is so named because of its correlation with the *qian* trigram of three unbroken lines. As every unbroken line symbolizes the *yang*, the entire symbol is thus named triple yang.

The God of the Woods takes a drive.
Warm breezes waft floral fragrance;
Light clouds renew the light of the sun.
Willows by the wayside spread their curvate green;
The rains give life; all things bear the looks of spring.

As master and disciples traveled slowly along the road, enjoying the scenery as they proceeded, they suddenly heard a loud cry that seemed the roar of ten thousand voices. Tripitaka Tang was so startled that he immediately pulled in his reins and refused to go forward. Turning back, he said, "Wukong, where did that terrible din come from?" "Yes, it sounded as if the earth were splitting apart and the mountains were toppling," said Bajie. "More like the crack of thunder I'd say," said Sha Monk. Tripitaka said, "I still think it's men shouting or horses neighing." With a chuckle, Pilgrim Sun said, "None of you has guessed correctly. Stop here and let old Monkey go take a look."

Dear Pilgrim! He leaped up at once and rose into midair, treading on the cloudy luminosity. He peered into the distance and discovered a moated city; when he looked more carefully, he saw that it was veiled by auspicious luminosity after all and not by any baleful vapor. This is a nice place, Pilgrim thought to himself. Why should there be such an ear-splitting roar? There are no banners or spears in sight in the city, and what we heard couldn't possibly be the roar of cannons. Why is it then that we hear this hubbub of men and horses? As he was thus thinking to himself, a large group of monks came into his sight: on a sandy beach outside the city gate they were trying to pull a cart up a steep ridge. As they strained and tugged, they cried out in unison to call on the name of the Bodhisattva King Powerful for help, and this was the noise that startled the Tang monk. Pilgrim lowered his cloud gradually to take a closer look. Aha! The cart was loaded with bricks, tiles, timber, earth clods, and the like. The ridge was exceedingly tall, and leading up to it was a small narrow path flanked by two perpendicular passes, with walls like two giant cliffs. How could the cart possibly be dragged up there? Though it was such a fine warm day that one would expect people to dress lightly, what the monks had on were virtually rags. They looked destitute indeed! Pilgrim thought to himself: "I suppose they must be trying to build or repair a monastery, and since a region like this undoubtedly yields a bountiful harvest, it must be difficult for them to find part-time laborers. That's why these monks themselves have to work so hard." As he was thus speculating, he saw two young Daoists swagger out of the city gate. "How were they dressed?" you ask.

Star caps crowned their heads;
Brocades draped their bodies;
Luminous star caps crowned their heads;
Colorful brocades draped their bodies.
Cloud-headed boots² held up their feet;
Fine silk sashes tied up their waists.
Like full moons their faces were handsome and bright;
They had the fair forms of jade-Heaven gods.

When the monks saw the two Daoists, they were terrified; every one of them redoubled his effort to pull desperately at the cart. "So, that's it!" said Pilgrim, comprehending the situation all at once. "These monks must be awfully afraid of the Daoists, for if not, why should they be tugging so hard at the carts? I have heard someone say that there is a place on the road to the West where Daoism is revered and Buddhism is set for destruction. This must be the place. I would like to go back and report this to Master, but I still don't know the whole truth and he might blame me for bringing him surmises, saying that even a smart person like me can't be counted on for a reliable report. Let me go down there and question them thoroughly before I give Master an answer."

"Whom would he question?" you ask. Dear Great Sage! He lowered his cloud and with a shake of his torso, he changed at the foot of the city into a wandering Daoist of the Completed Authenticity sect, with an exorcist hamper hung on his left arm. Striking a hollow wooden fish with his hands and chanting lyrics of Daoist themes, he walked up to the two Daoists near the city gate. "Masters," he said, bowing, "this humble Daoist raises his hand." Returning his salute, one of the Daoists said, "Sir, where did you come from?" "This disciple," said Pilgrim, "has wandered to the corners of the sea and to the edges of Heaven. I arrived here this morning with the sole purpose of collecting subscriptions for good works. May I ask the two masters which street in this city is favorable towards the Dao, and which alley is inclined towards piety? This humble Daoist would like to go there and beg for some vegetarian food." Smiling, the Daoist said, "O Sir! Why do you speak in such a disgraceful manner?" "What do you mean by disgraceful?" said Pilgrim. "If you want to *beg* for vegetarian food," said the Daoist, "isn't that disgraceful?" Pilgrim said, "Those who have left the family live by begging. If I didn't beg, where would I have money to buy food?"

---

2. Cloud-headed boots: a reference to the patterned embroidery on their boots, the tops of which are made of silk.

Chuckling, the Daoist said, "You've come from afar, and you don't know anything about our city. In this city of ours, not only the civil and military officials are fond of the Dao, the rich merchants and men of prominence devoted to piety, but even the ordinary citizens, young and old, will bow to present us food once they see us. It is, in fact, a trivial matter, hardly worth mentioning. What's most important about our city is that His Majesty, the king, is also fond of the Dao and devoted to piety." "This humble cleric is first of all quite young," said Pilgrim, "and second, he is indeed from afar. In truth I'm ignorant of the situation here. May I trouble the two masters to tell me the name of this place and give me a thorough account of how the king has come to be so devoted to the cause of Dao—for the sake of fraternal feelings among us Daoists?" The Daoist said, "This city has the name of the Cart Slow Kingdom, and the ruler on the precious throne is a relative of ours."

When Pilgrim heard these words, he broke into loud guffaws, saying, "I suppose that a Daoist has become king." "No," said the Daoist. "What happened was that twenty years ago, this region had a drought, so severe that not a single drop of rain fell from the sky and all grains and plants perished. The king and his subjects, the rich as well as the poor—every person was burning incense and praying to Heaven for relief. Just when it seemed that nothing else could preserve their lives, three immortals suddenly descended from the sky and saved us all." "Who were these immortals?" asked Pilgrim. "Our masters," said the Daoist. "What are their names?" said Pilgrim. The Daoist replied, "The eldest master is called the Tiger-Strength Great Immortal; the second master, the Deer-Strength Great Immortal; and the third master, Goat-Strength Great Immortal." "What kinds of magic power do your esteemed teachers possess?" asked Pilgrim. The Daoist said, "Summoning the wind and the rain for my masters would be as easy as flipping over one's palms; they point at water and it will change into oil; they touch stones and change them into gold, as quickly as one turns over in bed. With this kind of magic power, they are thus able to rob the creative genius of Heaven and Earth, to alter the mysteries of the stars and constellations. The king and his subjects have such profound respect for them that all of us Daoists are claimed as royal kin." Pilgrim said, "This ruler is lucky, all right. After all, the proverb says, 'Magic moves ministers!' He certainly can't lose to claim kinship with your old masters, if they possess such powers. Alas! I wonder if I had even that tiniest spark of affinity, such that I could have an audience with the old masters?" Chuckling, the Daoist replied, "If you want to see our masters, it's not difficult at all. The two of us are their bosom disciples. Moreover, our masters are so devoted to the Way and so deferential to the pious that the mere mention of the word 'Dao' would bring them out of the door, full of welcome. If we two were to introduce you, we would need to exert ourselves no more vigorously than to blow away some ashes."

Bowing deeply, Pilgrim said, "I am indebted to you for your introduction. Let us go into the city then." "Let's wait a moment," said one of the Daoists. "You sit here while we two finish our official business first. Then we'll go with you." Pilgrim said, "Those of us who have left the family are without cares or ties; we are completely free. What do you mean by official business?" The Daoist pointed with his finger at the monks on the beach and said, "Their work happens to be the means of livelihood for us. Lest they become indolent, we have come to check them off the roll before we go with you." Smiling, Pilgrim said, "You must be mistaken, Masters. Buddhists and Daoists are all people who have left the family. For what reason are they working for our support? Why are they willing to submit to our roll call?"

The Daoist said, "You have no idea that in the year when we were all praying for rain, the monks bowed to Buddha on one side while the Daoists petitioned the Pole Star on the other, all for the sake of finding some food for the country. The monks, however, were useless, their empty chants of sūtras wholly without efficacy. As soon as our masters arrived on the scene, they summoned the wind and the rain and the bitter affliction was removed from the multitudes. It was then that the Court became terribly vexed at the monks, saying that they were completely ineffective and that they deserved to have their monasteries wrecked and their Buddha images destroyed. Their travel rescripts were revoked and they were not permitted to return to their native regions. His Majesty gave them to us instead and they were to serve as bondsmen: they are the ones who tend the fires in our temple, who sweep the grounds, and who guard the gates. Since we have some buildings in the rear which are not completely finished, we have ordered these monks here to haul bricks, tiles, and timber for the construction. But for fear of their mischief, indolence, and unwillingness to pull the cart, we have come to investigate and make the roll call."

When Pilgrim heard that, he tugged at the Daoist as tears rolled from his eyes. "I said that I might not have the good affinity to see your old masters," he said, "and true enough I don't." "Why not?" asked the Daoist. "This humble Daoist is making a wide tour of the world," said Pilgrim, "both for the sake of eking out a living and for finding a relative." "What sort of relative do you have?" said the Daoist. Pilgrim said, "I have an uncle, who since his youth had left the family and shorn his hair to become a monk.

Because of famine some years ago he had to go abroad to beg for alms and hadn't returned since. As I remembered our ancestral benevolence, I decided that I would make a special effort to find him along the way. It's very likely, I suppose, that he is detained here and cannot go home. I must find him somehow and get to see him before I can go inside the city with you." "That's easy," said the Daoist. "The two of us can sit here while you go down to the beach to make the roll call for us. There should be five hundred of them on the roll. Take a look and see if your uncle is among them. If he is, we'll let him go for the sake of the fact that you, too, are a fellow Daoist. Then we'll go inside the city with you. How about that?"

Pilgrim thanked them profusely, and with a deep bow he took leave of the Daoists. Striking up his wooden fish, he headed down to the beach, passing the double passes as he walked down the narrow path from the steep ridge. All those monks knelt down at once and kowtowed, saying in unison, "Father, we have not been indolent. Not even half a person from the five hundred is missing—we are all here pulling the cart." Snickering to himself, Pilgrim thought: "These monks must have been awfully abused by the Daoist. They are terrified even when they see a fake Daoist like me. If a real Daoist goes near them, they will probably die of fear." Waving his hand, Pilgrim said, "Get up, and don't be afraid! I'm not here to inspect your work, I'm here to find a relative." When those monks heard that he was looking for a relative, they surrounded him on all sides, everyone of them sticking out his head and coughing, hoping that he would be claimed as kin. "Which of us is his relative?" they said. After he had looked at them for a while, Pilgrim burst into laughter. "Father," said the monks, "you don't seem to have found your relative. Why are you laughing instead?" Pilgrim said, "You want to know why I'm laughing? I'm laughing at how immature you monks are! It was because of your having been born under an unlucky star that your parents, for fear of your bringing misfortune upon them or for not bringing with you additional brothers and sisters, turned you out of the family and made you priests. How could you then not follow the Three Jewels and not revere the law of Buddha? Why aren't you reading the sūtras and chanting the litanies? Why do you serve the Daoists and allow them to exploit you as bondsmen and slaves?" "Venerable Father," said the monks, "are you here to ridicule us? You must have come from abroad, and you have no idea of our plight." "Indeed I'm from abroad," said Pilgrim, "and I truly have no idea of what sort of plight you have."

As they began to weep, the monks said, "The ruler of our country is wicked and partial. All he cares for are those persons like you, Venerable

Father, and those whom he hates are us Buddhists." "Why is that?" asked
Pilgrim. "Because the need for wind and rain," said one of the monks,
"caused three immortal elders to come here. They deceived our ruler
and persuaded him to tear down our monasteries and revoke our travel
rescripts, forbidding us to return to our native regions. He would not,
moreover, permit us to serve even in any secular capacity except as slaves
in the household of those immortal elders. Our agony is unbearable! If
any Daoist mendicant shows up in this region, they would immediately
request the king to grant him an audience and a handsome reward; but if
a monk appears, regardless of whether he is from nearby or afar, he will
be seized and sent to be a servant in the house of the immortals." Pilgrim
said, "Could it be that those Daoists are truly in possession of some mighty
magic, potent enough to seduce the king? If it's only a matter of summoning the wind and the rain, then it is merely a trivial trick of heterodoxy.
How could it sway a ruler's heart?" The monks said, "They know how
to manipulate cinnabar and refine lead, to sit in meditation in order to
nourish their spirits. They point to water and it changes into oil; they
touch stones and transform them into pieces of gold. Now they are in the
process of building a huge temple for the Three Pure Ones, in which they
can perform rites to Heaven and Earth and read scriptures night and day,
to the end that the king will remain youthful for ten thousand years. Such
enterprise undoubtedly pleases the king."

"So that's how it is!" said Pilgrim. "Why don't you all run away and be
done with it?" "Father, we can't!" said the monks. "Those immortal elders
have obtained permission from the king to have our portraits painted and
hung up in all four quarters of the kingdom. Although the territory of this
Cart Slow Kingdom is quite large, there is a picture of monks displayed
in the marketplace of every village, town, county, and province. It bears
on top the royal inscription that any official who catches a monk will be
elevated three grades, and any private citizen who does so will receive a
reward of fifty taels of white silver. That's why we can never escape. Let's
not say monks—but even those who have cut their hair short or are getting
bald will find it difficult to get past the officials. They are everywhere, the
detectives and the runners! No matter what you do, you simply can't flee.
We have no alternative but to remain here and suffer."

"In that case," said Pilgrim, "you might as well give up and die." "Venerable Father," said the monks, "many of us have died. There were altogether
some two thousand monks caught and brought here: some six or seven
hundred of them have perished because they could not bear the suffering
and the persecution, or because they could not endure the cold or adjust

to the climate. Another seven or eight hundred committed suicide. Only we five hundred failed to die." "What do you mean by that?" said Pilgrim. The monks said, "When we tried to hang ourselves, the ropes snapped; when we tried to cut ourselves, the blades were blunt; when we hurled ourselves into the river, we floated back up instead; and when we took poison, nothing happened to us." Pilgrim said, "You are very lucky! Heaven must be desirous of prolonging your lives!" "The last word is not quite right, Venerable Father," said the monks, "for surely you mean prolonging our torments! Our daily meals are thin gruel made of the coarsest grains, and at night, we have nowhere to rest but this exposed piece of sandy beach. When we close our eyes, however, there will be deities here to protect us." "You mean the hard work during the day," said Pilgrim, "causes you to see ghosts at night." "Not ghosts," said the monks, "but the Six Gods of Darkness and the Six Gods of Light, together with the Guardians of Monasteries. When night falls, they will appear to protect us and, in fact, prevent those who want to die from dying."

Pilgrim said, "These gods are rather unreasonable. They should rather let you die early so that you could reach Heaven at once. Why are they guarding you like that?" The monks said, "They try to comfort us in our dreams, telling us not to seek death but to endure our suffering for a while until the arrival of the holy monk from the Great Tang in the Land of the East, the arhat who is journeying to the Western Heaven to acquire scriptures. Under him, we are told, there is a disciple who is the Great Sage, Equal to Heaven, and who has vast magic powers. He is, moreover, a person of rectitude and kindness, one who will avenge the injustices of the world, assist those who are needy and oppressed, and comfort the orphans and the widows. We are told to wait for his arrival, for he will reveal his power and destroy the Daoists, so that the teaching of Chan and complete poverty will be honored once more." When Pilgrim heard these words, he said silently to himself, smiling,

"Don't say old Monkey has no abilities,
For gods proclaim in advance his fame."

Turning quickly and striking up again the wooden fish, he left the monks to return to the city gate to meet the Daoists. "Sir," said the Daoists as they greeted him, "which of them is your relative?" "All five hundred of them are relatives of mine," said Pilgrim. Laughing, the two Daoists said, "How could you have that many relatives?" "One hundred are neighbors to my left," said Pilgrim, "and one hundred are neighbors to my right; one hundred belong to my father's side, and one hundred belong to my mother's side. Finally, one hundred happen to be my bond-brothers. If you are willing to let these five hundred persons go, I'll be willing to enter the city with you. If you are not, I won't go with you." The Daoists said, "You must be a little crazy, for all at once you are babbling! These monks happen to be gifts from the king. If we want to release even one or two of them, we will have to go first before our masters to report that they are ill. Then, we have to submit a death certificate before we can consider the matter closed. How could you ask us to release them all? Nonsense! Nonsense! Why, not to speak of the fact that we would be left without servants in our household, but even the court might be offended. The king might send some officials to look into the work here or he himself might come to investigate. How could we dare let them go?" "You won't release them?" said Pilgrim. "No, we won't!" said the Daoists. Pilgrim asked them three times and his anger flared up. Whipping out his iron rod from his ear, he squeezed it once in the wind and it had the thickness of a rice bowl. He tested it with his hand before slamming it down on the Daoists' heads. How pitiful! This one blow made

Their heads crack, their blood flow, their bodies fall;
Their skin split, their necks snap, their brains flow out!

Those monks on the beach, when they saw in the distance that he had slain the Daoists, all abandoned the cart and ran towards him, crying, "What disaster! You've just killed royal kin." "What royal kin?" said Pilgrim. The monks had him completely surrounded, crying, "Their masters would not bow when they walk into court, and when they walk out, they would not take leave of the king. His Majesty addresses them constantly as Royal Preceptors, Elder Brothers, and Masters. How could you cause such a terrible disaster? Their disciples came out here to supervise our work and they did not offend you. How could you beat them to death? If those immortal elders claimed that you were here only to supervise our labor and that we were the ones who took their lives, what would happen to us? We must go into the city with you and have you confess your guilt first." "Stop hollering, all of you," said Pilgrim, laughing. "I am no mendicant Daoist of the Completed Authenticity sect. I'm here to save you." "You have murdered two men," said the monks, "and we are likely to be blamed for it. Look what you have added to our burdens! How could you be our savior?"

Pilgrim said, "I am Pilgrim Sun Wukong, the disciple of the holy monk of the Great Tang. I have come especially to save your lives." "No! No!" cried the monks. "You can't be, for we can recognize that venerable father." "You haven't even met him," said Pilgrim, "so how could you recognize him?" The monks said, "We have met in our dreams an old man who identified himself as the Gold Star Venus. He told us over and over again how Pilgrim Sun was supposed to look so that we wouldn't make a mistake in identifying him." "What did he tell you?" said Pilgrim. The monks said, "He said that the Great Sage has

A bumpy brow, and golden eyes flashing;
A round head and a hairy face jowl-less;
Gaping teeth, pointed mouth, a character most sly;
He looks more weird than a thunder god.
An expert with a golden-hooped iron rod,
He once broke open Heaven's gates.
He now follows Truth and protects a monk,
Ever a savior from mankind's distress."

When Pilgrim heard these words, he was both pleased and annoyed; pleased, because the gods had spread wide his fame, but also annoyed, because those old rogues, he thought, had revealed to mortals his primal form. He blurted out all at once: "Indeed all of you can see that I am not Pilgrim Sun, but I am a disciple of his, just learning how to cause some trouble for fun! Look over there! Isn't that Pilgrim Sun who is approaching?" He pointed to the East with his finger and tricked the monks into turning their heads. As they did so, he revealed his true form, which the monks recognized immediately. Every one of them went to his knees, saying, "Father, we are of fleshly eyes and mortal stock, and we failed to know that you appeared to us in transformation. We beg Father to avenge our wrongs and dispel our woes by entering the city quickly and exterminating the demonic ones." "Follow me," said Pilgrim, and the monks all followed him closely.

The Great Sage walked to the beach and exerted his power: he picked up the cart and sent it hurtling through the two passes and up the steep ridge before crashing into pieces. He then tossed all those bricks, tiles, and timber down a ravine. "Go away!" he bellowed to the monks. "Don't crowd around me. Let me see the king tomorrow and destroy those Daoists." "O Father!" said those monks. "We dare not go very far away, for we fear that we might be caught by the officials. Then we would be brought back for beatings and for ransom, and there would be no end to our woes." "In that case," said Pilgrim, "let me give you some means of protection."

Dear Great Sage! He plucked a handful of hairs which he chewed into small pieces. To each of the monks he gave a piece with the instruction: "Stick it into the nail of your fourth finger and then make a fist. You can walk as far as you want. Don't do anything if no one comes to seize you, but if there should be someone trying to arrest you, hold your fist up tightly and cry, 'Great Sage, Equal to Heaven.' I will come at once to protect you." "Father," said the monks, "if we walk too far away and you can't see or hear us, what good will it do?" "Relax," said Pilgrim, "for even if you are ten thousand miles away, I guarantee you that nothing will happen to you."

One of the monks who was somewhat courageous indeed held up his fist and whispered: "Great Sage, Equal to Heaven." At once a thunder spirit stood in front of him, holding an iron rod. He looked so formidable that not even a thousand cavalry would dare charge near him. Several scores of the monks made the call also, and several scores of Great Sages at once appeared. The monks kowtowed, crying, "Father, truly an efficacious manifestation!" "When you want it to disappear," said Pilgrim, "all you have to say is the word, 'Cease.'" They cried, "Cease!" and the hairs appeared again in their nails. The monks were overjoyed and began to disperse. "Don't go too far away," said Pilgrim, "but listen for news of me in the city. If a proclamation requesting for monks to return to the city is published, you may then enter the city and give me back my hairs." Those five hundred monks then scattered in all directions, and we shall speak no more of them for the moment.

We tell you now instead about the Tang monk by the wayside. When he waited in vain for Pilgrim to come back with a report, he told Zhu Bajie to lead the horse forward toward the West. As they proceeded, they met some monks hurrying by, and when they drew near the city, they saw Pilgrim standing there with a dozen or so monks who had not dispersed. Reining in his horse, Tripitaka said, "Wukong, you were sent here to find out about the strange noise. Why did it take you so long and still you didn't return?" Leading those monks to bow before the Tang monk's horse, Pilgrim gave a thorough account of what had happened. Horrified, Tripitaka said, "If this is the situation, what shall we do?" "Please have no fear, Venerable Father," said those monks. "Father Great Sage Sun is an incarnation of a Heavenly god, and his vast magic powers will no doubt prevent you from coming to any harm. We are priests of the Wisdom Depth Monastery of this city, an edifice built by imperial command of the late king, the father of the present ruler. Since the image of the late king is still inside the monastery, it has not been torn down along with all the other monasteries, big and small, of the city. Let us invite the venerable father to go into the city and rest in our humble dwelling. We are certain that the Great Sage Sun will know what to do by the time of the morning court tomorrow." "What you say is quite right," said Pilgrim. "All right! We might as well enter the city first."

The elder dismounted and went up to the city gate. The sun was setting as they walked across the drawbridge and inside the triple gates. When people on the streets saw that priests from the Wisdom Depth Monastery were toting luggage and leading a horse, they all drew back and avoided them. Before long they reached the entrance of the monastery, where they saw hanging high above the gate a huge plaque on which was written in gold letters: "The Wisdom Depth Monastery, Built by Imperial Command." Pushing open the gates, the monks led them through the Vairocana Hall. They then opened the door to the main hall; the Tang monk draped the cassock over his body and prostrated himself before the golden image. Only after he had paid homage to Buddha in this manner did he walk inside the main hall. "Hey, you who are looking after the house!" cried the monks, and an old priest emerged. When he saw Pilgrim, he fell on his knees at once and cried, "Father, have you arrived?" "Who am I?" said Pilgrim. "Why should you address me and honor me in this manner?" "I recognize you to be the Great Sage, Equal to Heaven, the Father Sun," said the priest. "Every night we dream of you, for the Gold Star Venus frequently appears to us in our dreams, telling us that we can preserve our lives only when you come to us. Today, I can tell immediately that you are the one whom we saw in our dreams. O Father, I'm so glad that you have arrived in time. After one or two more days, we may all become ghosts!" "Please rise! Please rise!" said Pilgrim with laughter. "Tomorrow you will see some results!" The monks all went to prepare for them a vegetarian meal, after which they swept clean the abbot's residence for the pilgrims to rest.

Pilgrim, however, was so preoccupied that he could not sleep even by the time of the second watch. From somewhere nearby also came the sound of pipes and gongs, and he became so aroused that he rose quietly and slipped on his clothes. He leaped into midair to have a better look and at once discovered that there was the bright glare of lamps and torches due south of him. Lowering his cloud, he peered intently and found that the Daoists of the Three Pure Ones Temple were making supplications to the stars. He saw

> The spiritual realm of a tall chamber;
> The blessed place of a magic hall.
> The spiritual realm of a tall chamber,
> August like the features of Mount Penglai;
> The blessed place of a magic hall,
> Immaculate like the Palace of Transformed Joy.
> Daoists on both sides played their strings and pipes;
> Masters at the center held up their tablets of jade.
> They expounded the Woe-Dispelling Litany;
> They lectured on the Classic of the Way and Virtue.

To raise dust[3] a few times they wrote out their charms;
To make the supplication they prostrated themselves.
With spell and water they sent a dispatch
As flames of torches shot up to the Region Above.
They sought and questioned the stars
As fragrant incense rose through the azure sky.
Before the stands were fresh offerings;
On top of tables were victuals sumptuous.

On both sides of the hall's entrance was hung a pair of yellow silk scrolls on which the following parallel couplet in large characters was embroidered:

For wind and rain in due season,
We invoke the Honorable Divines' boundless power.
As the empire's peaceful and prosperous,
May our lord's reign exceed ten thousand years.

There were three old Daoists resplendent in their ritual robes, and Pilgrim thought they had to be the Tiger-Strength, Deer-Strength, and Goat-Strength Immortals. Below them there was a motley crew of some seven or eight hundred Daoists; lined up on opposite sides, they were beating drums and gongs, offering incense, and saying prayers. Secretly pleased, Pilgrim said to himself, "I would like to go down there and fool with them a bit, but as the proverb says,

A silk fiber is no thread;
A single hand cannot clap.

Let me go back and alert Bajie and Sha Monk. Then we can return and have some fun."

He dropped down from the auspicious cloud and went straight back to the abbot's hall, where he found Bajie and Sha Monk asleep head to foot in one bed. Pilgrim tried to wake Wujing first, and as he stirred, Sha Monk said, "Elder Brother, you aren't asleep yet?" "Get up now," said Pilgrim, "for you and I are going to enjoy ourselves." "In the dead of night," said Sha Monk, "how could we enjoy ourselves when our mouths are dried and our eyes won't stay open?" Pilgrim said, "There is indeed in this city a Temple of the Three Pure Ones. Right now the Daoists in the temple are conducting a mass, and their main hall is filled with all kinds of offerings. The buns are big as barrels, and their cakes must weigh fifty or sixty pounds each. There are also countless rice condiments and fresh fruits. Come with me and we'll go enjoy ourselves!" When Zhu Bajie heard in

3. Raise dust: a reference to the ability of immortals of (literally) "kicking up dust" in the midst of a body of water—i.e., transforming water into land.

his sleep that there were good things to eat, he immediately woke up, saying, "Elder Brother, aren't you going to take care of me too?" "Brother," said Pilgrim, "if you want to eat, don't make all these noises and wake up Master. Just follow me."

The two of them slipped on their clothes and walked quietly out the door. They trod on the cloud with Pilgrim and rose into the air. When Idiot saw the flare of lights, he wanted immediately to go down there had not Pilgrim pulled him back. "Don't be so impatient," said Pilgrim, "wait till they disperse. Then we can go down there." Bajie said, "But obviously they are having such a good time praying. Why would they want to disperse?" "Let me use a little magic," said Pilgrim, "and they will."

Dear Great Sage! He made the magic sign with his fingers and recited a spell before he drew in his breath facing the ground toward the southwest. Then he blew it out and at once a violent whirlwind assailed the Three Pure Ones Hall, smashing flower vases and candle stands and tearing up all the ex-votos hanging on the four walls. As lights and torches were all blown out, the Daoists became terrified. Tiger-Strength Immortal said, "Disciples, let's disperse. Since this divine wind has extinguished all our lamps, torches, and incense, each of us should retire. We can rise earlier tomorrow morning to recite a few more scrolls of scriptures and make up for what we miss tonight." The various Daoists indeed retreated.

Our Pilgrim leading Bajie and Sha Monk lowered the clouds and dashed up to the Three Pure Ones Hall. Without bothering to find out whether it was raw or cooked, Idiot grabbed one of the cakes and gave it a fierce bite. Pilgrim whipped out the iron rod and tried to give his hand a whack. Hastily withdrawing his hand to dodge the blow, Bajie said, "I haven't even found out the taste yet, and you're trying to hit me already?" "Don't be so rude," said Pilgrim. "Let's sit down with proper manners and then we may treat ourselves." "Aren't you embarrassed?" said Bajie. "You are stealing food, you know, and you still want proper manners! If you were invited here, what would you do then?" Pilgrim said, "Who are these bodhisattvas sitting up there?" "What do you mean by who are these bodhisattvas?" chuckled Bajie. "Can't you recognize the Three Pure Ones?" "Which Three Pure Ones?" said Pilgrim. "The one in the middle," said Bajie, "is the Honorable Divine of the Origin; the one on the left is the Enlightened Lord of Spiritual Treasures; and the one on the right is Laozi." Pilgrim said, "We have to take on their appearances. Only then can we eat safely and comfortably." When he caught hold of the delicious fragrance coming from the offerings, Idiot could wait no longer. Climbing up onto the tall platform, he gave the figure of Laozi a shove with his snout and pushed it to the floor, saying, "Old fellow, you have sat here long enough!

Now let old Hog take your place for a while!" So Bajie changed himself into Laozi, while Pilgrim took on the appearance of the Honorable Divine of the Origin and Sha Monk became the Enlightened Lord of Spiritual Treasures. All the original images were pushed down to the floor. The moment they sat down, Bajie began to gorge himself with the huge buns. "Could you wait one moment?" said Pilgrim. "Elder Brother," said Bajie, "we have changed into their forms. Why wait any longer?"

"Brother," said Pilgrim, "it's a small thing to eat, but giving ourselves away is no small matter! These holy images we pushed on the floor could be found by those Daoists who had to rise early to strike the bell or sweep the grounds. If they stumbled over them, wouldn't our secret be revealed? Why don't you see if you can hide them somewhere?" Bajie said, "This is an unfamiliar place, and I don't even know where to begin to look for a hiding spot." "Just now when we entered the hall," Pilgrim said, "I chanced to notice a little door on our right. Judging from the foul stench coming through it, I think it must be a Bureau of Five-Grain Transmigration. Send them in there."

Idiot, in truth, was rather good at crude labor! He leaped down, threw the three images over his shoulder, and carried them out of the hall. When he kicked open the door, he found a huge privy inside. Chuckling to himself he said, "This Bimawen truly has a way with words! He even bestows on a privy a sacred title! The Bureau of Five-Grain Transmigration, what a name!" Still hauling the images on his shoulders, Idiot began to mumble this prayer to them:

"O Pure Ones Three,
I'll confide in thee:
From afar we came,
Staunch foes of bogies.
We'd like a treat,
But nowhere's cozy.
We borrow your seats
For a while only.
You've sat too long,
Now go to the privy.
In times past you've enjoyed countless good things
By being pure and clean Daoists.
Today you can't avoid facing something dirty
When you become Honorable Divines Most Smelly!"

After he had made his supplication, he threw them inside with a splash and half of his robe was soiled by the muck. As he walked back into the hall, Pilgrim said, "Did you hide them well?" "Well enough," said Bajie, "but some of the filth stained my robe. It still stinks. I hope it won't make you retch." "Never mind," said Pilgrim, laughing, "you just come and enjoy yourself. I wonder if we could all make a clean getaway!" After Idiot changed back into the form of Laozi, the three of them took their seats and abandoned themselves to enjoyment. They ate the huge buns fist; then they gobbled down the side dishes, the rice condiments, the dumplings, the baked goods, the cakes, the deep-fried dishes, and the steamed pastries—regardless of whether these were hot or cold. Pilgrim Sun, however, was not too fond of anything cooked; all he had were a few pieces of fruit, just to keep the other two company. Meanwhile Bajie and Sha Monk went after the offerings like comets chasing the moon, like wind mopping up the clouds! In no time at all, they were completely devoured. When there was nothing left for them to eat, they, instead of leaving, remained seated there to chat and wait for the food to digest.

Alas! This was what had to happen! There was, you see, in the east corridor a young Daoist, who, just when he had lain down, scrambled up again all at once when he thought to himself: "I left my handbell in the hall. If I lost it, the masters would rebuke me tomorrow." He said to his companion, "You sleep first. I've got to go find something." Without even putting on his undergarments, he threw a shirt on himself and went to the main hall to search for his bell. Groping this way and that in the darkness, he finally found it. As he was turning to leave, he suddenly heard sounds of breathing. Terribly frightened, the Daoist began to rush out of the hall, and as he did so, he stepped on a lychee seed, which sent him crashing to the floor and the bell was smashed to pieces. Unable to restrain himself, Zhu Bajie burst into roars of laughter, frightening the little Daoist out of his wits. He scrambled up only to fall down once more; stumbling all over, he managed to reach the master residence. "Grand-Masters," he screamed as he pounded on the door, "It's terrible! Disaster!" The three old Daoists had not yet fallen asleep. They opened the door to ask: "What disaster?" Trembling all over, the young Daoist said, "Your disciple left behind his handbell, and he went to the main hall to search for it. I heard someone roaring with laughter, and it almost frightened me to death." When the old Daoists heard these words, they cried, "Bring some light. Let's see what kind of perverse creature is around." The Daoists sleeping along the two corridors, old and young, were all aroused, and they at once scrambled up to the main hall with lamps and torches. We do not know what was the result; let's listen to the explanation in the next chapter.

At the Three Pure Ones Temple the Great Sage leaves his name;
At the Cart Slow Kingdom the Monkey King reveals his power.

We now tell you about the Great Sage Sun, who used his left hand to give Sha Monk a pinch, and his right to give Zhu Bajie a pinch. Immediately understanding what he meant, the two of them fell silent and sat with lowered faces on their high seats. They allowed those Daoists to examine them back and front with uplifted lamps and torches, but the three of them seemed no more than idols made of clay and adorned with gold. "There are no thieves around," said the Tiger-Strength Immortal, "but then, why are all the offerings eaten?" "It definitely looks as if humans have eaten them," said the Deer-Strength Immortal. "Look how the fruits are skinned and their stones spat out. Why is it that we don't see any human form?" "Don't be too suspicious, Elder Brothers," said the Goat-Strength Immortal. "I think that our piety and sincerity and the fact that we are reciting scriptures and saying prayers here night and day, all in the name of the Court, must have aroused the Honorable Divines. The Venerable Fathers of the Three Pure Ones, I suppose, must have descended to earth and consumed these offerings. Why don't we take advantage of the fact that their holy train and crane carriages are still here and make supplication to the Honorable Divines? We should beg for some golden elixir and holy water with which we may present His Majesty. Wouldn't his long life and perpetual youth be in fact our merit?" "You are right," said the Tiger-Strength Immortal. "Disciples, start the music and recite the scriptures. Bring us our ritual robes. Let me tread the stars to make our supplication." Those little Daoists all obeyed and lined themselves up on both sides. At the sound of the gong, they all recited in unison the scroll of *True Scriptures of the Yellow Court*. After having put on his ritual robe, the Tiger-Strength Immortal held high his jade tablet and began to kick up the dust with dancing. Intermittently he would fall to the ground and prostrate himself. Then he intoned this petition:

"*In fear and dread,*
We bow most humbly.

To stir up our faith
We seek Purity.
Vile priests we quell
To honor the Way.
This hall we build
The king to obey.
Dragon flags we raise,
And off'rings display;
Torches by night,
Incense by day.
One thought sincere
Doth Heaven sway.
Chariots divine
Now come to stay.
Grant unto us some elixir and holy water,
Which we may give to His Majesty
That he may gain longevity."

When Bajie heard these words, he was filled with apprehension. "This is our fault! We've eaten the goods and should be on our way. Now, how shall we answer such supplication?" Pilgrim gave him another pinch before suddenly opening his mouth and speaking out loud: "You immortals of a younger generation, please stop your recitation. We have just returned from the Festival of Immortal Peaches, and we have not brought along any golden elixir or holy water. In another day we shall come to bestow them on you." When those Daoists, old and young, heard that the image had actually spoken, everyone of them trembled violently. "O Fathers!" they cried, "the living Honorable Divines have descended to earth. We must not let them go. We must insist on their giving us some sort of magic formula for eternal youth." Then the Deer-Strength Immortal went forward also to prostrate himself and intone this supplication:

"Our heads to the dust,
We pray earnestly.
Your subjects submit
To the Pure Ones Three.
Since we came here,
The Way was set free.
The king is pleased
To seek longevity.
This Heavenly Mass
Chants scriptures nightly.

We thank the Honorable Divines
For revealing their presence holy.
O hear our prayers!
We seek your glory!
Do leave some holy water behind,
That your disciples long life may find!"

Sha Monk gave Pilgrim a pinch and whispered fiercely, "Elder Brother! They are at it again! Just listen to the prayer!" "All right," said Pilgrim, "let's give them something." "Where could we find it?" muttered Bajie. "Just watch me," said Pilgrim, "and when you see that I have it, you'll have it too!" After those Daoists had finished their music and their prayers, Pilgrim again spoke out loud: "You immortals of a younger generation, there's no need for your bowing and praying any longer. I am rather reluctant to leave you some holy water, but I fear then that our posterity will die out. If I gave you some, however, it would seem to be too easy a boon." When those Daoists heard these words, they all prostrated themselves and kow-towed. "We beseech the Honorable Divines to have regard for the reverence of your disciples," they cried, "and we beg you to leave us some. We shall proclaim far and near the Way and Virtue. We shall memorialize to the king to give added honors to the Gate of Mystery." "In that case," said Pilgrim, "bring us some vessels." The Daoists all touched their heads to the ground to give thanks. Being the greediest, the Tiger-Strength Immortal hauled in a huge cistern and placed it in the hall. The Deer-Strength Immortal fetched an earthen-ware garden vase and put it on top of the offering table. The Goat-Strength Immortal pulled out the flowers from a flowerpot and placed it in the middle of the other two vessels. Then Pilgrim said to them, "Now leave the hall and close the shutters so that the Heavenly mysteries will not be seen by profane eyes. We shall leave you some holy water." The Daoists retreated from the hall and closed the doors, after which they all prostrated themselves before the vermilion steps.

Pilgrim stood up at once and, lifting up his tiger-skin kilt, filled the flowerpot with his stinking urine. Delighted by what he saw, Zhu Bajie said, "Elder Brother, you and I have been brothers these few years but we have never had fun like this before. Since I gorged myself just now, I have been feeling the urge to do this." Lifting up his clothes, our Idiot let loose such a torrent that it sounded as if the Lüliang Cascade had crashed onto some wooden boards! He pissed till he filled the whole garden vase. Sha Monk, too, left behind half a cistern. They then straightened their clothes and resumed their seats solemnly before they called out: "Little ones, receive your holy water."

Pushing open the shutters, those Daoists kowtowed repeatedly to give thanks. They carried the cistern out first, and then they poured the contents of the vase and the pot into the bigger vessel, mixing the liquids together. "Disciples," said the Tiger-Strength Immortal, "bring me a cup so that I can have a taste." A young Daoist immediately fetched a tea cup and handed it to the old Daoist. After bailing out a cup of it and gulping down a huge mouthful, the old Daoist kept wiping his mouth and puckering his lips. "Elder Brother," said the Deer-Strength Immortal, "is it good?" "Not very good," said the old Daoist, his lips still pouted, "the flavor is quite potent!" "Let me try it also," said the Goat-Strength Immortal, and he, too, downed a mouthful. Immediately he said, "It smells somewhat like hog urine!" Sitting high above them and hearing this remark, Pilgrim knew that he could no longer fool them. He thought to himself: "I might as well display my abilities and leave them our names too." He cried out in a loud voice:

"*O Daoists, Daoists,*
You are so silly!
Which Three Pure Ones
Would be so worldly?
Let our true names
Be told most clearly.
Monks of the Great Tang
Go West by decree.
We come to your place
This fine night carefree.
Your offerings eaten,
We sit and play.
Your bows and greetings
How could we repay?
That was no holy water you drank.
'Twas only the urine we pissed that stank!"

The moment the Daoists heard this, they barred the door. Picking up pitchforks, rakes, brooms, tiles, rocks, and whatever else they could put their hands on, they sent these hurtling inside the main hall to attack the impostors. Dear Pilgrim! Using his left hand to catch hold of Sha Monk and his right to take hold of Bajie, he crashed out of the door and mounted the cloudy luminosity to go straight back to the Wisdom Depth Monastery. When they arrived at the abbot's residence, they dared not disturb their master; each went to bed quietly and slept until the third quarter of the fifth watch. At that time, of course, the king began to hold his morning court, where two rows of civil and military officials—some four hundred of them—stood in attention. You see

Bright lamps and torches midst purple gauze;
Fragrant clouds rising from treasure tripods.

As soon as Tripitaka Tang woke up, he said, "Disciples, help me to go and have our travel rescript certified." Rising quickly, Pilgrim, Sha Monk, and Bajie slipped on their clothes and stood to one side to wait on their master. They said, "Let it be known to our master that this king truly believes only the Daoists and is eager to exalt the Way and to exterminate the Buddhists. We fear that any ill-spoken word may cause him to refuse to certify our rescript. Let us therefore accompany Master to enter the court."

Highly pleased, the Tang monk draped the brocaded cassock on himself while Pilgrim took out the travel rescript; Wujing was told to hold the alms bowl and Wuneng to take up the priestly staff. The luggage and the horse were placed in the care of the monks of the Wisdom Depth Monastery. They went before the Five-Phoenix Tower and saluted the Custodian of the Yellow Gate. Having identified themselves, they declared that they were scripture pilgrims from the Great Tang in the Land of the East, who wished to have their travel rescript certified and would therefore like the custodian to announce their arrival. The official of the gate went at once into court and prostrated himself before the golden steps to memorialize to the king, saying, "There are four Buddhist monks outside who claim that they are scripture pilgrims from the Great Tang in the Land of the East. They wish to have their travel rescript certified, and they now await Your Majesty's decree before the Five-Phoenix Tower." When the king heard this, he said, "These monks have nowhere to court death and, of all places, they have to do it here! Why didn't our constables arrest them at once and bring them here?" A Grand Preceptor before the throne stepped forward and said, "The Great Tang in the Land of the East is located in the South Jambūdvīpa Continent; it's the great nation of China, some ten thousand miles from here. As the way is infested with monsters and fiends, these monks must have considerable magic powers or they would not dare undertake this westward journey. I implore Your Majesty to invite them in and certify their rescript so that they may proceed, for the sake of the fact that they are the distant monks from China and for the sake of not destroying any goodly affinity."

The king gave his consent and summoned the Tang monk and his followers before the Hall of Golden Chimes. After master and disciples arrived before the steps, they presented the rescript to the king. The king opened the document and was about to read it, when the Custodian of the Yellow Gate appeared to announce: "The three National Preceptors have arrived." The king was so flustered that he put away the rescript hurriedly and left the dragon seat. After having ordered his attendants to set out some embroidered cushions, he bent his body to receive his visitors. When Tripitaka and his followers turned around to look, they saw those three great immortals swagger in, followed by a young acolyte with two tousled pigtails. Not daring even to lift their eyes, the two rows of officials all bowed deeply as they walked by. After they ascended the Hall of Golden Chimes, they did not even bother to salute the king. "National Preceptors," said the king, "we have not invited you. How is it that you are pleased to visit us today?" "We have something to tell you," said one of the old Daoists, "and that's why we're here. Those four monks down there, where do they come from?" The king said, "They were sent by the Great Tang in the Land of the East to fetch scriptures, and they presented themselves here to have their travel rescript certified."

Clapping their hands together, the three Daoists burst out laughing and said, "We thought they had fled. So they are still here!" Somewhat startled, the king said, "What do you mean, Preceptors? When we first heard of their arrival, we wanted to arrest them and send them to serve you, had not our Grand Preceptor on duty intervened and presented a most reasonable memorial. Since we had regard for the fact that they had traveled a great distance, and since we did not wish to destroy our goodly affinity with China, we summoned them in here to verify their rescript. We did not expect you to raise any question about them. Could it be that they have offended you in some way?"

"Your Majesty wouldn't know about this," said one of the Daoists, chuckling. "Hardly had they arrived yesterday when they slew two of our disciples outside the eastern gate. The five hundred Buddhist prisoners were all released and the cart was smashed to pieces. As if that weren't enough, they sneaked into our temple last night, vandalized the holy images of the Three Pure Ones, and devoured all the imperial offerings. We were fooled by them at first, thinking that the Honorable Divines had descended to Earth. We therefore even asked them to give us some golden elixir and holy water with which we might present Your Majesty, so that you would be blessed with eternal youth. We hardly expected that they would trick us by leaving us their urine. We found out all right, after each of us had tasted a mouthful! Just when we were about to seize them, they managed to escape. We didn't think that they would dare remain here today. As the proverb says, 'The road for fated enemies is narrow indeed'!"

When the king heard this, he became so irate that he would have had the four priests executed at once. Pressing his palms together, the Great Sage Sun cried out in a loud voice, saying, "Your Majesty, let your thunderlike wrath subside for the moment and permit this monk to present his memorial." "You offended the National Preceptors!" said the king. "Do you dare imply that their words might be erroneous?"

Pilgrim said, "He claimed that we slaughtered yesterday two of his disciples outside the city. But who could be a witness? Even if we were to confess to this crime, and that would be a gross injustice, only two of us need be asked to pay with our lives, and two of us should be released so that we might proceed to acquire the scriptures. He claimed further that we wrecked their cart and released their Buddhist prisoners. Again, there is no witness, and moreover, this is hardly a mortal offense and only one of us should be punished for this if it were true. Finally, he charged us with vandalizing the images of the Three Pure Ones and caused disturbance in their temple. This is clearly a trap they set for us." "How could you say that it's a trap?" said the king.

"We monks are from the Land of the East," said Pilgrim, "and we've just arrived in this region. We can't even tell one street from another. How could we know about the affairs of their temple, and at night no less? If we could leave them our urine, they should have been able to arrest us right then and there. Why did they wait until this morning to accuse us? In this whole wide world, there are countless people who use false identities. How could they know for certain that we are guilty? I beg Your Majesty to withhold your anger and make a thorough investigation." The king, after all, had always been rather muddle-headed. When he heard this lengthy speech by Pilgrim, he became more confused than ever.

Just then, the Custodian of the Yellow Gate again came to make this announcement: "Your Majesty, there are outside the gate many village elders who await your summons." "For what reason?" asked the king. He ordered them brought in, and thirty or forty village elders came before the hall. "Your Majesty," they said as they kowtowed, "there has been no rain this year for the entire spring, and we fear that there will be a famine if it remains dry like this through summer. We have come especially to request that one of the Holy Fathers, the National Preceptors, to pray for sweet rain that will succor the entire population." The king said, "Let the village elders withdraw. Rain will be forthcoming." The village elders gave thanks and left.

Then the king said, "You, priests of the Tang court, why do you think that we honor the Dao and seek to destroy Buddhism? It was because in years past, the monks of this dynasty attempted to pray for rain, and they could not produce even a single drop. It was our good fortune that these National Preceptors descended from Heaven and saved us from our bitter affliction. Now all of you have offended the National Preceptors no sooner than you arrived from a great distance, and you should be condemned. We shall pardon you for the moment, however, and ask whether you dare to have a rainmaking competition with our Preceptors. If your prayers could bring us the rain to assuage the needs of the people, we would pardon you, certify your rescript, and permit you to journey to the West. If you fail in your competition and no rain comes, all of you will be taken to the block and beheaded publicly." With a laugh, Pilgrim said, "This little priest has some knowledge of prayers, too!"

When the king heard this, he at once asked for an altar to be built. Meanwhile, he also gave the command that his carriage be brought out. "We want personally to ascend the Five-Phoenix Tower to watch," he said. Many officials followed the carriage up the tower and the king took his seat. Tripitaka Tang, followed by Pilgrim, Sha Monk, and Bajie, stood at attention down below, while the three Daoists also accompanied the king and took their seats on the tower. In a little while, an official came riding with the report: "The altar is ready. Let one of the Father National Preceptors ascend it."

Bowing with his hands folded before him, the Tiger-Strength Immortal took leave of the king and walked down the tower. "Sir," said Pilgrim, barring his way, "where are you going?" "To ascend the altar and pray for rain," said the Great Immortal. "You do have a sense of self-importance," said Pilgrim, "absolutely unwilling to defer to us monks who have come from a great distance. All right! As the proverb says, 'Even a strong dragon is no match for a local worm!' But if the master insists on proceeding first, then he must make a statement first before the king." "What statement?" said the Great Immortal. Pilgrim said, "Both you and I are supposed to ascend the altar to pray for rain. When it comes, how could anyone tell whether it's your rain or mine? Who could tell whose merit it is?" When the king above them heard this, he was secretly pleased and said, "The words of this little priest are quite gutsy!" When Sha Monk heard this, he said to himself, smiling, "You don't know that his stomach's full of gutsiness! He hasn't shown much of it yet!"

The Great Immortal said, "There's no need for me to make any statement. His Majesty is quite familiar with what I am about to do." "He may know it," said Pilgrim, "but I am a monk who came from a distant region. I have never met you and I'm not familiar with what you are about to do. I don't want us to end up accusing each other later, for that wouldn't be good business. We must settle this first before we act." "All right," said the Great Immortal, "when I ascend the altar, I shall use my ritual tablet as a sign. When I bang it loudly on the table once, wind will come; the second time, clouds will gather; the third time, there will be lightning and thunder; the fourth time, rain will come; and finally the fifth time, rain will stop and clouds will disperse." "Marvelous!" said Pilgrim, laughing. "I have never seen this before! Please go! Please go!"

With great strides, the Great Immortal walked forward, followed by Tripitaka and the rest. As they approached the altar, they saw that it was a platform about thirty feet tall. On all sides were flown banners with the names of the Twenty-Eight Constellations written on them. There was a table on top of the altar, and on the table was set an urn filled with burning incense. On both sides of the urn were two candle stands with huge, brightly lit candles. Leaning against the urn was a tablet made of gold, carved with the names of the thunder deities. Beneath the table were five huge cisterns full of clear water and afloat with willow branches. To the branches was attached a thin sheet of iron inscribed with the charms used to summon the agents of the Thunder Bureau. Five huge pillars were also set up around the table, and written on these pillars were the names of the barbarian thunder lords of Five Quarters. There were two Daoists standing on both sides of each pillar; each of the Daoists held an iron bludgeon used for pounding on the pillar. There were also many Daoists drawing up documents behind the altar. Before them there were set up a brazier for burning papers and several statues, all representing the messengers of charms, the local spirits, and patron deities.

The Great Immortal, without affecting the slightest degree of modesty, walked straight up to the altar and stood still. A young Daoist presented him with several charms written on yellow papers and a treasure sword. Holding the sword, the Great Immortal recited a spell and then burnt a charm on the flame of a candle. Down below several Daoists picked up a document and a statue holding a charm and had these burned also. With a bang the old Daoist high above brought down his ritual tablet on the table and at once a breeze could be felt in the air. "O dear! O dear!" muttered Bajie. "This Daoist is certainly quite capable! He bangs his tablet once and indeed the wind's rising." "Be quiet, Brother," said Pilgrim. "Don't speak to me anymore. Just stand guard over Master here and let me do my business."

Dear Great Sage! He pulled off a piece of hair and blew on it his immortal breath, saying, "Change!" It changed at once into a spurious Pilgrim, standing next to the Tang monk. His true body rose with his primal spirit into midair, where he shouted, "Who is in charge of the wind here?" He so startled the Old Woman of the Wind that she hugged her bag while the Second Boy of the Wind pulled tight the rope at the mouth of the bag. They stepped forward to salute Pilgrim, who said, "I am accompanying the holy monk of the Tang Court to go to acquire scriptures in the Western Heaven. We happen to pass through the Cart Slow Kingdom and are now waging a rainmaking contest with that deviant Daoist. How could you not help old Monkey and assist that Daoist instead? I'll pardon you this time, but you'd better call in the wind. If there's just the tiniest breeze to make the whiskers of the Daoist flutter, each of you will receive twenty strokes of the iron rod!" "We dare not! We dare not!" said the Old Woman of the Wind, and so, there was no sign of any wind. Unable to contain himself, Bajie began to holler: "You Sir, please step down! You've banged aloud the tablet. How is it that there's no wind? You come down, and let us go up there."

Holding high his tablet, the Daoist burned another charm before bringing down his tablet once more. Immediately, clouds and fog began to form in midair, but the Great Sage Sun shouted again, "Who is spreading the clouds?" He so startled the Cloud-Pushing Boy and the Fog-Spreading Lad that they hurriedly came forward to salute him. After Pilgrim had given his explanation as before, the Cloud Boy and the Mist Lad removed the clouds, so that

The sun came out and shone most brilliantly;
The sky was cloudless for ten thousand miles.

Laughing, Bajie said, "This master may deceive the king and befool his subjects. But he hasn't any real abilities! Why, the tablet has sounded twice! Why is it that we don't see any clouds forming?"

Becoming rather agitated, the Daoist loosened his hair, picked up his sword, and recited another spell as he burned a charm. Once more he brought down his tablet with a bang, and immediately the Heavenly Lord Deng arrived from the South Heaven Gate, trailed by the Squire of Thunder and the Mother of Lightning. When they saw Pilgrim in midair, they saluted him, and he gave his explanation as before. "What powerful summons," he said "brought you all here so quickly?" The Heavenly Lord said, "The magic of five thunder exercised by that Daoist was not faked. He issued the summons and burned the document, which alerted the Jade Emperor. The Jade Emperor sent his decree to the residence of the Primordial Honorable Divine of All-Pervading Thunderclap in the Ninefold Heaven. We in turn received his command to come here and assist with the rainmaking by providing thunder and lightning." "In that case," said

Pilgrim, "just wait a moment. You can help old Monkey instead." There was, therefore, neither the sound of thunder nor the flash of lightning.

In sheer desperation now, that Daoist added more incense, burned his charms, recited more spells, and struck his tablet more loudly than ever. In midair, the Dragon Kings of Four Oceans arrived all together, only to be met by Pilgrim, who shouted, "Aoguang, where do you think you're going?" Aoguang, Aoshun, Aoqin, and Aorun all went forward to salute him, and Pilgrim gave his explanation as before. He thanked the Dragon Kings moreover, saying, "I needed your help in times past, but we have not yet reached our goal. Today, I must rely on your assistance once more to help me achieve this merit right now. That Daoist has struck his tablet four times, and it's now old Monkey's turn to do business. But I don't know how to burn charms, issue summons, or strike any tablet. So all of you must play along with me."

The Heavenly Lord Deng said, "If the Great Sage gives us the order, who would dare disobey? You must, however, give us a sign, so that we may follow your instructions in an orderly manner. Otherwise, thunder and rain may be all mixed up, and that will not be to the credit of the Great Sage." Pilgrim said, "I'll use my rod as the sign." "O Dear Father!" cried the Squire of Thunder, horrified. "How could we take the rod?" "I'm not going to strike you," said Pilgrim, "all I want from you is to watch the rod. If I point it upwards once, you'll make the wind blow." "We'll make the wind blow!" snapped the Old Woman of the Wind and the Second Boy of the Wind in unison.

"When the rod points upward a second time, you'll spread the clouds." "We'll spread the clouds! We'll spread the clouds!" cried the Cloud-Pushing Boy and the Mist-Spreading Lad.

"When I point the rod upwards for the third time, I want thunder and lightning." "We'll provide the service! We'll provide the service!" said the Squire of Thunder and the Mother of Lightning.

"When I point the rod upwards the fourth time, I want rain." "We obey! We obey!" said the Dragon Kings.

"And when I point the rod upwards the fifth time, I want sunshine and fair weather. Don't make any mistake!"

After he had given all these instructions, Pilgrim dropped down from the clouds and retrieved his hair back to his body. Being of fleshly eyes and mortal stock, how could those people know the difference? Pilgrim then cried out with a loud voice, "Sir, please stop! You have struck aloud the tablet four times, but there's not the slightest sign of wind, cloud, thunder, or rain. You should let me take over." The Daoist had no choice but to leave his place and come down the altar for Pilgrim to take his turn. Pouting, he went back to the tower to see the throne. "Let me follow him," said Pilgrim, "and see what he has to say." He arrived and heard the king asking the Daoist, "We have been listening here most eagerly for the sounds of your tablet. Four times it struck and there was neither wind nor rain. Why is that?" The Daoist said, "Today the dragon deities are not home." Pilgrim shouted with a loud voice, "Your Majesty, the dragon deities are home all right, but the magic of your National Preceptor is not efficacious enough to bring them here. Allow us priests to summon them here for you to see." "Ascend the altar at once," said the king, "and we shall wait for the rain here."

Having received this decree, Pilgrim dashed back to the altar and tugged at the Tang monk, saying, "Master, please go up to the altar." "Disciple," said the Tang monk, "I don't know how to pray for rain." "He's trying to set you up," said Bajie, laughing. "If there's no rain, they'll put you on the pyre and finish you off with a fire." Pilgrim said, "Though you may not know how to pray for rain, you know how to recite scriptures. Let me help you." The elder indeed ascended the altar and solemnly took a seat on top. With complete concentration, he recited silently the Heart Sūtra. Suddenly an official came galloping on a horse with the question, "Why are you monks not striking the tablet and burning charms?" Pilgrim answered in a loud voice, "No need for that! Ours is the quiet work of fervent prayers." The official left to give this reply to the king, and we shall mention him no further.

When Pilgrim heard that his old master had finished reciting the sūtra, he took out his rod from his ear and one wave of it in the wind gave it a length of twelve feet and the thickness of a rice bowl. He pointed it upwards in the air; when the Old Woman of the Wind saw it, she immediately shook loose her bag as the Second Boy of the Wind untied the rope around its mouth. The roar of the wind could be heard instantly, as tiles and bricks flew up all over the city and stones and dust hurtled through the air. Just look at it! It was truly marvelous wind, not at all similar to any ordinary breeze. You saw

> Snapped willows and cracked flowers;
> Fallen trees and toppled woods;
> Nine-layered halls with chipped and broken walls;
> A Five-Phoenix Tower of shaken pillars and beams;
> The red sun losing its brightness in Heav'n;
> The yellow sand taking wings on Earth;
> Alarmed warriors before the martial hall;

Frightened ministers in the letters bower;
Girls of three palaces with frowzy locks;
Beauties of six chambers with tousled hair.
Tassels dropped from gold caps of marquis and earls;
The prime minister's black gauze did spread its wings.
Attendants had words but they dared not speak;
The Yellow Gate held papers which could not be sent.
Gold fishes and jade belts stood not in rows;
Ivory tablets and silk gowns had broken ranks.
Colored rooms and turquoise screens were all damaged;
Green windows and scarlet doors were all destroyed.
Tiles of Golden Chimes Hall flew off with bricks;
Carved doors of Brocade-Cloud Hall all fell apart.
This violent wind was violent indeed!
It blew till king and subjects, fathers and sons, could not meet,
Till all streets and markets were emptied of men,
And doors of ten thousand homes were tightly shut.

As this violent gust of wind arose, Pilgrim Sun further revealed his magic power. Giving his golden-hooped rod a twirl, he pointed it upwards a second time. You saw

The Cloud-Pushing Boy,
The Fog-Spreading Lad—
The Cloud-Pushing Boy showed his godly power
And a murky mass dropped down from Heaven;
The Fog-Spreading Lad displayed his magic might
And dense, soaring mists covered the Earth.
The three markets all grew dim;
The six avenues all turned dark.
With wind clouds left the seas
And Kunlun, trailing the rain.
Soon they filled Heav'n and Earth
And blackened this world of dust.
'Twas opaque like chaos of yore;
None could see Phoenix Tower's door.

As thick fog and dense clouds rolled in, Pilgrim Sun gave his golden-hooped rod another twirl and pointed it upwards a third time. You saw

The Squire of Thunder raging,
The Mother of Lightning irate—
The Squire of Thunder, raging,
Rode a fiery beast backward as he came from Heaven's pass;

The Mother of Lightning, irate,
Wielded gold snakes madly as she left the Dipper Hall.
Hu-la-la cracked the thunder,
Shattering the Iron Fork Mountain;
Xi-li-li flashed the scarlet sheets,
Flying out of the Eastern Ocean.
Loud rumbles of chariots came on and off;
Like fires and flames the grains and rice shot up.
Myriad things sprouted, their spirits revived.
Countless insects were from dormancy aroused.[1]
King and subjects both were terrified;
Traders and merchants were awed by the sound.

Ping-ping, Pang-pang, the thunder roared so ferociously that it seemed as if mountains were toppling and the earth was splitting apart. So terrified were the city's inhabitants that every house lighted incense, that every home burned paper money. "Old Deng," shouted Pilgrim. "Take care to look out for those greedy and corrupt officials, those churlish and disobedient sons. Strike down many of them for me to warn the public!" The peal of thunder grew louder than ever. Finally, Pilgrim pointed the iron rod once more and you saw

The dragons gave order,
And rain filled the world,
Strong as Heaven's river spilling o'er the dikes,
Quick as the clouds rushing through a channel.
It pattered on top of towers;
It splashed outside the windows.
The Silver Stream ran down from Heaven,
And whitecaps surged through the streets.
It spurted like vases upturned;
It gushed forth like basins poured out.
With houses almost drowned in hamlets,
The water rose to rural bridges' height.
Truly mulberry fields became vast oceans,
And billows all too soon raced through the land.
Dragon gods came to lend a helping hand
By lifting up the Yangzi and throwing it down!

1. The last four lines of the poem allude to the phenomenon of spring storm; hence the thunder is associated with "arousing the torpid (*jingche*)," the third of the twenty-four solar terms (approx. March 5–20), when insects come out of their dormancy or winter quarters as the spring equinox approaches.

The torrential rain began in the morning and did not stop even after the noon hour. So great was the downpour that all the streets and gulleys of the Cart Slow Kingdom were completely flooded. The king therefore issued this decree: "The rain's enough! If we had any more, it might damage the crops and that would have made things worse." An official messenger below the Five-Phoenix Tower at once galloped through the rain to make this announcement: "Holy monk, we have enough rain." When Pilgrim heard this, he pointed the golden-hooped rod upwards once more and, instantly, the thunder stopped and the wind subsided, the rain ended and the clouds dispersed. The king was filled with delight, and not one of the various civil and military officials could refrain from marveling, saying, "Marvelous priest! This is truly that 'for the strong, there's someone stronger still!' Even when our National Preceptors were capable of making the rain, a fine drizzle would go on for virtually half a day before it stopped completely. How is it that the weather can turn fair the moment the priest wants it to be fair? Look, the sun comes out instantly and there is not a speck of cloud anywhere!"

The king gave the command for the carriage to be returned to the palace, for he wanted to certify the travel rescript and permit the Tang monk to pass through. Just as he was about to use his treasure seal, the three Daoists all went forward and stopped him, saying, "Your Majesty, this downpour of rain cannot be regarded as the monk's merit, for it still owes its origin to the strength of Daoism." The king said, "You just claimed that the Dragon Kings were not home and that was why it didn't rain. He walked up there, exercised his quiet work of fervent prayers, and rain came down at once. How could you strive with him for credit?"

The Tiger-Strength Immortal said, "I issued my summons, burned my charms, and struck my tablets several times after I ascended the altar. Which Dragon King would have the courage to absent himself? It had to be that someone else somewhere was also requesting their service, and that was the reason that the Dragon Kings along with the officers of the other four bureaus—of wind, cloud, thunder, and lightning—did not show up at first. Once they heard my summons, however, they were in a hurry to get here, and by that time it happened that I was leaving the altar already. The priest, of course, made use of the opportunity and it rained. But if you thought about the matter from the beginning, the dragons were those which I summoned here and the rain was that which we called for. How could you regard this, therefore, as their meritorious fruit?" When that dim-witted king heard these words, he became again all confused.

Pilgrim walked one step forward, and pressing his palms together, he said, "Your Majesty, this trivial magic of heterodoxy is hardly to be considered anything of consequence. Let's not worry about whether it's his merit or ours. Let me tell you instead that there are in midair right now the Dragon Kings of the Four Oceans; because I have not dismissed them, they dare not withdraw. If that National Preceptor could order the Dragon Kings to reveal themselves, I would concede that this was his merit." Very pleased, the king said, "We have been on the throne for twenty-three years, but we have never laid eyes on a living dragon. Both of you can exercise your magic power, regard-less whether you are a monk or a Daoist. If you could ask them to reveal themselves, it would be your merit; if you couldn't, it would be your fault."

Those Daoists, of course, had no such power or authority. Even if they were to give the order, the Dragon Kings would never dare show themselves on account of the presence of the Great Sage. So, the Daoists said, "We can't do this. Why don't you try?"

Lifting his face toward the air, the Great Sage cried out in a loud voice: "Aoguang, where are you? All of you brothers, show your true selves!" When those Dragon Kings heard this call, they at once revealed their original forms—four dragons dancing through clouds and mists toward the Hall of Golden Chimes. You see them

> Soaring and transforming,
> Encircling clouds and mists.
> Like white hooks the jade claws hang;
> Like bright mirrors the silver scales shine.
> Whiskers float like white silk, each strand's distinct;
> Horns rise ruggedly, each prong is clear.
> Those craggy foreheads;
> Those brilliant round eyes.
> They, hidden or seen, can't be fathomed;
> They, flying or soaring, can't be described.
> Pray for rain, and rain comes instantly;
> Ask for fair sky, and it's here at once.
> Only these are the true dragon forms, most potent and holy,
> Their good aura surrounds the court profusely.

The king lighted incense in the hall, and the various officials bowed down before the steps. "It was most kind of you to show us your precious forms," said the king. "Please go back, and we shall say a special mass another day to thank you." "All of you deities may now retire," said Pilgrim, "for the king has promised to thank you with a special mass on another day." The Dragon Kings returned to the oceans, while the other deities all went back to Heaven. Thus this is

The true magic power, so boundless and vast;
The side door's cut down by nature most enlightened.[2]

We don't know how the deviant is finally exorcised; let's listen to the explanation in the next chapter.

2. Side door: a metaphor for heterodoxy.

Heresy flaunts its strength to mock orthodoxy;
Mind Monkey shows his saintliness to slay the deviates.

We were telling you that when the king saw Pilgrim Sun's ability to summon dragons and command sages, he immediately applied his treasure seal
to the travel rescript. He was about to hand it back to the Tang monk and
permit him to take up the journey once more, when the three Daoists went
forward and prostrated themselves before the steps of the Hall of Golden
Chimes. The king left his dragon throne hurriedly and tried to raise them
with his hands. "National Preceptors," he said, "why do you three go
through such a great ceremony with us today?" "Your Majesty," said the
Daoists, "we have been upholding your reign and providing security for
your people here for these twenty years. Today this priest has made use
of some paltry tricks of magic and robbed us of all our credit and ruined
our reputation. Just because of one rainstorm, Your Majesty has pardoned
even their crime of murder. Are we not being treated lightly? Let Your
Majesty withhold their rescript for the moment and allow us brothers to
wage another contest with them. We shall see what happens then."

That king was in truth a confused man: he would side with the east
when they mentioned east, and with the west when they mentioned west.
Indeed, putting away the travel rescript, he said, "National Preceptors,
what sort of contest do you wish to wage with them?" "A contest of
meditation," said the Tiger-Strength Great Immortal. "That's no good,"
said the king, "for the monk is reared in the religion of meditation. He
must be well trained in such mysteries before he dares receive the decree
to acquire scriptures. Why do you want to wage such a contest with him?"
"This contest," said the Great Immortal, "is not an ordinary one, for it has
the name of the Manifestation of Saintliness by the Cloud Pillar." "What
do you mean by that?" said the king. The Great Immortal said, "We need
one hundred tables, fifty of which will be made, by piling one on top of
the other, into an altar of meditation. Each contestant must ascend to the
top without using his hands or a ladder, but only with the help of a cloud.

We shall also agree on how many hours we shall remain immobile while sitting on the top of the altar."

When he learned that it was to be such a difficult contest, the king put the question to the pilgrims, saying, "Hey, monks! Our National Preceptor would like to wage with you a contest of meditation, called the Manifestation of Saintliness by the Cloud Pillar. Can anyone of you do it?" When Pilgrim heard this, he fell silent and gave no reply. "Elder Brother," said Bajie, "why aren't you saying anything?" "Brother, to tell you the truth," said Pilgrim, "I'm quite capable of performing such difficult feats as kicking down the sky or overturning wells, stirring up oceans or upending rivers, carrying mountains or chasing the moon, and altering the course of stars and planets. I'm not afraid, in fact, of even having my head split open or cut off, of having my stomach ripped open and my heart gouged out, or of any such strange manipulations. But if you ask me to sit and meditate, I'll lose the contest even before I begin! Where could I, tell me, acquire the nature to sit still? Even if you were to chain me to an iron pillar, I would still try to climb up and down. I can never manage to sit still."

"But *I* know how to sit and meditate," the Tang monk blurted out suddenly. "Marvelous! Just marvelous!" said Pilgrim, highly pleased. "How long can you do this?" "I met some lofty Chan masters when I was young," said Tripitaka, "who expounded to me the absolutely crucial foundation of quiescence and concentration in order to preserve my spirit. Shut up alone in the so-called Life-and-Death Meditative Confinement, I had managed to sit still for two or three years at least." "If you do that, Master," said Pilgrim, "we won't need to go acquire scriptures! At most, I don't think it will be necessary for you to sit for more than three hours here before you will be able to come down." "But Disciple," said Tripitaka, "I can't get up there." "You step forward and accept the challenge," said Pilgrim. "I'll send you up there." Indeed the elder pressed his palms together before his chest and said, "This humble priest knows how to sit in meditation." The king at once gave the order for the altars to be built. Truly, a nation has the strength to topple mountains! In less than half an hour, two altars were built on the left and right of the Hall of Golden Chimes.

Coming down from the hall, the Tiger-Strength Great Immortal went to the middle of the courtyard. He leaped into the air and at once a mat of clouds formed under his feet and took him up to the altar to the west, where he sat down. Pilgrim meanwhile pulled off one strand of his hair and caused it to change into a spurious form of himself, standing down below to accompany Bajie and Sha Monk. He himself changed into an auspicious cloud of five colors to carry the Tang monk into the air and lift him to sit on the altar to the east. He then changed himself into a tiny mole-cricket and flew to alight on Bajie's ear to whisper to him, "Brother, look up and watch Master with care. Don't speak to the substitute of old Monkey!" Laughing, Idiot said, "I know! I know!"

We tell you now about the Deer-Strength Great Immortal sitting on the embroidered cushion in the hall, where he watched the two contestants for a long time and found them quite equally matched. This Daoist decided to give his elder brother some help: pulling a stubby piece of hair from the back of his head, he rolled it with his fingers into a tiny ball and filliped it on to the head of the Tang monk. The piece of hair changed into a huge bedbug and began to bite the elder. At first, the elder felt an itch, after which it changed to pain. Now, one of the rules in meditation is that one cannot move one's hands; when one does, it is an immediate admission of defeat. As the elder found the itch and pain to be quite unbearable, he sought to find relief by wriggling his head against the collar of his robe. "O dear!" said Bajie. "Master is going to have a fit!" "No," said Sha Monk, "he might be having a headache." Hearing this, Pilgrim said, "My master is an honest gentleman. If he said he knew how to practice meditation, he would be able to do it. A gentleman does not lie! Stop speculating, the two of you, and let me go up to take a look."

Dear Pilgrim! He buzzed up there and alighted on the head of the Tang monk, where he discovered a bedbug about the size of a bean biting the elder. Hurriedly, he removed it with his hand, and then he gave his master a few gentle scratches. His itch and pain relieved, the elder once more sat motionless on the altar. "The bald head of a priest," thought Pilgrim to himself, "can't even hold a louse! How could a bedbug get into it? It must be, I suppose, a stunt of that Daoist, trying to harm my master. Ha! Ha! Since they haven't quite reached a decision yet in this contest, let old Monkey give him a taste of his own tricks!" Flying up into the air until he reached a height beyond the roof of the palace, he shook his body and changed at once into a centipede at least seven inches in length. It dropped down from the sky and landed on the Daoist's upper lip before his nostrils, where it gave him a terrific bite. Unable to sit still any longer, the Daoist fell backwards from the altar head over heels and almost lost his life. He was fortunate enough to have all the officials rush forward to pull him up. The horrified king at once asked the Grand Preceptor before the Throne to help him go to the Pavilion of Cultural Florescence to be washed and combed. Pilgrim, meanwhile, changed himself again into the auspicious cloud to carry his master down to the courtyard before the steps, where he was declared the winner.

The king wanted to let them go, but the Deer-Strength Great Immortal again said to him, "Your Majesty, my elder brother has been suffering from a suppressed chill; when he goes up to a high place, the cold wind he's exposed to will bring on his old sickness. That was why the monk was able to gain the upper hand. Let me now wage with them a contest of guessing what's behind the boards." "What do you mean by that?" asked the king. Deer-Strength said, "This humble Daoist has the ability to gain knowledge of things even if they were placed behind boards. Let's see if those monks are able to do the same. If they could outguess me, let them go; but if not, then let them be punished according to Your Majesty's wishes so that our fraternal distress may be avenged and that our services to the kingdom for these twenty years may remain untainted."

Truly that king is exceedingly confused! Swayed by such fraudulent words, he at once gave the order for a red lacquered chest to be brought to the inner palace. The queen was asked to place a treasure in the chest before it was carried out again and set before the white-jade steps. The king said to the monks and the Daoists, "Let both sides wage your contest now and see who can guess the treasure inside the chest." "Disciple," said Tripitaka, "how could we know what's in the chest?" Pilgrim changed again into a mole-cricket and flew up to the head of the Tang monk. "Relax, Master," he said, "let me go take a look." Dear Great Sage! Unnoticed by anyone, he flew up to the chest and found a crack at the base, through which he crept inside. On a red lacquered tray he found a set of palace robes: they were the empire blouse and cosmic skirt. Quickly he picked them up and shook them loose; then he bit open the tip of his tongue and spat a mouthful of blood onto the garments, crying, "Change!" They changed instantly into a torn and worn-out cassock; before he left, however, he soaked it with his bubbly and stinking urine. After crawling out again through the crack, he flew back to alight on the Tang monk's ear and said, "Master, you may guess that it is a torn and worn-out cassock." "He said that it was some kind of treasure," said Tripitaka. "How could such a thing be a treasure?" "Never mind," said Pilgrim, "for what's important is that you guess correctly."

As the Tang monk took a step forward to announce what he guessed was in the chest, the Deer-Strength Great Immortal said, "I'll guess first. The chest contains an empire blouse and a cosmic skirt." "No! No!" cried the Tang monk. "There's only a torn and worn-out cassock in the chest." "How dare he?" said the king. "This priest thinks that there is no treasure in our kingdom. What's this worn-out cassock that he speaks of? Seize him!" The two rows of palace guards immediately wanted to raise their hands, and the Tang monk became so terrified that he pressed his palms together and shouted, "Your Majesty, please pardon this humble priest for the moment. Open the chest; if it were indeed a treasure, this humble priest would accept his punishment. But if it were not, wouldn't you have wrongly accused me?" The king had the chest opened, and when the attendant to the throne lifted out the lacquered tray, sitting on it was indeed one torn and worn-out cassock! "Who put this thing here?" cried the king, highly incensed, and from behind the dragon seat the queen of the three palaces came forward. "My lord," she said, "it was I who personally placed the empire blouse and the cosmic skirt inside the chest. How could they change into something like this?" "Let my royal wife retire," said the king, "for we are well aware of the fact that all the things used in the palace are made of the finest silk and embroidered materials. How could there be such an object?" He then said to his attendants: "Bring us the chest. We ourselves will hide something in it and try again."

The king went to his imperial garden in the rear and picked from his orchard a huge peach, about the size of a rice bowl, which he placed in the chest. The chest was brought out and the two parties were told to guess once more. "Disciples," said the Tang monk, "he wants us to guess again." "Relax," said Pilgrim, "let me go and take another look." With a buzz, he flew away and crawled inside the chest as before. Nothing could have been more agreeable to him than what he found: a peach. Changing back into his original form, he sat in the chest and ate the fruit so heartily that every morsel on both sides of the groove was picked clean. Leaving the stone behind, he changed back into the mole-cricket and flew back onto the Tang monk's ear, saying, "Master, say that it's a peach's pit." "Disciple," said the elder, "don't make a fool of me! If I weren't so quick with my mouth just now, I would have been seized and punished. This time we must say it's some kind of treasure. How could a peach's pit be a treasure?" "Have no fear," said Pilgrim. "You'll win, and that's all that matters!"

Tripitaka was just about to speak when the Goat-Strength Great Immortal said, "This humble Daoist will guess first: it is a peach." "Not a peach," said Tripitaka, "but a fleshless peach's pit." "It's a peach we put in ourselves," bellowed the king. "How could it be a pit? Our third National Preceptor has guessed correctly." "Your Majesty," said Tripitaka, "please open the chest and see for yourself." The attendant before the throne went to open the chest and lifted up the tray: it was in truth a pit, entirely without any peel or flesh. When the king saw this, he became quite frightened and said, "O National Preceptors, don't wage any more contests with them. Let them go! The peach was picked by our own hands, and now it turns out to be a pit. Who could have eaten it? The spirits and gods must be giving them secret assistance." When Bajie heard the words, he smiled sardonically to Sha Monk, saying, "Little does he realize how many years of peach eating are behind this!"

Just then, the Tiger-Strength Great Immortal walked out from the Pavilion of Cultural Florescence after he had been washed and combed. "Your Majesty," he said as he walked up the hall, "this monk knows the magic of object removal. Give me the chest, and I'll destroy his magic. Then we can have another contest with him." "What do you want to do?" said the king. Tiger-Strength said, "His magic can remove only lifeless objects but not a human body. Put this Daoist youth in the chest, and he'll never be able to remove him." The youth indeed was hidden in the chest, which was then brought down again from the hall to be placed before the steps. "You, monk," said the king, "guess again what sort of treasure we have inside." Tripitaka said, "Here it comes again!" "Let me go and have another look." said Pilgrim. With a buzz, he flew off and crawled inside, where he found a Daoist lad. Marvelous Great Sage! What readiness of mind! Truly

Such agility is rare in the world!
Such cleverness is uncommon indeed!

Shaking his body once, he changed himself into the form of one of those old Daoists, whispering as he entered the chest, "Disciple."

"Master," said the lad, "how did you come in here?" "With the magic of invisibility," said Pilgrim. The lad said, "Do you have some instructions for me?" "The priest saw you enter the chest," said Pilgrim, "and if he made his guess a Daoist lad, wouldn't we lose to him again? That's why I came here to discuss the matter with you. Let's shave your head, and we'll then make the guess that you are a monk." The Daoist lad said, "Do whatever you want, Master, just so that we win. For if we lose to them again, not only our reputation will be ruined, but the court also may no longer revere us." "Exactly," said Pilgrim. "Come over here, my child. When we defeat them, I'll reward you handsomely." He changed his golden-hooped rod into a sharp razor, and hugging the lad, he said, "Darling, try to endure the pain for a moment. Don't make any noise! I'll shave your head." In a little while, the lad's hair was completely shorn, rolled into a ball, and stuffed into one of the corners of the chest. He put away the razor, and rubbing the lad's bald head, he said, "My child, your head looks like a monk's all right, but your clothes don't fit. Take them off and let me change them for you." What the Daoist lad had on was a crane's-down robe of spring-onion white silk, embroidered with the cloud pattern and trimmed with brocade. When he took it off, Pilgrim blew on it his immortal breath, crying, "Change!" It changed instantly into a monk shirt of brown color, which Pilgrim helped him put on. He then pulled off two pieces of hair which he changed into a wooden fish and a tap. "Disciple," said Pilgrim, as he handed over the fish and the tap to the lad, "you must listen carefully. If you hear someone call for the Daoist youth, don't ever leave this chest. If someone calls 'Monk,' then you may push open the chest door, strike up the wooden fish, and walk out chanting a Buddhist sūtra. Then it'll be complete success for us." "I only know," said the lad, "how to recite the *Three Officials Scripture*, the *Northern Dipper Scripture*, or the *Woe-Dispelling Scripture*. I don't know how to recite any Buddhist sūtra." Pilgrim said, "Can you chant the name of Buddha?" "You mean Amitābha," said the lad. "Who doesn't know that?" "Good enough! Good enough!" said Pilgrim. "You may chant the name of Buddha. It'll spare me from having to teach you anything new. Remember what I've told you. I'm leaving." He changed back into a mole-cricket and crawled out, after which, he flew back to the ear of the Tang monk and said, "Master, just guess it's a monk." Tripitaka said, "This time I know I'll win." "How could you be so sure?" said Pilgrim, and Tripitaka replied, "The sūtras said, 'The Buddha, the Dharma, and the Saṅgha are the Three Jewels.' A monk therefore is a treasure."

As they were thus talking among themselves, the Tiger-Strength Great Immortal said, "Your Majesty, this third time it is a Daoist youth." He made the declaration several times, but nothing happened nor did anyone make an appearance. Pressing his palms together, Tripitaka said, "It's a monk." With all his might, Bajie screamed: "It's a monk in the chest!" All at once the youth kicked open the chest and walked out, striking the wooden fish and chanting the name of Buddha. So delighted were the two rows of civil and military officials that they shouted bravos repeatedly; so astonished were the three Daoists that they could not utter a sound. "These priests must have the assistance from spirits and gods," said the king. "How could a Daoist enter the chest and come out a monk? Even if he had an attendant with him, he might have been able to have his head shaved. How could he know how to take up the chanting of Buddha's name? O Preceptors! Please let them go!"

"Your Majesty," said the Tiger-Strength Great Immortal, "as the proverb says, 'The warrior has found his equal, the chess player his match.' We might as well make use of what we learned in our youth at Zhongnan Mountain and challenge them to a greater competition." "What did you learn?" said the king. Tiger-Strength said, "We three brothers all have acquired some magic abilities: cut off our heads, and we can put them back on our necks; open our chests and gouge out our hearts, and they will grow back again; inside a cauldron of boiling oil, we can take baths." Highly startled, the king said, "These three things are all roads leading to certain death!" "Only because we have such magic power," said Tiger-Strength, "do we dare make so bold a claim. We won't quit until we have waged this contest with them." The king said in a loud voice, "You priests from the Land of the East, our National Preceptors are unwilling to let you go. They wish to wage one more contest with you in head cutting, stomach ripping, and going into a cauldron of boiling oil to take a bath."

Pilgrim was still assuming the form of the mole-cricket, flying back and forth to make his secret report. When he heard this, he retrieved his hair which had been changed into his substitute, and he himself changed at once back into his true form. "Lucky! Lucky!" he cried with loud guffaws. "Business has come to my door!" "These three things," said Bajie, "will certainly make you lose your life. How could you say that business has come to your door?" "You still have no idea of my abilities!" said Pilgrim. "Elder Brother," said Bajie, "you are quite clever, quite capable in those transformations. Aren't those skills something already? What more abilities do you have?" Pilgrim said,

"Cut off my head and I still can speak.
Sever my arms, I still can beat you up!
My legs amputated, I still can walk.
My belly, ripped open, will heal again,
Smooth and snug as a wonton people make:
A tiny pinch and it's completely formed.
To bathe in boiling oil is easier still;
It's like warm liquid cleansing me of dirt."

When Bajie and Sha Monk heard these words, they roared with laughter. Pilgrim went forward and said, "Your Majesty, this young priest knows how to have his head cut off." "How did you acquire such an ability?" asked the king. "When I was practicing austerities in a monastery some years ago," said Pilgrim, "I met a mendicant Chan master, who taught me the magic of head cutting. I don't know whether it works or not, and that's why I want to try it out right now." "This priest is so young and ignorant!" said the king, chuckling. "Is head cutting something to try out? The head is, after all, the very fountain of the six kinds of *yang* energies in one's body. If you cut it off, you'll die." "That's what we want," said Tiger-Strength. "Only then can our feelings be relieved!" Besotted by the Daoist's words, the foolish ruler immediately gave the decree for an execution site to be prepared.

Once the command was given, three thousand imperial guards took up their positions outside the gate of the court. The king said, "Monk, go and cut off your head first." "I'll go first! I'll go first!" said Pilgrim merrily. He folded his hands before his chest and shouted, "National Preceptors, pardon my presumption for taking my turn first!" He turned swiftly and was about to dash out. The Tang monk grabbed him, saying, "O Disciple! Be careful! Where you are going isn't a playground!" "No fear!" said Pilgrim. "Take off your hands! Let me go!"

The Great Sage went straight to the execution site, where he was caught hold of by the executioner and bound with ropes. He was then led to a tall mound and pinned down on top of it. At the cry "Kill," his head came off with a swishing sound. Then the executioner gave the head a kick, and it rolled off like a watermelon to a distance of some forty paces away. No blood, however, spurted from the neck of Pilgrim. Instead, a voice came from inside his stomach, crying, "Come, head!" So alarmed was the Deer-Strength Great Immortal by the sight of such ability that he at once recited a spell and gave this charge to the local spirit and patron deity: "Hold down that head. When I have defeated the monk, I'll persuade the king to turn your little shrines into huge temples, your idols of clay into true bodies of gold." The local spirit and the god, you see, had to serve him since he knew the magic of the five thunders. Secretly, they indeed held Pilgrim's head down. Once more Pilgrim cried, "Come, head!" But the head stayed on the ground as if it had taken root; it would not move at all. Somewhat anxious, Pilgrim rolled his hands into fists and wrenched his body violently. The ropes all snapped and fell off; at the cry "Grow," a head sprang up instantly from his neck. Every one of the executioners and every member of the imperial guards became terrified, while the officer in charge of the execution dashed inside the court to make this report: "Your Majesty, that young priest had his head cut off, but another head has grown up." "Sha Monk," said Bajie, giggling, "we truly had no idea that Elder Brother has this kind of talent!" "If he knows seventy-two ways of transformation," said Sha Monk, "he may have altogether seventy-two heads!"

Hardly had he finished speaking when Pilgrim came walking back, saying, "Master." Exceedingly pleased, Tripitaka said, "Disciple, did it hurt?" "Hardly," said Pilgrim, "it's sort of fun!" "Elder Brother," said Bajie, "do you need ointment for the scar?" "Touch me," said Pilgrim, "and see if there's any scar." Idiot touched him and he was dumbfounded. "Marvelous! Marvelous!" he giggled. "It healed perfectly. You can't feel even the slightest scar!"

As the brothers were chatting happily among themselves, they heard the king say, "Receive your rescript. We give you a complete pardon. Go away!" Pilgrim said, "We'll take the rescript all right, but we want the National Preceptor to go there and cut his head off too! He should try something new!" "Great National Preceptor," said the king, "the priest is not willing to pass you up. If you want to compete with him, please try not to frighten us." Tiger-Strength had no choice but to go up to the site, where he was bound and pinned to the ground by several executioners. One of them lifted the sword and cut off his head, which was then kicked some thirty paces away. Blood did not spurt from his trunk either, and he, too, gave a cry, "Come, head!" Hurriedly pulling off a piece of hair, Pilgrim blew on it his immortal breath, crying, "Change!" It changed into a yellow hound, which dashed into the execution site, picked up the Daoist's head with its mouth, and ran to drop it into the imperial moat. The Daoist, meanwhile, called for his head three times without success. He did not, you see, have the ability of Pilgrim, and there was no possibility that he could produce another head. All at once, bright crimson gushed out from his trunk. Alas!

Though he could send for wind and call for rain,
How could he match an immortal of the right fruit?

In a moment, he fell to the dust, and those gathered about him discovered that he was actually a headless tiger with yellow fur.

The officer in charge of the execution went again to memorialize. "Your Majesty," he said, "the Great National Preceptor's head was cut off, but it could not grow back again. He perished in the dust and then he became a headless tiger with yellow fur." On hearing this, the king paled with fright and stared at the remaining two Daoists with unblinking eyes. Rising from his cushion, Deer-Strength said, "My Elder Brother must have been fated to die at this particular moment. But how could he be a yellow tiger? This has to be that monk's roguery. He is using some kind of deceptive magic to change my elder brother into a beast. I won't spare him now. I insist on having a competition of stomach ripping and heart gouging."

When the king heard this, he calmed down and said, "Little priest, our Second National Preceptor wants to wage another contest with you." "This little priest," said Pilgrim, "has not eaten much prepared food for a long time. The other day when we were journeying to the West, a kind patron kept asking us to eat and I stuffed myself with more pieces of steamed bread than I should have taken. I have been having a stomachache since, and I fear that I may have worms. This contest, therefore, can't be more timely, since I want very much to borrow Your Majesty's knife to rip open my stomach, so that I may take out my viscera and clean out my stomach

and spleen before I dare proceed to see Buddha in the Western Heaven."
When the king heard this, he gave the order: "Take him to the execution
site." A throng of captains and guards came forward to pull and tug at
Pilgrim, who pushed them back, saying, "I don't need people to hold me.
I'm going to walk there myself. There's one thing, however. I don't want
my hands tied, for I want to wash and clean out my viscera." The king at
once gave the order: "Don't tie his hands."

With a swagger, Pilgrim walked down to the execution site. Leaning
himself on a huge pillar, he untied his robe and revealed his stomach. The
executioner used a rope and tied his neck to the pillar; down below, another
rope strapped his two legs also to the pillar. Then he wielded a sharp dagger
and ripped Pilgrim's chest downward, all the way to his lower abdomen.
Pilgrim used both his hands to push open his belly, and then he took out
his intestines which he examined one by one. After a long pause, he put
them back inside, coil for coil exactly as before. Grasping the skins of his
belly and bringing them together with his hands, he blew his magic breath
on his abdomen, crying, "Grow!" At once his belly closed up completely.
So astonished was the king that he presented with both his hands the rescript to Pilgrim, saying, "Holy monk, please do not delay your westward
journey any further. Take your rescript and leave." "The rescript is a small
matter," said Pilgrim, chuckling. "How about asking Second National
Preceptor to go through with the cutting and ripping?" "Don't put the
blame on us," said the king to Deer-Strength. "It's you who wanted to be
his opponent. Please go! Please go!" "Relax!" said Deer-Strength. "I don't
think I'll ever lose to him!"

Look at him! He even imitated the swagger of Pilgrim Sun as he headed
for the execution site. There he was bound with ropes, and then his stomach was also ripped open by the dagger of the executioner. He, too, took
out his guts and manipulated them with his hands. Pilgrim at once pulled
off a piece of his hair, on which he blew a mouthful of his divine breath,
crying, "Change." It changed into a hungry hawk; spreading its wings and
claws, it flew up to the Daoist and snatched him clean of his guts. Then
it flew off to somewhere to enjoy its catch leisurely, while the Daoist was
reduced to

> A drippy ghost of torn belly and empty trunk,
> An aimless soul with less innards and no guts!

Kicking down the pillar, the executioner dragged the corpse over to have
a closer look. Ah! It was actually a white-coated deer with horns.

The officer in charge of the execution again ran hurriedly to make the
report: "Second National Preceptor is most unlucky! After his stomach was

ripped open, his viscera were snatched away by a hungry hawk. After he perished, his corpse changed into a white-coated deer with horns." More and more alarmed, the king said, "How could he turn into a deer with horns?" The Goat-Strength Great Immortal said, "Yes, how could my elder brother die and turn into the form of a beast? It has to be the magic of that monk, used by him to plot against us. Let me avenge the deaths of my elder brothers." "With what magic can you triumph over him?" said the king, and Goat-Strength replied, "I'm going to wage with him the contest of bathing in a cauldron of hot oil." The king indeed sent for a huge cauldron filled with fragrant oil and told them to begin the contest. "I thank you for your kindness," said Pilgrim, "for this young priest has not had a bath for a long time. My skin, in fact, has been rather dried and itchy these past two days, and I must have it scalded to take away the irritation."

The attendant before the throne indeed lighted a great fire on a huge pile of wood, and the oil in the cauldron was heated to boiling. When he was asked to step into it, Pilgrim pressed his palms together in front of him and asked: "Will it be a civil or a military bath?" "What's the difference?" asked the king. Pilgrim said, "A civil bath means that I shall not remove my clothing. With my hands on my hips, I'll jump in and jump out again after one little roll, so swiftly in fact that the clothes are not permitted to be soiled. If there's the tiniest speck of oil on the garments, I lose. A military bath, however, will require a clothes rack and a towel. I'll undress before I dive in, and I shall be permitted to play in there as I wish, including doing somersaults and cartwheels." The king said to Goat-Strength, "How do you want to compete with him? A civil or a military bath?" "If we take the civil bath," said Goat-Strength, "I fear that his robes may have been treated so that oil will slide off him. Let's have the military bath." Stepping forward instantly, Pilgrim said, "Pardon me again for the presumption of taking my turn first." Look at him! He took off his shirt and untied his tiger-skin kilt. With a bound, he leaped straight into the cauldron, splashing and frolicking in the boiling oil as if he were swimming in it.

When Bajie saw this, he bit his finger and said to Sha Monk, "We truly have misjudged this ape! During those sarcastic exchanges and the banter between us all this time, I thought he was simply joking! Little did I realize that he really had such ability!" They could hardly refrain from their marveling, but when Pilgrim saw them whispering back and forth to each other, he became highly suspicious and thought to himself: "That Idiot must be laughing at me! This is what the proverb means: 'Intelligence has its work and incompetence its leisure.' Old Monkey has to go through all this, and he's quite comfortable over there! Let me put some ropes on him and see whether he'll be more cautious!" As he bathed himself, he suddenly dove towards the bottom of the cauldron with a splash. There he changed himself into a small tack and all but disappeared.

The officer in charge of the proceedings went forward again to make the report: "Your Majesty, the young priest has been fried to death by the boiling oil." Delighted, the king gave the order for the bones to be fished out for him to see, and the executioner went forward to rake the oil with an iron strainer. The holes in the strainer, however, were quite large, whereas the tack into which Pilgrim had changed himself was very tiny, and repeatedly, it fell through the holes after it had been scooped up. The officer had no choice but to come back with this word:"The priest's body is tender and his bones are frail. He seems to have melted completely!"

The king at once shouted: "Seize those three monks!" Seeing how savage were the looks of Bajie, the palace guards rushed at him first and threw him to the ground, tying both of his hands behind his back. Tripitaka was so terrified that he cried out in a loud voice: "Your Majesty, please pardon this humble cleric for the moment. Since that disciple of mine embraced our faith, he has made merit again and again. Today his affront to the National Preceptor has led to his death in a cauldron of oil, and this humble cleric certainly has no desire to cling to my own life. Moreover, just as the officials are ruling over the people, so are you the ruler above all, and if you as king ask me, your subject, to die, how could I dare not die? But the one who died first has already become a spirit, and this is the reason I beg you for a moment's grace. Grant me half a cup of cold water or a bowl of thin gruel; give me also three paper horses and permit me to go before the cauldron to present these offerings and to express my regard for him as a disciple. Then I will accept whatever punishment you have for me." On hearing this, the king said, "All right! The Chinese are a very loyal people indeed!" He asked that the Tang monk be given the rice gruel and paper money.

The Tang monk requested that Sha Monk go with him below the steps, while a few of the guards dragged Bajie by the ears up to the cauldron. Facing it, the Tang monk offered the following invocation:

"My dear disciple, Sun Wukong!
Since taking your precepts at the grove of Chan,
What deep love you showed me on our westward way.
We hoped to reach together the Great Dao.
How could I know you would perish this day!
You lived for finding scriptures when alive;
In death you must on Buddha fix your mind.

Though far away your gallant soul should wait,
Your ghost from darkness will go to Thunderclap."

On hearing this prayer, Bajie said, "Master, that's not the proper invocation. Sha Monk, hold up the rice offering for me. Let me pray!" Bound
and pinned to the ground, Idiot panted out these words:

"You brazen, disaster-courting ape!
You ignorant Bimawen.
You brazen, death-deserving ape!
You deep-fried Bimawen!
The monkey's finished!
The mawen's undone!"

Pilgrim Sun was, of course, still in the bottom of the cauldron. When he
heard these castigations from Idiot, he could no longer restrain himself
and at once changed back into his original form. Standing up stark naked
in the cauldron, he shouted, "You overstuffed coolie! Whom are you cas-
tigating?" "Disciple," said the Tang monk when he saw Pilgrim, "you
almost frightened me to death!" Sha Monk said, "Elder Brother simply
loves to play dead!" The civil and military officials all rushed up the steps
to report: "Your Majesty, that priest did not die. He has emerged again
from the cauldron." Fearing that he might be found guilty of making a
false report to the throne, the officer in charge of execution said, "He is
dead all right. But today happens to be a rather inauspicious day and the
ghost of that young priest is now manifesting itself."

Maddened by what he heard, Pilgrim leaped out of the cauldron, dried
himself from the oil, and threw on his clothes. Dragging that officer over,
he whipped out his iron rod and one blow on the head reduced him to
a meat patty. "What ghost is this who's manifesting itself?" he huffed.
Those officials were so terrified that they freed Bajie at once and knelt on
the ground, pleading, "Pardon us! Pardon us!" The king, too, wanted to
leave his dragon throne, but he was caught by Pilgrim, who said, "Your
Majesty, don't walk away. Tell your third National Preceptor to go into
the cauldron also." Trembling all over, the king said, "Third National
Preceptor, save our life. Go into the cauldron quickly so that the monk
won't hit us." Goat-Strength went down the steps from the hall and took
off his clothes like Pilgrim. Leaping into the cauldron of boiling oil, he
began to cavort and bathe himself.

Letting go of the king, Pilgrim approached the cauldron and told the
fire tenders to add more wood while he put his hand into the oil. Aha! That
boiling oil felt ice cold. He thought to himself: "It was very hot when I took
the bath, but feel how cold it is now that he's washing in there. I know. It

has to be some dragon king who is giving him protection here." Leaping into the air, he recited a spell which began with the letter *Oṁ* and instantly summoned the Dragon King of the Northern Ocean to his side. "You horn-growing earthworm!" said Pilgrim to him. "You scaly lizard! How dare you assist that Daoist by coiling a cold dragon around the bottom of the cauldron? You want him to display his power and gain the upper hand on me?" Terribly intimidated, the Dragon King stammered out his answer: "Aoshun dares not do that! Perhaps the Great Sage has no knowledge of this: this cursed beast did go through quite an austere process of self-cultivation, to the point where he was able to cast off his original shell. He has acquired the true magic of the five thunders, while the rest of the magic powers he has are all those developed by heterodoxy, none fit to lead him to the true way of the immortals. The powers of both his associates have already been destroyed by the Great Sage and they had to reveal their original forms. The performance of this one right now is also part of the Great Illusion which he has learned in the Little Mao Mountain, a cold dragon which he has managed to cultivate by himself. This can deceive the worldly folks, but it can never deceive the Great Sage. I shall arrest that cold dragon at once, and you can be certain that he will be deep-fried—bones, skins, and all!" "Take him away," said Pilgrim, "and you'll be spared a whipping!" Changing into a violent gust of wind, the Dragon King swooped down to the cauldron and dragged the cold dragon back to the ocean.

Pilgrim dropped down from the air and stood again before the steps with Tripitaka, Bajie, and Sha Monk. They saw that the Daoist was bobbing up and down in the oil, but his desperate efforts to get out were all to no avail. Every time he climbed up the wall of the cauldron, he would slip back down; in no time at all, his flesh dissolved, his skin was charred, and his bones left his body. "Your Majesty," another officer in charge of execution went forward to report, "the Third National Preceptor has passed away!" As tears streamed from his eyes, the king clutched at the imperial table before him and sobbed uncontrollably, crying:

"The human form is hard, hard indeed, to get!
Make no elixir when there's no true guide.
You have the charms and water to send for gods,
But not the pill to lengthen, protect your life.
If perfection's undone,
Could Nirvāṇa be won?
Your life's precarious, your efforts are vain.
If you knew before such hardships you'd meet,
Why not abstain, stay safely in the mount?"

Truly

To touch gold, to refine lead—of what use are they?
To summon wind, to call for rain—still all is vain!

The king,[1] leaning on his dragon table, wept without ceasing until
night fell, his tears gushing forth like a stream. Finally, Pilgrim went up to
him and shouted: "How could you be so dim-witted? Look at the corpses
of those Daoists: one happens to be that of a tiger and the other, a deer.
Goat-Strength was, in fact, an antelope. If you don't believe me, ask them
to fish out his bones for you to see. How could humans have skeletons like
that? They were all mountain beasts which had become spirits, united in
their efforts to come here and plot against you. When they saw that your
ascendancy was still strong, they dared not harm you as yet; but after two
or more years when your ascendancy would be in decline, they would have
taken your life and your entire kingdom would have been theirs. It was
fortunate that we came in time to exterminate these deviates and save your
life. And you are still weeping? What for? Bring us our rescript at once and
send us on our way." Only when he had heard this from Pilgrim did the
king return to his senses. The civil and military officials also went forward
to speak to him, saying, "The dead indeed turn out to be a white deer and
a yellow tiger, while bones in the cauldron do belong to an antelope. It is
unwise not to listen to the words of the sage monk." "In that case," said
the king, "we are grateful to the sage monk. It's late already. Let the Grand
Preceptor escort the sage monks back to Wisdom Depth Monastery to
rest. During early court tomorrow, we shall open up the Eastern Pavilion
and command the Court of Imperial Entertainments to prepare a huge
vegetarian banquet to thank them." The priests were escorted back to the
monastery.

At the time of the fifth watch the following morning, the king held
court for many officials. He at once issued a decree to summon the Buddhist
monks to return to the city, and this decree was to be posted on every road
and on all four gates. After giving the order also for the preparation of a
huge banquet, he sent his imperial chariot to the Wisdom Depth Monastery
to invite Tripitaka and followers back to the Eastern Pavilion for the feast,
and we shall speak no more of that.

We tell you now instead about those monks who succeeded in escaping
with their lives. When they heard of the decree that was promulgated,
every one of them was delighted and began to return to the city to search

---

1. The remaining portion of the chapter is taken from the beginning of chapter
47 in the full-length edition.

for the Great Sage Sun, to thank him, and to return his hairs. Meanwhile, the elder, after the banquet was over, obtained the rescript from the king, who led the queen, the concubines, and two rows of civil and military officials out the gate of the court to see the priests off. As they came out, they found many monks kneeling on both sides of the road, saying "Father Great Sage, Equal to Heaven, we are the monks who escaped with our lives on the beach. When we heard that Father had wiped out the demons and rescued us, and when we further heard that our king had issued a decree commanding our return, we came here to present to you the hairs and to thank you for your Heavenly grace." "How many of you came back?" asked Pilgrim, chuckling, and they replied, "All five hundred. None's missing." Pilgrim shook his body once and immediately retrieved his hairs. Then he said to the king and the laypeople, "These monks indeed were released by old Monkey. The cart was smashed after old Monkey tossed it through the double passes and up the steep ridge, and it was Monkey also who beat to death those two perverse Daoists. After such pestilence has been exterminated this day, you should realize that the true way is the gate of Chan. Hereafter you should never believe in false doctrines. I hope you will honor the unity of the Three Religions: revere the monks, revere also the Daoists, and take care to nurture the talented. Your kingdom, I assure you, will be secure forever." The king gave his assent and his thanks repeatedly before he escorted the Tang monk out of the city. And so, this was the purpose of their journey:

A diligent search for the three canons;
A strenuous quest for the primal light.

We do not know what will happen to master and disciples; let's listen to the explanation in the next chapter.

The Chan Master, taking food, is demonically conceived;
Yellow Hag brings water to dissolve the perverse pregnancy.

We were telling you that master and disciples were on their way once more. Thus it was that
  With mind purged of care, they conform to Buddha's wisdom;
  They dine on wind and rest on water to journey west.
After traveling for a long time, it was again early spring and they heard
  Purple swallows murmuring
  And orioles warbling.
  Purple swallows murmur, tiring their scented beaks;
  Orioles warble, their artful notes persist.
  The ground full of fallen petals like brocade spread out;
  The whole mountain sprouting colors like cushion-piles.
  On the peak green plums are budding;
  By the cliff old cedars detain the clouds.
  Faint, misty lights o'er the meadows;
  Sandbars warmed by bright sunshine.
  In several gardens flowers begin to bloom;
  The sun comes back to Earth, willow sprouts anew
As they walked along, they came upon a small river of cool, limpid currents. The elder Tang reined in his horse to look around and saw in the distance several thatched huts beneath willows hanging jadelike. Pointing in that direction, Pilgrim said, "There must be someone running a ferryboat in those houses." "It's likely," said Tripitaka, "but since I haven't seen a boat, I don't dare open my mouth." Dropping down the luggage, Bajie screamed: "Hey, ferryman! Punt your boat over here." He yelled several times and indeed, from beneath the shade of willows a boat emerged, creaking as it was punted. In a little while, it approached the shore while master and disciples stared at it. Truly,
  As a paddle parts the foam,
  A light boat floats on the waves,

With olive cabins brightly painted
And a deck made of flat, level boards.
On the bow, iron cords encircle;
At the stern, a shining rudder stem.
Though it may be a reed of a boat,
It will sail the lakes and the seas;
Though without fancy cables and tall masts,
It has, in fact, oars of cedar and pine.
It's unlike the divine ship of great distance,
But it can traverse a river's width.
It comes and goes only between two banks;
It moves only in and out of ancient fords.

In a moment, the boat touched the bank, and the person punting called out: "If you want to cross the river, come over here." Tripitaka urged his horse forward to take a look at the boatman and saw that the person had

On the head a woolen wrap
And on the feet, two black silk shoes.
The body wore cotton coat and pants patched a hundred times;
A thousand-stitched, dirty cloth-skirt hugged the waist.
Though the wrists had coarse skin and the tendons, strength,
The eyes were dim, the brows knitted, and the features aged.
The voice was soft and coy like an oriole's,
But a closer look disclosed an old woman.

Walking to the side of the boat, Pilgrim said, "You are the one ferrying the boat?" "Yes," said the woman. "Why is the ferryman not here?" asked Pilgrim. "Why is the ferrywoman punting the boat?" The woman smiled and did not reply; she pulled out the gangplank instead and set it up. Sha Monk then poled the luggage into the boat, followed by the master holding onto Pilgrim. Then they moved the boat sideways so that Bajie could lead the horse to step into it. After the gangplank was put away, the woman punted the boat away from shore and, in a moment, rowed it across the river.

After they reached the western shore, the elder asked Sha Monk to untie one of the wraps and take out a few pennies for the woman. Without disputing the price, the woman tied the boat to a wooden pillar by the water and walked into one of the village huts nearby, giggling loudly all the time. When Tripitaka saw how clear the water was, he felt thirsty and told Bajie: "Get the almsbowl and fetch some water for me to drink." "I was just about to drink some myself," said Idiot, who took out the almsbowl and bailed out a full bowl of water to hand over to the master. The master drank less than half of the water, and when Idiot took the bowl back, he drank the rest of it in one gulp before he helped his master to mount the horse once more.

After master and disciples resumed their journey to the West, they had hardly traveled half an hour when the elder began to groan as he rode. "Stomachache!" he said, and Bajie behind him also said, "I have a stomachache, too." Sha Monk said, "It must be the cold water you drank." But before he even finished speaking, the elder cried out: "The pain's awful!" Bajie also screamed: "The pain's awful!" As the two of them struggled with this unbearable pain, their bellies began to swell in size steadily. Inside their abdomens, there seemed to be a clot of blood or a lump of flesh, which could be felt clearly by the hand, kicking and jumping wildly about. Tripitaka was in great discomfort when they came upon a small village by the road; two bundles of hay were tied to some branches on a tall tree nearby. "Master, that's good!" said Pilgrim. "The house over there must be an inn. Let me go over there to beg some hot liquid for you. I'll ask them also whether there is an apothecary around, so that I can get some ointment for your stomachache."

Delighted by what he heard, Tripitaka whipped his white horse and soon arrived at the village. As he dismounted, he saw an old woman sitting on a grass mound outside the village gate and knitting hemp. Pilgrim went forward and bowed to her with palms pressed together saying, "Popo,[1] this poor monk has come from the Great Tang in the Land of the East. My master is the royal brother of the Tang court. Because he drank some water from the river back there after we crossed it, he is having a stomachache." Breaking into loud guffaws, the woman said, "You people drank some water from the river?" "Yes," replied Pilgrim, "we drank some of the clean river water east of here." Giggling loudly, the old woman said, "What a joke! What a joke! Come in, all of you. I'll explain to you."

Pilgrim went to take hold of Tang monk while Sha Monk held up Bajie; moaning with every step the two sick men walked into the thatched hut to take a seat, their stomachs protruding and their faces turning yellow from the pain. "Popo," Pilgrim kept saying, "please make some hot liquid for my master. We'll thank you." Instead of boiling water, however, the old woman dashed inside, laughing and yelling, "Come and look, all of you!"

With loud clip-clops, several middle-aged women ran out from within

---

1. The word *po* in Chinese can mean an old woman in general or the maternal grandmother. Since neither "old lady" or "old woman" has quite the same flavor, I have kept the original.

to stare at the Tang monk, grinning stupidly all the time. Enraged, Pilgrim gave a yell and ground his teeth together, so frightening the whole crowd of them that they turned to flee, stumbling all over. Pilgrim darted forward and caught hold of the old woman, crying, "Boil some water quick and I'll spare you!" "O Father!" said the old woman, shaking violently, "boiling water is useless, because it won't cure their stomachaches. Let me go, and I'll tell you." Pilgrim released her, and she said, "This is the Nation of Women of Western Liang.[2] There are only women in our country, and not even a single male can be found here. That's why we were amused when we saw you. That water your master drank is not the best, for the river is called Child-and-Mother River. Outside our capital we also have a Male Reception Post-house, by the side of which there is also a Pregnancy Reflection Stream. Only after reaching her twentieth year would someone from this region dare go and drink that river's water, for she would feel the pain of conception soon after she took a drink. After three days, she would go to the Male Reception Post-house and look at her reflection in the stream. If a double reflection appears, it means that she will give birth to a child. Since your master drank some water from the Child-and-Mother River, he too has become pregnant and will give birth to a child. How could hot water cure him?"

When Tripitaka heard this, he paled with fright. "O disciple," he cried, "what shall we do?" "O father!" groaned Bajie as he twisted to spread his legs further apart, "we are men, and we have to give birth to babies? Where can we find a birth canal? How could the fetus come out?" With a chuckle Pilgrim said, "According to the ancients, 'A ripe melon will fall by itself.' When the time comes, you may have a gaping hole at your armpit and the baby will crawl out."

When Bajie heard this, he shook with fright, and that made the pain all the more unbearable. "Finished! Finished!" he cried. "I'm dead! I'm dead!" "Second Elder Brother," said Sha Monk, laughing, "stop writhing! Stop writhing! You may hurt the umbilical cord and end up with some sort of prenatal sickness." Our Idiot became more alarmed than ever. Tears welling up in his eyes, he tugged at Pilgrim and said, "Elder Brother, please ask the Popo to see if they have some midwives here who are not too heavy-handed. Let's find a few right away. The movement inside is becoming more frequent now. It must be labor pain. It's coming! It's coming!" Again

2. Nation of Women: in the *Record of the Western Territories of the Great Tang* (*Da Tang xiyuji*) authored by the historical Xuanzang, chapter 11 has a reference to a Kingdom of Western Women.

Sha Monk said chuckling, "Second Elder Brother, if it's labor pain, you'd better sit still. I fear you may puncture the water bag."

"O Popo," said Tripitaka with a moan, "do you have a physician here? I'll ask my disciple to go there and ask for a prescription. We'll take the drug and have an abortion." "Even drugs are useless," said the old woman, "but due south of here there is a Male-Undoing Mountain. In it there is a Child Destruction Cave, and inside the cave there is an Abortion Stream. You must drink a mouthful of water from the stream before the pregnancy can be terminated. But nowadays, it's not easy to get that water. Last year, a Daoist by the name of True Immortal Compliant came on the scene and he changed the name of the Child Destruction Cave to the Shrine of Immortal Assembly. Claiming the water from the Abortion Stream as his possession, he refused to give it out freely. Anyone who wants the water must present monetary offerings together with meats, wines, and fruit baskets. After bowing to him in complete reverence, you will receive a tiny bowl of the water. But all of you are mendicants. Where could you find the kind of money you need to spend for something like this? You might as well suffer here and wait for the births." When Pilgrim heard this, he was filled with delight. "Popo," he said, "how far is it from here to the Male-Undoing Mountain?" "About three thousand miles," replied the old woman. "Excellent! Excellent!" said Pilgrim. "Relax, Master! Let old Monkey go and fetch some of that water for you to drink."

Dear Great Sage! He gave this instruction to Sha Monk: "Take good care of Master. If this family ill behaves and tries to hurt him, bring out your old thuggery and scare them a little. Let me go fetch the water." Sha Monk obeyed. The old woman then took out a large porcelain bowl to hand over to Pilgrim, saying, "Take this bowl and try to get as much water as possible. We can save some for an emergency." Indeed Pilgrim took over the bowl, left that thatched hut, and mounted the cloud to leave. Only then did the old woman fall to her knees, bowing to the air, and cry, "O father! This monk knows how to ride the clouds!" She went inside and told the other women to come out to kowtow to the Tang monk, all addressing him as arhat or bodhisattva. Then they began to boil water and prepare rice to present to the pilgrims, and we shall leave them for the moment.

We tell you now about the Great Sage Sun on his cloud-somersault; in a little while, he saw the peak of a mountain blocking his path. Dropping down from his cloudy luminosity, he opened wide his eyes to look around. Marvelous mountain! He saw

Rare flowers spreading brocade;
Wild grass unrolling blue;

Plunging streams—one after another;
Brooks and clouds, both leisurely.
Canyons, packed together, rank with creepers and vines;
Ranges, stretching afar, dense with forests and trees.
Birds call, and wild geese glide by;
Deer drink, and monkeys clamber.
A mountain green like a jade screen;
A ridge blue like locks of hair.
Difficult indeed to reach from this world of dust!
Rocks and water splashing, a sight that never tires!
One often sees immortal lads leave, picking herbs.
One often meets woodsmen come, bearing loads.
Truly it's almost the scenery of Tiantai,
Surpassing perhaps the three peaks of Mount Hua.

As the Great Sage stared at the scenery, he discovered also a building
with its back on the dark side of the mountain and from where the sound
of a dog barking could be heard. Going down the mountain, the Great
Sage went toward the building, which was a rather nice place, too. Look
at the

Stream piercing a small bridge;
Thatched huts nestling a green hill.
A dog barks near the lonely fence;
The recluse comes and goes at will.

In a moment he came up to the gate, where he found an old Daoist sitting
cross-legged on the green lawn. When the Great Sage put down his porcelain bowl to bow to him, the Daoist rose slightly to return his greeting,
saying, "Where did you come from? For what purpose have you come
to this humble shrine?" Pilgrim replied, "This poor monk is a scripture
pilgrim sent by imperial commission of the Great Tang in the Land of
the East. Because my master mistakenly drank water from the Child-and-
Mother River, he is suffering from a swollen belly and unbearable pain.
We asked the natives there and learned that the pregnancy thus formed
has no cure. We are told, however, that there is an Abortion Stream in the
Child Destruction Cave of the Male-Undoing Mountain, and its water
can eliminate the conception. This is why I have come especially to see the
True Immortal Compliant, in order to beg from him some water to save
my master. May I trouble the old Daoist to lead me to him?" "This used to
be the Child Destruction Cave," said the Daoist, chuckling, "but it's now
changed to the Shrine of Immortal Assembly. I am none other than the
eldest disciple of the venerable father, True Immortal Compliant. What's
your name? Tell me so I can announce you." "I am the eldest disciple of

Tripitaka Tang, master of the Law," said Pilgrim, "and my vulgar name is Sun Wukong." "Where are your monetary gifts," asked the Daoist, "your offerings of wine?" Pilgrim said, "We are mendicants on a journey, and we haven't prepared them."

"You are quite mad!" said the Daoist, chuckling again. "My old master is now the protector of this mountain stream, and he has never given its water free to anyone. You go back and bring some gifts, and I'll announce you. Otherwise, please leave. Don't think about the water!" Pilgrim said, "Goodwill can be more powerful than an imperial edict. If you go and announce the name of old Monkey, I am sure that he will express his goodwill. Perhaps he will turn over the entire well of water to me."

This statement of Pilgrim gave the Daoist little alternative but to go inside to make the announcement. As the True Immortal was just playing the lute, the Daoist had to wait until he finished playing before saying, "Master, there is a Buddhist monk outside, who claims to be Sun Wukong, the eldest disciple of Tripitaka Tang. He wants some water from the Abortion Stream to save his master." It would have been better if the True Immortal had not heard the name, for the moment he came upon those words, "Wukong,"

Anger flared in his heart,
Wrath sprouted from his gall.

Jumping down quickly from his lute couch, he took off his casual garment and put on his Daoist robe. He picked up a compliant hook and leaped out of the door of the shrine. "Where is Sun Wukong?" he shouted. Pilgrim turned his head to see how that True Immortal was dressed.

A star cap of bright colors crowned his head;
He wore a red magic robe with golden threads.
His cloud shoes were topped by patterned brocade;
An elegant treasure belt wrapped around his waist.
A pair of stockings of embroidered silk;
Half visible, a patterned woolen kilt.
His hands held a compliant golden hook:
The blade, sharp; the handle, long and dragonlike.
Phoenix eyes glowed with brows going straight up;
Sharp, steely teeth within a blood-red mouth.
A beard soared like bright flames beneath his chin;
Like rushes flared his temple's scarlet hair.
His form seemed as violent as Marshal Wen's,[3]
Although their clothing was not the same.

3. One of the four grand marshals of the Daoist Heaven.

When Pilgrim saw him, he pressed his palms together before him and bowed, saying, "This poor monk is Sun Wukong." "Are you the real Sun Wukong," said the master with a laugh, "or are you merely assuming his name and surname?" "Look at the way the master speaks!" said Pilgrim. "As the proverb says, 'A gentleman changes neither his name when he stands, nor his surname when he sits.' What would be the reason for me to assume someone else's name?" The master asked, "Do you recognize me?" "Since I made repentance in the Buddhist gate and embraced with all sincerity the teaching of the monks," said Pilgrim, "I have only been climbing mountains and fording waters. I have lost contact with all the friends of my youth. Because I have never been able to visit you, I have never beheld your honorable countenance before. When we asked for our way in a village household west of the Child-and-Mother River, they told me that the master is called the True Immortal Compliant. That's how I know your name." The master said, "You are walking on your way, and I'm cultivating my realized immortality. Why did you come to visit me?" "Because my master drank by mistake the water of the Child-and-Mother River," replied Pilgrim, "and his stomachache turned into a pregnancy. I came especially to your immortal mansion to beg you for a bowl of water from the Abortion Stream, in order that my master might be freed from this ordeal."

"Is your master Tripitaka Tang?" asked the master, his eyes glowering. "Yes, indeed!" answered Pilgrim. Grinding his teeth together, the master said spitefully, "Have you run into a Great King Holy Child?"[4] "That's the nickname of the fiend, Red Boy," said Pilgrim, "who lived in the Fiery Cloud Cave by the Dried Pine Stream, in the Roaring Mountain. Why does the True Immortal ask after him?" "He happens to be my nephew," replied the master, "and the Bull Demon King is my brother. Some time ago my elder brother told me in a letter that Sun Wukong, the eldest disciple of Tripitaka Tang, was such a rascal that he brought his son great harm. I didn't know where to find you for vengeance, but you came instead to seek me out. And you're asking me for water?" Trying to placate him with a smile, Pilgrim said, "You are wrong, Sir. Your elder brother used to be my friend, for both of us belonged to a league of seven bond brothers when we were young. I just didn't know about you, and so I did not come to pay my respect in your mansion. Your nephew is very well off, for he is now the attendant of the Bodhisattva Guanyin. He has become

4. The dialogue here refers to chapters 40–42 of the hundred-chapter novel, which are not included in this edition.

the Boy of Goodly Wealth, with whom even we cannot compare. Why do you blame me instead?"

"You brazen monkey!" shouted the master. "Still waxing your tongue! Is my nephew better off being a king by himself, or being a slave to someone? Stop this insolence and have a taste of my hook!" Using the iron rod to parry the blow, the Great Sage said, "Please don't use the language of war, Sir. Give me some water and I'll leave." "Brazen monkey!" scolded the master. "You don't know any better! If you can withstand me for three rounds, I'll give you the water. If not, I'll chop you up as meat sauce to avenge my nephew." "You damned fool!" scolded Pilgrim. "You don't know what's good for you! If you want to fight, get up here and watch my rod!" The master at once countered with his compliant hook, and the two of them had quite a fight before the Shrine of Immortal Assembly.

> The sage monk drinks from this procreant stream,
> And Pilgrim must th'Immortal Compliant seek.
> Who knows the True Immortal is a fiend,
> Who safeguards by force the Abortion Stream?
> When these two meet, they speak as enemies
> Feuding, and resolved not to give one whit.
> The words thus traded engender distress;
> Rancor and malice so bent on revenge.
> This one, whose master's life is threatened, comes seeking water;
> That one for losing his nephew refuses to yield.
> Fierce as a scorpion's the compliant hook;
> Wild like a dragon's the golden-hooped rod.
> Madly it stabs the chest, what savagery!
> Aslant, it hooks the legs, what subtlety!
> The rod aiming down there[5] inflicts grave wounds;
> The hook, passing shoulders, will whip the head.
> The rod slaps the waist——"a hawk holds a bird."
> The hook swipes the head——"a mantis hits its prey."
> They move here and there, both striving to win;
> They turn and close in again and again.
> The hook hooks, the rod strikes, without letup——
> On either side victory cannot be seen.

The master fought the Great Sage for over ten rounds and then he began to weaken. The Great Sage, however, grew fiercer, the blows of his rod descended on his opponent's head like a meteor shower. His strength all

---

5. Down there: i.e., the genitals.

gone, the master fled toward the mountain with his compliant hook trailing behind him.

Instead of chasing after him, the Great Sage wanted to go into the shrine to look for the water, but the Daoist had long had the door tightly shut. Holding the porcelain bowl, the Great Sage dashed up to the door and kicked it down with all his might. He rushed inside and saw the Daoist leaning on the well, covering its mouth with his body. The Great Sage lifted high his rod and shouted that he was about to strike, causing the Daoist to flee to the rear. Then he found a bucket, and just as he tried to bail some water, the master dashed out from the rear and caught hold of one of his legs with the compliant hook. One hard tug sent the Great Sage tumbling beak-first to the ground. Clambering up, the Great Sage at once attacked with his iron rod, but the master only retreated to one side. With hook in hand, he cried, "See if you could take away my water!"

"Come up here! Come up here!" yelled the Great Sage. "I'll beat you to death!" But the master refused to go forward to fight; he just stood there and refused to permit the Great Sage to bail out the water. When the Great Sage saw that his enemy was motionless, he wielded his iron rod with his left hand while his right hand tried to let the rope down the well. Before the pulley had made several turns, however, the master again struck with his hook. As the Great Sage could hardly protect himself with only one hand, the hook once more caught hold of one of his legs, causing him to stumble and the rope to fall into the well, bucket and all. "This fellow is quite rude!" said the Great Sage, who clambered up and, holding the iron rod now with both hands, showered his opponent's body and head with blows. Not daring to face him and fight, the master fled away as before. Again the Great Sage wanted to get the water, but this time he had no bucket, and moreover, he was afraid that the master would return to attack him. He thought to himself: "I must go and find a helper."

Dear Great Sage! He mounted the clouds and went straight back to the village hut, crying, "Sha Monk." Inside Tripitaka was moaning to endure the pain, while the groans of Bajie were continuous. Delighted by the call, they said, "Sha Monk, Wukong's back." Sha Monk hurried out the door to ask, "Big Brother, have you brought water?" The Great Sage entered and gave a thorough account to the Tang monk. Shedding tears, Tripitaka said, "O disciple! How is this going to end?" "I came back," said the Great Sage, "to ask Brother Sha to go with me. When we reach the shrine, old Monkey will fight with that fellow and Sha Monk can use the opportunity to get that water to save you." Tripitaka said, "Both of you who are healthy will be gone, leaving behind the two of us who are sick.

Who will look after us?" The old woman waiting on them said, "Relax, old arhat. You don't need your disciples. We will serve you and take care of you. When you first arrived, we were already fond of you. Then we saw how this bodhisattva traveled by cloud and fog, and we knew that you had to be an arhat or bodhisattva. We'll never dare to harm you again."

"You are all women here," snapped Pilgrim. "Whom do you dare to harm?" "O dear father!" said the old woman, giggling. "You're lucky to have come to my house. If you had gone to another one, none of you would have remained whole." "What do you mean," said Bajie, still groaning, "by not remaining whole?" The old woman replied: "The four or five of us in this family are all getting on in years. We have given up the activities of love. If you go to another family, there may be more youthful members than old ones. You think the young ones will let you go? They will want to have intercourse with you, and if you refuse, they will take your lives. Then they will cut you up to use your flesh to make fragrant bags." "In that case," said Bajie, "I won't be hurt. They all smell nice, and they'll be good for fragrant bags. I'm a stinking hog, and even when I'm cut up, I still stink. That's why I can't be hurt." "Don't be so talkative!" said Pilgrim, chuckling. "Save your strength, so you can give birth." The old woman said, "No need for delay. Go quickly to get the water." "Do you have a bucket in your house?" asked Pilgrim. "Please lend us one." The old woman went to the back to take out a bucket and rope to hand over to Sha Monk, who said, "Let's bring two ropes. We may need them if the well is deep."

After Sha Monk received the bucket and the ropes, he followed the Great Sage out of the village hut and they left together, mounting the clouds. In less than half an hour, they arrived at the Male-Undoing Mountain. As they lowered their clouds to go before the shrine, the Great Sage gave Sha Monk this instruction: "Take the bucket with the ropes and hide yourself. Old Monkey will go and provoke battle. When we are in the thick of fighting, you can use the opportunity to go inside, get the water, and leave." Sha Monk obeyed.

Wielding his iron rod, the Great Sage Sun approached the door and shouted: "Open the door! Open the door!" The Daoist who stood guard at the door hurried inside to report: "Master, that Sun Wukong is here again." Greatly angered, the master said, "This brazen ape is insolent indeed! I have always heard that he has considerable abilities, and today I know it's true. That rod of his is quite difficult to withstand." "Master," said the Daoist, "his abilities may be great, but yours are not inferior. You are, in fact, exactly his match." "But twice before," said the master, "I lost to him." "Only in a contest of sheer violence," said the Daoist. "Later, when he tried to bail water, your hook made him fall twice. Haven't you equalized the situation? He had little alternative but to leave at first, and now he's back. It must be that Tripitaka's pregnancy is so advanced and his body so heavy that his complaints have driven this monkey to return, against his better judgment. He must feel rather contemptuous toward his master, and I'm sure that you will win." When the True Immortal heard these words, he became

Delighted and filled with elation;
Full of smiles and brimming with power.

Holding straight his compliant hook, he walked out of the door and shouted, "Brazen simian! Why are you here again?" "Only to fetch water," answered the Great Sage.

"That water," said the True Immortal, "happens to be in my well. Even if you are a king or a prime minister, you must come begging with offerings of meat and wines, and then I will only give you a little. You are my enemy no less, and you dare to ask for it with empty hands?" "You really refuse to give it to me?" asked the Great Sage, and the True Immortal replied, "Yes! Yes!" "You damned fool!" scolded the Great Sage. "If you don't give me the water, watch my rod!" He opened up at once and rushed at the True Immortal, bringing down the rod hard on his head. Stepping aside quickly to dodge the blow, the True Immortal met him with the hook and fought back. This time, it was even more ferocious a battle than last time. What a fight!

Golden-hooped rod,
Compliant hook,
Two angry men so full of enmity.
The cosmos darkens as sand and rocks fly up;
Sun and moon sadden as dirt and dust soar high.
The Great Sage seeks water to save his master,
Denied by the fiend for his nephew's sake.
The two exert their strength
To wage a contest there.
Teeth are ground together
To strive for a victory.
More and more alert,
They arouse themselves.
They belch cloud and fog to sadden ghosts and gods.
Bing-bing and bang-bang clash both hook and rod,
Their cries, their shouts shake up the mountain range.

The fierce wind, howling, ravages the woods;
The violent airs surge past the dipper stars.
The Great Sage grows happier as he strives;
The True Immortal's gladder as he fights.
They do this battle with their whole hearts and minds;
They will not give up until someone dies.

The two of them began their fighting outside the shrine, and as they struggled and danced together, they gradually moved to the mountain slope below. We shall leave this bitter contest for a moment.

We tell you instead about our Sha Monk, who crashed inside the door, holding the bucket. He was met by the Daoist, who barred the way at the well and said, "Who are you that you dare come to get our water?" Dropping the bucket, Sha Monk took out his fiend-routing treasure staff and, without a word, brought it down on the Daoist's head. The Daoist was unable to dodge fast enough, and his left arm and shoulder were broken by this one blow. Falling to the ground, he lay there struggling for his life. "I wanted to slaughter you, cursed beast," scolded Sha Monk, "but you are, after all, a human being. I still have some pity for you, and I'll spare you. Let me bail out the water." Crying for Heaven and Earth to help him, the Daoist crawled slowly to the rear, while Sha Monk lowered the bucket into the well and filled it to the brim. He then walked out of the shrine and mounted the cloud and fog before he shouted to Pilgrim, "Big Brother, I have gotten the water and I'm leaving. Spare him! Spare him!" When the Great Sage heard this, he stopped the hook with his iron rod and said, "I was about to exterminate you, but you have not committed a crime. Moreover, I still have regard for the feelings of your brother, the Bull Demon King. When I first came here, I was hooked by you twice and I didn't get my water. When I returned, I came with the trick of enticing the tiger to leave the mountain and deceived you into fighting me, so that my brother could go inside to get the water. If old Monkey is willing to use his real abilities to fight with you, don't say there is only one of you so-called True Immortal Compliant; even if there were several of you, I would beat you all to death. But to kill is not as good as to let live, and so I'm going to spare you and permit you to have a few more years. From now on if anyone wishes to obtain the water, you must not blackmail the person."

Not knowing anything better, that bogus immortal brandished his hook and once more attempted to catch Pilgrim's legs. The Great Sage evaded the blade of his hook and then rushed forward, crying, "Don't run!" The bogus immortal was caught unprepared and he was pushed head over heels to the ground, unable to get up. Grabbing the compliant hook the Great Sage snapped it in two; then he bundled the pieces together and, with another bend, broke them into four segments. Throwing them on the ground, he said, "Brazen, cursed beast! Still dare to be unruly?" Trembling all over, the bogus immortal took the insult and dared not utter a word. Our Great Sage, in peals of laughter, mounted the cloud to rise into the air, and we have a testimonial poem. The poem says:

> You need true water to smelt true lead;
> With dried mercury true water mixes well.
> True mercury and lead have no maternal breath;
> Elixir is divine drug and cinnabar.
> In vain the child conceived attains a form;
> Earth Mother has achieved merit with ease.
> Heresy pushed down, right faith's affirmed;
> The lord of the mind, all smiles, now goes back.

Mounting the auspicious luminosity, the Great Sage caught up with Sha Monk. Having acquired the true water, they were filled with delight as they returned to where they belonged. After they lowered the clouds and went up to the village hut, they found Zhu Bajie leaning on the door post and groaning, his belly huge and protruding. Walking quietly up to him, Pilgrim said, "Idiot, when did you enter the delivery room?" Horrified, Idiot said, "Elder Brother, don't make fun of me. Did you bring the water?" Pilgrim was about to tease him some more when Sha Monk followed him in, laughing as he said, "Water's coming! Water's coming!" Enduring the pain, Tripitaka rose slightly and said, "O disciples, I've caused you a lot of trouble." That old woman, too, was most delighted, and all of her relatives came out to kowtow, crying, "O bodhisattva! This is our luck! This is our luck!" She took a goblet of flowered porcelain, filled it half full, and handed it to Tripitaka, saying, "Old master, drink it slowly. All you need is a mouthful and the pregnancy will dissolve." "I don't need any goblet," said Bajie, "I'll just finish the bucket." "O Venerable Father, don't scare people to death!" said the old woman. "If you drink this bucket of water, your stomach and your intestines will all be dissolved."

Idiot was so taken aback that he dared not misbehave; he drank only half a goblet. In less than the time of a meal, the two of them experienced sharp pain and cramps in their bellies, and then their intestines growled four or five times. After that, Idiot could no longer contain himself: both waste and urine poured out of him. The Tang monk, too, felt the urge to relieve himself and wanted to go to a quiet place. "Master," said Pilgrim, "you mustn't go out to a place where there is a draft. If you are exposed to the wind, I fear that you may catch some postnatal illness." At once the old woman brought to them two night pots so that the two of them could find relief. After several bowel movements, the pain stopped and the swelling of their bellies gradually subsided as the lump of blood and flesh dissolved. The relatives of the old woman also boiled some white rice congee and presented it to them to strengthen their postnatal weakness.

"Popo," said Bajie, "I have a healthy constitution, and I have no need to strengthen any postnatal weakness. You go and boil me some water, so that I can take a bath before I eat the congee." "Second Elder Brother," said Sha Monk, "you can't take a bath. If water gets inside someone within a month after birth, the person will be sick." Bajie said, "But I have not given proper birth to anything; at most, I only have had a miscarriage. What's there to be afraid of? I must wash and clean up." Indeed, the old woman prepared some hot water for them to clean their hands and feet. The Tang monk then ate about two bowls of congee, but Bajie consumed over fifteen bowls and he still wanted more. "Coolie," chuckled Pilgrim, "don't eat so much. If you get a sandbag belly, you'll look quite awful." "Don't worry, don't worry," replied Bajie. "I'm no female hog. So, what's there to be afraid of?" The family members indeed went to prepare some more rice.

The old woman then said to the Tang monk, "Old master, please bestow this water on me." Pilgrim said, "Idiot, you are not drinking the water anymore?" "My stomachache is gone," said Bajie, "and the pregnancy, I suppose, must be dissolved. I'm quite fine now. Why should I drink any more water?" "Since the two of them have recovered," said Pilgrim, "we'll give this water to your family." After thanking Pilgrim, the old woman poured what was left of the water into a porcelain jar, which she buried in the rear garden. She said to the rest of the family, "This jar of water will take care of my funeral expenses." Everyone in that family, young and old, was delighted. A vegetarian meal was prepared and tables were set out to serve to the Tang monk. He and his disciples had a leisurely dinner and then rested.

At dawn the next day, they thanked the old woman and her family before leaving the village. Tripitaka Tang mounted up, Sha Monk toted the luggage, Zhu Bajie held the reins, and the Great Sage Sun led the way in front. So, this is how it should be:

The mouth washed of its sins, the self is clean;
Worldly conception dissolved, the body's fit.

We don't know what sort of affairs they must attend to when they reach the capital; let's listen to the explanation in the next chapter.

Dharma-nature, going west, reaches the Women Nation;
Mind Monkey devises a plan to flee the fair sex.

We tell you now about Tripitaka and his disciples, who left the household at the village and followed the road westward. In less than forty miles, they came upon the boundary of Western Liang. Pointing ahead as he rode along, the Tang monk said, "Wukong, we are approaching a city, and from the noise and hubbub coming from the markets, I suppose it must be the Nation of Women. All of you must take care to behave properly. Keep your desires under control and don't let them violate the teachings of our gate of Law." When the three disciples heard this, they obeyed the strict admonition. Soon they reached the head of the street that opened to the eastern gate. The people there, with long skirts and short blouses, powdered faces and oily heads, were all women regardless of whether they were young or old. Many of them were doing business on the streets, and when they saw the four of them walking by, they all clapped their hands in acclaim and laughed aloud, crying happily, "Human seeds are coming! Human seeds are coming!" Tripitaka was so startled that he reined in his horse; all at once the street was blocked, completely filled with women, and all you could hear were laughter and chatter. Bajie began to holler wildly: "I'm a pig for sale! I'm a pig for sale!" "Idiot," said Pilgrim, "stop this nonsense. Bring out your old features, that's all!" Indeed, Bajie shook his head a couple of times and stuck up his two rush-leaf fan ears; then he wriggled his lips like two hanging lotus roots and gave a yell, so frightening those women that they all fell and stumbled. We have a testimonial poem, and the poem says:

> *The sage monk, seeking Buddha, reached Western Liang,*
> *A land full of females but without one male.*
> *Farmers, scholars, workers, and those in trade,*
> *The fishers and plowers were women all.*
> *Maidens lined the streets, crying "Human seeds!"*
> *Young girls filled the roads to greet the comely men.*

If Wuneng did not show his ugly face,
The siege by the fair sex would be pain indeed.

In this way, the people became frightened and none dared go forward; everyone was rubbing her hands and squatting down. They shook their heads, bit their fingers, and crowded both sides of the street, trembling all over but still eager to stare at the Tang monk. The Great Sage Sun had to display his hideous face in order to open up the road, while Sha Monk, too, played monster to keep order. Leading the horse, Bajie stuck out his snout and waved his ears. As the whole entourage proceeded, the pilgrims discovered that the houses in the city were built in orderly rows while the shops had lavish displays. There were merchants selling rice and salt; there were wine and tea houses.

There were bell and drum towers with goods piled high;
Bannered pavilions with screens hung low.

As master and disciples followed the street through its several turns, they came upon a woman official standing in the street and crying, "Visitors from afar should not enter the city gate without permission. Please go to the post-house and enter your names on the register. Allow this humble official to announce you to the Throne. After your rescript is certified, you will be permitted to pass through." Hearing this, Tripitaka dismounted; then he saw a horizontal plaque hung over the gate of an official mansion nearby, and on the plaque were the three words, Male Reception Post-house. "Wukong," said the elder; "what that family in the village said is true. There is indeed a Male Reception Post-house." "Second Elder Brother," said Sha Monk, laughing, "go and show yourself at the Pregnancy Reflection Stream and see if there's a double reflection." Bajie replied, "Don't play with me! Since I drank that cup of water from the Abortion Stream, the pregnancy has been dissolved. Why should I show myself?" Turning around, Tripitaka said to him, "Wuneng, be careful with your words." He then went forward to greet the woman official, who led them inside the post-house.

After they took their seats in the main hall, the official asked for tea to be served. All the servants working here combed their hair into three braids, and their garments were worn in two sections. Look at them! Even those serving tea were giggling. In a moment, they finished tea, and the official rose and asked, "Where did the visitors come from?" Pilgrim replied, "We are people from the Land of the East, sent by imperial commission of the Great Tang Emperor to worship Buddha in the Western Heaven and to seek scriptures. My master, the royal brother of the Tang emperor, bears the title of Tripitaka Tang. I'm Sun Wukong, his eldest disciple, and these two—Zhu Wuneng and Sha Wujing—are my brothers. There are five of us altogether, including the horse. We have with us a travel rescript, and we beg you to certify it so that we may pass through." After the woman official wrote this in the register with a brush, she came forward to kowtow, saying, "Venerable Fathers, please pardon me. This humble official is the clerk at the Male Reception Post-house. I did not know that such dignitaries from a noble nation were on their way, and therefore I did not go to a distance to meet you." After she kowtowed, she rose and immediately gave an order to the housekeeper to prepare food and drink. "Let the venerable fathers sit here for a while," she said, "and this humble official will enter the capital to present a memorial to our ruler. We will certify your rescript and use our seals, so that you can be sent on your way to the West." Delighted, Tripitaka sat down and we shall leave him for the moment.

We tell you now about that clerk of the post-house, who, after she had put on the proper attire, went to the Five Phoenix Tower inside the capital and said to the Custodian of the Yellow Gate: "I'm the clerk of the Male Reception Post-house, and I must have an audience with the Throne." The Yellow Gate at once presented the memorial, and the clerk was summoned up to the main palace hall. The queen asked: "Why does the Clerk of the post-house wish to see us?" "Your humble subject," said the clerk, "has just received in the post-house Tripitaka Tang, the royal brother of the Great Tang Emperor in the Land of the East. He has three disciples by the names of Sun Wukong, Zhu Wuneng, and Sha Wujing; there are altogether five of them, including a horse. They are on their way to seek scriptures from the Buddha in the Western Heaven. I have come especially to report this to my queen and to ask whether they may have their travel rescript certified and the permission to pass through." When the queen heard this report, she was filled with delight. "Last night," she said to the civil and military officials, "we dreamed that

Luminous hues grew from the screens of gold,
Refulgent rays spread from the mirrors of jade.

That had to be a good omen for today." "Mistress," said the women officials in unison as they prostrated themselves before the vermilion steps, "how could you tell that it was a good omen?" The queen said, "This man from the Land of the East is a royal brother of the Tang court. In our country, the rulers of various generations since the time when chaos divided had never seen a man come here. Now the royal brother of the Tang emperor has arrived, and he must be a gift from Heaven. We will use the wealth of an entire nation to ask this royal brother to be king; we are willing to be his queen. Such a sexual union will produce children and grandchildren, and the perpetuity of our kingdom will be assured. When you consider this, is not our dream a good omen?" The women officials all kowtowed to express their delight and acclaim.

Then the clerk of the post-house said, "What our mistress has proposed is good for extending the familial line to ten thousand generations. But those three disciples of the royal brother are savage men; their appearances are most unsightly." "According to what you have seen, worthy subject, how does that royal brother look?" asked the queen. "And how do his disciples look?" "The royal brother," said the clerk, "has features most dignified and handsome, truly befitting a man who belongs to the Heavenly court of a noble nation, the China of South Jambūdvīpa. His three disciples, however, have such savage looks that they appear to be spirits." "In that case," said the queen, "let us provide his disciples with some supplies and certify the travel rescript for them. We shall send them off to the Western Heaven, and only the royal brother will remain here. Anything wrong with that?" Again the officials bowed to say, "The words of our mistress are most appropriate, and your subjects obey your instruction. The affair of marriage, however, requires a matchmaker, for as the ancients have declared,

The marriage contract depends on red leaves;[1]
A couple's joined by the moon-man's scarlet threads."[2]

"We shall follow the counsel of our subjects," replied the queen. "Let the present Grand Preceptor serve as our marriage go-between, and the clerk of the Male Reception Post-house as the one who officiates the ceremony. Let them go first to the post-house to propose to the royal brother. If he consents, we shall take our carriage out of the capital to receive him." The Grand Preceptor and the clerk accepted this decree and left the court.

We now tell you about Tripitaka and his disciples, who were just enjoying their vegetarian meal at the hall of the post-house when someone came in to report: "The Grand Preceptor and our own governess have arrived." Tripitaka said, "Why does the Grand Preceptor come here?" "Perhaps the

1. Red leaves: a reference to a story of the Tang in which a palace woman wrote a poem on a red leaf that floated out of the palace in the current of the moat. Picked up by a scholar, another poem on a red leaf was sent back to the palace when it was dropped in the moat's upper reach. The two of them eventually married when the emperor released thousands of palace concubines, for the red leaves they kept in secret were discovered and acknowledged as pledges.

2. Red threads: the Old Man in the Moon, the marriage broker par excellence in Chinese mythology, is supposed to tie the feet of fated lovers with scarlet threads to indicate a lasting relationship.

queen wants to give us an invitation," said Bajie. "If not that," said Pilgrim, "then to offer a proposal of marriage." "Wukong," said Tripitaka, "if they hold us and want to force us to marry them, what shall we do?" "Master," replied Pilgrim, "just say Yes to them. Old Monkey will take care of the matter."

They had hardly finished speaking when the two women officials arrived and bowed deeply to the elder, who returned their salutations one by one, saying, "This humble cleric is someone who has left the family. What virtue or talent do I have that I dare let you bow to me?" When the Grand Preceptor saw how impressive the elder looked, she was delighted and thought to herself: "Our nation is truly quite lucky! Such a man is most worthy to be the husband of our ruler." After the officials made their greetings, they stood on either side of the Tang monk and said, "Father royal brother, we wish you ten thousand happinesses!" "I'm someone who has left the family," replied Tripitaka. "Where do those happinesses come from?" Again bending low, the Grand Preceptor said, "This is the Nation of Women in the Western Liang, and since time immemorial, there is not a single male in our country. We are lucky at this time to have the arrival of father royal brother. Your subject, by the decree of my ruler, has come especially to offer a proposal of marriage." "My goodness! My goodness!" said Tripitaka. "This poor monk has arrived at your esteemed region all by himself, without the attendance of either son or daughter. I have with me only three mischievous disciples, and I wonder to which of us is offered this marriage proposal." The post-house clerk said, "Your lowly official just now went into court to present my report, and my ruler, in great delight, told us of an auspicious dream she had last night. She dreamed that

Luminous hues grew from the screens of gold,
Refulgent rays spread from the mirrors of jade.

When she learned that the royal brother is a man from the noble nation of China, she was willing to use the wealth of her entire nation to ask you to be her live-in husband. You would take the royal seat facing south to be called the man set apart from others,[3] and our ruler would be the queen. That was why she gave the decree for the Grand Preceptor to serve as the marriage go-between and this lowly official to officiate at the wedding. We came especially to offer you this proposal." When Tripitaka heard these words, he bowed his head and fell into complete silence. "When a man finds the time propitious," said the Grand Preceptor, "he should not

---

3. The man set apart from others or the lone man is another euphemistic title for the emperor.

pass up such an opportunity. Though there is, to be sure, such a thing in the world as asking a husband to live in the wife's family, the dowry of a nation's wealth is rare indeed. May we ask the royal brother to give his quick consent, so that we may report to our ruler." The elder, however, became more dumb and deaf than ever.

Sticking out his pestlelike snout, Bajie shouted, "Grand Preceptor, go back and tell your ruler that my master happens to be an arhat who has attained the Way after a long process of cultivation. He will never fall in love with the dowry of a nation's wealth, nor will he be enamored with even beauty that can topple an empire. You may as well certify the travel rescript quickly and send them off to the West. Let me stay here to be the live-in husband. How's that?" When the Grand Preceptor heard this, her heart quivered and her gall shook, unable to answer at all. The clerk of the post-house said, "Though you may be a male, your looks are hideous. Our ruler will not find you attractive." "You are much too inflexible," said Bajie, laughing. "As the proverb says,

The thick willow's a basket, the thin, a barrel—
Who in the world will take a man as an ugly fellow?"

Pilgrim said, "Idiot, stop this foolish talk. Let Master make up his mind: if he wants to leave, let him leave, and if he wants to stay, let him stay. Let's not waste the time of the marriage go-between."

"Wukong," said Tripitaka, "What do you think I ought to do?" "In old Monkey's opinion," replied Pilgrim, "perhaps it's good that you stay here. As the ancients said, 'One thread can tie up a distant marriage.' Where will you ever find such a marvelous opportunity?" Tripitaka said, "Disciple, if we remain here to dote on riches and glory, who will go to acquire scriptures in the Western Heaven? Won't the waiting kill my emperor of the Great Tang?" The Grand Preceptor said, "In the presence of the royal brother, your humble official dares not hide the truth. The wish of our ruler is only to offer you the proposal of marriage. After your disciples have attended the wedding banquet, provisions will be given them and the travel rescript will be certified, so that they may proceed to the Western Heaven to acquire the scriptures." "What the Grand Preceptor said is most reasonable," said Pilgrim, "and we need not be difficult about this. We are willing to let our master remain here to become the husband of your mistress. Certify our rescript quickly and send us off to the West. When we have acquired the scriptures, we will return here to visit father and mother and ask for travel expenses so that we may go back to the Great Tang." Both the Grand Preceptor and the clerk of the post-house bowed to Pilgrim as they said, "We thank this teacher for his kind assistance in concluding this marriage." Bajie said, "Grand Preceptor, don't use only your mouth to set the table! Since we have given our consent, tell your mistress to prepare us a banquet first. Let us have an engagement drink. How about it?" "Of course! Of course!" said the Grand Preceptor. "We'll send you a feast at once." In great delight, the Grand Preceptor left with the clerk of the post-house.

We tell you now about our elder Tang, who caught hold of Pilgrim immediately and berated him, crying, "Monkey head! Your tricks are killing me! How could you say such things and ask me to get married here while you people go to the Western Heaven to see Buddha? Even if I were to die, I would not dare do this." "Relax, Master," said Pilgrim, "old Monkey's not ignorant of how you feel. But since we have reached this place and met this kind of people, we have no alternative but to meet plot with plot." "What do you mean by that?" asked Tripitaka.

Pilgrim said, "If you persist in refusing them, they will not certify our travel rescript nor will they permit us to pass through. If they grow vicious and order many people to cut you up and use your flesh to make those so-called fragrant bags, do you think that we will treat them with kindness? We will, of course, bring out our abilities which are meant to subdue demons and dispel fiends. Our hands and feet are quite heavy, you know, and our weapons ferocious. Once we lift our hands, the people of this entire nation will be wiped out. But you must think of this, however. Although they are now blocking our path, they are no fiendish creatures or monster-spirits; all of them in this country are humans. And you have always been a man committed to kindness and compassion, refusing to hurt even one sentient being on our way. If we slaughter all these common folk here, can you bear it? That would be true wickedness."

When Tripitaka heard this, he said, "Wukong, what you have just said is most virtuous. But I fear that if the queen asks me to enter the palace, she will want me to perform the conjugal rite with her. How could I consent to lose my original *yang* and destroy the virtue of Buddhism, to leak my true sperm and fall from the humanity of our faith?" "Once we have agreed to the marriage," said Pilgrim, "she will no doubt follow royal etiquette and send her carriage out of the capital to receive you. Don't refuse her. Take a ride in her phoenix carriage and dragon chariot to go up to the treasure hall, and then sit down on the throne facing south. Ask the queen to take out her imperial seal and summon us brothers to go into court. After you have stamped the seal on the rescript, tell the queen to sign the document also and give it back to us. Meanwhile, you can also tell them to prepare a huge banquet; call it a wedding feast as well as a farewell party for us.

After the banquet, ask for the chariot once more on the excuse that you want to see us off outside the capital before you return to consummate the marriage with the queen. In this way, both ruler and subjects will be duped into false happiness; they will no longer try to block our way, nor will they have any cause to become vicious. Once we reach the outskirts of the capital, you will come down from the dragon chariot and Sha Monk will help you to mount the white horse immediately. Old Monkey will then use his magic of immobility to make all of them, ruler and subjects, unable to move. We can then follow the main road to the West. After one day and one night, I will recite a spell to recall the magic and release all of them, so that they can wake up and return to the city. For one thing, their lives will be preserved, and for another, your primal soul will not be hurt. This is a plot called Fleeing the Net by a False Marriage. Isn't it a doubly advantageous act?" When Tripitaka heard these words, he seemed as if he were snapping out of a stupor or waking up from a dream. So delighted was he that he forgot all his worries and thanked Pilgrim profusely, saying, "I'm deeply grateful for my worthy disciple's lofty intelligence." And so, the four of them were united in their decision, and we shall leave them for the moment.

We tell you now about that Grand Preceptor and the clerk of the post-house, who dashed inside the gate of the court without even waiting for summons and went before the white-jade steps. "The auspicious dream of our mistress is most accurate," they cried, "and nuptial bliss will soon be yours." When the queen heard this report, she had the pearly screen rolled up; descending from the dragon couch, she opened her cherry lips to reveal her silvery teeth and asked, full of smiles and in a most seductive voice, "What did the royal brother say after our worthy subjects saw him?" "After your subjects reached the post-house," said the Grand Preceptor, "and bowed to the royal brother, we immediately presented to him our proposal of marriage. The royal brother still expressed some reluctance, but it was fortunate that his eldest disciple gave his consent for them without hesitation. He was willing to let his master become the husband of our ruler and call himself king, facing south. All he wanted was to have their travel rescript certified so that the three of them could leave for the West. On their way back after acquiring the scriptures, they will come here to bow to father and mother and ask for travel expenses to go back to the Great Tang." "Did the royal brother say anything more?" asked the queen, smiling. The Grand Preceptor said, "The royal brother did not say anything more, but he seemed to be willing to marry our mistress. His second disciple, however, wanted to drink to their consent first."

When the queen heard this, she at once ordered the Court of Imperial Entertainments to prepare a banquet. She also requested that her imperial cortege be readied so that she might go out of the capital to receive her husband. The various women officials, in obedience to the queen's command, began to sweep and clean the palaces and to prepare the banquet with the utmost haste. Look at them! Though this Nation of Western Liang is a nation of women, the carriage and chariot are not less opulent than those of China. You see

Six dragons belching colors—
Two phoenixes bringing luck—
Six dragons, belching colors, support the chariot;
Two phoenixes, bringing luck, lift up the carriage.
Strange fragrance in endless waves;
Auspicious airs continuously rise.
Fish-pendants of gold or jade worn by many ministers;
Rows and rows of lovely locks and bejeweled hair.
A royal carriage shielded by mandarin-duck fans;
Through pearly screens glisten the phoenix hairpins.
Melodic pipes,
Harmonious strings.
What great sense of joy reaching to the sky!
What boundless bliss leaving the Estrade Numina.[4]
Three-layered canopies wave above the royal house;
Five-colored banners light up the imperial steps.
This land has ne'er seen the nuptial cup exchanged;
Today the queen marries a gifted man.

In a moment, the imperial cortege left the capital and arrived at the Male Reception Post-house. Someone went inside to announce to Tripitaka and his disciples: "The imperial cortege has arrived." On hearing this, Tripitaka straightened out his clothes and left the main hall with the three disciples to meet the carriage. As the queen rolled up the screen to descend from the carriage, she asked, "Which is the royal brother of the Tang court?" Pointing with her finger, the Grand Preceptor said, "The one in a clerical robe standing behind the incense table outside the post-house gate." Lifting her moth-brows and opening wide her phoenix-eyes, the queen stared at him and found that this was an uncommon figure indeed. Look at him!

4. Estrade Numina or *lingtai*, the name for an astronomical observatory established supposedly in the ancient Zhou period.

What handsome features!
What dignified looks!
Teeth white like silver bricks,
Ruddy lips and a square mouth.
His head's flat-topped, his forehead, wide and full;
Lovely eyes, neat eyebrows, and a chin that's long.
Two well-rounded ears betoken someone brave.
He is all elegance, a gifted man.
What a youthful and comely son of love,
So worthy to wed the pretty girl of Western Liang!

Utterly ravished by what she saw, the queen was swept away by amorous passion. Opening her tiny, cherrylike mouth, she cried out: "Royal brother of the Great Tang, aren't you coming to take and ride the phoenix?" When Tripitaka heard these words, his ears turned red and his face, scarlet; filled with embarrassment, he dared not lift his head at all.

On one side, however, Zhu Bajie stuck up his snout and stared with glassy eyes at the queen, who was quite beguiling herself. Truly she had

Brows like kingfisher hair,
And flesh like mutton jade.
Peach petals bedeck her face;
Her bun piles gold-phoenix hair.
Her eyes' cool, liquid gaze—such seductive charm.
Her hands' young, tender shoots—such dainty form.
Colors flutter from a red sash hung aslant;
Bright gleams flash forth from jade and pearl pinned high.
Don't speak of the beauty of Zhaojun,
She indeed surpasses even Xi Shi.[5]
The willow waist bends slightly to gold-pendant sounds;
The light, lotus steps move the jadelike limbs.
The lunar goddess cannot come up to her,
Nor can the maids of Heaven compare with her.
This fair, palatial style's no common kind;
She's like Queen Mother who comes from Jasper Pool.

As our Idiot gazed at this pleasing figure, he could not restrain the saliva from drooling out of his mouth and the deer pounding at his heart. All at once, he grew weak and numb and simply melted away like a snow lion faced with fire!

The queen went forward and caught hold of Tripitaka. In a most se-

5. Zhaojun and Xi Shi were legendary beauties of antiquity.

ductive voice, she said, "Royal brother darling, please ascend the dragon chariot so that we may go to the Treasure Hall of Golden Chimes and become husband and wife." Shaking so hard that he could barely stand up, our elder behaved as if he were drunk or mesmerized. Pilgrim on one side whispered to him, "Master, don't be too modest. Please get in the carriage with our mistress. Go and have our rescript certified quickly so that we may proceed to fetch the scriptures." The elder did not dare reply; he tugged at Pilgrim a couple of times and he could no longer stop the tears from falling down. "Master, you must not be distressed," said Pilgrim. "Look at all these riches! If you don't enjoy them now, when are you going to do it?" Tripitaka had little alternative but to acquiesce. Wiping away his tears, he forced himself to appear happy and joined the queen, as they,

> Holding hands together,
> Rode the dragon carriage.
> In great delight the queen wanted to get married;
> In great fear the elder wished only to worship Buddha.
> One desired amorous play in the bridal chamber;
> One sought to see the World-Honored One at Mount Spirit.
> The queen was sincere;
> The monk pretended,
> The queen was sincere,
> Hoping to reach old age in harmony.
> The monk pretended,
> Guarding his feelings to nurse his primal spirit.
> One was so glad to see a man
> That she would couple with him in broad daylight.
> One dreaded to meet a woman
> And thought only to flee and go to Thunderclap.
> The two mounted together the chariot.
> Who knew the Tang monk had something else in mind!

When those civil and military officials saw that their ruler and the Tang monk had ascended the phoenix carriage and sat side by side together, every one of them beamed with pleasure. The entire entourage turned around and went back into the capital.

Meanwhile, the Great Sage Sun told Sha Monk to pole the luggage and lead the white horse to follow the imperial cortege. Zhu Bajie, however, scurried ahead and ran madly up to the Tower of Five Phoenixes first, shouting all the while, "What comfort! What an opportunity! But this can't be done until we have drunk the wedding wine and presented ourselves to the kinfolk first." Those officials who were attending the cortege were so terrified that they went to the chariot and said, "My Lady, that monk who has a long snout and huge ears is shouting in front of the Five Phoenix Towers for wedding wine to drink." When the queen heard this, she leaned her fragrant shoulder over to the elder and put her peachlike cheeks up to his face. Opening her scented mouth, she said softly, "Royal brother darling, which disciple of yours is that one with a long snout and huge ears?" "He's my second disciple," said Tripitaka, "and he has a huge appetite. In fact, he loves to indulge his mouth throughout his life. He must be given some food and drink first before we can proceed with our business." The queen asked hurriedly, "Has the Court of Imperial Entertainments finished preparing the banquet?" "It has," reported one of the officials, "There are both meat and vegetarian dishes set up in the East Hall." "Why both?" asked the queen again. "We fear that the royal brother of the Tang court," said the official, "and his disciples are accustomed to keeping a vegetarian diet. That is why we have both meat and vegetarian dishes." Full of smiles, the queen again snuggled close to the elder and said, "Royal brother darling, do you eat meat, or are you keeping a vegetarian diet?" Tripitaka said, "This humble priest observes a vegetarian diet, but my disciples have not abstained from wine. My second disciple would like very much to have a few cups of dietary wine."

They had not finished speaking when the Grand Preceptor approached them and said, "Please go to the East Hall to attend the banquet. Today is an auspicious day, and Your Majesty can marry the venerable royal brother. Tomorrow Heaven will reveal the Yellow Road,[6] and we shall invite the venerable royal brother to ascend the treasure hall and face south. He can then designate the name of his reign and assume the throne." Highly pleased, the queen held hands with the elder to descend from the dragon chariot and enter the main palace gate. They were met by

Music divine, wind-wafted from the towers,
As the jade throne moved through the palace gates.
Phoenix doors flung wide to bright flares of light;
The palace now opened with rows of brocade.
The unicorn hall was draped o'er by incense smoke;
Bright corridors wound around the peacock screens.
Towers rose rugged like the noble state's,
With jade halls and gold horses more wondrous still.
When they reached the East Hall,

6. The Yellow Road is the ecliptic. The term is a traditional metaphor for a lucky or auspicious day.

They heard a choir of melodious strings and pipes;
They saw two rows of winsome, graceful maids.

Two kinds of sumptuous repast were set up in the central hall: on the head table to the left was the vegetarian spread, whereas meat dishes were placed on the right. Two rows of single tables were also set up toward the front of the hall. Rolling up her sleeves to reveal her dainty, pointed fingers, the queen immediately picked up a jade cup to toast her guests. Pilgrim went forward to say: "We are all keeping a vegetarian diet. Let our master be seated at the head table on the left. Then we three brothers may take the single tables on both sides of him." "Yes! Yes!" said the Grand Preceptor in delight. "Master and disciples are just like father and sons. They should not sit side by side." The various officials hurriedly set up the tables in proper order, after which the queen toasted each of them as he took his seat. Thereafter, Pilgrim gave the Tang monk a look, indicating to his master to return the salutation. Tripitaka, therefore, left his seat and, holding the jade goblet, also toasted the queen. The other civil and military officials all knelt to thank the imperial favor before they took the other seats on both sides according to their ranks. The music stopped and they began to drink and eat.

As Bajie was bent on satisfying his stomach, he had little regard for consequence. It did not matter that the food before him was corn, steamed breads, sweet pastries, button mushrooms, black mushrooms, tender bamboo shoots, wood-ears, Chinese cabbage, seaweed, laver, green turnips, taros, white turnips, yams, or yellow sperms—in big gulps, he finished them all, washing down the food with seven or eight cups of wine. "Bring us more food!" he hollered. "Bring some big steins! After we drink a few more steins, each of us will attend to our business." "Such a fine feast and you don't want to enjoy some more?" asked Sha Monk. "What sort of business do you want to attend to?" With a laugh, our Idiot said, "As the ancients said,

Let the bow-maker make his bow,
The arrow-maker his arrow.

At this time, those of us who want to take a wife may take a wife, and those of us who want to marry a husband may marry a husband. Those who want to acquire scriptures need to be on their way to acquire scriptures. We can't let the coveted cup delay our affairs. Let's have our rescript certified quickly. As the saying goes,

If the general does not dismount,
Every man will go his own way."

When the queen heard this, she asked for big cups, and the attendants quickly took out several parrot cups, cormorant-shaped ladles, gold beakers, silver chalices, glass goblets, crystal basins, Penglai bowls, and amber steins. They filled these with the mellowest of wines and all of the disciples drank a round.

Tripitaka then rose from the table and bowed to the queen with hands folded, saying, "Your Majesty, thank you for this lavish feast. We have drunk quite enough. Please ascend the treasure hall and certify our rescript. While there is still light, let us send the three of them on their way." The queen agreed. After the banquet had been dismissed, she led the elder by the hand up to the Hall of Golden Chimes and immediately wanted the elder to take the throne. "No! No!" said Tripitaka. "Just now the Grand Preceptor said that tomorrow would be the proper auspicious day, and only then would this poor monk dare assume the throne and call myself the man set apart. Today you should use your seal on the rescript so that they may be sent away." Again the queen agreed and sat down on the dragon couch. A golden high-backed chair was placed on the left of the couch for the Tang monk to sit on. Then the disciples were asked to bring forth the travel rescript. After Sha Monk untied the wrap and took it out, the Great Sage presented the rescript with both hands to the queen. When she examined it, she found on the document the marks of nine treasure seals of the Great Tang Emperor, together with the seals of the Precious Image Kingdom, the Black Rooster Kingdom, and the Cart Slow Kingdom. After the queen had looked at the document, she said again, smiling seductively, "So royal brother darling also bears the name of Chen?" "That is the surname of my secular family," said Tripitaka, "and my religious name is Xuanzang. Because the Tang emperor in his imperial kindness took me as his brother, he bestowed on me the name of Tang." "Why is it," asked the queen, "that the rescript does not contain the names of your disciples?" "My three mischievous disciples," replied Tripitaka, "are not people from the Tang court." "If they are not," asked the queen once more, "how is it that they are willing to follow you on your journey?"

"My eldest disciple," answered Tripitaka, "comes from the Aolai Country in the East Pūrvavideha Continent; the second disciple, from a village in Tibet in the West Aparagodānīya Continent; and the third, from the River of Flowing Sand. All three of them had transgressed the decrees of Heaven. The Bodhisattva Guanshiyin, however, liberated them from their sufferings, as a result of which they were willing to make submission and hold fast the good. So that their merits might atone for their sins, they resolved to accompany me and protect me on my journey to the Western Heaven to acquire scriptures. Since they became my disciples when I was already on my way, their names therefore had not been recorded on the rescript." "Let me add them on for you, all right?" asked the queen, and Tripitaka said, "Your Majesty may do as you please." The queen asked at once for brush and ink; after the ink had been rubbed out and the brush nicely soaked in it, she wrote at the end of the rescript declaration the names of Sun Wukong, Zhu Wuneng, and Sha Wujing. Then she took out her imperial seal with which she neatly stamped the rescript before she signed her own name. The document was passed down again to the Great Sage Sun, who gave it to Sha Monk to put into the wrap. Picking up a tray of small pieces of gold and silver, the queen left the dragon couch to hand it to Pilgrim, saying, "Take this, the three of you, as travel money, and may you reach the Western Heaven at an early date. When you return after you have acquired the scriptures, we shall have greater rewards for you." Pilgrim said, "We are those who have left the family, and we cannot accept gold or silver. There will be places on our way where we may beg for our living." When the queen saw that he refused, she took out ten bales of silk brocade and said to Pilgrim, "Since you are rushing away, there's no time for measurement or sewing. Take this and have some clothes made on the way to protect you from the cold." "Those who have left the family," said Pilgrim, "are not permitted to wear silk brocade. We have cloth garments to cover our bodies." When the queen saw that he refused again, she gave this order: "Take three pints of imperial rice, and you can use it for a meal on the road." When Bajie heard the word "meal," he at once accepted it and put the rice in the wrap. "Brother," said Pilgrim, "the luggage is getting heavier. You have the strength to pole it?" "You wouldn't know," chuckled Bajie, "but what's good about rice is that it's a product for daily consumption. One meal will finish it off." They all pressed their palms together to thank the queen.

Tripitaka said, "Let Your Majesty take the trouble to accompany this poor monk, who will send them off outside the capital. Let me give them a few instructions so that they may leave for the West. I will return and then I can enjoy forever with Your Majesty riches and glory. Only without such burdens or cares can we enter into conjugal bliss." The queen, of course, did not know that this was a trick, and she asked at once for the imperial cortege. Leaning her fragrant shoulder on Tripitaka, she ascended the phoenix carriage with him and proceeded to the west of the capital. At that time, all the people in the capital lined the streets with containers filled with clean water and urns with the finest incense. Wishing to see the cortege of the queen and the male form of the royal brother were all powdered faces and cloudlike hair; old and young, they crowded into the streets. In a moment, the imperial cortege went out of the capital and stopped before the western gate.

After putting everything in order, Pilgrim, Bajie, and Sha Monk faced the imperial carriage and cried out in unison, "The queen need not go any further. We shall take our leave now." Descending slowly from the dragon chariot, the elder raised his hands toward the queen and said, "Please go back, Your Majesty, and let this poor monk go to acquire scriptures." When the queen heard this, she paled with fright and tugged at the Tang monk. "Royal brother darling," she cried, "I'm willing to use the wealth of my entire nation to ask you to be my husband. Tomorrow you shall ascend the tall treasure throne to call yourself king, and I am to be your queen. You have even eaten the wedding feast. Why are you changing your mind now?" When Bajie heard what she said, he became slightly mad. Pouting his snout and flapping his ears wildly, he charged up to the carriage, shouting, "How could we monks marry a powdered skeleton like you? Let my master go on his journey!" When the queen saw that hideous face and ugly behavior, she was scared out of her wits and fell back into the carriage. Sha Monk pulled Tripitaka out of the crowd and was just helping him to mount the horse when another girl dashed out from somewhere and shouted, "Royal brother Tang, where are you going? Let's you and I make some love!" "You stupid hussy!" cried Sha Monk and, whipping out his treasure staff, brought it down hard on the head of the girl. Suddenly calling up a cyclone, the girl carried away the Tang monk with a loud whoosh and both of them vanished without a trace. Alas! Thus it was that

Having just left the fair sex net,
Then the demon of love he met.

We do not know whether that girl is a human or a fiend, or whether the old master will die or live; let's listen to the explanation in the next chapter.

Deviant form makes lustful play for Tripitaka Tang;
Upright nature safeguards the uncorrupted self.

We were just telling you of the Great Sage Sun and Zhu Bajie, who were about to use magic to render those women immobile when they heard the shouts of Sha Monk and the howl of the wind. They turned quickly to look, only to discover that the Tang monk had vanished. "Who is it that has abducted Master?" asked Pilgrim, and Sha Monk said, "It's a girl. She called up a cyclone and whizzed Master away." When Pilgrim heard this, he leaped straight up to the edge of the clouds; using his hand to shade his eyes, he peered all around and found a roiling mass of wind and dust hurtling toward the northwest. "Brothers," he shouted to them down below, "mount the clouds quickly to pursue Master with me." Bajie and Sha Monk tied the luggage to the horse, and with a whoosh they all shot up to midair and left.

Those women of the State of Western Liang, ruler and subjects, were so terrified that they knelt on the ground, all crying, "So these are arhats who can ascend to Heaven in broad daylight!" Then the officials said to the queen, "Let not our ruler be frightened or vexed any more. The royal brother of Tang has to be a Buddhist monk who has attained the Way. Since none of us possesses true discernment, we could not recognize these Chinese men for what they are and all our schemings have been wasted. Let our mistress ascend the carriage to go back to court." The queen herself became quite embarrassed, and as she went back to the capital with all her officials, we shall leave them for the moment.

We tell you instead about the Great Sage Sun with his two brothers, who trod on air and fog to give chase to that cyclone. In a little while, they came upon a tall mountain, where they saw the dust had died down and the wind subsided. Not knowing where the fiend had gone to, the three brothers lowered their clouds and began to search for the way. It was then that they saw on the side of the mountain a huge slab of stone, all shiny and green, that looked like a screen. The three of them led the horse to the back of the screen and discovered two stone doors, on which there was in large letters the following inscription: Toxic Foe Mountain, Cave of the Lute. As he had always been rather stupid, Bajie immediately wanted to break down the doors with his rake, but he was quickly stopped by Pilgrim. "Don't be so hasty, Brother," he said. "After we followed the cyclone here, we had to search for a while before we found these doors. We don't even know the long and short of the matter. Suppose this is the wrong door. Won't your action offend the owner? I think the two of you should look after the horse and wait in front of that stone screen. Let old Monkey go inside to do some detection before we start anything." Greatly pleased by what he heard, Sha Monk said, "Very good! This is what I call caution in recklessness, composure in urgency." So, the two of them led the horse away.

The Great Sage Sun, meanwhile, displayed his divine power: making the magic sign with his fingers, he recited a spell and with one shake of his body changed into a bee—truly agile and light. Look at him!

His thin wings go soft with wind;
His waist in sunlight is trim.
A mouth once sweetened by flowers;
A tail that stripe-toads has tamed.
What merit in honey-making!
How modest his home-returning!
A smart plan he now conceives
To soar past both doors and eaves.

Crawling inside through a crack in the door, Pilgrim flew past the second-level door and came upon a flower arbor in the middle of which sat a female fiend. Attending her on both sides were several young girls dressed in colored silk and with parted bangs on their foreheads. All of them appeared to be in a most pleasant mood, talking with great animation about something. Ever so lightly our Pilgrim flew up there and alighted on the trellis of the arbor. As he cocked his ear to listen, he saw two other girls with disheveled hair walking up to the arbor, each holding a plate of steaming hot pastries. "Madam," they said, "on this plate are buns stuffed with human flesh, and on the other buns stuffed with red bean paste." "Little ones," said the female fiend with a giggle, "help the royal brother of Tang to come out." The girls dressed in colored silk went to one of the rear chambers and led the Tang monk out by his hands. The master's face, however, had turned yellow and his lips, white; his eyes were red and brimming with tears. "Master has been poisoned!" sighed Pilgrim to himself.

The fiend walked out of the arbor and extended her dainty, spring-onion-like fingers to catch hold of the elder, saying, "Relax, royal brother!

Though our place here is not like the palace of the Nation of Women of Western Liang and cannot compare with their wealth and luxury, it is actually less hectic and more comfortable. You will find it perfect for chanting the name of Buddha and reading scriptures. I'll be your companion on the Way, and we'll enjoy a harmonious union until old age." Tripitaka would not utter a word. "Stop worrying," said the fiend again. "I know that you didn't eat much when you attended the banquet in the Nation of Women. Here are two kinds of flour goods, meat and vegetarian, and you may take whatever you want, just to calm your fear."

Tripitaka thought to himself: "I can remain silent and refuse to eat anything, but this fiend is not like the queen. The queen, after all, is a human being whose action is governed by propriety. This fiend is a monster-spirit most capable of hurting me. What shall I do? I wonder if my three disciples know that I am held in custody here. If she does harm me because of my stubborness, wouldn't I have thrown away my life?" As he questioned his mind with mind like that, he had no alternative but to force himself to open his mouth. "What's the meat made of and what's the vegetarian made of?" he asked. The fiend said, "The meat bun has human flesh stuffing, while the vegetarian has red bean paste stuffing." "This poor monk," said Tripitaka, "keeps a vegetarian diet." "Girls," said the female fiend, giggling, "bring us some hot tea so that the elder of your household can eat the vegetarian buns."

One of the girls indeed brought out a cup of fragrant tea and placed it in front of the elder. Picking up a vegetarian bun, the fiend broke it in half and handed the pieces to Tripitaka, who in turn took a meat bun and presented it whole to the fiend. "Royal brother," asked the fiend, laughing, "why didn't you break it first before you handed it to me?" Tripitaka pressed his palms together before he replied: "As someone who has left the family, I dare not break open food made with meat." "If you as someone who has left the family dare not break open food made with meat," said the fiend, "how is it that you were willing to eat water pudding[1] the other day at the Child-and-Mother Stream? Having done that, do you still insist on eating red bean paste stuffing today?" Tripitaka replied:

"At high tide a boat leaves quickly;
In sand traps a horse trots slowly."

1. The fiend is punning on the sounds of water pudding and high tide, both using the phonemes of *shuigao* but different graphs. The Tang monk's subsequent reply also makes use of a pun between bean-paste stuffing (*dousha xian*) and sand traps (*shaxian*).

Pilgrim on the trellis heard everything; fearing that such banter might confound the real nature of his master, he could no longer contain himself. He revealed his true form at once and whipped out his iron rod. "Cursed beast!" he shouted. "You're so unruly!" When the female fiend saw him, she blew out immediately from her mouth a ray of misty light to cover up the entire arbor. "Little ones," she cried, "take away the royal brother!" Picking up a steel trident, she leaped out of the arbor and yelled, "Lawless simian rascal! How dare you sneak into my house and play Peeping Tom? Don't run away! Have a taste of your mamma's trident!" Using the iron rod to parry her blows, the Great Sage fought back as he retreated.

The two of them fought their way out of the cave. Bajie and Sha Monk were waiting in front of the stone screen; when they saw the combatants emerging, Bajie hurriedly pulled the white horse out of the way, saying, "Sha Monk, you guard the horse and the luggage. Let old Hog go and help with the fight." Dear Idiot! Lifting high the rake with both his hands, he rushed forward and shouted, "Elder Brother, stay back! Let me beat up this bitch!" When the fiend saw Bajie approaching, she summoned up some more of her abilities. With one snort fire spurted out from her nostrils as smoke licked out from her mouth. She shook her body once and there were now three tridents dancing and thrusting in the air, wielded by who knows how many hands. As she charged like a cyclone into the fray, she was met by Pilgrim and Bajie on both sides.

"Sun Wukong," cried the fiend, "you really have no judgment! I recognize you, but you can't recognize me. But even your Buddha Tathāgata at the Thunderclap Monastery is afraid of me. Two clumsy oafs like you, you think you'll get anywhere! Come on up, both of you, and I'll give each of you a beating!" "How was this battle?" you ask.

> The female fiend's power expanded;
> The Monkey King's vigor increased.
> The Heavenly Reeds Marshal, striving for merit,
> Wielded wildly his rake to show his vim.
> That one with many hands and fast tridents the misty light encircled;
> From these two—impulsive, with strong weapons—foggy air rose up.
> The fiend wished only to seek a mate;
> The monk refused to leak his primal sperm.
> Yin and yang at odds now clashed together,
> Each flaunting its might in this bitter strife.
> Quiet yin, to nourish being, quickened in lust;
> Tranquil yang purged desires to guard its health.
> To these two parties thus came discord;

A contest was waged by trident, rake, and rod.
This one's rod was strong,
The rake, more potent—
But the fiend's trident met them blow for blow.
Three unyielding persons before Mount Toxic Foe;
Two ruthless factions outside the Cave of the Lute.
That one was pleased to seize the Tang monk as her spouse;
These two with the elder resolved to seek true scriptures.
To do battle they stirred up Heaven and Earth
And fought till sun and moon darkened and planets moved.

The three of them fought for a long time and no decision was reached. Leaping suddenly into the air, the female fiend resorted to the Horse-Felling Poisoned Stake and gave the Great Sage a terrific stab on his head. "Oh, misery!" cried Pilgrim and at once fled in severe pain. When Bajie saw that the tide was turning, he too retreated with the rake trailing behind him. The fiend thus retrieved her tridents and returned in triumph.

Gripping his head, with brows contracted and face woe-laden, Pilgrim kept crying, "Horror! Horror!" Bajie went up to him and asked: "Elder Brother, how is it that, when you were just enjoying the fight, you suddenly ran away, whining up a storm?" Pilgrim gripped his head and could only say, "It hurts! It hurts!" "It must be your migraine," said Sha Monk. "No! No!" cried Pilgrim, jumping up and down. "Elder Brother," said Bajie, "I didn't see that you were wounded. But now your head hurts. Why?" "Lord, it's terrible!" said Pilgrim with a groan. "I was just fighting with her. When she saw that I was breaking through her defense with the trident, she suddenly leaped into the air. I don't know what kind of weapon it was that gave my head a stab, but the pain is unbearable. That was why I ran away."

"You have always bragged about that head of yours when things were quiet," said Bajie with a laugh, "saying that it has gone through such a long process of cultivation. How is it now that it can't even take a stab?" "Indeed," replied Pilgrim. "Since I achieved the art of realized immortality, and since I stole and ate the immortal peaches, celestial wine, and the golden elixir of Laozi, this head of mine cannot be harmed. When I caused great disturbance in Heaven, the Jade Emperor sent the Demon King Powerful and the Twenty-Eight Constellations to take me outside the Dipper Star Palace and have me executed. What those divine warriors used on me were swords, axes, scimitars, bludgeons, thunderbolts, and fire. Thereafter Laozi placed me within his brazier of eight trigrams and smelted me for forty-nine days. But there wasn't even a scratch on my head. I don't know what sort of weapon this woman used today, but she certainly wounded old Monkey!"

"Take away your hands," said Sha Monk, "and let me see if the skin has been torn." "No, it hasn't," replied Pilgrim.

"I'll go to the State of Western Liang and ask for some ointment to tape on you," said Bajie. Pilgrim said, "There's no swelling, and it's not an open wound. Why should you want to tape ointment on it?"

"Brother," said Bajie, chuckling, "I didn't come down with any pre- or postnatal illness, but you are getting a brain tumor." "Stop joking, Second Elder Brother," said Sha Monk. "It's getting late! Big Brother's head has been hurt and we don't know whether Master is dead or alive. What shall we do?"

"Master's all right," said Pilgrim with a groan. "I changed into a bee to fly inside, and I found that woman sitting inside a flower arbor. In a little while, two maids brought out two plates of buns: one had human flesh for stuffing and the other, red bean paste. Then she asked two other maids to help Master out to eat, just to calm his fear. She also said something about her desire to be Master's companion on the Way. At first, Master did not say anything to the woman, nor did he eat the buns. Later, perhaps it was because of all her sweet talk or some other odd reason, he began to speak with her and told her that he kept a vegetarian diet. The woman broke one of those vegetarian buns into halves to hand to Master, and he presented her with a meat one whole. 'Why didn't you break it?' the woman asked, and Master said, 'Those who have left the family dare not break into something made with meat.' 'In that case,' asked the woman, 'how was it that you were willing to eat water pudding the other day? And you still insist on eating stuffing made of red bean paste?' Master didn't quite understand her puns, and he replied:

'At high tide a boat leaves quickly;
In sand traps a horse trots slowly.'

I heard everything on the trellis, and I was afraid that Master's nature might be confounded. That was when I revealed my true form and attacked her with my iron rod. She, too, used her magic power; blowing out some mist or fog to cover the arbor, she shouted for the girls to take away the 'royal brother' before she picked up her steel trident and fought her way out of the cave with old Monkey." When Sha Monk heard this, he bit his finger and said, "We've been picked up and followed by this bitch from who knows where, but she certainly has knowledge of what has happened to us recently."

"If you put it that way," said Bajie, "it looks as if we wouldn't be able to rest, doesn't it? Let's not worry if it's dusk or midnight. Let's go up to her door and provoke battle. At least our hubbub will prevent them from sleeping, so that she can't pull a fast one on our master." "My head hurts," said Pilgrim. "I can't go!" Sha Monk said, "No need to provoke battle. In the first place, Elder Brother has a headache, and in the second, our master is a true monk. He won't allow either form or emptiness to confound his nature. Let us sit here for the night beneath the mountain slope where there's no draft and regain our energy. Then we can decide what to do by morning." And so, the three brothers, after having tied up the white horse firmly, rested beneath the mountain slope, guarding the luggage.

We now tell you about that female fiend, who banished violence from her mind and once again took on a pleasant appearance. "Little ones," she said, "shut the front and back doors tightly." Two little fiends were instructed to stand watch against the intrusion of Pilgrim. If there were any sound at all at the door, they were told to report at once. Then she gave this order also: "Maids, fix up the bedroom nicely. After you have lit the candles and the incense, go and invite royal brother Tang to come here. I want to make love with him." They therefore brought out the elder from the rear. Putting on her most seductive charms, she caught hold of the Tang monk and said, "As the proverb says,

> Though gold may have its price,
> Our pleasure's more worthwhile.

Let's you and I play husband and wife and have some fun!"

Gritting his teeth, our elder would not permit even a sound to escape from his mouth. He was about to refuse her invitation, but he was afraid that she might decide to take his life. He had no alternative but to follow her into the perfumed room, trembling all the while. Completely in a stupor, he raised neither his eyes nor his head; he did not see what sort of coverlets or bedding there was in the room, nor was he eager to find out what kinds of furniture or dresser were placed therein. As for all the amorous declaration and sultry speech of the female fiend, he did not hear a word. Marvelous monk! Truly

> His eyes saw no evil form;
> His ears heard no lustful sound;
> He regarded as dirt and dung this coy, silken face,
> This pearl-like beauty as ashes and dust.
> His one love in life was to practice Chan,
> Unwilling to step once beyond Buddha-land.
> How could he show affection and pity
> When all he knew was religion and truth?

That fiend, all vibrant
With boundless passion;
Our elder, most deadpan
And filled with Buddhist zeal.
One was like soft jade and warm perfume;
One seemed like cold ashes or dried wood.
That person undid her collar,
Her passion overflowing;
This person tied up his robe,
His resolve unswerving.
That one wanted to mate, breast to breast with thighs entwined;
This one wished to face the wall and seek Bodhidharma in the mount.
The fiend loosened her clothes
To display her fine, scented flesh;
The Tang monk bundled up his cloak
To hide his coarse and thickset skin.
The fiend said, "My sheets and pillows are ready, why don't you sleep!"
The Tang monk said, "How could my bald head and strange attire join you
      there!"
That one said, "I'm willing to be the former period's Liu Cuicui."²
This one said, "This humble monk is not a lovesick priest!"
The fiend said, "I'm pretty as Xi Shi and e'en more lissome."
The Tang monk said, "Like King Yue I have long been mortified!"
The fiend said, "Royal brother, remember
He who dies beneath the flowers;
E'en his ghost's a happy lover."
The Tang monk said, "My true yang is treasure most precious.
How could I give it to a powdered cadaver?"

The two of them prattled on like that deep into the night, but the elder Tang showed no sign whatever that he had been aroused. Though the female fiend tugged and pulled at him and refused to let go, our master doggedly rejected her advances. By midnight, all this hassle made the fiend mad, and she shouted, "Little ones, bring me a rope!" Alas! The dearly beloved was at once trussed up until he looked like a shaggy ape! After telling her subordinates to drag the monk back to the corridor, she blew out the lamps and all of them retired.

Soon the cock crowed three times, and beneath the mountain slope our

2. Name of a famous courtesan in Hangzhou at the time of the Southern Song.

Great Sage Sun rose up, saying, "I had a headache for quite a while, but now my head feels neither painful nor numb. In fact, I have a little itch." "If you have an itch," chuckled Bajie, "how about asking her to give you another stab?" Pilgrim spat at him and said, "Go! Go! Go!" Bajie laughed again and replied, "Go! Go! Go! But it was Master last night who went wild! Wild! Wild!" "Stop gabbing, the two of you," said Sha Monk. "It's light. Go quickly to catch the monster." "Brother," said Pilgrim, "stay here to guard the horse and don't move. Zhu Bajie will go with me."

Arousing himself, our Idiot straightened out his black-silk shirt and followed Pilgrim; they took their weapons and leaped up to the mountain ledge to go before the stone screen. "Stand here," said Pilgrim to Bajie, "for I fear that the fiend might have harmed Master during the night. Let me go inside to snoop around a bit. If Master truly had lost his primal *yang* and his virtue because of her deception, then all of us could scatter. If he has not been confounded and if his Chan mind has remained unmoved, then we could in all diligence fight to the end, slaughter the monster-spirit, and rescue Master to go to the West." "You are quite numbskulled!" said Bajie. "As the proverb says, 'Could dried fish be used for a cat's pillows?' Like it or not, it would receive a few scratches!" Pilgrim said, "Stop babbling! I'll go and see."

Dear Great Sage! He left Bajie in front of the stone screen and shook his body again to change into a bee. After he flew inside, he found two maids sleeping, their heads resting on the watch-rattles. He went up to the flower arbor to look around. The monster-spirit, you see, had struggled for half the night; she and her attendants were all very tired. Everyone was still fast asleep, not knowing that it was dawn already. Flying to the rear, Pilgrim began to hear the faint moans of the Tang monk, and then he saw that the priest was left, hogtied, in the corridor. Pilgrim gently alighted on his head and whispered, "Master." Recognizing the voice, the Tang monk said, "Have you come, Wukong? Save my life, quick!" "How were the night's activities?" asked Pilgrim. Tripitaka, clenching his teeth, replied: "I would rather die than do anything of that sort!" "I thought," said Pilgrim, "I saw her showing you a good deal of tenderness yesterday. How is it that she is putting you through such torment today?"

"She pestered me for half the night," answered Tripitaka, "but I did not even loosen my clothes or touch her bed. When she saw that I refused to yield to her, she had me tied up like this. Please rescue me, so that I can go acquire the scriptures." As master and disciples spoke to each other like that, they woke up the monster-spirit. Though she was furious at the Tang monk, she was still very fond of him. When she stirred and heard something about going to acquire scriptures, she rolled off the bed at once and shouted: "You mean to tell me that you don't want to get married and still want to go and seek scriptures?"

Pilgrim was so startled that he abandoned his master, spread his wings, and flew out of the cave. "Bajie," he cried, and our Idiot came around the stone screen, saying, "Has that thing been concluded?" "Not yet! Not yet!" said Pilgrim, laughing. "She worked on the old master for quite some time, but he refused. She got mad and had him hogtied. He was just telling me all this when the fiend woke up, and I became so startled that I came back out here." Bajie said, "What did Master actually say?" "He said," replied Pilgrim, "that he did not even loosen his clothes nor did he touch her bed." "Good! Very good!" chuckled Bajie. "He's still a true monk! Let's go rescue him!"

As he had always been a roughneck, our Idiot did not wait for further discussion. Lifting high his muckrake, he brought it down on the stone doors with all his might, and with a loud crash they broke into many pieces. The two maids sleeping on the watch-rattles were so terrified that they ran back to the second-level door and screamed: "Open up! Those two ugly men of yesterday have come again and smashed our doors!" The female fiend was just leaving her room. "Little ones," she cried, "bring some hot water for me to wash my face. Carry the royal brother, all tied up like that, and hide him in the rear room. I'm going out to fight them."

Dear monster-spirit! She ran out with her trident uplifted and shouted: "Brazen ape! Wild boar! You don't know when to stop, do you? How dare you break my doors?" "You filthy bitch!" scolded Bajie. "You have our master imprisoned, and you still dare to talk with such insolence? Our master was only your kidnapped husband! Send him out quickly, and I'll spare you. If you dare but utter half a no, the blows of old Hog's rake will level even your mountain."

The monster-spirit, of course, did not permit such words to intimidate her. With enormous energy and using magic as before, she attacked with her steel trident while her nose and mouth belched fire and smoke. Bajie leaped aside to dodge her blow before striking back with his rake, helped by the Great Sage Sun and his iron rod on the other side. The power of that fiend was tremendous indeed! All at once she seemed to have acquired who knows how many hands, waving and parrying left and right. After they fought for several rounds, she again used some kind of weapon and gave the lip of Bajie a stab. His rake trailing behind him and his lips pouting, our Idiot fled in pain for his life. Pilgrim also became somewhat envious of him; making one false blow with the rod, he, too, fled in defeat. After the fiend returned in triumph, she told her little ones to place rock piles in front of the door.

We now tell you about Sha Monk, who was grazing the horse before the mountain slope when he heard some hog-grunting. As he raised his head, he saw Bajie dashing back, lips pouted and grunting as he ran. "What in the world . . . ?" said Sha Monk, and our Idiot blurted out: "It's awful! It's awful! This pain! This pain!" Hardly had he finished speaking when Pilgrim also arrived. "Dear Idiot!" he chuckled. "Yesterday you said I had a brain tumor, but now you are suffering from the plague of the swollen lip!" "I can't bear it!" cried Bajie. "The pain's acute! It's terrible! It's terrible!"

The three of them were thus in sad straits when they saw an old woman approaching from the south on the mountain road, her left hand carrying a little bamboo basket with vegetables in it. "Big Brother," said Sha Monk, "look at that old lady approaching. Let me find out from her what sort of a monster-spirit this is and what kind of weapon she has that can inflict a wound like this." "You stay where you are," said Pilgrim, "and let old Monkey question her." When Pilgrim stared at the old woman carefully, he saw that there were auspicious clouds covering her head and fragrant mists encircling her body. Recognizing all at once who she was, Pilgrim shouted, "Brothers, kowtow quickly! The lady is Bodhisattva!" Ignoring his pain, Bajie hurriedly went to his knees while Sha Monk bent low, still holding the reins of the horse. The Great Sage Sun, too, pressed his palms together and knelt down, all crying, "We submit to the great and compassionate, the efficacious savior, Bodhisattva Guanshiyin."

When the Bodhisattva saw that they recognized her primal light, she at once trod on the auspicious clouds and rose to midair to reveal her true form, the one which carried the fish basket. Pilgrim rushed up there also to say to her, bowing, "Bodhisattva, pardon us for not receiving you properly. We were desperately trying to rescue our master and we had no idea that the Bodhisattva was descending to earth. Our present demonic ordeal is hard to overcome indeed, and we beg the Bodhisattva to help us." "This monster-spirit," said the Bodhisattva, "is most formidable. Those tridents of hers happen to be two front claws, and what gave you such a painful stab is actually a stinger on her tail. It's called the Horse-Felling Poison, for she herself is a scorpion spirit. Once upon a time she happened to be listening to a lecture in the Thunderclap Monastery. When Tathāgata saw her, he wanted to push her away with his hand, but she turned around and gave the left thumb of the Buddha a stab. Even Tathāgata found the pain unbearable! When he ordered the arhats to seize her, she fled here. If you want to rescue the Tang monk, you must find a special friend of mine, for even I cannot go near her." Bowing again, Pilgrim said, "I beg the Bodhisattva to reveal to whom it is that your disciple should go to ask for assistance." "Go to the East Heaven Gate," replied the Bodhisattva, "and ask for help from the Star Lord Orionis[3] in the Luminescent Palace. He is the one to subdue this monster-spirit." When she finished speaking, she changed into a beam of golden light to return to South Sea.

Dropping down from the clouds, the Great Sage Sun said to Bajie and Sha Monk, "Relax, Brothers, we've found someone to rescue Master." "From where?" asked Sha Monk, and Pilgrim replied, "Just now the Bodhisattva told me to seek the assistance of the Star Lord Orionis. Old Monkey will go immediately." With swollen lips, Bajie grunted: "Elder Brother, please ask the god for some medicine for the pain." "No need for medicine," said Pilgrim with a laugh. "After one night, the pain will go away like mine." "Stop talking," said Sha Monk. "Go quickly!"

Dear Pilgrim! Mounting his cloud-somersault, he arrived instantly at the East Heaven Gate, where he was met by the Devarāja Virūḍhaka. "Great Sage," said the devarāja, bowing, "where are you going?" "On our way to acquire scriptures in the West," replied Pilgrim, "the Tang monk ran into another demonic obstacle. I must go to the Luminescent Palace to find the Star God of the Rising Sun." As he spoke, Tao, Zhang, Xin, and Deng, the four Grand Marshals, also approached him to ask where he was going. "I have to find the Star Lord Orionis," said Pilgrim, "and ask him to rescue my master from a monster-spirit." One of the grand marshals said, "By the decree of the Jade Emperor this morning, the god went to patrol the Star-Gazing Terrace." "Is that true?" asked Pilgrim. "All of us humble warriors," replied Grand Marshal Xin, "left the Dipper Palace with him at the same time. Would we dare speak falsehood?" "It has been a long time," said Grand Marshal Tao, "and he might be back already. The Great Sage should go to the Luminescent Palace first, and if he's not there, then you can go to the Star-Gazing Terrace."

Delighted, the Great Sage took leave of them and arrived at the gate of the Luminescent Palace. Indeed, there was no one in sight, and as he turned to leave, he saw a troop of soldiers approaching, followed by the god, who still had on his court regalia made of golden threads. Look at

His cap of five folds ablaze with gold;
His court tablet of most lustrous jade.
A seven-star sword, cloud patterned, hung from his robe;
An eight-treasure belt, lucent, wrapped around his waist.

3. One of the twenty-eight constellations.

His pendant jangled as if striking a tune;
It rang like a bell in a strong gust of wind.
Kingfisher fans parted and Orionis came
As celestial fragrance the courtyard filled.

Those soldiers walking in front saw Pilgrim standing outside the Luminescent Palace, and they turned quickly to report: "My lord, the Great Sage Sun is here." Stopping his cloud and straightening his court attire, the god ordered the soldiers to stand on both sides in two rows while he went forward to salute his visitor, saying, "Why has the Great Sage come here?"

"I have come here," replied Pilgrim, "especially to ask you to save my master from an ordeal." "Which ordeal," asked the god, "and where?" "In the Cave of the Lute at the Toxic Foe Mountain," Pilgrim answered, "which is located in the State of Western Liang." "What sort of monster is there in the cave," asked the god again, "that has made it necessary for you to call on this humble deity?"

Pilgrim said, "Just now the Bodhisattva Guanyin, in her epiphany, revealed to us that it was a scorpion spirit. She told us further that only you, sir, could overcome it. That is why I have come to call on you." "I should first go back and report to the Jade Emperor," said the god, "but the Great Sage is already here, and you have, moreover, the Bodhisattva's recommendation. Since I don't want to cause you delay, I dare not ask you for tea. I shall go with you to subdue the monster-spirit first before I report to the Throne."

When the Great Sage heard this, he at once went out of the East Heaven Gate with the god and sped to the State of Western Liang. Seeing the mountain ahead, Pilgrim pointed at it and said, "This is it." The god lowered his cloud and walked with Pilgrim up to the stone screen beneath the mountain slope. When Sha Monk saw them, he said, "Second Elder Brother, please rise. Big Brother has brought back the star god." His lips still pouting, Idiot said, "Pardon! Pardon! I'm ill, and I cannot salute you." "You are a man who practices self-cultivation," said the star god. "What kind of sickness do you have?" "Earlier in the morning," replied Bajie, "we fought with the monster-spirit, who gave me a stab on my lip. It still hurts."

The star god said, "Come up here, and I'll cure it for you." Taking his hand away from his snout, Idiot said, "I beg you to cure it, and I'll thank you most heartily." The star god used his hand to give Bajie's lip a stroke before blowing a mouthful of breath on it. At once, the pain ceased. In great delight, our Idiot went to his knees, crying, "Marvelous! Marvelous!" "May I trouble the star god to touch the top of my head also?" said Pilgrim with a grin. "You weren't poisoned," said the star god. "Why should I touch you?" Pilgrim replied, "Yesterday, I was poisoned, but after one night the pain is gone. The spot, however, still feels somewhat numb and itchy, and I fear that it may act up when the weather changes. Please cure it for me." The star god indeed touched the top of his head and blew a mouthful of breath on it. The remaining poison was thus eliminated, and Pilgrim no longer felt the numbness or the itch. "Elder Brother," said Bajie, growing ferocious, "let's go and beat up that bitch!" "Exactly!" said the star god. "You provoke her to come out, the two of you, and I'll subdue her."

Leaping up the mountain slope, Pilgrim and Bajie again went behind the stone screen. With his mouth spewing abuses and his hands working like a pair of fuel-gatherer hooks, our Idiot used his rake to remove the rocks piled up in front of the cave in no time at all. He then dashed up to the second-level door, and one blow of his rake reduced it to powder. The little fiends inside were so terrified that they fled inside to report: "Madam, those two ugly men have destroyed even our second-level door!" The fiend was just about to untie the Tang monk so that he could be fed some tea and rice. When she heard that the door had been broken down, she jumped out of the flower arbor and stabbed Bajie with the trident. Bajie met her with the rake, while Pilgrim assisted him with his iron rod. Rushing at her opponents, the fiend wanted to use her poisonous trick again, but Pilgrim and Bajie perceived her intentions and retreated immediately.

The fiend chased them beyond the stone screen, and Pilgrim shouted: "Orionis, where are you?" Standing erect on the mountain slope, the star god revealed his true form. He was, you see, actually a huge, double-combed rooster, about seven feet tall when he held up his head. He faced the fiend and crowed once: immediately the fiend revealed her true form, which was that of a scorpion about the size of a lute. The star god crowed again, and the fiend, whose whole body became paralyzed, died before the slope. We have a testimonial poem for you, and the poem says:

Like tasseled balls his embroidered neck and comb,
With long, hard claws and angry, bulging eyes,
He perfects the Five Virtues forcefully;
His three crows are done heroically.
No common, clucking fowl about the hut,
He's Heaven's star showing his holy name.
In vain the scorpion seeks the human ways;
She now her true, original form displays.

Bajie went forward and placed one foot on the back of the creature, saying, "Cursed beast! You can't use your Horse-Felling Poison this time!" Unable to make even a twitch, the fiend was pounded into a paste by the rake of the Idiot. Gathering up again his golden beams, the star god mounted the clouds and left, while Pilgrim led Bajie and Sha Monk to bow to the sky, saying, "Sorry for all your inconvenience! In another day, we shall go to your palace to thank you in person."

After the three of them gave thanks, they took the luggage and the horse into the cave, where they were met by those maids, who knelt on both sides to receive them. "Fathers," they cried, "we are not fiends. We are all women from the State of Western Liang who have been kidnapped by this monster-spirit some time ago. Right now your master is weeping in a scented room in the rear." On hearing this, Pilgrim stared at them and saw that there was indeed no demonic aura about them. He therefore went to the rear, crying, "Master!" When the Tang monk saw them, he was very pleased. "Worthy disciples," he said, "I have caused you a lot of trouble. What happened to that woman?" "She was a huge female scorpion," replied Bajie. "We are fortunate to have received the revelation from the Bodhisattva Guanyin, whereupon Big Brother went to Heaven to acquire the assistance of the Star Lord Orionis. He came here and subdued her, and she has been reduced to mud by old Hog. Only then did we dare walk in here to see your face." The Tang monk could not end his thanks to them. Then they found some rice and noodles with which they prepared a meal, after which they showed the way home to those girls who had been taken captive. Lighting up a fire, they burned out the entire cave-dwelling before they found the main road to the West once more. Thus it was that

They cut worldly ties to leave beauty and form;
They drained the gold sea to know the mind of Chan.

We do not know how many more years they still need in order to perfect the art of realized immortality; let's listen to the explanation in the next chapter.

The true Pilgrim lays bare his woes at Mount Potalaka;
The false Monkey King transcribes documents at Water-Curtain Cave.

[Ed.: The initiating incident of this episode recalls the events of both chapters 14 and 27 of the full-length novel, when Sun Wukong, whether by killing six bandits or attacking the Cadaver Demon encountered on the way, deeply offended the human Tripitaka. Regarding his disciple's action as needless life-taking, the monk indulged in prolonged recitation of the Tight-Fillet Spell to punish Sun. Finally, as before, Sun was banished from the pilgrimage.]

We were telling you about a heavy-hearted Great Sage Sun, who rose into midair. He was about to return to the Water-Curtain Cave of the Flower-Fruit Mountain, but he was afraid that those little fiends might laugh at him, for how could he be a true hero if he could betray his own word. He thought of seeking shelter in the celestial palace, but he feared that he would not be given permission to stay there long. He next thought of the islands in the sea, but then he was ashamed to face the resident immortals. Finally, he considered the dragon palace, but he could not stomach the idea of approaching the dragon kings as a suppliant. Truly, he had absolutely no place to go, and he thought sadly to himself: "All right! All right! All right! I'll go to see my master again, for only that is the right fruit."

He dropped down from the clouds and went before the horse of Tripi-taka, saying, "Master, please forgive this disciple one more time! I'll never dare work violence again. I promise I'll accept all your admonitions, and I beg you to let me accompany you to the Western Heaven." When the Tang monk saw him, however, he even refused to reply. As soon as he reined in the horse, he recited the Tight-Fillet Spell. Over and over again, he went through it for more than twenty times until the Great Sage fell prostrate to the ground, the fillet cutting an inch into his flesh. Only then did the elder stop and say, "Why don't you leave? Why have you come to bother me again?"

Pilgrim could only reply: "Don't recite anymore! Don't recite anymore!

I can spend my days somewhere, but without me I fear that you can't reach the Western Heaven." Growing angry, Tripitaka said, "You are a murderous ape! Heaven knows how many times you've brought troubles on me! I absolutely don't want you anymore. Whether I can reach there or not, it's no concern of yours. Leave quickly! If you don't, I'll start the magic word again, and this time, I won't stop—not until your brains are squeezed out!" When the Great Sage saw that his master refused to change his mind, and as the pain was truly unbearable, he had no alternative but to mount his cloud-somersault once more and rise into the air. Then he was struck by the thought: "If this monk is so ungrateful to me, I'll go to the Bodhisattva Guanyin at Mount Potalaka and tell on him."

Dear Great Sage! He turned his somersault around and in less than an hour reached the Great Southern Ocean. Lowering his auspicious luminosity, he descended on the Potalaka Mountain and sped at once into the purple bamboo grove. There he was met by the disciple Mokṣa, who greeted him, saying, "Where is the Great Sage going?" "I must see the Bodhisattva," replied Pilgrim. Mokṣa led him to the entrance of the Tidal Sound Cave, where the Boy of Goodly Wealth also greeted him, saying, "Why has the Great Sage come here?" "I have something to tell on the Bodhisattva," Pilgrim said.

When he heard the words "to tell on,"[1] Goodly Wealth laughed and said, "What a smart-mouthed ape! You think you can oppress people just like the time I caught the Tang monk.[2] Our Bodhisattva is a holy and righteous goddess, one who is of great compassion, great promise, and great conveyance, one who with boundless power saves us from our sufferings. What has she done that you want to bring an accusation against her?" Pilgrim was already deeply depressed; what he heard only aroused him to anger and he gave such a snarl that the Boy of Goodly Wealth backed off at once. "You wicked, ungrateful little beast!" he shouted. "You are so dim-witted! You were once a fiend, a spirit, but it was I who asked the Bodhisattva to take you in. Since you have made your submission to the Right, you have been enjoying true liberty and long life—an age as everlasting, in fact, as Heaven's. Instead of thanking me, how dare you be so insulting? I said that

1. The brief exchange between Pilgrim and Guanyin's attendant puns on the word *gao*, which can mean to report to, tell on, or to accuse in the legal sense of filing suit against someone.

2. The Boy of Goodly Wealth, prior to his submission to Guanyin, was a monster named Red Boy, and he was the son of the Bull Monster King. For the incidents referred to in his statement here, see chapters 40–42 in *The Journey to the West*, of which the present book is an abridgment.

I was going to tell something on the Bodhisattva. How dare you say that I'm smart-mouthed?" Trying to placate him with a smile, Goodly Wealth said, "You're still an impulsive ape! I was just teasing you. Why do you change color so suddenly?"

As they were thus conversing, a white cockatoo came into view, flying back and forth before them for a couple of times, and they knew that this was the summons of the Bodhisattva. Whereupon Mokṣa and Goodly Wealth led the way to the treasure lotus platform. As Pilgrim went to his knees to bow to the Bodhisattva, he could no longer restrain the tears from gushing forth and he wailed loudly. Asking Mokṣa to lift him up, the Bodhisattva said, "Wukong, tell me plainly what's causing you such great sorrow. Stop crying! I'll bring relief to your suffering and dispel your woe."

Pilgrim, still weeping, bowed again before he said, "In previous years, when has your disciple ever consented to be snubbed by anyone? When, however, I was liberated by the Bodhisattva from my Heaven-sent calamity, and when I took the vow of complete poverty to accompany the Tang monk on his way to see Buddha for scriptures in the Western Heaven, I was willing to risk my very life. To rescue him from his demonic obstacles was like

Snatching a tender bone from the tiger's mouth,
Scraping off one scale, live, from a dragon's back.

My only hope was to be able to return to the Real and attain the right fruit, to cleanse myself of sins and destroy the deviates. How could I know that this elder could be so ungrateful! He cannot recognize any virtuous cause, nor can he distinguish between black and white."

"Tell me," said the Bodhisattva, "a little about the black and white." Whereupon Pilgrim gave a thorough account of how he had beaten to death the brigands, which provoked the misgivings of the Tang monk; how without distinguishing black and white, the Tang monk had used the Tight-Fillet Spell to banish him several times; and how he had come to lay bare his woes to the Bodhisattva because there was no place on Earth or in Heaven where he could find shelter. Then the Bodhisattva said to him: "When Tripitaka Tang received the imperial decree to journey to the West, his sole intention was to be a virtuous monk, and therefore he most certainly would not lightly take away a human life. With your limitless magic power, why should you beat to death these many bandits? The bandits are no good, to be sure, but they are, after all, human beings and they don't deserve such punishment. They are not like those fiendish fowl or monstrous beasts, those demons or griffins. If you kill or slaughter those things, it's your merit, but when you take human lives, then it's your wickedness. Just frighten them away, and you would still be able to protect your master. In my opinion, therefore, you have not acted in a virtuous manner."

Still tearful, Pilgrim kowtowed and said, "Though I may not have acted in a virtuous manner, I should have been given a chance to use my merit to atone for my sins. I don't deserve to be banished like this. I beg now the Bodhisattva to have compassion on me and recite the Loose-Fillet Spell. Let me be released from the golden fillet and I'll give it back to you. Let me go back to the Water-Curtain Cave with my life." Smiling at him, the Bodhisattva replied: "The Tight-Fillet Spell was imparted to me originally by Tathāgata, who sent me in that year to go find a scripture pilgrim in the Land of the East. He gave me three kinds of treasure: the brocade cassock, the nine-ringed priestly staff, and three fillets named the golden, the tight, and the prohibitive. I was also taught in secret three different spells, but there was no such thing as the Loose-Fillet Spell."

"In that case," said Pilgrim, "let me take leave of the Bodhisattva." The Bodhisattva asked, "Where are you going?" "To the Western Heaven," replied Pilgrim, "where I'll beg Tathāgata to recite the Loose-Fillet Spell." "Wait a moment," said the Bodhisattva, "and let me scan the fortune for you." "No need for that," said Pilgrim. "This sort of misfortune is all I can take!" "I'm not scanning yours," said the Bodhisattva, "but the Tang monk's."

Dear Bodhisattva! As she sat solemnly on the lotus platform, her mind penetrated the three realms and her eyes of wisdom surveyed from a distance the entire universe. In a moment, she opened her mouth and said, "Wukong, your master will soon encounter a fatal ordeal. Before long, he will be looking for you, and I will tell him then to take you back so that both of you can acquire the scriptures to attain the right fruit." The Great Sage Sun had no choice but to obey; not daring to misbehave, he stood at attention beneath the lotus platform where we shall leave him for the moment.

We tell you now about the elder Tang, who, after he had banished Pilgrim, told Bajie to lead the horse and Sha Monk to pole the luggage. All four of them headed toward the West. When they had traveled some fifty miles, Tripitaka stopped the horse and said, "Disciples, we left the village at the early hour of the fifth watch, and then that Bimawen made me terribly upset. After this half a day, I'm quite hungry and thirsty. Which of you will go beg me some food?" "Please dismount, Master," said Bajie, "and let me see if there's a village nearby for me to do so." On hearing this,

Tripitaka climbed down from the horse, while Idiot rose on the clouds. As he stared all around, he found mountains everywhere, but there was not a single house in sight. Dropping down, Bajie said to Tripitaka, "There's no place to beg food. I couldn't see a village anywhere." "If there's no place to beg food," said Tripitaka, "let's get some water for my thirst." Bajie said, "I'll go fetch some water from the brooklet south of the mountain." Sha Monk therefore handed the almsbowl over to him, and supporting it with his palm, Bajie left on the clouds and fog. The elder sat by the road to wait for him, but after a long while, he still did not return. The bitter thirst, alas, was becoming quite unbearable, for which we have a testimonial poem. The poem says:

> To nourish breath and spirit's the essential thing:
> Feelings and nature are formally the same.
> Ailments arise from spirit and mind distraught;
> The Way's o'erturned when form and sperm decline.
> When the Three Flowers fail, your labor is vain;
> When the Four Greats[3] decay, you strive for naught.
> Earth and wood sterile, metal and water decease.
> True body's sluggish, when will it reach perfection?

When Sha Monk saw how greatly Tripitaka was suffering from his hunger and thirst, and Bajie still had not returned with the water, he had no alternative but to put down the wraps and tie up the white horse. Then he said, "Master, please sit here for a moment; let me go and see if I can hurry him back with the water." Tears welling up in his eyes, the elder could only nod his head to give his reply. Quickly mounting the cloudy luminosity, Sha Monk also headed for the south of the mountain.

As he sat there all by himself enduring his agonies, the elder suddenly heard a loud noise near him. He was so startled that he jumped up, and then he saw that Pilgrim Sun was kneeling on one side of the road, his two hands holding high a porcelain cup. "Master," he said, "without old Monkey, you don't even have water. This is a cup of nice, cool water. Drink it to relieve your thirst, and let me then go beg some food for you." "I won't drink your water!" replied the elder. "If I die of thirst on the spot, I'll consider this my martyrdom! I don't want you anymore! Leave me!" "Without me," said Pilgrim, "you can't go to the Western Heaven."

3. Four Greats: in Buddhism, the term usually refers to the four *tanmātra* or elements of earth, water, fire, and wir (wind) that join to form the human body. When these elements are improperly balanced (thus the expression *sida butiao*), all kinds of sicknesses will arise.

"Whether I can or not," said Tripitaka, "is no business of yours! Lawless ape! Why are you bothering me again?" Changing his color all at once, that Pilgrim became incensed and shouted at the elder, "You cruel bonze! How you humiliate me!" He threw away the porcelain cup and slammed the iron rod on the back of the elder, who fainted immediately on the ground. Picking up the two blue woolen wraps, the monkey mounted his cloud somersault and went off to some place.

We now tell you about Bajie, who went to the south slope of the mountain with his almsbowl. As he passed the fold of the mountain, a thatched hut, the sight of which had been blocked previously by the mountain, came into view. He walked up to it and discovered that this was some sort of human residence. Idiot thought to himself: "I have such an ugly face. They will no doubt be afraid of me and refuse to give me any food. I must use transformation . . ."

Dear Idiot! Making the magic sign with his fingers, he recited a spell and shook his body seven or eight times. At last he changed into a yellowish, consumptive monk, still rather stoutish. Moaning and groaning, he staggered up to the door and called out: "Patron,

If your kitchen has surplus rice,
Let it starved wayfarers suffice.

This humble cleric is from the Land of the East, on his way to seek scriptures in the Western Heaven. My master, now sitting by the road, is hungry and thirsty. If you have any cold rice or burnt crusts, I beg you to give us some."

Now, the men of the household, you see, had all gone to plant the fields, and only two women remained behind. They had just finished cooking lunch and filled two large bowls with rice to be sent to the fields, while some rice and crusts were still in the pot. When they saw his sickly appearance, and when they heard all that muttering about going to the Western Heaven from the Land of the East, they thought that he was babbling because of his illness. Afraid, moreover, that he might fall dead right before their door, the women hurriedly packed the almsbowl with the leftovers, crust and all, which Idiot gladly received. After he left on the road from which he came, he changed back into his original form.

As he proceeded, he heard someone calling, "Bajie!" Raising his head, he found that it was Sha Monk, standing on a cliff and shouting, "Come this way! Come this way!" Then he leaped down from the cliff and approached Bajie, saying, "There's lovely, clean water here in the brook. Why didn't you bail some? Where did you run off to?" "When I reached here," said Bajie, chuckling, "I saw a house in the fold of the mountain. I went there and succeeded in begging from them this bowl of dried rice." "We can use that," said Sha Monk, "but Master is terribly thirsty. How can we bring back some water?" "That's easy," replied Bajie. "Fold up the hem of your robe, and we'll use that to hold the rice. I'll take the almsbowl to bail some water."

In great spirits, the two of them went back to the spot by the road, where they saw Tripitaka lying down with his face hugging the earth. The reins were loosened, and the white horse was rearing up and neighing repeatedly by the road. The pole with the luggage, however, was nowhere to be seen. Bajie was so shaken that he stamped his feet and beat his breast, shouting, "This has to be it! This has to be it! The cohorts of those bandits whom Pilgrim Sun beat to death must have returned to kill Master and take the luggage." "Let's tie up the horse first," said Sha Monk, and then he too began to shout: "What shall we do? What shall we do? This is truly the failure that comes in midway!" As he turned to call but once "Master," tears streamed down his face and he wept bitterly. "Brother," said Bajie, "stop crying. When we have reached this stage of affairs, let's not talk about that scripture business. You watch over Master's corpse, and let me ride to some village store in whatever county or district nearby and see if I can buy a coffin. Let's bury Master and then we can disperse."

Unwilling, however, to give up on his master, Sha Monk turned the Tang monk over on his back and put his own face up to the corpse's face. "My poor master!" he wailed, and presently, the elder's mouth and nose began to belch hot air as a little warmth could also be felt on his chest. "Bajie," cried Sha Monk hurriedly, "come over here. Master's not dead!" Our Idiot approached them and lifted up the elder, who woke up slowly, groaning all the time. "You lawless ape!" he exclaimed. "You've just about struck me dead!" "Which ape is this?" asked both Sha Monk and Bajie, and the elder could do nothing more than to sigh. Only after he drank several gulps of water did he say, "Disciples, soon after both of you left, that Wukong came to bother me again. Because I adamantly refused to take him back, he gave me a blow with his rod and took away our blue woolen wraps."

When Bajie heard this, he clenched his teeth as fire leaped up from his heart. "This brazen ape!" he said. "How could he be so insolent? Sha Monk, you look after Master and let me go to his home to demand the wraps." "Stop being so angry," said Sha Monk. "We should take Master to that house in the fold of the mountain and beg for some hot liquids to warm up the rice we managed to get just now. Let's take care of Master first before you go look for him."

Bajie agreed; after having helped their master to mount up, they held the almsbowl and carried the cold rice up to the house's door, where they found only an old woman inside. Seeing them, she quickly wanted to hide. Sha Monk pressed his palms together and said, "Old Mama, we are those from the Land of the East sent by the Tang court to go to the Western Heaven. Our master is somewhat indisposed, and that is why we have come here especially to your house to beg some hot tea or water, so that he may eat some rice." "Just now," said the old woman, "there was a consumptive monk who claimed to have been sent from the Land of the East. We have already given him some food. How is it that you are also from the Land of the East? There's no one in the house. Please go to someplace else." On hearing this, the elder held onto Bajie and dismounted. Then he bent low and said, "Old Popo, I had originally three disciples, who were united in their efforts to accompany me to see Buddha for scriptures at the Great Thunderclap Monastery in India. My eldest disciple, whose name is Sun Wukong, has unfortunately practiced violence all his life and refused to follow the virtuous path. For this reason, I banished him. Little did I expect him to return in secret and give my back a blow with his rod. He even took our luggage and our clothing. I must now send a disciple to go find him and ask for our things, but the open road is no place to sit. Hence we have come to ask your permission to use your house as a temporary resting place. As soon as we get back our luggage, we'll leave, for we dare not linger."

"But there *was* a yellowish, consumptive monk just now," said the old woman, "who received our food. He also claimed to be part of a pilgrimage going to the Western Heaven from the Land of the East. How could there be so many of you?" Unable to restrain his giggles, Bajie said, "That was I. Because I have this long snout and huge ears, I was afraid that your family might be frightened and refuse me food. That was why I changed into the form of that monk. If you don't believe me, just take a look at what my brother's carrying in the fold of his robe. Isn't that your rice, crust and all?"

When the old woman saw that it was indeed the rice that she had given him, she no longer refused them and asked them to go inside and take a seat. She then prepared a pot of hot tea, which she gave to Sha Monk for him to mix with the rice. After the master had eaten several mouthfuls, he felt more calm and said, "Which of you will go ask for the luggage?" "In that year when Master sent him back there," said Bajie, "I went to look for him. So I know the way to his Flower-Fruit Mountain and the Water-Curtain Cave. Let me go! Let me go!" "You can't go!" replied the elder. "That monkey has never been friendly with you, and you are so rough with your words. A tiny slip when you talk to him and he may want to attack you. Let Wujing go."

"I'll go! I'll go!" said Sha Monk agreeably, whereupon the elder gave him this further instruction: "You must size up the situation as soon as you get there. If he's willing to give you our wraps, just pretend to thank him and take them. If he's unwilling, be sure not to argue or fight with him. Go directly to the Bodhisattva's place at the South Sea and tell her everything. Ask the Bodhisattva to demand the luggage from him." After he had listened most attentively, Sha Monk said to Bajie, "When I'm gone, you must not be slack in your care of Master. And don't cause any mischief in this family, for I fear that they would not serve you rice then. I'll be back soon." "I know," said Bajie, nodding. "But you must come back quickly, whether you succeed or not in getting our things back. I don't want something like 'Hauling firewood with a pointed pole: you lose at both ends' to happen!" And so, Sha Monk made the magic sign and mounted the cloudy luminosity to head for the East Pūrvavideha Continent. Truly,

Though body's present, spirit has left its home;
The brazier's fireless, how's elixir forged?
Yellow Hag leaves her lord to seek Metal Squire;
Wood Mother engages her teacher though he appears ill.
We know not when he'll return once he leaves,
Nor can we surmise his hour of return.
The Five Phases' mutual growth or conquest is not smooth.
Wait till Mind Monkey enters again the pass.[4]

Only after he had traveled in the air for three nights and days did Sha Monk finally reach the Great Eastern Ocean. As the sound of waves reached his ears, he lowered his head and saw that

Black fog swelling skyward makes the dark air dense;
The brine holds the sun to chill the light of dawn.

He was, of course, too preoccupied to enjoy the scenery. Passing the immortal island of Yingzhou, he hurried toward the Flower-Fruit Mountain, riding on the oceanic wind and tide.

After a long while, he saw towering peaks jutting up like rows of halberds and sheer cliffs like hanging screens. He dropped down on the highest

---

4. Daoist teachings sometimes use the metaphor of a frontier gate or a fortified pass (*guan*) to refer to certain narrows or passageways of the human body. In the ancient text *Huainanzi*, for example, the eyes, the ears, and the mouth are called the "three passes (*san guan*)," which are to be guarded with care against vain sights, sounds, and words.

summit and began to search for his way to the Water-Curtain Cave. As he drew near his destination, he began to hear a noisy din made by countless monkey spirits living in the mountain. Sha Monk walked closer and found Pilgrim Sun sitting high on a rock terrace, his two hands holding up a piece of paper from which he was reading aloud the following statement:

> Emperor Li, King of the Great Tang in the Land of the East, now commands the sage monk, Chen Xuanzang, royal brother before the Throne and master of the Law, to go to India in the West, and ask for scriptures in all sincerity from the Buddhist Patriarch, Tathāgata, in the Great Thunderclap Monastery on the Spirit Mountain.
>
> Because of grave illness invading our body, our soul departed for the region of Hades. It was our good fortune to have our life span unexpectedly lengthened, and the Kings of Darkness kindly returned us to life. Whereupon we convened a vast and goodly assembly to erect a plot of truth for the redemption of the dead. We were indebted to the salvific and woe-dispelling Bodhisattva Guanshiyin, who appeared to us in her golden form and revealed that there were both Buddha and scriptures in the West, which could deliver and redeem the lost souls of the dead. We have, therefore, commissioned Xuanzang, master of the Law, to traverse a thousand mountains in order to acquire such scriptures. When he reaches the various states of the Western region, we hope that they will not destroy such goodly affinity and allow him to pass through on the basis of this rescript.
>
> This is an imperial document promulgated on an auspicious day in the autumn of the thirteenth year in the Zhenguan reign period of the Great Tang.
>
> Since leaving my[5] noble nation, I have passed through several countries, and in midjourney, I have made three disciples: the eldest being Pilgrim Sun Wukong, the second being Zhu Wuneng Bajie, and the third being Sha Wujing Monk.

After he read it aloud once, he started again from the beginning. When Sha Monk realized that it was the travel rescript, he could no longer contain himself. Drawing near, he shouted: "Elder Brother, this is Master's rescript. Why are you reading it like that?" When that Pilgrim heard this, he raised his head but could not recognize Sha Monk. "Seize him! Seize

---

5. The change of voice here is intentional, since this section of the rescript has been added presumably by the queen of the Nation of Women previously.

him!" he yelled. The other monkeys immediately had Sha Monk surrounded; pulling and tugging at him, they hauled him before that Pilgrim, who bellowed: "Who are you, that you dare approach our immortal cave without permission?"

When Sha Monk saw how he had changed color and refused to recognize his own, he had little choice but to bow low and say, "Let me inform you, Elder Brother. Our master previously was rather impetuous and wrongly put the blame on you. He even cast the spell on you several times and banished you home. Your brothers did not really try to pacify Master for one thing, and for another, we soon had to look for water and beg for food because of Master's hunger and thirst. We didn't expect you to come back with all your good intentions. When you took offense at Master's adamant refusal to take you in again, you struck him down, left him fainted on the ground, and took the luggage. After we rescued him, I was sent to plead with you. If you no longer hate Master, and if you can recall his previous kindness in giving you freedom, please give us back the luggage and return with me to see Master. We can go to the Western Heaven together and accomplish the right fruit. But if your animosity is deep and you are unwilling to leave with me, please give me back the wraps at least. You can enjoy your old age in this mountain, and you will have done at the same time all of us a very good turn."

When he heard these words, that Pilgrim laughed scornfully and said, "Worthy Brother, what you said makes little sense to me. I struck the Tang monk and I took the luggage not because I didn't want to go to the West, nor because I loved to live in this place. I'm studying the rescript at the moment precisely because I want to go to the West all by myself to ask Buddha for the scriptures. When I deliver them to the Land of the East, it will be my success and no one else's. Those people of the South Jambūdvīpa Continent will honor me then as their patriarch and my fame will last for all posterity."

"You have spoken amiss, Elder Brother," said Sha Monk, smiling, "Why, we have never heard anyone speaking of 'Pilgrim Sun seeking scriptures'! When our Buddha Tathāgata created the three canons of true scriptures, he also told the Bodhisattva Guanyin to find a scripture pilgrim in the Land of the East. Then she wanted us to traverse a thousand hills and go through many nations as protectors of that pilgrim. The Bodhisattva once told us that the scripture pilgrim was originally Tathāgata's disciple, whose religious designation was the Elder Gold Cicada. Because he failed to listen attentively to the lectures of the Buddhist Patriarch, he was banished from the Spirit Mountain to be reborn in the Land of the East. He was then instructed to bear the right fruit in the West by cultivating once more the great Way. Since it was preordained that he should encounter many demonic obstacles in his journey, we three were liberated so that we might become his guardians. If Elder Brother does not wish to accompany the Tang monk in his quest, which Buddhist Patriarch would be willing to impart to you the scriptures? Haven't you dreamed up all this in vain?"

"Worthy Brother," said that Pilgrim, "you've always been rather block-ish! You know one thing, but you fail to perceive another. You claim that you have a Tang monk, who needs both of us to protect him. Do you really think that I don't have a Tang monk? I have already selected here a truly enlightened monk, who will go acquire the scriptures and old Monkey will only help him. Is there anything wrong with that? We have, in fact, decided that we'll begin the journey tomorrow. If you don't believe me, let me show you." He then cried: "Little ones, ask the old master to come out quickly please." The little fiends indeed ran inside and led out a white horse, followed by a Tripitaka Tang, a Bajie poling the luggage, and a Sha Monk carrying the priestly staff.

Enraged by the sight, Sha Monk cried, "Old Sand here changes neither his name when he walks nor his surname when he sits. How could there be another Sha Monk? Don't be impudent! Have a taste of my staff!"

Dear Sha Monk! Lifting high his fiend-routing staff with both his hands, he killed the specious Sha Monk with one blow on the head. He was actu-ally a monkey spirit. That Pilgrim, too, grew angry; wielding his golden-hooped rod, he led the other monkeys and had Sha Monk completely surrounded. Charging left and right, Sha Monk managed to fight his way out of the encirclement. As he fled for his life by mounting the cloud and fog, he said to himself: "This brazen ape is such a rogue! I'm going to see the Bodhisattva to tell on him!" When that Pilgrim saw that the Sha Monk had been forced to flee, he did not give chase. He went back to his cave instead and told his little ones to have the dead monkey skinned. Then his meat was taken to be fried and served as food along with coconut and grape wines. After they had their meal, that Pilgrim selected another monkey monster who knew transformation to change into a Sha Monk. He again gave them instructions on how to go to the West, and we shall leave them for the moment.

Once Sha Monk had left the Eastern Ocean by mounting the clouds, he reached the South Sea after journeying for a day and night. As he sped forward, he saw the Potalaka Mountain approaching, and he stopped his cloud to look around. Marvelous place it was! Truly

This secret spot of Heaven,
This hidden depth of Earth,
Where a hundred springs join to bathe both sun and stars,
Where the wind blows and the moon beams her rippling light.
When the tide rises, the big fishes change:
When the waves churn, the huge scorpaenids swim.
Here water joins the northwest sea,
Its billows the Eastern Ocean fuse.
Here the four seas are linked by the same pulse of Earth,
Though each isle immortal has its own fairy homes.
Speak not of Penglai's everywhere.
Let's look at Cave Potalaka.
What great scenery!
The peak's bright colors show prime essence strong.
Auspicious breeze wafts moonlight beneath the ridge.
Through groves of purple bamboo the peacocks fly;
On willow-branch a sentient parrot speaks.
Jade grass and flowers are every year fair:
Gold lotus, jewelled trees grow annually.
White cranes fly up to the peak several times;
To the mount arbor the phoenix often comes.
E'en fishes will seek th'immortal arts:
To listen to scriptures they o'erleap the waves.

Descending slowly from the Potalaka Mountain as he admired the scenery, he was met by the disciple, Mokṣa, who said to him, "Sha Wujing, why aren't you accompanying the Tang monk to procure scriptures? Why are you here?"

After Sha Monk returned his bow, he said, "I have a matter that requires my having an audience with the Bodhisattva. Please take the trouble to announce me." Mokṣa already knew that it had to do with his search for Pilgrim, but he did not mention it. He went instead inside first and said to the Bodhisattva, "The youngest disciple of the Tang monk, Sha Wujing, is outside seeking an audience." When Pilgrim Sun heard that beneath the platform, he chuckled and said, "This has to be that the Tang monk has met some kind of ordeal, and Sha Monk is here to seek the assistance of the Bodhisattva."

The Bodhisattva at once asked Mokṣa to call him in, and Sha Monk went to his knees to kowtow. After his bow, he raised his head and was about to tell the Bodhisattva what had happened, when all of a sudden he saw Pilgrim Sun standing on one side. Without even a word, Sha Monk whipped out his fiend-routing staff and aimed it at Pilgrim's face. Pilgrim, however, did not fight back; he only stepped aside to dodge the blow. "You brazen ape!" screamed Sha Monk. "You rebellious simian guilty of ten evil deeds! So, you are even here to hoodwink the Bodhisattva!" "Wujing!" shouted the Bodhisattva. "Don't raise your hands! If you have a complaint, tell it to me first."

Putting away his treasure staff, Sha Monk knelt down before the platform, and, still huffing, said to the Bodhisattva, "This monkey has performed countless violent acts along the way. The day before, he beat two highwaymen to death beneath the mountain slope, and Master already found fault with him. Little did we expect that that very night we had to live right in the bandit camp, and he slaughtered a whole band of them. As if that weren't enough, he took a bloody head back to show to Master, who was so aghast that he fell down from his horse. It was then that Master gave him a reprimand and banished him. After we separated, Master found the hunger and thirst unbearable at one place and told Bajie to go find water. When he didn't return after a long while, I was told to go find him. When Pilgrim Sun saw that we both had left, he sneaked back and gave Master a blow with his iron rod, after which he took away our two blue woolen wraps. When we finally returned, we managed to revive Master, and then I had to make a special trip to his Water-Curtain Cave to demand from him the wraps. How could I know that he would change his face and refuse to recognize me? Instead, he was reciting back and forth the travel rescript of Master. When I asked him why, he said that he was no longer willing to accompany the Tang monk. He wanted to go procure scriptures in the Western Heaven and take them all by himself to the Land of the East. That, he said, would be his sole merit, and the people would honor him as their patriarch while his fame would be everlasting. I told him: 'Without the Tang monk, who would be willing to give you scriptures?' He said then that he had already selected a true, enlightened monk, and he brought out a Tang monk, all right, including a white horse, followed by a Bajie and a Sha Monk for me to see. 'I'm the Sha Monk,' I said, 'so how could there be another Sha Monk?' I rushed up to this impostor and gave him a blow with my treasure staff; it turned out to be a monkey spirit. Then this ape led his followers to try to capture me, and that was when I fled and decided to come here to inform the Bodhisattva. He must have used his cloud-somersault and arrived first, and I don't know what sort of balderdash he has mouthed to dupe the Bodhisattva."

"Wujing," said the Bodhisattva, "don't blame another person wrongly. Wukong has been here for four days, and I haven't let him go anywhere.

How could he have gone to find another Tang monk to go fetch scriptures by themselves?" "But," said Sha Monk, "I saw a Pilgrim Sun in the Water-Curtain Cave. You think I'm lying?" "In that case," said the Bodhisattva, "don't get upset. I'll tell Wukong to go with you to take a look at the Flower-Fruit Mountain. Truth is indestructible, but falsehood can easily be eliminated. When you get there, you'll find out." On hearing this, our Great Sage and Sha Monk took leave at once of the Bodhisattva and left. And so, the result of their journey will be that

Before Mount Flower-Fruit black and white will be made distinct;
By the Water-Curtain Cave the true and perverse will be seen.

We don't know, however, how that will be accomplished; let's listen to the explanation in the next chapter.

Two Minds cause disturbance in the great cosmos;
It's hard for one substance to reach Perfect Rest.

After our Pilgrim and Sha Monk kowtowed to take leave of the Bodhisattva, they rose on two beams of auspicious light and departed from the South Sea. Now, the cloud-somersault of Pilgrim, you see, was much faster than the mere cloud-soaring of Sha Monk. He therefore wanted to speed ahead, but Sha Monk pulled him back, saying, "Elder Brother, you need not try to cover up or hide your tracks by getting there first. Let me travel right beside you." The Great Sage, of course, was full of good intentions, whereas Sha Monk at that moment was filled with suspicion.

So, the two of them rode the clouds together and in a little while, they spotted the Flower-Fruit Mountain. As they lowered their clouds to glance around, they found indeed outside the cave another Pilgrim, sitting high on a stone ledge and drinking merrily with a flock of monkeys. His looks were exactly the same as those of the Great Sage: he, too, had a gold fillet clamped to his brownish hair, a pair of fiery eyes with diamond pupils, a silk shirt on his body, a tiger kilt tied around his waist, a golden-hooped iron rod in one of his hands, and a pair of deerskin boots on his feet. He, too, had

A hairy face, a thunder god beak,
An empty jowl unlike Saturn's;
Two forked ears on a big, broad head,
And huge fangs that have outward grown.

His ire aroused, our Great Sage abandoned Sha Monk and rushed forward, wielding his iron rod and crying, "What sort of a fiend are you that you dare change into my appearance, take my descendants captive, occupy my immortal cave, and assume such airs?" When that Pilgrim saw him, he did not utter a word of reply; all he did was meet his opponent with the iron rod. The two Pilgrims closed in, and you could not distinguish the true one from the false. What a fight!

Two iron rods,
Two monkey sprites,

This fight of theirs is truly no light thing!
They both want to guard the royal brother of Tang,
Each seeking merit to acquire great fame.
The true ape accepts the poverty faith;
The specious fiend utters false Buddhist claims.
Their magic gives them transformations vast:
They're exact equals, that's the honest truth!
One is the Equal to Heaven Sage of the unified breath of Composite Prime;
One is a long-cultivated sentient spirit, able to shorten the ground.
This one is the compliant golden-hooped rod;
That one is the acquiescent staff of iron.
They block and parry and fight to a draw;
They buck and resist and neither can win.
They join hands at first outside the cave;
Soon they rise to do battle in midair.

Treading on the cloudy luminosity, the two of them rose into the sky to fight. On the side, Sha Monk did not have the courage to join the battle, for he found it truly difficult to distinguish between the two of them. He wanted very much to lend his assistance, but he feared that he might inadvertently inflict harm on the real Pilgrim. After waiting patiently for a long while, he leaped down from the mountain cliff and wielded his fiend-routing staff to disperse the various fiends outside the Water-Curtain Cave. He then overturned the stone benches and smashed to pieces all those eating and drinking utensils before searching for his two blue woolen wraps. They were, however, nowhere to be seen. The cave, you see, was located actually behind a huge waterfall, which had the entrance neatly hidden as if it were behind a white curtain. That was the reason for the name, Water-Curtain Cave. Sha Monk, of course, had no idea of its history or its layout, and it was therefore difficult for him to make his search.

Unable to recover his wraps, Sha Monk again mounted the clouds to rush up to midair. He held high his treasure staff, but he simply dared not strike at either of the combatants. "Sha Monk," said the Great Sage, "if you can't help me, go back to Master and tell him about our situation. Let old Monkey do battle with this fiend all the way to the Potalaka Mountain of South Sea so that the Bodhisattva can distinguish the true from the false." When he finished speaking, the other Pilgrim also said the same thing. Since both of them had exactly the same appearance and there was not even the slightest difference even in their voices, Sha Monk could not distinguish one from the other. He had no choice but to change the direction of his cloud and go back to report to the Tang monk. We shall now leave him for the moment.

Look at those two Pilgrims instead! They fought as they journeyed; soon they arrived at the Potalaka Mountain in the South Sea, trading blows and insults all the time. All the continuous uproar quickly alerted the various guardian deities, who rushed inside the Tidal Sound Cave to say, "Bodhisattva, there are indeed two Sun Wukongs who have arrived, fighting!" The Bodhisattva immediately descended from her lotus platform to go out of the cave with her disciples Mokṣa, the Boy of Goodly Wealth, and the Dragon Girl. "Cursed beasts," she cried, "where do you two think you are going?" Still entangled together, one of them said, "Bodhisattva, this fellow indeed resembles your disciple. We started our battle from the Water-Curtain Cave, but we have not yet reached a decision even after such a long bout. The fleshy eyes of Sha Wujing were too dim and dull to tell us apart, and thus he couldn't help us even if he had the strength. Your disciple told him to go back to the road to the West and report to my master. I have fought with this fellow up to your treasure mountain because I want you to lend us your eyes of wisdom. Please help your disciple to distinguish the true from the false, the real from the perverse." When he finished speaking, the other Pilgrim also repeated the same words. The various deities and the Bodhisattva stared at the two for a long time, but none could tell them apart. "Stop fighting," said the Bodhisattva, "and stand apart. Let me look at both of you once more." They indeed let go of each other and stood on opposite sides. "I'm the real one," said one side. "He's a fake!" said the other.

Asking Mokṣa and Goodly Wealth to approach her, the Bodhisattva whispered to them this instruction: "Each of you take hold of one of them firmly, and let me start reciting in secret the Tight-Fillet Spell. The one whose head hurts is the real monkey; the one who has no pain is specious." Indeed, the two disciples took hold of the two Pilgrims as the Bodhisattva recited in silence the magic words. At once the two of them gripped their heads and rolled on the ground, both screaming, "Don't recite! Don't recite!" The Bodhisattva stopped her recital, and the two of them again became entangled together, fighting and shouting as before. Unable to think of anything else, the Bodhisattva asked the various deities and Mokṣa to go forward to help, but the gods were afraid that they might hurt the real person and they, therefore, dared not raise their hands. "Sun Wukong," called the Bodhisattva, and the two of them answered in unison. "When you were appointed Bimawen," she said, "and when you brought chaos to Heaven, all those celestial warriors could certainly recognize you. You go up to the Region Above now and they should be able to distinguish between the two of you." This Great Sage thanked her and the other Pilgrim also thanked her.

Tugging and pulling at each other, screaming and hollering at each other, the two of them went before the South Heaven Gate. The Devarāja Virūpākṣa was so startled that he led Ma, Zhao, Wen, and Guan, the four great celestial warriors, and the rest of the divine gate attendants to bar the way with their weapons. "Where are you two going?" they cried. "Is this a place for fighting?"

The Great Sage said, "I was accompanying the Tang monk on his way to acquire scriptures in the Western Heaven. Because I slayed some thieves on the way, that Tripitaka banished me, and I went to tell my troubles to the Bodhisattva Guanyin at the Potalaka Mountain. I have no idea when this monster-spirit assumed my form, struck down my master, and robbed us of our wraps. Sha Monk went to look for our things at the Flower-Fruit Mountain and discovered that this monster-spirit had taken over my lair. Thereafter, he went to seek the assistance of the Bodhisattva, and when he saw me standing at attention beneath the platform, he falsely accused me of using my cloud-somersault in order to cover up my faults. The Bodhisattva, fortunately, was righteous and perceptive; she didn't listen to Sha Monk and told me to go with him instead to examine the evidence at the Flower-Fruit Mountain. I discovered there that this monster-spirit indeed resembled old Monkey. We fought just now from the Water-Curtain Cave to the place of the Bodhisattva, but even she found it difficult to tell us apart. That's why we came here. Let all of you deities take the trouble of using your perception and make distinction between the two of us." When he finished speaking, that Pilgrim also gave exactly the same account. Though the various gods stared at them for a long time, they could not tell the difference. "If all of you can't recognize us," the two of them shouted, "stand aside and let us go see the Jade Emperor!"

Unable to resist them, the various deities had to let them through the Heaven Gate, and they went straight up to the Treasure Hall of Divine Mists. Marshal Ma dashed inside with Zhang, Ge, Xu, and Qiu, the Four Celestial Masters, to memorialize, saying, "There are two Sun Wukongs from the Region Below who have fought their way into the Heaven Gate. They claim they want to see the Emperor." Hardly had they finished speaking when the two monkeys brawled their way in. The Jade Emperor was so taken aback that he stood up and came down the treasure hall to ask, "For what reason did the two of you enter the celestial palace without permission? Are you seeking death with your brawling before us?"

"Your Majesty! Your Majesty!" cried our Great Sage. "Your subject has already made submission and embraced the vow of poverty. I would never dare be so audacious as to mock your authority again. But because this monster-spirit has changed into the form of your subject, . . ." where-upon he gave a thorough account of what had taken place, ending with the words, "I beg you to do this for your subject and distinguish between the two of us." That Pilgrim also gave exactly the same account.

Issuing a decree at once to summon Devarāja Li, the Pagoda-Bearer, the Jade Emperor commanded: "Let us look at those two fellows through the imp-reflecting mirror, so that the false may perish and the true endure." The devarāja took out the mirror immediately and asked the Jade Emperor to watch with the various celestial deities. What appeared in the mirror were two reflections of Sun Wukong: there was not the slightest difference between their golden fillets, their clothing, and even their hair. Since the Jade Emperor found it impossible to distinguish them, he ordered them chased out of the hall.

Our Great Sage was laughing scornfully, while that Pilgrim also guf-fawed jovially as they grabbed each other's head and neck once more to fight their way out of the Heaven Gate. Dropping down to the road to the West, they shouted at each other: "I'll go see Master with you! I'll go see Master with you!"

We now tell you about that Sha Monk, who since leaving them at the Flower-Fruit Mountain, traveled again for three nights and days before he arrived at the mountain hut. After he told the Tang monk all that had taken place, the elder was filled with regret, saying, "I thought at that time that it was Sun Wukong who gave me a blow with his rod and who robbed us of our wraps. How could I know that it was a monster-spirit who had assumed the form of Pilgrim?" "Not only did that fiend do that," said Sha Monk, "but he had someone change into an elder, and another into Bajie poling our wraps. In addition to a white horse also, there was still another fiend who changed into the likeness of me. I couldn't restrain my anger and killed him with one blow of my staff. He was actually a monkey spirit. I left in a hurry to go to inform the Bodhisattva, who then asked Elder Brother to go with me to see for ourselves back at the Water-Curtain Cave. When we arrived, we discovered that that fiend was indeed an exact copy of Elder Brother. I couldn't tell them apart and it was difficult, therefore, for me to lend any assistance. That's why I came back first to report to you." On hearing this, Tripitaka paled with fright, but Bajie laughed uproariously, saying, "Fine! Fine! Fine! The Popo of our patron's house has spoken true! She said that there had to be several groups of pilgrims going to procure scriptures. Isn't this another group?"

The members of that family, old and young, all came to ask Sha Monk: "Where have you been these last few days? Did you go off to seek travel money?" "I went to the place of my Big Brother," said Sha Monk with a laugh, "at the Flower-Fruit Mountain of the East Pūrvavideha Continent to look for our luggage. Next I went to have an audience with the Bodhisattva Guanyin at the Potalaka Mountain of South Sea. Then I had to go back to the Flower-Fruit Mountain again before I came back here."

"What was the distance that you had to travel?" asked an old man again. "Back and forth," replied Sha Monk, "it had to be about two hundred thousand miles." "Oh, Sire," said the old man, "you mean to tell me that you have covered all that distance in these few days? You must have soared on the clouds, or you would never have made it." "If he didn't soar on the clouds," said Bajie, "how could he cross the sea?" "We haven't covered any distance," said Sha Monk. "If it were my Big Brother, it would take only a couple of days for him to get there and return." When those family members heard what he said, they all claimed that their visitors had to be immortals. "We are not immortals," said Bajie, "but the immortals are really our juniors!"

As they were speaking, they suddenly heard a great uproar in the middle of the sky. They were so startled that they came out to look, and they found two Pilgrims locked in battle as they drew near. On seeing them, Bajie's hands began to itch, and he said, "Let me see if I can tell them apart."

Dear Idiot! He leaped into the air and cried, "Elder Brother, don't fret! Old Hog's here!" The two Pilgrims cried out at the same time, "Brother, come and beat up this monster-spirit!" The old man was so astonished by the sight that he said to himself: "So we have in our house several arhats who can ride the clouds and mount the fog! Even if I had made a vow to feed the monks, I might not have been able to find this kind of noble people." Without bothering to think of the cost, he wanted at once to bring out more tea and rice to present to his visitors. Then he muttered to himself: "But I fear that no good can come out of these two Pilgrims, fighting like that. They will overturn Heaven and Earth and cause terrible calamity who knows where!"

When Tripitaka saw that the old man was openly pleased, though he was, at the same time, full of secret anxiety, he said to him, "Please do not worry, old Patron, and don't start any lamentation. When this humble cleric succeeds in subduing his disciple and in inducing the wicked to return to virtue, he will most certainly thank you." "Please don't mention it! Please don't mention it!" said the old man repeatedly. "Please don't say anything more, Patron," said Sha Monk. "Master, you sit here while I go up there with Second Elder Brother. Each of us will pull before you one of them, and you can start reciting that little something. We'll be able to tell, for whoever has pain will be the real Pilgrim." "You are absolutely right," said Tripitaka.

Sha Monk indeed rose to midair and said, "Stop fighting, the two of you, and we'll go with you to Master and let him distinguish the true from the false." Our Great Sage desisted, and that Pilgrim also dropped his hands. Sha Monk took hold of one of them and said, "Second Elder Brother, you take the other one." They dropped down from the clouds and went before the thatched hut. As soon as he saw them, Tripitaka began reciting the Tight-Fillet Spell, and the two of them immediately screamed, "We've been fighting so bitterly already. How could you still cast that spell on us? Stop it! Stop it!" As his disposition had always been kind, the elder at once stopped his recitation, but he could not tell them apart at all. Shrugging off the hold of Sha Monk and Bajie, the two of them were again locked in battle. "Brothers," said our Great Sage, "take care of Master, and let me go before King Yama with him to see if there could be any way of discriminating us." That Pilgrim also spoke to them in the same manner. Tugging and pulling at each other, the two of them soon vanished from sight.

"Sha Monk," said Bajie meanwhile, "when you saw the false Bajie poling the luggage in the Water-Curtain Cave, why didn't you take it away?" Sha Monk said, "When that monster-spirit saw me slaying his false Sha Monk with my treasure staff, he and his followers surrounded me and wanted to seize me. I had to flee for my life, you know. After I told the Bodhisattva and went back to the entrance of the cave with Pilgrim, the two of them fought in midair while I went to overturn their stone benches and scattered the little fiends. All I saw then was a huge cascade flowing into a stream, but I could not find the cave entrance anywhere nor could I locate the luggage. That's why I came back to Master empty-handed." "You really couldn't have known this," said Bajie. "When I went to ask him to return that year,[1] I met him first outside the cave. After I succeeded in persuading him to come, he said he wanted to go inside to change clothes. That was when I saw him diving right through the water, for the cascade is actually the cave entrance. That fiend, I suppose, must have hidden our wraps in there." "If you know where the entrance is," said Tripitaka, "you should go there now while he is absent and take out our wraps. Then we can go to the Western Heaven by ourselves. Even if he should want to join us again, I won't use him." "I'll go," answered Bajie. "Second Elder Brother," said

---

1. A reference to incidents recounted in chapters 30–31 of the full-length novel.

Sha Monk, "there are over a thousand little monkeys in that cave of his. You may not be able to handle them all by yourself." "No fear, no fear," said Bajie, laughing. He dashed out of the door, mounted the cloud and fog, and headed straight for the Flower-Fruit Mountain to search for the luggage.

We tell you now instead about those two Pilgrims, who brawled all the way to the rear of the Mountain of Perpetual Shade. All those spirits on the mountain were so terrified that they, shaking and quaking, tried desperately to hide themselves. A few managed to escape first and they rushed inside the fortified pass of the nether region and reported in the Treasure Hall of Darkness: "Great Kings, there are two Great Sages, Equal to Heaven, who are fighting their way down from the Mountain of Perpetual Shade." King Qinguang of the First Chamber was so terrified that he at once passed the word to King of the Beginning River in the Second Chamber, King of the Song Emperor in the Third Chamber, King of Complete Change in the Fourth Chamber, King Yama in the Fifth Chamber, King of Equal Ranks in the Sixth Chamber, King of Tai Mountain in the Seventh Chamber, King of City Markets in the Eighth Chamber, King of Avenging Ministers in the Ninth Chamber, and King of the Turning Wheel in the Tenth Chamber. Soon after the word had passed through each chamber, the ten kings assembled together and they also sent an urgent message to King Kṣitigarbha to meet them at the Hall of Darkness. At the same time, they called up all the soldiers of darkness to prepare to capture both the true and the false. In a moment, they felt a gush of strong wind and then they saw dense, dark fog rolling in, in the midst of which were two Pilgrims tumbling and fighting together.

The Rulers of Darkness went forth to stop them, saying, "For what purpose are the Great Sages causing trouble in our nether region?" "I had to pass through the State of Western Liang," replied our Great Sage, "because I was accompanying the Tang monk on his way to procure scriptures in the Western Heaven. We reached a mountain shortly thereafter, where brigands attempted to rob my master. Old Monkey slaughtered a few of them, but my master took offense and banished me. I went instead to the Bodhisattva at South Sea to make known my difficulties. I have no idea how this monster-spirit got wind of it, but somehow he changed into my likeness, struck down my master in midjourney, and robbed him of his luggage. My younger brother, Sha Monk, went to my native mountain to demand the wraps, but this fiend falsely claimed that he wished to go to seek scriptures in the Western Heaven in the name of Master. Fleeing to South Sea, Sha Monk informed the Bodhisattva when I was standing right there. The Bodhisattva then told me to go with him to look for myself at the Flower-Fruit Mountain, and I discovered that indeed my old lair was occupied by this fellow. I strove with him until we reached the place of the Bodhisattva, but in truth his appearance, his speech, and the like are exactly like mine. Even the Bodhisattva found it hard to distinguish us. Then we fought our way up to Heaven, and the gods couldn't tell us apart. We next went to see my master, and when he recited the Tight-Fillet Spell to test us, this fellow's head hurt just like mine. That's why we brawl down to the nether region, in hopes that you Rulers of Darkness will examine for me the Register of Life and Death and determine what is the origin of the specious Pilgrim. Snatch away his soul at once, so that there will not be the confusion of two Minds." After he finished speaking, the fiend also repeated what he said in exactly the same manner.

On hearing this, the Rulers of Darkness summoned the judge in charge of the register to examine it from the beginning, but there was, of course, nothing written down that had the name "specious Pilgrim." He then studied the volume on hairy creatures, but the one hundred and thirty some entries under the name "monkey," you see, had already been crossed out by the Great Sage Sun with one stroke of the brush, in that year when he caused great havoc in the region of darkness after he had attained the Way. Ever since that time, the name of any species of monkey was not recorded in the register. After he finished examining the volume, he went back to the hall to make his report. Picking up their court tablets to show their solemn intentions, the Rulers of Darkness said to both of the Pilgrims, "Great Sages, there is nowhere in the nether region for you to look up the impostor's name. You must seek discrimination in the world of light."

Hardly had they finished speaking when the Bodhisattva Kṣitigarbha said, "Wait a moment! Wait a moment! Let me ask Investigative Hearing to listen for you." That Investigative Hearing, you see, happens to be a beast which usually lies beneath the desk of Kṣitigarbha. When he crouches on the ground, he can in an instant perceive the true and the false, the virtuous and the wicked among all short-haired creatures, scaly creatures, hairy creatures, winged creatures, and crawling creatures, and among all the celestial immortals, the earthly immortals, the divine immortals, the human immortals, and the spirit immortals resident in all the cave Heavens and blessed lands in the various shrines, rivers, and mountains of the Four Great Continents. In obedience, therefore, to the command of Kṣitigarbha, the beast prostrated himself in the courtyard of the Hall of Darkness, and in a little while, he raised his head to say to his master, "I have the name of the fiend, but I cannot announce it in his presence. Nor can we give assistance in capturing him." "What would happen," asked Kṣitigarbha, "if you were to announce his name?" "I fear then," replied Investigative Hearing, "that the monster-spirit might unleash his violence to disturb our treasure hall and ruin the peace of the office of darkness."

"But why," asked his master again, "can't we give assistance in capturing him?" Investigative Hearing said, "The magic power of that monster-spirit is no different from the Great Sage Sun's. How much power do the gods of the nether region possess? That's why we cannot capture him." "How, then, shall we do away with him?" said Kṣitigarbha, and Investigative Hearing answered: "The power of Buddha is limitless." Waking up all at once, Kṣitigarbha said to the two Pilgrims, "Your forms are like a single person, and your powers are exactly the same. If you want clear distinction between the two of you, you must go to the Thunderclap Monastery, the abode of Śākyamuni." "You are right! You are right!" shouted both of them in unison. "We'll go to have this thing settled before the Buddhist Patriarch in the Western Heaven." The Rulers of Darkness of all Ten Chambers accompanied them out of the hall before they thanked Kṣitigarbha, who returned to the Jade Cloud Palace. The ghost attendants were then told to close up the fortified passes of the nether region, and we shall leave them for the moment.

Look at those two Pilgrims! Soaring on cloud and darting on fog, they fought their way up to the Western Heaven, and we have a testimonial poem. The poem says:

If one has two minds, disasters he'll breed;
He'll guess and conjecture both far and near.
He seeks a good horse or the Three Dukes'[2] office,
Or the seat of first rank there in Golden Chimes.
He'll war unceasing in the north and south;
He'll not keep still assailing both east and west.
You must learn of no mind in the gate of Chan,
And let the holy babe[3] be formed thus quietly.

Tugging and pulling at each other, the two of them brawled in midair as they proceeded, and finally, they reached the Thunderclap Treasure Monastery on the Spirit Vulture Mountain in the great Western Heaven.

At that time the Four Great Bodhisattvas, the Eight Great Diamond Kings, the five hundred arhats, the three thousand guardians of the faith, the mendi-

2. The Three Dukes are the three ministers of state.
3. Holy babe: in alchemical lore, realized immortality is often referred to as the baby (*ying'er*) or the holy embryo (*shengtai*).

cant nuns and the mendicant monks, the upāsakas and the upāsikās—all this holy multitude was gathered beneath the lotus seat of seven jewels to listen to a lecture by Tathāgata. His discourse had just reached the point on

The existent in the nonexistent;
The nonexistent in the non-nonexistent;
The form in the formlessness;
The emptiness in the nonemptiness.
For the nonexistent is the existent,
And the non-nonexistent is the nonexistent.
Formlessness is verily form;
Nonemptiness is verily emptiness.
Emptiness is indeed emptiness;
Form is indeed form.
Form has no fixed form;
Thus form is emptiness.
Emptiness has no fixed emptiness;
Thus emptiness is form.
The knowledge of emptiness is not emptiness;
The knowledge of form is not form.
When names and action mutually illuminate,
Then one has reached the wondrous sound.

As the multitude bowed their heads in submission and chanted in unison these words of the Buddha, Tathāgata caused celestial flowers to descend upon them in profusion. Then he said to the congregation: "You are all of one mind, but take a look at two Minds in competition and strife arriving here."

When the congregation looked up, there were indeed two Pilgrims locked in a clamorous battle as they approached the noble region of Thunderclap. The Eight Great Diamond Kings were so aghast that they went forward to bar the way, crying, "Where do you two think you are going?"

"A monster-spirit," replied our Great Sage, "has assumed my appearance. I want to go below the treasure lotus platform and ask Tathāgata to make distinction between us." The Diamond Kings could not restrain them, and the two monkeys brawled up to the platform. "Your disciple," said our Great Sage as he knelt before the Buddhist Patriarch, "was accompanying the Tang monk to journey to your treasure mountain and to beg you for true scriptures. I have exerted I don't know how much energy on our way in order to smelt demons and bind fiends. Some time ago, we ran into some bandits trying to rob us, and in truth, your disciple on two occasions did take a few lives. Master took offense and banished me, refusing to allow me to bow with him to the golden form of Tathāgata. I had no choice but to flee to South Sea and tell Guanyin of my woes. Little did I anticipate that this monster-spirit would falsely assume my voice and my appearance and then strike down Master, taking away even our luggage. My younger brother, Wujing, followed him to my native mountain, only to be told by the crafty words of this fiend that he had another true monk ready to be the scripture pilgrim. Wujing managed to escape to South Sea to inform Guanyin of everything. Whereupon the Bodhisattva told your disciple to return with Wujing to my mountain, as a result of which the two of us fought our way to South Sea and then to the celestial palace. We went also to see the Tang monk as well as the Rulers of Darkness, but no one could tell us apart. For this reason I make bold to come here, and I beg you in your great compassion to fling wide the great gate of means. Grant unto your disciple your discernment of the right and the perverse, so that I may again accompany the Tang monk to bow to your golden form in person, acquire the scriptures to bring back to the Land of the East, and forever exalt the great faith."

What the congregation heard was one statement made by two mouths in exactly the same voice, and none of them could distinguish between the two Pilgrims. Tathāgata, however, was the only one who had the perception; he was about to make his revelation when a pinkish cloud floating up from the south brought to them Guanyin, who bowed to the Buddha.

Pressing his palms together, our Buddha said, "Guanyin, the Honored One, can you tell which is the true Pilgrim and which is the false one?" "They came to your disciple's humble region the other day," replied the Bodhisattva, "but I truly could not distinguish between them. They then went to both the Palace of Heaven and the Office of Earth, but even there they could not be recognized. I have come, therefore, especially to beg Tathāgata to do this on the true Pilgrim's behalf."

Smiling, Tathāgata said, "Though all of you possess vast dharma power and are able to observe the events of the whole universe, you cannot know all the things therein, nor do you have the knowledge of all the species." When the Bodhisattva asked for further revelation, Tathāgata said, "There are five kinds of immortals in the universe, and they are: the celestial, the earthly, the divine, the human, and the spirit. There are also five kinds of creatures, and they are: the short-haired, the scaly, the hairy, the winged, and the crawling. This fellow belongs to none of these. But there are, however, four kinds of monkeys which also do not belong to any of these ten species." "May I inquire," said the Bodhisattva, "which four kinds they are?"

"The first," said Tathāgata, "is the intelligent stone monkey, who

Knows transformations,
Recognizes the seasons,
Discerns the advantages of earth,
And is able to alter the course of planets and stars.

The second is the red-buttocked baboon, who

Has knowledge of yin and yang,
Understands human affairs,
Is adept in its daily life
And able to avoid death and lengthen its life.

The third is the bare-armed gibbon, who can

Seize the sun and the moon,
Shorten a thousand mountains,
Distinguish the auspicious from the inauspicious,
And manipulate planets and stars.

The fourth is the six-eared macaque,[4] who has

A sensitive ear,
Discernment of fundamental principles,
Knowledge of past and future,
And comprehension of all things.

These four kinds of monkeys are not classified in the ten species, nor are they contained in the names between Heaven and Earth. As I see the matter, that specious Wukong must be a six-eared macaque, for even if this monkey stands in one place, he can possess the knowledge of events a thousand miles away and whatever a man may say in that distance. That is why I describe him as a creature who has

A sensitive ear,
Discernment of fundamental principles,
Knowledge of past and future,
And comprehension of all things.

The one who has the same appearance and the same voice as the true Wukong is a six-eared macaque."

When the macaque heard how Tathāgata had announced his original form, he shook with fear; leaping up quickly, he tried to flee. Tathāgata, however, at once ordered the Four Bodhisattvas, the Eight Diamond Kings, the five hundred arhats, the three thousand guardians of the faith, the men-

---

4. The name of this kind of monkey is puzzling, but it may have been derived from the common Buddhist saying, "The dharma is not to be transmitted to the sixth ear [i.e., the third pair or person]."

dicant monks, the mendicant nuns, the upāsakas, the upāsikās, Guanyin, and Mokṣa to have him completely encircled. The Great Sage Sun also wanted to rush forward, but Tathāgata said, "Wukong, don't move. Let me capture him for you." The macaque's hair stood on end, for he supposed that he would not be able to escape. Shaking his body quickly, he changed at once into a bee, flying straight up. Tathāgata threw up into the air a golden almsbowl, which caught the bee and brought it down. Not perceiving that, the congregation thought the macaque had escaped. With a smile, Tathāgata said, "Be silent, all of you. The monster-spirit hasn't escaped. He's underneath this almsbowl of mine." The congregation surged forward and lifted up the almsbowl; a six-eared macaque in his original form indeed appeared. Unable to contain himself anymore, the Great Sage Sun raised his iron rod and killed it with one blow on the head. To this day this species of monkey has remained extinct.

Moved to pity by the sight, Tathāgata exclaimed: "My goodness! My goodness!" "You should not have compassion on him, Tathāgata," said our Great Sage. "He wounded my master and robbed us of our wraps. Even according to the law, he was guilty of assault and robbery in broad daylight. He should have been executed." Tathāgata said, "Now you go back quickly to accompany the Tang monk here to seek the scriptures."

As he kowtowed to thank the Buddha, the Great Sage said, "Let me inform Tathāgata, that it is certain that my master will not want me back. If I go to him now and he rejects me, it's simply a waste of effort. I beg you to recite the Loose-Fillet Spell instead so that I can give back your golden fillet. Let me return to secular life." "Stop such foolish thought," said Tathāgata, "and don't be mischievous! If I ask Guanyin to take you back to your master, you should have no fear that he will reject you. Take care to protect him on his journey, and in due time

When merit's done and Nirvāṇa's home,
You, too, will sit on a lotus throne."

When she heard that, Guanyin pressed together her palms to thank the sage's grace, after which she led Wukong away by mounting the clouds. They were followed at once by her disciple, Mokṣa, and the white cockatoo. Soon, they arrived at the thatched hut, and when Sha Monk saw them, he quickly asked his master to bow at the door to receive them. "Tang monk," said the Bodhisattva, "the one who struck you the other day was a specious Pilgrim, a six-eared macaque. It was our good fortune that Tathāgata recognized him, and subsequently he was slain by Wukong. You must now take him back, for the demonic barriers on your journey are by no means entirely overcome, and only with his protection can you reach the Spirit Mountain and see the Buddha for scriptures. Don't be angry with him anymore." Kowtowing, Tripitaka replied, "I obey your instruction."

At that moment when he and Sha Monk were thanking the Bodhisattva, they heard a violent gust of wind blowing in from the east: it was Zhu Bajie, who returned riding the wind with two wraps on his back. When Idiot saw the Bodhisattva, he fell on his knees to bow to her, saying, "Your disciple took leave of my master the other day and went to the Water-Curtain Cave of the Flower-Fruit Mountain to look for our luggage. I saw indeed a specious Tang monk and another specious Bajie, both of whom I struck dead. They were two monkeys. Then I went inside and found the wraps, and examination revealed that nothing was missing. I mounted the wind to return here. What, may I ask, has happened to the two Pilgrims?" The Bodhisattva thereupon gave him a complete account of how Tathāgata had revealed the origin of the fiend, and Idiot was thoroughly delighted. Master and disciples all bowed to give thanks. As the Bodhisattva went back to South Sea, the pilgrims were again united in their hearts and minds, their animosity and anger all dissolved. After they also thanked the village household, they put in order their luggage and the horse to find their way to the West once more. Thus it is that

Parting in midway disturbs the Five Phases;
The fiend's defeat fuses the primal light.
Spirit returns to Mind and Chan can be still.
The six senses subdued, elixir's made.

We do not know when Tripitaka will be able to face the Buddha and ask for the scriptures; let's listen to the explanation in the next chapter.

Priests are hard to destroy—that's great awakening;
The Dharma-king perfects the right, his body's naturalized.

We were telling you about Tripitaka, who obeyed the instruction of the Bodhisattva and took back Pilgrim. As he followed his disciples to head for the West, it was soon again the time of summer, when warm breezes freshly stirred, and rain of the plum season drizzled down in fine strands. Marvelous scenery, it is:

Lush and dense is the green shade;
In light breeze young swallows parade.
New lilies unfold on the ponds;
Old bamboos spread slowly their fronds.
The sky joins the meadows in green;
Mountain blooms o'er the ground are seen.
Swordlike, rushes stand by the brook;
Pomegranates redden this sketchbook.

Master and diciples, the four of them, had to endure the heat, of course.

As they proceeded, they came upon two rows of tall willows flanking the road; from within the willow shade an old woman suddenly walked out, leading a young child by the hand. "Priest," she cried aloud to the Tang monk, "you must stop right now! Turn your horse around and return to the East quickly! The road to the West leads only to death!"

So startled was Tripitaka that he leaped down from the horse and bowed to her, saying, "Old Bodhisattva, as the ancients have said,

The ocean is wide so fishes may leap;
The sky is empty so birds may fly.

How could it be that a road to the West is lacking?"

Pointing westward with her finger, the old woman said, "About five or six miles from here is the Dharma-Destroying Kingdom. In some previous incarnation somewhere the king must have contracted evil karma so that in this life he sins without cause. Two years ago he made a stupendous vow that he would kill ten thousand Buddhist priests. Until now he has succeeded in slughtering nine thousand, nine hundred, and ninety-six name-less monks. All he is waiting for now are four more monks, preferably with names, and the perfect score of ten thousand will be reached. If you people arrive at his city, you will all become life-giving king bodhisattvas!"

Terror-stricken by these words, Tripitaka said, trembling all over, "Old Bodhisattva, I'm profoundly grateful for your kindness, and I can't thank you enough. May I ask whether there is another road that conveniently bypasses the city? This poor monk will gladly take such a road and proceed."

With a giggle, the old woman replied, "You can't bypass the city! You simply can't! You might do so only if you could fly!"

At once Bajie began to wag his tongue and said, "Mama, don't speak such scary words! We're all able to fly!" With his fiery eyes and diamond pupils, however, Pilgrim was the only one who could discern the truth: the old woman and the child were actually the Bodhisattva Guanyin and the Boy of Goodly Wealth. So alarmed was he that he went to his knees immediately and cried, "Bodhisattva, pardon your disciples for failing to meet you!"

Gently the bodhisattva rose on a petal of pink cloud, so astounding the elder Tang that he did not quite know where to stand. All he could do was to fall on his knees to kowtow, and Bajie and Sha Monk too went hurriedly to their knees to bow to the sky. In a moment, the auspicious cloud drifted away to return to South Sea. Pilgrim got up and raised his master, saying "Please rise, the bodhisattva has returned to her treasure mountain."

As he got up, Tripitaka said, "Wukong, if you had recognized the bodhisattva, why didn't you tell us sooner?"

"You couldn't stop asking questions," replied Pilgrim, laughing, "whereas I immediately went to my knees. Wasn't that soon enough?" Bajie and Sha Monk then said to Pilgrim, "Thanks to the bodhisattva's revelation, what lies before us has to be the Dharma-Destroying King-dom. What are we all going to do when there's this determination to kill monks?"

"Idiot, don't be afraid!" said Pilgrim. "We have met quite a few vicious demons and savage fiends, and we have gone through tiger lairs and dragon lagoons, but we have never been hurt. What we have to face here is a kingdom of common people. Why should we fear them? Our only trouble right now is that this is no place to stay. Besides, it's getting late, and if any villagers returning from business in the city catch sight of us priests and begin to spread the news, that won't be very convenient. Let's lead Master away from the main road and find a more secluded spot. We can then make further plans."

Tripitaka indeed followed his suggestion; all of them left the main road and went over to a small ditch, in which they sat down. "Brothers," said Pilgrim, "the two of you stay here and guard Master. Let old Monkey go in transformation to look over the city. Perhaps I can find a road that's out of the way, which will take us through the region this very night." "O Disciple!" urged the Tang monk. "Don't take this lightly, for you're going against the law of a king. Do be careful!"

"Relax! Relax!" replied Pilgrim with a smile. "Old Monkey will manage!" Dear Great Sage! When he finished speaking, he leaped into the air with a loud whistle. How fantastic!

Neither pulled from above by strings,
Nor supported below by cranes,
Like us all, two parents he owns,
But only he has lighter bones.

Standing at the edge of the clouds, he peered below and saw that the city was flooded by airs of gladness and auspicious luminosity. "What a lovely place!" Pilgrim said. "Why does it want to destroy the dharma?" As he stared at the place, it gradually grew dark. He saw that

At letter-ten crossings[1] lamps flared brightly;
At nine-tiered halls incense rose and bells tolled.
Seven glowing stars lit up the blue sky;
In eight quarters travelers dropped their gear.
From the six-corps camps
The painted bugles just faintly sounded;
In the five-watch tower,
Drop by drop the copper pot 'gan dripping.
On four sides night fog thickened;
At three marts chilly mist spread out.
Spouses, in twos, entered the silken drapes,
When one bright moon ascended the east.

He thought to himself: "I would like to go down to the business districts to look over the roadways, but with a face like mine, people will undoubtedly holler that I'm a priest if they see me. I'll transform myself." Making the magic sign and reciting a spell, he changed with one shake of his body into a moth:

1. Letter-ten crossings: crossroads in the shape of the Chinese graph ten (*shi*). I have translated quite literally to retain the numerical word play of the poem.

A small shape with light, agile wings,
He dives to snuff candles and lamps.
By metamorphosis he gains his true form,
Most active midst rotted grasses.
He strikes flames for love of hot light,
Flying, circling without ceasing.
Purple-robed, fragrant-winged, chasing the fireflies,
He likes most the deep windless night.

You see him soaring and turning as he flew toward those six boulevards and three marts, passing eaves and rafters. As he proceeded, he suddenly caught sight of a row of houses at the corner of the street ahead, each house having a lantern hung above its door.

"These families," he thought to himself, "must be celebrating the annual Lantern Feast. Why would they have lighted lanterns by the row?" Stiffening his wings, he flew near and looked carefully. The house in the very middle had a square lantern, on which these words were written: Rest for the Traveling Merchant. Below there were also the words: Steward Wang's Inn. Pilgrim knew therefore that it was a hotel.

When he stretched out his neck to look further, he saw that there were some eight or nine people, who had all finished their dinner. Having loosened their clothes, taken off their head wraps, and washed their hands and feet, they had taken to their beds to sleep. Secretly pleased, Pilgrim said, "Master may pass through, after all!" "How did he know so readily that his master might pass through?" you ask. He was about to follow a wicked scheme: waiting until those people were asleep, he would steal their clothes and wraps so that master and disciples could disguise themselves as secular folks to enter the city.

Alas! There had to be this disagreeable development! As he was deliberating by himself, the steward went forward and gave this instruction to his guests: "Sirs, do be careful, for our place caters to both gentlemen and rogues. I'd like to ask each of you to take care of your clothing and luggage." Think of it! People doing business abroad, would they not be careful with everything? When they heard such intruction from the innkeeper, they became more cautious than ever. Hastening to their feet, they said, "The proprietor is quite right. Those of us fatigued by travel may not easily wake up once we're asleep. If we lose our things, what are we going to do? Please take our clothes, our head wraps, and our money bags inside. When we get up in the morning, you may return them to us." Steward Wang accordingly took all of their clothes and belongings into his own residence.

By nature impulsive, Pilgrim at once spread his wings to fly there also and alighted on one of the head-wrap stands. Then he saw Steward Wang going to the front door to take down the lantern, lower the cloth curtain, and close the door and windows. Only then did Wang return to his room to take off his own clothes and lie down. The steward, however, also had a wife sleeping with two children, and they were still making so much noise that none of them could go to sleep right away. The wife, too, was patching some garment and refused to retire.

"If I wait until this woman sleeps," thought Pilgrim to himself, "won't Master be delayed?" Fearing also that the city gates might be closed later in the night, he could no longer refrain from flying down there and threw himself on the taper. Truly

He risked his life to dive into flames;
He scorched his brow to temp his fate.

The taper immediately went out. With one shake of his body he changed again into a rat. After a squeak or two he leaped down, took the garments and head wraps, and began to drag them out. Panic-stricken, the woman said, "Old man, things are bad! A rat has turned into a spirit!"

On hearing this, Pilgrim flaunted his abilities some more. Stopping at the door, he cried out in a loud voice, "Steward Wang, don't listen to the babblings of your woman. I'm no rodent-spirit. Since a man of light does not engage in shady dealings, I must tell you that I'm the Great Sage, Equal to Heaven, who has descended to earth to accompany the Tang monk on his way to seek scriptures in the Western Heaven. Because your king is without principles, I've come especially to borrow these caps and gowns to adorn my master. Once we've passed through the city, I'll return them." Hearing that, Steward Wang scrambled up at once. It was, of course, pitch black, and he was in a hurry besides. He grabbed his pants, thinking he had his shirt; but no matter how hard he tried, slipping them on this way and that, he could not put them on.

Using his magic of abduction, the Great Sage had already mounted the clouds to leave the city and return to the ditch by the road. In the bright light of the stars and moon, Tripitaka was standing there staring when he saw Pilgrim approaching. "Disciple," he asked, "can we go through the Dharma-Destroying Kingdom?"

Walking forward and putting down the garments, Pilgrim said, "Master, if you want to go through the Dharma-Destroying Kingdom, you can't remain a priest." "Elder Brother," said Bajie, "whom are you trying to fool? It's easy not to remain a priest: just don't shave your head for half a year, and you hair will grow." "We can't wait for half a year!" said Pilgrim. "We must become laymen right now!"

Horrified, our Idiot said, "The way you talk is most unreasonable, as always! We are all priests, and you want us to become laymen this instant! How could we even wear a head wrap? Even if we tighten the edges, we have nothing on our heads to tie the strings with!"

"Stop the wisecracks!" snapped Tripitaka. "Let's do what's proper! Wukong, what *is* your plan?"

"Master," said Pilgrim, "I have inspected the city here. Though the king is unprincipled enough to slaughter monks, he is nevertheless a genuine son of Heaven, for his city is filled with joyful and auspicious air. I can recognize the streets in the city, and I can converse in the local dialect. A moment ago I borrowed several garments and head wraps from a hotel. We must disguise ourselves as laymen and enter the city to ask for lodging. At the fourth watch we should rise and ask the innkeeper to prepare us a meal—vegetarian, of course. By about the hour of the fifth watch, we will walk close to the wall of the city-gate and find the main road to the West. If we run into anyone who tries to detain us, we can still give the explanation that we have been commissioned by the court of a superior state. The Dharma-Destroying King would not dare hinder us. He'll let us go." Sha Monk said, "Elder Brother's plan is most proper. Let's do as he tells us."

Indeed, the elder had little choice but to shed his monk's robe and his clerical cap and to put on the garment and head wrap of a layman. Sha Monk too changed his clothes. Bajie, however, had such a huge head that he could not wear the wrap as it was. Pilgrim had to rip open two wraps and sew them together with needle and thread to make one wrap and drape it over his head. A larger garment was selected for him to put on, after which Pilgrim himself also changed into a different set of clothing. "Once we get moving," he said, "you all must put away the words 'master and disciples.'"

"Without these terms," said Bajie, "how shall we address ourselves?"

Pilgrim said, "We should do so as if we were in a fraternal order: Master shall be called Grand Master Tang, you shall be Third Master Zhu, Sha Monk shall be called Fourth Master Sha, and I shall be called Second Master Sun. When we reach the hotel, however, none of you should talk; let me do all the talking. If they ask us what sort of business we're in, I'll say that we're horse traders, using this white horse of ours as a sample. I'll tell them that there are altogether ten of us in this fraternal order, but the four of us have come first to rent a room in the hotel and sell our horse. The innkeeper will certainly take care of us. If we receive his hospitality, I'll pick up by the time we leave some bits or pieces of broken titles and

change them into silver to thank him. Then we'll get on with our journey."
The elder had no alternative but to comply reluctantly.

The four of them, leading the horse and toting the luggage, hurried into the city. It was fortunate that this happened to be a peaceful region, so that the city gates had not yet been closed even as the time of the night watch began. When they reached the door of the Steward Wang's Hotel, they heard noises from inside, crying, "I've lost my head wrap!" Another person cried, "I've lost my clothes." Feigning ignorance, Pilgrim led them to another hotel, catercorner from this one. Since that hotel had not yet even taken down its lantern, Pilgrim walked up to the door and called out: "Innkeeper, do you have a room for us to stay in?"

Some woman inside replied at once, "Yes! Yes! Yes! Let the masters go up to the second floor." She had hardly finished speaking when a man arrived to take the horse, which Pilgrim handed over to him. He himself led his master behind the lamplight and up to the door of the second floor, where lounge tables and chairs had been placed. He pushed open the shutters, and moonlight streamed in as they took their seats. Someone came up with lighted lamps, but Pilgrim barred the door and blew out the lamps with one breath. "We don't need lamps when the moon's so bright," he said.

After the person with the lamps had been sent away, another maid brought up four bowls of pure tea, which Pilgrim accepted. From below, a woman about fifty-seven or fifty-eight years old came straight up to the second floor. Standing to one side, she asked, "Gentlemen, where have you come from? What treasure merchandise do you have?"

"We came from the north," replied Pilgrim, "and we have a few ordinary horses to sell."

"Well," said the woman, "we haven't seen many guests who sell horses."

"This one is Grand Master Tang," said Pilgrim, "this one is Third Master Zhu, and this one is Fourth Master Sha. Your humble student here is Second Master Sun."

"All different surnames," said the woman with a giggle.

"Indeed, all different surnames but living together," said Pilgrim. "There are altogether ten of us in our fraternal order; we four have come first to seek lodging at your hotel, and the six others are resting outside the city. With a herd of horses, they don't dare enter the city at such an hour. When we have located the proper place for them to stay, they'll come in tomorrow morning. Once we have sold the horses, we'll leave."

"How many horses are there in your herd?" asked the woman.

"Big and small, there are over a hundred," said Pilgrim, "all very much like the horse we have here. Only their colors vary."

Giggling some more, the woman said, "Second Master Sun is indeed a merchant in every way! It's a good thing that you've come to our place, for any other household would not dare receive you. We happen to have a large courtyard here, complete with stalls and stocked with feed. Even if you had several hundred horses, we can take care of them. You should be aware, too, that our hotel has been here for years and has gained quite a reputation. My late husband, who unfortunately died long ago, had the surname of Zhao, and that's why this hotel is named Widow Zhao's Inn. We have three classes of accommodation here. If you will kindly allow impoliteness to precede courtesy, I will discuss the room rates with you, so I'll know what to charge you."

"What you say is quite right," said Pilgrim. "What three classes of accommodation do you have in your hotel? As the saying goes,

High, medium, and low, are three prices of goods,
Guests, far and near, are not treated the same.

Tell me a little of your three classes of accommodation."

Widow Zhao said, "What we have here are the superior, moderate, and inferior classes of accommodation. For the superior, we will prepare a banquet of five kinds of fruits and five courses, topped by lion-head puddings and peck-candies. There will be two persons per table, and young hostesses will be invited to drink and rest with you. The charge per person is five coins of silver, and this includes the room."

"What a bargain!" said Pilgrim, chuckling. "Where I came from, five coins of silver won't even pay for the young ladies!"

"For the moderate," said the widow again, "all of you will share one table, and you'll get only fruits and hot wine. You yourselves may establish your drinking rules and play your finger-guessing games, but no young hostesses will be present. For this, we charge two coins of silver per person."

"That's even more of a bargain," said Pilgrim. "What's the inferior class like?"

"I dare not describe that in front of honored guests," replied the woman.

"You may tell us," said Pilgrim. "We'll find our bargain and do our thing."

The woman said, "In the inferior class there's no one to serve you. You may eat whatever rice there is in the pot, and when you've had your fill, you can get some straw and make yourself a bed on the ground. Find yourself a place to sleep, and in the morning you may give us a few pennies for the rice. We won't haggle with you."

On hearing this, Bajie said, "Lucky! Lucky! That's old Hog's kind of bargain! Let me stand in front of the pot and stuff myself with rice. Then I'll have a nice damn snooze in front of the hearth!" "Brother," said Pilgrim, "what are you saying? You and I, after all, have managed to earn a few ounces of silver here and there in the world, haven't we? Give us the superior class!"

Filled with delight, the woman cried, "Bring some fine tea! Tell the chefs to start their preparations." She dashed downstairs and shouted some more: "Slaughter some chickens and geese. Have them cooked or cured to go with the rice. Slaughter a pig and a lamb too; even if we can't use them today, we may use them tomorrow. Get the good wine. Cook white-grain rice, and take bleached flour to make biscuits."

When he heard her from upstairs, Tripitaka said, "Second Master Sun, what shall we do? She is planning to slaughter chickens, geese, a pig, and a lamb. When she brings these things up, which one of us, keepers of a perpetual vegetarian diet that we are, dare take one bite?"

"I know what to do," replied Pilgrim, and he went to the head of the stairs and tapped the floor with his foot. "Mama Zhao, please come up here," he said. The mama came up and said, "What instructions do you have for me, Second Master?" "Don't slaughter anything today," said Pilgrim, "for we're keeping a vegetarian diet."

Astonished, the widow said, "Do the masters keep a perpetual diet or a monthly diet?" "Neither," replied Pilgrim, "for ours is named the *geng-shen* diet. Since the cyclical combination for today is, in fact, *gengshen*, we must keep the diet. Once the hour of the third watch is past, it will be the day of *xinyou*, and we'll be able to eat meat. You may do the slaughtering tomorrow. Please go now and prepare us some vegetarian dishes. We'll pay you the price of the superior class just the same."

The woman was more delighted than ever. She dashed downstairs to say, "Don't slaughter anything! Don't slaughter anything! Take some woodears, Fujian bamboo-shoots, bean curds, wheat glutens, and pull some greens from our garden to make vermicelli soup. Let the dough rise so that we can steam some rolls. We can cook the white-grain rice and brew fragrant tea also." Aha! Those chefs in the kitchen, accustomed to do this every day, finished their preparations in no time at all. The food was brought upstairs, along with ready-made lion-puddings and candied fruits, so that the four could enjoy themselves to their hearts' content.

"Do you take dietary wine?" the woman asked again. Pilgrim said,

"Only Grand Master Tang doesn't drink, but the rest of us can use a few cups." The widow then brought up a bottle of hot wine. Hardly had the three of them finished pouring when they heard loud bangings on the floor down below.

"Mama," said Pilgrim, "did something fall downstairs?"

"No," replied the widow. "A few hired hands from our humble village who arrived rather late tonight with their monthly payment of rice were told to sleep downstairs. Since you masters have come, and we haven't enough help right now, I've asked them to take the carriages to go fetch the young hostesses here to keep you company. The poles on the carriages must have accidentally backed into the boards of the staircase."

"It's a good thing that you mention this," said Pilgrim. "Quickly tell them not to go. For one thing we're still keeping the diet, and for another our brothers have not yet arrived. Wait till they come in tomorrow, then we'll invite some call girls for the whole order to have some fun right here. After we've sold our horses, we'll leave."

"Good man! Good man!" said the widow. "You've not destroyed the peace, but you've saved your own energy at the same time!" She called out, "Bring back the carriages. No need to fetch the girls." After the four had finished the wine and rice, the utensils were taken away, and the attendants left.

Tripitaka whispered behind Pilgrim's ear, "Where shall we sleep?" "Up here," replied Pilgrim. "It's not quite safe," said Tripitaka. "All of us are rather tired. When we're asleep, if someone from this household chances to come by to fix things up and notices our bald heads if our caps roll off, they will see that we're monks. What shall we do if they begin yelling?"

"Indeed!" replied Pilgim. He went again to the head of the stairs to tap his foot, and the widow came up once more to ask: "What does Master Sun want?"

"Where shall we sleep?" asked Pilgrim. "Why, up here, of course!" said the woman. "There are no mosquitoes. You may open wide the windows, and with a nice southerly breeze, it's perfect for you to sleep."

"No, we can't," said Pilgrim. "Our Third Master Zhu here is somewhat allergic to dampness, and Fourth Master Sha has arthritic shoulders. Big Brother Tang can only sleep in the dark, and I, too, am rather sensitive to light. This is no place to sleep." The mama walked downstairs and, leaning on the counter, began to sigh. A daughter of hers, carrying a child, approached and said, "Mother, as the proverb says,

For ten days you sit on the shore;
In one day you may pass nine beaches.

Since this is the hot season, we haven't much business, but by the time of the fall, business may increase so much that we can't even cope with it. Why are you sighing?"

"Child," replied the woman, "I'm not worrying about lack of business, for at dusk today I was ready to close shop. But at the hour when the night watch began, four horse traders came to rent a room. Since they wanted the superior-class accommodation, I was hoping to make a few pennies profit from them. But they keep a vegetarian diet, and that completely dashes my hopes. That's why I'm sighing."

Her daughter said, "If they have eaten our rice, they can't leave and go to another household. Tomorrow we can prepare meat and wine for them. Why can't we make our profit then?" "But they are all sick," said the woman again, "afraid of draft, sensitive to light; they all want to sleep in a dark place. Come to think of it, all the buildings in our household are covered by single-tiered transparent titles. Where are we going to find a dark enough place for them? I think we'd better consider donating the meal to them and ask them to go someplace else."

"Mother," said her daughter, "there's a dark place in my building, and it has no draft. It's perfect!"

"Where is that?" asked the woman. The daughter said, "When father was alive, he made a huge wardrobe trunk about four feet wide, seven feet long, and at least three feet deep. Six or seven people can probably sleep in it. Tell them to go inside the wardrobe and sleep there." "I wonder if it's acceptable," said the woman. "Let me ask them. Hey, Master Sun, our humble dwelling is terribly small, and there is no dark place. We have only a huge wardrobe trunk which neither wind nor light can get through. How about sleeping in that?"

"Fine! Fine! Fine!" replied Pilgrim. Several of the hired hands were asked at once to haul out the wardrobe and remove the door before they were told to go downstairs. With Pilgrim leading his master and Sha Monk picking up the pole of luggage, they walked behind the lamplight to the wardrobe. Without regard for good or ill, Bajie immediately crawled in. After handing him the luggage, Sha Monk helped the Tang monk in before entering himself.

"Where's our horse?" said Pilgrim. One of the attendants on the side said, "It's tethered at the rear of the house and feeding."

"Bring it, along with the feed," said Pilgrim, "and tether it tightly beside the wardrobe." Only then did he himself enter the wardrobe. He cried, "Mama Zhao, put on the door, stick in the bolt and lock it up. Then take a look for us and see whether there are any holes anywhere that light may get through. Paste them up with paper. Tomorrow, come early and open the wardrobe." "You're much too careful!" said the widow. Thereafter everyone left to close the doors and sleep, and we shall leave those people for the moment.

We tell you now about the four of them inside the wardrobe. How pitiful! For one thing, it was the first time they had ever worn head wraps; for another, the weather was hot. Moreover, it was very stuffy because no breeze could get in. They all took off their wraps and their clothes, but without fans they could only wave their monk caps a little. Crowding and leaning on one another, they all began to doze by about the hour of the second watch.

Pilgrim, however, was determined to be mischievous! As he was the only one who could not sleep, he stretched out his hand and gave Bajie's leg a pinch. Pulling back his leg, our Idiot mumbled, "Go to sleep! Look how miserable we are! And you still find it interesting to pinch people's arms and legs for fun?" As a lark, Pilgrim began to say, "We originally had five thousand taels of silver. We sold some horses previously for three thousand taels, and right now, there are still four thousand taels left in the money bags. We can also sell our present herd of horses for three thousand taels, and we'll have both capital and profit. That's enough! That's enough!" Bajie, of course, was a man intent on sleeping, and he refused to answer him.

Little did they know that the waiters, the water haulers, and the fire tenders of this hotel had always been part of a band of thieves. When they heard Pilgrim speaking of so much silver, some of them slipped out at once and called up some twenty other thieves, who arrived with torches and staffs to rob the horse traders. As they rushed in, Widow Zhao and her daughter were so terrified that they slammed shut the door of their own building and let the thieves do what they pleased. Those bandits, you see, did not want anything from the hotel; all they desired was to find the guests. When they saw no trace of them upstairs, they searched everywhere with torches and came upon the huge wardrobe in the courtyard. To one of the legs a white horse was tethered. The wardrobe was tightly locked, and they could not pry open the door.

The thieves said, "Worldly people like us have to be observant! If this wardrobe is so heavy, there must be luggage and riches locked inside. What if we steal the horse, haul the wardrobe outside the city, break it up, and divide the contents among ourselves—wouldn't that be nice?" Indeed, those thieves did find some ropes and poles, with which they proceeded to haul the wardrobe out of the hotel. As they walked, the load swayed from side to side.

Waking up with a start, Bajie said, "O Elder Brother, please go to sleep! Why are you shaking us?" "Don't talk!" said Pilgrim. "No one's shaking you." Tripitaka and Sha Monk also woke up and cried, "Who is carrying us?" "Don't shout! Don't shout!" said Pilgrim. "Let them carry us. If they haul us all the way to the Western Heaven, it'll save us some walking!"

When those thieves succeeded in getting away from the hotel, they did not head for the West; instead, they hauled the chest toward the east of the city, where they broke out after killing some of the guards at the city gate. That disturbance, of course, alerted people in the six boulevards and three marts, the firemen and guards living in various stations. The reports went quickly to the Regional Patrol Commander and the East City Warden's office. Since this was an affair for which they had to assume responsibility, the commander and the warden at once summoned the cavalry and archers to pursue the thieves out of the city. When the thieves saw how strong the government troops were, they dared not contend with them. Putting down the huge wardrobe and abandoning the white horse, they fled in every direction. The government troops did not manage even to catch half a thief, but they did take the wardrobe and caught the horse, and they returned in triumph. As he looked at the horse beneath the lights, the commander saw that it was a fine creature indeed:

> Its mane parts like silver threads;
> Its tail dangles as strips of jade.
> Why mention the Eight Noble Dragon Steeds?[2]
> This one surpasses Suxiang's[3] slow trotting.
> Its bones would fetch a thousand gold,
> This wind-chaser through ten thousand miles.
> He climbs mountains oft to join the green clouds,
> Neighs at the moon, and fuses with white snow.
> Truly a dragon that has left the isles,
> A jade unicorn that man loves to own!

The commander, instead of riding his own horse, mounted this white horse to lead his troops back into the city. The wardrobe was hauled into his official residence, where it was then sealed with an official tape issued jointly by him and the warden. Soldiers were to guard it until dawn, when they could memorialize to the king to see about its disposal. As the other troops retired, we shall leave them for the moment.

We tell you instead about the elder Tang inside the wardrobe, who

2. Famous horses associated with various rulers.
3. Suxiang: the name of one of the Eight Noble Steeds.

complained to Pilgrim saying, "You ape-head! You've just about put me to death! If we had stayed outside and been caught and sent before the king of the Dharma-Destroying Kingdom, we could still argue with him. Now are locked up in a wardrobe, abducted by thieves, and then recovered by government troops. When we see the king tomorrow, we'll be ready-made victims for him to complete his number of ten thousand!"

Pilgrim said, "There are people outside right now! If they open the wardrobe and take us out, we'll either be bound or hanged! Do try to be more patient, so that we don't have to face the ropes. When we see that befuddled king tomorrow, old Monkey has his own way of answering him. I promise you that you'll not be harmed one whit. Now relax and sleep."

By about the hour of the third watch, Pilgrim exercised his ability and eased his rod out. Blowing his immortal breath on it, he cried, "Change!" and it changed into a three-pointed drill. He drilled along the bottom edge of the wardrobe two or three times and made a small hole. Retrieving the drill, he changed with one shake of his body into an ant and crawled out. Then he changed back into his original form to soar on the clouds into the royal palace. The king at that moment was sleeping soundly.

Using the Grand Magic of Body-Division in the Assembly of Gods, Pilgrim ripped off all the hairs on his left arm. He blew his immortal breath on them, crying, "Change!" They all changed into tiny Pilgrims. From his right arm he pulled off all the hairs, too, and blew his immortal breath on them, crying, "Change!" They changed into sleep-inducing insects. Then he recited another magic spell which began with the letter *Oṁ*, to summon the local spirits of the region into his presence. They were told to lead the small Pilgrims so that they could scatter throughout the royal palace, the Five Military Commissions, the Six Ministries, and the residences of officials high and low. Anyone with rank and appointment would be given a sleep-inducing insect, so that he would sleep soundly without even turning over.

Pilgrim also took up his golden-hooped rod; with a sqeeze and a wave, he cried, "Treasure, change!" It changed at once into hundreds and thousands of razor blades. He took one of them, and he told the tiny Pilgrims each to take one, so that they could go into the palace, the commissions, and the ministries to shave heads. Ah! This is how it was:

Dharma-king would the boundless dharma destroy,
Which fills the world and reaches the great Way.
All dharma-causes are of substance one;
Trīyana's wondrous forms are all the same.

The jade cupboard's drilled through, the truth is known;
Gold hairs are scattered and blindness is removed.
Dharma-king will surely the right fruit attain:
Birthless and deathless, he'll live in the void.

The shaving activities which went on for half the night were completely successful. Thereafter Pilgrim recited his spell to dismiss the local spirits. With one shake of his body he retrieved the hairs of both his arms. The razor blades he squeezed back into their true and original form—one golden-hooped rod—which he then reduced in size to store in his ear once more. He next assumed the form of an ant to crawl back into the wardrobe before changing into his original appearance to accompany the Tang monk in his confinement. There we shall leave them for the moment.

We tell you now about those palace maidens and harem girls in the inner chambers of the royal palace, who rose before dawn to wash and do their hair. Everyone of them had lost her hair. The hair of all the palace eunuchs, young and old, had also vanished. They crowded outside the palatial bed-chambers to start the music for waking the royal couple, all fighting hard to hold back their tears and not daring to report their mishap.

In a little while, the queen of the three palaces awoke, and she too found that her hair was gone. Hurriedly she moved a lamp to glance at the dragon bed: there in the midst of the silk coverlets a monk was sleeping![4] Unable to contain herself, the queen began to speak and her words awoke the king. When the king opened his eyes, all he saw was the bald head of the queen. Sitting bolt upright, he said, "My queen, why do you look like this?

"But my lord is also like this!" replied the queen. One touch of his own head sent the king into sheer panic, crying "What has become of us?" In that moment of desperation, the consorts of six halls, the palace maidens, and the eunuchs young and old all entered with bald heads. They knelt down and said, "Our lord, we have all become Buddhist priests!"

When the king saw them, tears fell from his eyes. "It must be the result of our slaughtering the monks," he said. Whereupon he gave this decree: "You are forbidden, all of you, to mention your loss of hair, for we fear that the civil and military officials would criticize the unrighteousness of the state. Let's prepare to hold court at the main hall."

We tell you now about all those officials, high and low, in the Five

4. This entire comic episode is built on the pun of the words *dharma* and hair, both of which in Chinese are vocalized as *fa*. The dharma-destroying king thus meets his reversal as the king who has lost his hair overnight.

Commissions and Six Ministries, who were about to have an audience with the Throne at dawn. As each one of them, you see, had also lost his hair during the night, they were all busily preparing memorials to report the incident. Thus you could hear that

Three times the whip struck as they faced the king:
The cause of their shorn hair they would make known.

In doing so, the many military officials presented their memorials saying, "Our lord, please pardon your subjects for being remiss in their manners."[5]

"Our worthy ministers have not departed from their customary good deportment," replied the king. "What is remiss in your manners?'

"O Our Lord!" said the various ministers, "we do not know the reason, but during the night all your subjects lost their hair." Clutching those memorials that complained of hair loss, the king descended from his dragon couch to say to his subjects, "Indeed we do not know the reason either, but we and the other members of the royal palace, high and low, also lost all our hair." As tears gushed from their eyes, ruler and subjects said to one another, "From now on, we wouldn't dare slaughter monks!"

Then the king ascended his dragon couch once more as the officials returned to standing in ranks. The king said, "Let those who have any business leave their ranks to present their memorials; if there is no further business, the let the screen be rolled up so that the court may retire." From the ranks of military officials the city patrol commander stepped out, and from the ranks of the civil officials the East City Warden walked forward. Both came up to the steps to kowtow and say, "By your sage decree your subjects were on patrol last night, and we succeeded in recovering the stolen goods of one wardrobe and one white horse. Your lowly subjects dare not dispose of these by our own authority, and we beg you to render a decision." Highly pleased, the king said, "Bring us both horse and wardrobe."

As soon as the two officials went back to their offices, they immediately summoned their troops to haul out the wardrobe. Locked inside, Tripitaka became so terrified that his soul was about to leave his body. "Disciples," he said, "what do we say once we appear before the king?"

Laughing, Pilgrim said, "Stop fussing! I have made the proper arrangements! When they open the wardrobe, they'll bow to us as their teachers. Just tell Bajie not to wrangle over seniority!" "To be spared from execution," said Bajie, "is already boundless blessing! You think I dare wrangle!"

5. The remaining portion of this chapter is taken actually from the beginning of chapter 85 of the full-length novel.

Hardly had they finished talking when the wardrobe was hauled to the court; the soldiers carried it inside the Five-Phoenix Tower and placed it before the vermilion steps.

When the subjects asked the king to inspect the wardrobe, he immediately commanded that it be opened. The moment the cover was lifted, however, Zhu Bajie could not refrain from leaping out, so terrifying the various officials that they were all struck dumb. Then they saw the Tang monk emerging, supported by Pilgrim Sun, while Sha Monk brought out the luggage. When Bajie caught sight of the commander holding the horse, he rushed forward and bellowed: "The horse is ours! Give it to me!" The commander was so frightened that he fell backward head over heels.

As the four of them stood on the steps, the king noticed that they were all Buddhist priests. Hurrying down from his dragon couch, the king asked all his consorts of the three palaces to join his subjects in descending from the Treasure Hall of Golden Chimes and bowing with him to the clerics. "Where did the elders come from?" the king asked.

Tripitaka said, "We are those sent by the Throne of the Great Tang in the Land of the East to go to India's Great Thunderclap Monastery in the West to seek true scriptures from the living Buddha."

"If the Venerable Master had come from such a great distance," said the king, "for what reason did you choose to rest in a wardrobe?"

"Your humble cleric," replied Tripitaka, "had learned of Your Majesty's vow to slaughter monks. We therefore dared not approach your superior state openly. Disguising ourselves as laymen, we came by night to an inn in your treasure region to ask for lodging. As we were afraid that people might still recognize our true identity, we chose to sleep in the wardrobe, which unfortunately was stolen by thieves. It was then recovered by the commander and brought here. Now that I am privileged to behold the dragon countenance of Your Majesty, I feel as if I had caught sight of the sun after the clouds had parted. I beg Your Majesty to extend your grace and favor wide as the sea to pardon and release this humble cleric."

"The Venerable Master is a noble priest from the Heavenly court of a superior state," replied the king, "and it is we who have been remiss in our welcome. The reason for our vow to slaughter monks stems from the fact that we were slandered by certain priests in years past. We therefore vowed to Heaven to kill ten thousand monks as a figure of perfection. Little did we anticipate that we would be forced to become monks instead, for all of us—ruler and subjects, king and consorts—now have had our hair shorn off. We, in turn, beg the Venerable Master not to be sparing in your great virtue and accept us as your disciples."

When Bajie heard these words, he roard with laughter, saying, "If you want to be our disciples, what sort of presentation gifts do you have for us?" "If the Master is willing," said the king, "we would be prepared to offer you the treasures and wealth of the state." "Don't mention treasures and wealth," said Pilgrim, "for we are the sort of monks who keep to our principles. Only certify our travel rescript and escort us out of the city. We promise you that your kingdom will be secure forever, and you will be endowed with blessings and long life in abundance."

When the king heard that, he at once ordered the Court of Imperial Entertainments to prepare a huge banquet. Ruler and subjects, meanwhile, prostrated themselves to return to the One. The travel rescript was certified immediately, and then the king requested the masters to change the name of his kingdom. "Your Majesty," said Pilgrim, "the name of Dharma Kingdom is an excellent one; it's only the word 'Destroying' that's inadequate. Since we have passed through this region, you may change its name to Dharma-Honoring Kingdom. We promise that you will

In calm sea and river prosper a thousand years
With rain and wind in season and in all quarters peace."

After thanking Pilgrim, the king asked for the imperial cortege and the entire court to escort master and disciples out of the city so they could leave for the West. Then ruler and subjects held fast to virtue to return to the truth, and we shall speak no more of them.

We tell you now about the elder, who took leave of the king of the Dharma-Honoring Kingdom. As he rode along, he said in great delight, "Wukong, you've employed an excellent method this time, and you've achieved a great merit."

"O Elder Brother," said Sha Monk, "where did you find so many barbers to shave off so many heads during the night?" Thereupon Pilgrim gave a thorough account of how he underwent transformations and exercised magic powers. Master and disciples laughed so hard they could hardly get their mouths shut. We do not know what happened thereafter; let's listen to the explanation in the next chapter.

Only when ape and horse are tamed will shells be cast;
With merit and work perfected, they see the Real.

We shall now tell you about the Tang monk and his three disciples, who set out on the main road.

In truth the land of Buddha in the West was quite different from other regions. What they saw everywhere were gemlike flowers and jasperlike grasses, aged cypresses and hoary pines. In the regions they passed through, every family was devoted to good works, and every household would feed the monks.

They met people in cultivation beneath the hills
And saw travellers reciting sūtras in the woods.

Resting at night and journeying at dawn, master and disciples proceeded for some six or seven days when they suddenly caught sight of a row of tall buildings and noble lofts. Truly

They soar skyward a hundred feet,
Tall and towering in the air.
You look down to see the setting sun
And reach out to pluck the shooting stars.
Spacious windows engulf the universe;
Lofty pillars join with the cloudy screens.
Yellow cranes bring letters[1] as autumn trees age;
Phoenix-sheets come with the cool evening breeze.
These are the treasure arches of a spirit palace,
The pearly courts and jeweled edifices,
The immortal hall where the Way is preached,
The cosmos where sūtras are taught.
The flowers bloom in the spring;
Pines grow green after the rain.

1. Immortals are thought to send their communications by means of magic birds like yellow cranes and blue phoenixes.

Purple agaric and divine fruits, fresh every year.

Phoenixes gambol, potent in every manner.

Lifting his whip to point ahead, Tripitaka said, "Wukong, what a lovely place!"

"Master," said Pilgrim, "you insisted on bowing down even in a specious region, before false images of Buddha. Today you have arrived at a true region with real images of Buddha, and you still haven't dismounted. What's your excuse?"

So taken aback was Tripitaka when he heard these words that he leaped down from the horse. Soon they arrived at the entrance to the buildings. A Daoist lad, standing before the gate, called out, "Are you the scripture seeker from the Land of the East?" Hurriedly tidying his clothes, the elder raised his head and looked at his interrogator.

He wore a robe of silk
And held a jade duster.
He wore a robe of silk
Often to feast at treasure lofts and jasper pools;
He held a jade yak's-tail
To wave and dust in the purple mansions.
From his arm hangs a sacred register,
And his feet are shod in sandals.
He floats—a true feathered-one;[2]
He's winsome—indeed uncanny!
Long life attained, he lives in this fine place;
Immortal, he can leave the world of dust.
The sage monk knows not our Mount Spirit guest:
The Immortal Golden Head of former years.[3]

The Great Sage, however, recognized the person. "Master," he cried, "this is the Great Immortal of the Golden Head, who resides in the Yuzhen Daoist Temple at the foot of the Spirit Mountain."

Only then did Tripitaka realize the truth, and he walked forward to make his bow. With laughter, the great immortal said, "So the sage monk has finally arrived this year. I have been deceived by the Bodhisattva Guanyin. When she received the gold decree from Buddha over ten years ago to find a scripture seeker in the Land of the East, she told me that he would be

2. From antiquity, it has been customary to refer to immortals or transcendents (and later, most Daoists) as feathered scholars (*yushi*) or feathered travelers (*yuke*). Upon success in cultivation, according to textual accounts, the adept would sprout feathers all over his body, sometimes even wings like Christian angels, so that they could ascend to Heaven.

3. Former years: the narrative here refers back to the account in chapter 8.

here after two or three years. I waited year after year for you, but no news came at all. Hardly have I anticipated that I would meet you this year!"

Pressing his palms together, Tripitaka said, "I'm greatly indebted to the great immortal's kindness. Thank you! Thank you!" The four pilgrims, leading the horse and toting the luggage, all went inside the temple before each of them greeted the great immortal once more. Tea and a vegetarian meal were ordered. The immortal also asked the lads to heat some scented liquid for the sage monk to bathe, so that he could ascend the land of Buddha. Truly,

It's good to bathe when merit and work are done,
When nature's tamed and the natural state is won.
All toils and labors are now at rest;
Law and obedience have renewed their zest.
At māra's end they reach indeed Buddha-land;
Their woes dispelled, before Śramaṇa they stand.
Unstained, they are washed of all filth and dust.
To a diamond body[4] return they must.

After master and disciples had bathed, it became late and they rested in the Yuzhen Temple.

Next morning the Tang monk changed his clothing and put on his brocade cassock and his Vairocana hat. Holding the priestly staff, he ascended the main hall to take leave of the great immortal. "Yesterday you seemed rather dowdy," said the great immortal, chuckling, "but today everything is fresh and bright. As I look at you now, you are a true of son of Buddha!" After a bow, Tripitaka wanted to set out at once.

"Wait a moment," said the great immortal. "Allow me to escort you." "There's no need for that," said Pilgrim. "Old Monkey knows the way."

"What you know happens to be the way in the clouds," said the great immortal, "a means of travel to which the sage monk has not yet been elevated. You must still stick to the main road."

"What you say is quite right," replied Pilgrim. "Though old Monkey has been to this place several times, he has always come and gone on the clouds and he has never stepped on the ground. If we must stick to the main road, we must trouble you to escort us a distance. My master's most eager to bow to Buddha. Let's not dally." Smiling broadly, the great immortal held the Tang monk's hand

To lead Candana up the gate of Law.

The way that they had to go, you see, did not lead back to the front gate. Instead, they had to go through the central hall of the temple to go

---

4. Here a reference to the diamond incorruptible body of Buddhahood.

out the rear door. Immediately behind the temple, in fact, was the Spirit Mountain, to which the great immortal pointed and said, "Sage Monk, look at the spot halfway up the sky, shrouded by auspicious luminosity of five colors and a thousand folds of hallowed mists. That's the tall Spirit Vulture Peak, the holy region of the Buddhist Patriarch."

The moment the Tang monk saw it, he began to bend low. With a chuckle, Pilgrim said, "Master, you haven't reached that place where you should bow down. As the proverb says, 'Even within sight of a mountain you can ride a horse to death!' You are still quite far from that principality. Why do you want to bow down now? How many times does your head need to touch the ground if you kowtow all the way to the summit?"

"Sage Monk," said the great immortal, "you, along with the Great Sage, Heavenly Reeds, and Curtain-Raising, have arrived at the blessed land when you can see Mount Spirit. I'm going back." Thereupon Tripitaka bowed to take leave of him.

The Great Sage led the Tang monk and his disciples slowly up the mountain. They had not gone for more than five or six miles when they came upon a torrent of water, eight or nine miles wide. There was no trace of human activity all around. Alarmed by the sight, Tripitaka said, "Wukong, this must be the wrong way! Could the great immortal have made a mistake? Look how wide and swift this river is! Without a boat, how could we get across?"

"There's no mistake!" said Pilgrim, chuckling. "Look over there! Isn't that a large bridge? You have to walk across that bridge before you can perfect the right fruit." The elder walked up to the bridge and saw beside it a tablet, on which was the inscription "Cloud-Transcending Stream." The bridge was actually a single log. Truly

Afar off, it's like a jade beam in the sky;
Near, a dried stump that o'er the water lies.
To bind up oceans it would easier seem.
How could one walk a single log or beam
Shrouded by rainbows of ten thousand feet,
By a thousand layers of silk-white sheet?
Too slipp'ry and small for all to cross its spread
Except those who on colored mists can tread.

Quivering all over, Tripitaka said, "Wukong, this bridge is not for human beings to cross. Let's find some other way."

"This is the way! This is the way!" said Pilgrim, laughing.

"If this is the way," said Bajie, horrified, "who dares walk on it? The water's so wide and rough. There's only a single log here, and it's so narrow and slippery. How could I move my legs?"

"Stand still, all of you," said Pilgrim. "Let old Monkey take a walk for you to see." Dear Great Sage! In big strides he bounded on to the single-log bridge. Swaying from side to side, he ran across it in no time at all. On the other side he shouted: "Come across! Come across!"

The Tang monk waved his hands, while Bajie and Sha Monk bit their fingers, all crying, "Hard! Hard! Hard!"

Pilgrim dashed back from the other side and pulled at Bajie, saying, "Idiot! Follow me! Follow me!" Lying flat on the ground, Bajie said, "It's much too slippery! Much too slippery! Let me go, please! Let me mount the wind and fog to get over there." Pushing him down, Pilgrim said, "What sort of a place do you think this is that you are permitted to mount wind and fog! Unless you walk across this bridge, you'll never become a Buddha." "O Elder Brother!" said Bajie. "It's okay with me if I don't become a Buddha. But I'm not going on that bridge!"

Right beside the bridge, the two of them started a tug-of-war. Only Sha Monk's admonitions managed to separate them. Tripitaka happened to turn his head, and he suddenly caught sight of someone punting a boat upstream and crying, "Ahoy! Ahoy!"

Highly pleased, the elder said, "Disciples, stop your frivolity! There's a boat coming." The three of them leaped up and stood still to stare at the boat. When it drew near, they found that it was a bottomless one. With his fiery eyes and diamond pupils, Pilgrim at once recognized that the ferryman was in fact the Conductor Buddha, also named the Light of Ratnadhvaja. Without revealing the Buddha's identity, however, Pilgrim simply said, "Over here! Punt it this way!"

Immediately the boatman punted it up to the shore. "Ahoy! Ahoy!" he cried. Terrified by what he saw, Tripitaka said, "How could this bottomless boat of yours carry anybody?" The Buddhist Patriarch said, "This boat of mine

Since creation's dawn has achieved great fame;
Punted by me, it has e'er been the same.
Upon the wind and wave it's still secure:
With no end or beginning its joy is sure.
It can return to One, completely clean,
Through ten thousand kalpas a sail serene.
Though bottomless boats may ne'er cross the sea,
This ferries all souls through eternity."

Pressing his palms together to thank him, the Great Sage Sun said, "I thank you for your great kindness in coming to receive and lead my master. Master, get on the boat. Though it is bottomless, it is safe. Even if there are wind and waves, it will not capsize."

The elder still hesistated, but Pilgrim took him by the shoulder and gave him a shove. With nothing to stand on, that master tumbled straight into the water, but the boatman swiftly pulled him out. As he stood on the side of the boat, the master kept shaking out his clothes and stamping his feet as he grumbled at Pilgrim. Pilgrim, however, helped Sha Monk and Bajie to lead the horse and tote the luggage into the boat. As they all stood on the gunwale, the Buddhist Patriarch gently punted the vessel away from shore. All at once they saw a corpse floating down the upstream, the sight of which filled the elder with terror.

"Don't be afraid, Master," said Pilgrim, laughing. "It's actually you!"

"It's you! It's you!" said Bajie also.

Clapping his hands, Sha Monk also said, "It's you! It's you!"

Adding his voice to the chorus, the boatman also said, "That's you! Congratulations! Congratulations!" Then the three disciples repeated this chanting in unison as the boat was punted across the water. In no time at all, they crossed the Divine Cloud-Transcending Stream all safe and sound. Only then did Tripitaka turn and skip lightly onto the other shore. We have here a testimonial poem, which says:

Delivered from their mortal flesh and bone,
A primal spirit of mutual love has grown.
Their work done, they become Buddhas this day,
Free of their former six-six senses'[5] sway.

Truly this is what is meant by the profound wisdom and the boundless dharma which enable a person to reach the other shore.

The moment the four pilgrims went ashore and turned around, the boatman and even the bottomless boat had disappeared. Only then did Pilgrim point out that it was the Conductor Buddha, and immediately Tripitaka awoke to the truth. Turning quickly, he thanked his three disciples instead.

Pilgrim said, "We two parties need not thank each other, for we are meant to support each other. We are indebted to our master for our liberation, through which we have found the gateway to the making of merit, and fortunately we have achieved the right fruit. Our master also has to rely on our protection so that he may be firm in keeping both law and faith to find the happy deliverance from this mortal stock. Master, look at this surpassing scenery of flowers and grass, pines and bamboos, phoenixes, cranes, and deer. Compared with those places of illusion manufactured by

5. Six-six senses: the intensive form of the six impure qualities engendered by the objects and organs of sense: sight, sound, smell, taste, touch, and idea.

monsters and deviates, which ones do you think are pleasant and which ones bad? Which ones are good and which evil?" Tripitaka expressed his thanks repeatedly as every one of them with lightness and agility walked up the Spirit Mountain. Soon this was the aged Thunderclap Monastery which came into view:

Its top touches the firmament;
Its root joins the Sumeru range.
Wondrous peaks in rows;
Strange boulders rugged.
Beneath the cliffs, jade-grass and jasper-flowers;
By the path, purple agaric and scented orchid.
Divine apes plucking fruits in the peach orchard
Seem like fire-burnished gold;
White cranes perching on the tips of pine branches
Resemble mist-shrouded jade.
Male phoenixes in pairs—
Female phoenixes in twos—
Male phoenixes in pairs
Make one call facing the sun to bless the world;
Female phoenixes in twos
Whose radiant dance in the wind is rarely seen
You see too those mandarin duck tiles of lustrous gold,
And luminous, patterned bricks cornelian-gilt.
In the east
And in the west
Stand rows of scented halls and pearly arches;
To the north
And to the south,
An endless sight of treasure lofts and precious towers.
The Devarāja Hall emits lambent mists;
The Dharma-guarding Hall sends forth purple flames.
The stūpa's clear form;
The Utpala's fragrance.
Truly a fine place similar to Heaven
With lazy clouds to make the day long.
The causes cease, red dust can't come at all:
Safe from all kalpas is this great Dharma Hall.

Footloose and carefree, master and disciples walked to the summit of Mount Spirit, where under a forest of green pines they saw a group of upāsikās and rows of worshipers in the midst of verdant cypresses. Immediately the elder bowed to them, so startling the upāsakas and upāsikās, the monks and the nuns, that they all pressed their palms together, saying, "Sage Monk, you should not render us such homage. Wait till you see Śākyamuni, and then you may come to exchange greetings with us."

"He is *always* in such a hurry!" said Pilgrim, laughing. "Let's go to bow to those seated at the top!" His arms and legs dancing with excitement, the elder followed Pilgrim straight up to the gate of the Thunderclap Monastery. There they were met by the Four Great Vajra Guardians, who said, "Has the sage monk arrived?"

Bending low, Tripitaka said, "Yes, your disciple Xuanzang has arrived." No sooner had he given this reply than he wanted to go inside. "Please wait a moment, Sage Monk," said the Vajra Guardians. "Allow us to announce your arrival first before you enter." One of the Vajra Guardians was asked to report to the other Four Great Vajra Guardians stationed at the second gate, and one of those porters passed the news of the Tang monk's arrival to the third gate. Those guarding the third gate happened to be divine monks who served at the great altar. When they heard the news, they quickly went to the Great Hero Hall to announce to Tathāgata, the Most Honored One, also named Buddha Śākyamuni, "The sage monk from the Tang court has arrived in this treasure monastery. He has come to fetch the scriptures."

Highly pleased, Holy Father Buddha at once asked the Eight Bodhisattvas, the Four Vajra Guardians, the Five Hundred Arhats, the Three Thousand Guardians, the Eleven Great Orbs, and the Eighteen Guardians of Monasteries to form two rows for the reception. Then he issued the golden decree to summon in the Tang monk. Again the word was passed from section to section, from gate to gate: "Let the sage monk enter." Meticulously observing the rules of ritual propriety, our Tang monk walked through the monastery gate with Wukong, Wuneng, and Wujing, still leading the horse and toting the luggage. Thus it was that

Commissioned that year, a resolve he made
To leave with rescript the royal steps of jade.
The hills he'd climb to face the morning dew
Or rest on a boulder when the twilight fades.
He totes his faith to ford three thousand streams,
His staff trailing o'er endless palisades.
His every thought's on seeking the right fruit.
Homage to Buddha will this day be paid.

The four pilgrims, on reaching the Great Hero Treasure Hall, prostrated themselves before Tathāgata. Thereafter, they bowed to all the attendants of Buddha on the left and right. This they repeated three times before kneeling again before the Buddhist Patriarch to present their traveling rescript to him. After reading it carefully, Tathāgata handed it back to Tripitaka, who touched his head to the ground once more to say, "By the decree of the Great Tang Emperor in the Land of the East, your disciple Xuanzang has come to this treasure monastery to beg you for the true scriptures for the redemption of the multitude. I implore the Buddhist Patriarch to vouchsafe his grace and grant me my wish, so that I may soon return to my country."

To express the compassion of his heart, Tathāgata opened his mouth of mercy and said to Tripitaka, "Your Land of the East belongs to the South Jambūdvīpa Continent. Because of your size and your fertile land, your prosperity and population, there is a great deal of greed and killing, lust and lying, oppression and deceit. People neither honor the teachings of Buddha nor cultivate virtuous karma; they neither revere the three lights nor respect the five grains. They are disloyal and unfilial, unrighteous and unkind, unscrupulous and self-deceiving. Through all manners of injustice and taking of lives, they have committed boundless transgressions. The fullness of their iniquities therefore has brought on them the ordeal of hell and sent them into eternal darkness and perdition to suffer the pains of pounding and grinding and of being transformed into beasts. Many of them will assume the forms of creatures with fur and horns; in this manner they will repay their debts by having their flesh made for food for mankind. These are the reasons for their eternal perdition in Avīci without deliverance.

"Though Confucius had promoted his teachings of benevolence, righteousness, ritual, and wisdom, and though a succession of kings and emperors had established such penalties as transportation, banishment, hanging, and beheading, these institutions had little effect on the foolish and the blind, the reckless and the antinomian.

"Now, I have here three baskets of scriptures which can deliver humanity from its afflictions and dispel its calamities. There is one basket of vinaya, which speak of Heaven; a basket of śāstras, which tell of the Earth; and a basket of sūtras, which redeem the damned. Altogether these three baskets of scriptures contain thirty-five titles written in fifteen thousand one hundred and forty-four scrolls. They are truly the pathway to the realization of immortality and the gate to ultimate virtue. Every concern of astronomy, geography, biography, flora and fauna, utensils, and human affairs within the Four Great Continents of this world is recorded therein. Since all of you have traveled such a great distance to come here, I would have liked to give the entire set to you. Unfortunately, the people of your region are both stupid and headstrong. Mocking the true words, they refuse to recognize the profound significance of our teachings of Śramaṇa."

Then Buddha turned to call out: "Ānanda and Kāśyapa, take the four of them to the space beneath the precious tower. Give them a vegetarian meal first. After the maigre, open our treasure loft for them and select a few scrolls from each of the thirty-five divisions of our three canons, so that they may take them back to the Land of the East as a perpetual token of grace."

The two Honored Ones obeyed and took the four pilgrims to the space beneath the tower, where countless rare dainties and exotic treasures were laid out in a seemingly endless spread. Those deities in charge of offerings and sacrifices began to serve a magnificent feast of divine food, tea, and fruit—viands of a hundred flavors completely different from those of the mortal world. After master and disciples had bowed to give thanks to Buddha, they abandoned themselves to enjoyment. In truth

Treasure flames, gold beams on their eyes have shined;
Strange fragrance and feed even more refined.
Boundlessly fair the tow'r of gold appears;
There's immortal music that clears the ears.
Such divine fare and flower humans rarely see;
Long life's attained through strange food and fragrant tea.
Long have they endured a thousand forms of pain.
This day in glory the Way they're glad to gain.

This time it was Bajie who was in luck and Sha Monk who had the advantage, for what the Buddhist Patriarch had provided for their complete enjoyment was nothing less than such viands as could grant them longevity and health and enable them to transform their mortal substance into immortal flesh and bones.

When the four pilgrims had finished their meal, the two Honored Ones who had kept them company led them up to the treasure loft. The moment the door was opened, they found the room enveloped in a thousand layers of auspicious air and magic beams, in ten thousand folds of colored fog and hallowed clouds. On the sūtra cases and jeweled chests red labels were attached, on which the titles of the books were written in clerkly script. After Ānanda and Kāśyapa had shown all the titles to the Tang monk, they said to him, "Sage Monk, having come all this distance from the Land of the East, what sort of small gifts have you brought for us? Take them out quickly! We'll be pleased to hand over the scriptures to you."

On hearing this, Tripitaka said, "Because of the great distance, your disciple, Xuanzang, has not been able to make such preparation."

"How nice! How nice!" said the two Honored Ones, snickering. "If we imparted the scriptures to you gratis, our posterity would starve to death!"

When Pilgrim saw them fidgeting and fussing, refusing to hand over the scriptures, he could not refrain from yelling, "Master, let's go tell Tathāgata about this! Let's make him come himself and hand over the scriptures to old Monkey!"

"Stop shouting!" said Ānanda. "Where do you think you are that you dare indulge in such mischief and waggery? Get over here and receive the scriptures!" Controlling their annoyance, Bajie and Sha Monk managed to restrain Pilgrim before they turned to receive the books. Scroll after scroll were wrapped and laid on the horse. Four additional luggage wraps were bundled up for Bajie and Sha Monk to tote, after which the pilgrims went before the jeweled throne again to kowtow and thank Tathāgata. As they walked out the gates of the monastery, they bowed twice whenever they came upon a Buddhist Patriarch or a Bodhisattva. When they reached the main gate, they also bowed to take leave of the priests and nuns, the upāsakas and upāsikās, before descending the mountain. We shall now leave them for the moment.

We tell you now that there was up in the treasure loft the aged Dīpaṁkara, also named the Buddha of the Past, who overheard everything and understood immediately that Ānanda and Kāśyapa had handed over to the pilgrims scrolls of scriptures that were actually wordless. Chuckling to himself, he said, "Most of the priests in the Land of the East are so stupid and blind that they will not recognize the value of these wordless scriptures. When that happens, won't it have made this long trek of our sage monk completely worthless?" Then he asked, "Who is here beside my throne?"

The White Heroic Honored One at once stepped forth, and the aged Buddha gave him this instruction: "You must exercise your magic powers and catch up with the Tang monk immediately. Take away those wordless scriptures from him, so that he will be forced to return for the true scriptures with words." Mounting a violent gust of wind, the White Heroic Honored One swept out of the gate of the Thunderclap Monastery. As he called up his vast magic powers, the wind was strong indeed! Truly

A stalwart Servant of Buddha
Is not like any common wind god;
The wrathful cries of an immortal
Far surpass a young girl's whistle!
This mighty gust

Causes fishes and dragons to lose their lairs
And angry waves in the rivers and seas.
Black apes find it hard to present their fruits;
Yellow cranes turn around to seek their nests.
The phoenix's pure cries have lost their songs;
The pheasant's callings turn most boisterous.
Green pine-branches snap;
Blue lotus-blossoms soar.
Stalk by stalk, verdant bamboos fall;
Petal by petal, gold lotus quakes.
Bell tones drift away to three thousand miles;
The scripture chants o'er countless gorges fly.
Beneath the cliff rare flowers' colors fade;
Fresh, jadelike grasses lie down by the road.
Phoenixes can't stretch their wings;
White deer hide on the ledge.
Vast waves of strange fragrance now fill the world
As cool, clear breezes penetrate the Heavens.

The elder Tang was walking along when he encountered this churning fragrant wind. Thinking that this was only an auspicious portent sent by the Buddhist Patriarch, he was completely off guard when, with a loud crack in midair, a hand descended. The scriptures that were loaded on the horse were lifted away with no effort at all. The sight left Tripitaka yelling in terror and beating his breast, while Bajie rolled off in pursuit on the ground and Sha Monk stood rigid to guard the empty pannier. Pilgrim Sun vaulted into the air. When that White Heroic Honored One saw him closing in rapidly, he feared that Pilgrim's rod might strike out blindly without regard for good or ill to cause him injury. He therefore ripped the scriptures open and threw them toward the ground. When Pilgrim saw that the scripture wrappers were torn and their contents scattered all over by the fragrant wind, he lowered the direction of his cloud to go after the books instead and stopped his pursuit. The White Heroic Honored One retrieved the wind and fog and returned to report to the Buddha of the Past.

As Bajie sped along, he saw the holy books dropping down from the sky. Soon he was joined by Pilgrim, and the two of them gathered up the scrolls to go back to the Tang monk. His eyes brimming with tears, the Tang monk said, "O Disciples! We are bullied by vicious demons even in this land of ultimate bliss!" When Sha Monk opened up a scroll of scripture which the other two disciples were clutching, his eyes perceived only snow-white paper without a trace of so much as half a letter on it.

Hurriedly he presented it to Tripitaka, saying, "Master, this scroll is wordless!" Pilgrim also opened a scroll and it, too, was wordless. Then Bajie opened still another scroll, and it was also wordless. "Open all of them!" cried Tripitaka. Every scroll had only blank paper.

Heaving big sighs, the elder said, "Our people in the Land of the East simply have no luck! What good is it to take back a wordless, empty volume like this? How could I possibly face the Tang emperor? The crime of mocking one's ruler is greater than one punishable by execution!"

Already perceiving the truth of the matter, Pilgrim said to the Tang monk, "Master, there's no need for further talk. This has all come about because we had no gifts for these fellows, Ānanda and Kāśyapa. That's why we were given these wordless texts. Let's go back quickly to Tathāgata and charge them with fraud and solicitation for a bribe."

"Exactly! Exactly!" yelled Bajie. "Let's go and charge them!" The four pilgrims turned and, with painful steps, once more ascended Thunderclap.

In a little while they reached the temple gates, where they were met by the multitude with hands folded in their sleeves. "Has the sage monk returned to ask for an exchange of scriptures?" they asked, laughing. Tripitaka nodded his affirmation, and the Vajra Guardians permitted them to go straight inside. When they arrived before the Great Hero Hall, Pilgrim shouted, "Tathāgata, we master and disciples had to experience ten thousand stings and a thousand demons in order to come bowing from the Land of the East. After you had specifically ordered the scriptures to be given to us, Ānanda and Kāśyapa sought a bribe from us; when they didn't succeed, they conspired in fraud and deliberately handed over wordless texts to us. Even if we took them, what good would they do? Pardon me, Tathāgata, but you must deal with this matter!"

"Stop shouting!" said the Buddhist Patriarch with a chuckle. "I knew already that the two of them would ask you for a little present. After all, the holy scriptures are not to be given lightly, nor are they to be received gratis. Some time ago, in fact, a few of our sage priests went down the mountain and recited these scriptures in the house of one Elder Zhao in the Kingdom of Śrāvastī, so that the living in his family would all be protected from harm and the deceased redeemed from perdition. For all that service they managed to charge him only three pecks and three pints of rice. I told them that they had made far too cheap a sale and that their posterity would have no money to spend. Since you people came with empty hands to acquire scriptures, blank texts were handed over to you. But these blank texts are actually true, wordless scriptures, and they are just as good as those with words. However, those creatures in your Land of the East are so foolish and unenlightened that I have no choice but to impart to you now the texts with words."

"Ānanda and Kāśyapa," he then called out, "quickly select for them a few scrolls from each of the titles of true scriptures with words, and then come back to me to report the total number."

The two Honored Ones again led the four pilgrims to the treasure loft, where they once more demanded a gift from the Tang monk. Since he had virtually nothing to offer, Tripitaka told Sha Monk to take out the alms bowl of purple gold. With both hands he presented it to the Honored Ones, saying, "Your disciple in truth has not brought with him any gift, owing to the great distance and my own poverty. This alms bowl, however, was bestowed by the Tang emperor in person, in order that I could use it to beg for my maigre, throughout the journey. As the humblest token of my gratitude, I am presenting it to you now, and I beg the Honored Ones to accept it. When I return to the court and make my report to the Tang emperor, a generous reward will certainly be forthcoming. Only grant us the true scriptures with words, so that His Majesty's goodwill will not be thwarted nor the labor of this lengthy journey be wasted." With a gentle smile, Ānanda took the alms bowl. All those vīra who guarded the precious towers, the kitchen helpers in charge of sacrifices and incense, and the Honored Ones who worked in the treasure loft began to clap one another on the back and tickle one another on the face. Snapping their fingers and curling their lips, every one of them said, "How shameless! How shameless! Asking the scripture seeker for a present!"

After a while, the two Honored Ones became rather embarrassed, though Ānanda continued to clutch firmly at the alms bowl. Kāśyapa, however, went into the loft to select the scrolls and handed them item by item to Tripitaka. "Disciples," said Tripitaka, "take a good look at these, and make sure that they are not like the earlier ones."

The three disciples examined each scroll as they received it, and this time all the scrolls had words written on them. Altogether they were given five thousand and forty-eight scrolls, making up the number of a single canon. After being properly packed, the scriptures were loaded onto the horse. An additional load was made for Bajie to tote, while their own luggage was toted by Sha Monk. As Pilgrim led the horse, the Tang monk took up his priestly staff and gave his Vairocana hat a press and his brocade cassock a shake. In delight they once more went before our Buddha Tathāgata. Thus it is that

> Sweet is the taste of the Great Piṭaka,
> Product most refined of Tathāgata.

Note how Xuanzang has climbed the mount with pain.
Pity Ānanda who has but love of gain.
Their blindness removed by Buddha of the Past,
The truth now received peace they have at last—
Glad to bring scriptures back to the East,
Where all may partake of this gracious feast.

Ānanda and Kāśyapa led the Tang monk before Tathāgata, who ascended the lofty lotus throne. He ordered Dragon-Tamer and Tiger-Subduer, the two arhats, to strike up the cloudy stone-chime to assemble all the divinities, including the three thousand Buddhas, the three thousand guardians, the Eight Vajra Guardians, the five hundred arhats, the eight hundred nuns and priests, the upāsakas and upāsikās, the Honored Ones from every Heaven and cave-dwelling, from every blessed land and spirit mountain. Those who ought to be seated were asked to ascend their treasure thrones, while those who should stand were told to make two columns on both sides. In a moment celestial music filled the air as layers of auspicious luminosity and hallowed mist loomed up in the sky. After all the Buddhas had assembled, they bowed to greet Tathāgata.

Then Tathāgata asked, "Ānanda and Kāśyapa, how many scrolls of scriptures have you passed on to him? Give me an itemized report."

The two Honored Ones said, "We have turned over to the Tang court the following:

1.	The Nirvāṇa Sūtra	400 scrolls
2.	The Ākāśagarbha-bodhisattva-dharmi Sūtra	20 scrolls
3.	The Gracious Will Sūtra, Major Collection	40 scrolls
4.	The Prajñāpāramitā-saṁkaya gāthā Sūtra	20 scrolls
5.	The Homage to Bhūtatathātā Sūtra	20 scrolls
6.	The Anakṣara-granthaka-rocana-garbha Sūtra	50 scrolls
7.	The Vimalakīrti-nirdeśa Sūtra	30 scrolls
8.	The Vajracchedika-prajñāpāramitā Sūtra	1 scroll
9.	The Buddha-carita-kāvya Sūtra	116 scrolls
10.	The Bodhisattva-piṭaka Sūtra	360 scrolls
11.	The Sūraṅgama-samādhi Sūtra	30 scrolls
12.	The Arthaviniścaya-dharmaparyāya Sūtra	40 scrolls
13.	The Avataṁsaka Sūtra	81 scrolls
14.	The Mahāprajñā-pāramitā Sūtra	600 scrolls
15.	The Abūta-dharma Sūtra	550 scrolls
16.	The Other Mādhyamika Sūtra	42 scrolls
17.	The Kāśyapa-parivarta Sūtra	20 scrolls
18.	The Pañca-nāga Sūtra	20 scrolls

19. *The Bodhisattva-caryā-nirdeśa Sūtra*	60 scrolls
20. *The Magadha Sūtra*	140 scrolls
21. *The Māyā-dālamahātantra mahāyāna-gambhīra nāya-guhya-paraśi Sūtra*	30 scrolls
22. *The Western Heaven Śāstra*	30 scrolls
23. *The Buddha-kṣetra Sūtra*	1,638 scrolls
24. *The Mahāprajñāpāramitā Śāstra*	90 scrolls
25. *The Original Loft Sūtra*	56 scrolls
26. *The Mahāmayūrī-vidyārajñī Sūtra*	14 scrolls
27. *The Abhidharma-kośa Śāstra*	10 scrolls
28. *The Mahāsaṃghata Sūtra*	30 scrolls
29. *The Saddharma-puṇḍarika Sūtra*	10 scrolls
30. *The Precious Permanence Sūtra*	170 scrolls
31. *The Sāṅghika-vinaya Sūtra*	110 scrolls
32. *The Mahāyāna-śraddhotpāda Śāstra*	50 scrolls
33. *The Precious Authority Sūtra*	140 scrolls
34. *The Correct Commandment Sūtra*	10 scrolls
35. *The Vidyā-mātra-siddhi Śāstra*	10 scrolls

From the thirty-five titles of scriptures that are in the treasury, we have selected altogether five thousand and forty-eight scrolls for the sage monk to take back to the Tang in the Land of the East. Most of these have been properly packed and loaded on the horse, and a few have also been arranged in a pannier. The pilgrims now wish to express their thanks to you."

Having tethered the horse and set down the poles, Tripitaka led his three disciples to bow to Buddha, each pressing his palms together in front of him. Tathāgata said to the Tang monk, "The efficacy of these scriptures cannot be measured. Not only are they the mirror of our faith, but they are also the source of the Three Religions. They must not be lightly handled, especially when you return to your South Jambūdvīpa Continent and display them to the multitude. No one should open a scroll without fasting and bathing first. Treasure them! Honor them! Therein will be found the mysteries of gaining immortality and comprehending the Way, the wondrous formulas for the execution of the thousand transformations." Tripitaka kowtowed to thank him and to express his faith and obedience. As before, he prostrated himself in homage three times to the Buddhist Patriarch with all earnestness and sincerity before he took the scriptures and left. As he went through the three monastery gates, he again thanked each of the sages, and we shall speak no more of him for the moment.

After he had sent away the Tang monk, Tathāgata dismissed the assembly for the transmission of scriptures. From one side stepped forth the Bodhisattva Guanshiyin, who pressed her palms together to say to the Buddhist Patriarch, "This disciple received your golden decree that year to search for someone in the Land of the East to be a scripture seeker. Today he has succeeded. Altogether, his journey took fourteen years or five thousand and forty days. Eight more days and the perfect canonical number will be attained. Would you permit me to surrender in return your golden decree?"

Highly pleased, Tathāgata said, "What you said is most appropriate. You are certainly permitted to surrender my golden decree." He then gave this instruction to the Eight Vajra Guardians: "Quickly exercise your magic powers to lift the sage monk back to the East. As soon as he has imparted the true scriptures to the people there, bring him back here to the West. You must accomplish all this within eight days, so as to fulfill the perfect canonical number of five thousand and forty-eight. Do not delay." The Vajra Guardians at once caught up with the Tang monk, crying, "Scripture seekers, follow us!" The Tang monk and his companions, all with healthy frames and buoyant bodies, followed the Vajra Guardians to rise in the air astride the clouds. Truly

Their minds enlightened, they bowed to Buddha;

Merit perfected, they ascended on high.

We do not know how they will pass on the scriptures after they have returned to the Land of the East; let's listen to the explanation in the next chapter.

Nine times nine ends the count and Māra's all destroyed;
The work of three times three¹ done, the Dao reverts to its root.

We shall not speak of the Eight Vajra Guardians escorting the Tang monk
back to his nation. We turn instead to those Guardians of the Five Quarters,
the Four Sentinels, the Six Gods of Darkness and the Six Gods of Light, and
the Guardians of Monasteries, who appeared before the triple gates and said
to the Bodhisattva Guanyin, "Your disciples had received the Bodhisattva's
dharma decree to give secret protection to the sage monk. Now that the
work of the sage monk is completed, and the Bodhisattva has returned
the Buddhist Patriarch's golden decree to him, we too request permission
from the Bodhisattva to return your dharma decree to you."

Highly pleased also, the Bodhisattva said, "Yes, yes! You have my permission." Then she asked, "What was the disposition of the four pilgrims
during their journey?"

"They showed genuine devotion and determination," replied the various deities, "which could hardly have escaped the penetrating observation
of the Bodhisattva. The Tang monk, after all, had endured unspeakable
sufferings. Indeed, all the ordeals which he had to undergo throughout
his journey have been recorded by your disciples. Here is the complete
account." The Bodhisattva started to read the registry from its beginning,
and this was the content:

The Guardians in obedience to your decree
Record with care the Tang monk's calamities.
Gold Cicada banished is the first ordeal [see chap. 8];²
Being almost killed after birth is the second ordeal [chap. 9];

1. Double three, or three times three, which equals nine, the number of perfection that is used in both Buddhist and Daoist (especially alchemical lore that utilizes
hexagramatical symbols derived from the *Classic of Change*) writings.
2. Chapter numbers throughout this catalog refer to those of the full-length
novel, *The Journey to the West*, 4 vols., trans. and ed. Anthony C. Yu (Chicago: University of Chicago Press, 1977–83).

Being thrown in the river hardly a month old is the third ordeal
[chap. 9];
Seeking parents and their vengeance is the fourth ordeal [chap. 9];
Meeting a tiger after leaving the city is the fifth ordeal [chap. 13];
Falling into a pit and losing followers is the sixth ordeal [chap. 13];
The Double-Fork Ridge is the seventh ordeal [chap. 13];
The Mountain of Two Frontiers is the eighth ordeal [chap. 13];
Changing horse at a steep brook is the ninth ordeal [chap. 15];
Burning by fire at night is the tenth ordeal [chap. 16];
Losing the cassock is the eleventh ordeal [chap. 16];
Bringing Bajie to submission is the twelfth ordeal [chaps. 18–19];
Being blocked by the Yellow Wind Fiend is the thirteenth ordeal
[chap. 20];
Seeking aid with Lingji is the fourteenth ordeal [chap. 21];
Hard to cross Flowing-Sand is the fifteenth ordeal [chap. 22];
Taking in Sha Monk is the sixteenth ordeal [chap. 22];
The Four Sages' epiphany is the seventeenth ordeal [chap. 23];
The Five Villages Temple is the eighteenth ordeal [chap. 24];
The ginseng hard to revive is the nineteenth ordeal [chap. 26];
Banishing the Mind Monkey is the twentieth ordeal [chap. 27];
Getting lost at Black Pine Forest is the twenty-first ordeal [chap. 28];
Sending a letter to Precious Image Kingdom is the twenty-second
ordeal [chap. 29];
Changing into a tiger at the Golden Chimes Hall is the twenty-third
ordeal[chap. 30];
Meeting demons at Level-Top Mountain is the twenty-fourth ordeal
[chap. 32];
Being hung high at Lotus-Flower Cave is the twenty-fifth ordeal
[chap. 33];
Saving the ruler of Black Rooster Kingdom is the twenty-sixth
ordeal [chap. 37];
Running into a demon's transformed body is the twenty-seventh
ordeal [chap. 37];
Meeting a fiend in Roaring Mountain is the twenty-eighth ordeal
[chap. 40];
The sage monk abducted by wind is the twenty-ninth ordeal [chap.
40];
The Mind Monkey being injured is the thirtieth ordeal [chap. 41];
Asking the sage to subdue monsters is the thirty-first ordeal [chap.
42];

Sinking in the Black River is the thirty-second ordeal [chap. 43];

Hauling at Cart Slow Kingdom is the thirty-third ordeal [chap. 44];

A mighty contest is the thirty-fourth ordeal [chaps. 45–46];

Expelling Daoists to prosper Buddhists is the thirty-fifth ordeal
[chap. 47];

Meeting a great water on the road is the thirty-sixth ordeal [chap.
47];

Falling into the Heaven-Reaching River is the thirty-seventh ordeal
[chap. 48];

The Fish-Basket revealing her body is the thirty-eighth ordeal [chap.
49];

Meeting a fiend at Golden Helmet Mountain is the thirty-ninth
ordeal [chap. 50];

Heaven's gods find it hard to win is the fortieth ordeal [chaps. 51–52];

Asking the Buddha for the source is the forty-first ordeal [chap. 52];

Being poisoned after drinking water is the forty-second ordeal [chap.
53];

Detained for marriage at Western Liang Kingdom is the forty-third
ordeal [chap. 54];

Suffering at the Cave of the Lute is the forty-fourth ordeal [chap.
55];

Banishing again the Mind Monkey is the forty-fifth ordeal [chap. 56];

The macaque hard to distinguish is the forty-sixth ordeal [chaps.
57–58];

The road blocked at the Mountain of Flames is the forty-seventh
ordeal [chap. 59];

Seeking the palm-leaf fan is the forty-eighth ordeal [chaps. 59–60];

Binding the demon king is the forty-ninth ordeal [chap. 61];

Sweeping the pagoda at Sacrifice Kingdom is the fiftieth ordeal [chap.
62];

Recovering the treasure to save the monks is the fifty-first ordeal
[chap. 63];

Chanting poetry at the Brambled Forest is the fifty-second ordeal
[chap. 64];

Meeting disaster at Little Thunderclap is the fifty-third ordeal [chap.
65];

The celestial gods being imprisoned is the fifty-fourth ordeal [chap.
66];

Being blocked by filth at Pulpy Persimmon Alley is the fifty-fifth
ordeal [chap. 67];

Applying medication at the Scarlet-Purple Kingdom is the fifty-sixth
ordeal [chaps. 68–69];

Healing fatigue and infirmity is the fifty-seventh ordeal [chaps.
68–69];

Subduing monster to recover a queen is the fifty-eighth ordeal
[chaps. 69–71];

Delusion by the seven passions is the fifty-ninth ordeal [chap. 72];

Being wounded by Many Eyes is the sixtieth ordeal [chap. 73];

The way blocked at the Lion-Camel Kingdom is the sixty-first ordeal
[chaps. 74–75];

The fiends divided into three colors is the sixty-second ordeal [chaps.
74–77];

Meeting calamity in the city is the sixty-third ordeal [chaps. 76–77];

Requesting Buddha to subdue the demons is the sixty-fourth ordeal
[chap. 77];

Rescuing the lads at Bhikṣu is the sixty-fifth ordeal [chap. 78];

Distinguishing the true from the deviate is the sixty-sixth ordeal
[chap. 79];

Saving a fiend at a pine forest is the sixty-seventh ordeal [chap. 80]:

Falling sick in a priestly chamber is the sixty-eighth ordeal [chap.
81];

Being imprisoned at the Bottomless Cave is the sixty-ninth ordeal
[chaps. 81–83];

Difficulty in going through Dharma-Destroying Kingdom is the
seventieth ordeal [chap. 84];

Meeting demons at Mist-Concealing Mountain is the seventy-first
ordeal [chaps. 85–86];

Seeking rain at Phoenix-Immortal Prefecture is the seventy-second
ordeal [chap. 87];

Losing their weapons is the seventy-third ordeal [chap. 88];

The festival of the rake is the seventy-fourth ordeal [chap. 89];

Meeting disaster at Bamboo-Knot Mountain is the seventy-fifth
ordeal [chap. 90];

Suffering at Mysterious Flower Cave is the seventy-sixth ordeal
[chap. 91];

Capturing the rhinoceroses is the seventy-seventh ordeal [chap. 92];

Being forced to marry at India is the seventy-eighth ordeal [chaps.
93–95];

Jailed at Bronze Terrace Prefecture is the seventy-ninth ordeal [chap.
97];

Delivered of mortal stock at Cloud-Transcending Stream is the
    eightieth ordeal [chap. 98];
The journey: one hundred and eight thousand miles.
The sage monk's ordeals are clearly on file.

After the Bodhisattva had read through the entire registry of ordeals, she
said hurriedly, "Within our order of Buddhism, nine times nine is the
crucial means by which one returns to immortality. The sage monk has
undergone eighty ordeals. Because one ordeal, therefore, is still lacking,
the sacred number is not yet complete."

At once she gave this order to one of the Guardians: "Catch the Vajra
Guardians and create one more ordeal." Having received this command,
the Guardian soared toward the east astride the clouds. After a night and
a day he caught the Vajra Guardians and whispered in their ears, "Do this
and this . . . ! Don't fail to obey the dharma decree of the Bodhisattva."
On hearing these words, the Eight Vajra Guardians immediately retrieved
the wind that had borne aloft the four pilgrims, dropping them and the
horse bearing the scriptures to the ground. Alas! Truly such is

Nine times nine, hard task of immortality!
Firmness of will yields the mysterious key.
By bitter toil you must the demons spurn;
Cultivation will the proper way return.
Regard not the scriptures as easy things.
So many are the sage monk's sufferings!
Learn of the old, wondrous Kinship of the Three:[3]
Elixir won't gel if there's slight errancy.

When his feet touched profane ground, Tripitaka became terribly frightened. Bajie, however, roared with laughter, saying, "Good! Good! Good!
This is exactly a case of 'More haste, less speed'!"

"Good! Good! Good!" said Sha Monk. "Because we've speeded up too
much, they want us to take a little rest here." "Have no worry," said the
Great Sage. "As the proverb says,

For ten days you sit on the shore;
In one day you may pass nine beaches."

"Stop matching your wits, you three!" said Tripitaka. "Let's see if we
can tell where we are." Looking all around, Sha Monk said, "I know the
place! I know the place! Master, listen to the sound of water!"

Pilgrim said, "The sound of water, I suppose, reminds you of your

---

3. *Kinship of the Three*: reputedly the earliest book on alchemical theory, by Wei
Boyang of the second century CE.

ancestral home." "Which is the Flowing-Sand River," said Bajie. "No! No!" said Sha Monk. "This happens to be the Heaven-Reaching River." Tripitaka said, "O Disciples! Take a careful look and see which side of the river we're on."

Vaulting into the air, Pilgrim shielded his eyes with his hand and took a careful survey of the place before dropping down once more. "Master," he said, "this is the west bank of the Heaven-Reaching River."

"Now I remember,"[4] said Tripitaka. "There was a Chen Village on the east bank. When we arrived here that year, you rescued their son and daughter. In their gratitude to us, they wanted to make a boat to take us across. Eventually we were fortunate enough to get across on the back of a white turtle. I recall, too, that there was no human habitation whatever on the west bank. What shall we do this time?"

"I thought that only profane people would practice this sort of fraud," said Bajie. "Now I know that even the Vajra Guardians before the face of Buddha can practice fraud! Buddha commanded them to take us back east. How could they just abandon us in mid-journey? Now we're in quite a bind! How are we going to get across?" "Stop grumbling, Second Elder Brother!" said Sha Monk. "Our master has already attained the Way, for he had already been delivered from his mortal frame previously at the Cloud-Transcending Stream. This time he can't possibly sink in water. Let's all of us exercise our magic of Displacement and take Master across."

"You can't take him over! You can't take him over!" said Pilgrim, chuckling to himself. Now, why did he say that? If he were willing to exercise his magic powers and reveal the mystery of flight, master and disciples could cross even a thousand rivers. He knew, however, that the Tang monk had not yet perfected the sacred number of nine times nine. That one remaining ordeal made it necessary for them to be detained at the spot.

As master and disciples conversed and walked slowly up to the edge of the water, they suddenly heard someone calling, "Tang Sage Monk! Tang Sage Monk! Come this way! Come this way!" Startled, the four of them looked all around but could not see any sign of a human being or a boat. Then they caught sight of a huge, white, scabby-headed turtle at the shoreline. "Old Master," he cried with outstretched neck, "I have waited for you for so many years! Have you returned only at this time?"

"Old Turtle," replied Pilgrim, smiling, "we troubled you in a year past, and today we meet again." Tripitaka, Bajie, and Sha Monk could not have been more pleased. "If indeed you want to serve us," said Pilgrim,

---

4. Tripitaka is recalling incidents of the episode narrated in chapters 47–49.

"come up on the shore." The turtle crawled up the bank. Pilgrim told his companions to guide the horse onto the turtle's back. As before, Bajie squatted at the rear of the horse, while the Tang monk and Sha Monk took up positions to the left and to the right of the horse. With one foot on the turtle's head and another on his neck, Pilgrim said, "Old Turtle, go steadily."

His four legs outstretched, the old turtle moved through the water as if he were on dry level ground, carrying all five of them—master, disciples, and the horse—straight toward the eastern shore. Thus it is that

In Advaya's[5] gate the dharma profound
Reveals Heav'n and Earth and demons confounds.
The original visage now they see;
Causes find perfection in one body.
Freely they move when Triyāna's won,
And when the elixir's nine turns are done.
The luggage and the staff there's no need to tote,
Glad to return on old turtle afloat.

Carrying the pilgrims on his back, the old turtle trod on the waves and proceeded for more than half a day. Late in the afternoon they were near the eastern shore when he suddenly asked this question: "Old Master, in that year when I took you across, I begged you to question Tathāgata, once you got to see him, when I would find my sought-after refuge and how much longer would I live. Did you do that?"

Now, that elder, since his arrival at the Western Heaven, had been preoccupied with bathing in the Yuzhen Temple, being renewed at Cloud-Transcending Stream, and bowing to the various sage monks, Bodhisattvas, and Buddhas. When he walked up the Spirit Mountain, he fixed his thought on the worship of Buddha and on the acquisition of scriptures, completely banishing from his mind all other concerns. He did not, of course, ask about the allotted age of the old turtle. Not daring to lie, however, he fell silent and did not answer the question for a long time. Perceiving that Tripitaka had not asked the Buddha for him, the old turtle shook his body once and dove with a splash into the depths. The four pilgrims, the horse, and the scriptures all fell into the water as well. Ah! It was fortunate that the Tang monk had cast off his mortal frame and attained the Way. If he were like the person he had been before, he would have sunk straight to the bottom. The white horse, moreover, was originally a dragon, while Bajie and Sha

5. Advaya: Chinese, *buer*, no second or nonduality; the one and undivided reality of the Buddha-nature.

Monk both were quite at home in the water. Smiling broadly, Pilgrim made a great display of his magic powers by hauling the Tang monk right out of the water and onto the eastern shore. But the scriptures, the clothing, and the saddle were completely soaked.

Master and disciples had just climbed up the riverbank when suddenly a violent gale arose; the sky darkened immediately and both thunder and lightning began as rocks and grit flew everywhere. What they felt was

One gust of wind
And the whole world teetered;
One clap of thunder
And both mountains and streams shuddered.
One flash of lightning
Shot flames through the clouds;
One sky of fog
Enveloped this great Earth.
The wind's mighty howl;
The thunder's violent roar;
The lightning's scarlet streaks;
The fog blanking moon and stars.
The wind hurtled dust and dirt at their faces;
The thunder sent tigers and leopards into hiding;
The lightning raised among the fowl a ruckus;
The fog made the woods and trees disappear.
That wind caused waves in the Heaven–Reaching River to toss and churn;
That lightning lit up the Heaven–Reaching River down to its bottom;
That thunder terrified the Heaven–Reaching River's dragons and fishes;
That fog covered the shores of Heaven–Reaching River with a shroud of
    darkness.
Marvelous wind!
Mountains cracked as pines and bamboos toppled.
Marvelous thunder!
Its power stirred insects and injured humans.
Marvelous lightning!
Like a gold snake it brightened both land and sky.
Marvelous fog!
It surged through the air to screen the Ninefold Heaven.

So terrified were the pilgrims that Tripitaka held firmly to the scripture wraps and Sha Monk threw himself on the poles. While Bajie clung to the white horse, Pilgrim wielded his iron rod with both hands to give protection left and right. That wind, fog, thunder, and lightning, you see, had been a storm brought on by invisible demons, who wanted to snatch away the scriptures the pilgrims had acquired. The commotion lasted all night, and only by morning did the storm subside. Soaked from top to bottom and shaking all over, the elder said, "Wukong, how did this storm come about?"

"Master, you don't seem to understand," said Pilgrim, panting heavily, "that when we escorted you to acquire these scriptures, we had, in fact, robbed Heaven and Earth of their creative powers. For our success meant that we could share the age of the universe; like the light of the sun and moon, we would enjoy life everlasting for we had put on an incorruptible body. Our success, however, had also incurred the envy of Heaven and Earth, the jealousy of both demons and gods, who wanted to snatch away the scriptures from us. They could not do so only because the scriptures were thoroughly wet and because they had been shielded by your rectified dharma-body, which could not be harmed by thunder, lightning, or fog. Moreover, old Monkey was brandishing his iron rod to exercise the nature of pure yang and give you protection. Now that it is morning, the forces of yang are evermore in ascendancy, and the demons cannot prevail."

Only then did Tripitaka, Bajie, and Sha Monk realize what had taken place, and they all thanked Pilgrim repeatedly. In a little while, the sun was way up in the sky, and they moved the scriptures to high ground so that the wraps could be opened and their contents dried. To this day the boulders have remained on which the scriptures were spread out and sunned. By the side of the boulders they also spread out their own clothing and shoes. As they stood, sat, or jumped about, truly this was their situation:

The one pure yang body facing the light
Has put invisible demons all to flight.
Know that true scriptures will o'er water prevail.
They fear not the thunder-and-lightning assail.
Henceforth to Sambodhi they'll go in peace,
And to fairy land they'll return with ease.
Rocks for sunning scriptures are still found here,
Though no demon would ever dare come near.

The four of them were examining the scriptures scroll by scroll to see if they had completely dried when some fishermen arrived at the shore. When they saw the pilgrims, one of the fishermen recognized them and said, "Old Masters, aren't you the ones who crossed this river some years ago on your way to the Western Heaven to seek scriptures?"

"Indeed, we are!" replied Bajie. "Where are you from? How is it that you recognize us?"

"We are from the Chen Village," said the fisherman. "How far is the village from here?" asked Bajie. The fisherman said, "Due south of this canal, about twenty miles."

"Master," said Bajie, "let's move the scriptures to the Chen Village and dry them there. They have a place for us to sit and food for us to eat. We can even ask their family to starch our clothing. Isn't that better than staying here?"

"Let's not go there," replied Tripitaka. "As soon as the scriptures are dried here, we can collect them and be on our way."

The fishermen, however, went back south of the canal and ran right into Chen Cheng. "Number Two," they cried, "the masters who offered themselves as sacrifice-substitutes for your children years ago have returned." "Where did you see them?" asked Chen Cheng. Pointing with their hands, the fishermen said, "Near the boulders over there, where they're sunning scrolls of scriptures."

Chen Cheng took some of his farmhands and ran past the canal. When he caught sight of the pilgrims, he hurriedly went to his knees and said, "Venerable Fathers, now that you have returned, having accomplished your work and merit of acquiring scriptures, why did you not come straight to our home? Why are you loitering here instead? Please, please come to our home!"

"Wait till we've dried the scriptures in the sun," said Pilgrim, "and we'll go with you." "How is it," asked Chen Cheng again, "that the clothing and scriptures of the venerable fathers are soaking wet?"

"In that previous year," replied Tripitaka, "we were indebted to a white turtle for taking us on his back to the western shore. This time he again offered to carry us back to the eastern shore. When we were about to reach the bank, he asked me whether I had remembered to inquire of Buddha for him about how much longer it would take for him to achieve human form. I had actually forgotten about the matter, and he dove into the water. That was how we got wet."

After Tripitaka had thus given a thorough account of what had taken place, Chen Cheng kowtowed and urged them to go back to the house. At length Tripitaka gave in, and they began to collect the scriptures together. They did not expect, however, that several scrolls of the *Buddha-carita-kāvya Sūtra* would be stuck to the rocks, and a part of the sūtra's ending was torn off. This is why the sūtra today is not a complete text, and the top of that particular boulder on which the sūtra had dried still retains some traces of writing. "We've been very careless!" said Tripitaka sorrowfully. "We should have been more vigilant."

"Hardly! Hardly!" said Pilgrim, laughing. "After all, even Heaven and Earth are not perfect. This sūtra may have been perfect, but a part of it has been torn off precisely because only in that condition will it correspond to the profound mystery of nonperfection. What happened isn't something human power could anticipate or change!" After master and disciples had finished packing up the scriptures, they headed for the village with Chen Cheng.

The news of the pilgrims' arrival was passed from one person to ten, from ten to a hundred, and from a hundred to a thousand, till all the people, old and young, came to receive them. When Chen Qing got the news, he immediately set up an incense altar in front of his door and called for drummers and musicians to play. The moment they arrived, Chen led his entire household to kowtow to the pilgrims so as to thank them once more for their previous kindness of saving their children. Then he ordered tea and maigre for them.

Since Tripitaka had partaken of the immortal victuals prepared for him by the Buddhist Patriarch, and since he had been delivered from his mortal frame to become a Buddha, he had no desire at all for profane food. The two old men begged and begged, and only to please them did he pick up the merest morsel. The Great Sage Sun, who never ate much cooked food anyway, said almost immediately, "Enough!" Sha Monk did not show much appetite either. As for Bajie, even he did not resemble his former self, for he soon put down his bowl.

"Idiot, aren't you eating anymore?" asked Pilgrim.

"I don't know why," said Bajie, "but my stomach seems to have weakened all at once!" They therefore put away the food, and the two old men asked about the enterprise of scripture seeking. Tripitaka gave a thorough account of how they bathed at the Yuzhen Temple first, how their bodies turned light and agile at the Cloud-Transcending Stream, how they bowed to Tathāgata at Thunderclap, and how they were feted beneath the precious tower and received scriptures at the treasure loft. He then went on to tell how the two Honored Ones, failing to obtain a gift at first, gave them wordless scriptures instead, how the second audience with Tathāgata had resulted in acquiring a canonical sum of scriptures, how the white turtle dove into the water, and how invisible demons tried to rob them. After this detailed rehearsal, he immediately wanted to leave.

The entire household of the two old men, of course, absolutely refused to let them go. "We could never have repaid," they said, "your profound kindness in saving the lives of our son and daughter except by building a temple to your memory. We have named it the Life-Saving Monastery so that we might offer you the perpetual sacrifice of incense." Then they called Chen Guanbao and One Load of Gold, the son and daughter for whom Pilgrim and Bajie originally served as substitutes on that occasion of child-sacrifice, to come out to kowtow again to their benefactors before they invited the pilgrims to view the monastery.

Leaving the scripture-wraps in front of their family hall, Tripitaka recited a scroll of the *Precious Permanence Sūtra* for their entire household. When they reached the monastery, food had already been laid out there by the Chen family. Hardly had they been seated than another banquet was sent in by another family. Before they could even raise their chopsticks, still another banquet was brought in. There seemed, in fact, to be an unending stream of visitors and food vying for the pilgrims' attention. Not wishing to decline such sincere display of the people's hospitality, Tripitaka forced himself to make some show of tasting what was set before him. That monastery, by the way, was a handsome building indeed.

The temple's bright red-painted doors
Reflect the work of all donors.
From that moment one edifice would rise
With two porticoes adding to its size.
Screens and casements scarlet;
Seven treasures exquisite.
Incense and clouds interlace
As pure light floods the airy space.
A few young cypresses need water still:
Pines have yet to form clusters on the hill.
A living stream in front
Reaches Heaven with its tossing billows;
A tall ridge behind,
The mountain range through which the earth pulse flows.

After he had looked at the monastery from the outside, Tripitaka then went up to the tall tower, where he found the four statues of himself and his disciples.

When Bajie saw these, he gave Pilgrim a tug and said, "Your statue looks very much like you!" "Second Elder Brother," said Sha Monk, "yours has great resemblance, too. But Master's seems to look even more handsome." "It's about right! It's about right!" said Tripitaka, and they descended the tower. In the front hall and the rear corridor, more vegetarian dishes were laid out for them.

Pilgrim asked the Chens, "What ever happened to the shrine of that Great King?"

"It was pulled down that very year," replied the two old men. "Since this monastery was built, Venerable Father, we have been enjoying a rich harvest every year. This has to be the blessing you bestowed on us."

"It's actually the gift of Heaven!" said Pilgrim, chuckling. "We have nothing to do with it. But after we leave this time, we shall try to give you all the protection we can, so that the families of your entire village may enjoy abundant posterity, the peaceful births of the six beasts, and annually wind and rain in due season." All the people kowtowed again to express their thanks.

Before and behind the monastery, there seemed to have gathered a numberless crowd all wanting to offer fruits and maigre to their benefactors. With a giggle Bajie said, "It's just my lousy luck! At the time when I could eat, there wasn't a single household that would give me ten meals. Today I have no appetite, but one family after another is pressing me with invitations." Though he felt stuffed, he raised his hands slightly and once more devoured eight or nine platters of vegetarian food. Though he claimed his stomach had weakened, he nonetheless put away twenty or thirty buns. The pilgrims all ate to their fullest capacity, but still there were other households waiting to invite them. "What contribution have these disciples made," said Tripitaka, "that we should receive such great outpouring of your affection? I beg you all to call a halt tonight. Wait till tomorrow and we shall be glad to be the recipients again."

It was already deep in the night. As he wanted to guard the true scriptures, Tripitaka dared not leave. He remained seated below the tower and meditated, so as to watch his possessions. By about the hour of the third watch, Tripitaka whispered, "Wukong, the people here have already perceived that we have finished our enterprise and attained the Way. As the ancients put it,

The adept does not show himself;
He who shows himself's no adept.

If they detain us too long, I fear that we may lose out in our main enterprise."

"What you say is quite right, Master," replied Pilgrim. "While it is still deep in the night and people are all sound asleep, let us leave quietly." Bajie now had become quite alert, and Sha Monk was most understanding. Even the white horse seemed to know their thoughts. They all arose, silently loaded the packs on the saddle, took up the poles, and toted their belongings through the corridor. When they reached the monastery gate, they found it padlocked. Using his magic, Pilgrim opened the locks on both the second-level gate and the main gate. As they were searching for the way toward the East, a voice rang out in midair. "You who are fleeing," cried the Eight Vajra Guardians, "follow us!"

As the elder smelled a strange fragrance, he rose with the others into the wind. Truly

Elixir's formed, he knows the original face;

His healthy frame, easy and free, bows to his lord.

We do not know how he finally managed to see the Tang emperor; let's listen to the explanation in the next chapter.

They return to the Land of the East;
The five sages attain immortality.

Let us not say anything more about how the four pilgrims departed by mounting the wind with the Vajra Guardians. We tell you instead about the multitude in the Life-Saving Monastery at the Chen Village, who rose at dawn and went at once to offer fruits and other food to their benefactors. When they arrived at the space beneath the tower, however, they found that the Tang monk had disappeared. Thereupon all of them hunted everywhere, but without success. They were so upset that they did not quite know what to do except to wail aloud, "We have allowed a Living Buddha to walk away!"

After a while, the entire household realized that they had no better alternative than to pile all the food and gifts on the altar up in the tower and offer them as sacrifices along with the burning of paper cash. Thereafter they made four great sacrifices and twenty-four smaller ones each year. Moreover, those who wanted to pray for healing, for safety on a journey, for the gift of a spouse, for wealth or children, and to make a vow appeared daily at every hour to present their offerings and incense. Truly,

The gold censer continued a thousand years' fire;
The jade chalice brightened with an eternal lamp.

In that condition we shall leave them.

We tell you now instead about the Eight Vajra Guardians, who employed the second gust of fragrant wind to carry the four pilgrims back to the Land of the East. In less than a day, the capital, Chang'an, gradually came into view. That Emperor Taizong, you see, had escorted the Tang monk out of the city three days before the full moon in the ninth month of the thirteenth year of the Zhenguan reign period. By the sixteenth year, he had already asked the Bureau of Labor to erect a Scripture-Watch Tower outside the Western-Peace Pass to receive the holy books. Each year Taizong would go personally to that place for a visit. It so happened that he had gone again to the tower that day when he caught sight of a skyful of auspicious mists drifting near from the West, and he noticed at the same time strong gusts of fragrant wind.

Halting in midair, the Vajra Guardians cried, "Sage Monk, this is the city Chang'an. It's not convenient for us to go down there, for the people of this region are quite intelligent, and our true identity may become known to them. Even the Great Sage Sun and his two companions needn't go; you yourself can go, hand over the scriptures, and return at once. We'll wait for you in the air so that we may all go back to report to Buddha."

"What the Honored Ones say may be most appropriate," said the Great Sage, "but how could my master tote all those scriptures? How could he lead the horse at the same time? We will have to escort him down there. May we trouble you to wait a while in the air? We dare not tarry."

"When the Bodhisattva Guanyin spoke to Tathāgata the other day," said the Vajra Guardians, "she assured him that the whole trip should take only eight days, so that the canonical number would be fulfilled. It's already more than four days now. We fear that Bajie might become so enamored of the riches down below that we will not be able to meet our appointed schedule."

"When Master attains Buddhahood," said Bajie, chuckling, "I, too, will attain Buddhahood. How could I become enamored of riches down below? Stupid old ruffians! Wait for me here, all of you! As soon as we have handed over the scriptures, I'll return with you and be canonized." Idiot took up the pole, Sha Monk led the horse, and Pilgrim supported the sage monk. Lowering their cloud, they dropped down beside the Scripture-Watch Tower.

When Taizong and his officials saw them, they all descended the tower to receive them. "Has the royal brother returned?" said the emperor. The Tang monk immediately prostrated himself, but he was raised by the emperor's own hands. "Who are these three persons?" asked the emperor once more.

"They are my disciples made during our journey," replied the Tang monk. Highly pleased, Taizong at once ordered his attendants, "Saddle one of our chariot horses for our royal brother to ride. We'll go back to the court together." The Tang monk thanked him and mounted the horse, closely followed by the Great Sage wielding his golden-hooped rod and by Bajie and Sha Monk toting the luggage and supporting the other horse. The entire entourage thus entered together the city of Chang'an. Truly

A banquet of peace was held years ago.
When lords, civil and martial, made a grand show.
A priest preached the law in a great event;

From Golden Chimes the king his subject sent.
Tripitaka was given a royal rescript,
For Five Phases matched the cause of holy script.
Through bitter smelting all demons were purged.
Merit done, they now on the court converged.

The Tang monk and his three disciples followed the Throne into the court, and soon there was not a single person in the city of Chang'an who had not learned of the scripture seekers' return.

We tell you now about those priests, young and old, of the Temple of Great Blessing, which was also the old residence of the Tang monk in Chang'an. That day they suddenly discovered that the branches of a few pine trees within the temple gate were pointing eastward. Astonished, they cried, "Strange! Strange! There was no strong wind to speak of last night. Why are all the tops of these trees twisted in this manner?"

One of the former disciples of Tripitaka said, "Quickly, let's get our proper clerical garb. The old master who went away to acquire scriptures must have returned."

"How do you know that?" asked the other priests.

"At the time of his departure," the old disciple said, "he made the remark that he might be away for two or three years, or for six or seven years. Whenever we noticed that these pine-tree tops were pointing to the east, it would mean that he has returned. Since my master spoke the holy words of a true Buddha, I know that the truth has been confirmed this day."

They put on their clothing hurriedly and left; by the time they reached the street to the west, people were already saying that the scripture seeker had just arrived and been received into the city by His Majesty. When they heard the news, the various monks dashed forward and ran right into the imperial chariot. Not daring to approach the emperor, they followed the entourage instead to the gate of the court. The Tang monk dismounted and entered the court with the emperor. The dragon horse, the scripture packs, Pilgrim, Bajie, and Sha Monk were all placed beneath the steps of jade, while Taizong commanded the royal brother to ascend the hall and take a seat.

After thanking the emperor and taking his seat, the Tang monk asked that the scripture scrolls be brought up. Pilgrim and his companions handed them over to the imperial attendants, who presented them in turn to the emperor for inspection. "How many scrolls of scriptures are there," asked Taizong, "and how did you acquire them?"

"When your subject arrived at the Spirit Mountain and bowed to the Buddhist Patriarch," replied Tripitaka, "he was kind enough to ask Ānanda and Kāśyapa, the two Honored Ones, to lead us to the precious tower first for a meal. Then we were brought to the treasure loft, where the scriptures were bestowed on us. Those Honored Ones asked for a gift, but we were not prepared and did not give them any. They gave us some scriptures anyway, and after thanking the Buddhist Patriarch, we headed east, but a monstrous wind snatched away the scriptures. My humble disciple fortunately had a little magic power; he gave chase at once, and the scriptures were thrown and scattered all over. When we unrolled the scrolls, we saw that they were all wordless, blank texts. Your subjects in great fear went again to bow and plead before Buddha. The Buddhist Patriarch said, 'When these scriptures were created, some Bhikṣu sage monks left the monastery and recited some scrolls for one Elder Zhao in the Śrāvastī Kingdom. As a result, the living members of that family were granted safety and protection, while the deceased attained redemption. For such great service they only managed to ask the elder for three pecks and three pints of rice and a little gold. I told them that it was too cheap a sale, and that their descendants would have no money to spend.' Since we learned that even the Buddhist Patriarch anticipated that the two Honored Ones would demand a gift, we had little choice but to offer them that alms bowl of purple gold which Your Majesty had bestowed on me. Only then did they willingly turn over the true scriptures with writing to us. There are thirty-five titles of these scriptures, and several scrolls were selected from each title. Altogether, there are now five thousand and forty-eight scrolls, the number of which makes up one canonical sum."

More delighted than ever, Taizong gave this command: "Let the Court of Imperial Entertainments prepare a banquet in the East Hall so that we may thank our royal brother." Then he happened to notice Tripitaka's three disciples standing beneath the steps, all with extraordinary looks, and he therefore asked, "Are your noble disciples foreigners?"

Prostrating himself, the elder said, "My eldest disciple has the surname of Sun, and his religious name is Wukong. Your subject also addresses him as Pilgrim Sun. He comes from the Water Curtain Cave of the Flower-Fruit Mountain, located in the Aolai Country in the East Pūrvavideha Continent. Because he caused great disturbance in the Celestial Palace, he was imprisoned in a stone box by the Buddhist Patriarch and pressed beneath the Mountain of Two Frontiers in the region of the Western barbarians. Thanks to the admonitions of the Bodhisattva Guanyin, he was converted to Buddhism and became my disciple when I freed him. Throughout my journey I relied heavily on his protection.

"My second disciple has the surname of Zhu, and his religious name is Wuneng. Your subject also addresses him as Zhu Bajie. He comes from the Cloudy Paths Cave of Fuling Mountain. He was playing the fiend at the Old Gao Village of Tibet when the admonitions of the Bodhisattva and the power of the Pilgrim caused him to become my disciple. He made his merit on our journey by toting the luggage and helping us to ford the waters.

"My third disciple has the surname of Sha, and his religious name is Wujing. Your subject also addresses him as Sha Monk. Originally he was a fiend at the Flowing-Sand River. Again the admonitions of the Bodhisattva persuaded him to take the vows of Buddhism. By the way, the horse is not the one my Lord bestowed on me."

Taizong said, "The color and the coat seem all the same. Why isn't it the same horse?"

"When your subject reached the Eagle Grief Stream in the Serpent Coil Mountain and tried to cross it," replied Tripitaka, "the original horse was devoured by this horse. Pilgrim managed to learn from the Bodhisattva that this horse was originally the prince of the Dragon King of the Western Ocean. Convicted of a crime, he would have been executed had it not been for the intervention of the Bodhisattva, who ordered him to be the steed of your subject. It was then that he changed into a horse with exactly the same coat as that of my original mount. I am greatly indebted to him for taking me over mountains and summits and through the most treacherous passages. Whether it be carrying me on my way there or bearing the scriptures upon our return, we are much beholden to his strength."

On hearing these words, Taizong complimented him profusely before asking again, "This long trek to the Western Region, exactly how far is it?"

Tripitaka said, "I recall that the Bodhisattva told us that the distance was a hundred and eight thousand miles. I did not make a careful record on the way. All I know is that we have experienced fourteen seasons of heat and cold. We encountered mountains and ridges daily; the forests we came upon were not small, and the waters we met were wide and swift. We also went through many kingdoms, whose rulers had affixed their seals and signatures on our document." Then he called out: "Disciples, bring up the travel rescript and present it to our Lord."

It was handed over immediately. Taizong took a look and realized that the document had been issued on the third day before the full moon, in the ninth month of the thirteenth year during the Zhenguan reign period. Smiling, Taizong said, "We have caused you the trouble of taking a long journey. This is now the twenty-seventh year of the Zhenguan period!" The travel rescript bore the seals of the Precious Image Kingdom, the Black

Rooster Kingdom, the Cart Slow Kingdom, the Kingdom of Women in Western Liang, the Sacrifice Kingdom, the Scarlet-Purple Kingdom, the Bhikṣu Kingdom, the Dharma-Destroying Kingdom. There were also the seals of the Phoenix-Immortal Prefecture, the Jade-Flower County, and the Gold-Level Prefecture. After reading through the document, Taizong put it away.

Soon the officer in attendance to the Throne arrived to invite them to the banquet. As the emperor took the hand of Tripitaka and walked down the steps of the hall, he asked once more, "Are your noble disciples familiar with the etiquette of the court?"

"My humble disciples," replied Tripitaka, "all began their careers as monsters deep in the wilds or a mountain village, and they have never been instructed in the etiquette of China's sage court. I beg my Lord to pardon them."

Smiling, Taizong said, "We won't blame them! We won't blame them! Let's all go to the feast set up in the East Hall." Tripitaka thanked him once more before calling for his three disciples to join them. Upon their arrival at the hall, they saw that the opulence of the great nation of China was indeed different from all ordinary kingdoms. You see

The doorway o'erhung with brocade.
The floor adorned with red carpets,
The whirls of exotic incense,
And fresh victuals most rare.
The amber cups
And crystal goblets
Are gold-trimmed and jade-set;
The gold platters
And white-jade bowls
Are patterned and silver-rimmed.
The tubers thoroughly cooked,
The taros sugar-coated;
Sweet, lovely button mushrooms,
Unusual, pure seaweeds.
Bamboo shoots, ginger-spiced, are served a few times;
Malva leafs, honey-drenched, are mixed several ways.
Wheat-glutens fried with xiangchun leaves:[1]
Wood-ears cooked with bean-curd skins.
Rock ferns and fairy plants;

1. Xiangchun: a kind of fragrant, slightly spicy plant.

Fern flour and dried wei-leaves.
Radishes cooked with Sichuan peppercorns;
Melon strands stirred with mustard powder.
These few vegetarian dishes are so-so,
But the many rare fruits quite steal the show!
Walnuts and persimmons,
Lung-ans and lychees.
The chestnuts of Yizhou and Shandong's dates;
The South's ginko fruits and hare-head pears.
Pine-seeds, lotus-seeds, and giant grapes;
Fei-nuts, melon seeds, and water chestnuts.
"Chinese olives"[2] and wild apples;
Crabapples and Pyrus-pears;
Tender stalks and young lotus roots;
Crisp plums and "Chinese strawberries."
Not one species is missing;
Not one kind is wanting.
There are, moreover, the steamed mille-feuilles, honeyed pastries, and fine
*   viands;*
And there are also the lovely wines, fragrant teas, and strange dainties.
An endless spread of a hundred flavors, true noble fare.
Western barbarians with great China can never compare!

Master and three disciples were grouped together with the officials, both civil and military, on both sides of the emperor Taizong, who took the seat in the middle. The dancing and the music proceeded in an orderly and solemn manner, and in this way they enjoyed themselves thoroughly for one whole day. Truly

The royal banquet rivals the sage kings':
True scriptures acquired excess blessings bring.
Forever these will prosper and remain
As Buddha's light shines on the king's domain.

When it became late, the officials thanked the emperor; while Taizong withdrew into his palace, the various officials returned to their residences. The Tang monk and his disciples, however, went to the Temple of Great Blessing, where they were met by the resident priests kowtowing. As they entered the temple gate, the priests said, "Master, the top of these trees were all suddenly pointing eastward this morning. We remembered your

---

2. Chinese olives: *ganlan* or *Canarium*. Oblong and pointed, either green or shriveled during drying, these fruits do not quite resemble the Mediterranean variety.

words and hurried out to the city to meet you. Indeed, you did arrive!" The elder could not have been more pleased as they were ushered into the abbot's quarters. By then, Bajie was not clamoring at all for food or tea, nor did he indulge in any mischief. Both Pilgrim and Sha Monk behaved most properly, for they had become naturally quiet and reserved since the Dao in them had come to fruition. They rested that night.

Taizong held court next morning and said to the officials, "We did not sleep the whole night when we reflected on how great and profound has been the merit of our brother, such that no compensation is quite adequate. We finally composed in our head several homely sentences as a mere token of our gratitude, but they have not yet been written down." Calling for one of the secretaries from the Central Drafting Office, he said, "Come, let us recite our composition for you, and you take it down sentence by sentence." The composition[3] was as follows:

We have heard how the Two Primary Forces[4] which manifest themselves in Heaven and Earth in the production of life are represented by images, whereas the invisible powers of the four seasons bring about transformation of things through the hidden action of heat and cold. By scanning Heaven and Earth, even the most ignorant may perceive their rudimentary laws. Even the thorough understanding of *yin* and *yang*, however, has seldom enabled the worthy and wise to comprehend fully their ultimate principle. It is easy to recognize that Heaven and Earth do contain *yin* and *yang* because there are images. It is difficult to comprehend fully how *yin* and *yang* pervade Heaven and Earth because the forces themselves are invisible. That images may manifest the minute is a fact that does not perplex even the foolish, whereas forms hidden in what is invisible are what confuses even the learned.

How much more difficult it is, therefore, to understand the way of Buddhism, which exalts the void, uses the dark, and exploits the silent in order to succor the myriad grades of living things and exercise control over the entire world. Its spiritual authority is the highest, and its divine potency has no equal. Its magnitude impregnates the entire cosmos; there is no space so tiny that it does not permeate it. Birthless and deathless, it

3. The composition refers to the "Preface to the Holy Religion (*Shengjiaoxu*)," authored by the emperor historically in 648 CE, in gratitude for the newly completed translation by the monk Xuanzang of the entire *Yogācārya-bhūmi Śāstra*.

4. Two Primary Forces: most likely a reference to the forces of darkness and light (i.e., *yin* and *yang*), themselves also regarded by the Chinese as symbolic of the female and male.

does not age after a thousand kalpas; half-hidden and half-manifest, it brings a hundred blessings even now. A wondrous way most mysterious, those who follow it cannot know its limit. A law flowing silent and deep, those who draw on it cannot fathom its source. How, therefore, could those benighted ordinary mortals not be perplexed if they tried to plumb its depths?

Now, this great Religion arose in the Land of the West. It soared to the court of the Han period in the form of a radiant dream,[5] which flowed with its mercy to enlighten the Eastern territory. In antiquity, during the time when form and abstraction were clearly distinguished, the words of the Buddha, even before spreading, had already established their goodly influence. In a generation when he was both frequently active in and withdrawn from the world, the people beheld his virtue and honored it. But when he returned to Nirvāṇa and generations passed by, the golden images concealed his true form and did not reflect the light of the universe. The beautiful paintings, though unfolding lovely portraits, vainly held up the figure of thirty-two marks.[6] Nonetheless his subtle doctrines spread far and wide to save men and beasts from the three unhappy paths, and his traditions were widely proclaimed to lead all creatures through the ten stages toward Buddhahood. Moreover, the Buddha made scriptures, which could be divided into the Great and the Small Vehicles. He also possessed the Law, which could be transmitted either in the correct or in the deviant method.

Our priest Xuanzang, a Master of the Law, is a leader within the Gate of Law. Devoted and intelligent as a youth, he realized at an early age the merit of the three forms of immateriality. When grown he comprehended the principles of the spiritual, including first the practice of the four forms of patience.[7] Neither the pine in the wind nor the moon mirrored in water can compare with his purity and radiance. Even the dew of Heaven and luminous gems cannot surpass the clarity and refinement of his person.

5. A radiant dream: a reference to the story of Emperor Ming (r. 58–75 CE), who dreamed that a golden deity was flying in front of his palace. Asked to explain its meaning the following morning, one of his ministers deciphered the dream representation as the flying Buddha from India. The emperor accepted this interpretation and decided to make further investigation, resulting in his eventual acceptance of the Buddhist religion.

6. Thirty-two marks: the body of Buddha, a "wheel-king (*cakravarti*)," is said to have thirty-two *lakṣaṇas* or special physical marks or signs.

7. Four forms of patience: i.e., the *siren* or four kinds of *kṣānti*, or the endurance under shame, hatred, physical hardship, and in pursuit of faith.

His intelligence encompassed even those elements which seemingly had no relations, and his spirit could perceive that which had yet to take visible forms. Having transcended the lure of the six senses, he was such an outstanding figure that in all the past he had no rival. He concentrated his mind on the internal verities, mourning all the time the mutilation of the correct doctrines. Worrying over the mysteries, he lamented that even the most profound treatises had errors.

He thought of revising the teachings and reviving certain arguments, so as to disseminate what he had received to a wider audience. He would, moreover, strike out the erroneous and preserve the true to enlighten the students. For this reason he longed for the Pure Land and a pilgrimage to the Western Territories. Risking dangers he set out on a long journey, with only his staff for his companion on this solitary expedition. Snow drifts in the morning would blanket his roadway; sand storms at dusk would blot out the horizon. Over ten thousand miles of mountains and streams he proceeded, pushing aside mist and smoke. Through a thousand alternations of heat and cold he advanced amidst frost and rain. As his zeal was great, he considered his task a light one, for he was determined to succeed.

He toured throughout the Western World for fourteen years,[8] going to all the foreign nations in quest of the proper doctrines. He led the life of an ascetic beneath twin śāla trees[9] and by the eight rivers of India. At the Deer Park and on the Vulture Peak he beheld the strange and searched out the different. He received ultimate truths from the senior sages and was taught the true doctrines by the highest worthies. Penetrating into the mysteries, he mastered the most profound lessons. The way of the Triyāna and Six Commandments he learned by heart; a hundred cases of scriptures forming the canon flowed like waves from his lips.

Though the countries he visited were innumerable, the scriptures he succeeded in acquiring had a definite number. Of those important texts of the Mahāyāna he received, there are thirty-five titles in altogether five thousand and forty-eight scrolls. When they are translated and spread through China, they will proclaim the surpassing merit of Buddhism, drawing the cloud of mercy from the Western extremity to shower the dharma-rain on the Eastern region. The Holy Religion, once incomplete, is now returned to perfection. The multitudes, once full of sins, are now brought back to

8. Perhaps a deliberate deviation, on the part of the full-length novel, from the nearly seventeen years of the pilgrimage given in the historical sources.

9. Trees beneath which Buddha himself was said to have attained enlightenment.

blessing. Like that which quenches the fire in a burning house, Buddhism works to save humanity lost on its way to perdition. Like a golden beam shining on darkened waters, it leads the voyagers to climb the other shore safely.

Thus we know that the wicked will fall because of their iniquities, but the virtuous will rise because of their affinities. The causes of such rise and fall are all self-made by man. Consider the cinnamon flourishing high on the mountain, its flowers nourished by cloud and mist, or the lotus growing atop the green waves, its leaves unsoiled by dust. This is not because the lotus is by nature clean or because the cinnamon itself is chaste, but because what the cinnamon depends on for its existence is lofty, and thus it will not be weighed down by trivia; and because what the lotus relies on is pure, and thus impurity cannot stain it. Since even the vegetable kingdom, which is itself without intelligence, knows that excellence comes from an environment of excellence, how can humans who understand the great relations not search for well-being by following well-being?

May these scriptures abide forever as the sun and moon and may the blessings they confer spread throughout the universe!

After the secretary had finished writing this treatise, the sage monk was summoned. At the time, the elder was already waiting outside the gate of the court. When he heard the summons, he hurried inside and prostrated himself to pay homage to the emperor.

Taizong asked him to ascend the hall and handed him the document. When he had finished reading it, the priest went to his knees again to express his gratitude. "The style and rhetoric of my Lord," said the priest, "are lofty and classical, while the reasoning in the treatise is both profound and subtle. I would like to know, however, whether a title has been chosen for this composition."

"We composed it orally last night,"[10] replied Taizong, "as a token of thanks to our royal brother. Will it be acceptable if I title this 'Preface to the Holy Religion'?" The elder kowtowed and thanked him profusely. Once more Taizong said,

"Our talents pale before the imperial tablets,
And our words cannot match the bronze and stone inscriptions.
As for the esoteric texts,
Our ignorance thereof is even greater.

10. The emperor's declaration here was actually a note written in reply to a formal memorial of thanks submitted by the historical Xuanzang.

Our treatise orally composed
Is actually quite unpolished—
Like mere spilled ink on tablets of gold.
Or broken tiles in a forest of pearls.
Writing it in self-interest,
We have quite ignored even embarrassment.
It is not worth your notice,
And you should not thank us."

All the officials present, however, congratulated the emperor and made arrangements immediately to promulgate the royal essay on Holy Religion inside and outside the capital.

Taizong said, "We would like to ask the royal brother to recite the true scriptures for us. How about it?"

"My Lord," said the elder, "if you want me to recite the true scriptures, we must find the proper religious site. The treasure palace is no place for recitation." Exceedingly pleased, Taizong asked his attendants, "Among the monasteries of Chang'an, which is the purest one?"

From among the ranks stepped forth the Grand Secretary, Xiao Yu, who said, "The Wild-Goose Pagoda Temple in the city is purest of all." At once Taizong gave this command to the various officials: "Each of you take several scrolls of these true scriptures and go reverently with us to the Wild-Goose Pagoda Temple. We want to ask our royal brother to expound the scriptures to us." Each of the officials indeed took up several scrolls and followed the emperor's carriage to the temple. A lofty platform with proper appointments was then erected. As before, the elder told Bajie and Sha Monk to hold the dragon horse and mind the luggage, while Pilgrim was to serve him by his side. Then he said to Taizong, "If my Lord would like to circulate the true scriptures throughout his empire, copies should be made before they are dispersed. We should treasure the originals and not handle them lightly."

Smiling, Taizong said, "The words of our royal brother are most appropriate! Most appropriate!" He thereupon ordered the officials in the Hanlin Academy and the Central Drafting Office to make copies of the true scriptures. For them he also erected another temple east of the capital and named it the Temple for Imperial Transcription.

The elder had already taken several scrolls of scriptures and mounted the platform. He was just about to recite them when he felt a gust of fragrant wind. In midair the Eight Vajra Guardians revealed themselves and cried, "Recitants, drop your scripture scrolls and follow us back to the West." From below Pilgrim and his two companions together with the white horse immediately rose into the air. The elder, too, abandoned the scriptures and rose from the platform. They all left soaring through the air. So startled were Taizong and the many officials that they all bowed down toward the sky. Thus it was that

Since scriptures were the sage monk's ardent quest,
He went on fourteen years throughout the West
A bitter journey full of trials and woes,
With many streams and mountains as his foes.
Nine merits more were added to eight times nine;
His three thousand works did on the great world shine.
The wondrous texts brought back to the noble state
Would in the East until now circulate.

After Taizong and many officials had finished their worship, they immediately set about the selection of high priests so that a Grand Mass of Land and Water could be held right in that Wild-Goose Pagoda Temple. Furthermore, they were to read and recite the true scriptures from the Great Canon in order that the damned spirits would be delivered from nether darkness and the celebration of good works be multiplied. The copies of transcribed scriptures would also be promulgated throughout the empire, and of this we shall speak no more.

We must tell you now about those Eight Great Vajra Guardians, who mounted the fragrant wind to lead the elder, his three disciples, and the white horse back to Spirit Mountain. The round trip was made precisely within a period of eight days. At that time the various divinities of Spirit Mountain were all assembled before Buddha to listen to his lecture. Ushering master and disciples before his presence, the Eight Vajra Guardians said, "Your disciples by your golden decree have escorted the sage monk and his companions back to the Tang nation. The scriptures have been handed over. We now return to surrender your decree." The Tang monk and his disciples were then told to approach the throne of Buddha to receive their appointments.

"Sage Monk," said Tathāgata, "in your previous incarnation you were originally my second disciple named Master Gold Cicada. Because you failed to listen to my exposition of the law and slighted my great teaching, your true spirit was banished to find another incarnation in the Land of the East. Happily you submitted and, by remaining faithful to our teaching, succeeded in acquiring the true scriptures. For such magnificent merit, you will receive a great promotion to become the Buddha of Candana Merit.

"Sun Wukong, when you caused great disturbance at the Celestial Palace, I had to exercise enormous dharma power to have you pressed beneath the Mountain of Five Phases. Fortunately your Heaven-sent calamity came to an end, and you embraced the Buddhist religion. I am pleased even more by the fact that you were devoted to the scourging of evil and the exaltation of good. Throughout your journey you made great merit by smelting the demons and defeating the fiends. For being faithful in the end as you were in the beginning, I hereby give you the grand promotion and appoint you the Buddha Victorious in Strife.

"Zhu Wuneng, you were originally an aquatic deity of the Heavenly River, the Marshal of Heavenly Reeds. For getting drunk during the Festival of Immortal Peaches and insulting the divine maiden, you were banished to an incarnation in the Region Below which would give you the body of a beast. Fortunately you still cherished and loved the human form, so that even when you sinned at the Cloudy Paths Cave in Fuling Mountain, you eventually submitted to our great religion and embraced our vows. Although you protected the sage monk on his way, you were still quite mischievous, for greed and lust were never wholly extinguished in you. For the merit of toting the luggage, however, I hereby grant you promotion and appoint you Janitor of the Altars."

"They have all become Buddhas!" shouted Bajie. "Why am I alone made Janitor of the Altars?"

"Because you are still talkative and lazy," replied Tathāgata, "and you retain an enormous appetite. Within the four great continents of the world, there are many people who observe our religion. Whenever there are Buddhist services, you will be asked to clear the altars. That's an appointment which offers you plenty of enjoyment. How could it be bad?

"Sha Wujing, you were originally the Great Curtain-Raising Captain. Because you broke a crystal chalice during the Festival of Immortal Peaches, you were banished to the Region Below, where at the River of Flowing-Sand you sinned by devouring humans. Fortunately you submitted to our religion and remained firm in your faith. As you escorted the sage monk, you made merit by leading his horse over all those mountains. I hereby grant you promotion and appoint you the Golden-Bodied Arhat."

Then he said to the white horse, "You were originally the prince of Dragon King Guangjin of the Western Ocean. Because you disobeyed your father's command and committed the crime of unfiliality, you were to be executed. Fortunately you made submission to the Law and accepted our vows. Because you carried the sage monk daily on your back during his journey to the West and because you also took the holy scriptures back to the East, you too have made merit. I hereby grant you promotion and appoint you one of the dragons belonging to the Eight Classes of Supernatural Beings."

The elder, his three disciples, and the horse all kowtowed to thank the Buddha, who ordered some of the guardians to take the horse to the Dragon-Transforming Pool at the back of the Spirit Mountain. After being pushed into the pool, the horse stretched himself, and in a little while he shed his coat, horns began to grow on his head, golden scales appeared all over his body, and silver whiskers emerged on his cheeks. His whole body shrouded in auspicious air and his four paws wrapped in hallowed clouds, he soared out of the pool and circled inside the monastery gate, on top of one of the Pillars that Support Heaven.

As the various Buddhas gave praise to the great dharma of Tathāgata, Pilgrim Sun said also to the Tang monk, "Master, I've become a Buddha now, just like you. It can't be that I still must wear a golden fillet! And you wouldn't want to clamp my head still by reciting that so-called Tight-Fillet Spell, would you? Recite the Loose-Fillet Spell quickly and get it off my head. I'm going to smash it to pieces, so that that so-called Bodhisattva can't use it anymore to play tricks on other people."

"Because you were difficult to control previously," said the Tang monk, "this method had to be used to keep you in hand. Now that you have become a Buddha, naturally it will be gone. How could it be still on your head? Try touching your head and see." Pilgrim raised his hand and felt along his head, and indeed the fillet had vanished. So at that time, Buddha Candana, Buddha Victorious in Strife, Janitor of the Altars, and Golden-Bodied Arhat all assumed the position of their own rightful fruition. The Heavenly dragon-horse too returned to immortality, and we have a testimonial poem for them. The poem says:

> One reality fallen to the dusty plain
> Fuses with Four Signs and cultivates self again.
> In Five Phases terms forms are but silent and void;
> The hundred fiends' false names one should all avoid.
> The great Bodhi's the right Candana fruition;
> Appointments complete their rise from perdition.
> When scriptures spread throughout the world the gracious light,
> Henceforth five sages live within Advaya's heights.

At the time when these five sages assumed their positions, the various Buddhist Patriarchs, Bodhisattvas, sage priests, arhats, guardians, bhikṣus, upāsakas and upāsikās, the immortals of various mountains and caves, the grand divinities, the Gods of Darkness and Light, the Sentinels, the Guardians of Monasteries, and all the immortals and preceptors who had attained the Way all came to listen to the proclamation before retiring to their proper stations. Look now at

Colored mists crowding the Spirit Vulture Peak,
And hallowed clouds gathered in the world of bliss.
Gold dragons safely sleeping,
Jade tigers resting in peace;
Black hares scampering freely,
Snakes and turtles circling at will.
Phoenixes, red and blue, gambol pleasantly;
Black apes and white deer saunter happily.
Strange flowers of eight periods,
Divine fruits of four seasons,
Hoary pines and old junipers,
Jade cypresses and aged bamboos.
Five-colored plums often blossoming and bearing fruit;
Millennial peaches frequently ripening and fresh.
A thousand flowers and fruits vying for beauty;
A whole sky full of auspicious mists.

Pressing their palms together to indicate their devotion, the holy congregation all chanted:

I submit to Dīpaṁkara, the Buddha of Antiquity.
I submit to Bhaiṣajya-vaiḍūrya-prabhāṣa, the Physician and Buddha
of Crystal Lights.
I submit to the Buddha Śākyamuni.
I submit to the Buddha of the Past, Present, and Future.
I submit to the Buddha of Pure Joy.
I submit to the Buddha Vairocana.
I submit to the Buddha, King of the Precious Banner.
I submit to the Maitreya, the Honored Buddha.
I submit to the Buddha Amitābha.
I submit to Sukhāvativyūha, the Buddha of Infinite Life.
I submit to the Buddha who Receives and Leads to Immorality.
I submit to the Buddha of Diamond Indestructibility.
I submit to Sūrya, the Buddha of Precious Light.
I submit to Mañjuśrī, the Buddha of the Race of Honorable Dragon
Kings.
I submit to the Buddha of Zealous Progress and Virtue.
I submit to Candraprabha, the Buddha of Precious Moonlight.
I submit to the Buddha of Presence without Ignorance.
I submit to Varuna, the Buddha of Sky and Water.
I submit to the Buddha Nārāyaṇa.
I submit to the Buddha of Radiant Meritorious Works.

I submit to the Buddha of Talented Meritorious Works.
I submit to Svāgata, the Buddha of the Well-Departed.
I submit to the Buddha of Candana Light.
I submit to the Buddha of Jeweled Banner.
I submit to the Buddha of the Light of Wisdom Torch.
I submit to the Buddha of the Light of Sea-Virtue.
I submit to the Buddha of Great Mercy Light.
I submit to the Buddha, King of Compassion-Power.
I submit to the Buddha, Leader of the Sages.
I submit to the Buddha of Vast Solemnity.
I submit to the Buddha of Golden Radiance.
I submit to the Buddha of Luminous Gifts.
I submit to the Buddha Victorious in Wisdom.
I submit to the Buddha, Quiescent Light of the World.
I submit to the Buddha, Light of the Sun and Moon.
I submit to the Buddha, Light of the Sun-and-Moon Pearl.
I submit to the Buddha, King of the Victorious Banner.
I submit to the Buddha of Wondrous Tone and Sound.
I submit to the Buddha, Banner of Permanent Light.
I submit to the Buddha, Lamp that Scans the World.
I submit to the Buddha, King of Surpassing Dharma.
I submit to the Buddha of Sumeru Light.
I submit to the Buddha, King of Great Wisdom.
I submit to the Buddha of Golden Sea Light.
I submit to the Buddha of Great Perfect Light.
I submit to the Buddha of the Gift of Light.
I submit to the Buddha of Candana Merit.
I submit to the Buddha Victorious in Strife.
I submit to the Bodhisattva Guanshiyin.
I submit to the Bodhisattva, Great Power-Coming.
I submit to the Bodhisattva Mañjuśrī.
I submit to the Bodhisattva Viśvabhadra and other Bodhisattvas.
I submit to the various Bodhisattvas of the Great Pure Ocean.
I submit to the Bodhisattva, the Buddha of Lotus Pool and Ocean
    Assembly.
I submit to the various Bodhisattvas in the Western Heaven of
    Ultimate Bliss.
I submit to the Great Bodhisattvas, the Three Thousand Guardians.
I submit to the Great Bodhisattvas, the Five Hundred Arhats.
I submit to the Bodhisattva, Bhikṣu-īkṣṇi.

I submit to the Bodhisattva of Boundless and Limitless Dharma.

I submit to the Bodhisattva, Diamond Great Scholar-Sage.

I submit to the Bodhisattva, Janitor of the Altars.

I submit to the Bodhisattva, Golden-Bodied Arhat of Eight Jewels.

I submit to the Bodhisattva of Vast Strength, the Heavenly Dragon
   of Eight Divisions of Supernatural Beings.

Such are these various Buddhas in all the worlds.

I wish to use these merits
To adorn Buddha's pure land—.
To repay fourfold grace above
And save those on three paths below.
If there are those who see and hear,
Their minds will find enlightenment.
Their births with us in paradise
Will be this body's recompense.
All the Buddhas of past, present, future in all the world,
The various Honored Bodhisattvas and Mahāsattvas,
Mahā-prajñā-pāramitā!

Made in United States
North Haven, CT
21 January 2024

47722408R00307